Nothing Could Quench
the Leaping Bright Fire
of Their Passion.

"I have never met anyone so stubborn," Francho railed at Dolores, as they stood by the river.

She stamped hard on his boot. "How can you expect me to accept apologies when you are shouting at me, *bribón!*" she cried as he jerked his foot back.

Francho reached out and brushed away the silky locks of auburn hair from where they blew against her mouth. His touch made her tremble. She could not drop her eyes from his, those amused, compelling eyes that haunted her dreams.

With a groan he pulled her into his arms and held her close to him. "What do you do to me? Why can't I leave you alone?" he moaned into her hair.

Transfixed and betrayed by her own helpless desire, Dolores melted into his embrace, molding herself against his tall body and muscled thighs, her hair whipping about them both. . . .

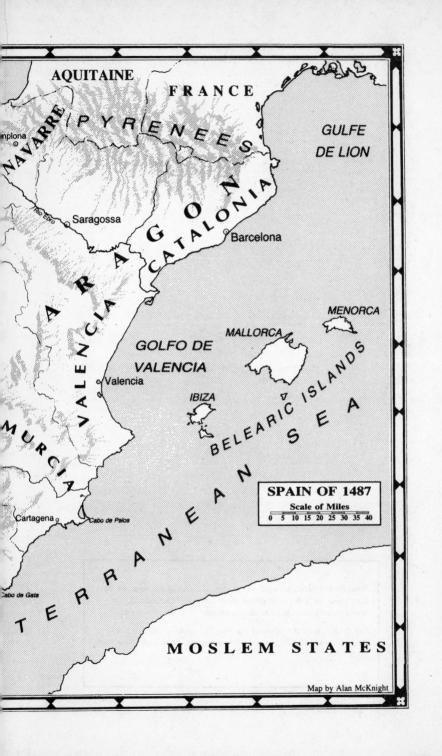

AQUITAINE

FRANCE

NAVARRE

PYRENEES

GULFE DE LION

A R A G O N

CATALONIA

ṃplona

Rio Ebro

Saragossa

Barcelona

VALENCIA

MENORCA

MALLORCA

GOLFO DE VALENCIA

Valencia

IBIZA

BELEARIC ISLANDS

M U R C I A

TERRANEAN SEA

Cartagena

Cabo de Palos

Cabo de Gata

SPAIN OF 1487

Scale of Miles

0 5 10 15 20 25 30 35 40

MOSLEM STATES

Map by Alan McKnight

Jasmine On The Wind

Mallory Dorn Hart

PUBLISHED BY POCKET BOOKS NEW YORK

Another *Original* publication of POCKET BOOKS

POCKET BOOKS, a division of Simon & Schuster, Inc.
1230 Avenue of the Americas, New York, N.Y. 10020

ISBN: 0-671-62302-8

First Pocket Books trade paperback printing October, 1986

10 9 8 7 6 5 4 3 2 1

POCKET and colophon are registered trademarks
of Simon & Schuster, Inc.

Printed in the U.S.A.

*In loving memory of Marie and Jack
without whom this book
could not have been written.*

Castile

❧ *Chapter 1* ❧

THE USUAL BUSTLE of merchants, farmers from the countryside, housewives and servants, travelers, vendors, and loiterers milled through the stalls of the city's big market square. The morning sun was halfway to noon when the loud thumping of a drum and tootle of a flute could be heard over the din of commerce and people began flocking from all the aisles of displays, carts, and crates to see the itinerant entertainers.

Dolores had already selected her mark and given Pepi the nod, but she was pleased that the woman left off her sniffing and prodding at the cheese before her and sailed off to follow the crowd. For Dolores's work, crowds were perfect. And this time she'd picked her victim more carefully. Last month she'd had to run for her life to make her "rat hole" and then had to slip back into the inn all smelly and dirty—just because the young woman whose silver pomade ball she coveted didn't happen to be wearing anything at all under her satin gown, the lewd bawd. As lightly as Dolores's hand had slid under the skirt to slit the pocket where the pomander rested, the woman had felt the feather touch on her bare legs and shrieked.

At least this time her mark was decently dressed, a stout, prosperous-looking matron in a white wimple whose gown was fashionably raised in front to display a heavy underskirt

3

and whose sleeves, slit at the elbow, showed the snowy fabric of a full-length chemise underneath. From her unobtrusive post at the side of the cheese stall, Dolores had made a quick but careful scan and determined where a laden pocket made the fabric of the gown ripple on one side with just a slight more downward pull than on the other. The lady even obligingly carried a cloth-covered market basket on one arm with the leafy tops of greens sticking out.

She swallowed the last bit of the honey cake she had filched, wiped her hands down her short, coarse-woven tunic, and peeled away from the canvas side of the stall to follow the woman as she joined the stream of people hastening to create a throng around the man with tinkling bells sewn to his tunic who nonchalantly slid burning brands down his throat as his cohorts played a gay jig. From the corner of her eye she saw Pepi slide off the crate of geese he sat on and attach himself to the mark from another angle. She hoped he wasn't going to gawk at the fire-eater himself before he got busy because she didn't believe in stringing things out. She liked to work her mark and be gone, and no more than two in a morning, for the more marks gulled the greater risk of "Thief! Thief! I've been robbed" splitting the air and then everyone became suspect, even a timid and innocent-looking thirteen-year-old girl.

Let Carlos and Francho take the chance of an alerted crowd grabbing to stop them or the Hermandad guards racing close on their tails, they loved that, the strutters. She didn't anymore, not since she'd grown too big to duck under an arm handily. Anyhow, Papa didn't complain about what she returned him in coin and salable goods. What she did, she did well.

Pepi was her "stall" today, and she watched him slip in just ahead of the mark, who was approaching the improvised stage. Pepi was small and now disappeared from her sight, blotted out by the stout woman's girth, but it didn't matter. As soon as the excited crowd began to tighten into a large knot, pushing and craning to see over each other, Pepi would create the diversion she needed. Innocently Dolores shuffled along just to the side of the woman, a great-chested dame whose eagerness to see the entertainment was making her careless. She decided at that point she would not need the tiny, curved knife forged to a band that fitted on the first joint of her forefinger. She judged the pocket shallow enough just to dip.

The crowd, shouting dares and encouragement at the posturing, jingling fire-eater whipping his burning brands around, was getting dense. The mark, bobbing her coiffed head to see the incredible sight of a man sliding searing orange flames down his gullet, was surrounded by jostling people, one of whom, Dolores thought impatiently, should be an eleven-year-old boy getting ready to— Whomp! The market basket flew up, knocked into the air by a staggering Pepi pretending to have been pushed into it by careless onlookers, onions, turnips, and beets tumbling out to the tune of the woman's dismayed cry. Cursing at Pepi's clumsiness, the dame moved to heave herself into a stoop and retrieve her vegetables before they were trampled or stolen, but the apologetic boy, trying to help her gather the erratically rolling onions, only hindered her more by his clumsiness, his back and shoulder getting in her way and immobilizing her against the people behind her for a second, all Dolores needed.

Clucking with sympathy at the woman's side Dolores stooped too, along with others around, to gather up what vegetables were salvageable. A lightening dip of her slim fingers and a small drawstring purse was nimbly withdrawn by its gathered top and speedily palmed. With a disgusted squawk the matron shoved Pepi aside and dove for her provisions, popping whatever she could find into the basket, the more honest people about her tossing in various bruised globes, even Dolores, who handed her a ragged bunch of beets, which she took with a nod and a dark mutter about wild and barbaric boys. Distracted by the loss of her provisions, the mark forgot about the fire-eater, shoved her wide back against the murmuring, fascinated throng pushing her forward, and began to fight her way out of the fire-eater's audience and back to her housewifely duties.

Dolores pushed her way from the crowd too, but in another direction. Actually she made no haste. Even if the woman felt in her pocket now and screamed her head off, even in the unlikely event she herself could be collared as the hook, she had passed the purse to Pepi as he had squeezed past her to slip away through the crowd. She was clean. She would meet Pepi at home and they would take a few coins before delivering the purse to Papa. She had felt copper maravedis inside the soft leather, but also at least six or so silver reales. She glanced sideways at a foolish and vain woman who wore her embroidered purse and a little scissors dangling on leather

5

cords from her belt, fine candidates for Dolores's tiny knife. But no. She'd gotten an expensive lace-trimmed satin kerchief today and a purse that was heavy for all it was small. Plenty for one morning, and the fortnightly market lasted two days; there was always tomorrow. Papa would only give her a few maravedis, anyhow, enough for a ribbon of shiny stuff or a cone of raffia matting holding honeyed fruits, and she could only clip so much from each haul. Her greedy father didn't part with enough to inspire her to work too hard.

She emerged from the square and took a shortcut alley to get back to the inn, scratching vigorously at some bug bites on her arm, which reminded her of how glad she was not to have to endure the fleas in her "rat hole"—actually a cat's nest in a plank shed nearby to the market square, with a prominent and stout iron lock on the door but with a loose plank in back that could be manipulated aside for quick entry and then pushed back again. Here she crouched, in the stink of the cats—whom she fed from time to time—and waited until whomever was chasing her had given up. This was the part of thieving she wasn't too happy with anymore, the fun was evaporating from getting scratched and filthy and scared.

But today she was pleased with herself; she tossed her kerchiefed head like some of the merchants' wives did, very proud and uppity, and her wide mouth curled in a grin at herself. Such airs, her Aunt Esperanza would snort. Not that Dolores wouldn't have been better pleased if she'd loosed a gold locket from its moorings or stealthily undid a good brooch. From a little girl on she'd been fascinated by the flash and glitter of jewelry, although any of it she got went to Papa. What would *she* do with it? Her new height stood her in good stead with jewelry though, for she was almost as tall as many adult women and could easily slip a ribbon knot and slide off a necklace without the wearer's neck even feeling the breeze.

There was still some sweetness on her lips from the honey cake and she wished she had another, but she didn't feel it was right to steal too much from the same vendor; they had to make their living too. Copying the erect but graceful walk of the decently dressed woman with two little children just ahead of her, Dolores sauntered down a narrow street, dropping her exaggerated sway when necessary to dodge splashes from mounted riders and carts spraying the dirty water that trickled down the center of the road. Oh well, some days the pickings were not as exciting as others; tomorrow she'd try for a gold brooch.

By 1483 the small city of Ciudad Real, set down in the rocky, sunbaked stretches of the Castilian plain, had grown to an important crossroad for commerce traveling north from Andalusia and Moorish Granada, and goods going south from the reaches of Catholic Spain. The city had a number of open squares to separate its torturous tangle of narrow streets and boasted not only a major market square for itinerant traders but also an impressive plaza, where local merchants and vendors did business in the shadow of a newly constructed, splendid Gothic church.

With all its burgeoning wealth and vitality, the city supported a number of hostelries, some mean, some excellent, but all with their partisans who would not think of spending their coins elsewhere.

Papa el Mono's two-story, thatched-roof, rundown establishment squatted behind its old wall on a small square not far from the city gates. The proprietor sold drink and passable food and kept wenches accessible for those whose purse sometimes matched their love of pleasure. Papa el Mono had achieved a modest reputation for having something for everyone: a cheap wine or flagon of ale for the muleteer; a blear-eyed woman for the raucous soldier; a decent roast hare or cold bird with some fiery spirit for the merchant or moneyed traveler; and transients could find beds in an upstairs dormitory, hardly fancy but cleaner than most.

The stoop-shouldered innkeeper looked like the pet monkeys sometimes carried by wealthy ladies, hence the wooden carving of a monkey hanging above the inn's wooden gates. His little eyes peered anxiously from his wizened face, his manner was hesitant, his attitude toward those who could not pay for what they had received more reproachful than angry as his huge peacekeeper 'Fredo booted the merchants into the stableyard dust. His patrons deemed him no more or less dishonest than any of his brethren, all of whom practiced petty chicanery when they could get away with it. But Papa el Mono had a quick eye for detail, such as on which side a man wore his purse and whether the bulge in it might mean copper, silver, or, less likely, gold; and where such a guest might be going when he left the premises, and in what sobriety. He carefully nurtured the relaxed opinion his customers held of him and considered himself a master of deception.

When there were few overnight guests upstairs to be breakfasted and ushered on their way by their host, Papa el Mono slept late, leaving his sister Esperanza to purchase food and to supervise the kitchen and the cleaning up from the night before, and affording his daughter the luxury of putting off her chores until he awoke to cuff her.

"Gently, *chiquita,* gently, *madre mía,* look at me, I am all wet." Tía Esperanza looked down at the expanse of her water-spotted tunic and heavily hitched her creaking three-legged stool away from the tub in which her young niece disported herself.

"It would take more than a few drops of water to get you all wet, Tía," Dolores giggled with an affectionate glance at her ponderous aunt sitting with a snow of white feathers at her feet from the half-plucked goose lying in her lap. "I have to rub hard to get off the soot. But it was surely worth it to get so dirty—and you had better keep your wagging tongue sewn down." She smiled to herself, thinking triumphantly of the silver coin she had rooted out of the ashes behind the hearthspit this morning, having noted where the drunk traveler had flung it the night before. She would add it to her little cache, and the devil with her duty to Papa. It would make a nice addition to the lace-trimmed satin kerchief she had squirreled away two days before.

"I have seen nothing, I know nothing," her aunt mumbled, crossing her vast bosom and rolling her eyes up to heaven to atone for the lie. On the way down her eyes squinted with calculation at the early morning sun slanting through the yellowing leaves of the old oak tree growing against the wall of the little yard, an area screened from the inn's entry by the tree's huge trunk and a fieldstone barrier. She was not going to be seduced by the warm tranquility of the morning, over which hung the pervasive smell from the inn's ramshackle stables. The hour was advancing, and she had more important things to do than guard the privacy of her niece's bath. "So. How many more minutes must I spend watching you scrub off your skin?" she demanded.

"Why is scrubbing so terrible, old grump? How can I expect a gallant and handsome *caballero* to notice me if I am smeared with dirt from head to toe?"

The wisp of mustache on Esperanza's upper lip was beaded with fine sweat. "Handsome *caballero*, indeed. Thirteen years old and your head stuffed full of romantic tales and silly wild dreams." she huffed. She knew the source of these fancy notions, she too had heard the scapegrace Francho warbling his rondelets of hoity-toit knightly chivalry and impractical pure young love. *Dios* only knew where he picked them up. Just the sort of meat her impressionable Dolores found good to dine on. She attacked the limp goose again, feathers flying as if she were rooting out all such foolishness then and there. "You are just like your mother," she lectured her niece. "You had less than a year when she died yet her mooning remains in you. *Sí,* and her temper too, for that matter."

Dolores grinned. "But since you raised me, *you* really have been my mother. And that's why I'm so stubborn."

Tía Esperanza refused to be teased. She cocked an eyebrow and regarded the piquant head and shoulders, which was all she could see of her young niece over the rim of the deep tub. "And didn't I raise you all up, in fact, and teach you to honor your father and to pray to God? A good job too, for a fat old woman." She nodded in satisfaction, shaking her chins, proud of herself.

"Tía, tell me about my mother, tell me how beautiful she was," Dolores begged, swishing her hair about in the water, her eyes closed against the sun.

"I have told you a hundred times that she was beautiful. She had curling hair which hung to her knees when she unbound it—with not so reddish a cast as yours. She was small, with a tiny waist. . . ." Esperanza droned on, patient with the oft-repeated litany.

Raising her wet head again Dolores opened eyes which she deliberately made very big and innocent. "Ah, that's what I have wondered, Tía. Why am I tall if my mother was not, nor Papa either? Doesn't that seem very strange to you?"

"What foolishness. It sometimes happens that way. Look at your brother Carlos. He is tall too."

"But crazy Luda said . . ."

Her aunt's heavy eyebrows frowned together her eyes. "Crazy Luda is crazy!" She stumped her legs under her as if she were going to get up. "Girl, you waste the good morning. Wash, wash all the time lately, like a fish. You will surely come down with the ague."

Dolores gave up the always hopeless quest for information

about her mother, but in revenge she teased her aunt. "Better to wash like a fish than stink like a goat. Men—gentlemen, that is—don't like goats, Auntie."

Her aunt pursed her lips and wrinkled a sweaty forehead plastered with wisps of hair. Dolores was yet a child. How did she come to speak in such a manner? Yes, she had noticed the lengthening leg, the budding chest. She had even provided Dolores with some soft, clean rags the day her monthly bleeding commenced. But *Díos mío,* that was only some months ago. . . .

Touched by her aunt's dismayed expression, Dolores relented. Quickly ducking herself she came up streaming and laughing. "Ah, Tía, don't worry. Do you know what I think of boys—young men—the pack of them, *idiotas?* This! Pouf!" She clapped her hands in the water, splashing a geyser all around and loosing a peal of girlish laughter that pulled the corners of her aunt's mouth up into her fat cheeks again.

Tía Esperanza was relieved. That was more like Dolores. This bathing, this concern about a little excess dirt, didn't yet mean her little girl had fled forever. She simply liked to dandle about in the water. She saw Dolores's brown tunic, which reached only to the girl's bare knees, lying in a heap on the packed earth of the yard, and there was a momentary sadness in her heart. Poor, unskilled in any honest way, for she could neither weave a basket nor sew a seam, Dolores was destined to marry at most some artisan's apprentice. Papa el Mono's money would never go into the decent dowry which might attract a shopkeeper, for instance. Ah yes, gentlemen, indeed.

She ripped out the last few feathers, and there was the goose, plucked naked. "Dolores, come out of there!" she ordered. "I cannot leave the imbeciles in the kitchen too long to their own devices."

"One more minute, Auntie, one more," Dolores entreated her indulgent aunt, unwilling to leave the silky feel of the water against her skin. Nevertheless she quit her lolling and began to wash seriously. She rubbed a piece of coarse soap against the small breasts that had finally appeared on her chest this year. It felt peculiarly good. . . .

She raised a glistening arm to wash underneath and became fascinated by the progression of sparkling drops beading down its length. Supposing they were jewels, she dreamed, the baubles of Queen Isabella. They would be sapphires and pearls, in fact her whole arm would be shimmering in cloth of

10

silver sewn with jewels, as once she had seen when the Court had ridden through Ciudad Real. Like the proud ruler of Castile and Leon, she would raise a gold-hilted sword to the shoulder of the gallant young knight who knelt worshipfully at her feet. . . .

Two youths sauntered around the corner of the scullery, the gleam of mischief hardly hidden in their elaborately casual glances. Dolores's soaring moment was shattered. She quickly refocused her eyes and pulled her queenly arm back into the water. In fact, she narrowed her eyes, being experienced with the two of them, and crouched deeper into the cloudy water.

Her brother Carlos moved his tall, spare body with economy, but Francho, the orphan her aunt had taken in years ago, approached with an easy grace, almost a swagger. He gripped in his hand the neck of a small lute he had robbed from a group of musicians and from whose worn strings, by dint of dogged practice and a natural ear for melody, he was able to coax a number of popular ballads. He had lately taken to composing doggerel of his own, too. He considered the battered instrument one of his dearest possessions and was rarely without it unless he was working. His smile was all innocence now as he cradled his lute, twanged a few chords, and impudently improvised in a clear, pleasant voice that had begun to deepen:

> There once was a mistress, a mistress there was
> With visage bedizened with dirt and with fuzz,
> She danced for the Devil and fearing his wrath
> Leaped into a barrel and took her a bath!

Both youths choked back their laughter, although Carlos tried to seem grave, but Dolores knew that the anticipatory gleam in Francho's cerulean blue eyes meant her no good, and as they started toward her again she shrilled, "Stop! Don't come any closer."

"Carlos! Francho!" Tía Esperanza warned, coming to a sudden decision there and then that Dolores had outgrown these sorts of rough pranks that even she had once laughed at.

The boys halted where they were and looked at each other, then back at Dolores, who sat so temptingly in a barrel which could be dumped over in a second.

"Hombre." Francho poked the lean Carlos in the ribs. "What is this? A fiesta day? A saint's day? If Dolores is

11

washing herself there must be a special event coming up, otherwise she doesn't care how dirty her face is."

Carlos smiled in his peculiar, reserved manner, with only half his mouth turning up. *"Sí, hombre,"* he drawled, "and if she washes her face how will we ever know her from all the other wenches? That way at least she was easy to recognize."

"Perros!" Dolores yelled at them, suspecting the worst. "Maybe your faces are so clean, *los bajos?* Get out of here."

Tía Esperanza shook her three chins at them. *"Sí,* and what matter if her face be dirty? Soon enough the tosspots at the wine keg will be looking under the dirt." Or under her skirt, the aunt thought to herself darkly.

His aunt's remark had sharpened Francho's attention on the pert, sun-browned face from which tilted gray eyes watched him warily over the barrel rim. She looked the same to him as always, didn't she, only cleaner? And yet—his smile did not falter but he felt a small shock of surprise. The baby roundness of her cheeks and of her indented chin had some-how melted away, for the familiar face seemed more finely contoured along the delicate bones. It occurred to him that the pink lips had acquired a sort of definite molding, and more width. His eyes followed the tangled strands of wet hair to the tops of her shoulders, which glistened in the sun and which seemed to have lost their sharpness, and the arm she shot from the water to shake an angry, clenched fist at them had rounded out, no longer resembling a frail twig.

Francho had never much thought of Dolores as female or pretty, she was just Dolores, someone to tease and tussle with when things were dull, an unintimidated hoyden who made a passable cutpurse. From his vantage point of a half-year past fifteen he still considered her a child. Nevertheless, the more sculpted outline of her features could not be denied. He watched Dolores's lips hurl epithets but he scarcely heard. It suddenly was obvious to him that the young girl in the tub could be praised for more than her deft fingers, and some-where behind this thought he knew he'd already noted her prettiness and hadn't wanted to accept it. He was amazed at how quickly girls changed.

Frowning ominously at the mischief seekers who still stood leering at the angry girl, Tía Esperanza nevertheless found her thoughts occupied by how fast they had all grown from children to adults. Dolores was her favorite, a lively and, until lately, a grubby child. Carlos was close-mouthed, aloof, he always made her a little uncomfortable because it was hard to tell what he was thinking. Pepi, the youngest, whose hard birth had killed their mother, was the image of his father, a wiry boy with a stutter and a grin. And then there was her foundling, Francho. She watched him teasingly strum a few more chords while Dolores fumed, and remembered—was it already over six years ago?—that hot day when she had battled with Papa el Mono to keep the starved and heatsick little boy who lay in a stupor on a bench in the scullery.

". . . Santa Maria, Santa Ana, San Raimundo, they will all know of your heartless deed. . . . The Devil will come for you as his own . . . you will be forsaken. . . ." She remembered pleading, "You cannot put this feverish child into the heat, into the dust, without a mouthful of water, cruel man. No, I will not let you. The poor little soul, see how little and skinny he is, he has no father, he has no mother, no—"

Papa el Mono had clapped his hands over his ears and screwed up his face. "Hold! Hold, you screaming woman, you are knocking a hole in my head. Enough! Succor your doxy's bastard, give him some gruel, whatever will shut up your trap, and send him away. And be it on your head if he steals every coin we have." Shaking his head in disgust, the innkeep shuffled off to see why the evening's roast pig had not been spitted yet.

From the moment the little boy opened eyes shockingly blue in his pale-olive face, and, crooning at him, she pushed the damp, black curls off his forehead, Esperanza knew that God had sent this particular little tatterdemalion for her to take care of. When the child recovered a bit he said his name was Francisco, that he was nine years old, that he was homeless and had wandered from a place farther north for many weeks. And then he stubbornly set his mouth against saying any more. She kept him mostly out of Papa's sight and spun out the time it took to put a little meat on his bones. In turn he was wide-eyed at life in the hostelry and seemed willing to stay on, and so, a few weeks later, she once more accosted her brother to convince him that the child would be a good addition to the small band of cutpurses he was training.

"I assure you, *hermano mío,* he is very smart—small and quick and not only that but he can read. Every day he reads to me the public notices the guards knock to our gates," Tía declared in wonder.

The innkeep's shoulders rounded in self-defense. "I don't

know. Who is he? Where is he from? How does it happen that he has such learning?"

Tía shrugged. "What does that matter? He will not tell me much. Perhaps he is ashamed." Her fat face began to fold up and she wrung her apron. "Believe me, brother, he will make a fine pupil, he will bring us a mountain of *reales,* wait, you will see. Carlos likes him. He is going tonight with Carlos to the *plaza major,* just to watch—"

Papa jerked his head around. "He already knows? What crack-brained *loco* idiocy, woman, you will ruin us. How do we know he will not run right to the Hermandad and betray us for a few pennies' reward?"

"No, no, he would not do that, you don't know how polite and shy he is. This lad is an angel from God. I beg you, brother, just talk with him, let 'Fredo teach him—"

"Basta! Enough, woman, I will think of it." Papa el Mono whined and shuffled away, worrying the inside of his ear with a finger. "I need to take a little siesta in this cursed heat, and you bray like twelve asses, a man has nowhere to turn for peace under his own roof. . . ."

A buzzing fly landed on Tía Esperanza's oily nose and brought the present back with a rush, breaking her few moments of musing. She shook off the annoying insect, frowned at her three charges, still confronting each other with insults. The raw-boned and stone-faced Carlos, a man of seventeen, already was breaking into the dangerous but lucrative business of stealing and selling horses. As for Francho, it was hard to see that small, undernourished, and strangely naive streetchild in this broad-shouldered, self-assured youth with the spark of deviltry in his black-fringed, azure eyes. She relished the fact that his hulking instructor 'Fredo boasted often to Papa how easily Francho eluded both outraged citizens and city guards alike. He was maturing, his worn tunic was tight across his chest, and his voice had lowered, but he was a good boy, one who could read and write and even sing, and he came to High Mass with her every week.

And Dolores? Tía considered the glowering girl. Dolores would often climb into her aunt's great lap to give her a big, hard hug of affection. Who knows, Tía Esperanza mused, getting lost in her own daydreams, Dolores might yet turn out to be a real beauty and be noticed by some man of worth who would keep her well. Perhaps even the Alcalde of the city, whose roving eye was well known. If she became the mayor's mistress, Dolores would live in a fine house with her own serving wench. And then perhaps the favored mistress would remember her old auntie with a valuable trinket . . . some money . . . a place in a pilgrim's caravan to Santiago de Campostela. . . .

Francho decided they'd traded enough smart remarks with Dolores and lowered his lute. Grinning, he nudged Carlos and gestured toward the angry bather with his head. Carlos nodded, very solemn, and they moved forward together, intoning:

"Oh, what a splash if we turned over the whole barrel. . . ."

"Dolores would float down the courtyard on the tide. . . ."

"And minstrels would write ballads about it, the song of the naked nymph, backside up on the tiles. . . ."

"Flowing over the wall and into the horsetrough for another dunk." They doubled over with laughter at their victim's helpless scrabbling to find a hiding place in the water.

"Tía!" Dolores shrieked to her aunt, who was sitting gathering wool. "Stop them. Dogs! Animals! Dirty scum! Your scullery maids will show you their nakedness, not I. I'll slit your throats, whoresons!" Her voice hit a high note.

Tía Esperanza heaved herself up and waddled toward them like an avenging avalanche, ready to swing the plucked goose by its neck, muttering darkly.

The avalanche and the goose would have descended on their heads if they hadn't heard Pepi calling from the stableyard, his voice insistent and shrill with excitement, obviously something more important brewing than this little pastime. With an assenting glance at each other they abandoned the game, dodged away from Tía Esperanza's slaps, and loped to duck around the corner of the building.

"I'll make you sorry, you slop-tails," Dolores yelled after them. "You'll be sorry you ever tried that, I promise you, cow dung . . . vile snakes . . . ! Her voice rose to a screech, and she hurled her hunk of soap at them as they disappeared.

"*Ay, madre mía,* that witch will burst her throat one day," Carlos remarked mildly.

"Or our heads," Francho added, but his grin had faded. He had turned to look back just as Dolores in her fury forgot herself, rose up to throw the soap, and inadvertently gave him a view of her glistening wet, small, pointed, and pink-tipped breasts, jutting out as her arm went back. A jolt lurched through his stomach and into his groin, a pleasant feeling even though it caught at his breath. It wasn't new to him, he was no virgin, but he clamped his jaw and tried to erase the feeling and the lingering picture of that pale, soft flesh. It was Dolores and Dolores was Dolores, not a girl . . .

They intercepted Pepi and strained to hear the news, which he jabbered so fast, his monkey face screwed up so intently that they were forced to pull him away from the early customers straggling through the gates, and into a secluded corner of the stable so he could repeat it more slowly and coherently.

"The constable, I heard the c-constable tell it to the s-smith near the Alcalde's house," Pepi stuttered doggedly. "They are expecting an im-m-portant party to arrive tonight. The C-C-Count of Tendilla, he said." Pepi's eyes grew big as he mentioned the name of the nobleman admired through the length and breadth of Spain and Granada. "The C-Count of Tendilla, riding with his household and m-men-at-arms. A rich c-caravan, fine horses, everything!"

Carlos's hand shaking his arm calmed him down. "Did you happen to find out where they would camp?"

"*S-sí,* to the north, off the road to Manzanares. But not the C-Count. The c-constable said the Count would be the guest of the w-w-whoreson scum Alcalde."

His listeners smiled, knowing that the endearing terms were more likely Pepi's than the constable's.

Carlos hunkered down, picking up a straw and chewing on it reflectively. In his memory only one royal cortege and few *ricos hombres* had visited Ciudad Real, even the Duke of Infantada, who owned castle and property but ten leagues distant, preferred not to spend time in the harsh climate of this part of Castile. Ciudad Real was not big enough to attract the visits of members of the Court, who preferred to pass through Valdepena and Alcazar de San Juan on their way north or south. So a large, noble party was a special event.

Francho joined him in a crouch, unable to restrain the eagerness in his eyes. "Listen, *amigo,* a fat, noble purse would at least be worthy of our efforts. We take our chances in the church and at the fairs for a few trinkets and what amounts to a few gold ducats at best. But this means real booty, purses full of gold and chains and jewelry worth our time and lord grand *ricos hombre* won't even miss them. What do you think?

There'll be plenty of confusion when so large a company arrives. I can easily slip in and—"

"Not so fast, El Cid," Carlos interrupted, biting on his straw. "Personal soldiers are different from the stupid city guards. They have to have eyes in their heads if they want to keep their fancy tabards. You'll have to carefully pick just the right time and place and make sure your legs are in working order if you don't want to end up with the rats in the Alcalde's dungeons."

Francho flashed his engaging smile. He knew Carlos enjoyed the role of senior advisor and that he was right about the alertness of personal guards versus the lazy Hermandad riffraff whose vigilance in guarding the citizens was never too expert. But he felt Carlos ignored how experienced he was. Six years of successful stickyfingers counted for something. . . . "Don't worry. You know I could steal the pillow from under the bishop's fat tail without him skipping a single *Deus Benitus.*" He punched Carlos in the arm lightly. "I'll have my souvenirs and they won't even know I was there. I'm thinking the time to move is when they arrive, that should be about sundown if Pepi has heard correctly. Not dark enough, true, but they'll be tired and unwary, and it seems the best occasion to have a stab at them before they disappear behind the Alcalde's gates."

Carlos listened to him calmly, and Pepi was hardly breathing. Confidently he continued. "As for place, it will have to be wherever I see there is an opportunity to separate a prize from its owner. If Pepi makes a diversion I can be on them and gone in one second. It will be easy, like flicking the hat from a blind man's head."

"That's the sort of reckless optimism that could be the ruin of you, my friend. Nothing that results in gain is easy, remember that, especially where you risk getting a lance in your ribs for any misstep or ill luck. Still, you have courage and brashness, and most likely they will see you through. They always have."

The black-eyed gaze locked with the blue one. Carlos decided Francho had not grown overly much yet, even though his shoulders were broadening and his neck had thickened; he was still built slim enough to disappear through a crowd. The youth was smart, and in fact Carlos gave him a silent respect for his ability to read and write and to think quickly. There was an ease with which he approached the world which sometimes made Carlos envious. But Francho was often cocky and imprudent, taking unnecessary risks for the exhilaration of it.

One corner of Carlos's mouth twitched. "Listen, Francho, think twice tonight if no opportunity looks worth the risk. You'll possibly have another chance at them before they ride out. We do not want to lose you. Seriously, *amigo.*"

Francho's smile held affection. He knew it was to Carlos's benefit to caution against excess, for if any one of them were caught and lashed or had a few bones snapped by the guard captain they might implicate the whole family. Yet the boy felt his friend was concerned more for his safety at this moment, and it touched him.

"*Sí,* seriously, Carlos. I give you my word to use good sense. I don't relish being taken, either."

Carlos turned his attention to Pepi. "Did you hear how many ride with the Count?"

"Y-yes, many, so the constable said. He told the smith to get his fire good and hot for they are riding all the way from S-Seville. At least thirty horsemen and more beside that on mule and foot, a lady's litter and ten well-loaded wagons."

"You're correct, *amigo.*" Carlos transferred his gaze and inclined his head at Francho. "This looks too rich to pass up. It occurs to me that the illustrious Count of Tendilla must have fine horseflesh under his men, and there will be no moon tonight. If the main party camping outside the walls is close to the Playenda gully, we can run the horses off and into our cave between the guards' snores. The bigger the party the more likely someone will wake up to piss and discover us, but not even Ferdinand the Royal gets God's safe conduct through this life, eh, *hombres?*" His solemn wink at Francho acknowledged what his face hadn't shown; he was just as avid as his companions to raid this treasure trove which had suddenly hove into view.

Carlos and some friends had discovered years ago a large, hidden cave under the banks of a meandering river a few scraggly bushed leagues across the plain from Ciudad Real. It had made a perfect stash for purloined animals awaiting the middlemen who would take them to distant towns for sale. The Playenda gully, an almost dry offshoot of the same river with banks overgrown with brush and tall reeds, would conveniently act as a screened highway direct to the cave.

Pepi, who, in imitation of his brother, was also chewing on

a straw, watched Carlos unfold his lanky bones and stand up to brush clinging straw bits from the skirt of his knee-length tunic and black wool hosen. "Where d-do you go now, C-Carlos?" the boy asked hopefully, even though he knew that he wouldn't be invited.

"To talk with Estaban and Diego Patiza and arrange for tonight. But Pepi, don't tell Dolores about this one or I will cut off your monkey nose."

"Why?"

"Because if there are any noblewomen riding in the train they will be festooned with gems enough to make your head reel. Dolores is excited by glitter. She'll get careless and with private guards that is dangerous."

"She'll learn of it anyhow," Francho shrugged. "The party probably rides by close to our doors. Or she'll hear word of it."

"That we can't help, but better later, after they've reached the Alcalde's house, than sooner."

"She'll open your veins for you when she finds out," Francho chuckled, "and mine too."

Carlos's thin lips slid into the suspicion of a smile. "None of us lives forever. I'll alert Papa and Alfredo." He clapped Francho on the shoulder and ruffled Pepi's hair at the same time. With a brief nod of the head and crackle of straw underfoot, he strode between them and was gone.

"I wish I w-was old enough to steal horses," Pepi confided wistfully as he watched Francho bite at the corner of his thumbnail, brows drawn together in thought. "Then I would take the fastest one for myself, a great charger with red velvet reins, and r-r-ride quick as the wind like a fearsome knight—"

"Sí, and they would ride you quick to the dungeons, estúpido, if they found a beggar like you mounted on a rich man's horse. I'm going up to sharpen my knife. How is yours? Dull as usual?"

"I'll go get it," said Pepi, his button eyes brightening.

❧ *Chapter 2* ❧

FRANCHO SAT ON his straw pallet under the low, second-story ceiling and ground his small knife carefully against a whetstone, which he held between his knees, drawing the blade up and down against the oiled stone with precise strokes. His dark brows were drawn together under the unruly black curls falling damply on his forehead with the heat, and he whistled softly through his teeth. Musing, he was unmindful of the stuffy air or of his aunt's faint but strident cries rising from the clatter of the kitchen a floor below.

His thoughts flowed around a possible strategy for the evening's work, but they were soon blunted under the hypnotic rhythm of his task. A distant church bell ringing out noon drifted him into an uncharacteristic reverie, and he recalled, as if the years were just days, the solemn pealing of the bells at Santo Domingo del Campo gathering the pious brothers to their worship all through the day and night.

Images rose in his mind's eye of the gloomy, thick-walled monastery where he had been abandoned as a baby and which he had left when he was nine: of patient, gray-haired Frey Ignacio, ah, was he still alive; of bumbling Jorge, the other foundling baby raised along with him; and of the old but beautiful Roman-arched church, where his child's dreams and budding love of music had soared along with the brothers' exalted voices.

Some of the memories were not so pleasant: of endless polishing of silver candlesticks and reliquaries; of the many Latin prayers to be memorized word for word and repeated constantly (and almost forgotten now, he realized wryly); of the austere little cell in which he and Jorge slept, bitterly cold in winter, suffocating in summer, and filled with an ear-ringing silence that nagged at the nerves of a small boy who yearned to shout until the stone walls echoed.

There were good memories, too. There was a field behind the refectory, where he and Jorge had played, running and shouting and tumbling as they pleased, with no care for the ragged jerkins that covered them. And evening vespers . . .

He closed his eyes for a moment and saw the high-vaulted, shadowed church, its nave lit with hundreds of flickering winks of fire that shed warm yellow light on the great silver crucifix over the altar and the white-robed brothers with their tonsured heads. How he had loved the church, the singing, the rich tonalities of the chant. Even as a child it had seemed to seep beneath his skin and fill him up, and he remembered the beautiful painted-wood Madonna with shiny lips who looked down on him from a high niche, smiling and urging him to sing too. . . .

It occurred to Francho, as he considered his short past, that it was strange that a nine year old raised from infancy inside a cloister had felt so compelling a need for excitement that he had finally run away. And he wondered if his urge to live in the outside world had been born in him as a heritage from the unknown man who'd sired him.

Francho had to smile to think of how strongly he had wanted to become a soldier, how innocently he thought the Christians' commanders were waiting just for him to save Spain from the Moors and become a greater hero than El Cid himself.

The good brothers had undertaken to raise a wailing babe who had been abandoned at their gate wrapped in a fine wool blanket and dressed in a linen gown, obviously not the child of a common whore. The name "Francisco" was scrawled on a parchment scrap, and after due deliberation the abbot decided this name was God's will, even though Domingo, he felt, would have been more suitable.

Francho was nurtured and instructed until he was nine, with the eventual goal of passing him through his novitiate and into the community of brothers. But the boy had discovered that by clambering up a chestnut tree growing against the monastery wall and lying along a broad limb he could drink in the sights and sounds of the vivid life on the road below, where not only locals and travelers passed by but also contingents of troops raised by Ferdinand and Isabella. With trumpets blaring they clattered south by the thousands in order to lend their arms to the long and bloody Christian siege occurring outside the Moorish city of Alhama.

In front of Francho's astonished eyes unrolled long cavalcades of men of high rank and experience, the cream of Castilian and Catalan nobility proud in their shining cuirasses. They were followed by ranks of cantering knights and squires and the tramping, sweating foot soldiers attached to their personal houses, as well as levies of impressed regulars from the cities. In the rear rumbled lumbering, heavily loaded supply carts, the drivers urging their mules on with whips and purple curses.

And in addition, to further this secular seduction, there was Rodrigo, a penniless mercenary who finally died on the eve of San Simon, suffering in the damp cell made available to him by the kind brothers who had honored his wish to breathe his last on holy ground. A small boy had been appointed to bring him drink and what food he could swallow, and the luckless man made friends with the child. It helped him pass the time as he wrestled with the dark angel of death.

'Drigo told Francho there were two kinds of men on earth: the fighters and the prayers, the doers and the thinkers, the ones who accomplish and the ones who accept. Solemnly regarding the thin little form before his fevered eyes, he told Francho he was sure that he was meant to be a fighter, ward of God or no, just as he was sure that Francho's sire, whoever he might have been, was a soldier.

"But how do you know that?" questioned the child, his heart thumping with excitement as he imagined having a father who was a glorious soldier in a plumed casque. "How do you know I should be a soldier?"

"I can tell it, lad, by just looking into your eyes, so blue and steady. The common man here does not have eyes the color of the sky, lad, your people must have been of those fierce ones from the north. But yours are the eyes that should belong to a worldly man, not a monk—one with a strong right arm and a powerful fist. You are young yet, and still stringy, but believe what Rodrigo says, lad, for I have seen boys and I have seen men and I have looked more keenly through them than their confessors. It is my way."

Rodrigo's leg was gangrenous. It was discolored and swollen and smelled bad. It should have been cut off, but while the man hurled black curses at the overturned wagon which had so badly crushed his limb, he preferred to die rather than let the chirurgeon amputate it.

Francho liked 'Drigo, even though he was coarse and a little frightening, with his dark, matted beard and powerful voice. The boy stole away from his duties every chance he got, to sit by the injured man's pallet and hear his tales of bloody battles and bravery, such as the story of how Rodrigo had once hacked thirty men to pieces with murderous swings of his double-edged sword until he fell half dead with three crossbow bolts in him, whereupon he used his remaining strength to hack open the belly of a horse and crawl inside the corpse to hide until the battle was over.

The older Francho could still hear the sonorous voice, surprisingly strong for a man whose end was near, growling at him, *"Vive Dios,* have you seen nothing but Latin books and psalms all your life? When I was your age I could handle a sword with no trouble and had tasted the honey of a pretty wench, and I fear me that by fourteen there was already blood on my hands. These priests, what do they know? God . . . and God, that is all. Good enough for some men, I'll warrant, but not for you, boy, you have too much blood in your gorge for that, I can tell. How old are you? Eight? Nine? Time enough to begin to learn how to grip life by the tail."

Francho, sitting cross-legged, leaned forward eagerly, a hundred questions burning to be asked. " 'Drigo, are the gentlemen that ride by with shiny breastplates and gold rings on every finger, are they . . . I mean, do they fight—"

Interrupting the stammering child, 'Drigo bellowed, "God's blood, are they good soldiers? Well . . . yes and no. Most of them have good training, fighting men through and through, ready to lead their troops into battle and ask no quarter. I tell you I have seen some valiant acts that would make you glad to call some of these nobles liege lord. Aha! But some of them sit shivering in their fancy feathers and venture not a toe from the camp until someone takes pity on their fainting souls and sends them back to their ladies, where they play the hero to the sickening.''

He frowned, surveying his rapt audience. "Why do you ask this?"

Francho hesitated for a moment under that stern look, then squared his thin shoulders and went on anyway. "Because if I were a soldier I would like to be a knight, with a gold saddlecloth on my horse and a big velvet hat with a plume. I would like to have a jeweled dagger, too. But I would be courageous like you, 'Drigo, and not run away from the enemy. Should I see a Moor, I would lop off his head with my sword and wipe the blood off on his tunic.'' The very thought brought a wolfish grin to the smooth-cheeked, olive-skinned face.

"Oho!" the sick man exclaimed. "A soldier in fine trappings, is that the lay of it?''

"I watch them every day from the big tree next to the wall. The *caballeros* water their horses at the trough, and I can hear them talking of places like Seville, and Valencia, and Toledo. Those must be great cities, 'Drigo, filled with knights and lords and bishops, even the King and Queen and the cardinals. 'Drigo, do you really think I could be a soldier?'' Without pausing for an answer Francho leaned closer, glancing around as if someone could hear. "Listen . . .''

Realizing there was a confidence coming, Rodrigo forced his pain-lined face into an expression of close attention.

"Being a friar is all right for Jorge—that's the other boy who lives here. He says he loves God too much to leave His service and he doesn't care about anything else. I love God too, but I could love Him while I was a soldier, just as much, couldn't I? I wouldn't make a good religious anyhow because Frey Ignacio says I lack patience. So I have made up my mind. I am going to be a soldier, not a monk.''

"All very well, lad. But how are you going to go about such a business?''

"Well, one night I shall swing myself over the wall and go to the town and offer myself as a soldier, ready to fight the heathen in the King's name. And in God's,'' he added quickly.

Rodrigo scratched at his heavy beard, noting the determined chin and serious blue gaze. "The Devil's belly, my little lad, you would make a handsome knight to woo a woman, but can you ride a steed? Can you duel with a broadsword? Or

24

heavy distaff? Can you use a pike? Or shoot an arquebus? Or draw a bow?"

Francho was not abashed by his lack of worldly attainments. "No, I can't. But I can learn, and quickly too. Frey Ignacio says I have a very agile mind. And I can wrestle. Jorge and I sometimes battle behind the stables just for fun. He is bigger than me but sometimes I win because I butt him in the stomach with my head and trip him. He never learns to watch out for that."

"Do you want me to tell you how to swing a broadsword, Francho?"

The boy nodded, a smile lighting his face.

"Then come back tomorrow with a broad stick about so long, and about so far down nail a smaller crosspiece. You shall be my pupil. But not a word of this to Frey Ignacio. He would broil your hide for you."

"No, not a word," promised Francho, entranced. The door to Paradise seemed to be swinging open.

"Ah, lad, I shall teach you things that will make you the scourge of the Moslem. I, Rodrigo, shall have a pupil. I shall pour into you all that has made me what I am, and you shall be even more," the dying warrior swore. He waited until the youngster left before falling back exhausted on the small bundle of clothes he used for a pillow, sweat gleaming on his forehead, his teeth clamped.

Francho went to sleep that night with his ears still holding the sound of Rodrigo's bass voice: ". . . scourge of the Moors . . . to the glory of God and Christ . . . Francho, the courageous . . ."

But alas, the lessons were never to be, for Francho could not sneak back to his friend for two days, and when he did Rodrigo was in high fever and half delirious. The silent monk who tended him padded out to join vespers services and Francho slipped in.

Rodrigo was muttering about omens and signs and insisted that there had been a sign he was to die soon. A black crow had flown through the window of the cell (except that there was no window), had circled the room, and had lit briefly at the foot of the man's pallet, finally flapping out again with an evil cry.

Rodrigo was flushed and hot, his black eyes burned, the great booming voice was reduced to a croak, which fought its way up through his chest with an effort. Drops of sweat stood out on his forehead, and now and then a deep groan escaped him. His leg, oozing under its soaked wrappings, was monstrously swollen, and the odor in the room was nauseating.

Francho gagged and wanted to run away. Ashamed of his fear and revulsion, he pressed his lips together hard and forced himself to draw nearer to the man. In a pitying effort to divert the sufferer from his pain, Francho pulled down the wide neckline of his jerkin and directed Rodrigo's attention to a puckered scar on his left shoulder blade, a mark about an inch and a half long, white against the olive skin. It was shaped like a cross, Frey Ignacio said, but Jorge had drawn him a picture of it and Francho knew it was shaped like a dagger with a down-curved hilt.

"What do you think, 'Drigo? Is this an omen too? Does it mean something?"

Rodrigo stared at the mark uncomprehendingly and then at the boy. His vision wavered and blurred and cleared again, and the boy before him had become twice as big, a man, while the white mark glowed ivorylike in the light of the candle set on the floor. Again everything swayed and shivered and it seemed to him the ivory dagger floated in space, writhing and twisting, and writing invisible words in black blood. He heard a terrible cry rend the air, a cry of disaster, a scream of despair, or was it a groan? Abruptly his head cleared and he saw Francho kneeling on the floor beside him, regarding him over his shoulder with pity and horror, and the dagger was merely a puckered scar on the child's thin back.

"Francisco," he whispered, and Francho turned and had to lean close to hear him, trying not to mind the putrid smell of the dying man's breath. "You will be a soldier, lad, destined to fight for Castile and for Leon. I have seen it written in letters of blood drawn by the dagger God has traced on your body. You are a secular servant of the Good Lord, boy, and not a priest. Listen to Rodrigo . . . he can read your omen. . . ."

He struggled to a half-sitting position and fumbled about in the bundle of possessions, then fell back grimacing and moaning, but in his hairy hand he grasped a small dagger in a wrought silver sheath. He shoved it through the rope belt holding Francho's jerkin close and then dropped his hand heavily, closing his eyes.

"Take it," he muttered weakly. "I have nothing else. Sword

was stolen from me by whoreson thieves in camp. This little blade has a clean and deadly thrust. Found it on a battlefield. . . in Brittany . . . belonged to a noble . . . you are my little friend . . . friend . . . the resurrection and the light . . . *ora pro nobis . . ."* Rodrigo's mind had wandered away. He breathed in short, shallow grunts.

Francho pulled the slim weapon from its sheath and leaned to the flickering candle to scrutinize it closer. The blade was long, narrow, and razor sharp; the tempered steel shone blue. The silver handle, above the wings of the guard, was twisted into the shape of a serpent's head, with tiny, glittering rubies for eyes. It was surprisingly light, even with the sheath, which had a hooded, coiled snake hammered into it of a type totally different from the few Francho had ever encountered in the fields. The whole weapon was only about twice the length of his small hand.

"Oh." Francho breathed to himself, thrilled, turning the gift over and over and examining it for long moments before finally slipping it back into its close-fitting sheath. He raised a face lit with rapture to find Rodrigo staring at him with eyes briefly aware.

"With that little sticker you go for the heart, lad, just slip it in above the top rib and you're done. 'Twill scarce make a slit. A slit . . . no wider than a maiden's . . ." The agonized eyes squeezed closed again.

Francho wanted to tell 'Drigo how he would cherish this munificent gift, that he would never part with it, that it would accompany him on all his forays against the Moslems, but he was so overwhelmed the words would hardly come.

" 'Drigo . . . ?"

Rodrigo groaned and didn't open his eyes. The flames of Hell were slowly roasting his body and licking at his heart. But his pride forbade him company even in dying. He wanted this last acquaintance's memory of him to be otherwise than this fearful pain.

"Leave me, boy, I am weary," he ordered. "Go, now, and leave me be."

"But 'Drigo, I want to stay with you."

"No . . . God, tell you, I wish it. Francisco . . . Francisco . . . good lad, call the dispenser to me . . . tell him to bring his poppy tincture . . . right away . . . pray for me, young soldier, pray for me." The groaning breath again came in short gasps.

Grateful to reach the fresh night air again, Francho gulped in deep breaths. He ran quickly to tell the dispensary monk the dying man needed medicine to ease his pain.

Later on, slipping around a corner of the courtyard and momentarily hidden from any eyes, Francho fished under his tunic and pulled the dagger from where he had stuck it in his loincloth. As he slipped it from its sheath a sliver of moonlight leaped down the blade and spilled off the sharp tip, and the snake's ruby eyes sparkled darkly in his open hand. A delicious shiver ran down his spine as the light blade balanced perfectly on one finger. "This is mine . . . this is mine," he whispered to himself and to the shadows of the night, which whispered back. "It is a sign. It is an omen."

He put the blade back in its sheath and ran lightly across the silent yard, for most of the monks were already snoring away their few hours of sleep between vespers and compline. He reached the second-story window of the small cell he shared with Jorge by means of an overturned tun and a strong vine. That night he slept under his threadbare blanket with the hard joy of the silver sheath pressing against his side.

A few days later, hearing again the rattle of drums and flourish of trumpets as another armed column announced their approach to the town of Tijuna, Francho scooted to his vantage point in the heavily leafed tree, this time, thanks to the silver stiletto he had carefully hidden, feeling almost like a member of the exalted company going past.

The gentlemen were gorgeously dressed, with polished steel breastplates gleaming over silk doublets wrought in every color of the peacock's tail, and with short, jaunty velvet capes flung over their shoulders. Their hands flashed with rings, and gold and silver threads ran through their hosen. Their steel helmets, though, and greaves and sollerets were all packed away on baggage mules because the weather was too warm for such martial display and the enemy too far off, something of a disappointment to the little boy who gazed down on the warriors with such rapture. But the elegance of their plumed toques and hats like folded, velvet turbans, the embroidered and tasseled trappings of their great horses, and the brilliance of the heraldic and church banners fluttering proudly over their heads was more than enough to set a child's heart hammering with excitement.

As he watched, words kept running through his mind, what he had said to poor 'Drigo and what the man had said to him;

he knew that the solemn, dedicated life at Santo Domingo had crept entirely away from his heart; that he was sick of polishing candlesticks and saying prayers and reading Latin and scrubbing the abbot's floors. Why not run away now, tonight, he thought. Why not? There are the doers and the thinkers. Why not—

Suddenly he heard a twig on the ground crackle and realized the cortege had already passed by. Twisting his head around he saw Frey Ignacio standing below, purple with indignation.

"Francisco! Come down from there! Come down instantly, you scapegrace! May God forgive you for your impunities. Villain, descend, I say!"

Slowly Francho disentangled himself from the branches, sighing sadly. The tree had been a good hiding place in summer. Its leaves provided cover and the brothers usually walked with eyes downcast anyhow. It would be the first place Frey Ignacio would look for him now. He glanced once more at the beautiful, secular world over the wall to strengthen his resolve, then shinned down the trunk to land lightly at the friar's feet, head hanging, guiltily awaiting the storm.

Sitting on his pallet at Papa el Mono's, the daydreaming Francho shifted his weight as if he could still feel the sting of that beating on his buttocks, a punishment he must have surely deserved, he thought wryly from a more mature viewpoint, if the kindly old man had been driven to such anger. Absently, with an experienced thumb, he tested the curved-tip knife he was honing, then laid it aside and took up Pepi's to sharpen.

Francho felt he was lucky to have fainted on Papa el Mono's doorsill a few weeks after he had run away, for the family had taken him in and trained him for a trade—not as distinguished or honest as soldiering, but just as exciting. He had become so fascinated with the kaleidoscope of patrons and travelers and the constant commotion at the inn that all thought of continuing his lonely quest to find the war was forgotten.

Coached by Papa's cohort, the huge and ugly Alfredo, he had soon become quite dexterous with the little curved knife they gave him. As a pickpocket and cutpurse he grew to be a great success, wringing tears of happiness from Tía Esperanza's eyes and even grudging nods of approval from Papa. He was allowed to keep a few maravedis in each haul, and sometimes he held back from turning over a trinket or so that he particularly liked. Soon he was amazed at his own wealth.

By his last count it was the sum of six silver reales, a gold buckle, a small ivory cross—particularly valuable and rare— his silver stiletto with the snake's head hilt, and his lute, all hidden cunningly, except for the lute, under a plank in the floor.

The sin of stealing—a great evil, according to Frey Ignacio —he had rationalized out of existence with the fact that Tía Esperanza was a very pious woman and she said that stealing was merely a forced charity to the poor, earning blessings for both thief and victim alike. He stubbornly resisted looking any further into it because he liked his life, because he knew if he listened too hard the Latin student inside would begin to wag a mental finger at him and to whisper stern moral lectures learned from a cloistered monk in a rich order who knew nothing of having to earn one's bread.

He was proud of the loot he had accumulated, although he kept it well hidden away, especially from Dolores, who would steal the eyes from a blind man. He was shruggingly aware of the danger in his trade, but his contempt for the Hermandad, the city guards, had grown as he tricked and evaded them time and again.

His luck lay in the fact that he was clever and slippery as an eel. Pepi too, moving up from pickpocket to cutpurse, was able to strike and melt away before the victim knew what had befallen him. Dolores delighted in preying upon women, but they discovered lately she also made a fine stall. She'd get in front of a male mark and accidentally—so the mark thought —press her backside into his groin, swaying away and then doing it again as the crush of bodies presumably pushed her, keeping the startled, flattered, and interested mark nailed in place for the few seconds it took for the hook's light-fingered skill to clip the man's purse, even if it were chained, and move away undetected. The fools who grabbed at her buttocks got their feet stomped on or her sharp elbow wanged into their gut, to the laughter of those around who saw the crude byplay. The first and only time Dolores was nabbed, when she was about ten, he'd seen her battle and kick her way out of the embrace of a grunting guard like a spitting cat.

Francho was happy enough. He had a bed, friends, some coins in his pocket, and a daring life, perhaps escalating one day to horsethief, like Carlos. Six years for the transformation from altar acolyte to petty thief, from innocent scholar to wily rascal! He tested Pepi's knife on an old piece of stiff leather as voices below, laughter, the clack of wooden trenchers being stacked impinged on his train of thought. I wonder, he mused, if I have changed so much so fast, might I not change again? And to what, next time? Why does it even come into my mind that I shall leave here someday?

For a moment he listened to a whispery interior voice that rustled, "Who am I?" And his mind brushed against all the unanswered questions of his birth and the mysterious, unaccountable, sometimes guilty-feeling person who tramped around in his head once in a while. But immediately he slapped the thoughts away like annoying, buzzing insects. They made him angry because he had no answers, and so he dismissed them.

❧ *Chapter 3* ❧

THE SUN WAS close to dipping behind the walls of the inn as Francho reached the ladder serving as staircase into a back passageway. He drew back as he saw, standing below, Dolores and Carlos, who had returned from his original mission and seemed to be leaving again.

Dolores had a blue cloth wrapped around her head which fastened behind and under the single thick braid of reddish hair falling down her back. The usual stray strands which often wisped into her eyes were now caught back under the headcloth so that her sooty-lashed gray eyes, wide and tilted, stood out clearly. She wore a clean homespun bodice with a skirt which reached her ankles. She grasped at Carlos's arm, her bare feet planted solidly on the floor, her manner openly suspicious.

"Where do you go, Carlos?" she challenged him. "You flaunt such high and mighty airs today, as if you know something I don't. Why are you in such a hurry?"

"Leave hold, Dolo. When do I have to account to you for my actions?"

With lifted chin and one hand on her narrow hip she complained, "I thought we all worked together, but I can see, now you are such a gentleman with a silver buckle to your belt, that we are not good enough for you anymore."

"Perhaps, and perhaps it is because I do things my way, sister, and we only work together when I say we do." He twitched his arm from her grasp. "Take yourself into the kitchen, girl. Tía probably needs you. And stop following me like a sniffing hound on the trail. . . ."

The choice of words was unfortunate. A deeper color suffused Dolores' sun-browned cheeks. "Hound?" she erupted. "It's you who are the beast. Going behind the stable with the fat Philita, aren't you? Don't think I haven't seen you squeezing her. Bah! *Qué bobería!*" To Dolores, who both admired and feared her brother, his interest in females, which meant the scullions and barmaids in the area, was silliness she couldn't understand. She thought a successful horsethief should be above bothering with giggling women.

Carlos's lean face darkened. "Mind your own business, *perrita*," he warned, his low voice threatening. "If you don't learn how I'll give you a lesson. Remember the last time, you couldn't sit for a week. Now get back to your chores, *pronto.*" He seized her arm in a grip forestalling argument and propelled her in the direction of the kitchen.

Dolores went, with a defiant jerk of her arm from his grip and a flip of her shoulder, cursing under her breath. But she went.

Watching from above Francho shook his head in admiration for Carlos's ability to squelch Dolores. The brother sometimes slapped her around when she transgressed but in no way that would really hurt her, for there was a bond of real affection among the innkeep's wife's three children. Still, when Carlos fixed Dolores or Pepi with his hard stare, they obeyed him. Hailing Carlos to wait up, Francho quickly clambered down the ladder.

Shortly after, a still sulky Dolores, poised in the door of the scullery ready to slop out a bucket of greasy water, lowered it instead as she spied Francho making his way around an untidy trash heap to a little door in the back wall half hidden by heaped up kindling wood. She was almost certain they were cutting her out of a fair gull, although she couldn't imagine what since today was no special day when a big crowd might gather. Watching Francho she unconsciously put up one hand to smooth down her hair, then remembered she had braided it and covered it with her next-to-best kerchief. But maybe she had meant to smooth her tangled thoughts, she considered, for lately she was always so anxious to be somewhere around Francho, in spite of his teasing, and when he was near there was that giddy—that excited sort of feeling—that left her confused, anxious to cling to the more familiar emotions that had so far ruled her young life—and yet greedy to feel more of the pleasant shivers that she felt when he turned his startlingly blue eyes on her.

Irritated at how even this small glimpse of him caused an accelerated beating of her heart, she stuck her tongue out at the spot where her aunt's foster son had been and heaved away the water in her bucket with enough vehemence to drown the entire world.

She turned back to the kitchen, where she would help Tía shell almonds, suddenly not even caring anymore to follow her sneaky cohorts. She advised herself to think about the silver coin she had acquired that morning and not about how those lice had tried to humiliate her in her bath as if she were a dragtail child. She was certainly not going to think about how handsome Francho had grown; could it be because his height had suddenly outdistanced hers? The Devil with him. It was more satisfying and less upsetting to think of the silver coin as it lay gleaming in her hand. She had special plans for all the coins she could safely separate from her duty as honest daughter to Papa.

On the north end of the *plaza major* rose the impressive new church, rendered in high Gothic style and set upon a base of broad but shallow steps facing in three directions. Forming the other side of the large plaza, from which radiated five main streets, were three-story buildings providing roofed arcades which sheltered shops, letter writers' booths, money-lenders, food vendors, harness makers, apothecaries, beggars, idlers, and assorted townspeople.

It was a universal custom for travelers upon first entering a town for the night to visit the church to give thanks for a safe journey. Banking on the Count's party making this stop, Francho lurked in a deep recess of one of the church's elaborately carved and ribbed Gothic doorways, a felt cap pulled low over his ears and eyes to partially hide his face. He had finally decided that his best chance—perhaps only chance—of success would be at the church, where the travelers would have to dismount, for if they returned to pray tomorrow they would be too rested and alert.

There was still activity about in the early twilight. Vendors banged closed their shutters, tired apprentices and journey-men headed toward their homes, a group of black-robed religious trod the cobbles slowly toward the church, some ragged peasants strained to move a heavy cart with a splin-tered axle. And at the far end, opposite the church, four or five helmeted city guards with pikes made ready to start on their nightly rounds. Francho sniffed and wiped his nose on his sleeve. The setting wasn't exactly ideal; close-packed, dis-tracted crowds such as on execution days were better, but since seldom would he find the opportunity to separate a grandee from his purse, the prize seemed worth the extra risk of an exposed position. The gathering darkness helped. He sent up a short prayer to San Bismas.

From one of the feeder streets a small retinue of horsemen clopped smartly into the plaza, the jingling of bells on the horses' emblazoned furnishings causing heads in the immedi-ate vicinity to turn. The party proceeded to the church steps and dismounted. Peering from behind his embrasure's heavy stone piers, Francho gratefully saw that most of the Count's retainers had been left outside of town to make camp, leaving only five men-at-arms, wearing crested tabards over chain mail shirts, to contend with. He would have been disappointed—Pepi's information was exaggerated obviously since only two noblemen swung off their horses—but both of these were richly dressed and had purses suspended from their belts. Either one would do, but something told him the taller one was the illustrious Count. The smallness of the party made him curse the stupidity of not taking Dolores along. They could have gotten both purses. . . .

Two guards led the horses away to water them at the trough; the other three followed the Count and his companion up the steps at a respectful distance.

". . . and not only that, but the pain in my right thigh has become worse, so that I sit crooked in the saddle. God's mercy, but this has been a bone-rattling trip."

The Count of Tendilla, smoothing the rumpled maroon velvet of his fur-trimmed tunic, glanced with reserved amuse-ment at the small, finely attired man glumly limping up the steps beside him. "It would seem from the account of your various aches and pains, my poor Pietro, that you are rapidly falling to pieces. We came but fifteen leagues today."

"*E verro,* My Lord, but can one call that jumble a road? And at the mad pace we took it? The human body, even so hardy a one as mine"—he worked a silk-clad shoulder around to relieve the muscles—"is not meant to take such grueling punishment."

"Fie, maestro, I have seen you do three times fifteen leagues and remain as fresh as the mountain air—when you had your heart in it."

"Ah, there is the crux," the Italian scholar agreed. "I am disappointed to have left the delights of Cordoba to go north at this moment. With the winter scarce here yet, with the Moslem crowing over our defeat at Loja and gathering forces for another attack, with my war chronicles in a state of chaos and incompleteness . . ."

Tendilla took up the litany ". . . and with Louis of France poised with an army to the north in Navarre, the Court preparing to move to Madrid in a month, and your patron's estates and revenues calling for attention, I assure you life will not be dull, my friend, just because the Moor has been left behind."

Di Lido's lips pursed as if he had just eaten a lemon. "Bah! Madrid, a rural little village. Why not, at least, Valladolid, or Burgos?"

"In time, in time, maestro. Methinks the pain in your leg has made you liverish," Tendilla remarked dryly.

"Might I say, Excellence, that in view of the fact that the Marquis of Cadiz has heretofore coveted your position next the throne, and that an . . . *Diavolo!*"

A brown streak had detached itself from a side doorway, slamming into the Count and knocking him off his balance and into his astonished companion. Flailing to recover himself before they both went tumbling down the steps, Tendilla had the impression of a flash of steel, a swift tug, a muffled clink. Securing his footing he whirled about, but the thief was off, having bolted under his arm and down the steps like a panicked hare, faster than the men-at-arms could react.

The shrill voice of the little Italian seemed to pierce Francho's back as he leaped the steps three at a time: *"Al ladro, al ladro! Rubatore!"* A pike whizzed past his shoulder to clatter on the stones, just missing a group of open-mouthed citizens arriving early for evening mass, who stood arrested between one step and another as he fled past them. "There he goes," voices cried behind him to the scattered people in the square. "Catch him, catch him!"

Francho streaked for the escape he had mapped out, dodging a grabbing hand, jumping a jutting leg, his head down, legs pumping, showing the pursuing men-at-arms a clean pair of heels. Instinct warned him to weave away as a city guard who'd been behind the cart with the broken axle jumped into his path, but the man managed to catch his arm and swing him around. His frantic kick to the man's groin broke the insecure grip and he wrenched away, bolting toward a narrow alley with the Count's men no more than ten sword lengths behind him and the Hermandad guards behind them. The pound of their boots was so close he was sure he felt their breath on the back of his neck as they furiously cursed and yelled at him to halt.

Zigzagging through clefts between houses he purposely chose the narrowest and most rubble-strewn to eliminate anyone on horseback or zealous citizens who might try to help the guards. He ran around the corner of a building and used the seconds when they couldn't see him to evaporate into another narrow alley going back the way he had come, a point at which he usually lost the Hermandad, who figured him to have gone forward into a twisting passage showing across the street. But the Count's men were swifter and not so easily shaken off, one somehow saw him and hollered, and then they were behind him again. He emerged briefly into a square and, hurtling aside some startled residents who happened to be in his path, reached the opposite side to dart once more into a dank alley. Lying heavily within his tunic was the purse embroidered with the Mendoza coat-of-arms. He'd be broiled in Hell if he gave up such a prize.

His chest was tight and his breath came in rasps, sweat was pouring into his eyes; he whipped off his cap to dash it away. It was getting hard to see, a point in his favor, for he knew this warren of tight passages and they didn't. He dashed from a side street, lungs straining, praying to San Bismas between gasps of breath, and heard a sword slide from its scabbard behind him as his pursuers pounded in his wake. They were gaining. He didn't dare a backward glance. Leaping a small pile of bricks left by builders he fought down panic and scuttled into an odiferous little slit between two uncompleted buildings, slipping on something disgusting but recovering himself. A sharp pain stabbed through his chest as he realized he'd mistaken the buildings, he didn't know this passage. He stumbled suddenly over a half-buried rock and fell forward on one knee, his outstretched palm landing on something sharp, but he frantically scrambled up and lurched on, barely escaping the point of the leading guard's sword.

He windmilled forward only a short way in the gloom before only his sixth sense and an outstretched arm saved him from ramming into a blank wall barring his way.

The closest pursuer pounced on him, spinning him around and flinging him against the wall where he was held by muscle and the point of a sword until the man could catch his heaving breath. Francho gulped air, struggling unsuccessfully against the brawny grip, cursing with what wind he had.

"Give it over, gutter spawn," the furious soldier wheezed, laboring to speak. "Hand over that purse before I slit your filthy gizzard."

Two other of Tendilla's guards panted up, pikes lowered. Stubbornly Francho shook his head. A lump rose in his throat with the bitterness of his defeat, with the fear that his luck had run out. Momentarily he glared at them, but his eyes darted to either side and he noticed a crevice between the houses to his right, narrow, cramped, short enough so just at that moment he glimpsed a muleteer, waggling his whip, pass before the far opening on the street. His heart leaped—

The exhausted soldier made a grab for the tell-tale bulge of the purse under Francho's tunic, his sword point lowering as he did so, and with a sudden downward plunge Francho ducked under the man's arm, swiveled past the other two, who thought their prey had been cornered, and slid into the God-sent passage like a bug into a crack, passing through it sideways and emerging onto the narrow street just in time to skitter in front of the lead mules of a caravan.

The outraged guards followed, scraping their broader forms through the narrow slit only to find themselves bottled up in the crack by a long line of doubly hitched mules plodding stolidly past in spite of the crack of an impatient whip over their heads. The frustrated men started to hack wildly through the traces to get to the other side of the flare-lit street, cursing the slow-moving animals, cursing the muleteer, who, astonished at this sudden attack, yelled and tried to drive them off with cracks of his long whip. Frightened by the attempts of flailing men to climb over their huge burdens, the animals backed up and knocked over one of the guards, who had to be rescued from the tangle of reins by his mates. The leader, roaring with fury, attempted to climb over the animals' lumpily packed backs but was pulled off by the red-faced muleteer, who had squeezed his way up to them.

By the time they reached the alley down which their prey had fled, Francho was nowhere to be seen, and the few onlookers shrugged their shoulders. The bulky guard with the sword sheathed his weapon with a clang and swore a disgusted oath.

Lying prone to peer over the edge of a flat tile roof not far away, Francho gripped his arms about himself tightly to hold in his laughter over the ridiculous scene he had just witnessed and watched as the guards glumly pulled themselves together and turned to go back to the *plaza major*. Actually he was weak with relief, and as soon as they left he lay on his back on the still-warm red tiles and breathed deeply, trying to relax the tension in his muscles. He'd never had so close a call. He could still feel the prick of the sword point aimed at his gullet, the squeeze of fright in his gut when he thought it was all over. He scrubbed at the dust in his eyes with his sleeve. The cut on his palm was bleeding and stung, and his imagination produced the dank stink of the Alcalde's dungeons—or was that only his shoes, where he'd raced through the litter of rubbish and excrement.

Closing weary eyes, he smiled. He had come a hair's breadth from grief but he had his purse. He rested for a while before feeling his way down the gnarled vine which had helped him to the roof of the building—part of a ceramics works it would seem from the smell of clay and paint. His chest puffed out. The contents of the purse he had snatched would buy him more than a painted plate.

The evening was still early as he slipped back through the little door in the scullery yard, filled a bucket at the well, and avoided the stair from the common room and various eyes by scrambling up the rear ladder to the hostel's top floor.

In his tiny cubicle he unbuckled his belt, and the heavy purse fell to the floor with a loud, metallic jangle. Aching to open it, he forced himself to wait, savoring the anticipation while he first kicked off his malodorous shoes, then cleaned the small cut on his palm, which had stopped bleeding. He pulled off his clothes, wrung out a rag in the water to wash his

39

face and then the sweat and grime from his body, giving himself a going-over befitting the new owner of such a splendid purse. He splashed some water to smooth down the unruly dark hair curling into his eyes, donned his other tunic and hosen, and shoved his feet into worn straw slippers. Taking the bucket from his cubicle to a small window overlooking a back alley he yelled, "'Way, below!" and slung the dirty water out.

Only then, back in his lair, did he finally give himself the pleasure of slipping two fingers into the satin-lined purse and pulling open the drawstring.

Famished, he pounded down the ladder again to the kitchen room where an old hag squatted at a hearth basting and turning braces of sizzling fowl. She greeted him with a cackle. "Where is everyone?" he asked her, meaning the family, meanwhile grabbing a piece of bread and a hunk of hard cheese from a littered board up on wooden horses. The ancient, enjoying the warmth of the fire, wagged her head toward the common room. "Hee, hee, hee . . . full house tonight."

Francho wolfed his snack with a couple of swallows of leftover wine from a used cup, then went to peer from behind the tied-back leather curtain at the kitchen entry, a vantage spot where he could see the patrons without being seen. The common room was the same noisy mixture of babble, guffaws, and coarse people as it had been when he first viewed it six years ago, a long, airless chamber with a low, whitewashed ceiling supported by rough-cut beams, and a worn plank floor. Delicious smells emanated from a smoke-blackened hearth, where Tía Esperanza alternated her attention between a sleepy Pepi, who was turning the spit, and the task of basting the fat-dripping pig impaled over the fire. A ragged minstrel sat on a three-legged stool plinking the strings of a Moorish guembri. Snatches of song were hurled at him from all over the room, and Papa el Mono and several barmaids made their smiling way among the noisy throng, the full pitchers of wine in their hands held high to avoid being spilled.

There was a blind beggar back of the stack of wine barrels munching on a bone and grinning into his black world, and loud gamblers in a corner, rattling big dice over a pile of copper coins. Wet-lipped women sat on laps and giggled and drank as much as the men; already one lolled boneless across a long table, croaking nonsense. A table of merchants was slightly separated from the rest, around which the hungry diners stuffed their mouths and wiped their greasy fingers on their good tunics. A blowsy creature with bouncing breasts purposely loosed the strings on her bodice and made a lewd suggestion as she flounced past them.

Francho's spirits were slightly dampened. Tía and Papa were busy serving, Pepi turned the spit, Dolores seemed nowhere around, and Carlos, he knew, was with Esteban in a cart, delivering to the nobleman's encampment a barrel of cheap wine, which they would pass off as a welcoming gift from the Alcalde, and which they hoped would help the company sleep soundly that night. He pressed his elbow against the purse, once more hidden under his tunic, which was bagged out over his belt. He frowned his annoyance. Here he was eager to show off his treasure and tell the tale of his hair's breadth escape and there was no one to hear it.

He mooched across the entry court aimlessly, kicked at a rusty nail, got out of the way of some patrons leading their mounts through the gate, and was considering going back for more to eat when his frown cleared as he spied Dolores just coming from the stable.

His shrill, short whistle stopped Dolores in her tracks, and she waited for him under a lantern hung from an iron arm on the side of the building. She tapped her foot with fake impatience for she was actually glad to see him, bored with the evening's run-of-the-mill patrons and curious to know where he'd been. She could almost see the gleam in his bold, blue eyes as he loped toward her, a big grin splitting his face. He was now taller than she, but that had happened only recently and not by much—although Tía said his legs were long and when his full height came he'd be useless as a cutpurse. Dolores wished he wouldn't outgrow her, she didn't care to look up at him when for so long they had been equals. She framed a scathing reply in her mind in case he had come to tease her.

"Well, what is it, *picaro?* Can't you see I am busy?" she demanded, her peevish tone reflecting the morning's contretemps.

"Not as busy as I've been, I'll wager. I want to show you something."

Dolores indicated her armload of straw. "That stupid Lina spilled a pan of hot grease all over the floor and broiled her arm besides. Tía put an herb poultice on her burn, and I'm bringing this to spread fresh on the floor."

They both leaped aside as a couple of inebriated horsemen clopped up to the stable halooing for the one harried hostler to take their mounts. "Wait until you see the loot I just hooked, you'll have trouble keeping your eyes in your head," he crowed. "I'd be kicking on a rope for this one, and almost was, too. But not here, it's too busy."

She could feel the excitement he could scarcely bottle up and her eyes widened. There were dire punishments for thievery, but hanging was reserved for the worst offenses. "What? What is it? Francho, show me."

"Hold a minute and I'll show you. Where? Here, this way, in here." Pulling her along by the wrist he ducked into the stables and kept going past the few animals tethered near the door and down to the rear of the long, dark, and dusty structure. He shoved her into an empty stall where a stream of light from the hanging lantern outside came through a rent in the boards forming the upper wall. They could see motes of dust dancing where the flickering rays pushed a path through the gloom and spread onto the scattered straw underfoot.

Francho knelt on the dirty straw and pulled the velvet purse from his tunic, pushing it into the light where the silver- and gold-embroidered noble emblem gleamed dully. He looked up and his eyebrows arched with rascal pleasure at the look of awe on her face.

Dolores's mouth hung open in wonder. *"Ay, mi madre!* It has a blazon on it!"* she breathed. She reached two tentative fingers to touch the coat of arms and then drew them back quickly. "It's—it's the coronet of a count, I think," she added, casting back in her memory to a long ago day when 'Fredo, who had once been a mercenary to an Aragonese nobleman, amused himself by teaching her what he knew of heraldry. "The blessed saints save us, if they had caught you, Francho, you'd have been beaten to death. But where did you get it? Oh, what a chance you took. . . ."

He was enjoying the mingled admiration and fright on her face. "But they didn't catch me, did they, or I wouldn't be here, goose. And when I tell you how I got away, you'll see it wasn't so simple." A short snort of laughter escaped him at the memory of the guards slashing at the mules' traces and cursing. "Those idiotic men-at-arms. Stupid, like cats watching at the wrong mousehole."

"But whose purse is it?"

His broad shoulders squared back. "The Count of Tendilla. The Queen's man on her right hand. He is laying over at the Alcalde's house tonight, on his way north with his household."

Dolores sat back on her heels, hands on hips, totally exasperated. "Aha! I *knew* something was offering. That miserable Carlos. Worse than he considers he is my master, he thinks that I don't know what I'm about, the sloptail. The putrid—" Francho broke her rising ire by wiggling the bag till it jingled, riveting her attention again on the well-filled reticule lying in the stream of light. "How much is there in it?" she asked breathlessly. Forgetting her indignation, she stared as if she expected the purse to get up on two legs and dance. The tip of her pink tongue darting out to moisten her lips.

Moving to sit cross-legged across from her, Francho shot his bolt with an expansive gesture. "How much, *hermanita?* A small fortune, that's how much. Enough to buy this whole hostelry and the Alcalde's house besides. Fifteen excellentes, five reales, six gold Italian ducats, and some coppers. I'll give Papa the excellentes, that should please his itching palm, but the rest is all mine, I'm keeping it, and if you spill a word I'll pull your thumbs from their sockets and jam them into your ears."

Dolores had wiggled herself closer to the purse. Francho could see her clearly now in her blue headcloth, her tipped gray eyes wide and lit with worshipful admiration. "Oh, I would never tell, Francho. Did we not take oath, the four of us, never to blab on each other? *Dios mío,* a *ricos hombre* has many guards, you have to tell me how you hooked this. Sometimes I think you're as smart as Carlos. And brave too. To get away without a scratch. With half the city after you . . ." She edged closer to the purse.

Unaccustomed to such flattery from Dolores, Francho basked in the praise and tried to put some modesty in his shrug. He was willing to tell her all about it, but she was still giving all her attention to the purse. Her eyes shone as she put forward her hand.

"Let me just touch it, Francho. Never have I touched anything belonging to a grandee."

That tickled him. "And had you, it would not have belonged to the grandee for very long." He chuckled. But his guard was down. He picked up the clinking purse and held it out to her.

As quick as a striking snake she snatched the purse from his hand, jumped up, and hid it behind her, stepping back slowly and giggling, and now the sparkle in her eyes meant mischief.

"Dolores, don't be funny."

"That's what I said this morning when you tried to throw me out of my bath, remember?"

Francho came to his knees, his mouth grinning in warning. "Dolores, give me that purse. Give it here, you sneaky brat."

"Hola, listen to him, the great lord. I told you this morning I'd get even. Maybe you're bigger than I am now, but I can still run faster. And now you'll know better than to vex me, *estúpido."*

She whirled to run but she had misjudged the length of his arms and wasn't fast enough. With one lunge he grabbed the back of her skirt, yanking her to the ground with a heavy thump. Squealing, she rolled over, the arm holding the purse shielded underneath her and kicked at him forcefully, catching him in the ribs with the toe of her shoe.

The silly presumption that led her to think she could get away with his loot had diverted him, but now his irritation mounted. He wasn't interested in playing children's games with a purse full of silver and gold. He fell on top of her, knocking the wind out of her lungs in a grunt. Holding her down he yanked hard at the arm underneath her, but she gritted her teeth and opposed him, pressing her weight down on it. Wrestling wasn't new to them, they'd often disputed physically in the past, even over a copper maravedi, and when they were much younger she could sometimes win, by dint of biting.

"Trampista!"

"Puerco!"

"Drop it or I'll tear your arm from its joint—"

"Never!" Dolores panted in his ears. "I'm going to give it to Papa. You dungpicker—" She surprised him with a solid heave which almost rolled him off of her, but he recovered and pinned her down again. She clawed at his face like a cat and, when he blocked that, tried to bite his hand, but he remembered her old tricks. He finally managed to capture her wildly striking free arm and then held her head down by twining his other hand in her thick braid and pulling cruelly. Her headcloth had fallen off; her hair, wisping around her piquant face, gleamed deep copper in the spray of light from the lantern outside. She had let up struggling for a moment, and he could see that her eyes were squeezed closed in pain. He tried to nudge her over with his elbow, but she stiffened and wouldn't budge.

He yanked meanly on the braid. "If you don't give up my purse I'll punch you in the mouth," he threatened, angry. "You'll see I mean what I say when you spit teeth."

Dolores answered what he thought she would. "No. I won't, I won't, you garbage. Next time you leave me in peace when I bathe." Stubborn to the end. But, unexpectedly, her voice trailed off very small.

It was because her voice was so oddly weak that he paused and peered down at her, wondering if he had really hurt her. It didn't sound like Dolores.

She lay still, her breath coming shallowly because almost half his weight was on her. Frowning, he studied her face for some clue to her behavior, not trusting what seemed like capitulation. But what presented itself, suddenly, was an acute awareness of her newly matured body soft underneath him. He could feel a slim flare of hips where lately there were none at all, and her small breasts were pressing against his chest with a firm presence that caused an excited stirring in his loins. His gaze moved to the pale skin of her bare shoulder where the neckline of her bodice had slipped sideways, the warm flesh gleaming so silky smooth in the flickering of lantern light that he was astonished to feel an urge to taste it by pressing his lips there.

Even in the musty straw a faint odor of field blossoms rose from her skin, and there was heat coming from her body. His heart thumped in his chest, and against his will his anger melted away under the onslaught of another emotion he had no name for, sweet and intense—

He stared at the young girl he had forced into immobility as if he had never seen her before, and in truth he never had in just this way. Even though Dolores was a little girl of seven when Tía Esperanza had taken him in and he called her *hermanita*—little sister—like all the rest, he had never really thought of her as a foster sister; sisters, he imagined, were sweet and lovable. Dolores was just Dolores, an unpredictable, impudent female child, a member of her own clan. And now she had gone her own peculiar way again and grown up. With no warning.

He did not consider himself a novice when it came to women. The year before a married woman five years his senior had amused herself by seducing him and for a while allowed his newly awakened and insatiable appetite free rein, teaching him just what to do when inexperience made him awkward and showing him where it pleased her for him to touch. Since then there were several young wenches in the neighborhood who enjoyed occasional dalliance and vied for his attention, which he was not adverse to give. But although he enjoyed sexual encounters and thought that lying with a pretty wench was even more exciting than stealing, he had never experienced so intensely the lure of the flesh under his fingers or felt such a commotion whirling in his stomach. And with Dolores, yesterday's runny-nosed brat!

Watching the sooty lashes flutter on the tender cheek he wondered if she even knew that she could no longer wrestle with him like a child, giving and receiving bruises for insults done; that suddenly she was capable of arousing his maleness.

Dolores opened her eyes, not understanding why Francho had relaxed his grip on her hair, and feeling his body tremble. She found him gazing down at her with an odd expression, his brows slightly drawn in the habitual half-scowl he used when he was concentrating on a thought. She could have pulled her arm away from him now, but she didn't really want to strike at him anymore. A heated sensation washed through her, catching at her breath and making her tremble too under his stare. She found herself wishing he would smile at her in the roguish way he had, and that he would admire her with those clear and intense blue eyes. She felt his warm breath on her neck, and an involuntary and pleasurable tightening of the muscles in her belly answered. Her heart began to flutter like a bird in her chest, and she wondered if he would kiss her and what it would be like.

She tried to calm herself and she drew a deep breath, but this pressed her yet closer to him. A tiny whimper escaped her at the strange, delicious bliss this contact caused. It was a whimper of fear, but not of him. She sensed a loss, the retreating refuge of innocent childhood, whose door would be closed forever if she allowed her pounding heart to lead her—for she recognized the startling, mysterious new attraction that had sprung up between her and her brotherlike companion and realized her welcome of it.

Silently she stared into his eyes for a long moment, the luminous gray plumbing the deep blue, and she saw flickering about the edges of his gaze the same distrust of that adult road which was beckoning them to explore its wondrous reaches. But then his arm tightened about her and there was an intriguing, tender strength to the fingers gripping her shoulder. She was becoming overwhelmed by strange, provocative sensations stirring up her blood.

Francho's eyes traced the pert cleft in her chin, the new fullness to her lower lip. He saw her soft, pink lips part with apprehension. Still not sure she understood that the wrestling was over, he tried to put a rein on his own uneven breathing. "I want to kiss you," he whispered. "Will you let me?"

She blushed, lowered her lashes and responded, "Yes. But . . . but I don't know what to do with my nose." It was a situation that had puzzled her ever since she had begun to think about kissing. She glanced up hesitantly, afraid he might mock her.

But Francho remembered his own awkwardness the first time he had kissed a girl, and his expression was solemn. "Don't worry. Don't be afraid. You don't have to do anything. I'll show you."

He lowered his head and planted a kiss full on her mouth, so anxious to please her that it was a little rougher and harder than he intended and their teeth grated together. In a moment he pulled back, peering at her for a reaction. She lay still, eyes closed once more. Then she whimpered softly and tilted up her face to him. "Kiss me again, Francho—"

So she did know she had grown up.

Clumsily he untangled his hand from her braid and touched the sun-browned throat where the pulse was beating, beating. There was a clamor inside of him. He let go of the arm he had been pinning above her, and immediately she wound it about his neck. He bent his head to her. This time his kiss was gentler and longer, and he felt her lips quiver under his. At first her mouth was deliciously innocent, passive, but soon she began to respond to him and then she was eagerly returning the pressure of his kiss. Immensely excited, feeling her breath sweet on his cheek, he made the third ardent kiss last as long as he could before they both needed air.

The purse forgotten, her other arm came from beneath her back and went around his neck too. She smiled shyly up at him, her eyes shadowed, but her breathing was shallow and quick and her lips still sought more. Flame began to pour through him, and the hardness between his thighs swelled in response to the innocent desire gripping the pretty girl who moved him more than any other maid he had fondled.

He shifted his weight off of her. His eager hand slid along her smooth shoulder and into the wide neck of her bodice, gently cupping over a small, pear-shaped breast. He suspected that this caress would startle her, and he was not mistaken.

"No!" She tried to push herself up.

"Let me, Dolores, don't be a baby. It feels good, doesn't it?"

"No, let me up." Dolores pushed at him in vain, trying to dislodge his persistent hand from her breast, although the incredible sensations that radiated through her body made her toes curl. Panicking because she sensed this was her last chance to retreat before her helpless need allowed the wondrous tide to engulf her, she struggled.

Although he was trying to be gentle and not frighten her, Francho couldn't help a light grin. Her resistance was much more like the Dolores that he knew, yet it intensified his excited feeling of sexual domination. "You'll have to learn from someone not to brawl with men. This is what happens, eh?" he told her hoarsely, holding her down. He saw a shadow of grief in her wide eyes, and the grin faded into a softer, understanding smile. "Everyone grows up, little sister. Better with me than with a strange man who cares nothing for you."

"You are not yet a man," she protested weakly.

Withdrawing his hand from the soft mound of flesh that had fed fuel to his fire, he sat up quickly, drew his legs under him and pulled her up to him as if she were a feather, gathering her in his arms before she knew what was happening, hugging her hard, wanting her to feel the male strength of his embrace.

Dolores felt it and more, her heart hammering in her throat, her bones seeming to melt in her body. She abandoned herself to the need to know, to unfold, to give, and so she offered her mouth to his kiss. She reveled in the young hardness of his slim body and that the arms about her were not crushing her ribs in play but holding her possessively as if she were something precious. She was so intoxicated her head swam. "This is the love of which the tales tell, of which the ballads sing," she thought deliriously. "I have a sweetheart!"

Feeling her surrender and relax in his arms, Francho applied a trembling hand to open the strings of her blouse and pushed wide the shirred edges to see her fresh beauty, for she wore no shift under her homespun garment.

For a second Dolores wanted to shrink to be so naked under his gaze but she did not, for she could see his hot blue stare was filled with admiration tinged, even, with awe. Suddenly she thought she should be proud of how her body had changed.

"Am I too skinny?" she asked timidly.

"No. You . . . you're very pretty," he stammered, stunned with the truth of it. The married woman had offered huge, round breasts that had often threatened to suffocate him with their amplitude, and his little laundresses were plump too. But Dolores's young breasts looked like small pears, round at the base and then narrowing so that the rosy area and pink nipple thrust forward at a tilt. He wanted to fondle, play with them, to put his lips on them, but he knew he had no time.

With his foot he thrust away the purse she had brought from underneath her. He pressed her back on the straw, fumbling at the same time with the string that laced together his hosen. He kissed her mouth again with hot urgency and then ran his hand in a coaxing caress over her bare shoulders and breasts, and little shudders took her. She looked at him so trustingly, her young body was so helplessly excited under his hands, that his heart squeezed together with love for her. He was her first lover. And her only one too, he silently vowed, sudden possessiveness sweeping him so strongly that she gasped under the hard pressure of his awkward hug.

His hand disappeared under her pushed up skirt, brushed along the firm, silky thighs, and found where she was warm and wet. She jerked as if a hot coal had touched her and moaned, fearful again.

"Only lie still, Dolores," he soothed her, whispering against her cheek. "Just lie still, sweet. No, let me, let me . . ."

Then, in a moment, "Do you like it?"

"Oh yes, yes, oh . . ."

She begged, "Will you hurt me? Please don't hurt me."

"I'll try not to, I swear. I will never want to hurt you." He meant it. He thought wildly that he loved her. His hand kept moving under her skirt, and now he bent his head to kiss the hard little tip of her breast and the earth seemed to whirl away from under him. He lost all control. He rolled on top of her, parting her legs with his knees, forcing himself into the dampness, ignoring her soft cries, and then the louder, sharp yelp when he pushed through her maidenhead, riding her overwhelmed body, and finally feeling himself shatter in a burst of mingled pain and pleasure such as he had never felt before. In a few seconds it was over.

Dolores knew he had rolled off of her because she could breathe again, in panting gasps. The incredible new part of her that he had discovered lay hurting but exultant. She wondered if her mortal soul would ever come to earth again, if her heart would finally stop bouncing about as if to jump out of her chest. Somewhere down below she felt burning, some pain, but it was not nearly so bad as she had imagined when she eavesdropped on the kitchen wenches giggling together one day and heard them recount with relish and pride the fear, the shock, the pain their first swains had caused them. Francho had hurt her but she cared little about it, she was so dazed and joyful over having pleased him, over the new feelings in her own body that he had released.

A sharp pang of jealousy invaded momentarily when she considered that he had not learned to love a female so confidently without practice, but she quickly quashed it. So much the better for her, at least she had not suffered for his lack of knowledge like the girls she'd heard talking, and what did the others matter now when he looked at her so reverently? She felt her heart swell with pride that the handsome and clever Francho was her sweetheart, but she longed to hear him say the lovely thing that had blossomed in their young world.

She raised herself up on one arm so she could better see his face as he lay there quietly. "Francho? Do you . . . do you love me?" she asked in a small, husky voice, feeling humble before the might of that magic word, her heart in her throat to see how tenderly he looked at her.

Floating on a cloud of thistledown, sated, Francho was tempted to tease her, but one glance at the shy expectancy on her face and he thought better of it. He turned on his side to face her, a bent arm raising his head to the height of hers.

"Yes, *hermanita,* I care about you. More than anyone in the world."

"Is that the same as love?"

"I think so," he answered honestly, touching his fingers to her flowerlike face. But the thought raced through his mind that, except for the verses of the few love songs he had learned to sing, what did he know about true love yet?

Her eyes were drawn to his mouth, which she noticed for the first time had a square underlip, and when he smiled, as he was doing now, tiny, flat circles, not quite dimples, appeared at its corners, fascinating her, physical reminders of his scapegrace charm.

"Do-lo-res!"

Gasping, they started, then scrambled to their feet, shocked and intimidated by the voice of Tía Esperanza somewhere outside bawling for her niece. Quickly they arranged their garments, finishing by energetically brushing the straw off each other. Dolores wanted to avoid Tía. She was anxious now to gain the small chamber she shared with her aunt and see if the wetness she felt on her thighs was blood, like the girls had murmured about. She blotted at the damp with her heavy skirt. Still clumsy with happiness, she tried to smooth her disheveled hair and then giggled at Francho's dubious look. "I'll say a drunken customer tried to manhandle me. Tía's been warning me to stay away from the stables lest some brute catch me and drag me off."

"And so do I warn you of that," cautioned Francho, newly anxious about the other males who would soon notice that she was blooming. "Except if you are with me," he added, breaking into a grin.

His caring thrilled her.

Francho picked up the nearly forgotten purse, plunged his hand into it to feel around among the coins, found what he wanted, and put it in Dolores's hand.

Confused, she drew back. "What is that? *Diantre!* Do you think I am a whore?"

"No, *mi dulce,* hold your temper. This is a keepsake between you and me. See, look . . ." Together, in the ray of light, they examined the small, square metal piece, tarnished black, with a square hole in the middle and strange figures and squiggles around the edges like a design. "I've never seen a coin like it. It must come from a land at the edge of the earth."

"I will put it on a ribbon and hang it around my neck,"

Dolores murmured, her eyes dancing. "Only you will know it's there. It will be a secret talisman." His swaggering, white grin washed over her.

"Tomorrow I'll buy you a pretty sash for your waist—a crimson silk one now I am so wealthy. Would you like that?"

She nodded vigorously, once more the old, acquisitive Dolores.

"Dolores! Dolores! *Donde estuvistes, picara . . . ?"* Tía Esperanza sounded angry.

"I'll go before she finds us here," Dolores said. "Francho, we must act as we always do when anyone is near. Otherwise they'll suspect that we . . . we love each other and they'll tease us. I will . . . meet you here tomorrow eve, if you'd like?" Her legs suddenly seemed to wobble, and she didn't wait for an answer but stretched up to quickly brush his lips with her own, then turned and fled down the aisle, past the few softly snorting horses, clutching the square coin in her warm palm.

A few minutes later, peering into the shadows surrounding the pools of light from the stableyard torches, Francho slipped after her. He reached his little cubicle and he carefully hid the purse under the loose plank which served as his guard-money. Then he lay on his pallet, hands behind his head, wrapped in a pleasant fog, marveling. He had never particularly cared what the girl who lay with him thought or what she felt, beyond heating her up so she would cooperate. Before, that is. But with Dolores he had wanted so much to please her, to reassure her, to make her happy with lying with him. And then there was that aching squeeze at his heart at the few frightened tears she had shed.

How strange that it was Dolores who had introduced him to passion that had a face and a soul and was more than just a body accepting his. The thought of her inexperienced but eager, sweet kisses and warm, smooth, skin stirred him even now. But he felt tender toward her, protective. The thought that any other male should touch her made him growl deep in his throat. Was that love? How did a man know? He recalled an old manuscript he'd sneaked peeks into at Santo Domingo, behind the back of the brother who was copying it. How did the good brother Abelard know that he truly loved Heloise? Or, from the popular ballads, the gallant El Cid know his undying affection for his lady Jimena?

He shook his head in confusion. He decided to leave the stuffy chamber to wait in the courtyard for Carlos to return and admire his blazoned purse. He felt wonderful and depressed at the same time. Becoming a man seemed to be like a puppy chasing after its own tail, one minute you feel strong and free, the next minute, you feel grown, responsible and— Dolores's trusting face with the small sprinkling of freckles over the cheeks shimmered before his eyes—even guilty.

She was hardly out of childhood and you have already taken her maidenhead, his conscience pricked him.

"'Tis no matter, that, I do care for her and I shall be her true swain," he offered up to San Bismas, who he suddenly felt, shamefacedly, was looking down in stern disapproval. "So she has done no wrong, only I, and I shall say fifty Paternosters come Sunday. And I will never abandon her," he swore, ignoring the certainty in his bones that there had to be more to his life than finally becoming a horsethief, or helping run the inn when Papa died.

Preoccupied, Francho strolled past the doorway of the common room with a careless lack of caution, not even registering the face of the man brushing past him to relieve himself outside. But, unfortunately, the Count of Tendilla's burly sergeant-at-arms recognized him, stopped in his tracks, and lunged at him from behind with a triumphant, "Ha, you scum!" With a swift movement the man twisted Francho's arm painfully behind his back, whirled him around, and pinioned his neck in a bearlike grip against his barrel chest.

Recovering from his stunned surprise, Francho tried to pry the guard's arm loose from under his Adam's apple, meanwhile struggling to kick backward as well as he could, but the big man had lifted him almost free of the ground and Francho's arm was agonizingly close to snapping with the added pressure of his weight.

"Ho, Manuel, Gaspar!" the sergeant boomed to his mates who had been looking over the crowd from just inside the door. "See what I kicked up in this dung heap! This is the one, the sewer rat that ran our legs off back there. I'd know that thievin' face in Hell, I tell you. Here you, *bergante,* leave off that wriggling or I'll tighten me arm and put an end to your miserable life. 'Twould be no matter, you'll swing for this little strike anyhow, mark me good."

The two other guards came running, daggers drawn, a noisy group collecting about them. *"Sí,* that's him sure enough," one of the guards corroborated, with oily pleasure. "Now we'll see how tough the wretch is. . . ."

"Where is it, scum, where's that money? Spit it up, damn you."

Francho's heart was black with curses at his own stupidity. "I don't have it. I threw it away," he gasped.

"Liar! Give it here, *rata,* or I'll crack you in two."

Francho's teeth gritted, and purple sparks swam before his eyes as the soldier forced his back to arch like a bow.

Tía Esperanza, peering with horror through the encircling onlookers, moaned aloud but dared not interfere with the soldiers. Papa el Mono, his face set in a grimace, hurried away unobtrusively. There was nothing to connect Francho with the inn, unless one of the regular patrons piped up, but should they ever decide to search the place, his goose was both spitted and cooked. . . .

"Where is it!" There was a vicious tug on Francho's twisted arm. The motley group yelled encouragement, some to the soldiers, some to the pickpocket.

"I don't know . . . it wasn't me. . . ."

"Liar! Are you going to find it for us or do we have to light a little fire under you?"

"I swear . . . I don't have it . . . I don't have it, see for yourself," Francho croaked.

"Yes, I have eyes in my head, filth. But where did you hide it away, in what rat's nest? Tell me! Out with it!"

"Hold, what happens here? What is the trouble, sergeant?" The stern, demanding voice gave the sergeant pause as Carlos pushed into the circle, impressing even the sweating Francho with his long, serious face under a feathered felt cap, his stark, black costume lit only with an enormous silver buckle.

The sergeant glared suspiciously, but allowed Francho some relief from the torture of his arm. "And who, pray, are you?" he growled.

"Son of the proprietor of this establishment. What has this fellow done?"

"Enough to get himself stretched from the gibbet, that's what. Stole the purse of my lord, Count of Tendilla . . ." There was an appreciative babble from the onlookers. ". . . and he'll return every last maravedi if I have to choke it out of him."

"A moment, *hombre.* Perhaps you are wrong. There are many thieves in the city. Maybe this is not the same rogue you are after?"

The burly sergeant wasn't intimidated by a young commoner with airs. "Wrong, eh? You trying to tell me that there's some other rascal running around with this one's face? Not likely! He's the culprit, all right, and he'll get his just desserts, whether he coughs it up or not." His eyes narrowed under his casque. "You know this one?"

Carlos's black eyes locked with Francho's. They understood each other. Carlos shrugged. "He loiters around here sometimes looking for drunks to pick. We boot him out."

The sergeant grunted. "Pah, we waste time. We'll make him sorry he was born. Out of my way, fellow." He motioned to his companions and began dragging Francho away, the gawkers opening a path before them.

"Ay, Santa Maria carisima, where are they taking my *muchacho?"* wailed Tía Esperanza from the common's room doorway. "Bring him back, villains, he is a good boy, he never steals . . ." she wept.

"Hold your tongue, woman," growled Papa el Mono, pinching her side cruelly. "Don't claim him, fool. Do you want to bring the entire Hermandad down on us? We have loot here. . . ."

But Tía Esperanza rushed out into the courtyard, groaning, "They will hang him, they will hang my handsome Francho, my little foundling. *Ay socorro,* Santa Maria, Santa Rosa, San Pedro, *Dios mío . . ."* Fortunately the swelled crowd of tavern revelers, following the soldiers, and boisterously shouting suggestions for the best place to loop up a rope, drowned her wails.

"There is nothing to be done here," Carlos whispered grimly to Papa. "But they surely will not hang him tonight. Tomorrow, if we can get a bribe to the turnkey—"

Papa turned on him, tiny eyes hard. "I care nothing for him, the idiot. I care for what he will tell them if they apply the screws to his thumbs. Whatever it was he stole, find it. Get it out of here, fast. And anything else that can be recognized for stolen, or we'll all be carrion for the crows," the frightened innkeep hissed.

To the disappointment of the rabble there was no hanging on the spot, for the soldiers' horses waited outside the stable and they mounted. Francho was slung on his belly in front of the sergeant, his hands secured behind him with a length of rein, his feet bound together, body pinned down in his captor's grip. His jaw was clenched in defiance, his only thought to show Carlos his courage and let him know he wouldn't crack. He refused to admit the sharp sliver of fear that was stabbing around his chest.

The Count's guards and their prisoner clattered out under the stone arch in a swirl of dust. Francho twisted his head quickly, hoping to catch Carlos's eye, certain his companion had a plan to help him, for Carlos had some access to the Alcalde's turnkey.

But Carlos was gone. In his place stood Dolores, hand pressed against her mouth, tear-filled eyes huge with horror.

❧ *Chapter 4* ❧

CLOSETED WITH HIS two guests before a small fire laid to take the early chill off the air, Señor Piroso, the Alcalde of Ciudad Real, wielded an ivory-handled knife with plump fingers, deftly removing the skin of an apple in one strip. Wishing he had not gone so far in his last statement to his most illustrious guest—who was, after all, a military commander for the Queen as well as her confidant—he addressed the apple to avoid the black eyes lazily trying to insinuate themselves into the very depths of his head.

He heard the Count clear his throat. "So then it is your opinion, Señor Alcalde, that by next summer's campaigns, Spain will not yet be ready to mount a full invasion of the Kingdom of Granada?"

"Ah, no, my lord, you put it a trifle strongly. Perhaps ready, yes, but not *as* ready as could be. The mighty and decisive blow it would require to forever rid our land of the Moslem scourge, even with what great sacrifices and toll of blood, must needs be carried out by a vast recruitment of men and provisions and armaments. Ah . . . with all deference to the wisdom of the royal advisors, it seems to my uninformed reckoning that we shall have to strain beyond possibility to produce such numbers."

"You have had problems raising your levy of troops for our last campaigns?"

"Problems, ah no, indeed, Ciudad Real has always easily met its quotas," the Alcalde said quickly, wishing it were true. "But food this year is everywhere in scant supply and dear because of the drought. How will such an army be fed? And one hears . . . rumors, of course . . . that the royal coffers are . . . ah . . . hardly filled."

"Has one also heard rumors that our northern borders are in unsettled condition?" the Count probed, his tone neutral.

Señor Piroso shifted uncomfortably in his chair. Shrugging, he proferred to his guest the quarters of peeled apple on a crystal plate. "Ah, to be sure, my lord, there is always talk. The threat from Navarre is not new, of course, only . . . one hears it has become acute and that there could be war in that quarter by spring." He licked his thick lips. "But, I assure you, as a loyal subject of the throne, my heart and my hand are behind anything Their Most Gracious Majesties see fit to do."

The Count of Tendilla, his lean frame resting in a tall, pillowed armchair across a small table from Piroso, skewered an apple quarter with his small dagger. He wanted to make the provincial official more comfortable. Ascertaining the leaning of those functionaries responsible for filling the royal ranks of soldiers was essential to military decisions. He smiled blandly, waving the morsel of apple at his host.

"Of course, of course, but don't retreat, good *señor*. It so happens I agree with you most strongly, which makes me unpopular among my colleagues. The resources we could send south this year would be minor compared to the might of Abul Hassan's legions arrayed against us, and his many thick-walled fortresses." He consumed the apple in two decisive bites. "But Her Majesty will not be swayed from her crusade, and the drums are beating throughout Aragon and Castile, as you know, to fill our lists and warehouses." He picked up his wine goblet from the small table at his side. "A pity. . . . I have always disapproved of premature wars."

Tendilla sighed, shifting his black gaze to sight moodily through the fine ruby-colored wineglass.

The fretting Alcalde was torn, eager for information yet thinking he should change the subject. He felt he was but an administrator, not a court diplomat, and he did not want to be surprised into saying what was really in his heart, that the Queen's vendetta against the Moslem was ill timed at present and smacked of fanaticism. The heathen had, after all, dwelt in Granada countless centuries. What would a few more years hurt, years in which Señor Piroso, at least, could certainly make his own nest a little softer.

The Count of Tendilla, as a powerful grandee of Spain, was in a position to express his opinion freely. But since the accession to the Castilian throne of the intense Isabella and her Aragonese consort, life could turn sour for those lesser lights who disagreed with royal desires.

Still, he was so small a fish, could he not risk keeping the conversation going and perhaps learn what might really be in the wind? He had hundreds of reales invested in business ventures which depended on the free flow of commerce between the cities of Granada and their northern markets.

His plump, beringed hand patted nervously at his graying hair, which he wore in the old-fashioned mode, long and straight, with short bangs over his fleshy brow. He ventured to break the Count's musing. "Ah . . . is it true, my lord Tendilla, that this summer's attack on the city of Loja has cost us . . . well, what is the incredible rumor?" His pale eyes bulged. "Fifteen thousand soldiers!" Not to mention the worst of the "rumor," the near capture and death of Ferdinand himself in that infamous Moslem ambush.

Pietro di Lido, nattily attired in a short brocade doublet with brown satin sleeves and brown-and-white striped hosen, approached from the other end of the long room, where he had been examining several shelves of large, bound manuscripts and some printed books.

"Let me make so bold as to answer that, Señor Piroso," he began in his mellifluous Spanish Italian-accented. "More to the truth, it was twenty thousand men, God save their souls. A rout, an inglorious defeat, a surprise stab in the back. Think you 'twas an easy matter to attempt to breach that great pile of stone walls manned by the very glory of Moorish knighthood and such fierce troops as we yet only dream of? Ah no, *señor,* but alas, even with the best chivalry of Spain pledged to capture Loja at all costs, we were outfought, and worse, outwitted by those wily Arabs. Whatever history may say of them, I see them to be the very incarnation of the ancient Greek warrior, brave, ferocious, and vastly cunning."

Piroso bristled. "Fie, Señor di Lido, I am aghast. Do you praise these heathen devils, these defilers of our Holy Church? Those murderers of innocent women and children? The spawn of Satan himself? I cannot believe you even consider them a respected enemy." *That* should show Tendilla where his loyalties lay.

"We too have done our share of bloody murdering, *señor,*" di Lido responded with relish, warming up to his favorite way to pass a dull evening.

Seeing the Alcalde sputtering, the amused Tendilla took pity on him. "I fear Maestro di Lido often makes startling remarks in order to provoke some lively discussion, *señor.* In truth, being an instructed Roman of the highest order, he is quite impartial in his respect for combatants, with a high regard for the clever and valorous of whatever stripe. A habit left over from the ancient gladiatorial contests, no doubt, where a particularly brave warrior was allowed to live, even though he had lost against Rome's champion; nay, was honored, even."

It was almost possible for Tendilla to see the indignation forming behind the Alcalde's forehead as di Lido, one eyebrow languidly raised to see if his challenge to discourse would be taken up, fanned himself with a showy handkerchief.

"Woman!" the Alcalde thought, raising his velvet sleeve to wipe his moist brow. "Silly little fop. He would faint at a stuck finger." Wondering what strange business would bring the dignified Count within the sphere of this mincing foreigner, nevertheless for courtesy's sake he clumsily changed the subject. "And how do you find my library, Señor di Lido? Naturally it must seem quite incomplete to a renowned scholar such as yourself?"

Di Lido nodded gracefully. "On the contrary, may I commend you, sir. You have a fine collection, chosen with much expertise. *Excelamente!* One rarely finds a complete copy of the *Scripta Theosophica* in private hands. And the illumination of your manuscript is superb, such magnificent tints, such detailed renderings. I am delighted to have come across it," the Italian enthused, quite genuinely.

The Alcalde smirked. Actually the books had belonged to his uncle, who had died without heirs, but it could do no harm to take credit for that late lamented's erudition, God rest his soul. And bless him, for the volumes were worth a fortune in money.

"It is not easy for a man of moderate means to come by fine volumes and in a lesser corner of the world. Therefore, never would I part with 'my children' as it were. But I must confess that I have had some luck in their acquisition," Piroso declaimed modestly. He leaned over to refill the Count's wineglass from a figured silver decanter, but stopped midway, frowning, as there came a loud knock on the heavy, arched door. Damn them, he had said there were to be no disturbances. What had gone wrong in the kitchen now? Plague take his drunken steward. . . . "Enter!"

But it was the Count's big sergeant-at-arms who entered, looking somewhat mussed, his helmet held under his arm. He saluted his patron respectfully. "My lord."

"What is it, Rondero?"

"We have the young thief, my lord, the one who got away from us earlier this evening."

"Good. Have you recovered my purse?"

"Ah . . . no, Your Excellency, he refuses to tell what he's done with it. And no amount of coaxing seems to help the scum to speak. Following your rule, my lord, we did not yet apply the strongest persuasions. He's certainly dropped it in some rathole in the city . . . your pardon, Señor Alcalde . . . and it is impossible to know where to look."

"Did you tell him he is liable to a hanging? Did that make no impression?"

"None, my lord. He is more stubborn than most street bastards would be under our hands."

"Well, that takes some sort of courage, however foolish. Yet the rascal did get away with a princely amount. And worse, a very rare coin from Cathay which I treasured." Tendilla considered for a moment. "'Tis a pity to just let it go, hang him or not. Bring him up here then and I will try to persuade him he will hang without his soul shriven if he persists in this foolishness. The money might as well buy us some amusement."

The Alcalde wrung his hands. "My lord, might I say again how I deplore that this should have happened in our fine city of Ciudad Real. If you will just turn the trash over to my constable we shall deal with him quickly."

The Count waved his hand. This might liven up the dull evening. "Nonsense, no apology is required, *señor*. Such thievery happens everywhere. Rondero?"

The guard hesitated. "My lord, I would not advise bringing him to this room. He is somewhat bloody, a bit, you see . . ."

"Quite right, my fastidious giant, we should not like to mar our good host's Moorish carpets. Where have you got him, in the gate house? Then come, Pietro, we will stretch our legs a bit before we dine. Señor Alcalde will permit . . . ?"

"But naturally, my lord, anything which pleases Your Excellence." Piroso rose, showing his bad teeth in an obsequious smile. "And if you will pardon my absence I will see that my chamberlain has had your rooms prepared for your every comfort."

He bowed deferentially and then followed them out, the hulking Rondero bringing up the rear.

When Francho finally managed to open one puffed eye it was to see the blurred, lively face of Pietro di Lido hanging over him. The face withdrew and the ruddy visage of Rondero took its place.

"So, you've still got some life in you, rascal. I'll teach you to steal! Stand up, stand up there and show some respect. On your feet, *estúpido . . .*" Francho felt himself hauled off the floor and stood up half-conscious before the Count, who was casually seated on the edge of a rude table. In the background the Count's men and some of the Alcalde's city guards were ranged against the damp wall of the low-ceilinged stone chamber, watching with interest.

Rondero gave the boy a good poke with the hilt of his sword to stop him from swaying. "This miserable ragpicker is the culprit, Your Excellence."

Other than a torch smoking in a holder by the door, the only light was from a thick candle on the table that sent flickering shadows onto Tendilla's face. Francho, wobbling uncertainly, blinked his swollen eyes at this new tormentor and weakly crossed himself, croaking under his breath, "María Santa . . ."

Di Lido understood why the frightened boy called on the Mother of God for protection. In the gloom, lit only from below by the leaping yellow flame, Iñigo Lopez de Mendoza, Count of Tendilla and lord of other rich dependencies, respected, favored, and admired courtier of Their Catholic Majesties, did most certainly bring the Devil himself to mind.

Tendilla's oval, aristocratic face was defined by sharply honed features: a long and narrow nose swooping between arrogant, shadowed cheekbones; thin lips so finely chiseled they hinted, with close study, of sensuousness rather than cruelty; a pointed chin adorned by a small triangle of dark beard, an affectation in a cleanshaven age.

But it was his black eyes, eyes which did not gaze but pierced, which made men uncomfortable. Women, conversely, vied to attract their attention, charmed by his elegance and subtlety, intrigued by his seeming imperviousness to feminine wiles.

Casually Tendilla's long, thin fingers toyed with a small, jeweled dagger which he had drawn from the belt of a velvet doublet so dark it absorbed all the light and threw his patrician face into shadowed, sinister relief.

Di Lido chuckled to himself; there was no telling *this* book by the leather of its cover. Although he knew that his patron enjoyed creating an awesome impression, he wished Tendilla could see himself as he appeared now, especially as he must seem to this poor wretched youth, who would pay a dear price for his indiscretion in robbing a grandee.

The Count could see blood welling from a bad gash in the boy's scalp, and there were ugly bruises and red, seeping welts on his bare arms and presumably on his back where his tunic had been ripped open. The youth slowly wiped his bloody nose with his arm. There was yet a stubborn glint in the one blue eye that could open and a set to the scraped, dirt-streaked jaw that showed no loss of defiance. Tendilla concealed his mild admiration for such tenacity and reminded himself of the sum of money the boy had snatched.

"Come, lad," he said suavely, "that money could not mean more to you than your life? Tell us where it is and we'll let you go with your life, since you've been this punished. My word on it."

Francho let his breath puff out. He had expected to hear the growl of Lucifer, but instead heard soft words and a surprisingly lenient bargain. But how could he reveal where the purse was hidden without putting his foster family at the inn in jeopardy? Those people had been good to him; he could not implicate them to pay for his carelessness.

"I don't know where it is," he mumbled. "I lost it."

"He's lying, Excellence, this pup is much too clever to lose a sum of money like that," Rondero burst out. "Be glad of your luck, you whelp," he commanded, shoving Francho again, "in that my lord does not believe how well a bit of stretching on the rack loosens tongues, or how a foot crushed bloody in the boot would make you damn well babble in a hurry—"

"Softly, Rondero," Tendilla chided. "I know he is lying. Speak up there, boy, I can't hear you. Come closer."

Rondero propelled Francho further forward into the light.

"I swear to you, I don't know where it is!" Francho croaked out, staring as steadily as he could at the heavy gold medallion on his captor's chest, afraid to meet the black eyes that might see his secret right through his forehead. He knew he was doomed. But he would not give away his friends.

Suddenly the black-clad leg stopped swinging aimlessly, and he glanced up to see Tendilla's face darkening under a frown. "So be it," Francho thought bleakly. "Unless Carlos works a miracle, I am as good as dead."

But all Tendilla did was to stare at him strangely and then beckon di Lido to his side. "Pietro." Indicating Francho with a motion of his chin, the Count leaned forward to whisper to his friend, "The face is battered, but study it. Do you recall someone? Of long ago?"

Di Lido squinted at Francho for a moment. The next moment his jaw dropped. But he quickly recovered, closed his mouth, and shrugged. "Ah, I see what you mean, my lord, a certain resemblance. One has to look closely. If his face were not so . . . damaged . . . perhaps. No. No, now I see there is not much there."

"But the shape of the head and jaw . . . the eyes. Once the thought entered my head it gripped like an incubus. I cannot escape seeing . . . the other, like a ghostly overlay. Curious!"

"But impossible, dear Count. After all . . ."

"Yes, I suppose you are right. My imagination plays tricks." But he did not sound convinced.

Francho's head throbbed unmercifully, his knees were weak, and he swayed in spite of his determination to stand straight and steady before the Count. Blood running from his nose trickled saltily into a corner of his mouth; he raised a trembling hand to wipe it away. *Dios mío,* the three of those vermin had punched and beaten him all over the room. There seemed to be a great bell ringing in his ears. A picture of Tía Esperanza rose before his bleary vision, great, comfortable, comforting Tía. He would never see her again.

"Well, boy, do you insist on being mule-headed? You are a fool!"

Francho shook his head, trying to clear his daze. "No . . . I don't . . . know . . . where . . ."

Tendilla lost patience and stood up, resheathing his dagger.

The sight of the battered youth did not amuse him at all, his stomach growled its hunger, and he was tired from his journey. He shrugged his elegant shoulders. "This is a farce, he is evidently an imbecile. Rondero, give him over to the Alcalde's constable. Although what good that money will do him ten feet high on the rope is more than I can comprehend. Come, maestro . . ."

One of the guards opened the door, letting in a swirl of leaves from the courtyard. Suddenly, in a frantic, final burst of resistance, Francho willed his legs to move and he lunged to dash past the Count, who had already turned his back, although knowing full well that even if he escaped the gate house, the main portal would be closed and locked. But with surprising swiftness a leg in bright hosen flashed out before him and tripped him up, and a hand grabbed him to keep him from falling headlong into Tendilla.

Francho twisted in despair to find the little Italian grinning into his face, holding on to his upper arm with a grip strong as an iron clamp.

"Calm yourself, my little lion," di Lido advised in his finest lecture tone as he passed Francho over to Rondero. "For every crime there must be a punishment, there will be expiation for every sin and an unpleasant end for every sinner—"

"Don Pietro!" Tendilla exclaimed sharply from where he stood to one side of them. "Look here, *por piedad!*" He pointed to a spot on Francho's back which was now turned toward the brighter flames from the flaring torch at the door. The Count's face had gone quite intense, the nostrils of his thin nose flaring.

Di Lido peered at the place indicated by Tendilla's long finger, and then his eyebrows flew up as if they would leave his narrow face. *"Mater Domini!"* he blurted, "This is a cicatrix I have seen before. Indeed. *Jesu, Jesu . . ."* He let his breath out in a soft whistle.

The two of them stared in wonder at the odd, puckered white scar, the small dagger shape on Francho's shoulder blade, which showed up clearly as he sagged in Rondero's grip. The other guards in the room, curious, moved closer.

"Can this possibly be the little holy grail for whom we quested so long?"

"There is a good chance," Tendilla muttered, recovering a measure of calm. "How many markings like this could there be in Spain? And look at his face, the unique resemblance we remarked before. Could coincidence be so wild?" He motioned to Rondero to bring the youth back to the table and with his foot shoved up a stool for the captive to sit on. In the close light of the candle all three intently studied Francho's pain-filled features as he swayed on his seat. The Italian wrung his hands in a transport of amazement. Tendilla took his silk kerchief and swabbed away the blood trickling down the side of Francho's face, the better to examine him.

Francho's eyes were closed. He felt weak and faint, and the pain from his cuts and welts and where he had been brutally kicked in the ribs racked through him in burning waves. The worst was the ringing in his ears that made him so dizzy. Yet something penetrated his befuddled brain so that he levered his good eye open, finally focusing on the saturnine nobleman standing before him. The man's mouth opened to speak.

"What is your name, boy?"

"Francisco," he croaked, with a large effort.

Tendilla started as if he had been stung by a nettle. "What more?" The man seemed to hold his breath.

"There is no more. I have no family. I live in the streets." Never, never would he betray his friends.

"Where were you born, do you know? Have you always lived in Ciudad Real? No? Where else?"

He did not know what to make of all the questions launched at him, but he reached back into his short past and told the truth, just so they would leave him be, let him rest. He was nauseated, dizzy. "Raised at the monastery of San Martín in Tijuna . . . left there as a baby," he muttered.

"Do the brothers know who left you?"

"N–no. They only said I was . . . abandoned in the fall—1468 . . ."

"God's mercy on us," di Lido breathed. "Exactly the time, my lord! And the name!"

Tendilla's mouth was compressed. "Of course. But how would it have occurred to us to search as far afield as Tijauna?"

Francho wanted to cry out at the sudden, buzzing purple mist that descended to blur out their faces and the stone wall behind them, but his tongue wouldn't move. Their voices over the spinning distance came to him like metallic clanging. The purple was devouring his consciousness. He toppled sideways off the stool, with hands reaching out too late to stop him. He

66

felt his head crack on the stone floor. Darkness swallowed him up.

Containing his own surprise at the tension gripping the two aristocrats, Rondero stolidly stepped forward at the Count's motion and scooped the boy up, brushing past the gawking men-at-arms to lay the limp body on a pallet in the corner. He nodded his head at Tendilla's orders to see that the boy's wounds were carefully tended and bound up and that he was made comfortable with a blanket against the chill. And above all, watched, so there was no escape, although Rondero doubted the rascal would be going anywhere with what were probably some broken ribs.

He watched the grandee and his learned companion stare down once more, in grave wonder, at the battered young cutpurse with blood-matted hair, lying limp and pale in his torn tunic.

"I worry that he is hurt. Ask Piroso to send for his physician, tell him any fable you wish. We will take the lad with us in the morning. Whatever doubts may remain in our minds can be dispelled with careful inquiry."

Di Lido's sharp-featured face mirrored excitement battling with skepticism. "It shall be as you say, *Excelencia*. But my thoughts are skittering around in my skull like little mice, trying to encompass this stunning event. As usual God works in his most mysterious ways."

Tendilla nodded. His stare again raked over Francho's face. "I do not like his color. See to him," he ordered. He turned on his heel and strode out of the gate house and into the night, eyes glazed and unseeing, his long, dark cloak billowing out behind him. Di Lido watched the stiff, retreating back, almost-forgotten, titillating speculations welling up anew in his mind and certainly perking up a dull evening.

❧ *Chapter 5* ❧

FRANCHO WAS A decent swimmer. 'Fredo had taught them all to swim in a cold and swiftly flowing stream in the countryside outside Ciudad Real. Now he was swimming, swimming, breasting his way up from turgid depths and battling to rise against the sucking current that was clutching again at his limbs and refusing to let him go. But this time, now, he seemed to be much stronger, he would not give up. He doubled his efforts to bring his head above the gray, swirling miasma.

And then—was it a moment or an hour—he knew he was awake. The weird, nightmare impressions of swaying and creaking, of wavering, unknown faces and strange, muted voices, of the odor of horses, dust, and dry wood, of shriveling heat that baked him and shivering cold that froze him, were gone. About him there was only silence. He felt cool and rested and at peace, as if he were floating in the calm after a bad storm. Light pressed softly on his eyelids.

Peacefully then he opened his eyes, only to quickly squint them against the bright of daylight. He lay flat on his back. He was staring up at what seemed to be an undulating blue ceiling. Gripped by languor he shifted his gaze to discover that he was partially enclosed by walls of the same dark blue, hanging in heavy folds. He turned his head and the realization

68

seeped slowly into his idling mind that he was ensconced in a great bed—a baronial bed with canopy and curtains.

His legs prickled. He moved them, wondering that they seemed so stiff and cramped. He stretched them out slowly and wriggled his shoulders around for they were also stiff. Still as if in a dream he slowly pushed away the feather-filled comforter from his chest, looked down, and was suddenly jolted into true wakefulness by sheer amazement.

No one wore garments to bed except the wealthy, the old, or the sick, but he was clothed in a prim, long nightrobe of white flannel with embroidery-edged sleeves tightened at the wrists by white ribbons. His incredulity deepened as he also realized that he was resting in a goosedown mattress with his head on a feather pillow. He had never in his life slept in a bedstead, much less on goosedown!

Was he dead? Had San Bismas interceded with the angels to bear him up to heaven? Or had he gone the other way and soon cruel Satan would spring a trap under the bed and drop him into the flames?

All at once his memories flooded back, filling up his head with misery, and he groaned as he recalled the burly, angry guard carrying him off from Papa el Mono's and the fear and subsequent pain of the beating and whipping to make him talk. The whoreson guards had used wide leather straps to beat him bloody and then had bounced him off the walls like a deflated ball, kicking him when he fell. No wonder he felt so feeble. His heart sank like a stone; what he did not remember was escaping their clutches, and so he must still be a captive.

Ignoring the weakness of his arms he struggled to a sitting position where he could see past the open bed curtains into the expanse of his cell. But the large chamber around which his eyes wandered uncomprehendingly made a peculiar prison. Opposite his bed there was a wide fireplace whose pyramid-shaped marble breast was carved with an escutcheon twined with ivy vines. On one wall a vivid tapestry of stylized birds and hounds came alive in shafts of sunlight streaming from two high but unbarred windows. A Savonarola x-chair with a tassled pillow and a similarly cushioned folding stool stood before the hearth, flanking a polished table that bore silver candlesticks, ink pot and reed pen, and a bowl of wildflowers. In one corner a prie-dieu stood expectantly, its velvet kneerest scuffed from years of supporting pious supplicants. In another corner sat a commodious, carved chest. The floor, of decorated tiles, was warmed near the bed by a fringed Eastern carpet of heavy wool.

Francho shook his head like a dog coming out of water. For all his natural optimism he understood that no one got installed in a luxurious chamber as a reward for distinguished thievery. In his puzzlement he decided he was suffering delirium from the crack on the head he had taken from the guards. But when he gingerly put his hand up to the dull ache on his crown he found the hair had been carefully cut away from the area and the cut was closed and crusted, healing.

The shrill, startling chirrup of a bird drew his attention to the windows. Slowly he edged his legs over the side of the bed and stood, clinging to the bed curtain to fight off a momentary blackness that buzzed into his eyes. Finally, he tottered across the chamber to verify his conclusion that, for some reason, he was locked in the Alcalde's own mansion to await his punishment. He leaned over the slanted ledge of the open window, looked down and then to each side, and was forced to swallow repeatedly to contain the nausea that rose in his chest as he realized that the fortress which surrounded him no more resembled the Alcalde's house than an eagle resembled a sparrow.

Solitary, stark, standing on the only rise of ground within leagues, the huge fortress-castle which stretched on either side of his high window commanded the arid plains around it like a grim colossus. Below him the breeze-ruffled dark water of the moat mirrored great, round-towered walls and a green-and-white banner fluttering gaily, incongruously, from the highest tower of the pile, signifying that the lord of the manor was in residence. Any watch patrolling the crenellated bastions had a far, clear view of the rutted road which wound its way from the Castilian uplands and through the nearby town huddling close to the strength and security of its centuries-old guardian, and then went on past boulder-dotted fields, where herdsmen guarded the castle's own great herds of sheep and those consigned to winter over in annual migrations from Galicia and the northern provinces.

A silvered, piping hawk wheeled alone in the boundless turquoise sky, swooping occasionally at the puffs of dust raised by peasants driving goats along the road. The bird held Francho's stare for a moment, causing a yearning in his breast to fly away and be that free.

He slid off the wide, slanting window ledge to subside in a weary heap on the floor. There was no doubt he was a prisoner of this frowning castle. But how could he escape if he couldn't even walk across the floor? Summoning a little energy, he managed to lurch back to the bed, seeking the comfort of the goosedown again, very tired from his small excursion. His disconnected thoughts rolled around in his brain like dice in a box as he waited to gather strength again. He had to take some action, if only to get something to wet his desperately parched throat. With a hostile eye he took in his rich surroundings. Surely they had some water in this place.

Hoisting himself up on one elbow he croaked wildly, "I want some water, *por piedad.* Water!" He waited a few moments, then strained to make it louder this time, *"Hola,* whoever you are, bring some drink. Answer me, someone! Help, help . . ."

He heard quick footsteps without, and then the heavy wood door to the chamber squeaked open and a lackey peeked in, looking like a startled goldfish. He glanced at the youth half sitting up in the bed, uttered a flustered "oh!" and withdrew, closing the door swiftly.

Annoyed, Francho let a few minutes pass and was just about to call out again when the door opened once more and the same servant bowed in a small gentleman, who came smiling and nodding across the carpet to Francho's bed, sniffing at a scented handkerchief. Francho immediately recognized him as the Count of Tendilla's foreign companion, and suddenly his arm tingled as he recalled the painfully strong grip that had closed on it when he had tried to make a break from the Alcalde's gate house. The puzzle of his whereabouts deepened.

"Well, my boy, I'd say you have much better color this matin. You gave us an awful fright, falling so ill. We knew not whether 'twas your fever or the blow to your head when you fell which kept you senseless so long, but the physician treated both." He held up a finger. "But not by bleeding, you may be sure. Neither the Count nor I favor it. How do you feel now?" the man asked cheerfully. "Do you wish to eat?"

"Water," Francho croaked. The lackey sprang to produce a ewer and goblet from a stool at the other side of the bed and gave a filled glass to Francho, who drank gratefully. Di Lido then motioned the servant out of the room.

"Who are you?" Francho demanded, wiping his mouth on his fancy sleeve, revived by the water. There was nothing for it but to take the bull by the horns.

The elegant eyebrows fluttered upward. "Who am I? A friend, dear lad, a friend. Pietro di Lido, humanist, historian, amateur physician, and Iñigo de Mendoza's sometime confidential secretary. 'Twas on my advice, as soon as your fever broke, that your windows were left unshuttered. I felt you would regain your strength sooner with fresh air and sunlight, a notion I acquired from the ancient Greeks and quite against the offices of these provincial Spanish doctors, of course. And from the looks of you, inherent intelligence has evidently triumphed once more."

"Where is this place?" Francho asked, suspiciously, discounting di Lido's cordial tone.

"Well, I could tell you but 'tis not my duty. You have endured a debilitating malady, Francisco. Do not trouble your head with details now. Just rest easy and wait. You will soon learn everything relevant to your situation."

"Do you intend to hang me?" Francho persisted boldly, although he held his breath for the answer.

Di Lido gaped at him, noting the slight shadow of fear in the defiant blue eyes. He opened his mouth to respond when a blare of horns, mingled with a rattling and clattering of horses crossing the ancient wooden drawbridge and the cries of hurrying grooms, drew him quickly to the window. He peered down with interest at the magnificently arrayed churchman on a milky white jennet just riding under the portcullis at the head of a large troop of stiff-backed, lance-carrying soldiers. The prelate was flanked by four lesser clerics in the white robes of the Dominican Order and preceded by liveried pages bearing his banner and cross.

The Italian smiled with pleasure. "Ah, his worship, the gentle Bishop of Avila. He visits his abbeys in the region and sometimes graces us with his presence. How fortuitous he should arrive at this moment. I must attend the Count and tell him the good news of your condition, and then I must make myself ready to greet the Bishop; he is a great stickler for the formal proprieties." Nodding in agreement with himself, he turned to leave, almost forgetting the boy who still glowered at him.

"Wait! I want to know where I am and why are you . . . why am I . . . what do you intend to do with me?"

Di Lido could not ignore the boy's distress, which he feared might cause a relapse into brain fever. He glided forward to the bed, hands pressed together as if in prayer and waggled them up and down. *"Dolce, dolce,* lad. Oh, the impatience of youth! You are at Castle Mondejar, an ancient family fortress belonging to the Count of Tendilla and Figueroa, a most illustrious member of the great Mendoza family."

"I see." Francho's voice turned dull. "His Grandness wanted his familiar comforts about him while the hangman puts my neck in the noose."

"Hangman?" Di Lido tittered in amusement. "God's mercy, boy. Do you count it the normal thing for gallow's bait to be laid up in a princely bed with doctors dancing in attendance and all his comforts seen to with dispatch? Look about you, then; you must realize there is no question of punishment beyond that which you have already endured. In fact, your roguish deed has been quite forgotten."

Francho clenched his teeth in frustration, still believing he was slated to provide a fatal entertainment, plagued by all this mysterious solicitude from men who but yesterday ordered him beaten and given over to the constable. "Will I be allowed to leave? To go back to Ciudad Real?" he tested.

"Now, why would you wish to return to that insufferable hole? In any case we are many days away from Ciudad Real, and you will find the atmosphere at Mondejar much more elevating and pleasant."

"Many days . . . ? Then I *am* a prisoner here."

"Oh, forbid, no prisoner at all. But be patient and you will know the hows and wherefores in good time, I pledge you. Now I must take my leave." He patted Francho's knee under the blanket, his small, sharp features warmed with a sincere expression. "Rest now and conserve your strength. I shall send someone in to attend you."

Francho gave up, too weary to press the man further. From the doorway di Lido eyed him brightly and with sympathy and recited a Latin homily on the rewards of abiding with patience, to which Francho automatically replied in good Latin with the reversal, "He who waits too long to drink, drains the dregs." He did not care that the scholar's brows raised up as he left the chamber and that a delighted smile touched the man's lips.

* * *

Tendilla's small study, sanctuary from the capacious proportions of Mondejar's public chambers, was a favorite withdrawing room for the Count, where he could study and meditate without distraction, surrounded by objects he enjoyed. One walnut-paneled wall was hung with intricately embellished dress armor and a collection of Toledo and Damascus swords and daggers. Along another a long bench supported use-worn musical instruments: cornettos, lutes, a rebec, and a portable organ. A niche in the wall held the Count's armillary sphere, quadrant, dividers, and triangle and plumb line. And everywhere there were books: stacks of bound and unbound manuscripts piled on table and floor, those on the writing table lying open with notes entered in their margin in a flowing script. The floor was warmed by a rich, patterned wool carpet. A fire in the corner hearth made the room cozy.

Looking around the well-lit space, the Bishop of Avila noted how well the objects it contained reflected the many-sided personality of its owner, and he was pleased, as always, to be one of the intimates allowed a glimpse into this very private man. It wafted across his mind that the three of them meeting in this sanctum represented the same puissant coalition of secular power, religious faith, and questing philosophy that had long ago propelled a small remnant of Visigothic Christians out of their mountain strongholds in Asturia to retake in only three centuries almost the whole of their native Iberian peninsula from the Moorish conquerers. It was a conceited thought, but he liked it.

Now the Count turned from a cupboard from which he had been extracting a coffer, candlelight gleaming off the rich silk of his amber brocade doublet frothed with the white of linen pulled out through the arm and elbow slits in the doublet's tight sleeves. Smiling, the grandee deposited his coffer on the table.

"If Your Worship is refreshed and rested from the rigors of the journey, would you care to hear of our most amazing discovery?"

Talavera shifted impatiently in his chair. "May the Almighty forgive you, Don Iñigo, you have been talking in riddles for many minutes, and if it is your cruel purpose to whet my curiosity, you have succeeded. Di Lido, have mercy on these old white hairs and settle yourself so that we may finally hear the pronouncement of this prodigious news."

"First a drop of spiritous wine, Your Worship?" the Italian, flamboyant in a large, crimson hat, offered as he also helped himself. "You may find you require it."

He smiled as the Bishop, plump and ruddy-faced, waved a jeweled hand. "Proceed, proceed, *señores,* deliver me from your clutches."

"Quite simply stated, my lord Bishop," Tendilla responded, arms folded casually, "I have found the missing Venegas child." He saw, with amusement, that Talavera reacted like a chubby cherub whose behind had been pinched. The faded brown eyes popped, the fingers spread wide with astonishment, the huge emerald ring on the prelate's thumb glittered green in the firelight. The rosy mouth worked, and finally the words sputtered out:

"No! It could not be possible. We had exhausted every effort. We decided finally the babe had been murdered."

"We were wrong. The boy is very much alive. We stumbled upon him not a fortnight ago."

"But . . . I am dumbfounded. It has been—fifteen years. But are you sure? And where is he?"

"In one of the chambers above," Tendilla replied, leaning back to sit, as was his habit, on the edge of the table. "He had recently an unfortunate accident which gave him a bang on the head and a fever. In fact his slow recovery has worried us, although Pietro tells me he is awake and greatly improved today. You will, I am sure, wish to see him?"

"Most certainly, most certainly. But you must tell me the details, Iñigo. I am struck with wonder at this incredible happening. Where did you find him?" This time the Bishop speedily accepted the goblet di Lido proffered and took a generous sip.

Briefly Tendilla recounted the circumstances which had brought the young cutpurse of Ciudad Real into his hands, relishing, now that his own emotions were under control, the incredulity with which Talavera greeted the story. At the end, with his rueful admission that the boy never did tell where he had hidden the stolen purse, they all broke into chuckles.

"Ah well, 'twas worth the money to find this remnant of the house of Venegas, merciful God give his father peace." Talavera's face, having creased into a broad smile, now became more thoughtful. "But, my lord, how can you be so positive that this youth is truly Juan de Venegas's issue? After all, we must be certain."

Tendilla patted the leather coffer he had put on the desk. "I have certain proofs here that I pray you to examine to clear your mind of doubt. Beyond this my strongest proof is the lad himself. Not only the close resemblance, but you will immediately recognize the singular scar we remarked on at the time of his baptism. Do you remember?"

"Yes, yes, ah indeed, I recall it even now. A small cicatrix, like a little dagger?"

"The curious mark of a dagger. His father believed it foretold of great military exploits for him."

They were silent for a moment, each involved with his own memories of the tragedy of so long ago. At length Talavera heaved himself up to slowly pace the room, his hand plucking at the huge silver cross which lay on his broad velvet bosom, his brow furrowed. As he came abreast of Tendilla he made a gesture of agitation.

"Might it not have been more charitable to leave him in peace, ignorant of his birthright? What can we do now for a child of Juan de Venegas? His estates, his grants, his patents have all been forfeited to the Crown. The very name Venegas is still anathema to Isabella, and she is guilty of the sin of pride. She does not forgive easily; her lust for vengeance is strong enough to extend even unto a youth who was a mere babe when she was acclaimed heir to the throne. My heart fears for this boy, who has been martyred on the wheel of his father's stupidity."

"And yet you loved his father well, good Bishop," Tendilla reminded him.

"Yes . . . I did. Before the Devil claimed him he was a generous, reverent man, innocent of guile. And for the sake of this memory and the gentle Jesu I shall take his son to my heart. But I tell you there is no hope of recovering the boy's patrimony. Of this I am certain."

"No more than I, Your Grace. I am well aware of the Queen's attitude toward the issue of the supposed murderer of her brother. Yet sit down, I beg you. We may still pull more than one chestnut from this vexing fire."

"Ha! I might have known you would have a clever plan, my dear Iñigo."

The Count absently balanced his little dagger off one fingertip. "No, not yet a detailed plan, Your Grace, but an idea, a speculation that might benefit us all."

Di Lido, lounging in a chair, eyes half-closed, punctuated his patron's words here and there with a silent but emphatic nod. Tendilla cleared his throat. His black eyes glittered, and two spots of color showed on the fine, high cheekbones.

"It is clear that our war with the Moors is rapidly gaining momentum and that the near future will see an ever more bitter and bloody battle to push the Moslems entirely out of Granada and out of Spain. However, although there is no doubt in my mind that the forces of Their Catholic Majesties will eventually prevail, I realize it will be at a fearful cost." He pushed off from the table and began to pace up and down the chamber, hands clasped behind his back.

"But when we do have Granada in our hands, Granada, so lush a Garden of Eden, the repository of many of civilization's greatest art treasures and scientific wonders—I mean to use every power I can muster to keep this magnificent prize from being ransacked by the governorship of the avaricious Medina-Sidonia, or the vengeful Cadiz. My purpose is to undermine their candidacy for the position, no matter how their great feats of valor in the field may impress the Crown."

"Not to be compared to the brilliance and bravery of the victor of Alcala, my lord," di Lido reminded him.

Tendilla waved away the compliment and continued, fixing the prelate with his piercing gaze. "If you suspect, Your Grace, that I am determined to be named, myself, first Christian Governor of Granada, so far in the future as the conquest may now seem, you are right. And, to administer along with me in the post of spiritual leader of the new territories, I would require a man of temperance and reason and justice, filled with Christ's boundless mercy for those to whom all wisdom was not given. A shepherd such as you, Father."

Although the Bishop's faded eyes were keenly focused on his host, his smile was rueful. "I thank you for words, my son. I shall but give them back to you. How few of the nobility follow, as you do, the precepts of Our Dear Jesu, to neither rob nor rape nor murder, to deal fairly with fellow human beings, to wield power with love and God in their hearts. Not many, Almighty save us, not many." He sighed deeply. "Not even among my fellow religious."

The Count circled Talavera's chair. "Then must we not actively prepare our campaign, using every subtlety we can command to place ourselves in a position to offer the most remarkable service in the struggle for Granada?" he asked intently.

"Indeed. But by what method do we proceed?" Talavera was confident the brilliant Tendilla had already decided this.

"Having worked hand in glove with me for many years, good Bishop, you are aware that often I am able to obtain, sub rosa, military and political information that has proved of great value to Ferdinand and Isabella. It is this unusual service, if spectacularly continued, which could ensure for me the governorship of Granada, along with the influence to have you appointed to the See." He paused to pour a bit more of the strong wine into his goblet.

"Yes, yes. Go on, Iñigo . . ."

"It is my hope to develop a fully reliable source of information emanating from the heart of the Kingdom of Granada, from the very Alhambra with the Sultan himself, as close to the seat of decision as possible, so that there is no enemy move contemplated that Their Majesties will not know, beforehand, through me." A touch of arrogance had colored the clipped, dry tone.

"Aha!" The Bishop echoed Tendilla's decisive tone, though not quite as calmly. "But *señor,* you are seeking a miracle of duplicity. The Moors have so heavy a penchant for lying and betrayal it makes our intriguers seem babes by comparison. To dupe them, where will you find so wily, resourceful, courageous, intelligent, and selfless an agent, who would also be bribe-proof and completely trustworthy? The sword of deception cuts with two edges. We could as well be undone by false information."

The Count folded his length into the high-backed chair behind the desk, expression concentrated into examining his own thinking as he spoke. "We have now a miraculous opportunity, see you. We have in our camp a boy, a person young enough to be completely trained and indoctrinated, a person who has already demonstrated a certain intrepidity by daring to steal my purse. He is a Venegas. His early education was with the brothers, and di Lido tells me he quotes Latin proverbs. God willing, he is not stupid. I believe, with work, we could shape him into the perfect instrument by which all of our plans may be realized."

Talavera blinked. He reflected a few seconds. Finally he grunted. "Perhaps this is so. Perhaps he presents a most tempting clay to be molded into a masterful spy—and let us call what is black, black. Why would he agree to such peril and the rigors of training for it?"

"To gain his own ends," Tendilla asserted. "If *he* were the source from which flowed priceless information which aided the armies of the Cross in a rapid conquest of Granada, would Their Generous Majesties not consider serving justice and repaying such loyalty by reinstating his titles and lands? What more glittering inducement to risk for an impecunious orphan?"

Talavera grunted again. "All presuming he has the ability to do what you devise for him." A beringed hand went up. "Nor do I wish to know the details. Your craftiness may yet provide this young person the means to recoup his family's honor, and for this I commend you." The rounded shoulders shrugged under the shimmering white satin robe. "The Lord will work his own will in the question of spiritual leadership of the territories reclaimed for Christ. But I would strongly like to see as temporal captain a man of your judicious nature, who is not ruled by greed or cruel passions. Therefore I say to you, plant your seeds in good time. And I shall pray that your confidence in this boy is not misplaced."

"Then we may count on you, should it be required for the Queen's confessor to whisper a gentle suggestion in the royal ear? Or should the need arise for a liaison acquainted with the whole story in the event I am not available?"

"I will help in whichever way I can that is not displeasing to God. I take it, it is just we three who are aware of this boy's identity?"

"Just so, and one other, my cousin Doña Maria de Zuniga, the past few years a member of my household and the nurse who has brought the lad back to health."

"Ah, yes, I recall her, a pious and discreet lady. The two of you have always enjoyed a close kinship."

Di Lido now came forward to the desk. "Your Worship, at Don Iñigo's request I have drawn up several documents pertaining to his relationship with this youth, and also a testimony of the boy's true parentage. After you have met the person in question, we hope you will be gracious enough to witness these and carry sealed copies with you into safekeeping." He extended a leather envelope, which Talavera took from him.

There was a gentle rapping at the door.

"That is my major-domo to tell us our supper is waiting," Tendilla announced genially, and rose. "Come, good sirs, we can all use some rich fare under our belts. Eh, Your Grace?"

"Amen," intoned Talavera, raising his hands in mock agreement. "I thought surely you were making me wait until breakfast."

All three laughed easily together, like the longtime friends they were.

The chamber was dark when Francho again opened his eyes. But now he felt stronger. And he was ravenously hungry. Realizing that footsteps without had awakened him, he sat up and looked toward the door with trepidation, half expecting a hooded hangman to enter, noose in hand.

Instead, a flare of cheerful light introduced a woman into the chamber, followed by two servants holding many-branched candelabra aloft in each hand and a third lackey bearing a bowl and a cup on a tray.

The woman, in her middle age, rustled toward him with a warm expression. Her gown was of a busy-patterned brocade, full-shirted, droopy-sleeved, and cinched with a tassled golden cord about the waist. A few gray hairs escaped from the confining coif which soared above her head like white butterfly's wings. Her eyes, shiny brown beads caught in a net of fine lines, evinced a gentle humor. "The blessed heart of Jesu be praised," she exclaimed in a soft contralto. "I can see for myself you are indeed much recovered." Unhesitatingly she placed a cool hand on his forehead. "Not a trace of fever. You must thank God you have an iron pate, lad, and a strong constitution. Many a grown man would have been laid in his coffin from such a terrible mauling."

For a moment she peered into his eyes intently, then smiled. "They told me you had eyes blue as the heavens. . . ."

She offered Francho a mug and he accepted it. It was cool, mulled wine mixed with water, and it coursed spicy and lively through his veins, reviving him. The woman watched him with a pleased smile, then directed the servant to put the tray with its bowl of steaming gruel and big spoon on Francho's lap. "We had to pour rich broth down your throat bit by bit while you lay senseless for so long. You shall have to eat hearty these next days to get some flesh on your bones." Her mouth, with its faintly pleated upper lip, twitched to see him fall upon the food. "I can see such a task will not overly try you," she murmured.

Francho wolfed down the cereal, blowing impatiently on each spoonful to cool it and scraping up every stray morsel. The lady, meanwhile, directed the servants to take the chill off the night air with a hearth fire and to smooth the bedclothes. She sent one valet running for a basin of water so that Francho could wash his hands and face. When the last of the gruel had disappeared and the washing had refreshed him, Francho returned his mind to his predicament.

"I thank you for your kindness, lady. But will you tell me what I am doing here? I don't understand . . . ?" Maybe she, at least, wouldn't talk in riddles like the little man who had visited him earlier.

But the dame simply stood still for a moment, cocking her head to listen to noises outside. "In a moment, Francisco, all your questions will be answered. You have visitors."

A lackey threw open the door to admit three gentlemen, while another servant quickly pushed a chair closer to the bed. Francho shoved himself fully erect, wincing at the soreness around his ribs and silently cursing the weakness that kept him from leaping off the bed. He faced them silently with what he hoped was a belligerent expression. He wanted to impress upon them that he was not frightened, although under his projected bravado he remained tense and wary. He also wished he had on his own clothes rather than the silly nightrobe.

Tendilla and di Lido he already recognized, so he centered his attention on the richly robed cleric accompanying them, whose purple skullcap, almost hidden in a halo of wispy white hair, and huge episcopal ring proclaimed him a high dignitary of the Church.

The ecclesiastic walked directly up to the bed and automatically made the sign of the cross over Francho's head, meanwhile drawing his white brows together in concentration. His faded eyes roved over Francho's face, studying his features carefully, an examination through which Francho sat unflinchingly, although he felt himself flush with discomfort. At last the Bishop murmured a soft *"Dominus Vobiscum"* and clasped Francho's hands together between his own warm ones for a moment.

"Et cum spiritu tuo, good Father," Francho mumbled back.

Talavera expelled a heavy breath and seemed to relax. "I

believe you are correct, Don Iñigo, although I still have a doubt or two. The resemblance, especially the eyes, is uncanny."

Tendilla stepped forward. "This will dispell any doubts, Your Grace. The most telling proof is the scar on his back. If you will allow me, Francisco?"

Francho stiffened, but the Count leveled upon him so severe a look he thought it wiser to conserve his energy and submit. He let the nobleman pull away the neck of his nightgown so that the churchman could stare myopically at the puckered white scar on his shoulder blade, and he was more puzzled than ever at their actions.

The men drew back, exchanging glances of satisfaction. The portly prelate turned away to seat himself thoughtfully in the chair before the bed.

The woman said calmly to her cousin, "Don Iñigo, the boy is sorely tried to know why he is at Mondejar."

"Indeed?" Tendilla's black eyes surveyed Francho with the air of a man who has just bought a questionable horse. Francho, unwavering under the scrutiny, stared back; he hoped the bobbing of his Adam's apple did not give evidence of his acute unease.

Tendilla allowed a slow smile to soften his saturnine features. "Even so," he murmured. "Courage, curiosity, and mulishness. Traits one might recognize all by themselves."

An odd expression flitted across the face of di Lido, sitting at the foot of the bed. But he merely snapped his fingers at the one flunky who had remained in attendance, and the man bowed out of the chamber.

The Count remained standing before Francho, fingering his bearded chin, one arm supporting his bent elbow. "You are known as Francisco, is that correct?"

"Yes . . . *Grandeza.*"

"I shall present you to my companions: His Grace, Hernando de Talavera, Bishop of Avila and the Royal Confessor; my most excellent cousin, Doña Maria de Zuniga, to whose kind ministrations your wounds and brain fever have yielded; and you have already met Italy's most renowned savant, Señor Pietro di Lido." They all acknowledged the introduction by beaming at the boy in the bed. Francho only nodded back stiffly.

Tendilla dropped his arms into a commending, akimbo

position. "You were raised at San Martín , a small monastery in Tijuna, true?"

"Yes . . . my lord."

"Then what were you doing in Ciudad Real?" the Count snapped.

"I ran away from the monastery. I lived with friends in Ciudad Real . . ."

". . . who taught you the meritorious art of stealing? Solicitous friends, indeed!"

"Perhaps not to some, but they were the only ones who cared whether I lived or died." Francho's eyes flashed blue fire. "They gave me a home when I had none, and for that I shall repay them someday."

Tendilla, although he was both amused and impressed by the boy's spirited defense of his lawless coterie, remained silent.

"And why do you ask me all these questions?" Francho stumbled ahead boldly. "What does it matter to you?" His voice cracked.

"You stole a nice sum of money from me. Surely that should allow me some interest in you? Are you not aware that I am within my rights to hang you for such offense?"

"It would be a just dessert for allowing myself to be caught by that flatfooted pigsticker of yours," Francho muttered, remembering the beating. "A one-legged girl could outrun him."

Tendilla's lips twitched. "Oh, but you will not be hanged. Great blind fortune as well as your penchant for crime, I suppose, has happily brought you to your true friends. See here, boy, *you* may not know your parentage and birthright, but we who are present here *do* know who you are." The grandee paused, unable to resist being dramatic as he saw the boy's eyes widen and his lips part in surprise.

"What? I don't follow you. . . ."

"You are Francisco Luis de Venegas, the Marquis of Olivenza."

The brittle silence that followed was suffocating. Francho sat staring, transfixed, convinced that the famous Tendilla was a lunatic. He glanced around at the others; but their faces mirrored only sympathy for his shock. No surprise, no objection. But—they're all mad, he decided, crazy ones escaped from a holding, pretending to be aristocrats.

"You think we are moonstruck, do you not?" the Count continued, as smoothly as if he had announced merely that Francho's name was not Francisco but Juan. "Let me assure you that during your illness we have taken rapid steps to be certain that you are the high-born infant of whom we lost track fifteen years ago. And we are satisfied of your identity." The smile that finally warmed his lean face seemed genuine to Francho's scrutiny. "Let me give you welcome to Mondejar, Don Francisco, lord of Olivenza." A hint of sympathy flickered in the black eyes.

Francho closed his mouth abruptly. Did they think he was an idiot? Marquis? Since when did a marquis get left naked on doorsills? He said rigidly, "I don't understand why you joke with me."

"Joke?" Tendilla rumbled. "By all the saints and devils, do I impress you as a bandier of words? Mark me well when I speak; I tell you the truth."

"His disbelief is understandable, my lord," di Lido interrupted. "It must be a resounding shock to discover one's true name after so long. And then to have it bear a noble escutcheon in the bargain . . ."

"Sí, my lord, it must be a difficult thing to encompass," Talavera agreed compassionately, rising from his chair to approach Francho. "Listen then to me, my son. Your father, Juan de Venegas, was a grandee of the realm. His rank of marquis is now yours, as his only heir. Your mother was Doña Elena de Lura, a sweet and noble lady and peeress in her own right, with title to the county of Monteroja. At the time of their unfortunate deaths, may the Redeemer have rescued both their immortal souls, you were taken away by a trusted retainer, who was to safely hide you until you could be delivered into friendly hands. Whatever misfortune befell him, the man was heard from no more; and when we took up a search, we could not find any clue as to what had become of you, a tiny babe."

The Count's voice took up the tale. "Nor do we know even now why he went to Tijuna. No matter. It is our present desire, just as then, to help you take your rightful place in the peerage. Because your sire . . . and your mother . . . were close to our hearts."

Doña Maria, warming her back at the fire, watched the flabbergasted boy struggle to find some composure, as if he were bracing against being pushed off the edge of a cliff. Poor fellow, she thought, he had learned to survive in his world, however mean, and now comes this revelation—astounding, bewildering, a monumental leap from the familiar. Her gaze swept his face. The high brow and square jaw were inherited from Don Juan, unquestionably. But the other features, a shock of dark ringlets spilling over his forehead, the sensitive mouth, and especially the intensely blue eyes, so startling against the pale olive complexion—those were Elena de Lura, almost as if that fey spirit had reappeared to face the world in sturdy male guise. Poor naive, unlucky Elena . . .

Doña Maria transferred her attention to her cousin, Tendilla. What bittersweet memories the finding of this boy must have loosed upon him, although he would not show it. Her musings were broken by Francho's desperate appeal to the Bishop of Avila, as the one he deemed least inclined to lie.

"Reverend Bishop, there are thousands of bastards left in the street every week. Perhaps it is not really me, Francisco no-name, whom you seek." But even as he protested Francho felt the stirrings of a fascinated willingness to believe. Alternating with a hysterical desire to laugh.

Talavera deferred to Tendilla, who responded, with a hint of impatience, "Are you absurd enough to think we would indiscriminately accept any waif as Don Juan's missing heir? There are a number of proofs. One, you strongly resemble your parents." He held up one tapered finger. "Two, you have the right name and the right age. Three, we have obtained by relay couriers several articles that were left with you at Santo Domingo—a blanket of fine wool such as would wrap the babe of a *ricos hombre,* and especially the ingenious and unique silver nursing cup your father invented for you when a wetnurse could not be obtained.

"These things are in my possession; you may examine them when you wish. But the last proof, to my mind, is the most conclusive. After your christening, when we had repaired to the castle's hall for the feast and celebration, your father called his friends about him to display to us a curious mark on the shoulder blade of his firstborn."

Lifting his head, Tendilla stared at a point straight ahead of him, as if seeing back into the past. "It was so unusual as to not be forgotten, a red and ragged tear which the Hebrew doctor had sewn up with fine silk, and which resembled, by chance alone, a hilted dagger. Your birth was hard. The doctor used a secret instrument to turn you in the womb, wounding you but saving both your life and your mother's. My friend Venegas was awed. He believed it was an omen, a sign that your arm would bring victory in the field and honor upon his house."

The dark stare dropped back to Francho. "The scar has turned white with age. But it is the same one we all gaped at fifteen years ago."

Unconsciously Francho's hand felt behind him, under his right shoulder blade.

"You must assimilate this. You *are* Don Francisco de Venegas."

Tendilla turned suddenly, deliberate as a stalking cat, and moved to the unshuttered window. He clasped his hands behind him and frowned out into the night. Doña Maria knew he was disturbed by the boy's eyes. But Tendilla spoke, and although it was toward the cloud-misted moon rising over the plains like a hesitant bride, his words, resonant and precise, rebounded from the walls of the quiet chamber. "Just for tonight, however."

Pietro di Lido sniffed his scented handkerchief. Talavera fingered the large cross at his bosom. Doña Maria looked down, busily smoothing her skirt. Francho glanced helplessly at each one, hoping to find some expression, some guide that would help him understand the tangle of statements and contradictions which they presented. He found nothing but kind sympathy.

He swiped at his moist forehead with the back of his beribboned wrist, then shoved back the blanket and swung his legs off the side of the bed.

"Where do you go, boy?" Doña Maria cried.

The Count turned his head without haste. "Are you leaving us, Don Francisco?" His voice was untroubled.

"Yes, if it is true I am not a prisoner. Why would I want to be a Venegas tonight and someone else tomorrow and maybe someone else after that? I'd rather be me, Francho, and go back to my own people and my own life in Ciudad Real." He scowled at them all and hoped he sounded in control of himself, for deep within he knew that whatever their game nothing would ever be the same again. If they let him go he would be forever haunted by these strange revelations and wondering were they true. "And even if I am who you say I am, what is that to me but a name? I don't know how to be a lord. I'm a cut . . . a member of the rabble, pure and simple."

Talavera shook his head. "God's mercy, my lord Tendilla," he chided. "It is cruel to bait the boy with ambiguous statements. Explain to him all of it, I beg you."

Tendilla lifted an eyebrow in apology to the prelate. "Forgive me, you are right, Your Grace. That was unworthy advantage. Pray, stay in your bed, Francho. You are still weak. I shall attempt to speak more plainly." He came across the chamber again to resume his stance before the bed.

Francho finally shrugged and got back under the comforter again since he had reached the same conclusion about his strength; his head ached faintly and he was glad to subside against the pillow once more. The idea began to grip his mind that, after all, these people seemed favorably inclined toward him. If they insisted he was the son of a *ricos hombre,* well, what was so terrible? A marquis? A marquis owned lands, vassals, riches, everything.

Tendilla's smile was thin. "You must believe you *are* Francisco de Venegas, born to Elena and Juan Alfonso de Venegas, nobility of the realm. Normally you would be heir to your father's extensive estate and income as well as your mother's. But—although it is your right to know this it becomes a cruelty, for the fact remains that your entire inheritance was confiscated by the Crown, as well as all your patents and titles. What is worse"—and here Tendilla rubbed a finger across the small triangle of beard on his chin—"is that your own life is an execration to your sovereigns.

"In time I shall tell you the reason for this, but let us go on for the moment—although mark me very well, not a person outside of those present in this room must know your real identity. If you value your life you will hold your tongue and keep your true name secret within you."

Francho fought to keep his voice from rising. "But if I cannot claim my natural name or rank, then what . . . who shall I be?"

"My son," Tendilla answered blandly.

"Y . . . your son?"

"Yes, an excellent subterfuge. Let us imagine that I had in my youth discreetly sired an illegitimate child by some unvirtuous but well-born lady, and that it has lately come to my attention that the good woman has expired, leaving the child alone. Having a marriage which no longer allows hope of any offspring, I now go to fetch my son by the bar sinister and bring him home to live with me, to be the means by which my line is perpetuated. Simple, is it not?"

And simple it was. The mortality rate of offspring being high, even Francho knew that the arrangement proposed by Tendilla was quite common. Bastard children of the nobility, officially installed as heirs or favorites, were recognized without question or prejudice.

"Therefore," the Count continued, pointing the hilt of his little dagger at Francho for emphasis, "you will now be known by the name of Francisco de Mendoza and will be entitled to the honor given the progeny of a grandee of the realm. My name will keep you safe. Yours will not. Do you understand?"

Not wanting to appear stupid, Francho nodded. But hesitantly.

Tendilla cocked an eyebrow. "You wish to question the arrangement?"

Francho cleared his throat. "Yes. Why would you do this for me?"

Again he was rewarded by the thin smile. "Good, you are discerning. Naught comes for naught, eh? Let me assure you that my intentions are most honorable and for your greatest benefit. And, as you correctly sense, for mine. You may trust me, Francisco. I shall shape a victorious future for us both."

Francho's glance traveled again from face to face, returning to meet Tendilla's eyes. "And if I do not want to stay?" he tested.

"If you cannot support the fine life of a gentleman you may go as soon as you wish, and freely, with no further argument. My word on it."

Francho believed him. His tense muscles relaxed. His stomach stopped roiling. He took a deep breath, a quavering one in spite of himself. "I will stay."

Tendilla nodded, sheathing his little dagger. Di Lido strode over to clap Francho's shoulder with friendly reassurance. "Bravo, bravo! Ah, what a list of cognomens you have knocking about your head, eh? Soon you will find them all too familiar."

Doña Maria clasped her hands before her, smiling. "You will be happy here, Don Francisco. This is where you belong."

Talavera, ruddy face beaming, approached to take Francho's hands and offer a blessing. *"Sanguis Domini nostri*

Jesu Christi custodiat. Trust in the greatness of God, my son, and he will lead you."

"Enough, enough for now. We shall further discuss the future, Francisco, when you are stronger. Come, my friends, let us retire and leave this newly begat hope of my house to regain his health and collect his thoughts." Tendilla's dark head in its velvet toque inclined stiffly, although a small smile still softened his aristocratic features. "I bid you a good night, Don Francisco de Mendoza," he murmured. He turned on his heel and strode to the portal, the others following behind him.

The sound of their footsteps as they closed the door and left sounded to Francho like the rustle of leaves whispering away in the wind.

A lackey entered to place a jug of water on a stool by his bed, extinguish the candles, and half close the bedcurtains, but Francho, worn out, hardly noticed the servant's entrance or departure. He slipped down under the cover and stretched out but then thrashed about, unable to find comfort. His ribs ached. His head spun.

Venegas . . . Mendoza . . . Olivenza . . . Marquis . . . the names churned about in his brain, the impressive, impossible names burning in letters of flame in front of his eyes. He rolled his head back and forth, and suddenly he was whispering into the dark, "No. I am Francho. I am a thief and an ordinary varlet. I am me. I want to go back to the hostel, to Tía Esperanza, to Carlos and Pepi and Dolores and big 'Fredo. I want to go home."

Ashamed of the tear that suddenly spilled down his cheek he strove to comfort himself. "Tomorrow. Tomorrow I will tell them no. Tomorrow I will get out of here and back to Ciudad Real. Somehow." At last, determined to leave, he fell asleep, fists clenched, brows drawn together, the dark ringlets damp on his forehead.

The clarion call of a trumpet awoke him to a bright morning full of the exciting sounds of bustle and clatter in the great courtyard below. Sliding out of the bed, he slowly walked over to the window on legs which carried him normally at last and climbed up to lean on the window ledge. Looking down he discovered he had an unimpeded view of a colorful hunting party which was just leaving the castle over the drawbridge and going against a stream of people coming the other way: supplicants, clerics, farmers with carts of grain or chickens, merchants with something to sell to the steward, neighboring townspeople to petition or to fawn, all drawn to Mondejar by the presence of the governing lord of the county—and for whose return from the hunt they would now have to wait in the yard or the great hall most of the day.

But Francho had eyes only for the stiff-backed Count of Tendilla in a burnished steel cuirass, riding out first on a high-stepping black stallion, the animal bedecked in argent and green trappings with silver tassels hanging from the wide, scalloped reins. Talavera rode beside him on a similarly bedecked horse, the prelate's large pectoral cross flashing in the early sunlight. A woman, possibly Doña Maria's lady-in-waiting, and Pietro di Lido followed, the lady sidesaddle on a chestnut mare, the fragile veil from her winged hat floating charmingly on the light breeze. Behind them came two tonsured members of Talavera's entourage in sedate robes, and these were followed by falconers supporting hooded birds on their padded fists, beaters with their dogs, armsbearers with crossbows and javelins, and a small squad of chain-mailed guards commanded by the unmistakable Rondero.

The hunting party clopped out over the bridge and then fell into a canter, stirring up dust along the road until the road curved and took them out of Francho's line of sight.

He slid down the ledge. Before his envious eyes still lingered the vision of Tendilla's easy seat and control of the spirited horse. With a twinge of homesickness, he mused that Carlos would give his soul to get such an animal. Yet, in the cheerful sunlight of morning his predicament seemed much less alarming, in fact the magnitude of his good luck finally leaped out at him. How craven it would be of him to flee back to Ciudad Real like a frightened rabbit. What had he to lose in learning to be a gentleman, and in a grandee's household, no less? He could always leave, later. He straightened his shoulders in resolution and banished the fear that had assailed him the night before.

A short knock and Doña Maria sailed in with a lackey, who silently placed a tray of food on the table. Her bright eyes surveyed him cordially from under her wimple-draped, rolled-brim turban. "So, Don Francisco, you are up and around. How nice. There is soup and bread and a fresh, white cheese for your breakfast. And how do you do, this matin?"

"Very well, my lady," he mumbled, suddenly shy.

She indicated the raiment which she carried draped over her arms. "Look here, I have brought you garments to wear while we wait for those which have been ordered from the costumer in Madrid. These are Pietro di Lido's, since he is closest to your size, and have been altered by a needlewoman in the village. I shall leave them here, and in a moment a valet will attend you. Now eat, my dear, eat. The soup will get cold."

She settled herself and sat for a while, contentedly watching him apply the cheese to a large slab of pale wheaten bread and wolf it down, along with the hot broth. Finally, lifting his gaze to hers, he asked offhandedly just to fill the silence, "Why did you not ride out with the hunt?"

Smiling, she shrugged. "Alas, I have a limb which pains me much with prolonged sitting in the saddle. But my companion, Doña Catalina, truly enjoys it, and so she is my emissary."

"And what will they bag?"

"Not much here, compared to the teeming forests near Don Iñigo's other properties. Some hare and red partridge for pies for our supper tonight, mayhap enough to also fill the bellies of the poor monks sheltering with us below on their way to Campostela." She rose, preparing to leave. Her smile was closedmouth because her teeth were bad, but it was friendly, as she took his chin and tilted up his face for closer inspection. "Good, your color is fine today; you were so deathly wan these weeks under those bruises, I feared for you. If you wish, you may explore the castle a bit to amuse yourself. It is a drafty old pile, but when I was your age I found it intriguing. It reminded me of the old times when knights were chivalrous and rescued distressed maidens and the mail-clad warriors to whom honor was all stood shoulder to shoulder defending these thick walls." She laughed at herself in a soft contralto as she pulled tighter the embroidered belt encircling her thickened waist to dangle in two tassels about her knees. "But I babble on about silly, young girl's fancies. I have tasks to accomplish. The major-domo here is sometimes negligent and the milk house is in a shambles. . . ."

"But what if I should come upon the guards who caught me in Ciudad Real?"

Turning from the door, she hastened to assure him. "Ah, but you will not, for they have been dismissed on some pretext or other—except for the big one, Rondero, who is the Count's most trusted servitor. The major-domo has informed the household that you are their master's natural son and that they are expected to show you due deference. So, whatever you should desire, you merely request it."

How incredible, those words!

Francho was still tasting the sweetness of them when an unctuous valet arrived to assist him with dressing. Since a full bath was bad for the recently ill, the fellow had brought with him a basin, hard soap, and a towel and insisted on sponging off Francho's thin young body, still showing the yellow and purple of fading bruises and the brown of welts. The servant asked no questions. He fluttered about his charge like an anxious nursemaid, handing him each garment, allowing him first to cover his nakedness with close-fitting underpants and a white, long-sleeved shirt, both of softest linen. Then Francho shoved his legs into skin-tight gray hosen, which the man drew up for him, and pulled the drawstring tight at the waist, ignoring his charge's embarrassment with the insistent help.

Over this went a gray-and-white doublet of fine wool, organpipe-pleated all around, belted with a silvered cord, and reaching to Francho's mid-thigh. His shoulders were broadened by wide-puffed sleeves, which then descended so tight to the wrist they had to be slashed at the elbow to allow movement, and for decorative effect the underfabric of his shirt was pulled through the slits. His feet went into purple leather shoes of new style, minus the exaggerated toes which had become passé with the fashionable, the valet thought it necessary to explain. The man attached to Francho's belt as a part of his costume a small dagger in a sheath and slipped a chain of plain gold links about his neck. He finished by extending a russet felt hat with a soft crown and rolled brim, frowned when it was clapped on carelessly, and himself resettled it properly on the dark curls, with a tilt.

The valet finally held up a glass mirror framed in gilt-painted wood. Francho had never seen himself in a mirror so clear and true, but the erstwhile cutpurse and pickpocket cockily assumed an attitude to peer at himself. He was immediately devastated at the astonishing image of a youth of refinement which jumped back at him; a well-dressed, unmistakable scion of privilege. Quickly he stopped goggling and introduced what he thought was a fitting air of hauteur into his expression, noting from the corner of his eye the valet's approval.

Hand on the hilt of his dagger, he sallied out of the chamber at last, not with his usual careless swagger but with a proud bearing imitating Tendilla's.

Roaming around the castle it didn't take him long to relish being addressed as Don Francisco by respectful, if curious, servitors as they went about their business. He was self-conscious at first, but he soon began to enjoy his exalted position and, taking his cue from earlier, brief observations of Tendilla and di Lido, just nodded at them imperiously.

The fact was that he turned somersaults inside when the guards stationed about the castle and before the door to Tendilla's private apartments struck their chests with a stiff forearm salute as he passed.

"Ay, María," he gloated, his glee unbounded, "not three weeks ago they would have spat on me. Now they must kiss my behind and bang their chests. Salute, you *bobiecas!* I can still steal the eyes from your head before you could blink."

He wandered happily about for a long time, passing through numerous chambers and climbing endless, twisting stairs in shadowy towers, which exuded dampness and cold from their stone walls. From the high slit windows he surveyed the gate house, the tidy stables where the Count's prize horses were pampered, the neat but sterile gardens and courts within the walls, the blacksmith's stall, from which a metallic clangor arose even to his aerie, the guard's barracks in a long building detached from the main house, and the square, moldering keep squatting to one side of the main court.

Exhausted, finally, he managed by some miracle to find his wing of the castle and his own chamber, tossed aside his hat, and gratefully fell upon the bed to rest.

When he woke up, with growling stomach, it was dusk and someone was knocking loudly on his door. The man who entered at his bidding was dressed more grandly than the ordinary lackey and had long, graying hair. This would be the major-domo, Francho thought, rubbing the sleep from his eyes.

"The Count requests you to attend him in his chambers, Don Francisco," the man said in a rusty voice. "If you would please to follow me?"

Smoothing his clothes and replacing his hat, Francho followed him, amused by the old retainer's bowlegged gait. Past the guarded door he was shown through a suite of fine rooms which at last led to Tendilla's study, where the major-domo knocked on the heavy door and then withdrew. "Enter," came the reply.

Francho pulled back his shoulders and opened the door. He felt this second interview would be easier for him now that he had grasped his position and adjusted his attitude. It remained to see what Tendilla really wanted and, just as important, to receive answers to the many questions that had nagged at him as he had loped through the stone reaches of the castle.

He thought he detected approval in Tendilla's brief scrutiny of him, but the Count said nothing, indicating with a tilt of his head and the tip of his feathered stylus that Francho was to wait while he finished a letter. Francho quietly strolled the paneled chamber, his self-conscious set of shoulders forgotten as he poked into the fascinating scientific bric-a-brac, manuscripts and military objects scattered about. Hands behind his back, he studied the mounted armor and weapons and tentatively touched the celestial orb.

But it was the marvelously inlaid eight-stringed lute that made his eyes glow as he came upon it. With reverence he lifted the lute from the bench and stroked the satiny wood of the bellied sound box for a moment, then he softly twanged the strings. He ran his thumb up and down the long, fretted neck and noted how lightly and how comfortably the instrument nestled into his body.

He didn't see Tendilla, still in the attitude of writing, watching him from under lowered brows.

"Can you play it?" the Count asked suddenly.

Francho started. He had been absorbed by the instrument. "A bit, my lord. I have had no formal lessons. I've just copied what I heard, and on no fine instrument such as this."

"Pluck it, then, I am fond of music. I shall not expect you to be expert."

The lute was a tenor, with dark, honey-toned resonance, and Francho's pleasure with the master-crafted instrument was evident as he plucked lightly at the strings and then tightened the screws on the angled head to bring the lute into pitch.

He wondered if perhaps he should show more modesty and

decline to exhibit his amateur talent, but the fancy passed; he would not give up the chance to try such a lute.

Finally he stroked a ballad which he had often heard at Papa el Mono's toward midnight, when the bleary-eyed company had played itself out, sitting sprawled in drunken stupor, sobbing along with the minstrel's song of unrequited love and a distant home.

Standing easy, with one leg raised on the low bench, he cradled the lute and at first played the mournful lay simply and without embellishment, trying for a controlled, sweet singing to flow through his fingers into the taut strings. Then, with a thrum, he changed into chorded figurations and took up the melody in his own supple voice, drawing out some of the words in order to weave vocal fugues around the instrumental notes.

> O amado mío, *hast thou not one tear*
> *For the sighing heart that wanders*
> > *o'er the wilds?*
> *Thou water, o, thou whispering wind,*
> *What message dost thou bring?*
> > *Shall my song e'er tell*
> *Of Life's revolving wheel, of sorrow*
> > *And penance,*
> *And sorrow again . . .*

Several stanzas later he ended in a minor key tremolo, letting the melancholy note die away wavering, to drift into silence. He had chosen the song for no reason except it was one he knew he could do well.

Tendilla sat quietly, staring at a corner of his writing table. Finally he raised his head, giving Francho a surprising glimpse of loneliness in the back of the dark eyes before the lids quickly flickered and impassivity resettled upon the aristocratic features.

"Bravo, Don Francisco. Well done, indeed. You have surprised me with your gift for music."

"Gracias, my lord."

"I think we shall see to it that you acquire even greater skill. This unsuspected talent could prove the key to the road you must follow. What other abilities have you developed in your short fifteen years?"

Francho shrugged. "I can read and write in both Latin and Castilian. I know by memory numerous prayers and saints' lives. I can stay on a horse, but just barely. That's all."

His candid appraisal amused Tendilla. "And—you have very crafty fingers and nimble legs, do you forget?"

Francho flushed, then grinned. He had no intention of apologizing for that. But he decided to speak up while his host seemed receptive.

"You give me fine clothes, your name, the freedom of your castle. What is it you want me to do in return?"

"For the first thing, learn to speak less directly," the Count responded. "By approaching a subject obliquely you oftimes can disarm your opponent into a more honest admission, or even a surprise blurting of the truth. Yet, in this instance you are right. Between us, at least, we shall have to have complete frankness if our purposes are to succeed." He pushed back his chair so he could cross his long, black-sheathed legs. "As your friend and advisor I shall speak to you always without guile. And I shall expect the same honesty from you."

Francho sat down in the x-chair the Count indicated at the side of his table. He nodded. "I have reflected much since yesterday, my lord, and I am willing to follow your advice. I will do anything I can to regain my own name and my right to my father's properties."

"Would you place your life in jeopardy?"

Francho did not hesitate. "If the prize is rich, yes. Once, when I was little, I dreamed of being a soldier, to fight against the Moors and have worth in the eyes of others. I forgot this for a while, but now . . . instead of fighting the Moors I will fight for my own legacy."

"You may do both, my cockerel, if you agree to act as I direct."

Francho nodded. He felt his heart beating quicker, in anticipation.

How serious his mien, with those azure eyes burning out from under that frown, Tendilla thought. How very much like her. . . . He yanked his thoughts from that path. "I shall give you a very brief history first, so you may understand the catastrophe which overtook your house. Queen Isabella's half-brother Henrique, who ruled as king before you were born, was called 'The Impotent' by the people because he was a corrupt, vacillating man who would not control the veniality and power feuds of his vassals. The epithet had another meaning as well: in twenty years and two queens he had had no issue, legitimate or otherwise. Then, suddenly, his Portuguese queen swelled and was delivered of a girl child. There was open accusation that the baby had been sired by Beltran de la Cueva, the royal favorite, an obnoxious, stupid man the King had allowed undue influence.

"There were those who desired to keep this child, this 'Beltraneja,' from any claim to the throne, nor could they tolerate any longer Henrique's disastrous domestic and foreign policies. Many of the grandees and nobility of Castile—and I was a leader, along with the Marquis of Villena and the warlike Archbishop of Toledo—openly demanded the King be deposed. In his place we wished to install his little half-brother, the eleven-year-old Prince Alfonso."

"I have heard tales of this prince," Francho said.

"No doubt. He was hailed as a savior by nobility and populace alike, and in fact he was an amiable and intelligent boy. Every noble chose a side, and for three years there was what amounted to a miserable civil war between the minions of Henrique and the Beltraneja, and us, the supporters of Alfonso."

"Was my father with you?"

"Yes, he was. He and I had been fast friends since our youngest years, we rode together in the . . . Well, now I must tell you of your father." Tendilla studied his long fingers drumming slowly on the table. "He was a brave man. Most personable, generous to a fault, an admirer of poetry and painting, a man of charm. But he had two failings which in the end undid him: an uncontrollable extravagance that made him the prey of rapacious moneylenders; and a stiff pride which would not allow him to approach his friends for help, or even advice, when his life seemed to be going askew."

Francho shifted in his chair. "What did he do?" he asked, reluctant to find out.

"During the power struggle I have just mentioned, the impractical Marquis of Olivenza fell into dire financial straits. His estates were potentially rich but managed poorly. He seemed to lose all perspective. He showered money and jewels and even land upon artistic hangers-on to whom he had become patron. Not one of us realized how profoundly in debt he was to the usurers of Toledo, how heavily his houses and properties were mortgaged. And then you were born—the celebration lasted four days—and evidently his empty purse precipitated a mood so black and desperate that he clutched at any way to recoup. Except to go to his friends . . ."

Francho sensed that under his cool exterior Tendilla was finding his tale uncomfortable. The Count pushed back his chair and commenced to pace the study.

"But there was someone much more astute at guessing Don Juan's situation than I, for I was embroiled at that time in my own personal distresses. You have heard of the Count of Haro? He was at that time Constable to Henrique, and it is my opinion, totally unprovable, that it was he who offered your father 200,000 maravedis for special services to the throne. And so the Marquis of Olivenza switched his allegiance to the Beltraneja. In secret, of course. We knew none of this until it was too late."

Tendilla turned to refocus his attention upon his listener and noticed the apprehension on the youth's face. He made an effort to soften his tone. "Look you, Francisco, your father in his normal mind would never have consented to such calumny. Something seemed to have gotten a grip on him. His behavior became gradually bizarre. His physicians finally diagnosed a nervous malady, but none could cure it and it was soon to cause his total collapse. It was grave illness that befuddled his senses."

Francho nodded to indicate he accepted the palliative.

"The unthinkable happened," the Count continued, returning to a more matter-of-fact manner. "The date will never leave me: July 5, 1468. The young Infante Alfonso of Castile and Leon was discovered dead in his bed, the victim of a meal of poisoned fish. The consternation of my faction was intense; we found ourselves a rebellious body without a head. We turned then to Alfonso's sister Isabella, who was then seventeen and a calm and commanding person, and we championed her in Alfonso's place. Those years, so distressful, were filled with uproar and betrayal. Finally, in her commendable wisdom, Isabella decided to reconcile with Henrique if he would recognize her rights. The Count of Haro, hearing the popular acclaim for Isabella and smelling her victory, defected to her. And to prove his loyalty the despicable toady denounced Juan de Venegas, naming him as the murderer of Alfonso and producing a receipt for the blood money scrawled with your father's signature. Haro never revealed where he got the receipt."

Francho found his fists clenched in his lap. Don Juan de Venegas was still just a name to him, he couldn't even picture the man, and yet—and yet . . .

Tendilla stepped up to the window, where he paused for a breath of air. Then he turned back to fix Francho with his hard stare. "Francisco. Never forget that Isabella of Castile and Leon is your sovereign and that you and I are her most loyal and devoted vassals. But rulers are human and amidst their nobler qualities they have grievous faults. Isabella was a young woman. She mourned inconsolably for her little brother, whom she had loved so well. The need for vengeance consumed her, and she sent her minions in pursuit of your father, who had just in time gathered up his wife and child and was fleeing north to the protection of the Mendozas. He had sworn to me he was innocent of the murder and I believed him, and I believed he had really just been a dupe. My family would have helped him to cross into France until it was safe for him to return."

"Would have?" Francho asked slowly. "Was my father caught and executed for treason, then?"

"He did not die by the axe," came the softer reply. "He foolishly made a stop at Toledo and there cleared his estates of all liens, but he became too sick to continue the journey north. Someone gave away his hiding place. He was found by the Queen's men and taken away into custody. But the Queen did not have her revenge. Don Juan fell mortally ill and died in a coma."

"And my mother?"

Tendilla shook his head and sighed. "Your mother? Your mother could have saved herself as you were saved, by being hidden. There had been warning just before the pursuers arrived, but the servants we questioned said she refused to leave her sick husband. I do not think she was killed, she had no knowledge of Olivenza's treachery and the de Luras are not powerful, they would not have made trouble for a son-in-law's death. But she was taken away with him and soon thereafter died. Of a chill . . . so it was reported."

The thin lips twisted. Francho saw a shadow pass over Tendilla's face.

"Who was it who betrayed their hiding place in Toledo?"

Tendilla cleared his throat. "I do not know."

"Then I will find out, somehow. . . ."

"And will your knowing bring back the dead? In any case it is an impossible quest; many who were involved are now dust these fifteen years and dust will not speak. What is more important now is the living—you. You cannot hope to prove whether your father committed murder or not. But you can regain honor for his name and carry forward his line. Can you see that this is more eloquent than avenging his death?"

After a moment's deep reflection, Francho nodded. To him came the duty of raising a house from its ruins, of forcing a new respect for his family's name. *His* name—incredibly—*his* heritage. The sudden sense of high purpose, of crusade, raised a thrill like little mice feet running along his spine.

"Gramercy to the empty condition of the Royal Treasury, we have time to develop my scheme," Tendilla continued dryly, rubbing his thumb across the jeweled hilt of the little dagger in his hand. "You are to be trained as an observer— more bluntly, a spy, to go among the Moors, achieve a sensitive position in the Sultan's train, and return information to me. So few words, it sounds so easy. It will not be. I will demand hard work from you and the deepest dedication, and a relatively solitary life at first to screen out prying eyes. And all this comes *before* the adventure, the intrigue that is zest to a young man's life." He came to stand before Francho and Francho rose. Tendilla put a firm hand on his shoulder and looked deeply into him, the black eyes boring through to his soul. "My instinct tells me you have all the ability we need. If you follow my orders implicitly, with God's help we will gain our ends."

Francho nodded, then boldly ventured, "But what is *your* end, my lord?"

Without wavering the reply came. "I wish to be Governor of the City and Territory of Granada when we have finally gained the might to conquer it."

"I promise you will have no cause to regret your faith in me." Francho's gaze was just as steady.

Tendilla extended his long, sensitive hand. "Give me your hand on it, Francisco, and we are bound."

The solemn handclasp, a seal of a bargain to aid each other's purposes, held firm. Francho regarded the noble before him gravely, trust and a deep respect welling in him. Tendilla smiled slightly.

"You shall take supper with us tonight, in my chamber," he

said, ringing a bell for a lackey. "The good Bishop would like a word with you before he departs for Madrid."

"Yes, my lord."

"See you don't give him Godspeed by lifting his jewelry."

Tendilla's dry chuckle spilled out afterward, when Francho had departed and closed the door.

❧ *Chapter 6* ❧

"THERE SEEMS NO doubt but that you must go, my daughter. It is your duty."

Blanca's delicate, strained face continued to reflect her reluctance. "But Reverend Mother, I have not yet finished my studies."

The tiny prioress, almost dwarfed by her winged coif and high-backed chair, folded her thin lips in the same manner as she folded her hands within her sleeves, dourly. To Dolores, standing back in the shadows of the vaulted audience room, the directress of the Convent of the Familia Santa y Santa Rosa resembled a vulture staring stark and uncompromising from a ruff of white feathers. It was obvious to her that Reverend Mother had no sympathy for Blanca's unwillingness to leave the small but sheltered world where the girl had spent her childhood.

"Doña Blanca, your grandsire's demand must come before your studies. He is dying, so we're told, and you are his only kin. You must hurry to attend him, and pray God to stay his flight to heaven until he can look upon you once more." The prioress's stern tone brooked no more argument.

Blanca hung her small head and sighed. Her long, gangly body was sheathed in a gown of gray brocade amongst whose supple folds she twisted her nail-bitten fingers. Her brown hair was parted in the middle, plaited and coiled about each ear, and then caught in a silken red net, and covering her head was a white chiffon scarf, which was no less pale than the color of her face at this painful juncture of her life.

The Reverend Mother studied her young charge for a moment out of cold eyes. "However, I am concerned that you must travel so far a distance north at this uncertain time of the year. The roads could turn to quagmires and become impassable, no matter all the assurances of the fellow who came to fetch you. You might have to tide over somewhere a few weeks until the spring settles in and the mud dries up. I do not like to think of a maiden of fourteen years traveling alone with only a male servitor to see to her. This is a problem."

Blanca muttered something into her chest.

"Speak up, child, I cannot hear you."

"My serving maid could go with me. I trust her. She is not lazy, and she is very resourceful."

The prioress directed her lashless gaze to the slim girl who stood in the background, hands folded under her apron.

"Stand forward, my child. Ah yes. It is—Dolores, is it not? The innkeeper's daughter? The one Father Julio of Ciudad Real brought to us two years ago?"

"Yes, Mother." Dolores's curtsey was not an ordinary bob up and down, but the deeper one practiced by the half-dozen young ladies being boarded and educated at the convent.

"Well. What think you? Do you wish to accompany Doña Blanca to her home? It is a long way from here. And your family, what would they have to say?"

"I have only two brothers and they are—far distant. They will not care where I go, or wish to say me nay. See, I have become used to serving Lady Blanca, and I would like to remain with her."

The girl's tone was pitched respectfully low, but there was a vibrant quality underlying it which the prioress thought made a good match to the wench's high coloring; the warm, peach complexion with its glowing cheeks as well as the tilted, luminous gray eyes which gazed so steadily into her own. She judged the girl to be about fifteen, not a robust peasant sort, if dainty wrists and a slim neck were any indication, but healthy and well knit. With sour approval she also noted the clean serge gown and the reddish hair, neatly coiled and knotted under a small, white cap firmly tied under the chin.

The hard-headed nun was not fooled by the present quiet,

serious demeanor of the serving maid before her. She had
often peered into the refectory to see whose laughter rang in
such peals as the chattering lay aides helped to arrange the
tables for the noonday meal. There was no doubt but this one
was a lively wench; certainly good as a balance to Blanca's
timidity.

Of all the servitors attending her damsels, this girl had
always struck her as being the least sneaky and ignorant. She
was indeed better than nothing.

The prioress nodded her head in stiff assent. "Go then, if
you so desire it. And look you both after each other." The two
girls now stood side by side before her. They were almost of a
height, the high-strung Blanca drooping and unhappy, her
serving maid calm and clear-eyed. "I shall see you provisioned for the start of the journey, and I have this for you,
Doña Blanca. . . ." She removed from a coffer at her chairside
a purse which jingled interestingly and proffered it. "Upon
admission of our young women *in statu pupillari*, we always
require a sum of money deposited, to be kept for their return
to their families. It is a wise precaution in such an age where
families squander their resources in feuds over a hectare of
land and dishonesty is everywhere. It will help ease your
journey. Go now and prepare yourselves. You must make
haste, Doña Blanca, if you are to see your grandsire alive."

She blessed them quickly, spent a thin smile, and then
turned to other affairs, finished with the business, not caring
about the relieved look that ran between the two girls as
Blanca hefted the full purse.

They left in the fogged-over morning. The girls perched on a
wooden seat fitted into a canvas-hooded, four-wheeled cart,
which was loaded with Blanca's iron-clasped chests and
walnut prie-dieu and Dolores's small bundle of possessions.
Miguel, the wiry old retainer who had come to fetch Blanca,
rode on the lead of the two mules hauling the cart, urging the
animals on by voice and whip over the difficult road.

Wrapped in a cloak and hood against the damp, and
swaying with the jolting vehicle, Dolores saw Blanca's downcast expression and determined to cheer her up, even though
her own heart was not light and she was still not sure she
wasn't sealing herself away forever into a remote barony, far
from the quest she had set for herself. Still, she believed it was

a step forward from the convent, from which she had already extracted much learning and good experience of the well-born classes, and which could do nothing further for her but assign her to a new mistress and circle her around to the beginning again.

Her goal was to avoid a life of common drudgery, or of living wild and coarse with Carlos in the mountains. Whatever might be squeezed from dwelling in the Baron de la Rocha's manse she would squeeze, although, without a *gitana* to read her signs, the Dear Lord only knew what her destiny would turn out to be. She sighed deeply. Even though it was already two years since the world fell out from under her feet, her heart still felt leaden to contemplate how alone and unprotected she was.

Ah well, what could not be helped must be cheerfully endured, as Tía had always said. Oh, how she missed the solid presence of her fat, comforting aunt. . . .

She squared back her shoulders and lifted her chin, curving her lips in a smile. She reached out to pat Blanca's gloved hand. "Just think, Doña, no more matins, no more nones and complines, no more bells ringing in the night to disturb your sleep, no more Sister Oberanga to pull your nose when your embroidery stitches run crooked . . ."

Blanca joined in, grudgingly, ". . . no more straw mattress, no more black bread, no more Latin verbs, no more thick stockings . . ." Her pale brown eyes lit, finally, and she finished, ". . . and no more meals of ugly blood puddings and chicken feet!"

"Dances, only dances from now on." Dolores laughed. "Your grandfather will give a great feast and dance in your honor and you will at last meet your betrothed. How exciting!"

Blanca quickly lost the small enthusiasm she had found. "My grandsire will do nothing of the sort. For one, he is dying. Nor would he, even if he were hale. He hates people. He would not spend a maravedi, even if he had any, for an entertainment."

"But, Blanca, he paid your place in the convent these many years and sent you coins of silver on your saint's day. You must think more kindly of him. Your memories, after all, are the view of a six-year-old child. Did you ever think that now you are grown and educated mayhap he will like you better?"

The young noblewoman was too chilled that morning to return her companion's cheerfulness. "Oh, you don't know what you are saying," she pouted. "Although you should, after all we've whispered about night after night until the candle burned out. I've told you—nay, in fact, warned you—when you said you would come north with me, that the Baron has been ill in his head since my father died. He dismissed his lumber cutters, he closed the mill and turned out the serfs, and whatever was in his coffers then has scarce been replenished. He will leave me near penniless, except for my dowry." She touched her chest, where the small key for her dowry box was suspended under her bodice. "In fact, Miguel says there is no male lackey left in attendance but him."

"But at least your grandfather is leaving you betrothed, and to a landed knight, according to Miguel. So you will not live alone, or poorly."

Blanca threw the serving maid who had become her friend a gloomy glance and chewed at her nail. "And who is he, this gallant knight, of whom I know nothing and who is my inferior in rank? Is he old or young, ugly as a dragon, feeble or fit? If he will accept *me* I suspect he stands in need of our small lands and my dowry. How would you like to be clasped in the arms of some greedy man who mayhap has already ten children by two wives he has already worn out?"

Dolores couldn't help laughing. "Ah, you are too full of doom. He is probably most presentable and young. And at any rate, since you have not yet signed the contract you may break the betrothal if your grandfather dies."

"I do not think that is true, Dolores." Blanca started in on another nail. "You make up the law."

"*Sí*, but it is so. I heard Doña Elvira de Padilla say it. When she was ten such a thing happened to her. Her father died before the contract was signed and her mother was able to put aside the promised betrothal when a loftier hand was offered."

"The Padillas are powerful and rich. Gold buys anyone off."

The high front wheel of the racketing cart hit a hole in the road, and the two girls cried out as they lurched into each other. But Blanca did not let Dolores go. She clutched to her concave bosom the serving maid who had been by chance assigned to her at the convent and who had quickly become her confidante and source of strength in exchange for being allowed to read the lessons along with her.

"I don't want to leave Santa Rosa," she wailed on Dolores's shoulder. "I will miss dear Sister Jesu-Maria, I will miss old Doña Elvira in spite of her foul breath, I will miss everything and everyone . . ." She began to sob.

Hugging back the boney frame of her unhappy mistress, Dolores's gray eyes focused upon the distance as she gazed over Blanca's shoulder, past Miguel's back, and along the indistinct, meandering road. She knew what it was to pine for what was over. Even yet she could hardly think of Tía Esperanza or Papa or her carefree childhood at the inn without tears stinging the backs of her eyes. Sympathetically she patted Blanca's back and silently rocked her back and forth until the girl finally stopped crying.

When they halted for their midday meal of bread and cold fowl, Dolores asked Miguel to remove a blanket from one of the chests. Then she spread it in the small space between the baggage and the bench where they sat so that when one of them was tired she could lie down and rest, albeit in a curled up position. Dolores had a feeling the trip was going to be hard on Blanca.

"Well, at least we have this," Blanca muttered later, patting the purse which hung at her belt. "The sum Miguel brought with him would not have bought even one meal a day for the three of us."

"Aha, you see, you knew naught of this money, and yet, there it was. Perhaps there are other pleasant surprises awaiting you when we reach Torrejoncillo." Dolores chucked her mistress under the chin like a baby.

"Not in that house," Blanca responded with unusual vehemence. "I hate that house, it is full of demons and imps, and the roof always leaked in my chamber." A scowl disfigured her small features. Yet, as the day wore on, it began slowly to vanish as the adventure of the trip took hold of her.

Just before dark they reached their first stopping place, an inn of not much distinction except for the promise of hot soup and a private chamber if they paid for the three other pallets in the room. They left the cart and the animals among others being sheltered, watered, and fed in the inn yard and gratefully stretched their cramped limbs before going inside. Their dress and equipage being unremarkable, they were able to take their supper at a long trestle table in the common room without any undue attention from the locals or travelers who ate with them, and in any case Miguel, who was old but still strong-appearing and unbent, kept in his belt a long, ugly knout.

He might have worn the Baron's blazon on a tabard over his tunic, so he had informed Blanca when she sniffed at the commonplace look of their little caravan, but he had decided against it: an insignia of rank would draw the attention of all the blackguards in Castile and Extremadura to their defenseless little party.

After supping, the girls went directly to their pallets. They barred the door, said their prayers, exchanged a few words about still feeling the rocking motion of the cart when they closed their eyes, and quickly fell into a weary sleep, as they would every night of their bone-rattling journey to the northwest.

In some overcrowded hostels they were forced to share a pallet between them. In some the chamber stunk and lacked a window, or offered such abundant vermin that they preferred to doze on the benches of the common room, watched over by a nodding Miguel. Oftimes, retreating from the stinking horror of a filthy and rotting latrine, they chose to use the shelter of the bushes along the road. And sometimes, if their route took them through a larger town, they were lucky and they found an inn offering good fare and decent accommodation—the knowledgeable innkeeper's daughter grateful for the landlord's humanity in spending some of his profits on the comfort of his guests.

They traveled as fast as was practicable over the badly marked roads, almost alone as they climbed and descended through mountain passes, other times sharing the flatter stretches with carts, mounted riders, herds of sheep or goats, and wayfarers on foot, or pulling aside to let pass the goods-laden caravans of merchants or wealthy persons moving their entire households between residences. They happily followed these long progressions, which included well-armed guards whose power to deter the numerous brigands preying on travelers rubbed off on all who accompanied them as well.

In their prayers every night they thanked God that the highwaymen had not noticed them and that the season of heavy rains seemed to be over; the roads were drying out and what might have been seas of mud at least held firm enough for their cart to pass. Although it remained chill, the revivifying smell of spring came on the wind. The trees held tiny April buds, and the sun often shone for several days at a time before clouds again masked the sky over the forests and fields they trundled past.

Dolores was impressed by Miguel's devotion to Blanca, whom, after all, he had not seen in eight years. He insisted his charge wrap her warm cloak around her angular body on cold mornings and peeped from the corner of his eyes when they supped to see if she ate hearty, which she never did anyway, usually giving Dolores part of the choicest portion of her meal because she just couldn't finish it. Miguel's one good eye blinked anxiously at Blanca's merest sneeze. If the place where they stopped the cart was muddy, the strong old man insisted on conveying Blanca pig-a-back until the ground was dryer for her to walk on, leaving Dolores, of course, to lift her serge skirt and squish along as best she could in the wooden clogs she wore over her shoes.

He said little. Most of what Dolores knew of him was from Blanca; that generations of his family had been in the de la Rochas' employ and that Miguel was already fifty years in service to the old Baron. And that he was all that remained to the household.

The best part of the trip was when they bumped through some of the larger towns to save the distance of going around. The noise and bustle in the main squares, the bumptious but colorfully dressed city dwellers hurrying on their endless errands, the loiterers, beggars, and peddlers, the riders and conveyances winding through the littered, cobbled streets, all these gave their eyes welcome relief from the tedious fields and quiet vistas of the road.

But after more than a fortnight had passed, the hard journey began to seem endless. Their spirits started to sag badly, so badly that when they finally crossed the Tagus River and reached Santanander—which meant that more than three-quarters of their journey had been accomplished—Blanca called a celebration and had Miguel ask directions to the very finest inn in the city, where they could lift up their weary bodies and souls, and hang the expense.

The girls reveled in a well-swept chamber with a glowing brazier to combat the damp and a real bed to spread their sheets on, not caring at all that the mattress was husk-filled. Sturdy boys carried in a double tub—one bath for both as a concession to their dwindling funds—filled it with buckets of hot water, and supplied a huge, flannel towel for their use.

Peeling off their stained garments, the two of them stepped gingerly into the wooden, iron-ringed tub. They squealed at the temperature of the water, but they lowered themselves an inch of skin at a time until finally they got used to the heat and sat, facing each other, groaning with pleasure. They washed themselves with a rough cloth and coarse soap, but neither could remember a luxury so welcome as this liquid warmth that drew the dirt off their skins and melted the fatigue from their bones.

"Turn about, I'll scrub your back for you," Dolores offered. "All the saints in Heaven, this water has turned black as a witch's dug."

Blanca looked askance. "And where did you learn that curse?"

Dolores made a silly twist with her mouth. "From Sister Sidonia," she joked, chuckling at the very thought of the gentle nun swearing. She had never elaborated to the naive Blanca on how colorful her past had really been at Papa el Mono's.

"I think we carried half the country along with us on our bodies," Blanca vowed, splashing water to wash off the soap. "Already I feel a hundredweight lighter." Gleaming between her small, wet breasts hung the dowry box key—the precious box with the ten silver excellentes—one thousand maravedis! —which her father had set aside to attract a good husband for her. The key was her talisman. She never took it off.

They had just dried themselves and donned flannel chemises when a wheezing woman brought bread and a stew of lamb and barley on a tray, along with an earthenware carafe of red wine. Famished, they fell upon the hearty fare with a will.

Dolores was scraping the last delicious morsels from her bowl when she caught Blanca's brown eyes on her speculatively and a somewhat sly expression resting on the ordinarily guileless face. She tossed back the still damp strands of auburn hair from her cheeks and tilted her head. Her stomach was filled, her body laundered, her face felt clean and glowing from the heat of the bath, and she was relaxed. "Well," she drawled. "Well, what? You are thinking something."

Blanca felt good. "*Sí*, indeed I am, and I have been thinking it for a while. You would be surprised," she teased.

"Is it sinful?" Dolores grinned. "Shall we put a blindfold on your eyes so you cannot see and daydream about the young men where they bulge fore and aft in their shameful, tiny-skirted doublets?"

"'Tis not I who looks, 'tis you," Blanca protested, a blush heating her pale cheeks nevertheless. "I've seen you often stare at them, both coming and going, and you smiled secretly when you thought no one was looking." She giggled and wagged a raw-bitten finger under Dolores's nose. "You cannot fool me. From how you act I know you have already had a man, although you say not. No virgin directs her gaze so unerringly at a codpiece as do you." The eager eyes opened wide, coaxing. "Now come on, confess. Do we not tell each other everything?"

Dolores laughed and shrugged casually. "He was not a man, he was a boy . . ." she admitted, for the trip had thrown them so closely together there was hardly a secret or yearning they had not revealed to each other, "although he did a man's job," she added, wickedly. But she wanted to make light of it, for she still couldn't share either the brief delight or the heart-break of Francho with anyone.

Still, it was a relief to speak, however lightly and irreverent-ly, of sexual ardor, the vivid memory of which invaded her dreams, sleeping or waking, with an emotion so sweet and so longing that it made her body quiver and her heart want to leap from her breast, and sometimes woke her in her bed, panting and moist. But to reveal, even to Blanca, the real strength of the love that still bound her to a youth long disappeared from her life, whose bluest eyes and dark curls overlay the face of every swaggering young man who from the distance looked even remotely like him, was embarrassing. And so she made light of it, the most beautiful experience of her whole life.

But Blanca didn't want to believe her anyhow, because to Blanca the awesome, reportedly painful experience of lying with a lover was nothing anyone would laugh at, nor did she care to think her serving maid had more experience of life than she, year older or not. "You lie," she chided her compan-ion. "You saw no men at the convent. And before that you were a mere child and told me you had a loving aunt who guarded you. It's more that you would *like* to hug and kiss and . . . and warm your backside in winter against somebody warm and strong."

"Well, wouldn't you?" Dolores grinned, seeing the yearning in Blanca's soft eyes.

"Yes!" Blanca blushed, and the ring of their joined, girlish laughter bounced from the wood-beamed ceiling.

"But, this is what I was really thinking," Blanca finally continued, as they wiped their eyes. "I have no idea who this monster may be, to whom I am betrothed, or maybe"—she bit her lip wistfully—"he will even *be* a gallant, and handsome. But no matter which, I don't wish to appear a poor mouse creeping home to marry him and flee my dreary life, lest he feel my low estate and lack of family entitled him to mistreat me. It would be better if I could show more wealth. But since that is not possible, I could at least emphasize my rank as heiress to a barony. I mean, appear more important? More elegant?" Blanca groped to express her meaning.

"A fine ambition, my lady, and you are right. But how? An elegant dame rides on a richly bedecked mare."

"True. And so shall I," Blanca stated, finally allowing her inspiration to light her face.

"An elegant dame has ladies in attendance. And you have none." Dolores continued to tick off what requirements she knew of social standing.

Blanca clapped her hands gleefully. "Ah, but I do, indeed!"

"You are addled. Who?"

"You!" Blanca cried, smiling broadly. Dolores's dark-fringed eyes flew wide. "See, Dolores, you have followed all my studies with me, you have skill in ciphering and spelling and reading of Latin and poetry, and you have even practiced with me the steps of the galliard and the pavane Doña Elvira taught me. You are comely, you bear yourself well, and you have not the look of a commoner. See, we are about the same height. I will give you a gown and a hat and there, you will be a lady."

Although she had to close her mouth and gulp, Dolores didn't waste time with false modesty. The fact was, she had always believed that the angel who parceled out children bent too low when he had distributed her. But her foolish yearnings, her formless plotting to raise herself up, were really just that—vague dreams on the periphery of reality—and here was Doña Blanca, in one moment and out of thin air, creating her a lady. She hesitated not a whit to grab the offer, empty of real meaning as she knew it was since she could be a lady only as long as Blanca allowed it.

Still she cried out gaily, "But I must have a name. And a past."

"And so we will devise one," Blanca agreed. "Yes, yes, you can be from the south, Andalusia somewhere, for no one in Torrejoncillo will have the least idea of southern families." Blanca jumped up excitedly and ran barefoot to the one chest Miguel had carried up, rummaging among the layers of clothing. Her silky brown hair, let loose to dry, rippled and gleamed in the candlelight.

"I know just which gown I will give you, ah, this one, the deep blue one with the square-cut, low neck—it was never becoming to me anyhow—and my third-best hat from which we shall drape this rose veil, and, let me see . . ." She drew out her small jewelry casket. ". . . the enamel locket with the black ribbon, that shall be yours." With breathless enthusiasm she ran back and pulled Dolores toward the little pile she had made and urged, "Put them on, put them on. I'll help you drape the veil."

Brimming with delight at her brilliant idea, Blanca danced around her grinning serving maid as Dolores dropped the deep blue, high-waisted gown over her head, then pulled tight the front bodice laces so that only a mere edging of her white chemise showed over the square, black-embroidered neckline. The neckline was lower than she had ever worn, exhibiting the firm rise of her satin-skinned breasts, which, Blanca declared with a touch of envy, did not even require a corselet to keep them high. And it was here, on this warm field, that Dolores nestled the round locket, enameled with fanciful birds and flowers, hanging it next to the strange, square coin suspended from her neck on a thin gold chain she had pinched years back.

With Blanca's help she draped the veil over the high, wide hennin, which did not look quite right since her burnished auburn hair waved loose beneath the hat instead of being totally tucked in, or at least coiled up around her ears. However, the idea was there, and except for a couple of inches too little at the hemline of the gown—"We can say it is an Andalusian fashion," Blanca giggled—they both decided that the effect was fine, that the transformation from serving maid to lady-in-waiting was made, in appearance, anyhow.

As Dolores craned to see the whole costume in Blanca's little mirror, they were interrupted by a soft knock on the door. Dolores went to unbar it, her step suddenly more stately, unable to contain a smile of pure pleasure as the veil rippled and the small train of the gown swished behind her.

113

She opened to Miguel, who immediately swept off his peaked felt hat and pulled his gray forelock politely.

"Just come to remind you, my lady, that we must make an earlier start tomorrow"—he goggled as he realized it was Dolores and not Blanca—"if we are to reach the only inn on our road before dark. . . ." He trailed off.

Laughing, they both at once pulled him into the chamber to explain Dolores's finery, for he must needs be part of the conspiracy too. Miguel could do little in the face of his mistress's insistence on the transformation but agree to go along with it. If it made his young mistress feel more confident, he considered, where was the harm? The gloomy Ganavet domicile could use the brightening up of two young ladies, and the wench Dolores would know better than to lord it over him.

"So then, when we reach home you will address her as a lady, as Doña Dolores. You do understand, Miguel, how this can but better impress my betrothed husband with our quality?" Blanca peered anxiously into the man's one good eye.

He nodded slowly, not wishing to upset her with the fact that having a lady in attendance would never fool anyone who could see even with one eye how deteriorated was her house and depleted the land. But he agreed, "Yes, Doña Blanca, it shall be as you say." Turning to Dolores he dropped a thick, gray eyebrow over his one eye and studied her. "*Sí.* You look the part of a gently reared damsel. But 'tis more than a gown that makes a lady." He grunted. "You must not forget your courtesies. My master may be old and close to death, but he is nobility and he can recognize such easily."

Her pride stung, Dolores faced him, chin lifted. "You have naught to worry, Miguel," she answered grandly. "I am a good mime and no actions of mine will give me away, even to the Baron."

"I shall hope so."

Casting one last sidelong glance at Dolores, the grooves deeper in his lined face, Miguel shrugged and left.

"You know," Blanca said as Dolores divested herself of both finery and chemise and knelt to say a quick prayer, "I remember a chest of my mother's garments and coifs still in the chamber where she slept. If the mice have not gotten them, we could make them over to be more fashionable for you."

114

She was already snuggled down, naked, under their own sheets and a blanket of colorful wool squares sewn together. "Although I noticed in Merida that the hennin is fast losing favor."

"But what of my name? My family history?" Dolores questioned, slipping into the other side of the bed, naked too. Doña Dolores, the Lady Dolores, she repeated to herself, she already loved the sound of that name.

Blanca smiled into the dark, hugging herself with the pleasure of their little deceit, her spirits much higher now with the end of the trip in sight and a lady of her own to carry her train. But she was tired. "Well, let's go to sleep now and we'll think on it as we travel. You're so clever at thinking up things, we should have a complete genealogy by the time we see Torrejoncillo." She giggled. There was silence between them for a moment. Suddenly Blanca slid over awkwardly and kissed Dolores on the cheek.

"What was that for?" Dolores wanted to know, surprised and touched, imagining the demure Blanca's face reddening.

"I . . . I suppose I can do that now that you are my lady," the girl stammered. And then, she breathed, in a rush, "Oh, Dolores, I am so glad you came with me. How should I have stood this awful journey without you, or what I must face at its end. I . . . I feel so blessed that the Good Lord fated us to come together. I know how hard you've tried to make my portion seem easier and how I've often been grumpy and unappreciative. But if I had a sister or kinswoman, I would have wished her to be just like you."

Shyness overtook her and she quickly slipped back to her own place, but Dolores caught at her hand and squeezed it warmly, swallowing the lump in her own throat, wordless for once. The erstwhile serving maid could finally only say, "Thank you. Thank you, dear Doña Blanca. I am grateful to you too."

"Good night, *amiga,*" came the soft response.

"Good night, my lady."

Dolores was forced to surrender her dream to the insistent noise that had been irritating her, and she woke. She was facing the unshuttered window, so that the first thing she saw on opening her eyes was the morning star glittering lonely in the cold blue of approaching day. Then the noise came again, a loud whimper. A shadow moved, and, adjusting her eyes, she saw Blanca's profile and indistinct shape outlined against the window.

"Blanca. What is it?"

"Oh, Dolores, a pain. I have a bad pain, here, in my right side. It woke me up a while ago and it won't go away. Oh!" the girl cried, bending over, "it is so sharp it makes me feel sick."

Dolores slid from the bed, ignoring the goose pimples as the chill air struck her warm body, pattering to where Blanca was leaning against the window embrasure, one hand pressed against the side of her belly. Putting an arm around the doubled-over girl, she tugged at her, "Come back to bed, Doña Blanca, come back to bed where it is warm. You'll see, it is nothing, it will go away."

"It feels like sharp knives," Blanca moaned, but she stumbled along, allowing Dolores to help her back to bed. "I have never had such a pain before. What is it? What has assailed me?" She shivered as Dolores tucked the blanket about her curled up form. "Oh, oh, it gets worse," she cried out, convulsively drawing up her knees to her chin.

Quickly Dolores slipped on her chemise and padded over to the iron brazier, where she touched a candle to the still glowing charcoal. Blanca was like a babe-in-arms. The least cut or scratch or bad stomach made her go pale with fear. "Don't be frightened, *doña*, 'tis only air, gas," she called over her shoulder, "I will massage it for you and it will pass. Perhaps the meat for our supper was spoiled."

She put the candle on a stool close to the bed. "See, chasing away the darkness will chase away your fears. A light has always helped me to calm when terrible beasts pursue me in a bad dream and I wake up terrified. You'll see, by morning you will be well." But when she stroked Blanca's brow she couldn't help frowning, for she felt too much warmth under the palm of her hand. The girl moaned and quivered, whimpering, "Holy Virgin, Holy Virgin, help me."

"Shh, now, it is only air, you will see, it will soon come out from one end or the other. Let me rub the spot. . . ." But at her gentlest touch on Blanca's lower right side the girl squealed with pain and knocked away her hand. "It will be cock's crow in a short while and the servants will be up. I will get you a clear, hot broth with some verjuice squeezed in, and the pain will dispell, I promise you," Dolores soothed, wishing she felt as confident as she sounded, for she had never known the sticking of air in the entrails to cause fever.

She wished she had known her mother, who was a healer as well as a baker and who would have taught her which herbs and balms to use when people fell sick. She wished she had spent more time in the convent dispensary learning from the nun who mixed the potions and made the compresses. But Dolores knew no more to do than to hold Blanca's hand tightly as the pain made the girl writhe and clench her body. They would have to wait for morning to seek medicine.

Yet, in an hour Blanca was better, lying limp but quiet on the bed, breathing wearily through her mouth. Although her head was still warm, the onslaught of pain seemed to have passed, and when Miguel knocked she was quite able to get up. Dolores helped her to wash her face and hands and to dress and plaited and coiled her hair for her, placing a turbanlike coif just so on the droopy head. But Blanca could only move stiffly, for her side was sore and tender to the touch.

Dolores had donned her own gray serge gown, which would suffice to take the stains and wear of travel until they were closer to their goal. She would save the blue velvet, for it was Blanca's plan to rent them some saddle animals in a town close to Torrejoncillo so they might ride to her home with greater dignity than that lent by an old cart.

Listless at the common room table, Blanca ate little of her breakfast, a spoonful of cooked oats and a bite of cheese, but Dolores purchased a substantial meat pie with some dried fruits for their midday meal and hoped the girl might find more appetite.

"What is the matter with her?" Miguel asked Dolores from the corner of his mouth, having noticed the glaze over Blanca's eyes and hearing her gasp and clutch at her side as he had to half-hoist her into the cart.

Dolores shrugged, but did not smile. "I think it is wind in the belly. She was even worse last night, but this morning she stopped her moaning and seemed able to continue on."

"I pray God she is not falling ill," Miguel grunted. He gestured at the meandering road they were traveling, hardly more than a trail, its boundaries indistinct from the surrounding woods and fields, its path full of stones and depressions. "There is naught between here and the hostel in Delbrava, and we must journey almost eight, ten hours to achieve that. And a bouncing ride, too. This is not the King's highway."

"Oh, she will be all right," Dolores said, hoping it would be true. "Just try not to drive us through every hole in Spain." Now she did smile faintly, joking to ease the old man's concern.

In fact, Blanca did seem more comfortable with each passing league, gasping only softly when the cart's rattling, wooden wheels joggled over jutting stones or a dead tree branch blown into the narrow path. Huddled in her cloak she leaned tiredly against the humped, wooden frame holding aloft the canvas. Her face was pale, but she would give Dolores a weak, reassuring smile now and then, and she insisted she felt much better. When they stopped to eat she even had a mouthful of the greasy meat pie Dolores and Miguel devoured, washing it down with water from a stoppered jug.

In mid-afternoon the fitful sun that had been warming the day disappeared altogether behind an overcast of low, gray-black clouds, which scudded swiftly through the sky above them. Soon jagged lightning flashed and deep rumblings echoed in the distance, spurring the few peasants who shared their path to turn off toward familiar shelters beyond the trees. But Miguel spied the red walls and turrets of a castle jutting up from the crest of a rocky hill, and he judged it was not too far. With a quick squint at the sky, he called back that they had time to reach it, for there they would surely be given shelter from the storm and perhaps even herbals to ease Blanca's bellyache. They jolted along, creaking and rattling and jingling as fast as the old man could make the mules pull the cart.

The horrendous clap of thunder right overhead and Blanca's sudden, terrible shriek of agony as she grabbed at her side occurred together, each as terrifying as the other. Dolores thought the poor girl was pitching from the cart and dove to hold her from falling out. But Blanca was vomiting, with a retching, gagging sound, vomiting and moaning, bent double on one side. Dolores scrambled to hold the burning forehead of the stricken girl, who was delivering up her guts over the side of the cart between breathless moans and gasps. Dolores was frightened now. This was not a simple case of indigestion.

Emptied, panting, Blanca fell back in her arms, turning up eyes bright with fever and terror. "Dolores, what is happening to me? *Ay, mi madre,* it hurts, make it stop, make it stop," she gasped out as Dolores groped with one arm for the water bottle to hold to Blanca's mouth. "I have never had such pain. My whole belly is on fire with the flames of Hell! I will die. I know it. *Ay, ay . . .*" she shrieked out, writhing to the floor of the cart, tears of pain spilling over her screwed up face.

Chewing her lip in consternation, Dolores yelled out to Miguel between the violent cracks of thunder. He came loping back to the cart, gray hair blowing in the rising wind. The careworn lines between his big nose and chin sunk deeper yet as he realized the serious situation.

Between them they maneuvered the screaming, retching girl onto the blanket on the floor of the cart, where she clenched herself into a tortured knot. There was just enough room for Dolores to hunker beside her. Miguel fished a blanket from the bundle of linen, while Dolores cut a strip from one of their sheets with the small eating knife she drew from the reticule hung from her belt. She wet the cloth with water from the jug and applied it to Blanca's burning forehead.

"How far to that castle?" she yelled at Miguel against the wind and the flapping of the canvas, as the first great drops splattered down into the swirling dust of the trail. "She needs shelter and medicines. Can we reach it?"

"I don't know," the old man yelled back, pulling the hood of his tunic up over his cap. "That castle could be further than I thought, mayhap an hour, and I can get little speed from these old mules. And if we are caught in a torrent the wheels will mire. But we'll try. Pray, girl, pray Jesu to overcome the evil demons that are attacking that poor child."

Dolores had just time to wonder if it was rain or tears she saw on his leathery cheeks before he hurried back to the mules.

The cart's canvas covering made little difference when the storm fully broke since the rain blew in from both open ends. Blanca was partially protected by the mound of chests and bundles blocking the back end, but Dolores's cloak-shrouded head and shoulders were soon dampened. She took no notice, all her attention taken up with trying to ease the screaming Blanca, wetting the cloth again and again, wiping sweat and tears from the grimacing face, holding tight to the clawing hands, bending to ears that turned this way and that to plead into them, "Take heart, Doña Blanca, the Lord will help you and the Holy Saints, for did we not pray and confess and

119

cleanse ourselves of sin before we left Santa Rosa? Have faith, sweet lady, soon we will reach shelter and Miguel will ride for a Jew physician to ease your torments. Don't cry, Blanca, don't cry . . ."

Blanca flung her head and retched again, a thin fluid. Her chest heaved and her eyes bulged with the anguish of the terrible pain that blazed in her gut.

Tears of helplessness leaked from Dolores's eyes. She turned her stricken face up to the murky, streaming sky outside and pleaded, "Holy Virgin, Mother of Jesu, I beg you, intercede with Our Father, take from this guiltless girl such torment and suffering and make her well again . . ." Entreating for God's mercy several times over again as they jolted on she promised to give her new locket to the poor if He would save the kind young noblewoman who had befriended her. Finally, after a while, she noticed that Blanca's agonized thrashing had lessened, the desperate grip of the narrow hand had relaxed, and the unseeing, hollow eyes had closed. The cart lurched to a stop, and a sodden, dripping Miguel squished back to her.

"It's getting too late and dark to go on," he cried over the clamor of the rain, and she realized she could hardly see him. "The castle was bound in mist, lost to my sight at the onset of the storm, we may have even passed it. But I have found a clearing here and some sort of hut. If the thatch is sound we can at least spend the night out of the rain." He disappeared before Dolores could protest, running a few moments later to report, "The roof scarce leaks at all, I think. It is barren of comforts but it is dry."

"But she needs herbals, bleeding, a potion to break her fever."

"So I know too, and her life is more dear to me than to you," Miguel shouted. "But I cannot see the trail or the holes and rocks which will break our axles. We must stay here the night, and at daybreak, the Saints protect us, we will go on." Hunched against the relentless, driving rain, he slogged back to grab the lines and lead the mules as close as possible to the shelter he had spotted just beyond a thin bank of trees.

The battered herder's hut whose rude door they shoved open smelled dank, of goats, dogs, and moldering straw. The failing light yet allowed them to see that there was neither hearth nor furnishings, but at least the hard-packed floor was swept clean. An ash-filled and blackened pit rimmed with a few rocks marked where a fire could be laid had they the fuel, but in any case rain dripped through the makeshift chimney punched through the roof above it. There were no windows.

With his tinder Miguel managed to light a couple of their candles in their iron holders so they could close the door against the storm. They rigged up a pallet from most of their bedding, and Miguel carried in and laid upon it a limp, moaning, stuporous Blanca, lips pallid, face glistening with the sweat of high fever, her gown drenched under the cloak. A spasm ran through her whole lanky body every few moments. Dolores wrestled off Blanca's cloak and gown, then wrapped her in dry sheets. She supported the sick girl's head with a pillow and wetted her lips with water while Miguel unhitched the mules and led in the dripping animals, tying their halters to a pole supporting the roof.

Stripped of their soaked outer garments and wrapped in blankets which still did not prevent the damp chill from seeping into their bones, the old peasant and the young serving maid so lately appointed lady sat huddled together against a wall and consumed the remains of the cold meat pie while they listened in misery to the moans and broken, delirious raving of poor Blanca.

"Why cries she out so piteously about the 'cave of sin repented'?" Dolores muttered to Miguel, whose lone eye was riveted upon the sick girl as if by will alone he could cure her. "What does that mean? Do you know?"

Miguel's hollow voice seemed to come from far away, although he sat next to her. There was resignation in his tone. "What matters it now that I should tell you of the cave? It is in my bones that my master is already dead and that his granddaughter, Doña Blanca, all who remains of the Ganavets, will die too. So . . ." He paused for a moment in sad contemplation, and then, with an effort, resumed. "Her father was murdered for adulterous sinning with the wife of a powerful lord in our district. His dead body was delivered to my master with the head parted from it, and so sore was my master stricken with this terrible deed that he swooned and the Devil took possession of him. And from that moment did his senses leave him.

"He caused the body of his only son to be laid in a stone sarcophagus in a dry cave not far from the manse—and soon after he laid there his daughter-in-law too. But the head—his son's head he put in a cage of mesh and chained this to a niche where he kept a perpetual lamp burning, and there it moldered and stunk until the flesh rotted away from the skull. And there, every day, did he drag his wretched and shrinking granddaughter to stand before this terrible relict with him and pray for her father's soul. The pitiful child dreaded that cave."

Dolores's throat constricted in disgust and pity. "Oh, poor Blanca! She never told me of this."

"Mayhap she forgot it. She was so young. And thin, like a little stick." Miguel shrugged, his eye never leaving the muttering Blanca. "And yet, she was fortunate. My master did not like her, so in her sixth year he sent her far away, to the convent where her mother had once sheltered. She was fortunate," he repeated. "She had not to endure the follies of an old man crazed in the head most of the time, venturing not even to the church nor permitting any visitors save the notary, the one who brought to him the offer for Blanca's hand, and sometimes the priest. He cared nothing that his servants robbed him and then left him. And now there is no one save myself and a dimwitted old townswoman who cares for him and who once warmed his bed when his body was still well."

Dolores stared at the man's craggy profile, harsh in the flickering light of the candles. "And you? Why do you stay in so morbid a house?"

"And where would I go, my lady?" he answered, using the address with sarcasm. "Torrejoncillo is my home, it is where I was born. And now I am old and tired, my sight is failing, with scarcely a coin to ease what days I have left. Who would give me work? Shelter? None!" he answered his own question. "At least at Torrejoncillo I have a sturdy cottage of my own and a bit of land to grow turnips and onions, and the Baron supplies me with a maravedi here and there in return for doing what I can with the place."

Suddenly he clasped his gnarled hands and beat the air before him, and his voice trembled with anger. "That is why she dare not die, this poor female into whose weak hands will be entrusted what small portion I have. For no matter that she marry or not, she remembers me of yore, I gave her sweet cakes and rode her about on my shoulders. She will not evict me. She will not take from me all I have."

Dolores finally understood his constant concern for Blanca's health. But she was not without sympathy, for it suddenly flashed into her mind that her own future was also in grave doubt. What would become of her should the suffering girl on the pallet give up the ghost? She would be stranded, with no purpose for continuing the journey, and with nowhere to go but back to the convent.

Feeling miserable and forlorn, she hugged her knees to her chest. What was she doing here, alone and so far from Ciudad Real, from Carlos and Pepi, from the silly dreams that had warmed her young life at the inn, from the foolish quest to find Francisco, the brash cutpurse who had stolen her virginity and her heart and who, if he was still alive, was certainly hundreds of leagues distant from this remote province anyway? Why had she even left Santa Rosa, where at least she was safe?

There was a thrashing from the pallet and a little shriek. "Ay, ay, help me, help me!" Blanca cried wildly. Then her voice dropped into a conversational mode. *"Ora, ora pro nobis* . . . see now, cross the stitch to the left . . . little flowers . . . knot, knot, knot, sister . . . ah, no, pack up my tapestry, we shall not leave it . . ."

Sighing, Dolores crawled to her, too tired to stand up. Blanca's cheeks were sunken, her eyes were open but staring, unfocused and unseeing, there was dribble coming out of her mouth. Dolores drew back the sheet and gently felt the right side of the shockingly swollen belly, but pulled back her hand immediately as Blanca jerked and screamed thinly at her touch.

"Grandfather, grandfather, I am afraid . . . the cave . . . Holy Virgin, cut off his head he has been bad . . . no, no . . . I am repentant, I repent . . ." Blanca wailed, her head rolling about in distress.

Dolores picked up the limp, hot hand with the pathetic, ragged nails and put it to her own cheek. She rocked back and forth, strands of auburn hair straggling from her felt cap to tangle on her blanketed shoulders. "Oh Blanca, Blanca," she despaired. "Oh Blanca, get well."

At last Blanca quieted. Her eyes fluttered closed. She continued breathing heavily through her mouth, uttering only an occasional soft groan, but Dolores thought the girl's skin felt a little cooler.

Wrapping herself up in her own blanket, Dolores finally stretched out on the hard ground as Miguel had already done, her head on her bent arm. She dropped off into an exhausted but shallow sleep so that she heard Miguel leave the hut some time later to relieve himself. She opened one eye just enough to cast a bleary look at Blanca, who now lay still, the breath whistling through her throat, and then closed it again.

The next time she woke—somehow she knew it was hours after—she was pulled into consciousness by the movements of the restless mules. Now it was Dolores who had to answer a call of nature. Shivering in her still damp cloak she stepped outside, only to blink in astonishment at the pale blue clarity of the rainless morning. She sniffed at the pleasant little breeze rippling the big puddles and decided the water would soon reflect the cheer of a rising sun and a dry, warm day that would harden the muddy road. Perhaps they could quickly reach a healer's help for Blanca. She refused to think they might need a priest.

A deep, long breath of the fresh, clean-washed air lifted her heart. She raised her mud-caked skirt, accomplished her mission quickly, and returned to check on Blanca, who, the Dear Lord willing, may have passed the worst of her illness during the night. She would also waken the snoring Miguel so they could be on their way, although she would have to lead the mules on foot so that Miguel could shoulder the cart from behind through the deep ruts. Her strength revived, she pushed open the crude door.

So quietly had Blanca slipped away from them.

She saw Miguel kneeling by the pallet, his back toward her, rocking and rocking back and forth and crying, "Jesu, Jesu, whyfor hast thou forsaken me . . ." Hearing Dolores's step he sobbed out to her, without turning, "She is dead. She is dead, I tell you. She breathes no more."

Dolores gasped, feeling that she had been struck a giant blow in the chest. She ran and sank to her knees beside the pallet where lay the dead body of young Blanca de la Rocha, ashen-skinned, mouth open, and head fallen to one side like a broken doll, a plait of sweat-dulled brown hair lying loose across the thin neck where no pulse was beating.

Burning tears sprang up and spilled from Dolores's gray eyes to roll down her cheeks as she gazed in disbelief at her lifeless friend, so lately smiling and laughing and scheming to appear more prosperous in spite of her lack of money; a shy and artless young person who had amiably shared two years of her short life with a serving maid greedy for learning. And now she was gone, like a light snuffed out, and all her little dreams and hopes and fears gone with her. Why, why? Why did God want to take poor Blanca?

Heavy with grief and bewilderment and horror, Dolores brushed the braid back off of Blanca's neck and tucked a lifeless hand back under the sheet. In the sudden blaze of a shaft of sunlight stabbing in from the doorway she bowed her head as she knelt there and brokenly began to intone the Latin prayer she'd heard the nuns repeat over their dead.

Dolores perched, swaying, on the wooden seat as Miguel led the beasts carefully along the least rutted and muddy part of the road. They had started off again on their endless odyssey, but now with a corpse wrapped and shrouded in the back of the wagon—only the corpse was not of the Lady Blanca, she who now sat straight-backed and unblinking in the slow-moving cart, but of her servant, a wench with no relations, from far to the south.

Dolores could still see Miguel's hand flinging the blanket over Blanca's face as they both rose from the deathbed. She could still hear Miguel's voice grating hoarsely as the tears dried on his cheeks. "Listen to me, girl. You must help the both of us," he told her, the body at his feet already dismissed. "And do not look so wretched. I have observed that you are a clever wench and you will see the merit in what I have to say.

"Now the Baron will die without an heir, do you understand?" The old servitor who had been so diffident pushed his craggy face aggressively into hers. "His goods and his land, what is left of them, will be forfeit to his liege lord, the Marquis of Escambura, who will keep the land or sell it, but who will surely kick me out like a dog, a useless cur. And you, girl, you will no longer have a mistress, nor anywhere to go save forward to the same fate as myself, for how can you return, by yourself and penniless, two hundred leagues back to Santa Rosa. True, is it not? True, everything I have said?" Miguel impatiently shook Dolores by the shoulders to evict the blank look from her eyes.

"Yes, yes, true," she gulped. "Yes. So then, what shall we do?" Still stunned, she was willing to let him be the leader.

A little more kindly, then, he grasped her hand and led her away from the pathetic corpse outside, where the fresh morning air washed over her in a purifying wave. He found an old bucket leaning against the hut. It was half-filled with clean rainwater, and he offered it to her. She cupped her hands and lifted the cold water to her mouth gratefully, and when she was finished, so did he. They both splashed water on their faces. Then, upending the bucket, he made her sit on it, wet wood or not.

"The only persons alive who could recognize Blanca de la Rocha from her childhood are myself and the Baron, he who can scarce hear or see and who is at death's mean door, if not already through it; the Prioress of Santa Rosa, too, of a certainty, and the nuns, but they are far distant and of no account. The priest who baptized Doña Blanca, the nurse who raised her—and her father before her—the servants once in my master's employ, are gone, all gone.

"So, who is to say *you* are not Blanca de la Rocha, granddaughter of the Baron, inheritor of his patents and estates!" Miguel rasped fiercely into her face, his one eye blazing.

He stopped her protest by clapping a leathery hand over her mouth. "Be quiet, *estúpida,* and listen. You have here all of little Blanca's effects, her clothes, her few jewels, her casket of letters and keepsakes. You have lived with her and women do prattle. You surely know enough of what *she* knew of her heritage to take her place, and what you do not know will be forgiven by any who may pry—a child of six years does not retain much. Attend me, girl!"

He chucked up her chin and stepped back from her to survey her, and his greasy gray locks fell on his forehead. He was an old man in wrinkled stockings and a worn tunic but with determination written strong on his lined face. "She carried herself no more nobly than you, so I realized when you had arrayed yourself in her garments, nor did she speak more delicately. Your coloring is not far distant from hers, and whatever distance there is could be charged off to the change from child to adult."

Speechless, Dolores shook her head.

Miguel clasped his hands before him in a transport of passion. "All you need do is wish it and in a twinkling, 'twixt this hut and the cart over there, you can become a titled lady, *sí,* with a title of centuries standing, barely a handful left in Spain now deemed as Baron, so my master has babbled. You have a new life to gain, girl, you, a mere common wench."

"But . . . but such deception . . ." Dolores choked out.

Miguel jerked his head toward the hut where lay the still,

blanketed body. "Will she care, rest in peace? Will my dying master care? Will even the Good Lord, praise to His name, care, since harm is done to no one?" he croaked out. "But I am an old man who fears to die homeless in a ditch, and you are a young woman with nothing. Together we can stay alive, and where, you tell me, where is the harm? I want little. You can have all the rest, whatever there is. Just let me live out my days in peace, in my own place, that is all I ask; and that my corpse be laid there by the side of my sainted sister, under the chestnut tree we planted fifty years ago when we were children."

Dolores's lips were stiff and white. "To be discovered in such chicanery would mean execution by the hangman, or worse, burning." She shuddered. "What do I know of you? It is clear you care not a whit for the poor mistress who shrieked and suffered away her life last night with a poison in her belly. All she meant to you was the promise of a haven for your old bones. Why should I put my trust, nay, my life, in your hands?"

Deliberately Miguel pulled his forelock and bobbed his head in a show of subservience. "Since I am the only one who vouchsafes you, to betray you would be to betray myself. What would be my aim?" he asked.

In spite of herself Dolores had to consider his words for a moment and finally agree. "'Tis true. There would seem no purpose for betrayal, either way. But what about Doña Blanca's betrothed?"

Miguel suddenly deflated, his shoulders sagged, and he turned his glance away from her, into the golden morning. "'Tis a problem only you may answer, whether to keep that bargain or nay. And perhaps you must marry, for the old Baron's coffers are near empty. But your lord will allow you to succor one poor old servant in his dotage. What man would not do such small bidding for a comely wife?" His voice suddenly wavered. "And say not that I cared little for her. When she was a child I carried her on my strong shoulders."

As his voice cracked and trailed away, Dolores started and jerked around, for she thought she heard another voice, lighter and higher, whisper in her ear, "Dolores, Dolores, take my name, I bequeath it to you. Take all of my goods, they are yours. But for the love of God, dear friend, let them bury me not in that cave of horror but in the sweet ground where the petals of roses fall. . . ."

Of course it was only the breeze of early morning rustling through the trees behind the hut, but Dolores's grief welled up again. She lowered her head and the tears began to seep. Yes, yes, dear Blanca, I will see you safely to a peaceful bed. . . .

Miguel turned to peer at her with a dull, glazed eye, his hands shaking as they fingered his felt cap. His face was gray and drawn, and the man who yesterday had seemed so hale for his age now stood stooped before her. She wiped her eyes on her sleeve and snuffled. Well, once a thief, always a thief, she shrugged, then thought with irony about how she was progressing in life. It was a large step from stealing a purse to stealing a name, but evidently not too large for her. In any case, she had decided. Her chin rose and her lips curved shallowly in the ghost of a smile.

Rising from the bucket she reached out and touched the old man's hand reassuringly. "Good Miguel, pray, carry in Doña Blanca's chest—" She drew in her breath sharply. ". . . *my* chest, Miguel, so I may divest myself of this muddied costume. There is a blue gown and a rose veil I would rather wear on this fine spring day. And wrap carefully the body of my poor serving maid. We shall lay her in a box at the first village we come to and carry her to Torrejoncillo for burial."

Miguel's one eye blazed with relief. He instantly followed along with her. "*Sí*, my lady, and if fortune favors us we shall soon come up on an inn to ease our hunger and a church in which to pray for this poor, dead child." He turned and shuffled toward the cart, more erect now, but paused for a moment to turn to her once again. "Do not be afraid, Doña Blanca," he said gruffly, reassuring in his turn. "There will be no problems. All will go well, you will see."

"Only God can know that, Miguel. But, in any case, address me as Doña Blanca only when you must, in case I should forget to answer to the name." She had never cared for the name of Blanca. Her name was Dolores and always would be. She was going to find some way to retain it.

The castle they had seen the day before grew closer and bigger, loomed over them and faded behind them. A half league further they discovered the hostel for which they had been bound. There they ate and then asked directions to whomever in the neighborhood would prepare a body for burial.

And that melancholy task done, they went on. Dolores felt

better, physically anyway. Her stomach was filled with a hot meal. Her nerves were less raw, for the swift draught of aguardiente she had upended had taken away her breath but given her back her courage. The warm sun spread its pleasant blessings upon her as she sat in the rose-veiled, stately hennin and the wide-skirted blue gown Blanca had so gaily chosen for her. In her pouch was the little key to Blanca's dowry box, as well as the short missive Santa Rosa's prioress had written to Baron de la Rocha to note the discharge of her student and the deliverance of the travel allowance into her hands.

She willed herself not to think of the hastily knocked together pine box and its burden in the cart behind her, nor to allow the sad, bereft feelings to escape from the depths of her heart, where she had banished them. She gave herself up to the jolting of the cart and thought of Torrejoncillo, creating pretty daydreams in her head of a pampered and petted existence— something like that lived by the Alcalde's mistress—and she stroked the soft, rich velvet of her gown to help her blank out reality.

In the few remaining days of the journey, as the mules eagerly jangled forward toward Torrejoncillo, sensing, some-how, the nearness of their own familiar domain, she almost came to believe her own inventions.

❧ *Chapter 7* ❧

THE PEBBLES HAD rattled against the outside wall of the bedchamber like an out-of-season hailstorm.

"What was it?" yawned Constanza, addressing the bare, muscular back that leaned over the window ledge as its owner peered down into the court two floors below.

"It's my arms instructor, Von Gormach," Francho answered, turning back into the warmly lit room and the rosy, disheveled young woman lying languidly on the bed. "Something's afoot and he signals me to come down."

"Now?" There was light dismay in her voice.

"Now."

"Ah, no, not yet, *carido,*" Constanza wheedled, turning on her side and propping up her artificially blond head. She reached a round arm toward him. "Surely there is time for one more little kiss? Just one more? I don't see you so often these days." She ran a hand down her voluptuous body, preening. "Or maybe you have found someone you like better than Constanza?" Her eyes greedily took in her gentleman lover, barechested, built like an inverted triangle, the hard muscles bunched in his thighs and calves. The sight of the tall and handsome Mendoza scion thrilled Constanza still, even after the many times that that strong body had clasped, impassioned, and taken her own.

But now he was sated. The same blue eyes that before had devoured her with undisguised hunger had now regained their usual glint of affectionate humor. He sauntered to the bed and leaned over her, flashing the warm but devastatingly dangerous smile that had seduced her in the first place.

"No more kisses, little glutton. I know you, you will draw me into that siren's net and chain me once more to your beauty, and I shall not escape you till dawn." As he spoke he brushed his warm fingers slowly along the raised hill of her naked hip and watched her close her eyes against the tingles he was raising on her skin. Demons take Von Gormach, Francho thought, for he was finding the arousal of her lusty desire hard to resist.

She shifted her plump body and seized his hand, cupping it on her full breast, where the nipple was already hardening at his touch. "Don't leave me so soon, *mi caro.* Can't you feel how my heart beats for you?" she murmured, wriggling seductively. She threw her arms about his neck, trying to draw him down to the tumbled bed where they had already pleasured each other twice.

Reluctantly he took his fingers from the hard, russet nipple they were automatically caressing and reached to break her grip from around his neck. The compliant tinker's wife had been all that stood between him and death by boredom this last year at Mondejar, and they had evolved a very satisfying physical friendship for which both of them were greedy. "You are insatiable. Do you wish to kill me, cruel wench? I am played out." He laughed. He pulled her up by the arms for a second kiss on the mouth, then let her drop with a bounce on the mattress. "Von Gormach wouldn't disturb me—or his own tryst for that matter—for anything that could wait." His smile turned wry. "I suppose we should be overjoyed that he didn't decide to need me an hour ago."

Constanza, realizing defeat, shrugged her shoulders and relaxed, pulling the sheet up part way. Admiringly she watched the muscles ripple under his smooth, pale olive skin as he poured water from an earthenware ewer into a bowl and washed quickly and vigorously. Francisco might complain of his long, hard tilts with Van Gormach and enduring the shock of the stocky German's fiercely propelled lance, of the strenuous dueling exercises with di Lido, whose sword was as flashy as his dress, or the demanding wrestling matches with his wiry instructor of history whose weight was about equal to his, but he also took a cocky male pride in the hard and bulging muscles all this obtained him.

Although his back was toward her she saw his features in her mind's eye, so handsome one could cry, bright blue eyes lighting his tanned face, humor-quirked mouth both firm and sensuous with a square, full underlip, and his black hair curling softly on his forehead. Constanza sighed contentedly. Perhaps tonight it had happened, perhaps tonight he had given her a son just like him. The old tinker to whom she was married, who discreetly stayed late in his little shop because he liked the silver coins the Count's son left with his wife, could never give her a babe. But neither would the old stud ever admit it and so a baby by Mendoza would certainly have a home and a proud father.

Dressed now, Francho came to kiss her goodbye, and she pushed her fingers through the dark ringlets on his forehead. "When will you come to me again?" she asked him.

Francho reacted with mild surprise. "As always, Friday hence. You know that."

She looked at him for a long moment, her dark eyes unfathomable. "It comes to my mind I will never see you again. Mayhap it is a presentiment? Is it true?"

"Estúpida!" He slapped her sheet-covered rump playfully. "Who then would I see in this village if not you?" He was impatient to go now. "Come on, Constanza, a little smile to send me back to my heavy labors. I promise you, *mi cara,* you will see me again and again and again. . . ." He tickled her rounded belly and joined in her laughter.

Giggling, she jumped up. She watched him as he threw a long leg over the window ledge and climbed out onto the tree that grew there. He clambered from branch to branch and finally leaped to the ground, where the stolid Von Gormach, a man as wide as he was tall, awaited him. She chuckled to herself as she scratched her bare bottom. There was nothing to keep him from going down the house's wooden stairs. He just liked to swing from trees. Played out, indeed!

"I sought you vere dead. Vot took zo long to zay goodbye?"

"You great ox, I keep telling you, a gentleman doesn't leave a lady without a dulcet expression of regret."

"Vell, she's no lady. You zay *adiós,* you don't make her vun of your poems."

"What's in your craw that you can't wait to tell me? No bad

tidings, I hope?" His mount was waiting beside Von Gormach's in the small, covered alley at the side of the house. They swung into their saddles and rode out into the dusty village street. Elderly women sitting and sewing at their front doors nodded at them and showed their gums, and then winked to each other once the nice young lord was past.

"No, not bad. For you, I sink, very gut. A courier has arrived chust now from His Excellence to Pietro, and de little man vas smiling ear to ear. Go, run, Von Gormach, fetch Don Vrancisco, he zays to me, and qvickly. And he push me out de portal."

"He did not say what was so urgent?" Francho found a few maravedis in his purse and tossed them at the delighted urchins playing about the village well while their mothers gossiped or slapped their laundry in a side trough.

"No." Von Gormach shrugged. "You know him. Ven he vant not to say, he don't say."

Passing the last house they broke into a canter. Excitement began to filter through Francho's blood. It *had* to be the summons he had been awaiting so long. Now, maybe now Tendilla would deem him ready to leave Mondejar, and maybe the arduous years of preparation were coming to an end.

When he thought back it seemed like ten years he had spent in the draughty old castle pounding his brains and his body in a shape to suit his teachers, and yet, it was only three. And poor di Lido must think it even longer. The Count came and went between Mondejar and the Court, but di Lido had been requested to remain at Mondejar to supervise the training of Don Francisco de Mendoza and so only rarely journeyed away.

In the beginning couriers were sent out seeking the services of several of Spain's most vaunted teachers. Those who were unencumbered by lecture schedules at Salamanca or Valladolid responded rapidly in the affirmative. They were flattered by Tendilla's attention, for he was the son of the late Marquis de Santillana, Spain's foremost author, and a patron of art and letters in his own right. Furthermore, he was most generous in his fees.

Between three academic tutors Francho was exposed to mathematics, astronomy, history, and geography. Additionally, another teacher was provided to drill him in the etiquette of the Court, proper modes of address, obeisance, precedence, bearing and demeanor, plus the histories and insignias of Spain's noble families.

Di Lido himself took on instruction in Spanish and Arabic literature, philosophy, and poetry. And, to Francho's astonishment, the precise little man also taught him swordsmanship, for anyone so rude as to goad the temper of this savant soon found themselves pinned by the tip of his flashing sword. Di Lido was a demanding teacher, insistent upon detail whether the definitive meaning of an obscure passage in Virgil or the exact position of the dagger hand during the sword's offensive motion. But his pleasure was so evident at Francho's quick grasp of the nuances of fighting with the sword and his lithe grace that Francho worked doubly hard to please him.

Von Gormach, a German knight turned mercenary, was an expert instructor of weapons. He taught the techniques of handling a hunting javelin, a heavy jousting lance or a mace, and how to wield these with balance and agility while wearing a sixty-pound suit of jointed steel. Teamed up with a riding master who taught seat and form on either a light jennet or great war horse, di Lido and Von Gormach exacted such heavy physical practice from Francho that for the first six months his legs and buttocks were constantly sore and he could hardly lift his arms to get himself dressed.

But, and considered the most important by Tendilla and di Lido, there were two additional masters who arrived just before winter settled gray on the plains: silent, effacing hooded clerics treading with downcast eyes, imported to instruct the Count's newly found son in theology and religion. To allow them the peace of meditation these two were quartered together in one of the further towers, and their meals brought to them.

Francho was hugely amused by this strange pair of monks in their muffling robes, for neither was a religious. When one threw back his cowl a scarred, hawk-nosed, dark-complexioned visage emerged. He was a Morisco, a Catholicized Moor named Esteban Ebarra who had been born a slave, freed by Tendilla, and then taken into the Count's household. Ebarra's mission to Mondejar was crucial: to teach Tendilla's son the Arabic-Berber tongue of Granada and render him fluent in all aspects and intonations of the language. Ebarra, a man of few words but much intelligence, would lay down his life for Tendilla; to him this assignment was simple, there was no question of failure.

The other pseudo-monk was Pedro Nunez, a middle-aged Andalusian of uncertain sobriety, puffy-eyed and stub-fingered, hired as an instructor of music because he was a most accomplished balladeer and musician—when not in his cups—and because he was not a frequenter of Isabella's refined court.

Nunez alternated evening sessions with Ebarra in one of the tower rooms, which had been sound- and light-proofed with thick rugs and tapestries over the walls and windows. Declin-ing to be curious about his wealthy patron's reason for such elaborate privacy, Nunez labored to impart some of his genius to Mendoza's son, instructing him in the lute and in the large body of Moorish and European music appropriate to it, as well as to the seven-stringed, flat-bodied African guitar, called the guembri. He had written down himself, in musical nota-tion on a six-lined staff, many of the songs that until then had been handed along only by voice and showed Francho how to translate the mysterious squiggles into sound.

Daydreaming of the past years, his mount so familiar with the road between Castle Mondejar and the village that the beast needed no guidance, Francho held an easy seat, his body seeming to flow along with the horse's gait. He chuckled to himself as he remembered demonstrating to Nunez what he thought was his considerable talent on the lute, only to see the man clap hands to his ears and wrinkle up his jowly face in pain. "No, no, you are strangling that poor instrument," Nunez protested, snatching away the lute from his abashed pupil. "First we will do finger exercises, over and over until your fingers are stretched and strengthened. But on a piece of wood, not on the strings."

Oh, those exercises! It had seemed to Francho his fingers did chord positions in his sleep. Yet, a year later, in his loose-lipped, casual way, Nunez remarked on Francho's keen musical ear and admitted that his job had been much eased by his pupil's natural flair for music. Anyway, the dogged prac-tice necessary for advanced fingering and speed was counted pleasure by Francho rather than drudgery, and he jealously guarded the time put aside for his music studies and practice. His mathematics tutor, who thought him an indifferent stu-dent, would have been astonished at his superiority in music and in that further study which also took a tuned ear, language.

His days fell into a strict pattern, with very little surcease from the continual grind of learning. Had he less ability or less proud desire to master whatever Mendoza indicated was necessary for him to know, the unceasing demands upon his mental capacity might have exhausted him. But he aired out his brains through physical action, tilting with Von Gormach, riding, or wrestling with his wiry instructor of history.

Friday night was reserved for a change of pace, a jaunt into the nearby village, when Von Gormach and Pietro di Lido (insisting he was present only as an observer of village life) took Francho to the crude tavern to drink and to dally with the local wenches. Von Gormach's capacity for mug after mug of a local wine, which he boastfully encouraged young Francho to match, was only halted by di Lido's incapacity to stay sober on the stuff, a "neutralizer," so he said, to all his various bodily complaints. The guards at the drawbridge were inured to the Friday night homecomings and managed not to grin at the tipsy trio, horses left slack-reined to make their own way home, clapping each other on the shoulders and roaring out the vulgar, offkey ditties they warbled at the moon.

The sour note sounded Saturday mornings, when Francho suffered his pounding head through an early morning recital of the Ptolemaic principle of universe and di Lido moaned in his study with a cup of bitter herb tea. Von Gormach, however, to the petty irritation of his less able drinking companions, always appeared at an early hour his usual bluff self, with no visible effects from the ocean of drink he had floated home on the night before.

Although Francho took his studies seriously, propelled by driving ambition to devote himself to excelling, the old streak of deviltry popped out now and then. Since he was certain his skill at thievery would come in handy sometime, he kept himself in practice by stealthily lifting the gold pomander off di Lido's belt, then returning it by stooping and offering it back with a bland-faced, "Your pardon, Maestro, but you seem to have dropped your perfumer."

Doña Maria's rosary beads, Von Gormach's leather gloves, which he wore stuck in his belt, the dance teacher's clappers for beating time, and the major-domo's keys suffered the same light-fingered fate from time to time and were returned with the same straight-faced composure, the victims mystified by their apparent repeated carelessness—except for di Lido, of course, who found his Roman risibilities so tickled by the puzzlement of the others that he did not mind Francho's pranks. In fact he approved. Stealing was the one useful skill for a spy in which his charge was already well trained. Di Lido included this in the regular dispatches he sent to the Count to inform him of Francho's progress in all his undertakings.

The Lord's days were left to Francho to do with as he pleased, and he spent them after mass in various pleasurable pursuits, hunting with his tutors, fishing, reading, composing intricate *cancioneros,* or dreaming. It was the only quiet time he had to think back to the past, what he now considered an aimless existence and which he no longer regretted leaving, although at first he was very homesick and sorely missed Tía Esperanza's maternal warmth and the friendship of Carlos, who was, after all, someone of his own age. Enjoying the sun in a corner of the ordered garden, he would reminisce to himself about the inn and his days of evading the law, and even sent his thoughts back to the gentle old monk at San Martín who had been both his mother and father in his babyhood.

But for a long while it was Dolores that he thought of the most, and not only on Sundays. Her piquant face with its wide, engaging eyes and pink lips was easy to conjure up, and so clearly could he see her even after months had passed that it seemed those full, smiling lips were moving and telling him something and that he should listen. The memory of their last meeting together, especially the sweet passion with which she had responded to him, sent ripples of pleasure through his body, even as it unsettled him by invading his mind at inconvenient moments with images of the soft, young breasts, a finally yielding body, and a shadowed face softening into helpless complicity. Dolores haunted him whenever he allowed his mind or body to flag. He even took to imagining how he would ride into Ciudad Real, the rich and elegant son of a grandee, and visit Papa el Mono's, where the ragged Dolores would gasp and gawk at him and he would make her a gift of money enough to buy her own hostelry and swear always to protect her and Carlos and Pepi, and she would take him into her bed and with tears of gratitude show him again those fragrant, pear-shaped, pink-tipped breasts. . . .

It was only after he had encountered and seduced the very accommodating, insatiable Constanza that the intrusive memories of Dolores and his yearnings for her moved to the back of his mind, neither faded nor forgotten, but laid away in the limbo of broken-off paths.

The sharp barking of the dogs who bounded out over the drawbridge to meet them snapped him from his reverie.

"Come on, Von Gormach," Francho yelled, rising in his stirrups. "A gold piece to the dungeon steps!"

"Ja, ja, I vin it!" the German hollered back, delighted, and sunk his spurs into his mount. The horses lunged forward and thundered over the road, necks stretched out, eyes bulging, surging across the shuddering bridge and under the iron portcullis to skid to a simultaneous cloud-of-dust halt before the hoary, square tower in the court, with both riders vaulting from the saddle to race to touch the pitted wooden portal. *"Basta!"* Francho flung at the grinning Von Gormach, "I think you read my mind. I cannot steal a minute's march on you."

He nodded to the grooms hurrying up to take their horses, and they strode off to find di Lido.

"Ah, ah, there you are, Francisco, come in, and you too, Von Gormach, why not?" the Italian cried exuberantly as they opened his chamber door. He held up several missives with their seals broken. "The outer world has deigned to remember us all at once, so it seems, and with glad tidings. So! And which would you like to hear first, Francisco, my fine news or yours?"

Eagerness blazed in Francho's eyes, but he had learned well his lessons in courtesy and forced his racing pulse to quiet. "Yours, Maestro, to be certain. It is surely of greater consequence," he deferred politely.

Di Lido's dark eyes gleamed in appreciation of Francho's restraint since he could hardly contain his own jubilation. "Very well, and I will not try you with the details. I have had recently an invitation to lecture on the divine Dante at Salamanca this winter, which I now feel free to accept. Moreover, His Excellence has requested of me a better translation of the glorious poet's *Vita Nuovo* and the *Convivio* into Castilian, as a present to his brother, the Grand Cardinal. And he agrees that I shall do this at Court, since Don Iñigo knows I do my best work only amidst the activity and hubbub occasioned by the Royal presence. So, see you, I am liberated from this vast pile of stone!" His eye caught a fleeting, injured expression on Francho's face and he arched his brows. "But my dear Francisco, that is not to say that I have not thoroughly enjoyed guiding so good a mind as yours into the higher realms of thought. It has been a great pleasure to see your progress—"

"You have been chafing with boredom, Maestro, especially since your last trip to Madrid," Francho interrupted amiably as he lolled on the end of his spine in an x-chair, the only sign of his controlled excitement an erratic swinging of one booted foot.

"True, true, very observant." Di Lido nodded and took a sip of wine from his fine, enameled glass goblet, a gift from Ludovico Sforza, who had heard his lectures at the university in Milan. Two bright spots on his pale cheeks indicated that he had been celebrating even while awaiting them. "But that does not mean I am pleased to leave you, Francisco, just when you have achieved some understanding of the elegance of Arabic metaphor. Still, in swordsmanship you most definitely have under control all the nuances of my technique. No one could ruin your style now. In fact, Von Gormach can take over and the change will afford you good experience."

Francho understood what he meant. Where di Lido's strokes were lightning fast and unexpected, the German's weapon hacked and slashed, requiring his opponent to use less brainwork and more sheer muscle. Although he felt that without his padded armor of lightweight leather he would have been slain more often by di Lido's new technique of a flurry of swift, lunging thrusts rather than Von Gormach's signaled onslaughts, he agreed his parrying of the whistling, murderous, double-edged slice needed strengthening.

For a moment his thoughts became absorbed with di Lido's departure and what would result from it. "You have given me a generous part of your life, Maestro, and never shall I forget it. If you are happy, then I am happy. Nevertheless, I shall miss you sorely. I wish I could be with you when you go to Seville this year," he added wistfully.

Di Lido triumphantly held up one of the letters, a broad smile illuminating his fine-boned face. "Aha, and so you will, my friend, and thereby hangs your good news. My Lord Tendilla indicates he wishes you to journey with the Court when it leaves for Seville in the spring, and"—he paused for effect—"thence into the field with him for the summer campaigns against the Moor. So full of praise have our reports been of your progress that your period of learning is over. Just a few more months and you are reborn!"

Francho launched himself from the chair like a missile from a catapult, knocking over his seat. *"Ola!"* he yelled, leaping into the air in joyous transport and brandishing clasped hands above his head, proving to di Lido that his advice to his patron had been correct. The young man was but eighteen, in the first flush of his manhood and filled to bursting with heavy instruction and tedious practice. He was ready, nay, needed, to preen his feathers amongst his peers.

Francho's white teeth flashed against his olive skin, and in his exuberance he whirled, drew his sword, and neatly skimmed the tops off all the candles in an iron candelabra standing nearby. "Saved! I'm saved, *amigos,"* he exulted as the stubs clattered to the floor. "I soon would have been baying at the moon with the hounds, quite mad, quite mad, I tell you."

"Und me alzo!" Von Gormach grunted happily, for Francho's departure would mean that he too was freed of Mondejar.

"And there is more." Di Lido tittered with amusement, sitting down abruptly and downing another mouthful of wine with a neat tilt of his head. "We shall soon have a delightful guest for several days. Doña Maria's daughter, Doña Leonora, has been appointed to the train of the Infanta, the Royal Princess Isabel. She is traveling to Madrid from the seminary, where she has spent the last four of her fifteen years being academically instructed according to the requirement for noblewomen laid down by our most progressive of Queens. She will pass by Mondejar on her way and bring a bit of grace and beauty to this ancient pile."

"Doña Maria must be most happy," Francho tossed in, still flushed from his burst of elation to know he was soon to join the world again. Doña Maria did not speak to him often of her daughter, and when she did it was in modest terms. But she missed the girl and was ambitious enough for her to have actively petitioned her highly placed relatives and the Queen herself for Leonora's placement in the royal household.

"Overjoyed, she is overjoyed," di Lido agreed pleasantly. "And so I am too, for I shall ride north with the young lady to Madrid, and thence on to Salamanca."

"Will you come back this way to go south to Seville with me?"

"*Sí*, if it is convenient. Would your old *cicerone* allow Daniel to walk by himself into the den of lions?" He chuckled at the uncertainty that settled on Francho's face. "Nay, Francisco, I but jest. You are more than prepared to take your place at Court. I do not pass you from these shackles lightly. In fact, so high is the curiosity and speculation ever since His Excellence made it known he has formally recognized a bastard that you will be lionized—devoured in that way, if you take my meaning, ha ha. You will make the ladies faint with desire. It will be a triumph."

Von Gormach bent to adjust his soft boot, which was too tight. "And another step forward," di Lido added, with a significant nod over the German's head, recalling the purpose of all this.

Leonora's mercenary-accompanied litter passed over the drawbridge and was waved on by the guard as Doña Maria threw on her cloak, ran down the steps, and stood waiting before the main portal. The little caravan rattled across the court and came to a halt, and Doña Maria's daughter stepped nimbly down from the curtained conveyance.

"Mother!"

"My dear daughter!"

Arms wide, mother and daughter embraced, tearfully, uttering cries of endearment, hugging and kissing until the first transport of reunion exhausted itself.

Doña Maria held Leonora away by the shoulders. "Let me look at you. I almost do not recognize you, you are so much a grown woman. You have filled out. But, you are beautiful!" the mother exclaimed, her eyes bright with happy tears.

Leonora put a loving hand to her mother's face, where there were wrinkles that had not been there before. Dimpling, she laughed. "But you have not seen me since my fourteenth saint's day, almost two years past, dearest madam. I was bound to change a bit in so long a time. Oh, and you are looking so well. These few years at Mondejar have done you so much good, mother."

Doña Maria drew a lace kerchief from her tight sleeve and dabbed at her eyes. "Yes, *querida*, I have finally overcome the sadness the death of your dear sire precipitated, the Lord give him rest." She crossed herself, then wrinkled her eyes in a smile. "But the fickleness of woman seems to prevail, and now I am finding the peaceful life tedious and would welcome a change. So I am considering a return to Court."

Leonora clapped her hands gleefully. "Oh mother, that is such good news! We will be able to gossip together like two old crones."

"But why are we standing here in the wind?" Doña Maria cried. "Come inside, let me give you a warm potion and food, and then we will unpack your chest together . . ."

"And I will show you all the new Court gowns that I ordered sewn in Cuenca, they are truly beautiful."

Doña Maria ordered refreshments brought to the carpeted, velvet-hung chamber assigned to Leonora and had the pleasure of seeing some fragrant meat pastries and hot broth bring roses back into the young woman's travel-pale face. Chattering and laughing, Leonora drew out one damask or velvet gown after another from her chest, whirling about the room to show them off to her mother and then handing them to a servant, who carefully hung them on pegs behind a curtain. Delighted with her prestigious appointment to the Infanta Isabel's small, select circle, happy to see her mother, relieved to be finished with the tedium of education, she kept Doña Maria entertained with all the events of the past months, leaving one sentence unfinished to switch breathlessly to another. Catching her elation, Doña Maria added her own news of Leonora's sister who was ten years older, married to an Italian duke, and living in Rome, and gossip of various friends and relatives learned by letter. Neither had been in a position to observe much of the tidings they chatted about, but what they didn't know firsthand they supplied from hearsay.

Watching her daughter's small, elegant head shine bright gold as she passed back and forth through a shaft of sunlight from the window, Doña Maria realized how much she had missed her youngest and resolved to ignore her own retiring nature and spend more time along with the Court. What was more, although she felt there would be suitors enough for Leonora's hand, the most advantageous matches often needed an on-the-spot parental guiding hand to come about.

Sinking finally onto an upholstered stool as the last gown and headdress was hung up or repacked by the servant, Leonora heaved an exaggerated sigh of exhaustion and popped a nutmeat from a bowl into her mouth. Crunching it she broached the subject uppermost in her mind.

"Tell me, *mi madre*, of Don Iñigo's bastard. Forgive me, I sometimes could not make out your hand in your letters. My curiosity is bursting. Has he been acknowledged heir?"

Doña Maria sat and fanned her face, which often flushed with the strange heat caused by the end of a woman's childbearing years. "No, not yet, my dear. He has merely been recognized and is soon to be presented at Court. That is enough for a while, according to Don Iñigo."

Leonora tilted her blond head pensively. "You know, mother, Don Iñigo once told me that because he was childless I would inherit his properties since his nephew, the Duke, owns so much of Castile already. 'Tis strange he did not ever mention a bastard child before." Her brown eyes were curious, but innocent of rancor.

Doña Maria was prepared and answered her daughter with a shrug. "Poof, that happens often. An unmarried youth whose blood runs hot begets a child on some poor mistress, then takes a wife, has legitimate issue, and forgets the very existence of the child born on the left side of the blanket, one among many, usually. It was by a whim—perhaps an angel had brushed a dream of mortality over my cousin's eyes—that he stopped to see his natural son in Ciudad Real just as the boy's mother lay dying."

"Was his mother a well-born woman then?"

"She was gently raised. Her father had been a silk merchant, but had lost all his ships in a storm. She lived on the charity of a penurious brother; her son was raised with little but a roof over his head. Seeing the boy was sturdy and bright, Don Iñigo was moved to claim him and give him all the advantages he lacked."

"Poor Carlotta. I wonder what she would think of this. After all, it should have been her child. . . ."

"Poor Carlotta thinks not of anything," Doña Maria said, a slight asperity in her voice. "Her madness has grown but worse through the years, and you know well she was barren."

So infrequently was Don Iñigo's wife mentioned, so completely was the curtain of superstitious dread drawn about the broken mind alternately drooping or raving for over a decade in a barred room of a cloistered nunnery, that Doña Maria was startled by her daughter's memory of the woman. She deemed it wiser now to turn the conversation into safer channels.

"You will like your new kinsman, Leonora. He is a handsome devil and a charmer. The young maids at Court will find him much to their taste."

"I see he has already won you, sweet mother," Leonora chided, her eyes dancing.

"And why not? My sight is not yet so dim nor my mind so ancient that I cannot see the beauty of young men." They giggled together like conspirators.

Together they chose the gown Leonora would wear at supper. It was of pale brown silk brocade, high-waisted and full-skirted, trimmed with a narrow edging of gray squirrel along the low, square neck and at the cuffs of the tight, elbow-slashed sleeves. They rejected the hennin headdress for this evening in favor of a little silk hat like a baby's cap. This knotted demurely under the chin and would show off Leonora's shining hair, tied back at the rear and streaming down her back. From her jewel casket they selected a slim necklace of sparkling garnets to encircle her white throat.

Doña Maria rose to leave. "Why don't you rest for a while, daughter. They will bring you a bath shortly and some lovely essence I made myself from last summer's lilies and roses. I will come for you later and we will go down together to the great hall. You look so fashionable. I must see if I have such a low-necked dress in my own chest so you will not outshine me."

"Oh mother!" Leonora laughed, putting a hand up to her bosom in mock modesty. She walked with Doña Maria to the door and hugged her in temporary farewell. "Thank you. Thank you, madam."

"Thank me for what, may I ask?" Doña Maria gazed lovingly into her daughter's warm, velvety eyes, their height level with her own.

A shy smile touched the girl's lips, and she plucked affectionately at Doña Maria's sleeve. "For being with me. For being you. Mother, I have missed you so."

Later, as they made their descent down the long main stair, Leonora gliding as if there were no legs under her skirt just as the good sisters had labored to teach her, Doña Maria laid a staying hand on her daughter's arm.

"*Querida*, do you regret the fact that Francisco de Mendoza may inherit from Don Iñigo?" she asked, keeping her tone mild.

"Regret?" Leonora queried, as if the thought had not occurred to her. "Indeed no, why should I regret? I have a noblewoman's dowry and will inherit my father's lands, I am amply provided for. I was but curious before. In fact, I am most happy that my cousin Tendilla has reclaimed a son to carry on his line."

The older woman knew her daughter; in spite of her denial there was a hint of resentment, a spark of calculation behind the lively interest in the velvety eyes. But the mother believed it only momentary pique. The truth was closer to what Leonora had voiced.

"I apologize, my dear. I meant no harm. I know you have always been most fond of Don Iñigo, from the time he jounced you on his knee as a baby and your little heels beat a tattoo on his leg." She patted her daughter's hand. Leonora's dimpled smile appeared and they continued down.

Doña Maria was proud of Leonora's charity in the situation and considered that the reward for such good nature would come. At the return of Francho's inheritance as a Venegas, Don Iñigo would again be without an heir and that would make Leonora de Zuniga one of the wealthiest women in Spain. What Tendilla promised, he accomplished. Doña Maria had no doubts he would see Francisco recover his patrimony, or that her daughters, when the time came, would be amply remembered by their illustrious cousin.

Jumping from his foam-flecked, blowing horse, Francho quickly patted the animal's damp nose, tossed the reins to a groom, and bounded up the stairs to his chamber, bawling for his valet. As soon as he had seen the strange men-at-arms in the courtyard among the host of other daily visitors, he knew Leonora de Zuniga must have arrived. And here he was, covered with dust and in the old doublet and felt cap he used to gallop across the countryside whenever he could escape from Ebarra and Nunez.

Finally, later, carefully bathed and combed, he felt cleaner but not calmer, and went twice through his wardrobe unable to decide what to wear. At last he chose a high-collared, velvet doublet of rich blue (Constanza had said it made his eyes more cerulean than the sky) embroidered with gold arabesques, its slashed sleeves showing the white of his linen shirt and its skirt so short it barely covered his buttocks. He left the front of the doublet open to show the embroidered shirt beneath but secured it at the neck with a gold cord. Over his muscled legs he had drawn up dark hosen, around his waist he fastened a thin belt from which hung his dagger, on his head he set a blue velvet hat with a jaunty white plume curling behind. He felt presentable, even though his hair, curling just at his collar, would not lie flat. He dropped his gold chain twice, his soft red leather boots were new and pinched his toes, and the valet had to be berated for jiggling the long, polished steel mirror that reflected his finery. But finally he was ready.

He descended to the great hall two steps at a time but slowed his pace at the bottom steps, where he threw back his shoulders and donned an expression of calm. In fact, to his great surprise, he suddenly was calm. He was a member of the elite, was he not, not only by training but by birth? And by all the ill-gotten coin at Papa el Mono's, he was going to act as such.

Entering the huge, banner-hung chamber, which was used for banquets, gatherings, entertainments, and the formal reception of visitors, he saw the group at the far end sitting or standing before the tremendous hearth, being served cups of Val de Penas wine by two valets with trays. Di Lido, Von Gormach, and several of his other tutors were there, but the person who drew his eyes like a magnet was the small, delicate young woman in a fur-trimmed gown whose golden hair lit the space around her like the sun and whose laugh pealed out like Pan pipes in a glade. In just the few moments that it took to come up quietly behind her as she regaled di Lido and her mother with a lively mimic of the acerbic prioress at the seminary, rearing back her head and pursing her lips in imitation of the nun's pressed mouth, his heart flopped over, ceased to beat for a moment, and then thumped in his chest like a bird pierced by an arrow.

"Ah, Master Francisco, there you are," di Lido called, and Leonora turned about. "Doña Leonora, I should like to present to you Francisco de Mendoza, a gentleman for whom I have much admiration, even after so many months of incarceration with him."

Francho saw Leonora's dancing golden eyes widen under the pale brows as they met his for a moment, and then she returned his bow with a graceful court curtsey. *"Señor,"* she murmured, acknowledging the introduction. And then, raising her sleek head, she flashed him a smile so warm and so charmingly bracketed by two adorable dimples that he fell instantaneously, impossibly, inconsolably, in love.

Afterward Francho could hardly remember what conversations sustained the evening, either then or when they went up to supper, which was laid in Doña Maria's quarters. All evening his eyes and his mind were on the living, breathing miracle that had happened to him. He found it impossible to follow courtesy and not stare at her, even though she seemed not to mind his impoliteness. She smiled at him and inquired about his studies and chatted about her own, or else turned from him to charm the other men present into a fatuous glow. When her attention was elsewhere Francho felt the room had gone dark. Yet, even as he gazed directly into her shining brown eyes and drank into his thirsting soul the sight of her enchanting dimples, ivory skin, and cascade of blond hair, the lovelorn Francho fought despair.

His thoughts were gloomy, although he conversed with what wit and intelligence he could muster. The exquisite Leonora would stay only a few nights at Mondejar, for she was already overdue at Madrid and could not linger.

The injustice of it infuriated him, to find his love and lose her, all in a few days, and lose her forever, perhaps, since the young men at Court had eyes in their heads too, and time enough to press their suits. What cruelty! How had he angered Providence that life so mocked him, giving him so astounding a gift and then taking it away.

The evening flew, the convivial supper was finished, the hour grew late, and Leonora's silken laugh rose above Von Gormach's stentorian tones as the German bowed low, kissed her fingers, and bade her rest well. Francho too kissed her warm fingers, loath to let them go, hoping she could read his admiration in his eyes, wondering if perhaps, behind the cousinly favor she displayed, there hid an answering regard.

He could not sleep that night but lay picturing her face in his mind, imagining what it would be like to hold her body against his, and his breathing came fast and shallow and was hardly conducive to slumber. An arrangement of tones floated into his head, and he began to compose a new *canción*, beginning it, "O wondrous fair, o earthly angel. . . ." Somewhere in the midst of it, his eyes finally closed.

Leonora stayed late in her chamber the next morning, so Francho caught no sight of her before his tutor of science and alchemy claimed him, following Tendilla's orders that nothing be allowed to disturb the routine of learning. Later, he had a glimpse of her blond head leaning over the stone balustrade above the dirt-floored indoor court where he and Von Gormach had been hacking away at each other with blunt-edged swords for almost two hours. Suddenly Francho's tiring body became rejuvenated, his blows landed more forcefully, and his offense became heavily aggressive. But when the hard-pressed puffing German finally called quarter and Francho bounded up the spiral steps to greet Leonora, he found the balcony empty.

Disconsolately he shrugged out of his padded armor and stalked off to clean up, and while he washed away the sweat and dust he consoled himself by describing his golden lady to himself in flowery Arabic, preparing for his session with Ebarra by transposing into the Moorish language the words of the love song he had composed the night before.

It was already late afternoon, his tutorial appointments over for the day, that he headed toward Doña Maria's wing of the castle and was drawn all the more swiftly by the sound of a flute and a deeper-toned whistle issuing gaily from that lady's chambers. At his knock, he was bidden enter.

"Oh, Don Francisco, do please join us," Doña Maria cried, her eyes bright as two polished beads. "I thought Doña Leonora might enjoy hearing these fellows"—she indicated two ragged, grinning village musicians who often tootled in the castle courtyard for whatever small coin was thrown them—"for they offer all the music we have hereabout." The little lie was delivered admirably blandly; she and di Lido had enjoyed many a secret concert in the padded tower room.

The two ladies had seated themselves with their needlework near the hearth of the commodious chamber which held Doña Maria's curtained bed, sundry chests and furniture, a Moorish carved table used both for dining and writing, her prized brass ewers and bowls displayed in an open cupboard, and salvers heaped with dried flower petals, which lent a faint perfume to the air.

Francho approached and bowed politely, his eyes filled with Leonora's lovely face under the pale white wings of a starched coif. He thought he had never imagined in all his dreams so perfect and delicate a nose, as if carved from the whitest and

smoothest of marble, nor so charming a small mouth, like a
rosy flower.

"I fear Doña Leonora will find Mondejar not only lacking
in music but in most entertainments, unfortunately, which
were deemed too distracting for both tutors and scholars."
Francho answered Doña Maria deprecatingly. "Here we live a
life replete with no events. But that was, of course, until
yesterday, when my lady Leonora entered this little world and
set every corner of it ablaze with her beauty. Even Doña
Maria's brilliant smile had too much to do to offset our
austere lives." He stepped up and took Leonora's small hand
and kissed it. "Your presence, *doña*, lends this old castle a
glory it has never seen before."

Pleased with himself, he watched a soft smile curve Leonora's mouth. "Why, you are too kind, sir. And I see that you
learn more here than just Latin and the Greek philosophers.
Does my cousin also have a tutor of flattery, mother?"

"He has no need for one, my dear." Doña Maria chuckled.
"Master Francisco has a natural aptitude for turning the right
phrase. And even Señor di Lido praises his talent for poesy."

Leonora bent her liquid amber-brown gaze upon her new
cousin. "Then you shall be much admired at Court, Don
Francisco. Queen Isabella, I hear, is extremely fond of the
more gentle talents."

"And you, *doña*?" Francho motioned toward the two intent
musicians piping away at a galliard in the background. "Are
you fond of music?"

"Indeed, *señor*, very much. I adore dancing. And I am told
that the Queen keeps many fine musicians at Court and that
there is wonderful music and dancing at every occasion." The
rise of her voice gave him a delighted glimpse of how excited
she was to be going to Court.

"No occasion at Court has yet been so sparkling as the first
one to be graced by your shining presence, my lady."

A dainty pink flushed Leonora's face. His smile was most
disarming, she thought, but it was his eager, bright azure gaze
that made her feel shy. She glanced down at the square of silk
she was embroidering. "My mother tells me you shall soon
repair to Court yourself. Are you excited about it?"

"Yes, very. But not because of the dancing," Francho
answered, and he assumed a rueful expression, recognizing a
fine opportunity to engage her more intimately. "The sad fact
is that although I've been taught the various steps, I've had

little chance to practice them. Doña Maria cannot, to my regret, honor me as a partner"—Leonora glanced over sympathetically at her mother, whose bad leg still caused her pain "—and Maestro di Lido does not make a very inspiring lady. I should probably trip over my own feet and bring disgrace on the Mendozas."

Her chimelike laughter enchanted his ear. Her eyes flickered over him as he leaned casually against one of the fat stone columns which supported the ceiling. "Oh, I scarcely think so, sir. I chanced to see you this morning at your dueling practice and you were most nimble and sure-footed."

"*Sí,* but wielding a sword against a great ox is not the same as handing a delicate lady into the proper figures without treading hard on her slippers or knocking off her hat." He grinned, shrugged. "I am afraid I am hopeless."

"Most tragic," she murmured. Then she tilted her head and smiled up archly, "However, if . . . if it please you, I would be happy to practice the steps with you. We had a fine master at the seminary but the same problem arose, there were only women to dance with. In fact, it would help my confidence, too."

Francho straightened and smiled broadly, swept off his tall, small-brimmed hat, and made a deep bow. "I shall be gladly and forever in your debt, *doña.* When, then?"

"Well, why not now? If they will play again the galliard they just finished, one could try a few steps right here."

The eavesdropping musicians exchanged glances, nodded, and swung once more into the measured but zestful dance that had become so popular throughout Europe. Although they lacked a drum, the whistle-player filled in by stamping his foot in rhythm.

Leonora rose and held out her small, soft hand, and Francho took it, devastated by her touch and by the sweet dimples that flashed into being at the corners of her mouth. With a graceful movement she stooped and swept up the short train of her dark green gown. He led her out onto the arabesqued carpet which covered almost half the chamber, still peeking sideways at her because he couldn't get enough of looking at her. Hands clasped and held high, they waited for the beat and began the pattern, walking slowly forward to the count of four, facing each other, still holding hands rotating in a stately, clockwise circle, facing each other, rotating counterclockwise. They faced each other again and made a quick step forward, coming so close together Francho could feel her sweet breath on his chin, took two steps back, and bowed. Then, going four more steps in the original direction, they repeated the entire pattern.

By the time they reached the end of the room, her accusing glance told him she had realized how good a dancer he was. But the amused smile that followed told him his ruse was forgiven, and as they stepped into a new figure where he could momentarily put his arm about her tiny waist he wondered if she could feel the involuntary quiver of his muscle as he tried not to sweep her into his arms.

"What else do you *not* do well, sir, so I will be advised not to offer you help you don't need?"

"Don't be angry, *doña*. It was the desperate ploy of a man who dreamt all night of the touch of your hand."

"Methinks you have stayed too long in this country castle and would find attractive even the ugliest damsel if she came to visit."

"Ah, cruel lady, you have pierced my heart to believe that. Even if I were in Paris and surrounded by all the beauties of the ancient world, you would be my Helen, the dazzling light by which all other lamps of beauty are extinguished. Look at me. Can't you tell how I am distracted by you?"

Having to follow the music they now bowed, then clasped raised hands and stepped in close to each other again. He saw a tiny flame leap in her amber eyes as she saw beyond his smile and read the sincerity in his regard. She flushed and quickly dropped her lashes over her telltale response, but to his pleasure she did not simper.

"Sir, you are too bold," she remonstrated, as the dance steps turned them back toward Doña Maria, the musicians happily outdoing themselves by inventing new measures to the music.

He squeezed her hand gently, for he thought he was not really displeasing her. "*Sí*, and I kneel at your feet for my precipitousness. But you have entered my life like the most luminous angel sent from Heaven and I am overwhelmed. It is desperation makes me speak so openly."

Hand on his hip he led her smoothly around the circle. Now her upward glance held mischief. "Desperation, *señor?* Whatever for?"

"For the fact that you will fly from here tomorrow and my deprived eyes will have to wait weary months to behold you again. And perhaps in that time Doña Maria will have promised you to some powerful grandee. . . ."

"Nay, I do not think my dear mother and my cousin Tendilla will so quickly decide on whom to bestow my hand."

"And would you have naught to say about it, should they?" he pressed.

"Women seldom do," she teased, smiling up into his furrowed brow.

He bent his dark head down to hers as they came to the final notes, murmuring in her ear, "Will you send me a letter from Court, kind angel, and not let me languish forgotten in this gloomy ward?"

She threw back her head and laughed, and his eyes drank in the marble smoothness of her throat and the soft, white rise of bosom from her gold-laced bodice. "And will you dream of me every night, Master Francisco?" she countered and both to his delight and consternation squeezed his hand back.

He pledged fervently as they circled one last time, "Every night and every day and four times on the Lord's day." He wondered whether to believe her oblique invitation. There were wiles of women he was not yet easy with, and he could not tell was she toying with him or was she really welcoming his suit. Not that it mattered. He was determined to pursue her, for what would be the good of all the wealth and titles in Christendom if he could not share them with this exquisite girl?

"Very well, good cuz," she answered cordially. "I will send you a letter and tell you all the news of Court."

"Three letters, four. And news of you is all I want."

"And news of me too," she promised, eyes smiling up at him through a veil of brown lashes. The music ended on a long, drawn out note, they bowed to each other, and he offered her his arm to walk the few paces back to her stool and the too busily sewing Doña Maria.

But she did not write several letters. She dispatched him, via a royal courier riding through to Valencia, only one, and that a short one, from Leon, where the Court had traveled to enable Their Majesties to handle pressing affairs in that province. She wrote little of a personal nature other than she was delighted with the liveliness of the Infanta's personal household, but he carried the letter under his doublet nevertheless and waylaid each arriving courier hopefully seeking more letters which never came. Doña Maria, however, heard from Leonora several times and each time informed Francho that her daughter sent wishes for his continuing health and successful studies. It was, perhaps, just a polite inclusion, but Francho consoled himself that at least she remembered his existence. He made a vow that the next time he was in her presence she would come away remembering much more than that.

The enervating heat of false summer during most of November soon passed into the bleak damp of winter, and Francho's former patience with his studies disappeared. He complained to Von Gormach that he felt as removed from life as a stylite living on a pillar and that he was full to the eyes with hunting, fishing, and thinking, and even with the pregnant Constanza. Especially he missed the lively presence and acerbic wit of di Lido and eagerly awaited the occasional letter the maestro wrote from the great university in Salamanca.

"'The young men insist on bringing their own private tutors to my lectures on history, and these pedants squirm with rage to hear their pet notions totally disproven,'" Francho read gleefully to Doña Maria, who had strained to make out di Lido's tiny hand. "And there's more, listen. 'Deeming my discourse on ancient philosophies too long, some rude and bored youths began scraping their feet on the floor and were thrown out bodily from the lecture chamber by my indignant supporters, who threatened the ruffians with a beating.'" Francho chuckled, just imagining his teacher's delight with the fracas. "And listen again. 'Imagine how great was the throng to hear my lecture on the satires of Juvenal that every street and path to the hall was blocked, and I had to be delivered to my lectern on the shoulders of my students!'" Both of them smiled broadly, transported in their minds to the narrow, clogged streets.

In addition to academic triumphs di Lido also thought to include in one letter the reports he had garnered of the past summer's hit-and-run battles in Granada, the blockade of various Moorish fortresses, and a description of the Spanish capture of the city of Ronda with the release of four hundred starved Christian captives from their heavy manacles—all of which served as fuel to Francho's discontent.

One by one Francho's tutors departed that third year,

deeming him well versed in their subjects. By January there remained at Mondejar only the faithful Von Gormach and Ebarra and Nunez, whose semi-confinement was relaxed in the small company.

Francho's studies of Arabic and music now filled more of his time, not only because his future might depend on them but because he enjoyed them. He conversed easily with Ebarra in the Berber dialect and read and wrote a fluent Arabic. Using as a textbook a smuggled Koran, he learned to reckon time from the year of the Hegira rather than the birth of Christ and committed to memory the dates and meanings of the Moslem religious holy days. Just as important, he caught from Ebarra a true glimpse of the Moslem character, for every so often the flame of Islam burned through what had been the man's forced conversion to Christianity.

As a product of the Moorish system of free education for all, Ebarra could recount in detail the histories of the great Arab houses that had ruled Spain and whose armies of the Crescent might have overrun all of Europe had not Charles Martel and the Franks stopped them at Poitiers. The invasion began in the eighth century, armies of Middle Eastern Arabs pouring across the straits from North Africa and in only a few short years conquering all of Spain, pushing what remained of the Christianized Iberians into a corner of the wild northern mountains. The whole peninsula belonged to the Arabs, called Moors from the invading Moroccan Berbers, for hundreds of years, until the land-hungry knights of the Cross strengthened enough to burst out of their strongholds and century by century retake their country, so that now only the territory of Granada remained Moslem.

The bitter pride Ebarra took in the ancient Moslem triumphs reflected the ideal of religious aggression held by many believers in Mohammed the Prophet. On the other hand he was just as proud of the glories of Arab architecture and arts and their amazing advances in science and medicine, to say nothing of their remarkable body of literature. Some of these writings included volumes on the art and exquisitely refined techniques of lovemaking, which, when Pietro di Lido described some of the passages he had committed to memory, held Francho's undivided attention.

In Don Iñigo's youth there had been peace between Spain and Granada, and the young bloods of both sides met and competed in important tourneys. This enabled Tendilla, in a long letter, to accurately describe to Francho the habits and manners of the Moorish aristocracy.

The distinctive, convoluted music of the Arab was Nunez's province to teach. Centuries of living side by side had eroded much of the difference between Christian and Moslem music, and the ubiquitous gypsy had stitched the two modes even more closely together. The wide repertoire Francho learned needed only a switch of language to be appropriate in either Court.

Restlessly he nursed his lovesick heart and daydreamed of Leonora, although he knew he had no right to covet her, not without first securing his own title and fortune. This, at least, gave him the impetus to continue honing his skills. He had only to think of her—curiously, he could not produce a steady image of her face; just when he got one feature clear in his mind's eye, the others blurred out—and resolve coursed through him like strong wine. The Mendoza name was borrowed. The only one that counted was the name he had a right to: Francisco Luis de Venegas, Marquis of Olivenza. Marquis! He would redeem it if he had to die.

The year turned and then once more it was spring, and the first crocus heads poked from the gray earth in the garden. On March 5—Francho would never forget the day—Mendoza's courier galloped under the raised portcullis bearing a dispatch bidding Francho join the Court in Toledo forthwith, from whence they would then travel south together to Seville. The long tutoring was over. Von Gormach, who had been in the village, returned much later to find Francho supine on his bed, an empty earthenware jug of aguardiente hugged to his chest, a silly smile on his drunken face. And slumped snoring on the carpet with another empty jug and similar smiles, Nunez and Ebarra.

Five days later, after a frenzy of packing and preparations which had the servants of every stripe panting, Francho and his companions consumed a hearty breakfast, retired one by one to Mondejar's chapel room to confess themselves to the black-robed village priest and were bid Godspeed by the saddened major-domo and his staff. In the courtyard, confusion reigned as retainers hurried and scurried about with last minute additions to the baggage and the excited horses snorted and stamped. Finally, to a cacophony of barking dogs and trumpet blasts to clear the steward's stream of daily petitioners from the path, the entourage cantered over the drawbridge and met a fresh breeze that snapped their flags like whips.

Two men-at-arms rode first with green-and-white tabards over their chain mail, one supporting a green standard with the white castle-and-bar emblem of the Mendozas, the other a fluttering, long-tailed oriflamme of dark blue, the color associated with Zunigas. Francho and Von Gormach rode next, Francho with a steel cuirass over his velvet doublet, a short, fur-edged cape over his shoulders, and a tall, feathered hat on his dark curls. There were silver spurs attached to his soft, high boots. He rode with one fist on his hip, the other gloved hand holding the reins of his arch-necked black stallion gripping a small whip as well. Beside him Von Gormach creaked in the ungainly, black-painted half-armor and plumed casque of the German knight.

Doña Maria traveled in a swaying gilt litter slung between two large mules, each ridden by a youth in green livery. The litter's damask curtains were stitched in gold and silver with the coronet of a viscountess and her crest showing the emblems of Mendoza, Zuniga, and a French lion couchant.

Behind her came the two monks on mules, riding silent and hooded, for the Count had insisted Nunez and Ebarra maintain their anonymity, and these were followed by a smart bodyguard of a dozen pikemen, and then as many overladen baggage mules and carts, carrying everything from beds to Von Gormach's pet bird in a wicker cage.

Francho was enthralled by his own elegance. In his heart there was still a place dedicated to the scapegrace who had haunted the back alleys of Ciudad Real and who had stared in awe at the mounted entourages of the upper classes as they rode grandly past him. Now the *pobres* made way for him and stood humbly with cap in hand along the side of the road as this proud young gentleman, his noble party, and his jangling escort went past in a halo of dignity and wealth.

He held his gaze aloof from the peasants, but that did not mean he did not see them. At one point, touched with pity, he hailed a bedraggled youth toiling along on a crutch, a heavy bundle strapped to his twisted back, and invited him to ride into the next village on their spare mule.

They passed Carabana, they passed the great castle at Maqueda that jutted against the sky, but otherwise the landscape was somber and monotonous. The first night they made camp in a field, enjoying the comfort of sturdy tents and the safeguard of their escort. The second night they presumed upon the hospitality of a gentleman known to Doña Maria, whose manse was just beyond Aranjuez.

On the third day, nearing Toledo, Francho reined in and waited until Doña Maria's litter came abreast. The lady, lying full length on her soft pillows, had pushed the emblazoned curtains back all the way, for the day was warm. She greeted him with a friendly smile, but after studying his set profile a few moments as he rode along beside her, decided to open the exchange he seemed to be having trouble commencing.

"What troubles you, Francisco? Do I detect some nervousness now we are nearing the Court?"

Francho threw her a rueful smile. "You seem to discover me so easily, Lady, as if you could look right into my head. I won't deny I am nervous at the thought of standing before the Royal Monarchs of Spain." He shrugged a deep breath into his lungs. "I know, I know, I have been more than competently rehearsed in the proper etiquette and speeches, but even so I am dry-mouthed at the prospect. I fear my tongue will tie itself in knots and I will bring disgrace to my lord Tendilla."

"Knots? Your silver tongue, my dear Francisco? Nonsense. Being presented to Their Majesties is an honor, not a torment. And most people live through it." She tucked an escaped lock of hair under her embroidered coif and shifted against her backrest.

"You have never described the Queen to me in much detail. Tell me again what she is like, I beg you."

"Willingly, although it has been over four years since I last attended Court, and perhaps she has changed a bit in the face, as we all do." Doña Maria smiled her closed-lipped smile, but her bright eyes twinkled with a relaxed humor. "The Queen is a handsome woman, of medium height and a proud, erect bearing. Her skin is the color of ivory, smooth, without wrinkles even when she smiles. Her eyes are blue, her hair brown with shadings of red, and uncoifed it hangs down past her waist."

"And her temperament?"

"Maestro di Lido in fact has described her as tranquil, but untamed. And indeed she is spirited; when I think of Isabella I think of her as she often rides, clad in armor and mounted on a snorting charger!"

"But what of her day-to-day nature?" Francho insisted,

fascinated. "For that is how I shall encounter her, on her throne and surrounded by her courtiers."

"Ah, Francisco, believe me there are as many opinions of our Queen's true nature as there are people in her Court. Some find her smile warm and frequent, some find it icy; some say she is pious and devout, some say fanatic; some say her pride comes from lofty nobility, some label it power-seeking vanity. She has been called bigoted; but there are those who deem this wisdom, and those who deem it calamity." Doña Maria shrugged and used her fan to create a cooling breeze on her face. "But I can tell you one certainty that all agree on, that she is just, to a fault. She protects the humblest in her kingdom as well as her dearest friends."

Doña Maria threw back her head and laughed, forgetting her bad teeth. "Oh, let me tell you, for I was there when it happened. Once, just after she had taken the Crown, we traveled through a village where they were holding a competition for the post of town crier, and the Queen, invited to listen, noted which humble man really had the bigger voice and then recommended him to the Alcalde. Since this was not the mayor's favorite, for in so small a place he surely wished to reward some brother or cousin with the post, you should have seen his face when there was naught for it but to comply with the Queen's justly arrived at conclusion." Laughter at the official's sour smile suffused her face.

"The thing is, my dear," Doña Maria became more sober, "never lose confidence, neither in yourself or in God." She saw the cockiness seeking to come back into his blue eyes. "Our faith in you is unshakable. Francisco de Mendoza is, after all, a most trained and polished gentleman." She dropped her chin, so that her eyes looked up at him from their network of tiny lines with a meaningful stare, and he knew she was silently adding, "So, too, is Francisco de Venegas."

"I thank you, my lady. I shall endeavor to be worthy of your faith. I thank you for your kind words." Her staunch encouragement helping him to shake off some of the anxiety which had suddenly assailed him, Francho gave her a grateful smile and a smart salute, then spurred his horse into a gallop to ride in advance of the party, picking up Von Gormach as he passed him.

Pupil and tutor galloped carefree through fields suddenly grown rockier and humped and jagged as they approached Toledo from its riverless north. "Look at me," Francho called in his mind to the laboring peasants in the field. "Look at my fast courser, my clothes, my escort! Do you know who I am? I am Francho, the cutpurse, the alley rat, and I shall soon stand before your exalted rulers. Do you believe it? Ha-yah!" Ebulliently he urged his speeding horse on, and the fresh wind blew away the rest of his unease.

❧ *Chapter 8* ❧

THE GRAY TOWERS and battlements which were Toledo sat upon a height above the black torrent of the Tagus River and rose as a sudden shock from the relatively flat plains around. Topping the city's hoary medieval walls a hodge-podge of drab, crammed together buildings climbed up the cliffs toward the spires of the soaring cathedral. But even a city of such somber and serious mien could not take the edge off the pageantry of a royal arrival.

The trumpets' clarion blares rang out loud and clear, the drums rattled, and a forest of banners and pennants flashed their vivid colors and snapped in the breeze as Los Reyes Católicos on white chargers entered Toledo by the ancient Moorish gate called Puerta de Visagra, from which they could get a good view of the lofty Moorish-built Alcazar palace, where they would reside for a month. Slowly the long and glittering procession in which Dolores rode wound its way upward through the coil of cobbled streets and plazas lined with the craning populace.

The buildings on either side were old and thus in Moorish style, with dirty, tiled designs for decoration and arabesque grills on the windows. Some of these gray hulks were being used as convents and seminaries, and a surprising number of them were old synagogues, most with blank, boarded windows or else in use for other purposes. It seemed to Dolores as she rode through, remembering the smaller but more open and bright Madrid, that Toledo was a city of gray, brown, and black, overfull of churches and chapels and old women sitting silent before shadowed doorways. Even the people who applauded the rich cavalcade as it clopped past them displayed more curiosity than excitement.

Luisa de Escobar glanced at the young woman who was riding by her side and thought that the Baroness de la Rocha looked particularly splendid today on her purple-and-green caparisoned horse, riding so erect on the sidesaddle, her shimmering satin cloak spread out on her mount's flanks and jeweled earrings flashing in her lobes. Luisa, who had been to Toledo before, thought she understood why her friend's usually wide smile had dwindled so small. She reached out to pat Dolores's shoulder and get her attention.

"You are thinking how bleak this city looks, am I right, Doña Dolores? But the palaces, at least, are most gorgeous. Just think on the gala banquet Cardinal Mendoza has announced for our stay and pay no attention to Toledo."

"But what ails these people that they are so glum?" Dolores questioned the round-faced little Countess, whose sharp eyes never missed much.

"My father told me that Toledo has staged so many bloody purges to rid itself of the stamp of Jew and Moor that the people have become mystics in their constant battle against the Anti-Christs. In fact the Queen received reports that the city just last month put to the flame fifty blasphemers at one time and that the air hung black with smoke and ash for hours afterward." She shrugged her plump, velvet-covered shoulders. "Such zealousness, I suppose, makes no cause for gaiety."

Just then they entered a large plaza, where an unusually large gallows held five swinging miscreants. Even the children throwing rocks at the swaying bodies had small enthusiasm, and the remains of the crowd who had just witnessed the executions now turned to the spectacle of the royal arrival with little chatter or comment to enliven their bows of welcome. Dolores suppressed a shudder and averted her eyes from the purple-faced, bulging-eyed corpses twisting in the breeze as she rode by and swallowed hard to quell the surge of nausea that assailed her. The rope had taken her father, after all, and avoid the thought as she might, it could also take her if her masquerade were ever discovered. The possibility was so remote it seldom worried her, but the fear was deep inside nevertheless and flashed to the surface at any sight or sound of fatal justice being meted out.

With a forced brightness she turned to Luisa. "You are right, *doña*. Who cares about this dour city?"

Luisa showed her jumbled teeth in an amiable smile. "Have you thought on which gown you will wear to the fiesta?"

Dolores neck-reined her horse so as not to crowd another of the Queen's large retinue of ladies riding before her. *"Sí,* but it depends on which shade Her Majesty chooses since we cannot wear the same color. Still, I pray she does not choose argent for that is my newest gown and quite in the Italian mode— with a very enticing bosom." She chuckled and winked at Luisa, whose smile broadened.

"Well, the Queen never wears purple so I shall wear my purple and gold brocade with the five slashes on each sleeve and gold welting at the waist. Then I shall be in the Italian style too, and if my corsage is not as low as yours there is still much more of me to fill the space allotted." Luisa laughed, then straightened her slumping back and slid her eyes side-ways. "Do you think the commanders bringing down the military levies from the north will reach Toledo in time for the Cardinal's party?"

Dolores suppressed a smile. "I would hope so," she replied. "We could hardly have a splendid evening without the charm-ing Count of Cifuentes or the Marquis of Villena or the elegant Count of Tendilla . . ."

"Or the chivalrous Duke of Medina-Sidonia?" Luisa prompted, hoping for a confidence.

"Yes, and his son, Felipe de Guzman," Dolores continued smoothly, although it made her laugh inside at how avidly everyone sought to confirm what they *thought* they already knew: that the powerful Medina-Sidonia not only had intro-duced the obscure but beauteous Baroness de la Rocha to Court and wangled her a good place among the Queen's younger attendants, but was her lover as well. Although the demeanor between the Duke and the young woman he spon-sored had been most decorous the past winter in Madrid, the gossips of the Court were quick to note the Duke's proprietary attitude toward this orphaned daughter of an old friend and the Duchess's silent sourness in the face of this newest rival.

Dolores had no wish to allay the whisperings and speculations. As his suspected mistress the Duke's stature at Court rubbed off on her, so that even though her title had little importance she had been treated with politeness and acceptance from the moment she arrived in Madrid with Medina-Sidonia's entourage. She was, after all, totally alone in the world. Nothing but luck and her wits had raised her so high from the seamy inn where she was born. Sometimes she had nightmares about running naked from a jeering crowd, her fine clothes ripped off and trampled in the mud, her jewels crushed, the back of everyone she knew turned against her. It was because of these fears that the security of her arrangement with Enrique de Guzman suited her very well.

The silly Maria Padilla, in a cloak trimmed with gray squirrel tails tied with satin bows and a rolled turban wider than any of the other women near her, urged her mount in between them as the street winding up to the Alcazar widened. She had overheard some of their conversation and wanted to be included. "Tell me, is it true, I heard Doña Beatrix mention that the Count of Tendilla is at last bringing his bastard to Court to be presented here in Toledo?" Her twittering voice turned into a giggle. "I also heard Leonora de Zuniga say that her new cousin is very, very handsome."

"You seem to hear so much. You must be blessed with ears sharp as a bat's." Luisa sniffed.

Undaunted, Maria continued, "These miserable wars carry off so many of our gallants every year; I fair cried when the Viscount Coruna and that sweet Luis Manta Alonza never returned alive from Ronda last summer. A new *caballero* is always welcome. Don't you think, Doña Dolores?"

Dolores had pulled her heart back from its sudden lurch. "Especially if he is handsome," she managed to agree sociably, in spite of the drying of her mouth. So. Finally she would know if the dismissed guard had spoken the truth to her so long ago in Ciudad Real or if her wild dreams were stupid. She had already been presented to the Count of Tendilla in Madrid, and now and then when they were thrown together in a group she chatted briefly and pleasantly with him. He was fascinating, she thought, with dark eyes inviolate to scrutiny and a certain inner tension which in spite of his reserve cast an aura of mystery about him that held strong appeal for women. But there had been no son with him in Madrid. Now it seemed as if there would be one in Toledo.

And what if her surmise about Francho was wrong, would it matter? She had already cast the dice, her path was chosen for good or ill. She paid little attention to the conversation around her as she rode straight ahead, ignoring the fluttering feeling in her stomach. But for a tiny moment she closed her eyes and prayed she would not remain altogether alone amidst the swirl and intrigue of the Spanish Court.

On Fridays Their Catholic Majesties held regular audience for any subject who wished to claim their ears as they sat enthroned upon a multicolored tile dais with the arms of Leon and Castile embroidered on gold damascened draperies behind them. The huge, Moorish-arched great hall of the Alcazar was filled with chatting, strolling *hidalgos* and their ladies, with clerics of every rank and order, and wealthy bourgeoisie, and through their numbers threaded liveried pages and lackeys bearing messages. Some conversed in small groups, some talked privately in tête-à-tête, many formed an audience before the dais to see and be seen, to view the proceedings and hear what news a stream of couriers delivered.

Dolores stood with a group close to the dais but to one side. Her hand was supported on the burly arm of Medina-Sidonia. She was regaling the Count and Countess of Cabra, Don Juan Garcia de Padilla, master of the military Order of Calatrava, and the Duke's son and heir, Don Felipe, with an account of the furor caused by two of the Queen's favorite ladies who coveted the same chamber, when a subtle murmur of interest swept through the throng. She stopped in mid-sentence as she noticed some heads turning.

"What is it?" the Countess of Cabra asked, too short to see past several backs to the space that had opened before the dais, but noticing the cessation of conversation between gentlemen who had been talking together on the platform's steps.

"Nothing," remarked Don Felipe, the Count of Perens, staring with pale eyes at the three men who had just arrived before their monarchs. "Tendilla and his newly recognized bastard."

No one noticed Dolores's eyes widen or heard her sharp intake of breath, for all gimlet-eyed curiosity was bent upon

the young man who stood with such confident grace between
Tendilla and Pietro di Lido. She thought that she might faint.
She thought she was going to laugh or cry. She finally, at least,
remembered to close her mouth.

He was slim yet muscular, taller than Tendilla but with hair
just as dark curling against his neck. Blue eyes flashed like
sapphires against a pale olive complexion, his determined
chin underlined a strong, sensuous mouth. A short, loose,
plum velvet jacket with fur-trimmed hem descended from
broad shoulders and had wide armholes that showed a tight
gray doublet underneath. Steel greaves pointed up the muscles
of his calves. A silver-hilted dagger rode one hip. He carried
his plumed cap under his arm, for only grandees were privileged to go hatted in the royal presence.

"Para todos los santos!" Dolores breathed out softly. So, it
was Francho. He had grown into a man, he projected the
composed haughtiness of a grandee's son, but it was a face
that had never left her thoughts, and after four years or forty
she would recognize him at the ends of the earth. Her head
swam as she stared at him and she blinked hard to dispel an
urge to tears.

Medina-Sidonia absently took her arm so they could move
closer, within earshot of the dais. She glanced up at the Duke's
intent profile. The large, heavy-jawed face endeavored to show
only ordinary interest, yet he was gripping her arm much too
hard, enough to bruise her. The rivalry between Tendilla and
Medina-Sidonia for military supremacy had been recounted
to her in Madrid, but this was her first real appreciation of its
virulence.

Ferdinand was holding a document just delivered to him by
the Grand Constable. He raised his eyes from scanning the
report as the three courtiers at the foot of the dais swept low
bows. "Ah, you have arrived at an excellent moment, Don
Iñigo," the Prince of Aragon and joint ruler of all Christian
Spain boomed out. "I have wonderful news here from the
foundry at Huesca on our heavy bombards." Still in his early
thirties and strongly built, although already carrying a
paunch, Ferdinand rose so that his voice would carry to others
of his military commanders who stood nearby. "My lords, our
cannon will be delivered in April, a full four weeks ahead of
schedule. Fifteen new cannon, each a fearful three ells in
length and capable of hurling marble shot weighing more than
a man." The hawk-nosed face had suffused with a triumphant

165

flush. "A great feat for our foundry! And an even greater surprise for our enemies."

Amidst the excited chatter that went up around the hall the military lords closest to the throne, Villena, Cordoba, Medina-Sidonia and Cardenas grinned like wolves.

Tendilla, dressed in black and silver, with a rolled-brim turban trailing its velvet tail down his elegant back, made a half bow, hand on heart. "Most excellent, Your Majesty, such news warms the blood. If it please you, I should like to peruse the reports of the foundry master." He smiled his approving but stiff smile.

"Certainly, my lord. I shall have them sent to you." The lines on either side of Ferdinand's mouth deepened and then relaxed again. "For once, sirs, we shall come before our objective fully armed and capable of blowing our enemy to their heathen hell should they be stupid enough to oppose us. I am tired of the antique weapons our chronic lack of funds has forced upon us."

Don Iñigo sought to continue Ferdinand's mood of jubilation. "This year will bring the enemy many unpleasant surprises, Sire. I have a communication from my dependence of Murilliano on our eastern border where until now the levies were light. This summer I am pledged at least two hundred more foot and thirty more horsemen in time for our early offensives."

"Good, good," Ferdinand nodded, reseating himself.

"But I beg your indulgence a moment, my lieges," and here Tendilla's suave address included both rulers, for the Queen's attention was also upon him. "With your kind permission it would honor me greatly to present to you my natural son, Francisco de Mendoza." And with his accustomed grace he now made a low bow.

Isabella's chestnut hair was caught in a gem-sparkled, stiffened gold coif that rose like a halo around her face. Her alert eyes surveyed this favored courtier with more than a hint of curiosity. Answering for both herself and her husband as she often did, she responded, "It is about time we were allowed a glimpse of this offspring certain tongues have been wagging about. We are pleased to receive him. Bring him forward, my good lord."

Tendilla turned to Francho and gestured for him to approach, and Francho was both surprised and pleased to see the gleam of pride in the Count's dark eyes. He moved forward smoothly, with the litheness of a well-trained gladiator, and sank upon both knees, head bowed. His heart was pounding so loudly he thought all must hear it, but he intended to acquit himself well.

"We welcome you to our Court, Francisco de Mendoza," Isabella's mellifluous voice sang out from before him, where she sat elevated on her gilt throne. He raised his head and smiled into the mild blue eyes that warmed the ivory oval of the Queen's comely, unlined face.

"Indeed, we are ever pleased to embrace the issue of the distinguished house of Mendoza," Ferdinand added. "Pray, rise up, young man."

With a fluid movement Francho rose, and he knew the picture of the two powerful monarchs before him would never be erased from his memory: Ferdinand in his gold-embroidered calf-length tunic sitting relaxed, as if appreciative of this calmer moment in his day, and the glittering Isabella leaning forward to peer with keen interest—or perhaps only because she was somewhat myopic. Their genial attention was focused upon him—upon him who might not have imagined such a circumstance in his wildest inventions, upon him, a cutpurse who would have been dead by the hangman's noose or by beating if a small mark on his back had not brought him to stand in honor before his rulers. A wave of gratitude flooded through him toward everyone in his life who had nurtured him, from the unknown servant who had spirited him away to San Martín Ignacio and Tía Esperanza, and Don Iñigo, now looking on so grave and proud. If the depth of his warm feeling for these friends shone from his eyes and was interpreted by his monarchs as the ardor of loyalty, so much the better.

He placed one hand to his heart in salute. "Gracious Majesties, it is my fervent prayer that you will accept my pledge of fealty and my promise to be your most humble and loyal vassal as long as I shall live. It will be my duty to serve you faithfully with the help of God and to address myself always to the honor and pride of Christian Spain." He spoke out firmly, his modulated baritone carrying to the ears of those who were watching.

Isabella looked into the intense blue eyes, studied the startlingly handsome face, and approved. Beauty at her Court pleased her, especially in those who could divert her prettier female subjects from coquetting with their King. "The pride

and honor of Spain are built upon such stalwart and courageous gentlemen as you, young sir. We gratefully accept your
pledge and extend to you the privileges of our Court," she
intoned. The formulas of courtesy being done with, she
shifted into a subject close to her heart. "We are informed by
your esteemed tutor Maestro di Lido that you have lately
completed a most rigorous course of studies and acquitted
yourself with excellence. We congratulate you upon this. If we
are to progress among the nations of Europe we must both
refine and add to the gentler aspect of our civilization. The
nobility is where the appreciation of knowledge must begin."

Francho relaxed slightly, one knee bent, a hand resting
lightly on the pommel of his dagger. "It pleased me to gratify
my instructors, Your Majesty. But I confess I gave equal effort
to perfecting my dexterity with weapons, that I might help
vanquish the Moorish scourge from our land." As he had
hoped, Ferdinand eyed him with greater interest.

"An admirable ambition," the King rumbled, "for in serving us you will have ample opportunity to indulge your
hankering for battle. We have a multitude of gallant *caballeros,* but not so many that another of their breed is not greatly
valued."

"I am an instrument of your wishes, Gracious Majesties,"
Francho murmured. "It will be my hoped for goal to excel
both on the battlefield and in the pursuit of erudition."

Ferdinand raised an eyebrow. "A tall order, methinks,
although one already accomplished by your sire, my lord
Tendilla. We wish you success in emulating so lofty a gentleman."

"Most kind, Sire," Tendilla murmured modestly.

Isabella favored Tendilla with her tranquil smile. "You are
fortunate to have discovered this amiable scion, Don Iñigo.
He pleases us well."

Ferdinand's attention had not left Francho. "We shall hope
to have you within the ranks of God's champions in this
season's campaigns, Francisco de Mendoza. The endeavor
heats up. With our new armaments and determination we will
show the world our power to finally drive the Moslem from
this continent."

"It is my most fervent wish to distinguish myself in your
eyes, my liege." The polished words just flowed of their own
accord from Francho's mouth. He was blooming under the
approval of both pairs of royal eyes.

"God have you in His holy keeping until next we meet, young sir." Isabella's measured tone seemed like a benediction. "And see you that no evil befalls your fair promise."

It was hard to believe, Francho thought, that this calm, intelligent woman of such gracious demeanor was the same implacable ruler who had years ago mercilessly condemned to death both a man and his tiny baby, but he forcibly relaxed the momentary stiffening of his smile and wiped clean his mind of such useless reflection.

The interview was at an end. Bowing and retreating backward Francho withdrew to the side with Tendilla and di Lido, amidst a soft buzz of conversation.

"He favors Tendilla in looks," Ferdinand observed to his wife.

"Yes he does. And no. There is something about the eyes that vaguely recalls someone. . . ."

"Is the mother known?"

"Don Iñigo is a man of honor. And a closed mouth. A country gentlewoman, my ladies gossip. Perhaps."

"I have an idea we shall not be deprived of incidents relating to that young man," Ferdinand muttered. "He has the look of a hotblood."

Isabella put a beringed hand on his arm. "He reminds me of you, dear husband, when first I laid eyes on the dashing young Infante of Aragon, so tall, so stalwart. Only you were much more handsome. And so you still are."

Ferdinand merely grunted through the indulgent smile on his lips and then gave his attention to another leather-clad courier who had slipped through the crowd and now strode to the dais, drawing a sealed parchment from his leather pouch.

"You spoke well, Francisco."

"I am happy I did not disgrace you, my lord. My knees were shaking."

"Then you are a facile dissembler, for you seemed quite calm. A good beginning, my cockerel. Their Majesties have marked you well."

"I feel like a butterfly just come from a cocoon," Francho grinned, but he had to save his other thoughts for later for they were descended upon by the first of the finely dressed courtiers wishing to pay their respects to the prestigious Tendilla and acquaint themselves with the new member of the Mendoza clan. He was presented to the Count of Cifuentes, the

Marquis of Villena, Cardenas, master of the great military Order of Santiago, the young, immensely rich Duke of Infantado, a nephew to Tendilla, the warlike Bishop of Jaen, the King's illegitimate brother who carried the title Duke of Villahermosa, and a number of others. Many were mighty names that he had heard celebrated for valor in the long Moorish campaigns, but disembodied names only until now when the men themselves stood before him courteously acknowledging the introduction.

He stood easy as he spoke to each one of them, but behind his fine manners he was still stunned to be in such exalted company.

"Cielo, I do suddenly feel faint," Dolores exclaimed, swaying a bit, certain her face was pale if only from the uncontrollable fluttering of her stomach. "It is much too warm in here. I should like to return to my chamber." She had noticed the Countess of Cabra, preparing to suggest they all go over to the circle around Tendilla. She had no intention of confronting Francho amidst all these people. He might even give her away in his astonishment. Actually the control of the situation was hers for the moment and she enjoyed the feeling. She would pick the time and place for their reunion. Something dramatic, of course. . . .

"You do look ashen, my dear," Don Enrique agreed, quickly offering his arm. His face had arranged itself into blander lines. "You should lie down. People have lately been taken with bad congestions and perhaps you have been exposed."

Behind him Dolores was aware of Felipe de Guzman's cold, pale eyes on her. The young nobleman flipped back the fringe of thin blond hair from his eyes with a characteristic gesture of his head. "Yes. It is always better to get off one's feet. If one is ill." The innuendo in his voice infuriated her, but she would give his veiled rudeness no satisfaction. She raised her chin and smiled, although she met his stare with gray eyes gone steely.

The Duke inclined his head toward Cabra. "You will excuse us, my lord. We will put off the pleasure of having Tendilla's son presented to us until another time," he declared. An imposing, heavy-jawed presence, Medina-Sidonia turned and with stately dignity led the drooping Dolores from the crowded hall.

His son, Perens, looked after them, no expression on his face. Then he strolled toward a knot of his friends, leaving Cabra to stand by himself irresolutely while his Countess bore down on Tendilla's group like a ship in full sail, the ample veil draped from her horned hat puffing out behind her.

Because they were the newest of the Queen's ladies, the chamber shared by Dolores and Luisa, the Countess of Zafra, was quite removed from the Queen's own apartments. Luisa's big, carved bed, which would soon contain both her and her husband until another chamber was found, was placed against a wall decorated with painted arabesques, while Dolores's bed, hung with green velvet drapes, took up another. As Dolores slipped through the door she was pleased to see that Luisa was elsewhere and that she had the cramped room all to herself. Grabbing up a pillow she flung herself stomach first on her bed, all unmindful of the delicate coif of stiffened and woven gold braid that was knocked off her top-knotted hair and rolled to the floor.

She hugged the pillow to her convulsively, uttering little squeaks of happiness, wallowing in the disbelief and joy of finding Francho again and trying to encompass the reality that Francho, her fellow pickpocket, had truly been a lost Mendoza, a byblow of the lofty Count of Tendilla.

Ay, mi madre, how he had grown tall and handsome. Not to mention broad-shouldered, proud, and rich. To think that the skinny urchin sick with heat and hunger that Tía Esperanza had picked off the floor of the inn, and who had become her childhood friend, hers and Carlos's and Pepi's, a slick rascal in a too-tight tunic and wrinkled hosen, was the present *caballero* Francisco de Mendoza! What would he say, what would he think when he saw her, herself so transformed? Would he remember with any of the tenderness, which had still not faded for her, of their last meeting in the gloom of the stable when she had given him her virginity?

Turning over on her back she stared thoughtfully at the stretched green velvet canopy. She had just attained seventeen years, and still the true love that women's hearts seek had eluded her. At Torrejoncillo there had been men who had wanted her, for one the crippled knight to whom poor Blanca had been promised, for another the poltroon steward representing Medina-Sidonia, not to mention the great Duke

171

himself when he finally decided to deal personally with this stick-in-the-spokes of his plans. And in the half year she had resided with the Court not a few titled gentlemen had slipped her longing poems of their own creation and claimed her jealously at dances, and looked deep and pleadingly into her eyes. But even though their ardor was somewhat furtive, since few wished to take on Medina-Sidonia, it delighted her vanity.

Still, she had felt no love for any of these, no sweet contractions of the heart like those she remembered from her one experience with her fifteen-year-old lover, no burst of adoration. Granted that was long ago and she had been a naive child; perhaps she had lived through too much travail since and sustained too many shocks and her capacity to love was gone. Perhaps she would never feel her body stir with as much desire for a grown man as it had done, that once, for a youth.

She squeezed her eyes closed to rid herself of that train of thought. Her goal was to hoard up enough money for a fine marriage dowry and make a secure life with some worthwhile, wealthy gentleman. Love was secondary.

She thought once again of Francho and pictured him as she had just seen him, standing poised and confident before Their Catholic Majesties, so different from her own tongue-tied introduction to the Queen. A wave of pride for him washed over her. He was a part of her decimated family. He was almost like a brother or a cousin. He was a lost love. And he was here.

A sudden jab of doubt darkened her gray eyes. What if he should want nothing to do with her? What if he gave her an icy reception, caring nothing for yesterdays? He was born with noble blood, after all, and now he was a young gentleman, polished, elegant. What had he to do with a smudge-faced, red-kneed pickpurse? He might even detest her deception and give her away, for, it suddenly came to her, he was one of the very few who knew the truth of her. Well, she would slap him hard right in his smug face, *el picaro! El perro!* The miserable scum, she would kick him hard in the gut, she would . . .

No! Where was her mind? Her long lashes fluttered as her eyes moved in swift caress over the green velvet curtains and the sturdy bed posters holding them up, and glided over her other furnishings and the tooled leather clothes chests on the floor beyond. *Dios mío,* there wasn't any Dolores the pickpocket. Now she would come before him as an honored lady of the Queen's train! She was Dolores Ganavet, the Baroness de la Rocha, as luxuriously attired as he, with a recognized coat-of-arms and an estate, and manners just as fine. What was there for him to despise?

The tension flowed out of her body and her lips curved upward again. She couldn't think the man had gone that far from the boy. Her eyes had taken in his same old swagger, however subdued, and caught the flash of his quick grin toward di Lido as he rejoined the throng in the audience hall. She was familiar with this jaunty gallant under the brocades and velvets, and he would be overjoyed to see her.

She must plan carefully, this would be a momentous meeting. A thrill coursed through her as she imagined his shock when he realized who she was. But there was so little privacy in the crowded world of privilege revolving about the Throne. It would have to be at a time when most members of the Court were distracted, and of course when she was looking her very best. Like the night of the Cardinal's grand fiesta, to be held in the middle of the Court's sojourn in Toledo? Could she wait a week? Although there were entertainments almost every night, musicians playing, poets declaiming, balladeers and magicians, and games of checkers and cards, the special banquet would be attended by everybody, and in the Cardinal's vast mansion there surely would be some remote and quiet place to talk. Yes. It would be worth waiting for. She would just have to be careful, avoid crossing his path, and keep turned away from his glance.

She savored the anticipation and the suspense. She was also flirting, like a fighter in the bullring waving his red cloth, with a tiny threat of danger which she felt but could not interpret.

Abruptly she sprang up from the bed and ran over the red tiles to one of her chests. Opening it she plunged in her hand and felt about, fruitlessly for a while, overturning layer after layer of clothing and objects, but finally her fingers closed on a ribbon-tied packet and her frown cleared. Yes, there it was. She heaved a sigh of happy relief. This was going to be fun.

In the Monarchs' wake as they descended the dais and made a stately progress through the aisle which people opened for them lumbered a rotund man, his lumpy nose canted, his mouth turned down as if he smelled something bad, but the plume in his hat was more gorgeous than any other in the room. The sight of the Count of Haro still narrowed Francho's eyes.

Tendilla laid a hand on Francho's arm. "Francisco. Take care. I advise you to let the past be the past. Haro's influence with Their Majesties is enormous. Antagonizing him will only gain you an enemy to oppose your future petition." His voice was low but came through with stern clarity.

"Si, my lord, I understand. I will comply, you have my word." Francho answered slowly, but never taking his eyes from the man who had betrayed Juan de Venegas. "Nonetheless, I detest him."

Tendilla nodded, but his stern black eyes continued to rivet his protégé. "To hate is your privilege—as long as no sign of it shows. Such indulgence could cost you dear."

A page appeared at the Count's elbow to summon him to a council meeting, and the warning tone shifted smoothly. "In any case, Francisco, convey my excuses to my illustrious brother the Cardinal, when you return to his residence. However, I am confident you will represent me at his table with all distinction. Your debut is over; now take your place as a courtier." With a hint of a smile at the corners of his mouth, Tendilla turned on his heel and strode off through the dispersing assembly.

For a moment Francho's gaze followed the imperious back as it disappeared through an oriental-arched portal. "If one could have affection for so reserved a man I suppose that I do," Francho admitted to himself, wryly. The Count had found him, helped him, molded him, and was trying for his future. Like a father. Francho knew he would always be loyal to him.

Di Lido, finally rid of some stout and overweening duchess who insisted on burdening his ear, now turned smiling to Francho again, but in a moment was staring over his shoulder across the great hall, his mouth pinched as if there were offal on his tongue. "There walks that evil blight, Torquemada," he grated. Francho tried to swing about, but the little Italian darted a restraining hand on his arm and then performed a subtle maneuver so that it was not obvious Francho's position had shifted. What he saw was a small knot of bent-headed clerics walking slowly to the egress, led by a heavy-set Dominican in snowy white robes whose meekly folded hands contrasted strongly with the hard face and burning eyes peering from under the humble cowl.

No other identification was needed. In a mere handful of years Frey Tomas de Torquemada, the Inquisitor-General, had already sent thousands of heretics and blasphemers into the searing flames, and it was plain that this was only the beginning of his holy war. Di Lido put up a discreet hand to shield his lips, although there was no chance the man could hear him. "They say he's so fearful of assassination he keeps a unicorn's horn to neutralize any poison in his food. A useless precaution. Superstition will not save him from answering to his Maker for all the tortured and maimed innocents his fanaticism has claimed."

Mesmerized like a fledgling bird before a snake, Francho could not draw his eyes away from the jowled face with its heavy shadow of dark beard. Even at Mondejar word had come of the dread autos-da-fé in Valencia and Burgos, where hundreds of coerced penitents in tall, pointed hats had stumbled in procession toward the ghastly poles and pyres that would purify their souls and provide fine entertainment for the citizenry.

"Never allow the glance of that Satan to fall directly or too often upon you, Francisco. He takes umbrage at certain faces and assigns sins to them of which they may be innocent."

Francho grimaced. "But—I do not understand, Maestro, how it is that the Queen, who is revered for her justice and benevolence, countenances his excesses?"

Di Lido answered with a soft snort. "Countenance those mass murders? Do not be naive, ignorant youth. Her piety is such that she condones them."

The sauntering approach of some young gentlemen, whose eyes were friendly yet measuring of the new buck in their arena, cut short the subject. It was not until later, having left the Alcazar and ridden some streets below the palace's lofty perch, and while they mounted together the marble steps of the Cardinal's residence, that Francho hesitated, frowning. "But the Queen . . . Tell me, Maestro, does not the Church advise that for the protection and advancement of the Faith all means are proper?"

Di Lido's eyes flashed with the intellectual's hatred of twisted truths. "Is it our sacred duty to commit crime in the name of God, do you mean?" But then his breath was expelled in a weary sigh and the narrow shoulders folded in on themselves. "I cannot think so, Francisco. I cannot forget the words of Our Saviour to his overzealous disciples: 'Ye know not what manner of spirit you are of. The Son of Man is not come to destroy men's lives, but to save them!' He would not save them by painfully breaking their bones and then turning them to ashes."

Noting Francho's disturbed expression, he added, "The fact I have mentioned, of the extent of the needless torture, is not general knowledge; the Holy Office cloaks its activities in secrecy and silence. As your teacher I only feel that I must inform you so that you may carefully consider such actions. But carefully. And in silence too."

They fell quiet as they continued up the broad entrance stair, and in a moment di Lido was sufficiently calm so that when they entered the ebb and flow of visitors waiting in the great hall hoping for audience with Cardinal Mendoza he had quite recovered his urbane, elegant self.

After the cold Gothic starkness of Mondejar the worldly opulence surrounding Pedro Gonzalez de Mendoza, Grand Cardinal of Spain, put Francho in mind of a pot of clover honey instead of a vinegar jug. The prelate's huge establishment, the tremendous numbers of retainers and soldiers he maintained, the magnificence of his furnishings and objets d'art, and the nightly feasts arrayed on gold plates on his table kept Francho in a perpetually awed state. The Cardinal, who resembled Don Iñigo only about the sharp-honed eyes and thin mouth, had already sired two children by two different noblewomen and would, no doubt, produce several more, for he was known to be a man of lusty appetites and followed the Holy Gospel *"cum grano salis."* Yet he was highly respected throughout Europe as a capable primary of the Church and in fact gave precedence of authority only to the Pope, Innocent VIII. He also carried tremendous weight with Los Reyes Católicos, for he served as a brilliant tactician in their power balance with the Holy See. He was, in fact, sometimes referred to as the "third monarch of Spain."

When they had first arrived, as Francho genuflected and kissed the great amethyst ring extended to him, he had glimpsed the red-robed Cardinal winking cozily over his head at Tendilla, pleased that his austere younger brother, unfortunately married to a barren, addled woman who had been sequestered for years, had had the foresight to impregnate a mistress with this handsome, promising son. When the Cardinal inquired whether Francho had any leaning toward a religious vocation, the hint was not lost upon Tendilla. "He was offering, of course, to further any plans I might have to place you in a politically strategic church position," the Count told Francho later. "A sinecure not to be sneezed at, certainly. But not strategic enough." None of which tepid water served to extinguish Francho's exhilaration at claiming the Grand Cardinal of Spain as his uncle.

Leonora was driving her kinsman to distraction. When Francisco de Mendoza's group had arrived at the Cardinal's palace where they were to reside, she had been eagerly waiting to greet her mother with hugs and kisses, but also, Francho would have wagered his life on it, to blush and give him her hand in greeting too. In fact, he could not let go of her soft hand as she looked up at him through her lashes, drowning him in sunlit pools of amber brown.

She had to excuse herself very soon after to resume her duties with the Infanta Isabel, but threw him so expressive and warm a glance over her shoulder as he handed her into her litter that he had to swallow hard and keep his booted feet from rising several ells off the ground.

Yet for all the good this promising arrival meeting did him he might have remained at Mondejar. Leonora, as all new brooms, was so busy as one of the Infanta's dressers and companions that a passing, dimpled smile and the new French affectation of a wiggling wave of the fingers was all the blond charmer could spare her brooding admirer. Beside the fact that the droopy, skinny young Princess was often indisposed and in need of coddling, the Infanta Isabel had also been taken with her new lady and liked her about. So Francho found small opportunity to draw Leonora away from the gay group of young nobility always surrounding the Princess. Even the afternoon of his presentation to Their Majesties had been marred by a quick note from Leonora saying the Princess had a bellyache and she could not leave her post to be there.

However, a surprising—to him—number of ladies, young and older, did seek his attention and coquetted and flirted

177

openly. Yet, except for his passing appreciation of the prettiest ones, they were little comfort. He wanted Leonora to look at him so, Leonora to obliquely suggest a walk in the palace gardens, Leonora to waft the scent of chypre under his nose, Leonora, his dazzling and dimpled delight. . . .

As the full and fascinating days in Toledo followed each other he worked off his frustration with physical competition, having been immediately challenged by his curious, aggressive peers and hesitating not a moment to don armor and in the arena match his skill and virility against the bluest bloods of Spain. Von Gormach had trained him to an exacting level; his rushing lance unseated three of their best champions before he himself was thrown from his charger to land in a bruising crash of steel plate. His almost nonchalant prowess and strength with the lance and the sword left no question of acceptance into this bold circle of knights, and he took easily to their banter and their staglike rivalries. These vigorous and headstrong men were flexing their muscles, primed and ready to head south for the seasonal attacks against the detested Moors, and so was he.

A few nights after his arrival in Toledo he had attended Tendilla, di Lido, and a bemused Bishop of Talavera in a chamber in a little-used wing of the Cardinal's palace, and there he held them rapt for two hours with his mastery of the lute and the guembri and his rich-voiced delivery of a repertoire of ballads. Further, he had to grin as even Tendilla's face mirrored admiration at his complex conversation with Ebarra in perfectly accented Arabic. But Tendilla and Talavera were agreed that the time was still distant when his special talents would be needed to accomplish the miracle they sought. In return they also agreed that now was certainly propitious for him to join the army being sent to attack the stronghold of Baza in May. The difference to him was only one of degree. He was pawing like a bull to bring his prowess to the battlefield, to blood his sword. But he solemnly promised to continue as well the practice of music and Arabic, and Tendilla presented to him the willing Esteban Ebarra as an equerry.

Dolores knew her excitement was causing her to look flushed, but she couldn't help it. She was always thrilled with the excesses of dress and glitter of the peacock nobility, and their noise and laughter and the mountains of food. The vast hall was ablaze with the light of thousands of tapers in standing candelabra around the tapestried walls and fat candles suspended from the painted ceilings in great iron chandeliers. The banquet tables were arranged in a great U-shape, with the Cardinal, his rulers, and his honored guests at the head on a dais. Big, square banners displaying the colors and insignias of all the religious orders of Europe hung in a forest overhead. The tables, covered with red damask, were so long and so crowded with several hundred guests seated on both sides of them that the army of liveried valets serving up myriad platters and pouring drink had scarce room to squeeze their jewel-decorated ewers between shoulders.

On the same side of the table but quite a distance down from her, Dolores had glimpsed Francho eating with Leonora de Zuniga, Antonio de la Cueva, and others of the Infanta's train; luckily they had not been assigned closer to her or opposite, where he might have been able to see her, even though the tables opposite were across a space almost wide enough for a tourney field.

Quick glimpse or not, she had still admired his appearance as he stood waiting for Leonora to seat herself, the very picture of the bravura courtier in a rich blue velvet surcoat which swung from his broad shoulders to barely below his hips and exhibited almost all of the particolored blue-and-white hosen that molded his strong legs and firm haunches. An orange felt hat with a jeweled ostrich plume was slanted dashingly on the black hair, which curled softly to the high collar of his doublet. He was elegant, and his confident stance and flash of white teeth bore this out.

Dolores thought it was sickening the way he devoured the little Zuniga with his eyes, all done up as she was in gold brocade and a high toque veiled in floating gold chiffon. In any case, she hoped that the intrusive competition of the Count of Perens, who was sitting on Leonora's other hand, would allow a minute when her message could be discreetly delivered to Tendilla's son.

The Duke, next to her, looked down his crooked nose and with his pinky jiggled her ringed hand lying on the table. "Well, Baroness, what manner of reverie do you entertain to take you so far away from this clamorous company?"

"My lord? Oh, I have no idea what I was thinking. Just a

momentary lapse. In truth, I have never attended such a splendid occasion, it quite takes my breath away."

He pushed a goblet brimming with wine toward her and inserted it in her hand. "Then drink up, my lady, for the evening is very young. Come, Aphrodite, drink with me," he challenged her, bitterness plain behind the bulbous, blinking eyes. He raised his own goblet and downed the wine in it in one draught, although he was already showing the effects of several consumed earlier. To please him she swallowed a long gulp of her own wine. He leaned his shoulder toward her and spoke intimately in her ear, although he did not look directly at her.

"Shall I tell you, Doña Dolores, you take my breath away this evening? Your radiance captivates me; you are like a rosy peach whose dewy flesh tantalizes one to take a bite. And your eyes . . . so luminous, those gray orbs, so magnetic . . ." There was a certain tightness under his casual drawl. "But I've told you this before. I hope I do not bore you."

Dolores slid a glance up at him through her sooty lashes and favored him with a brilliant smile. "Dear Don Enrique, no woman can ever hear enough of such flattery. We see ourselves only through the eyes of the distinguished gentlemen who admire us."

In answer the Duke pointed with his heavy chin. "Regard. The Ambassador from Lombardy sits opposite, on your left. He cannot take his eyes from you."

"Does that distress you, my lord?" She looked over at the chain-bedecked grayhead who was gazing brightly at her and nodded graciously, returning the man's smile.

"No. It is your due, after all, and who would prevent the chill of blood from worshipping the sun? But I sometimes think the Moors brilliant to hide their women behind veils."

She put a cozening hand on his heavily embroidered, slashed sleeve. "But everyone knows that though my eyes may on occasion flirt, my interest lies wholly with you, Don Enrique."

"Interest? Interests, *doña*. That says it more accurately."

"Why are you wroth with me, my lord? Do I not keep to the letter of our agreement?"

There was already a flush over his cheekbones from the wine. He turned his large face full to her, his protruding eyes wandering from the wavy auburn hair parted beneath her rolled-brim, jeweled coif to the warm plunge of satin-skinned bosom behind the silvery green silk bodice of her gown. His gaze finally came to rest somewhere below her chin, and she thought for one alarmed moment that he was drunkenly going to press his lips right then and there to the tender column of her throat.

Instead he grunted. "I am not wroth with you, *doña.* I merely want what I cannot have."

She kept her smile steady, for there were people all around who could see them if they could not hear. Her voice was cajoling as she tried to divert him, "Pray, Don Enrique, enjoy the banquet. I truly look forward to your leading me out in the dance. You turn so elegant a step."

His heavy-lidded smile held sarcasm. *"Sí, belleza,* I am very good at the dance. It will be my pleasure to soon hasten to oblige you." Again he handed her her wine cup and saluted her with his own. She took a smaller sip this time, determined to stay sober.

She gave her attention to the colorfully attired players on a balcony whose shawms, pipes, flutes, lutes, and drum had been floating music over the heads of the guests. She took a deep breath and opened wide her senses to all the grandiloquence of the Cardinal's celebration. She breathed in the expensive, heavy musk and amber perfumes worn by men and women alike. She fell to eating, savoring the several types of rich soups and devouring sizzling chunks of venison and roasted lamb, which she speared with her knife. A small, crackling-skinned fowl was placed on her golden plate, and she greedily pulled it apart with her hands. She took a bit of this and a bit of that from a dizzying succession of platters offered her, nibbled on some fine cheese shipped from France which the Duke proffered her on his knife, and perhaps drank more from her gold cup than she meant to of the aromatic wines. Lackeys passed her damp, perfumed cloths to wipe her greasy mouth and fingers.

The center of the banquet U was paced by poets declaiming their verses and singers plucking lutes and twining together the polyphonic beauty of their voices in tender ballads of love. The last courses were accompanied by the shenanigans of a team of dwarf acrobats, who threw each other through the air so handily and with such shrill shouts they woke up the sleepiest of overeaters.

Finally the smiling Queen, holding high her glittering arm as signal to the musicians, proclaimed the dance and turned a look of loving expectancy toward her husband, for they would lead the floor. The music began, a stately pavanne, and couples rose to dance, or to stroll the room or to find a cooler breath in the gardens outside. Servants hurried to push back the tables to make more room.

Now. The apprehensive fluttering began again in Dolores's stomach. She allowed herself another swallow of wine, grateful for the courtesy greeting that had taken the Duke and his Duchess toward the dais. Sinuous as a cat—or as the urchin who had insinuated herself so often through crowds offering tempting purses—she quickly slipped past the knots of guests and exited by a small side door. Behind this she found her serving woman waiting for her, handily helped by a bribed house servant who was quite used to the clandestine comings and goings of the libidinous nobility.

Francho wandered through several chambers occupied by groups in conversation or couples in various stages of amorous flirtation before discovering the little outside balcony where he could fill his lungs with fresh air and cool his jealousy until Leonora had danced her fill with Perens and her other gallants. It was only by good fortune that the diligently searching serving woman thought to glance out there and saw him half-sitting on the stone ledge and brooding into the dark, cool night.

"Don Francisco?" the servant inquired softly.

Francho started. He had been listening to the dance music emanating from the great hall and picturing with wine-heated yearning one golden stepper in particular, peevishly wondering if thwarted love could kill a man.

"*Sí.* What is it?" he growled, frowning into the gloom.

"I have a message, *señor,*" came the high, tiny voice.

Leonora! She needed him to rescue her from those louts, she had finally seen there was no one she cared more for . . .

"Say on," he demanded.

With a warning "sssh," the serving woman, head covered with a stiff linen kerchief, stepped out on the balcony and furtively offered him a wandlike object. Surprised, Francho reached out and took it. It was a soft leather bag rolled into a cylinder and tied with a thong. He frowned, puzzled. Could such be from Leonora? Something warned him that this wanted privacy. "I will step inside to the light," he told the servant. "Is there anyone in the chamber?"

The small woman shook her head.

"Good. You stand outside the door and see no one blunders in for the moment. But do not depart."

The shadowed room was hung with carved wooden sculptures and swags of red brocade, but contained only a table and chairs and some locked chests. Several fat candles on the table guttered in the breeze from the balcony, and in the light of these he examined the unremarkable bag and then turned it over to unroll it, feeling something hard and tapered beneath his fingers. Feverishly he pulled aside the remaining flap. And stood staring, transfixed. A reflected tongue of flame leaped in the candlelight, a flash of metal darted into the shadows.

He sucked in his breath. *Madre de Dios*, the snake-headed dagger! *His* dagger. There was no mistaking the elegant, ruby-eyed weapon the dying soldier Rodrigo had given to a restless little boy so long ago. He drew the slim blade from its heavily embossed sheath; a dollop of silver fire dripped from the wicked tip. *"Por Christo!"* he breathed. How often he had regretted having to abandon so artful a piece to whomever stumbled across his little cache at the hotel. For a second he blinked at the dagger, filled with the connection it gave him to his early years. And then it hit him. Someone was at Court who knew the real history of Francisco de Mendoza! More than that, well-wishers hardly sent messages of lost property in the midst of a Court gala. Swiftly he rewrapped the dagger and in two strides he reached the door, fearful the serving woman would be gone. But she waited without, patiently. "You! Who sent you? Who gave you this packet?"

"Will you come with me, *señor?*" The woman had a flare she had brought with her.

"To where?"

"To the one who has returned your property. There is a need for discretion, *señor,* and time is important. I can say no more." The woman's wrinkled lips pressed together adamantly.

He had no choice. He could not leave a mystery someone who might begin unraveling his carefully built up Mendoza heritage. Pressing his plumed hat firmly on his head and thrusting the packet into the belt under his surcoat, he motioned the servant ahead of him. "Lead on, woman." She lifted her flare.

He had vaguely expected to leave the house, but instead he was led deeper into the palace, through one dimly lit or dark room into another in a chain of corridorless, square, and high-ceilinged spaces. At last they did come to a cross-corridor, quiet, lit by bracketed torches, and overseen at the end by a solitary guard in the Cardinal's colors. In a few paces down the corridor the woman stopped before a carved portal and knocked. She then opened the door and motioned Francho in. "Enter, *señor, por favor.*"

"Whose quarters are these?" he asked. He had not been in this wing before.

"I cannot say, *señor.*"

"Who sent you?" he persisted.

"I cannot say, *señor,*" the woman whined, quailing. "But I swear, you will not come to any harm." Francho thought he heard a touch of irony in the little voice, but he stepped in and she backed away and closed the door softly behind him.

This was a small chamber, almost empty as usual, for it did not belong to any of the permanent household and visitors had always to bring their furnishings with them. There was, however, a table and a curtained bed, and light was provided by an oil lamp set on the table and tapers in a double-arm sconce. The room was unoccupied. The utter silence, the sense of mystery prickled at his nerve ends; automatically he loosened his dress dagger in its scabbard. Then the sudden loud squeak of the door opening in the far wall made him jump.

The woman who glided in had come only a few paces toward him, her face still in the shadows, when, uniquely, from her bearing, it leaped to his mind that this must be the bruited Baroness de la Rocha, although he had rarely seen her slim, swaying-hipped figure except to admire it from the back. Her necklace of sapphires and pearls sparkled as she gracefully leaned to gather the short train of her gown. He dropped his hand from his dagger hilt as wordlessly as she approached him, finally coming full into the circle of pale, yellow light, and for the first time he had a close view of her oval face. With a quickening of admiration he realized that Don Enrique de Guzman had good reason to be jealous of this woman.

Her beauty was sensuous, she was a true Spanish "cinnamon flower," rare, flamboyant, exciting. Clear gray eyes, wide, tilted, and sooty-lashed, gazed out at him from under winged brows; and they were provocative eyes, luminous with mystery and promise, even wit. Skin warm as a summer peach gleamed pale rose on the high cheekbones and stretched flawlessly over a straight, slim nose slightly spade-shaped at the tip. Her generous mouth which drew his stare like a magnet was pink-lipped, full and moist, and there was a seductive cleft in her firm chin. Her delicious coloring was enhanced by her darkly flaming cascade of waving hair, center-parted over a smooth forehead and held back by a rolled and beaded crownless coif.

The seductive lips parted. Her eyebrow quirked, as if she were waiting for something. "Sir?" she finally said in a breathy voice.

He bowed stiffly, but remembered to smile. "Don Francisco de Mendoza, *doña,* and so should you be aware since it appears you have requested my presence." Something tickled at him, in the back of his head. She reminded him of someone. Very much. But who?

The gleam in the woman's eyes deepened. She chuckled throatily. With a shrug of her brocaded shoulder she glided closer to him. "And you should know that if you are seen here with me in such suggestive rendezvous you might have to answer dearly for it," she murmured.

But Francho found himself harkening to the timber of her voice, the certain tone-set. He drew his brows together and regarded her sternly, refusing to be trifled with. "An object was delivered to me tonight, evidently by way of message from you or from someone you represent. I wish to know what is your purpose in this, and then I will quickly disembarrass you of my presence."

Dolores was enchanted with the situation. He just didn't recognize her, the ninny. But *she* had no trouble feeling comfortable with him, he was just the same, only bigger, the same crease between the brows and compelling blue eyes, the same curly dark hair and wide shoulders, the same insouciant, white smile against his pale olive skin—a smile not in evidence at this point, however. She was bursting to tell him who she was, but she couldn't resist toying with him for a few moments.

"Ah, but it is my intention to enlighten you, *señor.* And I was merely teasing you; you may rest easy, we are safely closeted here." Her breath seemed to come quicker under his suspicious gaze. "But what discourtesy from a gentleman of such high birth, sir. Do you not even greet a lady properly?" She extended her hand with regal dignity.

Her slim fingers were cool to his lips as he kissed them perfunctorily, to be polite. But her jasmine perfume tantalized his nostrils, her mobile, full lips kept drawing his eyes. And her curious air of familiarity with him was confounding; it made him uncomfortable. "I beg your forgiveness, lady, I did not wish to seem abrupt, but as you say, so private a meeting between us could prove precarious. Why have you summoned me, Baroness?"

"Ah, then you know who I am? I am most flattered, *señor*, since we have never met before. Have we?" She accompanied her question by suddenly putting her hands up to his shoulders and lifting her smiling face up to his, fixing the full force of her exotic eyes on him and so mesmerizing him he did not even think to back away from such astonishing intimacy.

Dumbstruck, he could only shake his head.

"But Francho, you blockhead, don't you know me?" she cried gaily.

Sangre de Dios! Francho? Who called him that now?

He stared down at the female crowding him and as he did so a wild, impossible answer came to him, born of the sudden superimposition in his mind of a piquant, dirt-streaked little girl's face over the face of the bewitching young woman.

Seeing light dawning in his eyes, she laughed. "Have you forgotten Papa el Mono's then, and Papa's daughter? Have you forgotten your old friends at the inn so soon, *picaro?*"

Francho's jaw dropped. "Dolores?" he breathed. And then, a second later he shouted, "Dolores, *per Dios!*" and grasped her hard by the elbows.

"Shhhh!" she giggled. "You'll wake up the dead. . . ."

"Diantre! Dolores, for the love of God, is it really you?" He shook her in delight.

"Yes, yes, it is me. *Ay, mi madre,* you are rattling my teeth!"

He stood her away from him while his stunned gaze traveled over her. She could almost see the myriad memories flashing through his mind. "But . . . but—" he stammered.

"But I have changed," she laughed and finished for him, "and you are shocked that I am no longer as I was. But then again, neither are you, eh, Francho? Look, see here, is this the ragged hoyden you remember?" She picked up her short train and pirouetted in front of him in a rustle of pale green and silver silk and a glitter of jewels, preening in the unabashed admiration shining from his eyes, and finishing with a low, mocking bow that inadvertently gave him an entrancing view of her lovely bosom.

He shook his head in wonder. "I don't believe it. The little nuisance that screeched like an eagle! Dolores? But . . . you are beautiful!"

"And you are handsome, as you always were," she teased him, amused by the quick blush that suffused his olive skin. "Yet I almost didn't recognize you either the first I saw you, here in Toledo. I saw from a distance this strong, dark-haired *caballero,* so intent upon his lady he had no thought for anything else, and I wondered who was the dashing gallant Leonora de Zuniga had captured in Toledo, for had I seen the set of those shoulders in Madrid I would have noted them. And then, when you were presented to Their Majesties I saw you close, and I knew you immediately. I purposely waited until there was a chance of us being alone and uninterrupted, and then I gave my serving maid the dagger which brought you to me. I had kept it all this time."

"I might have known. I might have surmised that if anyone found my secret little cache at the inn it would have to be Dolores."

"The clever and curious."

"The spying, you mean." He chuckled. "There were some open chinks in the wall of my cubby."

"But are you glad to see me?"

"Am I glad to see you? By all the Holy Saints, Dolores!" He grabbed her and hugged her, he lifted her off her feet like a feather and whirled her around in the air several times before setting her down. "Dolores, the most slippery lightfingers in all Ciudad Real! How many times I wondered how you did, and Carlos, and Tía—" He stopped as reality struck him, his high joy fading into confusion again. "But how did you come here, to the Court? And why are you called Baroness? And how did you—I mean, what is—"

"Oh Francho, you have me all out of breath," she gasped out and momentarily silenced him with a slim finger on his lips. Looking around and spying nothing to sit on but the bed, she took his hand and pulled him to it. "Propriety or not, we cannot stand up all night, and my serving maid shook the dust off the spread earlier. Come, let us settle and I'll tell you everything and so shall you tell me. Oh, are you not just dazzled with us? Haven't we had unbelievably good fortune, the two of us?" she exclaimed, and held joyously out her arms so he could span her slim waist to boost her up on the edge of the high bed, which was without a step.

He sat down close to her and she grabbed his hand affectionately, holding it in her lap like a sister. But assailed by her heady perfume, by her warm beauty, in spite of himself Francho was aware that she was *not* a sister, not real kin, nor had she acted so the last time they had been together, so he suddenly remembered. Disgusted with the faint stirring of lust within him, he cursed himself for a brute and closed off part of his mind to pay close attention to her tale.

Her tone had sobered now. "I shall never forget the night they dragged you away, Francho. I trembled with fear for you. My heart broke and my eyes swelled almost shut from wild weeping for I was sure you were forever gone from us, gone from me. The next morning Carlos went to inquire from his friend among the Alcalde's guards and was told the Count of Tendilla had already quitted Ciudad Real and taken you along with his party, slung in a litter, hurt or dying, and certainly being transported to be hung up somewhere as a warning to others contemplating robbing a grandee. I wailed and Pepi wailed and Tía Esperanza, oh, that woman wept an ocean, for you had become part of our little family. But what could we do?"

She squeezed his hand. "Yet I did not forget you, I lit a candle for you whenever I passed the church and I paid the priest to pray for your soul. Well, life went on. Carlos, Pepi, and I continued risking our skins to fill Papa's bottomless coffers, although we were chastened and much more cautious now. Some weeks later I heard a drunk in the common room blurt out that he had lately been a guard for the Count of Tendilla, and I cozened and flattered him and asked him questions until he recounted that he thought Tendilla had recovered a natural son right in Ciudad Real whom he had legally recognized and who was now living in his castle. I suffered his hairy paws on my shoulders until he remembered some description of the Count's son, and it was you, Francho! At least, it *could* have been you, I believed."

"You were always a master of worming information from

lips trying to be silent," he teased. But he squeezed her hand sympathetically.

Her thoughts seemed to turn inward, and the innocent hopes of a dreamy girl slipped onto her face. "I prayed from then on that you would return to Ciudad Real—oh, not to join us again, for surely you had become a grand gentleman and probably would not even speak to us, but just so I could see you again, see you in your rich clothes. I . . . I just wanted to see you again."

Francho protested, defending his loyalty. "What you thought was not true, *hermanita,* you know I would have swung you up on my horse and kissed you soundly in front of everyone."

She held up a hand. "Ah, but 'twas better that I was not so sure of your good heart, you see. Because then I began to grow angry—nay, more—terribly jealous, to think of your sudden elevation in the world and me? Not even good enough to rate a kind word from you. And mind you, this anger grew even though I was not really certain there had been some other youth found in Ciudad Real and Francho, my Francho, cold and dead. I have somewhat of a hot temper," she reflected, then grinned along with his hoot of laughter.

"I became restless, discontent with my homespun rags and hot little room over the scullery, disdainful of stupid Tía and disgusted with Papa's greed and selfishness, miserable with my lot. And then it ended, the 'lot' I was so unhappy with, in the blink of an eye it was gone."

He saw her gray eyes cloud over as she shrugged and sighed. "Papa's greed grew so enormous he began to do careless things. Just as we took you in, so he took in another boy of small stature. He felt he had to; Carlos had gone away with his small band of brigands and taken Pepi along with him, to a hideout in the mountains, many leagues distant. And who was there left? Only me—poof, a girl." She shrugged, her lip curling at the insult. "I hated that new cutpurse, a stupid rascal with a running nose and a hand always reaching for my breast. He gulled hard enough but he was too slow, and one day the Hermandad caught him. And after they'd used the strappado on him he jabbered like a magpie; they knew that where they caught one they'd catch others."

She drew in a deep breath. "The constable pounced, his men ransacked the inn, found some of the loot, and dragged everyone off to the dungeons. Except me. God helped me and I had run on an errand for Tía. When I returned, here was this great crowd about the gate, excited, boisterous, yelling epithets at the guards. But before I could elbow my way through, the priest saw me—you remember dear Father Julio?—and with a strength I had no idea he possessed he grabbed my arm and hustled me quickly away. For a few days I slept in the robing room of the church, and then he located a place for me to live and earn my keep, away from the city. It was as a serving maid to a young noblewoman. . . ."

"Once you told me you would never empty slops or carry bathwater for any female, even if you starved first. Remember?" Francho wanted to recall the stupid words the minute he had said them. Why embarrass her? Her story was sad enough and it touched his heart.

But she seemed not to mind. "But you see, I had a mad plan at the time, that's why I accepted the place. I had an idea that perhaps I would meet you again, if you were still alive, and I was ashamed of me. So I fetched and carried and brushed out the gowns of this girl and combed her hair. . . . She wasn't even pretty and her purse was very slim. But I learned. I watched how she walked, how she ate, what she said— everything she did I memorized and practiced. I could read, you know—you partially taught me, remember—and as I helped her to study her lessons I learned too. Everything she knew, this born lady, I knew!"

Moved by the pride and triumph in her eyes, Francho took her hand and put it to his lips in sudden tenderness, in tribute to her determined struggle.

She stopped for a moment, a momentary shyness overtaking her. "It's such a long story," she excused herself.

"Long or short, leave nothing out," he commanded gruffly, for he realized how alone she had been with her history, as indeed, in other ways, so was he with his own. "I want to know all that has befallen you in these years. Everything."

Lifting her eyes gratefully, Dolores nodded, and continued. She recounted to him the two years at the convent, her fast friendship with Blanca Ganavet de la Rocha, and the fateful trip to Torrejoncillo on which the poor little Baroness died of a stomach evil. And how it came about that she finished that journey in Blanca's place.

"The mad old Baron had died, in truth, leaving nothing but

a ruined manse and some hectares of forest land." Her voice was stronger now, as if reflecting the boldness she had summoned to carry out the deception. "There were some funds in Blanca's dowry box, but not nearly what she had told me. Evidently there had been another key," she speculated acidly.

"Was your identity questioned?"

"Never. Not once. And by whom, anyway? The woman who had cared for the Baron and had buried him in that monstrous cave was by no means as ancient or stupid as Miguel had made out, she was merely old and with no other roof to go over her head. She had never known Blanca. She is, in fact, the little servant who brought you here, and greatly loyal to Blanca—to me—for not having turned her out. And the notary, when he was summoned, merely told me how tall I had grown, and as soon as I had paid him from Blanca's dowry box the past and present fees due him—a reasonable amount, surprisingly—he produced documents of inheritance to sign. And so I signed them."

"But how do you come to be known as Doña Dolores, not Doña Blanca?"

She threw back her head a moment in delight; and he was enchanted by the pure line of her slim throat. "That bothered me too," Dolores continued, chuckling, "for I cannot abide the name Blanca, rest in peace my poor little friend. I just told him I preferred to be called Dolores, to honor a nun whom I revered, and with not so much as a blink of an eye he wrote it into the documents after the name Blanca, and said he would tell the priest to add it to the church registry of Blanca's birth. Just like that. After I broke my head for nights trying to think of a clever way to do it. . . ."

"And what happened to Blanca's betrothed?"

"He came to see me. But I told him there was no dowry left, nor was there any true, signed agreement, merely a promise to betroth. He pressed his suit anyhow and seemed not to care for the money or the land, but I discouraged him and at last he left." That the poor, gentle young man's back was humped and hearing impaired Dolores did not mention; her pride preferred Francho to think Don Diego a worthy suitor. "After all, at last I had the trappings of a lady and especially a title. What use to bury it all in the furthest reaches of Extremadura?"

191

"We interred Blanca under Miguel's tree in the full sun, and then and there I decided I would never let go of that land, wild as it was, for it was dear Blanca's legacy to me. There was just the little matter of having to live as poorly in that leaking manse as in Ciudad Real. And worse, isolated from the world. Not much improvement from the alleys, was it?"

She threw back her head again and laughed, and he thought the rich, fluting notes of her uninhibited mirth could make a leper grin. She recovered herself. "Patience, you wanted to hear it all, did you not? I have Miguel to thank for making me wise, for he pointed out that there was a gorge on the Baron's land over which flowed a small river to form the only strong fall of water in hundreds of leagues, and according to him the place was worth one hundred times the rest of the estate. A water mill was already located there, used years past to grind grain, but it was in ruins, of no use. As I cast about frantically in my head for a means to earn funds with which to leave that place—although I had nowhere to go—Medina-Sidonia's chief steward arrived with an offer to purchase the barony. But I refused."

Now Francho's eyebrows shot up. "Refused? But why? You said you had not a maravedi and here was an offer of money."

Her eyes flashed. "Ah yes, but without the land I held no title, and you must see, Francho," her tone turned mocking, "that the blue had been in my blood for so short a time that it was hard to give it up." He let his grin match her own. "I refused at least three offers."

"In any case, Miguel guessed it was the power of the riverfall that the Duke wanted, not the land or unimportant title, for he already had a dukedom's worth of property in the area. So I thought of something that might gain me everything, the land, the title, *and* some money. Hah! Little did the grasping steward realize that the young woman so hard to bargain with lived with her two servants for so many stubborn months on coarse bread and beer, some chickens, and a few greens and beans from Miguel's garden. Finally the Duke was in residence at La Natera, the steward said, soon to head north to join the Court in Madrid. And he was furious that I, a penniless woman of no importance, was thwarting his steward's plans to enrich him further."

"What plans?"

"I had little idea then and not much more now. Something

new, to do with making the paper on which books are printed and which requires a mill and a force of water capable of operating great beaters and cutters and other machinery." She shrugged. "And so the Duke himself arrived, in a cold rage at first. But then he became suddenly much gentler when I mentioned I would compromise and would rent to him the riverfall for an annual sum and for so many years, but rent only."

Abruptly she fell silent and dropped her eyes. In silence he contemplated her. Francho finally said softly, "He was much gentled because he clapped eyes on you, I think."

"And that is most of my story," she said, her chin coming up, and her mouth turned up at the corners again. He had decided he didn't want to know the rest, it was patently obvious anyway, and she seemed to sense that. "Now tell me about you," she demanded brightly, and with a pleasant sisterliness braced his shoulder to face her a little more. But he suddenly wanted to move about. He put aside her hands and stood up, stretching a bit. *"Dios mío,* how can I make four years of nothing but studies and training interesting to tell? Compared to yours my life has been a morass of serenity. Well—I promised. . . ."

Pacing, sweeping his hat off and placing it on the table, he began with his arrival at Mondejar and quickly described all that had been his life there, save, of course, whatever was connected to the secret of his own birthright and the plans to reestablish that. He enjoyed her laughter when he described practicing his light-fingered skills all over the castle; and they both became hilarious together as they imagined, now they were both on the scene, the reaction of people they knew at present to a mysterious rash of purse liftings and jewel thefts right in the bosom of the Court.

The laughter wiped away his discomfort with the untold end of her story. But the subject of stealing had led his thoughts back in a circle and a somber question finally struck him. He came and sat down beside her again as she dabbed at her eyes, her face warm and flushed from laughing. "Dolores. You never said what became of Tía and Papa. Or perhaps I feared to ask. Are they alive?" Her smile disappeared. "Are they dead?"

She saw the pucker appear between his eyes and looked down, sadly, picking at the silver-embroidered flowers on her gown. "I couldn't find many tears when they hung Papa; I was too numb."

"Ah, Dolores!"

"Yes, they strung him, what did you expect? Once the finger was pointed they found all the evidence they needed, there'd been no time to hide anything. They had to carry him to the gibbet, jerking and screaming in terror and wet with his own water." Her lower lip trembled. "It was horrible. And Tía Esperanza? The poor woman at least had God's mercy on her and died easily—her heart failed her as they were taken and I saw her as she lay sprawled in the street, lay there for hours until the guards fetched a big enough cart to remove her. Poor, dear Tía, she was so fat. But Father Julio had caught me and he held me tight, would not let me go near her for fear they would grab me too. My dear aunt, my only mother, and I could not even kiss her goodbye." Feeling grief again she swayed toward him and Francho took her in his arms to comfort her, and himself too for that matter, for he had also loved the fat woman.

Dolores rested her silken cheek against his shoulder. "God's children are all so frail, Francho," she murmured. "We are here a moment and then we are gone and nothing to show where our mortal feet have trod, or with what humors our hearts have beat." Her hand rested against his chest, she was like a child come to have a wound bound up. "I loved Tía Esperanza. She really was like my mother, she cared for me. And there was no one, no one at all to cry with me when she died."

Distressed with her pain Francho sought to ease her. "But she lives on in your heart, little sister, and in mine, and in the mind of God. Why should you sigh for a spirit that is so sweetly guarded?"

"But she died alone and unshriven. Perhaps she is burning in Hell?"

"No, no, do not think that. In purgatory only, awaiting God's mercy." He held her close and kissed the top of her head, a purely fraternal gesture meant to soothe and assure her, as his stroking hand was meant to calm her. For a few minutes they were silent. He could feel her breathing against his chest. Then she leaned back and lifted her gorgeous, tiger lily face to his.

Bells set up a sonorous clanging in his head.

Wistfully she said to him, "Sometimes I almost wish I could turn back the years. We were poor and ignorant, but were we not happy?"

Francho scarcely heard her. He was watching her wide, sensuous, full-lipped mouth, and he realized that the high, pointed bosom whose secret valley he'd had a stolen glimpse of before was pressed up against him, that he held in his arms one of the most desirable women in all Spain, and one of the most unusual. His good sense began to spin. Thus she had caught him in her net when he was fifteen, with her touch of innocence mingled with sheer, female magnetism, intensified now a hundredfold by beauty blossomed into irresistible seductiveness.

But the quickening in his groin dismayed him. She had come to meet him as a sister, as a friend, and he, God help him, he wanted to ravish her. He stood up, but still with his arms around her, and boldly supported her as she slipped down his body the small distance until her feet touched the floor, knowing she could feel his physical response to her. Her hands yet rested lightly against his chest, but her eyes were huge, deep pools of quicksilver drawing him in, nor would she take her gaze from his. Wordless, stricken, they stared at each other. Her generous mouth trembled slightly. Her lips parted.

"Francho . . ."

What ran through his head was the memory that he had been her first lover, the first to deflower this beautiful siren, and this awareness conspired against him; he suddenly felt a jealous sense of ownership—totally unfounded, totally unreasonable, but he felt it. She had given him that precious part of her she could never give away again, and so in some way she belonged to him. It wasn't love. He felt an affection for her, but he *loved* Leonora de Zuniga and only that sweet lady held his heart. Nevertheless, right now he wanted Dolores.

His face must have mirrored his galloping desire, for the light hands tensed on his chest. He felt her shiver, heard her quick indrawn breath, saw the throb of pulse in her neck. He could feel the warmth of her body through the silk of her gown, her sensuous body which curved so perfectly into his. Her perfume rose up and drowned him.

"Señor . . ." she whispered. Yet she did not push him away.

The whole chamber seemed to revolve and funnel down to that lily face lifted up to his and to the satiny, half-exposed bosom rising and falling under the glinting necklace. He was overwhelmed by the need to kiss her. Just one kiss, just one taste of those mobile, pink lips.

Swooping his head he took her mouth, and it seemed like nectar spreading under his lips. For a moment she was passive, allowing him to press his lips against the moist softness of hers, and his mouth fit on hers as if they had both been traced of one pattern. And then she responded, returning the pressure, and a shock wave ran through his body; he breathed in her breath, like the scent of clover, and he felt he was drinking deeply, greedily, from a honeyed cup that was pouring fire into his veins. Passion flooded through him. In a second what had begun gentle was turning to raging hunger.

Roughly he forced open her lips with a hard, thrusting tongue, ignoring her sudden struggle, holding her to him with arms like iron bands. She writhed in his grasp and unsuccessfully tried to push him away. She made squeaking, smothered, indignant noises. But then, gradually, she succumbed. Her arms locked about his neck and she clung to him, accepting his demanding, searching tongue, returning his kiss with a sudden ardor of her own. Not even the trumps of Gabriel could make him take his mouth from hers now, although his heart beat so madly he thought it would jump from his chest.

Dolores couldn't breathe but she cared nothing for it. The first touch of his lips seemed to have burned away a cocoon that had tight enclosed her, and now she was rising off the earth on wings she had never imagined. She gave him her lips, she molded her body to his muscled frame, she wanted to melt into him, and she did not even care for her abandon. From the moment he'd taken her into his arms to comfort her, from the shocking thrill that had run up her spine, she knew with crystal clarity that what had begun years ago was not yet finished. She knew it as she found herself unable to look away from the flare of craving in his vivid blue eyes, eyes that excited her, eyes that both caressed her and undressed her, erased her will, made her want to offer all of herself up to him like a priestess in a pagan temple.

His hard, demanding kiss poured fire into her belly. She could see against her closed eyelids the strong, square under-lip on which her gaze had lingered all the time they talked, and now as she kissed him back and clung to him she wanted to suck at that lip and bite it, and she was not even astounded with herself. What was driving her to destruction was a strange, enticing, musky male scent, a natural perfume that seemed to exude from his breath, from his skin, that turned her limbs into jelly and made her faint with need. Her head reeled. She tried to resist, to pull away, but there was no strength in her. When he forced her mouth open with his driving desire she easily gave up. Instinctively she met his restless, thrusting tongue with her own and tasted him in a deep kiss, inhaling that strange, compelling scent that was turning her delirious.

He released her mouth and lifted his head to breathe for a moment, his blue stare, half-lidded now, raking her face with an expression almost like pain. She felt his hands sliding warmly down to the small of her back and then lower, to her rounded bottom, to press her hips closer against him, so close the male hardness in his loins bruised her. She felt besotted. She was aware passion drooped her own lids too, that she breathed in pants. Somewhere inside her she was stunned with her wantonness and knew she was mad, mad, and yet she welcomed his mouth again because she was consumed by him. Her hand went under the curling dark hair to sensuously hold the back of his taut neck. Again he pulled his mouth from her clinging lips, but this time to place it burning on her thrown-back throat, on her delicate collarbones, descending, descending, and finally to press it ardently against the naked rise of her breast so that she gasped and quivered in his arms, and strained up against the hot mouth on her flesh.

Suddenly she knew why she was so shamelessly reveling in his wonderful embrace. Her heart was engulfed by the truth of it. She loved him. She always had, with no rhyme or reason for it, scarcely daring to dream she might find him again, the youth who had taken her girl's heart and body in the straw of a stable. And now here was the man, moving her still, demanding her heart again and she would give it. She loved him. With a sacred devotion, with a profane lust, but she loved him.

She scarcely heard his soft curse or felt him lift her off her feet and lay her on the bed, himself sitting so he could lean over her and, with a suddenly gentle hand, stroke her hair, stroke her face, murmuring *"querida"* over and over. He kissed her closed eyes, the tip of her nose. He drove her wild by running his finger delicately over her lips before he claimed her mouth again with his own, plundering it with his tongue, with his rampant desire until she moaned with delirium. But it was the feel of his hand, the heat of it cupping around her jutting, pear-shaped breast with its sensitive nipple pushing against the silk of her bodice that caused such voluptuous pleasure to surge through her that the very torrent terrified her, jolting her aware.

No. No, this was not right, tumbled about in her mind, even as his hand began a gentle squeezing. Wait, wait. There was more. There had to be more, there had to be love, there had to be the words that celebrated the twining of two spirits, that matched the fever of their bodies with the fervor of joyful promises. . . . Stop, stop. Still holding her lips in a kiss with his own, his fingers slipped under the silk covering her bosom and one fingertip just reached to her swollen nipple. The lightning that flashed through her nerves from the top of her head to her toes totally unstrung her. Her eyes flew open, she drew on every ounce of will she had and ripped her mouth away from his, gasping, frantic. Summoning up all her strength and taking him by surprise she pushed and twisted away from him, wriggling away to quickly slide off the opposite side of the bed. Recovering he lunged after her, reaching out to pull her back, but too late. He stared up at her, his face dark with desire.

She stood just out of reach and put out an unsteady hand to hold him off. "No, Francho, please. Please. Do not shame me," she whispered. Now, she prayed in her heart, watching the rapid play of emotions across his face, now say you love me truly, that never have you forgotten the discovery of love we shared in Ciudad Real and that God then and there pledged us to each other. Now. Disheveled, her chest heaving, her eyes wide and suppliant moving over his face, she waited for him to declare his love for her and then she would give herself joyously into his arms once more. Ah, sweet Virgin, make him know it, guide his heart. . . .

But—

He got up and came around the corner of the bed to where she stood. As if he thought she was teasing, the flat smile lines at the corners of his mouth deepened, and a gleam appeared in his eyes. He held out his strong, finely shaped hands to her again. She could not keep her glance from noticing that the tight hosen of his abbreviated costume left nothing of his physical hunger to the imagination.

"Dolores, come here, *querida*. Don't try to tease me. We found long ago a passion between us and still it lives, a miracle, a blessing. Dare we deny it? You are so beautiful, little sister. Come back to my arms, sweet, and let me love you." His voice was coaxing, seductive.

A sharp claw seemed to snag in her heart. Will you not say that which is more than passion, oh, will you not, her eyes begged.

As if not to frighten her he came only a pace closer. But she saw that the straight, square underlip which could brush so tenderly against hers, which she so wanted to kiss her to distraction, could also smile like this: hard, cruel. "Dolores, *querida,* do you think you can ignore what your gaze, your lips, your whole trembling body has already told me?" The blue heat in his eyes burned her, chilled her. "Why do you play at games when you have so bewitched me? Are we not old and good friends? Have we not already lain together—?"

"Enough!" Gulping, fighting tears, Dolores backed away, hearing her illusions shatter. She felt humiliated and a fool. It was all too obvious he held nothing for her but lust, no more than any other man. But what was worse, he seemed to think he was entitled to her, the despicable *puerco.* Her cheeks flamed, but she took a deep breath and drew herself up. "We seem to be not enough of old friends, Don Francisco. What do you take me for? A bedraggled trull who runs to your beckoning? A wench with whom you can take every liberty because you presume on a childhood we once shared?" Anger, blotting out the truth of how willingly she had entered his arms, how eagerly she had returned his kisses, loosened the hurt that tightened up her throat. "I think you forget, sir, whose protection I claim and that I am far from alone and vulnerable in this Court, or do you choose to ignore it? I warn you, that is dangerous." She deliberately threw the threat like a pail of cold water in his face.

The amorous glaze fled his eyes, replaced momentarily by an off-balance confusion.

Dolores stared at him defiantly, her chin up, her eyes stormy. "How dare you, sir, presume upon friendship and a female's helplessness? And indeed, you have overlooked my position. Or don't the current details pertaining to your old friend's success interest you?" she taunted.

Feeling as if she'd punched him hard in the stomach,

Francho growled back at her, "Now that you mention it, no. I have no interest in hearing about your liaison with that lecherous pig, Guzman. But it seems that you are quite faithful to him." He suddenly felt foolish and so he was surly.

Forcibly composing herself Dolores managed a short laugh. So he too, her old friend, preferred the most glib explanation of her connection with the Duke. Well, the Devil take him for caring nothing, she'd flaunt it in his stupid face then. "And why should I not be faithful to Don Enrique? He has been only generous and gallant toward me. I was without resources, without family or friend, and he was genuinely concerned by my plight. He cared." She flung this word at him accusingly, and then seeing that she was producing the desired effect, she injected a note of vivaciousness, tilting her head, hand on her hip. "Don Enrique accompanied me to Court and he used both money and strong influence to procure me a place with the Queen so I might have a greater allowance on which to live. He brought to me the best seamstresses and he even gave me a dancing master to perfect my steps, a simpering little Jew who repeated the same catechism over and over, listen, I can say it word for word: 'A damsel's bearing should be gentle and suave, her bodily movements humble and affable and display-ing a signorial dignity; and let her be light on her feet. Her glances should not be roving, gazing here and there, but lowered to the ground, and showing more modesty than a man. A lady must not allow her hand to be grasped except by the tips of the fingers. . . .'" There was a touch of hysteria in her light laugh. "Have you seen any of these Court dames dance with their eyes on the ground?"

He'd let her run on so he could cool down physically. Now he cut into her jibing. "You're nothing but a cold-blooded adventuress," he rasped.

"That's a step better than a scabby thief, is it not?" she flung back.

In two steps he had hooked his finger under her sapphire necklace and yanked so that she was forced up against him, forced to look into the blue flame of his anger. "How can you endure the touch of that pop-eyed, limping—"

She slapped his hand away smartly. "I told you—he is kind to me. He gives me presents, jewels, lace handkerchiefs, he even promises to lease me a small house of my own in Seville. Why should I care that he is homely?"

"You are—" He snapped his mouth shut on the ugly words.

His hand raised as if it itched to slap her mocking mouth, and then clenched.

"I am Papa el Mono's common daughter, a street rat, why don't you say it? And don't you feel powerful, o son of the mighty Tendilla? You could destroy me, you could tell the whole Court the truth of me. Then do it, if you despise me so much!"

"Never. Have your masquerade; I will not betray you. But not for your sake. For Tía's sake. Perhaps she would have approved of your method of binding a rich protector, perhaps not. But for her sake I will not hurt you."

Dolores tilted eyes narrowed like a spitting cat. "What would you have preferred me to do?" she shot back. "Starve on the streets? Beg on the cathedral steps? Marry a bumpkin squire in Torrejoncillo who would work me to exhaustion and give me ten children and an early grave?"

"Yes," he blurted, saying anything in his irritation. "Better than see you a concubine to a randy, homely goat."

"And what matter that! *He* did not take my honor from me, there was another, remember? And you would have renewed your conquest tonight, but *that* would not have counted as shameful because you are handsome, eh?" Her lip curled. "Go to, my newly born and chivalrous gentleman, your life merely fell in your lap. Mine I have to make. You can choose Leonora de Zuniga to lavish your heart on, I must take who offers me most." Now her smile grew sly. "And you adore your Leonora because she is sweet and innocent and pure, I suppose?"

He refused to be trapped by her feminine spite. Abruptly he veered the argument. "Have you let Carlos know where you are?"

She was startled at his quick switch but responded anyway. "No. Why should I? I had a message from him just before I left Santa Rosa saying he had set Pepi up at an inn near Montero and that I could reach him from there. But I'm not interested in spending my life in a louse-infested camp in the mountains, getting calluses on my hands from carting water buckets up the path." She stretched out her ringed fingers and mocked at him. "I like my hands the way they are—soft and fine and covered with jewels that were presented to me, not stolen."

"Greedy. You were always greedy. But at least you honored yourself."

Dolores had a split-second to wonder why she even stood and listened to him before her temper erupted. "How do you dare speak to me in such a fashion! What is it to you what I do? If we had not met here at Court, would you have ever given one thought to the tavernkeeper's daughter? Would you have cared if I had given myself to every tinker or muleteer that passed? Would you have even bothered to know whether I was dead or alive?" She had drawn blood.

The tense muscles in his face slackened for a moment; he blinked and she could see the truth had sunk in, but stubbornly he drove on.

"Very well then, 'tis as you say. Our paths diverged. But I speak now because of our childhood companionship, Dolores, and because of my past friendship with your brother. He would want you with a sincere and sober husband to look after you, to give you children—"

Her lips drew back from her even teeth, the sound she made more of a hoot than a laugh. "More likely he would pat me on the back for earning more riches than he's ever dreamed of. And the devil with Carlos! Do you think to hoodwink me with your prim morality, Francisco de Mendoza, late the scourge of the Hermandad? Or"—she tossed back her hair and saucily sauntered about him a few steps, and since he did not turn with her she had a good view of his taut jaw in profile—"or isn't it really that your pride is wounded, that you breathe dragonfire because Don Enrique has my favor whilst you I rebuff? That prig Zuniga will not give you the tip of her finger to kiss, while the woman you once taught the rudiments of lust would rather her crooked-nosed protector than you. Yes, rather! He at least will not ask why I don't prefer a life of carrying slop pails. *Picaro!* You are green with envy of him, as is every other gallant in the Court."

Holding her head proudly as she glided up to him, the smile on her mouth was as evil as she felt. "And since your tender sensibility for my mortal soul is only occasioned by your wounded male pride, I hope it really distresses you to hear that should a handsomer and richer duke or marquis offer more largess he would not have to be jealous of Guzman very long!"

He faced her squarely, unable to control his wrath with her, nor explain it. She flashed beautiful virago eyes at him, disheveled strands of long, auburn hair tangled across her shoulders. He was aching to slap the mocking smile off that honey-tasting mouth, but he realized through his anger that she was right, that there was no good reason for him so to revile her. That she gave herself was not uncommon for ambitious ladies with few means or male relatives, and after all, she was no kin of his, no family honor was involved. But— He grated, "You show very plainly where you come from; it's written all over your grasping heart. My advice still holds. Take the considerable spoils you must already have and find a grateful knight to marry. At least that way you will not be discarded when he is tired of you."

"Oh monster!" she flung back. "Go to your angelic Leonora and sigh for her every glance, which is all you'll get for your pains from that ice statue. Unless maybe last winter in Madrid her constant suitor, Felipe de Guzman, lowered her barriers. The Count of Perens is a persuasive lover, so I hear, and the little Zuniga also has her own ambitions—"

"You vixen!"

"Serpiente! Go. Leave my sight. And spare me your sanctimonious opinions, hereafter, you dealer in hypocrisy."

Dolores glared at him, and even in the dim and guttering light of the burnt down candles she could see very well the white anger pressing his mouth, the fury in his eyes. She was overjoyed that her feline swipe at Leonora, actually based on no more than instinct, had struck home.

"I'll leave you. With pleasure—Baroness," he hurled back. He snatched up his plumed hat and whirled on his heel. He flung open the door and stalked out, without giving any indication he had heard her final sarcastic, *"Buenos noches,* Señor Mendoza," as he slammed the door behind him.

Dolores stood like a statue, staring at the closed door. One hand crept up to press against her mouth as she tried to calm the turmoil inside of her. Finally, like a sleepwalker, she moved to the bed and clung to one of the slim posts for support, for her legs suddenly seemed not to want to carry her. Slowly she sank along the smooth wood until she had subsided to her knees. She felt the burn of tears spring to her eyes then, and the great, hot drops began to roll down her cheeks. Angrily she tried to brush them away but soon she just buried her face in her hands and the pained, angry tears flowed through her fingers to make dark splotches on her brocade gown.

There the birdlike Engracia found her and with a twitter of sympathy went to her old knees too. Asking no questions she held the lovely head on her withered bosom until the wild, hurt sobbing wore away.

❦ *Chapter 9* ❦

WHAM! THE CLENCHED, ringless fist struck the ornate table top with surprising force. Shocked at the outburst, the elderly Marquis of Cantado looked up from the parchment he had been reading aloud, uncertain whether to go on. His Queen's blue eyes had darkened with anger; her mouth was drawn into a tight line.

"Continue, continue, my lord," she cried. "The worst is yet to come. You must read it all aloud, to impress upon our minds that our plans and preparations, our sacrifices, seem to have been for naught, thrown into the winds like so much useless chaff." Her stormy glances took in Luis Porto-Carrero, Lord of Palma; Don Fadrique de Toledo, who had brought the upsetting dispatch; her confessor, Bishop Talavera; her loyal friend and confidante, Beatrix de Boabdilla, Marquesa of Moya; and several other trusted advisors, all closeted with her in the council chamber of the episcopal palace in the southern city of Jaen.

"Gently, my daughter, gently," Talavera tried to calm her, of all of them the least dismayed by her unusual show of temper. "The fevers have but lately left you. You must conserve your strength."

With an effort of will Isabella managed to cool the fire in her eyes and lower her voice. "Go on, Cantado," she ordered coldly.

The Marquis, the communication held out almost at arm's length, lowered his eyes and continued. ". . . and although our informants had reported that Baza was unprepared to withstand attack and would capitulate, the long delay of our armies in securing the frontier outposts allowed ample time for the city to summon from Almeria the commander Cidi Yahye with over ten thousand warriors, bringing their garrison strength to above thirty thousand men and adding huge supplies of munitions to their armory."

The Marquis looked up from his reading, turned down the corners of his wrinkled mouth, and then went on with the letter. "Our surrender demand being rejected, we decided to rigorously press our siege. This required several detachments to take control of the wide green labyrinth of orchards surrounding the city walls so that our artillery might move into position. Fearlessly they rode out, our gallant Christian *caballeros,* in the assurance that God and the strength of their arms would give them victory. But scarcely had they reached the verge of the orchards when, in a fearful din of trumpets and drums, a horde of Moorish warriors poured out of Baza's gates, led by the shouting Cidi Yahye himself, who exhorted them on.

"The two opposing forces met in the very midst of the overgrown groves. Our lances, crossbowmen, arquebusses, and swordsmen reaped bloody rewards for their bravery, but the confusing nature of the battlefield, cut up as it was by canals and streams and numerous storage towers and huts, and obscured by the closeness of the trees, gave greater advantage to the enemy, for our troops were mounted and they were on foot. The Hell-spawned Moors were able to lurk, to sally forth and attack, and then to retreat almost without loss."

A low groan ran around the table. Cantado raised questioning eyes to the Queen and she nodded. He continued. "Finally the Grand Master of Santiago and other of our noble captains ordered their horsemen to dismount and fight on foot, for we could make no advance. The orchards became a scene of carnage, so clouded with smoke from the burning towers that we could see little from our vantage point and our forces were hampered in our attempt to reinforce those areas where the battle went badly. For twelve hellish hours we fought to gain the groves. The eye saw columns of smoke in every direction, there was the constant thunder of the arquebusses and the ringing clash of arms against armor amidst the shouts of the combatants—and worse to our ears, the pitiful cries of the legion of wounded bespeaking the terrible toll in blood and pain of this unexpectedly difficult battle.

"Our weary Christians, unfamiliar with the terrain and its unsuitability to normal warfare, were fallen upon again and again by the Moors, whose light armor allowed them more agility, more adroitness. My heart aches to report, my queen, that our troops were slaughtered by the hundreds."

Beatrix de Boabdilla stifled a cough. Isabella's lips were pressed and grim.

"Yet, rejoice, for so many were the acts of great valor performed by our courageous warriors in the midst of such destruction that should I relate only two which I have seen personally it will lift up your heart. Our prized Don Juan de Luna stood over a fatally wounded young knight and alone defended him vigorously from six heathen warriors screaming for the man's head as a trophy, and in spite of his own heavy wounds de Luna held off the devils until he was relieved by the Count of Cabra's soldiers.

"And again: during the most furious part of the conflict the standard bearer for the Grand Cardinal's troops had his arm carried off by a cannonball. The standard of a prince of our Church was almost falling into the hands of the exulting heathen when out of a cloud of smoke Francisco de Mendoza, Tendilla's natural son, dashed to its rescue, riding through a shower of lances, arrows, and balls. He swooped up the standard and with bloody sword flashing rushed forward with it into the thick of the battle, followed by Tendilla's clamoring soldiery.

"Thus inch by inch we won those orchards and drove back the Moor inside their gates and so set up our camp at last. I will not burden your heart with the sights that greeted our reddened eyes the following daybreak; suffice it to say our position in the orchards was untenable.

"But I send you this account, Lady Queen, so you may know the tolls and sufferings that have decimated our divisions and will understand the frustrations of our present position."

Isabella tapped sharply on her table, interrupting the reading and making Cantado look up. She addressed Toledo.

"Don Fadrique, you were attached to our troops at the orchard encampment. Describe to us the situation after the battle."

The tired knight, who had ridden hard from Baza to Jaen to deliver the dispatch, cleared his throat. "A piteous spectacle, Your Majesty," he began, his face pale with the memory, for it had actually been his first campaign. "Our soldiers sat white and haggard, almost too weary to lift their heads, while outside the camp lay a multitude of dead and dying, heaped up in the terrible piles in which they had fallen during the night. The orchards beyond us . . ." He faltered, obviously searching for less gory words than the ones crowding his tongue.

"Do not be afraid for our tender sensibilities," Isabella ordered. "We have seen battlefields before."

Again clearing his throat nervously, the courier continued. "The orchards, my queen, were a shocking scene of horror and desolation. The towers and pavilions were smoking ruins; the canal and streams were dying with blood and choked with the bodies of the slain. The ground was chopped up men and horses, slimy and slippery with gore; and amidst the trampled shrubs and fruit lay the broken bodies of our men—of our enemy too, certainly—some still locked together in mortal ferocity. A few of the gutted horses still shrieked loudly in agony—"

"Enough!" Isabella's raised hand halted him. A vein pulsed in her neck. "Enough, my friend. Your eloquence is quite equal to your bravery, Don Fadrique."

"May we hear the remainder of His Majesty's report, my Queen?" quietly asked Porto-Carrero, his wiry, reddish hair bristling with outrage.

"Yes. Indeed." Isabella was suddenly weary. "You must know what you are riding toward." She signaled the Marquis to resume reading from the dispatch and leaned back in her chair, eyelids lowered. "If you will, my lord."

"The following day we resolved to abandon the orchards and extricate our army from so entangled a position, and although pressed and harassed by Cidi Yahye and a fresh legion of Moorish horse and foot, we withdrew in good order and, God be praised, without much further toll of life. The toll was in a disabling loss of supplies and munitions which had to be abandoned.

"Our camp now being too distant from Baza to inflict any harm on the city even with our new artillery, but close enough for the heathen to sally forth upon us and return through their damned groves without hindrance, we called our council to consider how to proceed. Our good Lord Cadiz advises abandoning the siege, the city being too well garrisoned and provisioned for us to assault it. The Marquis further argues the approach of the southern season of rainfall, which will expose our armies to suffering and disease and cause swelling rivers, which could imprison us for months in this territory. He recommends withdrawal now, followed by a policy of heavy predation upon their supply lines by our garrisons in neighboring territories, so that by next year we will be able to starve them into submission."

"Next year, next year," the Queen muttered.

"This reasonable opinion is concurred by the lords Medina-Sidonia, Cabra, Aguilar, Albuquerque, and Villena. But the Grand Master of Santiago, and Tendilla as well, urge the opposite of Cadiz, championing the vigorous prosecution of the siege now, so as not to give new energy to their commander in chief, El Zagal.

"But we reflected heavily upon our army's great losses and most especially upon the impossibility of obtaining regular supplies in winter across such length and leagues of rugged mountains as separate me from thee. And it was our conclusion that our humiliation and chagrin in ending this campaign without prize was little to endure in exchange for the lives of our subjects. And so we announced our decision to withdraw.

"Imagine, dear consort, our joy and silent thanks to God, when with one voice our entire and brave Christian soldiery entreated us not to abandon the siege until it was won! However, this show of brave unity furthered our indecision.

"We are sorely perplexed by the conflicting strong opinions of our commanders. We dispatch to you this account of our predicament confident that, as so often before, your wise counsel might help dispel our uncertainty.

"Subscribed, with all tender considerations for the well-being and tranquility of our most beloved Queen and Consort, this date 20 August 1489. Ferdinand."

Isabella's sharp tone was full of pique. "Tranquility? Now that it devolves upon *us* to decide the fate of our loyal troops?

Would that our good husband had thought to bespeak himself to God and allow the Holy Spirit to guide his fortunes rather than the opinion of his Queen, who is only a woman, not a learned general or oracle."

Doña Beatrix cast down her eyes, struggling to hide a smile. A woman yes . . . Isabella was certainly that, in her dainty femininity and her adoration of her husband. But the soft blue eyes and white bosom were merely velvet trappings for the iron determination of a general that underlay them, an aggressiveness more astute and demanding than many of Ferdinand's male commanders. Never in her life had Isabella displayed irresolution or fainting courage or timidity. Beatrix, over twenty years a loyal substitute mother to Castile's most beloved ruler, knew her better than she knew herself. And she knew—and hence the hidden smile—that Isabella's present irritation lay not at all with having to help make an important military decision but with the fact that Ferdinand once more had neglected to enclose the separate, loving, and intimate little letter meant for her eyes alone, a habit he had begun early in their marriage.

"My friends, how shall I take the responsibility of deciding this question? I am bitter with this unforeseen reversal. Our glorious aim to be on the threshold of victory in driving the Moslems from our shores by the turn of the decade may be lost, continue the siege of Baza or not, for the Egyptian Sultan may any day sail to the rescue of Granada. Such a defeat as we have had, both in lives and time, may mean we are not able to . . ."

A frown was darkening Talavera's round and saintly face as he interrupted her tirade. "This reversal is by the hand of God, my child. It is his indication that we must redouble our efforts and sacrifice to our utmost to unloose the Moslem grip on our land, and perhaps it is a sign of displeasure that we have not applied ourself fervently enough in advancing His will. God's ways are His mystery. Therefore will you abandon your faith and show Him anger when His works do not suit your schedule? Pray, daughter, for acceptance, for humility, for wisdom."

There was a few moments' silence while the pious Isabella sat back with closed eyes and her council exchanged beset glances. At last her eyelids rose, and to their relief a more normal calm shone in her steady blue eyes and she seemed more relaxed.

"Yes. Our Reverend Father leads us in the righteous path of contemplation. It would be a sin, I think, to leave the ground we have already bought so dearly."

"A word from you will surely raise up the enthusiasm of our tired King, my queen," suggested Beatrix. "Offer him your personal assurances of success, so that his heart will be strengthened."

Isabella pursed her lips for a moment, thinking. Then her forehead smoothed.

"I will offer him more than that, *doña,* I will offer him our greater aid," she announced. "I will return forthwith a dispatch stating my opinion that we might never be able to resume our operation on so formidable a manpower scale as the force he has now, for such a great legion, once disbanded for the winter might lose heart and be difficult to recruit again. Don't you agree, my lords? And I shall entreat him, Your Worship," and here she smiled placatingly at Talavera, "to trust in the providence of God in our battle with the followers of false prophets and to consider the sin of abandoning the gains purchased at so terrible a price. And—I will give him our assurances that if his captains and army are true to their duty they can rely upon us to most faithfully furnish the requisite supplies and money to bring them victoriously through a winter siege if such becomes necessary. A *winter* campaign, my friends, to confound our enemies and consign them to Hell!"

The color had come high on her cheeks again as she glanced around at the small, startled assembly. "Now send my scribe to me, if you will, Doña Beatrix."

Jaen, 5 September 1489

My beloved King and husband:
. . . it will be, as we previously outlined to you, a gigantic undertaking; to transport huge masses of supplies for the first army of winter in our history, sixty thousand men strong, but a task which we and our councillors willingly address.

Our first care has been the critical transport through the dangerous and broken mountain passes, for which we have hired fourteen thousand mules and horses along with one hundred fifty muleteers to lead them. To protect the trains from constant Moorish attack and plunder we have ap-

pointed the lords *Fernandez* and *Monte Mayor* to conscript as many hundred of mercenaries and soldiers as necessary to fend off raids.

The network of local administrators we have supported all these years now bend their backs to a vast task: gathering in grain, grinding and delivering it, purchasing and slaughtering large herds of cattle running in our eastern provinces, collecting other foodstuffs to be prepared, salted, dried, whatever is necessary for their preservation.

Be joyful, Sire, for we deem it no more than a fortnight before our first caravan reaches you, and thence daily over the route you have indicated. With prayers to the Almighty to keep the coming winter from totally closing the passes. . . .

Before Baza, 10 September 1489

Most gracious and beloved of all Queens:

. . . so to surround the enemy we have divided our encampment in two, the northern under the Marquis of Cadiz, and this one under our own command. Ten thousand men are sweating to cut timber from these huge orchards, which they either saw into planks to turn these flimsy siege tents into a more solid city offering greater shelter against the hard winter, or stack for fuel. We also build an immense depot into which to deposit the meal and foodstuffs you send us.

Dearest Lady, we are proud of your swift and efficient response to our need and await with excitement the arrival of your first mule train, this lifeline you throw over the wild and rugged Sierra de Serano. Amidst a cacophony of vigorous hammering, chopping, and sawing, we send you our gratitude . . .

Jaen, 2 October 1489

Most honored husband:

. . . expenditures have grown so enormous we have found our ordinary avenues for financing insufficient, in spite of tremendous donations from noble, prelate, merchant and wealthy bourgeois, and our sale of certain

Crown properties. Therefore, since God has seen fit to place such perplexity in the hands of a mere woman, we can only do what is left and we have caused to be collected all the gold and silver plate belonging to the Crown and, together with a casket of our personal jewels, have sent these to Valencia and Barcelona in pledge for ducats enough to see the enterprise through . . .

Baza winter camp, 16 October 1489

Dearest and most beloved of Queens:
. . . the walls and roofs of over one thousand sturdy dwellings and barracks rise above our wooden bulwarks, laid out along streets and squares as great and busy as any city. This must surely be of huge dismay to the prince Cidi Yahye, who surely has watched, pacing his battlements, the disappearance of our flimsy silk pavilions and the erection of these stubborn fortifications.

Our headquarters, in the center, displaying the proud royal standards of Castile and Aragon flying above, is both large and happily provided with many comforts unusual in the field, gramercy, my lady Queen, to your mountain-defying caravans. Already merchants and artificers from all parts of Spain have found us, and we have armorers, cloth merchants, furriers, tailors, and tradesmen of all ilk who see to it that our splendid Spanish cavaliers do not go unclothed and unembellished.

More somberly, Cidi Yahye's prime regiments daily attack our outposts in heavy, bloody skirmishes terrible of cost in lives. Their spirit and vigor made us fear they were well provisioned enough to survive through the winter until relief could arrive from Granada. But Don Iñigo de Mendoza's Morisco agents, who by some manner of magic gain entry and exit into the city, report Cidi Yahye's military chest has been drained of funds with which to pay his troops, nor are their stores of food so great as we once believed.

Still, since quick surrender will avert the exhaustion of our own resources and remove the chance that El Zagal and the Grand Sultan Boabdil may cease their bitter wrangling and together mount a rescue force, we have conceived a bold plan to shorten the siege by proving to the

*citizens of Baza that we intend to stay here until not one
soul remains alive in their city.*

*Our plan is this: We pray you, Madam, to arrive here at
our great camp in the highest pomp and with all your
Court, proud retinue and train, so to publicly and visibly
take up winter residence with your consort and your
army. Not even a heathen of lowest intelligence will
miss the ominous and pointed meaning of this confident
display . . .*

Privy: To Her Majesty's eyes alone:

*. . . the days are filled with reports and orders and
alarms. But the nights stretch lonely and I chafe without
my beloved and beautiful lady Queen to warm both my
heart and my body, my wife of so many tendernesses to
adorn my warrior's breast with the sweetness of her lovely
head . . .*

*And so I subscribe myself to you, your loving and
lovelorn husband,*

Ferdinand

So be it, thought Isabella with a satisfied smile. Two birds with
one stone. A recalcitrant city and a restless man . . .

Francho stared down at the peaceful villages slumbering not
far from each other in the valley and strained to make them
out more clearly in the wan light of predawn. Under those
roofs the Moslem villagers rested from their labors, quiet and
unsuspecting, and all the more vulnerable to attack because a
fold of hills blocked them from the view of the fortified city of
Gaudix on the other side of the plain. From his higher vantage
point in the mouth of a hidden defile through the mountains
which the large force halted behind him had negotiated by
starlight to avoid the Moorish patrols, Francho thought he
could see, were it lighter, the gilded tip of the tallest mosque
towers in El Zagal's nest.

Sitting his charger beside Francho, Antonio de la Cueva,
co-conspirator in this unauthorized foray into enemy territory, leaned forward in his saddle with a soft clink of armor
joints, peering to see if any military camps protected the
huddles of prosperous farmers and artisans below. "Incredible," de la Cueva muttered, as he scanned the valley. "That
half-breed told the truth. They lie like lambs to the knife."

Behind them came the snort and rattle of horses and arms, carefully muted by riders whose best advantage in this raid was stealth. Francho's blood began to warm in spite of the cold, and his mouth stretched in a wolfish grin. He turned about in his saddle. Excitement pumped through him to view the lengthy, motionless column of armored men sitting their mounts along the rugged, stony path, plumes and pennons stirring in the early morning breeze, flags fluttering but colorless still in the dim light, ready and eager to "bear off spoils from under the very nose of El Zagal and pluck the fiery Arab by the beard," as their Morisco scout had urged. This half-breed, his purse needing filling, had played on the boredom and suppressed energy of the most restless of the young *caballeros* in the Baza camp, and they, Francho, Antonio, Hernando, and some others, had rounded up without trouble two hundred other hot-blooded warriors and one hundred foot soldiers to beard the Eagle.

Francho could hardly credit the miracle of the column's silent midnight ride from camp without waking the more prudent leaders or eliciting any comment from the guards. Yet exit his troop did, primed and armed. And here they waited now, a pride of eager warriors following him and his friends to gain glory for the Cross and booty for themselves.

Francho motioned Hernando del Pulgar forward and when he came up said softly, "Our *aldalid* is correct. The villages lie unprotected by anything more than the patrols in the main pass."

"*Gracias a Dios.* Where is the guide now?"

"Just below," Antonio answered. "The trail down is not steep. If we negotiate it now we will reach level ground just as the sun rises. The nearest village is but half a league away, so it looks to me."

Pulgar guffawed. "We will fall upon them before they take their first piss."

"We ride onward then," Francho decided, "and we ride to the attack as soon as we clear the mountain. But pass back the word, again, Hernando, that we are here for conquest and for loot. Not murder. We kill only those who attack us. The rest we take prisoner for the Crown. Those are the orders."

Pulgar squinted in the brightening light at the tall, commanding rider whose gauntleted fist was locked around an upright lance flying the green-and-white Mendoza colors, with brave green-and-white plumes waving above his helmet. Then he grinned into the level stare of this late-come but instinctive leader. "*Ay, mi madre,* but you forbid the best part, *amigo.* What good conquest and pillage without a little blood to wash it down?" he complained, half serious. But he wheeled his huge, caparisoned horse back to join the column.

De la Cueva's wolfish expression matched Francho's. "This will be even easier than plucking the rose from a maid."

"*Sí*, Antonio, as long as we are swift. That is our advantage, to strike like lightning and quick away. If we return laden with booty and captives we are heroes, but if we are decimated by El Zagal's hordes we will have far worse to contend with from our own."

De la Cueva's visor was raised; Francho could almost see the sparkle in his companion's dark eyes, the heightened color in a boyish face now blotched from excitement. "God is with us—and we therefore will prevail," the young nobleman averred. He turned to the men behind him and held up one steel-covered arm as a signal to the cavalry to advance. Francho did the same, and they both turned down the gently descending scree, loose pebbles rattling away from under the hooves of the horses. The sky continued brightening.

From the moment they gave the attack signal, jamming spurs into their mounts and loosing a pounding horde of steel-plated demons to terrify stunned and gasping villagers with blood-curdling cries of "Santiago" and "Castile and Aragon" and "Hammer of God!" a rapid sequence of events passed before Francho's consciousness in flicks and flashes. He found himself everywhere at once on his rearing horse; leading the destructive sack of the houses for whatever coin, plate, bolts of cloth, and silver and gold jewelry the people had accumulated and loading them into any cart available; sweeping along the fields and orchards with crackling torches setting afire stubble and trees and outbuildings so that great columns of smoke rose up to the fresh and cloudless sky; helping direct the rounding up of herds of fat sheep and cattle and their drovers; overseeing the gathering and roping together of prisoners, all the male villagers they could find except those few who to protect their homes had attacked the soldiers with wooden pitchforks and died for it.

With a detachment appointed to guard the spoils, he and de la Cueva reformed the main body of their troops and led them in a wild dash toward the second, smaller village a few leagues distant. These people had taken alarm at the smoke darkening the sky to the north and were scurrying to hide or protect what they could, yet the first easy victory added such exhilaration to the Christian charge that Francho and his cohorts pounded in among them like great evil *djinns* with leveled lances, yelling for surrender. Francho's followers swirled about, looting the houses and shops, dragging sacks of grain, taking prisoners, burning, repeating the rapacious plundering of earlier in the morning.

"Do we ride on to the other hamlet, the one to the east with the tower?" Pulgar called, wheeling his horse about in a melee of frightened elders, barking dogs, soldiers bearing away booty, wailing children, and mounted knights herding captive men.

"No," Francho yelled back, indicating the sun with a raised fist, thumb cocked up. He had slammed his sword back into its scabbard, for the few men who had offered resistance were dead or captured. "We must assume that any villager who escaped us has now reached Gaudix or a patrol. We must go back."

A short, stocky knight with the Encantando blazon on the tabard over his armor rode up to them. "The men want more. They are disappointed with their take. They hear there is a mill in the next village, great stores of grain—"

"No!" Francho ordered. "Their greed will get them a Moorish bolt in their backs. We have been hours in this valley and our retreat will be clumsy and slowed by the herds, the prisoners, the wagons. There is plenty for all. We go back. Now."

Intimidated by the threatening line of drawn black brows and implacable tone of command from his leader, the knight responded, "*Sí, señor.* I will get the prisoners moving. Fast," he added for good measure.

De la Cueva trotted up, his helmet off and fastened to his saddle because the sun heated up the gold- and silver-trimmed steel casque considerably. "What is wrong?"

"The hour, Antonio. If we do not turn about now we are foolhardy, and tempting the Devil to bring El Zagal baying on our tail. We are overburdened with plunder . . ."

". . . and what's worse, plodding sheep and cattle and sullen captives," Pulgar agreed. He frowned into the distance in the direction of Gaudix.

"But the men grumble. There is a richer village to the east," Antonio said, shifting his seat, uncomfortable under many pounds of heat-trapping steel. He pulled off a gauntlet and wiped sweat from his forehead.

"To the Devil with them. Better one piece of booty less than the whole raid forfeit. Ho, Fortrano! de Bejas!" Francho shouted to nearby riders. "Call in your men. *Caballeros!* To us! We retreat!" The tug to thoroughly flout the enemy and rape the remaining villages was strong and Francho felt it too, elated as he was with the success of the foray. Great piles of agricultural booty and captured farmers dumped at the foot of the Spanish throne could only enhance his standing. But the same warning bell that had once signaled hold your hand, a Hermandad guard is too close, now pealed in his head that time had turned against him. Success could become disaster.

He and his main leaders rode up and down the retreating column keeping the procession of soldiers, captives, and beasts moving as fast as they could go, and in fact once turned homeward the grievances of the greedy disappeared and they joined the rest in hustling the train along.

At last they reached the hidden entry into the little-known pass. Bringing up the rear as the last of the column rattled along the scree, Francho turned to scan the valley, which was wreathed in ugly columns of smoke reaching to the blue sky, spying nothing of interest but the movements, tiny in the distance, of the women and children left in the nearer village. Appointing two riders to remain at the head of the trail until dark to watch for signs of pursuit, he plunged into the defile to catch up to de la Cueva, knowing they would not be safe until they emerged on the other side of the mountain, where their own forces patrolled.

The lumpy trail widened considerably and began a winding ascent over jagged hills as it cut a cleft in the mountain range. The awkward cortege plodded forward as quickly as it could be pressed on, until, squinting up at the slanting sun Francho judged they were more than halfway through the pass. But then there was a shout. A commotion rippled all along the line as a rider urged his mount forward, scattering whatever was in his way and yelling out to the horsemen and soldiers on either side of the column. Motioning the men at the head of the train to keep up the pace, Francho, his cohorts and other leaders wheeled around to gallop swiftly back and meet the rider.

Francho saw it was one of his rear pickets, now followed forward by thirty or forty other *caballeros.*

"A great cloud of dust, Senor Mendoza," the rider called out, "from the direction of Gaudix. El Zagal's men, riding like the wind. They would have reached the first village by now, or past it, perhaps!"

"How many riders?"

"Too far away to tell accurately. But from the plume of dust I think at least five hundred men."

A growl ran through the assembled knights as they faced the main leaders. "They are hot on our traces and they far outnumber us. And so encumbered are we that they will make short work of us!" a nearby rider spoke out in concern.

"*Sí,* they are fresh. We have been in the saddle since last midnight," agreed another voice. Francho heard de la Cueva's low grunt of disgust beside him, "Poltroons. They want to run."

Another man yelled from the crowd of horsemen, "I say we abandon the animals and the captives and ride our spurs out of this rocky trap!" There was a loud mutter of defiant agreement from the bone-weary cavalry for whom the earlier glamour of the expedition had faded into this harried, rag-tag retreat.

"*Sí,* we can surely make the safety of the camp if we ride now, and if we rid ourselves of these entanglements," urged another with red-rimmed eyes.

With an oath Francho flung up his arms for silence. "*Hombres! Señores!* I cannot believe what my ears are hearing. Is this the flower of Spain who speaks so cravenly? Is this the vaunted ranks of *caballeros* riding for Los Reyes Católicos, feared and respected by every Moslem from Malaga to Egypt? We began this venture in the quest of glory for the Cross, and now will you end it in dishonor?"

The last of the column of booty and captives clattered by them, followed by the rear guard, some of whom stopped to join the controversy.

"What dishonor is there to recognize when to retreat and so live to fight another day? We have had no sleep, no food, our mounts droop—"

"For shame, *señores!*" Francho roared, black brows drawn together in a fierce line. "Could you be suggesting then that we leave our own foot soldiers to the swords of the enemy? Which one would evermore trust their standard to your arms? We do not run, *caballeros,* we fight. We are not women fainting with fatigue, we are men and knights in the service of Castile and Aragon, of Christ and Our Lord, of Their Majesties Ferdinand and Isabella. We are pledged to a code of honor followed by every warrior since the mighty El Cid. No, I say, we do not leave our spoils and captives, captives who pay for the thousands of Christian souls that are rotting in Moorish dungeons. No! We stand and fight!"

Now there were some voices calling out in assent over the rumble of comment.

"A rider approaches," came a yell and in a few seconds the second rear picket galloped around a fall of rock and pulled to a sharp halt before the gathered leaders. "El Zagal's men have found the defile and entered it. They are not far behind us," he panted. "I counted four hundred horse."

"Aha, the gap has been narrowed, from five hundred to four!" de la Cueva declared ringingly. "What Christian fighter cannot account for the dispatch of at least two Moslem dogs with every sweep of his good sword?"

Already they could hear faintly the sound of hooves and the clink and rattle of cavalry ascending the pass at an urgent pace.

Francho called out, "Look back. No more than five or six men can face each other in that narrow neck behind us. And they must attack, they must throw themselves on our lances and swords while we stand," Francho pressed. "Even half of us can cut them down, and they will have to fight upon a growing mountain of their dead." The sounds of the pursuing force grew louder, and the enemy could be glimpsed below through the rocks lining the trail.

A sudden roar erupted from the heretofore silent but scowling Pulgar. "What soldiers are these? These are women! Hernando del Pulgar does not turn tail!" he yelled, and with his armored bulk half-standing in the stirrups he kneed his horse, bore down upon the wavering standard bearer, and snatched away the lance from him. Yanking from under his own thigh-piece a delicate red chiffon kerchief conferred upon him by some lady, he snagged it firmly over the Castilian insignia already on the lance head, hurled a black look at the irresolute raiders, and clanged down his visor. He spurred up his mount so fiercely that the animal bucked and reared before hurling himself and his rider forward at the vanguard of the enemy, which had already ridden into sight down the trail.

"Santiago!" he hollered, "Santia-a-go!" The kerchief streamed bravely from his aggressively lowered lance, and in no more than the blink of an eye his war cry was echoed by Francho, de la Cueva, and some others, who spurted after him like arrows from a bow. "Santia-a-go!" Francho yelled. He heard a growing thunder of hooves behind him and knew that the main body of Spanish *caballeros* had rallied, goaded by the courage of their leaders and the sight of the enemy bearing down on the narrow neck of rock. Now in their numbers they charged with him and shouted Santiago to the skies, their shamed consciences making their cry fiercer than ever. He smiled grimly behind his lowered visor.

A flood of energy pounded through Francho's veins. The Moors would not expect them to attack so precipitously; such ferocity could disorganize the enemy, cause a breaking of ranks, a panic. He was not going to lose his great column of booty now; in his position of disobedience death was preferable to dishonoring the gentleman known as Francisco de Mendoza. But he would not die. With God's help and his men's strong arms they would hack El Zagal's pursuing riders to pieces. Thundering forward shoulder to shoulder with de la Cueva and Pulgar, he sighted sharply through his visor slit and quickly picked out his mark, a black-and-purple-beplumed Moorish knight bearing down on them with jutting lance and curdling cries. He steadied his own heavy, iron-tipped lance with the sure and firm grip of a tourney champion and with his elbow tested to see his sword was loose in its scabbard.

Along with the other ringleaders of the raid, Francisco de Mendoza slouched on the rude wooden bench that ran around the perimeter of the anteroom to Ferdinand's audience chamber. The dusty, blood-spattered, grinning *caballeros* of yesterday, who had led their cavalcade in triumph into the Baza camp with Pulgar in the vanguard proudly bearing his red kerchief on a lance, had metamorphosed into this morning's fine courtiers, immaculately attired—and nervous.

For hours they had been left to cool their heels and await their monarch's pleasure, or displeasure, for in spite of the welcome riches they had contributed to the encampment, they had still ridden out without permission. Francho stared along the length of his leg and inspected the tip of his boots, entertaining his own thoughts, but it did register that the conversations among the group were growing edgier and edgier as they remained unsummoned.

"Think you the Queen and her ladies will arrive soon? 'Tis already mid-November."

"Surely before full winter closes in. The women could hardly be expected to journey through the mountain blizzards and the winter muck of this plain."

"Ah, can I hold my patience until they are here? What a joy to see a pretty face again and hear a female voice not coarsened with drink."

"Me, I am considering kicking my whore out on her fat behind. She snores. And with the Court on its way I can afford to be particular."

Muted guffaws. "God grant the Duchess of Najera brings all her fine daughters. Lucia, the prettiest one, looks quite kindly upon me."

There was a snicker and a voice said insinuatingly, "By the bones of St. Anthony here is a naive gallant! She looks kindly upon any *caballero* who fills out his codpiece hugely." More soft laughter.

A hand flew to the hilt of a sword, hackles rose, eyes glared.

"As for me," drawled another gentleman, "I shall pray Medina-Sidonia has summoned his red-headed mistress. A breathtaking piece, that one, and much too young for his aging joints. She'll look elsewhere for her fun this winter, I'll wager. . . ."

"Not at you, friend. Her eyes seem to favor those of us less windy and more suited to action. And better able to meet her expensive tastes, I might add."

Francho raised his eyes. He had to stay calm for the coming session with the King. But the conversation was beginning to rile him. It was crude and rude. For his part, when the Court reached Seville he had sent a truly abject note of apology to Dolores—for some reason it had taken him a few weeks to get over his strange anger at her—begging forgiveness for his boorish behavior and expressing the anxious hope that she would forgive him. Actually he had departed Seville almost as he arrived, accompanying the Count on a mission to the King of Portugal, and returning just in time to leave with the army for the summer campaign against the strategic city of Baza. So he could only hope that his genuinely contrite letter had moved her to forgive and forget the execrable episode in Toledo.

"And who is this vaunted *amada* you are all so hot about?" asked a very young gentleman who had only just joined his brother at Baza.

The first man answered, "Daughter of some petty Baron dead and moldering in the southern Extremadura, they say, but gently educated. Medina-Sidonia holds a county there, and the lady's lands interest him. And so, upon hearing of this poor, orphaned country lady's desire to go to Court, he finds it within his heart to add her to his cortege and present her to the Queen."

Another voice chimed in, "So the solicitous Duke takes the gentle maid's protection upon himself. No matter that she is a raving beauty with a lively manner to match. Just for pity's sake, you understand."

"And installed her in a small but fine house in Seville for when she is not on service with the Queen. Ah, the beneficence of pity!" mocked a third gallant.

"But her old servant told my sister's duenna that their entanglement was solely financial, her doddering old sire having left no instructions . . ."

The objecting voice was drowned out by guffaws all around. Francho listened stonily but silently, for what had they said that was not true? He credited the rage he felt beginning to gnaw at his innards as just the result of the suspense of awaiting Ferdinand's reaction.

The portiers were pushed aside and a latecomer entered. Abruptly the subject of conversation was changed.

Felipe de Guzman had been a member of the raiding party too, albeit a disgruntled and surly one since neither the idea nor the leadership was his. There was no doubt in Francho's mind that the Count of Perens and his coterie had gotten their share of marketable spoils, even though he had to admit Perens was one of the first to slam down his visor and spur his charger at the pursuing Moorish troops. Perens was not a coward. But he was an implacable rival for Leonora. Biting at the edge of his thumb, Francho withdrew again into his own musings, only half aware as Guzman greeted several of the group around the room and condescended to a few moments of aimless banter with them. Then Don Felipe seemed to address his main purpose and strolled over toward the group's ringleader with barely concealed antagonism.

223

Francho looked fully up to see the blond, clenched-jawed cavalier planted solidly before him, disdain lurking in the pale fox eyes.

"But soft, *amigos*," Felipe murmured. "Let us not disturb the sweet reveries of our friend Mendoza, pursuing vain dreams concerning his gentle cousin Doña Leonora, no doubt. Should we then intrude upon such hopeless fantasy?"

Francho unwound his frame with deliberate slowness, a cold light showing in his eyes. "So? Do you dare even mention my kinswoman in the same room where we have discussed your sire's *enamorata?*"

Felipe snapped his fingers loudly. "That! for my father's doxy. Should you disparage the Medina-Sidonia courage or military astuteness I would cut you down between two breaths, but the Duke's romantic liaisons move me not. And as for the lovely Zuniga," Perens continued, "her name is pure enough to remove the taint of coarseness from the room. But I advise you to dream no more, Mendoza, for the Court arrives here within the fortnight and the lady will shortly inform you her choice lies elsewhere."

"Upon you, no doubt?" Francho sneered. They stood glaring face to face, almost nose to nose.

"But of course. She merely plays with you to tease me, as any clever female would."

The hands of both men rested angrily upon the hilts of their swords. With a quick movement Francho unhooked the clasp of his short cape and flung it upon the bench behind him as Felipe almost casually undid the button of the high neck on his doublet. "And what makes you so certain of this, my lord Perens?" Francho growled. The other *caballeros*, aware of the intense rivalry between these two for the attentions of Leonora de Zuniga, fixed eager eyes upon one, then the other. "What makes you so certain that my sensible cousin would seriously consider so fabricating and posturing a churl as you?"

Perens ground out his answer. "And think you she'd rather a come-lately bravo who was tucked up like a trembling coward with his studies for years, while the rest of us took care the Moors did not disturb his trances?"

They sprung apart, swords snickering out of their scabbards. Francho advanced a pace, belligerent. "I'll push those words down your verminous gullet!"

Felipe twirled the point of his sword. "Take care, jester. I am aching to cut your pretty face. 'Twill give my lady pause even to look at you."

"Come on then, braggart, here is the sharp edge of my sword. Avoid it if you can."

Lumpy Juan Pimentel, Count of Bonavente, ranged himself behind Perens, an ugly smirk on his pocked face. "Go to, Don Felipe," he urged, "these new ones always need heavy persuasion to make them keep their place." Bonavente was twenty-seven and married, but rumor had it he kept his homely wife as pristine as a maiden and dallied instead with the servants' little boys.

Quietly Antonio de la Cueva stepped behind Francho. "This is not your battle, Bonavente. Nor even your place. You do much better in a nursery shucking unripe infants."

With a snarl Bonavente flashed his sword and launched a clumsy assault upon de la Cueva, who, weapon in hand, danced away and circled, as if baiting a stupid bear.

At the same instant Felipe struck out at Francho with a violent sideways slash designed to separate head from shoulders, but his stroke only rang loudly upon Francho's swift, strong blade, brought up and over as he jumped away from the blow. Felipe immediately pressed forward and launched another frontal assault.

The other men spread to the edges of the chamber to give the four duelists room and followed each stroke and parry with zestful attention. They had seen the pugnacious Perens wield his sword in other personal fights and knew his deadly ability. Francho had wiped his blade clean of Moorish blood numerous times and he had their respect for his daring in the field, but they had never assessed him in a private feud, where hate often deflected one's aim. Many of them were keen to discover how Pietro di Lido's pupil would fare against an opponent of Felipe de Guzman's experienced caliber.

But the enticing clash of steel upon steel and the juicy insults flung back and forth between the slashing protagonists were too much for some of the young bloods to bear passively. Luisa's detractor deliberately remarked within earshot of that maiden's swain that at least this duel was being fought over a woman whose honor was unquestionable, and for this effort was rewarded with a cry of rage and a spat out epithet. Two more weapons slithered from their scabbards. The circle widened.

Pressed savagely by Perens, Francho yielded, trying to gain enough time to be sure of his enemy's methods before launching his own offensive, cursing silently the other fighters who crowded him. Perens's technique seemed to pair ferocious attack with inviting recession, a combination meant to catch a clumsy opponent off guard for the ensuing, vicious onslaught. Francho, counting on his ability to parry the powerful slices, determined to stay on the defensive until Perens wore out a bit, and then he would strike back with di Lido's befuddling method of feint-sidestep-lunge to the heart.

Amidst cries of encouragement and advice the tension increased, threatening to turn the three small wars in which at first only injury was meant into more deadly contests.

At that moment the door curtains were roughly shoved aside and the Grand Constable barged in, his eyes popping with wrath, followed by three royal guards with lowered poleaxes. "Stop this! By the orders of Their Majesties, I say cease! Lay down your swords at once, gentlemen, or I shall arrest you all." He motioned to the guards to advance on the combatants. The swords were lowered grudgingly. The Count of Haro's face was purple. "How dare you break the King's law in his own house? A monstrous breach, *señores,* and were I not ashamed to inform His Majesty of this infantile behavior on the part of his noble gentlemen, I would clap you all in the dungeons to reflect on your temerity. How do you dare, sirs!"

The men who had been dueling scowled, resheathed their swords, and said nothing. The guards lifted their poleaxes, one not fast enough to suit the vicious Bonavente, who with a powerful blow and a curse knocked the weapon up in the man's hands. The spectators, though, were incensed, for although Haro was entirely within his office in stopping the imbroglio, he had no excuse to be so ruffled except his own pomposity. In spite of the royal edict against dueling, personal fights went on little abated even if sub rosa, and the Grand Constable knew it.

Now the thick door to the inner chamber opened and the King's chief secretary, Don Manuel Sorrolla, appeared and nodded at the twenty-odd *caballeros* in the anteroom. Resettling and brushing off their clothes, the duelists wiped the sullenness from their faces, and then, as a group, filed past Sorrolla and into the frowning royal presence.

Francho thought his ears would scorch under Ferdinand's

vehement lecture on insubordination. The angry ruler hurled his words like firebrands, burning his displeasure deep into their souls, the ten-minute storm even included a menacing description of the punishment awaiting anyone discovered engaging in private duels, for the muted sounds of swordplay had not escaped the royal notice.

The King finally wiped his brow with a silk kerchief and paused for breath, sternly surveying the contritely bowed heads battered by his tirade. Well, that was sufficient. They would remember his wrath for a long time. Now what he really wanted was to hear a detailed account of the spur-of-the-moment venture which had so enriched his larder and treasury. "Don Antonio de la Cueva. We would appreciate from you a full report of this midnight sortie, sir," he demanded.

Francho observed the relish with which Ferdinand listened to de la Cueva's colorful accounting of their foray, and in spite of his chastened condition his admiration waxed again for this king, who was, before all, a warrior. But he felt heat rise in his face each time Antonio cited him as leader during several crucial spots in the venture and the hooded royal stare shifted to him, as it finally also did to Hernando del Pulgar. After a vivid description of their violent surprise attack at the narrow part of the trail and the thundering clash with the Moors which threw the enemy into complete disarray and caused them to panic and turn tail, leaving their injured to be stripped and added to the shackled prisoners, de la Cueva's narrative came to an end. The young nobleman bowed and stepped back, but although his eyes were still chastened from the foregoing tongue-lashing, the pride in his voice and the set of his shoulders could not be missed.

There was a pause, and some uncomfortable shifting.

"My lords. Señores," Ferdinand finally rumbled. But the severity had left his tone, replaced by a more ringing pitch. And then, with a triumphant pound of his fist against his table and an elated grin from ear to ear, Ferdinand's fighting nature which so endeared him to his men emerged. "By Saint Anthony's bones, a splendid and victorious undertaking, gentlemen. I congratulate you all, each one of you, on your courage and audacity. And on the morrow in the ground before our manse, be it rain or no rain, we will cause a great ceremony to be held, to show the appreciation of your

Monarchs and your country for your great valor. *Señores,* I salute you!" And the King rose up with such vigor his heavy chair fell over backward.

Outside, as the relieved group of men dispersed to their well-earned midday meal, Antonio drawled to his cronies, "That furious outburst had me convinced we might barely escape the headsman."

Francho rubbed his neck wryly and began a cocky answer but let it die in his throat as the Count of Perens strode past. Francho's eyes locked with the malevolent, almost colorless pale blue ones in a hard stare.

"We are not yet finished, Mendoza," Perens grated from stiff lips.

"My pleasure, my lord," Francho growled in invitation. "At any time." His lip curled and he watched with undisguised dislike as Perens, followed by his cohorts, stalked on.

"You had scarce joined the Court when he decided you were anathema to him. Is it solely the hand of Doña Leonora that causes such rancor between the two of you?" Pulgar asked curiously as he stood beside Francho.

Francho raised his big shoulders in a slight shrug. "Perhaps he does not like the cut of my clothes. Who knows? I know of no other reason for enmity between us."

But he did and now it was on his own part. Along with his jealousy that the icy Count of Perens would even claim that Leonora showed him serious consideration, there was the sharp thrust of rage that had stabbed his breast when the viper had dared to call Dolores a doxy, a term reserved for the lowest whore. He would allow no one, no one to insult Papa el Mono's daughter. And so there were two causes, at least, prodding him to swear to himself to grind Felipe de Guzman's soulless face in the dirt one day.

⁓ *Chapter 10* ⁓

CIDI YAHYE, WIPING grease from his mustache with a linen napkin, contemplated the remains of the delicious midday meal of roast lamb and pepper sauce he had just enjoyed and realized disgruntledly that it was probably his last until the blockade was lifted. And it would be lifted, in spite of the enemy's brave show of provisioning the past few months. The Christians, he felt certain, would yet give up their unheard-of six-month siege and wearily depart to the comfort of their homes and families for the winter. Any day now, and certainly before the snow closed the passes.

At that moment footsteps pattered across the tiled floor of the arabesqued chamber where he dined, and he looked up to see his pantalooned aide and several of his captains hurrying toward him. "Yes, what is it?" he growled out.

"Your Excellence, please come quickly to the ramparts," his adjutant panted. "There is a strange Christian cavalcade coming down into the valley from the north. It is not merely one of their supply trains. You will want to see it for yourself."

Calmly putting down his napkin, the commander of the city of Baza rose from his cushions. "Very well, Ali Mansour. The Amatana Gate tower, our highest point, is where I shall view this apparition." He asked no questions, for since his adjutant

229

rarely became agitated it was best to consider immediately
what had so shaken him.

The jog up the hundreds of steps inside the great, square
tower was nothing to Yahye in spite of his girth; he made it a
practice to ascend in a run to the battlements several times a
day to survey the valley, although there was little to see
besides the smoke fires from the enemy camps and the daily
skirmishes his captains mounted to harass them. Skirmishes
only; his commanders were under orders to waste as few lives
as possible in these short battles. The city was fast running out
of food, true, but his people were with their families in
comfortable and familiar surroundings. *They* could last the
few weeks until bad weather, disease, fever, and restlessness
would surely drive the cooped up Spanish to retreat.

From the Amatana tower, however, his disbelieving eyes
told him a different story. And all about him, on the battlements, the tallest housetops, and mosque towers, the turbaned
inhabitants of Baza jostled pop-eyed to get a view of the great,
shining column of riders slowly coming from the northwest
hills toward the Christian camps.

The wind brought to his ears the distant flourishes of
trumpets, flutes, and bells which accompanied the Spanish
procession. Shading his eyes from the sun, Yahye made out in
the van, under the fluttering white tower-on-crimson of the
house of Trastemare, an imperious, magnificently robed lady
riding a large white mule, the animal so bedecked in golden
trappings that they brushed along the ground. "Their Queen,
Isabella," he muttered, feeling shaken, and experiencing a
sudden indigestion not brought on by the fatty lamb.

Familiar with the Christian Court, he believed that the
smaller figures riding on Isabella's right were her daughter, the
fourteen-year-old Infanta Isabel in shining satin and jewels,
and the Infante Juan, the little Prince of Asturias and heir to
the throne, clad in a miniature suit of armor. On the Queen's
left could only be the powerful Grand Cardinal Mendoza,
whose red robes and cloak spilled over his glossy black charger
like lapping fire, and whose steady hand supported a tall,
gilded pole topped with a gem-encrusted, golden cross. A long
train of splendidly dressed noblewomen followed, most of
them on horse or muleback but some traveling in brightly
painted litters with arms-emblazoned curtains. Many of the
ladies wore green- or red-dyed fur cloaks full enough to drape
over their animals' haunches.

An honor guard of armored, high-ranking *hidalgos* with plumed helmets and closed visors cantered as escort to the ladies, and behind all this rode hundreds of gentlemen, squires, soldiers, and pages in a long, straight line whose rear guard had barely gotten clear of the hills. Over their proud heads flew the multicolored banners and pennants and guidons of Christian Spain.

"May Allah preserve us," muttered one of Cidi Yahye's captains. "They bring their women to camp. And with baggage and hundreds of beasts of burden laden with extra supplies. What means this?"

With leaden heart Cidi Yahye continued to stare at the distant procession. Presently a company of cavaliers burst from the gates of the Christian camp to meet the Queen's train. These were soon followed by Ferdinand in great pomp, attended by his commanders and other grandees, many of whom Yahye had met as peer in long ago tourneys between Spain and Granada, when peace still held. From the Christian camp cries of joy pierced the air, and they could see caps and helms and headgear being flung to the sky in jubilation.

Yahye had viewed enough, and he turned away from the glittering message which Ferdinand had so clearly delivered him. He saw his captains watching him, waiting for some pronouncement. Swallowing hard he said, "You know as well as I what this portends: that the fate of Baza is decided. Warriors of the Crescent, pray Allah to show us mercy. The enemy intends never to leave our gates until he triumphs."

Ali Mansour quivered to see his Prince's eyes dead as stones. "Excellence! We can best them yet. At your order our entire force can ride out and throw themselves upon that arriving column; we can decimate them and beat back whatever army Ferdinand sends to their aid. We can—"

"No! I prohibit it!" Cidi Yahye's dark face sagged under the shadowy droop of his mustaches. "To what avail murder their women and old men? Their message is clear: they are so well provisioned they can maintain their whole Court in camp and not relent until we behind our walls are all dead of starvation. I am a Prince and Caliph of this city. I must think of my people. I will not bring retribution down on their heads."

Another captain groaned, "What about Gaudix or Granada? Perhaps if we hold out there will be succor . . . ?"

This, at least, brought a spark of outrage into Yahye's eyes. "You saw the communication we had from El Zagal. He is without an adequate force to break the blockade, so he says. He is powerless to save us. Or unwilling, if you will have the truth. Yet, perhaps the Sultan . . . But I am not a fool. I will not deceive myself about deliverance until all hope of lenient negotiation is past." Bitterly he surveyed his white-lipped captains. "Hear me, I forbid any attack or insult upon the Christian cavalcade. Their Queen, a lady of valor, is among them. Let us demonstrate that Moslems do not lack the courtesy of proud men. We do not war upon women."

To hide the tears of vexation that sprang to his eyes he turned again, with his mingled feelings of astonishment, grief, and awe, to the mighty demonstration of Ferdinand's confidence. The people of Baza too began to understand their predicament, and a low keening started from their throats. The muezzins in the mosque towers commenced wailing. *"Allah acbar . . . eched en la ila ella Allah, eched en Mohammed rasou Allah . . ."*

But the point of the horizon in the direction of Mecca toward which all of the frightened, turbaned faithful turned their eyes was unluckily directly in line with the grandiose Christian procession as it began to veer off toward the southern camp.

Francho was lucky. When the Court arrived he was at some distance beyond the camp, behind a small rise where he often went with his equerry, Ebarra, so they could converse in Arabic without being overheard in order to keep up his fluency. At the first glimpse of the spectacular cortege just emerging from the shadow of the mountains, he clapped on his helmet, leaped onto his horse, and galloped out to meet it. As he rode past the ranks of the procession he saluted the exuberant, gaily waving ladies, greeting the ones he knew, but he scanned their number carefully until he finally found the one he sought. Immediately he insinuated himself into the escort bordering the column, blessing his good fortune to be so well ahead of Ferdinand's official welcoming party—and his rival.

"Santa María Purissima! Where did you drop from, *señor?"* Leonora de Zuniga laughed, smiling up into devilish blue eyes shining from under the burnished steel of a plumed helmet.

For a moment Francho just drank in the delicate gold and white beauty of his lady, who was wrapped against the chill coming off the mountain in a cloak of pale brown fur, a few tendrils of honey-colored hair whipped back charmingly against her hood. He felt besotted with the very sight of Leonora's winsome face. The sound of her sweet voice enchanted him. Already he felt himself free from the depressing grip of a loneliness no blowsy campfollower could lessen.

"My lady," he began, wondering if the words would come out clearly from his paralyzed throat. "My dearest Doña Leonora, I have lurked behind every bush and rock in this valley for days on end, just awaiting the scent of your perfume to tell me you were near."

Her dimples flashed into being and turned him lightheaded with joy.

"Ah, knave, a very pretty story, but do you expect me to believe you would suffer the cold of night and the hard ground on my account? 'Tis very flattering."

"There is nothing, nothing I would not gladly suffer on your account, *doña,* and so do you know it. I have missed you, Leonora."

She blushed prettily and cast down her dancing amber eyes. "I understand you are to be addressed as *Don* Francisco now, and I am happy to congratulate you, cousin. I am truly sorry we were not in time for the knighting ceremony."

"*Sí,* and so am I, for it was splendid," Francho recalled, unable to hide his pride. "The King wore his grand robes of royal purple and ermine over his ceremonial armor, and our entire complement of grandees and *hidalgos* and prelates attended, even the old Archbishop of Seville in his teetering jeweled miter, and so every merchant, equerry, attendant, and common soldier in camp who could crane a neck to see past the gathered nobility. My friend Hernando del Pulgar was knighted by His Majesty as well, and assigned to bear on his arms a lance with a red kerchief. And as for Antonio de la Cueva, for he is already a Marquis and standing to inherit his father's dukedom, he was heavily praised for his leadership and presented with a most richly caparisoned, magnificent charger."

"Oh, could I have just witnessed it," Leonora enthused. "Especially as I have heard that the King praised you most fulsomely for rallying your wavering band against a superior force and turning those cravens into heroes. I was very proud of you."

For such tribute, for the admiration shining from her eyes, he would have attacked all four hundred Moors alone, even though her approval made color rise in his face. "Lady, how did you hear of this so fast? It happened only several days ago."

"You must not be so modest. Everyone has heard of the 'midnight foray.' Do you forget that our Monarchs are connected by swift couriers?"

A distant shout now took his attention, and he spied riders coming toward them from the camp. His time alone with Leonora was short. He leaned from his saddle to speak closer to her fur-enveloped ear, at the same time delighting his eyes with the smooth texture of her soft cheek, pink with cold. "You have grown more beautiful since I last saw you, *doña,* if such is possible." His voice was husky.

Leonora looked up at him sideways. "And I've grown more worldly too, *señor.* I no longer let pretty words and smooth phrases turn my head."

"I have never uttered a word to you I didn't mean sincerely, with all my heart."

She held on to the forward cantle of her saddle as her mule stumbled upon a rock. Recovering, she responded lightly, "But I have learned that of times the head is not completely in tune with the air the heart is singing."

It was meant to be a cryptic remark but Francho knew clearly what she meant. He had already professed his undying love to her, in Toledo, in Seville, but not a word further than that. Yet, how could he say more with his future so questionable? He was afraid she might believe that with his high-ranking name and Tendilla's large fortune to inherit perhaps he was seeking a more politically strong marriage. And did she love him? He thought so, but a maid of her station ordinarily would not declare her feelings without strong proof of a wooer's good faith and *Sangre de Dios,* he had never even kissed her, damn the watchful eyes of the old lady assigned to act as *duena* to her. The most they'd done was to sit and whisper on benches in the palace garden, furtively holding hands.

He resolved to make a quick, positive move to gain her, even if he had to reveal his thorny position. He reached out for one of her gloved hands, viewing her with his half-frown, hoping she could read his adoration of her in the depths of his eyes. "Some day, dear heart, I will sing my song so sweetly to you that even your marble heart will melt, and you will surely know who loves you best."

"Ah, indeed," she murmured, "I have always admired music, cuz." But she squeezed his gauntleted hand, and he did not miss her message.

The first of the welcoming party galloped up to salute the Queen, and the entire train halted. "Tomorrow night," Francho said to Leonora urgently, "tomorrow night we must meet privately for I have many things to tell you. And in this you dare not say me nay."

She withdrew her hand from his grip for decorum's sake, but her smile and the light in her eyes were warm. "And why would I want to say you nay, Don Francisco?" she flirted. Their eyes held. They smiled at each other, then rode on in companionable silence as the column moved forward again.

The cortege was escorted into camp amidst the noisy acclaim of *caballeros* and commoners alike, the ladies sitting their mounts proudly, delighted at the cheers of welcome from the jubilant men. They halted in the large square before Ferdinand's wooden headquarters, hardly a palace but a remarkably large building for a war camp and now even larger, with a newly built wing to accommodate the women in the train of the Queen and the Infanta. The rest of the female nobility had been assigned to quarters with their husbands or kinsmen, or, in coveys of two and three for propriety's sake, to the larger houses among the commanders.

The Queen was assisted to dismount, by means of a wooden stepstool, by her beaming husband and by the dukes of Medina-Sidonia and Albuquerque. The other nobles and *caballeros* saw to their wives and sisters and sweethearts, and a band of beaming monks and ecclesiastics surrounded the Grand Cardinal Mendoza. A billeting committee met the other arriving gentlemen and their servants.

Swinging from his saddle, Francho held up his arms to Leonora and she leaned toward him, laughing at the rakish quirk of his black eyebrow. He lifted her lightly down from her mule and blessed both their enveloping cloaks that allowed him to boldly slide her body along his without undue exhibition. He expected a rebuke for the irresistible liberty, but there came none. Now impatience grabbed him. "Leonora, I meant what I said. I must speak with you."

They stood quite close, for in the commotion no one noticed that his hands still spanned her waist under the fur cloak. He knew the pretty pink coloring her cheeks was not just from the wind.

"Speak then, sir; your words are always charming," she coquetted lightly.

"Not here, certainly," he grumbled, wanting first to shake her and then to hug her. "Tomorrow. Or the next night. Alone. I will arrange a meeting place. Surely you can manage to give your *duena* the blind eye for an hour?" They both noticed Felipe de Guzman approaching swiftly and they stepped apart.

But not before she quickly whispered, " 'Tis strange, sir, but my *duena* sleeps *most* soundly right after the copious wine served at a feast. Mayhap fetch me then?" With a saucy tilt of her head and a rustle of silk, Leonora turned the full force of her dimpled smile on the bare-headed, steel-chested Perens, who first glowered at Francho and then bent to press a lingering kiss to Leonora's gloved hand. There was a short, two-sided, and uncomfortable conversation in which Leonora spoke first to Felipe and then to Francho, while the two men carefully kept their eyes only on her. Then, spying Doña Maria being helped from her litter, Leonora fluttered, "I fear I must beg leave of your gallant company, *señores,* but I would speak to my mother before the Infanta claims my attendance."

Felipe took swift advantage. "I should be pleased to escort you to your distinguished dame, *doña,* if I may offer my arm?"

"Most kind, Don Felipe," Leonora accepted politely and laid her light hand on the velvet-covered ropy muscles of the Count of Perens's arm, which he held stiffly crooked for her. With a soft "Don Francisco" and a quick, meaningful smile of farewell, she moved off with Perens to join her mother.

Francho stood looking after them, wondering why he always felt so—incomplete, was the only word that came to his mind—after every encounter with Leonora. He resolved once and for all to define their situation clearly with her. His thoughts on what he was going to do were so riveted that de la Cueva, the amiable and brash, had to clap him twice on the shoulder to get his attention.

"There she is, more bewitching than ever. Did you see her? Did you see how he hustled her off?" Antonio's eyebrows wriggled with mock lust. "*Madre mía,* what delectable lips, what divine form . . ."

For a second Francho thought his friend meant Leonora. But he quickly erased his glare as he saw Antonio was looking in another direction. "Who?" he asked, his mood on the rise. "What poor virgin must run from your clutches now?"

"No maiden this, I'll wager, so all the more intriguing." Antonio flipped his head toward the retreating form of a cloaked and hooded lady attentively escorted by the Duke of Medina-Sidonia. The tall, graceful woman was trailed by an old *dueña* and four servants staggering with baggage.

"That looks to be the Baroness de la Rocha. I had no idea you were so smitten by her, my lord." Francho said this affably enough but in fact he was actually uncomfortable. He didn't like discussing Dolores, even with his good friend.

"Pah, Francisco, do you live cocooned in a woolen mitten? Granted you spent little time with the Court in Seville this spring, but she threatened to outdo even your Leonora in the count of admirers who wrote her poems and sang her ballads and would have been glad to lay themselves down beneath her feet. Me too. But my lord Medina-Sidonia is so jealous he watches her as carefully and dangerously as a starving mountain cat."

The truth was Francho had glimpsed Dolores earlier, for she had already arrived at the square just as he and Leonora rode in. She was being helped to dismount by several eager gentlemen, Medina-Sidonia finding it necessary to first greet his Duchess, and her eyes were wide and sparkling in the high color of her gorgeous, glowing face, reddish locks whipping from her hood in the wind. He saw her lips form words as she bantered with the delighted gallants who handed her down, and the quick memory of how passionately those lips could kiss had shaken him. He had an angry impulse to stalk over to the laughing group and lay about him with the flat of his sword to scatter the greedy bees that swarmed to the welcoming honeypot, but convulsively quashed both the recollection of her mouth and his reaction, with a furtive glance at Leonora who was fortunately looking elsewhere at the moment than at him. Yet he still felt ashamed of his previous cruelty to Dolores, and contrite, and he didn't count the short note he had written to her as enough. He really wanted her forgiveness. He would try to speak to her personally as soon as a moment presented itself.

Now he warned Antonio, "Beware, my friend, you almost didn't come out in one piece the last time you tasted somebody else's wine."

"Devil take it, if I'm going to be bludgeoned into marrying that silly Countess de Moulines for the sake of her relation to the French throne, I might as well enjoy myself while there's still a chance. But not with the beauteous Doña Dolores, believe me. I have no care to tangle with Medina-Sidonia."

Francho grinned, stamping his feet against the cold. The sun was disappearing behind a wall of gray clouds sailing in from the west; they could see their breath now on the damp, chill air. "No one could bludgeon you into anything, Antonio, even your worthy sire. The daughter of Monsieur l'Ambassadeur pleases you well enough, but you're too stubborn to admit it. And she's too well guarded to admit you!"

Antonio grinned back wryly. "Aha! I see my father has another voice of reason on his side. Well, come on, Mendoza, I can use some spiced wine to help me contemplate the swift approach of the marriage bonds. And this cursed damp is creeping into my bones."

"Lead on, friend, but not for too long. I have some arrangements to accomplish before tomorrow's grand fiesta." They strode off together, away from the square filled with the throng of the newly arrived and their welcomers and shouting servants endeavoring to sort out the baggage mules.

The ancient hand curved like a claw shot out to grab Dolores's wrist as she walked by the group perched on benches about a brocade-covered gaming table. She looked down to see the rice powder-coated visage of the Duchess of Dimonales grinning up at her, an elderly wheeze in a threadbare, droopy-sleeved gown thirty years out of date but with a large pile of gold coins heaped up at her place. "Ah, my dear pretty Doña Dolores, join us, join us, add your dear charming presence to our little party!" the insistent Doña Teresa spluttered, not releasing her hold on the slim wrist.

Dolores, feeling exquisitely fragile-looking that night in a becoming gown of pale lavender velvet embroidered with silver nettle leaves, her hair coiled under a turbanlike hat of matching silk, had no idea why the wealthy harridan had always seemed to favor her from the moment she joined the Court. In return Dolores had always taken pains to be pleasant to the poor old thing, whose tenacious grip on life seemed only occasioned by her greedy love for gambling. Dolores smiled at the invitation but thought she would say no. For one, her Queen had retired early, ostensibly to rest the remains of a chest croup, which had freed her ladies to mingle with the indefatigable courtiers greeting each other in the hall of the encampment's royal quarters. Dolores was being trailed about—in Medina-Sidonia's absence—by several gentlemen whom she traded banter with and who were happy for the least flirtatious glance from her.

For another she wasn't fond of gambling, although the gentlemen, so long away from frivolous pursuits, were full of siege talk tonight, which did not amuse her either. Bursts of happy laughter came from various parts of the big hall, rising over the piping harmonies of musicians on the wooden balcony, everyone so exhilarated at the reuniting of the Court that in spite of the grueling journey that had just ended that afternoon and the fact that a formal celebration was planned for the following night no one seemed tired. She wanted to keep flitting from one group to another, the better to accidently bump into Francisco de Mendoza, who seemed, so far, to be nowhere about. But then again, neither was the prim little Zuniga, although Dolores felt assured that was because the Infanta was always cranky and indisposed after a trip and kept her ladies about her in her quarters.

She was on the point of politely refusing when her glance took in the other players at the table, the rakish Count of Valencia; a sallow young prelate in a purple skullcap and brocade robe; a large, bluff man with a rugged face whom she thought was a da Silva, and— Her eyes locked momentarily with the pale blue, contemptuous gaze of Don Felipe de Guzman.

Perens rose with a sinuous movement, a thin smile on his lips, and surprised her by joining the old dame's coaxing. "It would give us great pleasure if you would enter our game, Doña Dolores. We are short one person to make the betting more interesting." He indicated a place on the bench next to Valencia, whose wide hat sported two peacock feathers quivering behind. "Honor us by being seated, if you will."

Caught off guard Dolores could only answer the oily invitation with an inane echo, "By being seated?"

His eyes glittered at her from under a lank blond fringe of hair that almost concealed them, but his rangy frame, clad in a short, fur-trimmed doublet, stood relaxed, and he projected a casual air. "Surely you know how to play Riba-bajo? Even in Extremadura they must teach it to the children. Your beauty, Baroness, added to Doña Teresa's"—and here he nodded

239

affably to the shrewd-eyed old number chewing on her gums
—"will bring radiance to our corner. Why not test your good
fortune then? No reason for it to desert you tonight."

In the face of his caustic smile Dolores found her balance
again. She understood his aim was to humiliate her by pitting
her relative inexperience—or so he thought—against these
facile players. He would be evilly pleased if she lost a large
sum. It was only lately she had realized that his barely
concealed hostility arose because of his father's expenditure
of what Felipe suspected was inordinate sums of money on
her, a policy the Duke had never been known to pursue before
and one that annoyed his often financially strapped heir. Her
gorge rose, as it always did around Felipe.

Still, she hesitated. She did not mind sitting with the other
ladies attending the Queen and playing cards, but only for
maravedis and with a modest limit, for she hated to lose and
so she couldn't help cheating. Papa el Mono's skill at palming
cards had gained him enough gold to buy the inn when he was
young until one day the business end of a knife skewered to
the table both his hand and the cards secreted in its curve,
crippling the hand and his gambling career together since he
did not like dice. But such harsh penalty for being detected
didn't deter him from showing the children he raised every
dishonest way he knew to assure the desired fall of the cards,
and he insisted they practice until they mastered them.
Dolores had turned out best at it for her hands were smaller
and quicker than the two older boys and she thought faster
than Pepi.

She saw Don Felipe still looking at her, challenge in the flare
of his narrow nostrils. Still she was torn. She could not afford
the slightest hint of taint of cheating on her reputation,
cheating was for peasants, she thought.

The Duchess dragged on her wrist again. "Come,
Doña . . ."

"Of course, if it would sorely distress your purse . . ."
Felipe drawled.

She began to lose her temper with his veiled intimidation.
So he thought he would clean her out, did he?

Her glance took in that the empty place at the table backed
up against a wall; there would be no one behind her. She
deliberately tossed her head with the careless vanity he
expected from her, retrieved her wrist, and slid past the
politely standing Valencia to take her seat. Pleased with

himself Felipe presented the two players she didn't know, the Bishop of Albi, who smiled at her to show two missing teeth, and Don Jaime da Silva, pleasantly hearty.

Widening her eyes Dolores told them, "I'm not very experienced with gambling, but I'll do my best not to hold up the play."

"But you are already," the Duchess complained, suddenly turning testy. "Come then, sirs, if you insist on inviting amateurs, wager up, wager up." Her hand, with its yellowed, dirt-embedded nails, hovered over her untidy heap of *excellentes* and silver *reales.*

In a belated afterthought Dolores fished the silk pouch from her pocket and was dashed to realize she hadn't nearly enough money in it to buy the time necessary to prepare her ambush of the offensive Perens. *Diantre!*

But Felipe hadn't taken his eyes off her. Red spots of color rode his pale cheeks. "Is there something that bothers you, my lady?"

"Well, perhaps I am not entirely prepared . . . I did not expect . . ."

"A signed note would be honored—"

"A—a—ah, my lord! We have determined we do not play with paper," the Duchess objected.

"Too easily abrogated in the confusion and danger of war," the slightly built Bishop explained softly, adding his smug, gapped smile.

Dolores bit the inside of her lip in vexation, but Felipe leaned forward and with too nonchalant an attitude indicated with his chin the brooch pinned on her bodice. "What about that? If you run out of funds you could wager with that bauble."

Dolores looked down at the beautiful brooch the Duke had presented her with, a tower wrought of gold laid against a crescent moon of diamonds, with a narrow band of diamonds at its base representing a moat and a teardrop-shaped pearl pendant below. She placed her hand over it defensively. "This is most valuable," she declared.

"That is no worry," Felipe countered smoothly. "When the time comes I promise you it will be most valuably matched."

"Don Felipe is a gentleman who always keeps his word," the old lady growled impatiently. "Let us then continue our business."

Dolores squared back her shoulders and gave Felipe a

disdainful smile. Very well. Since the weasel was so anxious to skin her alive she was going to let him think he could. She drew a gold coin from her bag and tossed it into the center, the Duchess cackled and followed suit and so did the others and the game began, idle spectators collecting about them. From time to time Dolores pulled her lace-trimmed kerchief from where it was tucked in the flared sleeve which overlapped her wrist and dabbed it delicately at her nose.

Riba-bajo was simplicity itself, with each person dealt three cards, two hidden and one showing, the object being to match the random "high" or "low," called before the deal by the person to the dealer's left, with the numerical score of one's cards. Betting was done before each card was dealt. It was a swift game of chance, the only skill required being the ability to fool opponents into thinking one held a better hand than they and forcing them out. It was a perfect pastime for inveterate gamblers who didn't care to think—and for manipulators who didn't care to lose, especially since the ace of the spade suit counted either as double fourteen or as one.

Dolores kept up a constant murmur of comment to herself as she played, wriggled in her seat, tapped her nails on the stiffened parchment of the small, square, handpainted cards. She was glad that Valencia had the annoying habit of humming under his breath and that Don Jaime's nervous foot tapping shook the table a little. She laughed, she groaned, she chattered brightly between deals about events on the trip, anything to be diverting. And she deliberately lost the first two games with very stupid bets. The Duchess looked at her with scorn, the Bishop with pity as he hauled in his winnings. Perens kept his gaze averted from her, but his hard mouth turned up slightly at the corners.

Doña Teresa shuffled and dealt. "Now that my lady de la Rocha has got her feet wet, let us open wider the spigot, so to speak," she wheezed, and raised her bet considerably.

Dolores began to feel hot. She needed to seem a witless player and a loser, but she also needed to stay with the game for a while, especially until she got the deal. The problem was she was going to run out of money. She'd have to win one of the better pots to stay alive. She prepared by nattering away to the disinterested gamblers about savages in Africa she'd heard used cards made of human skin. . . .

No one seemed to have good cards on the next deal, the

betting was small. Dolores dabbed at her nose, then retucked her kerchief. She was about out of money.

"Have you an ague of the head, my child?" the Bishop inquired pleasantly, drawing up more coins from his embroidered purse.

"It rained so heavily through most of our trip, Your Grace. Even the Queen, whose health is always so robust, Lord be thanked, suffered a bad croup."

"Tsk, tsk," the prelate clucked, but he was much more interested in what cards were coming his way.

Dolores kept glancing at Perens, as if she were trying to read from his face how good his cards were. She was glad to see he obliged her show of naiveté and passed a false expression across his features, as if his hand were not outstanding. She knew he was too good a player to show such giveaway reactions and she allowed herself an interior laugh. Tucking away her kerchief she bet the last of her money on a low call, with a two showing before her. When the last card was dealt and she showed her hand she had won, with a four. Don Jaime grabbed a goblet of wine from a passing lackey's tray to help him mourn his near miss with a five. Felipe flicked Dolores a coldly amused look. "You seem to be learning to play this game, *doña*. How clever of you," he rasped softly.

"Women are good at playing games, my lord. That is all we are allowed to do," she sniffed.

She'd won twenty-four gold excellentes and eight reales, enough to buy herself three new gowns, but she was only beginning. It was going to take at least several deals to palm the cards she needed and slip them up her sleeve via the handkerchief, a glass-smooth, lightning-quick sleight-of-hand she helped cover by clucking at her cards, giggling, smiling seductively at the men, keeping her opponents attention off balance with chatter about the games she'd played during her convent years. She lost several times again, showing not much better gambling luck than before.

She received the deal finally, fumbled the shuffle (and, as if it were invisible, the powerful ace of spades disappeared into the curve of her palm). With the deck in hand she wiggled around on her stool, carried away by excitement (a king, minutely marked in the middle of the deck by her little finger, found its way to the top of the pile and in a second joined the ace) and then awkwardly tried to deal as fast as the others had

243

with an embarrassed laugh (giving herself undetected two cards together, one of which joined the others in the same place where she had kept the two aces that had won her the excellentes).

She did nothing more unusual on this deal and Don Felipe took the stakes. Now she had only two excellentes on the table before her. Shrugging ruefully she turned up her hands to signify she was out and then placed them on the table edge to lever herself up from the narrow space.

"I will not let you go from us empty-handed, Baroness. Surely another few deals will bring back your luck?" Don Felipe stayed her from rising by putting a hand over hers. She repressed an urge to jerk away. "Have you not the courage to lay your brooch on the table then, *doña?"* he challenged her.

"This brooch is worth over a thousand ducats," Dolores told him, frowning.

"Yes. I know that." His chilly stare was steady.

Valencia yawned. "Well. You can count me out, I haven't that much about me. In fact, does anyone?" He looked around the table and shrugged. No one did, and the Duchess made no move to remember the rings on her fingers. Dolores started to get up, but Felipe kept her hand pinned down.

"Wait. I do. This should make it worth your while and more." The Count of Perens rose and unbuckled the dagger belt around his waist, which brought all eyes and those of the casual onlookers standing behind them to the magnificent buckle securing the belt, a large, heavy fastening of gold with a wide silver tongue, paved all around with large, colored gemstones inlaid to spell G U Z on top, M A N on bottom. He drew the dagger, used the sharp blade to slit the leather strap and free the buckle, and then held the buckle out to her. "Here is *another* Guzman piece, my lady. Surely you will find it worthy a wager for yours. Two games out of three."

But Dolores's attention clung to what he'd said. "Another . . . ?"

Felipe continued favoring her with his insolent smile. "The brooch you wear. It is strangely identical with an heirloom jewel inherited by my father from his dear mother. Of course, it could not be such. Just a slip of the tongue, *doña* . . ."

But there were murmurings among the onlookers, a laugh, several giggles, and Don Jaime grinned.

Dolores saw black. She'd no idea the Duke had given her a Guzman family treasure, nor, she thought, had anyone else at

Court suspected such until now. The Duke was insensitive, his son a cad. All the joy was out of owning the lovely piece. She almost pricked her finger in her fumbling haste to undo it. She tossed it on the cloth, next to his buckle and then looked around boldly at the other players. "But why should we cut these fine companions from our game, eh, my lord? Why not let them bet with us to share in what money comes along with the stakes?" She shoved her last two excellentes beside the brooch.

Don Jaime banged the table with his fist. "Excellent idea, my lady, you are a most noble gamestress. What say you, Perens?"

Felipe hesitated a tiny second, looking at Dolores with a flicker of suspicion brought on by the sudden strength in her voice. But logic ruled. He shrugged and his expression became normal. "By all means . . ." And with a stiff little bow he acknowledged the toothlessly grinning Doña Teresa and took his seat. The old lady tossed out a ducat and the others followed with equivalent sums.

All around them the large hall reverberated with the sounds of music and chatter and laughter, even the deep barking of the King's hounds being teased with tidbits—a loud hum and swirl from which their own small corner seemed suddenly blanketed. On the cut of the deck Dolores won the deal. The interested idlers looking over their shoulders went quiet.

She was now controlling the game, no matter what happened, but she won the first game honestly, to some encouraging finger-snapping from her gallants. She felt the sweat trickle between her breasts and dampen the velvet bodice beneath her armpits. Her face felt moist. It was so *hot* in the crowded hall. At the same time she was exhilarated, delighted to know she hadn't lost her light-fingered dexterity, praying she was going to stitch the hateful Felipe's ears to his head. The giggle of a naughty child bubbled up inside of her.

She did not have to try to lose the second game, her cards were terrible. But she saw Felipe's hard mouth split into a smile as he handed her the shuffled deck, and so bright was the accompanying glitter of his eyes that she was taken aback for a second. He was such a scoundrel, it was not impossible that he had slipped a card from the deck too. Carefully smiling back with the silly confidence that had marked all her bad bets, she crushed her tiny bout with panic by remembering that after all she had the ace of spades. She pulled out her kerchief to pat her damp face and then picked up the deck to deal the third and last game.

"High," he rapped out. She dealt him the first card off the top for his open card. It was a high ace, as she had suspected it would be from his momentary indulgence in gloating. There was an excited murmur all around. "*Cielo*, Don Felipe, you have made the call well," she said, keeping up her patter.

Her own open card turned out to be a three, but that was all right, anything would do. She was glad for the Duchess of Dimonales's usual distracting antics, for when that worthy wasn't clapping her claws at another chance to bet she was hawking and spitting on the straw-strewn plank floor. As everyone began to sense Dolores a loser, the other players shoved more gold into the pot, betting with Don Felipe. Surprisingly, the usually canny Duchess bet with her, but Dolores had no time to wonder why.

Dolores dealt the last cards, then put down the deck, tucked her kerchief away, consulted her cards, and looked at Felipe.

His pale face glistened, and she could see a dark sweat stain on his velvet doublet when he raised his arm. Slowly he put down his two hidden cards face up on the table. First an ace, then another ace, added to the one already on the cloth, forty-two points. A gasp went up and muffled cries of excitement. Valencia laughed. Don Jaime's grin couldn't have been wider. But Doña Teresa hissed out, "Silencio! The play is not over," and for sympathy as much as courtesy all eyes turned to Dolores, who was showing only a three.

Her pulse was pounding in her temples like a hammer. She forced herself to a dignified demeanor, but she wanted to jump up and down with triumph. Raising her eyes from Felipe's almost unbeatable three aces, she kept up her pretense by smiling a little unsteadily at him. His mocking sneer was out in the open now. Relishing the drama she laid down one card next to her three, a king. The onlookers stirred. The Count of Perens's expression did not change, there was no way she could top his score.

Except one. To the wild beating of her heart she laid down next to the king the double-scored ace of spades, and her total was forty-four. She sat back, still smiling, but now there was a wicked sparkle in her eyes. Up went a universal gasp immediately turning into stunned cries and shouts of glee, and then all about her clapping and finger-snapping and congratulations.

"Lord, Lord, Thy ways are wondrous to behold," the little Bishop sighed over his lost money and gazed skyward.

"I love you, dear pretty lady," Doña Teresa shrieked, bobbing up and knocking her huge, old-fashioned hennin askew on the chin of an overhanging spectator. The old one raked the gold over to her and began to divide the money between Dolores and herself. The buckle and the brooch were left on the red brocade to glint in the bright light of the dozens of fat candles in the chandelier above.

Perens's abrasive personality had made him more enemies than friends at Court; he had never been well liked. He had learned to hold his emotions close to him. The first open-mouthed shock passed from his face in an instant, to be displaced by fury which was swiftly overlaid by his usual pale steeliness, and even Dolores had to admire the will it took for such poised recovery, for the jewel-studded buckle was no small loss. The Count of Perens, she suspected, would never allow a woman to think she had discomfited him. He stood up slowly and leaned over to casually riffle her winning cards with a long forefinger, which didn't bother her since the lower cards for which she'd substituted the king and ace she'd slipped safely back in the deck, along with the two in case he'd called "low." Then he stared into her eyes, and the malevolence that struck her made her almost sorry she had taken him on.

"Very well, *doña*, you have won," he conceded stonily. He indicated the buckle. "That is a keepsake I would rather not part with. I will send my valet to you tomorrow with the money to buy it back. That is, if you will permit?"

"Of course, my lord," Dolores nodded, in spite of herself unable to keep a certain preening from her voice. The fine gentleman tried to outcheat her? Weasel!

Pale-lashed lids blinked over his baleful stare. "Then I bid you good night, *doña*." He swept the money before him into his purse. "Doña Teresa? Gentlemen? Your Grace?" With a tilt of his head to the other gamers, Felipe spun about and pushed past the spectators to stride away, immediately joined on either side by two twittering, sympathetic ladies, who were eager to console him.

The people around began to lose interest and drift off. Dolores noticed the young Viscount of Mirabel quietly waiting for her off to one side, admiration and doglike devotion in his attitude. She rose, hastily sweeping the brooch, buckle, and coins into her kerchief. Now that it was over she wondered how smart it had been to have publicly bested the Duke's son, even just in a game of chance. Don Enrique seemed unaware of Felipe's dislike for her, and she had always felt it was best not to call the Duke's attention to this. Hoping Felipe would continue, for whatever reasons he had, to keep his feelings to himself, she made her apologies to the disappointed other three players for not giving them a chance to win something back and even though she'd been playing only twenty minutes, she claimed fatigue because it was true.

Tying up the corners of the kerchief she looked around to decide which way she would go, and consternation fell upon her like a disoriented flutter of wings, for even at a distance she could see the accusation in the pair of vivid blue eyes boring into hers. There was Francho, standing to her right, visible now that some others had drifted away. Virgin help her! How long had he been watching? She saw his head move back and forth in a barely perceptible but definite gesture of disapproval, and his cynically quirked eyebrow didn't help. His lips were pressed together in what could be taken for utter disgust. "The *gusano!*" she thought with guilty defiance. "Instead of judging me he should be impressed. That was a flashy bit of finger work, anybody would say." But she dropped her eyes quickly for this was not how she had thought she would meet him again.

Slipping the heavy kerchief into her pocket she bid the players and some new bettors who had joined them good night and then, with head held high, nose atilt, and an unnaturally brilliant smile, she glided off to the peace of her bed, in the opposite direction from the one person in the room who knew how ill gotten her gains were. She would just pretend he didn't exist.

Francho watched her go, and the mirth he'd been straining to hold in sputtered out of him. He threw back his head and laughed. What a skinning she'd given Perens. He sobered after a moment, though. He had absolutely no sympathy for her victim, of course, but what bothered him was why Dolores seemed willing to stick her hand in the wasp's nest of Felipe's personality. His laughter turned into an annoyed sigh. She had no idea of what she was about. He'd have to keep an eye out to see she didn't get stung too badly.

* * *

Francho's nose was out of joint. The headquarters hall for communal feasting had been hastily enlarged for the banquet but even so there was not enough room for all to be accommodated at the long U-shaped tables and so almost one hundred of the newer knights and untitled younger sons were asked to arrive later to dance and watch the entertainment. Francho was one of these.

When he was finally admitted to the hall it was already stuffy with the odors of the many-coursed meal, the cloying perfumes of the guests, and the flat smell of a vast number of tallow candles. The Queen, of course, had brought with her all the royal accoutrements of luxury and so the tables were covered in silver damask sprinkled with rose water, the service was of heavy, gleaming wrought silver, and after each course of delicacies—roast peacock, seared hare, venison with leeks, pickled swans' tongues, and spicy curries—golden basins of perfumed water and lace-edged napkins were offered the greasy-fingered diners by scurrying and sweating lackeys. Above their heads from the rudely hewn rafters stirred the silken banners of all the great houses and orders of Spain in a profusion of colorful chevrons, bars, castles, lions, gazelles, casques, coronets, fleurs-de-lys, and crosses; insignias of pride, courage, and the determination to prevail.

Francho ground his teeth in chagrin when a quick scan of the crowded tables showed him Leonora seated with the Count of Perens—Felipe de Guzman. What did he care for the antics of the Queen's jester or her ugly Nubian dwarf, for the jugglers and their hoops, or the gaudy gypsy dancers festooned with beads who stamped and swirled to the insistent music of tambourines and castanets, or the poet who fought against the boisterous din of chatter and laughter, drawing arpeggios from his minstrel's harp and intoning his passionate verses of welcome to the Queen, "To stand as high, as high to stand, Isabella as Ferdinand . . . "?

What did he care about anything except that Leonora was chatting so animatedly into the cool, stiff-lipped insolence of the damnable Perens? There were several ladies at the tables trying to catch his eye, but he did nothing but bite the edge of his thumb and wish the cursed entertainment over with.

At last from the overhead balcony the recorders and viols struck up a dance. Everyone rose from the tables, which were then carried back out of the way. Isabella, looking especially attractive in a flowing brocade gown and miniver-edged tabard, her chiffon-draped hair crowned only with a small, jeweled tiara, was led forth in the grave and graceful pace by a very solicitous Ferdinand, followed by a number of ladies and gentlemen.

To Francho's relief he saw Felipe lean toward Leonora and say something to which she smiled only politely, after which the man rose and made for the entry to the hall. Francho's grin was wolfish again. One couldn't drink wine and ale all night and not need to visit a convenience, a circumstance he had been counting on to clear his field. Immediately he pushed his way through the throng to Leonora's side. She was dazzling in an amber velvet gown clasped with a tasseled belt strewn with topazes. Her honey hair was coiled into an openwork amber velvet cap encrusted with seed pearls, leaving bare her graceful neck and smooth, white shoulders. She was delicate and appealing, and her sunny, dimpled smile was drawing gallants from various parts of the room like a fragrant blossom draws bees. But Francho reached her first.

He offered his arm. "Will you honor me, Doña Leonora?"

"With much pleasure, Don Francisco." She nodded, and pink crept up her ivory skin as she took his arm.

The music changed and they joined the lightly stepping dancers in a galliard, moving down the room to the sprightly tempo. Francho swore to her, "I have existed all day on your promise of the first dance, and the bedeviled day seemed like a year." His tender glance spoke volumes as he gazed down at her.

"Well, it was naught but mere curiosity, sir, that kept me thinking of you. You were my pupil in stepping this dance at Castle Mondejar, remember? And so I was wondering if you had forgotten the measure," she teased him, expecting a playful answer.

But Francho's sense of humor was wanting that evening. He was so determined to talk to her privately he had no time for playing. "Leonora," he plunged in, "tomorrow night there is a requiem mass. Pretend you are ill and you won't have to attend. At nine of the clock the guard's hut to the left of the small portal in this building's west wall—'tis the same side as the wall over there where hangs the tapestry of Diana the Huntress—that hut will be unoccupied for a short time. Will you meet me there?"

"At night? But my *dueña?*"

As they switched hands on a crossover step he quickly and unobtrusively drew a tiny packet from his tight sleeve and pressed it into her hand, with silent thanks to Pietro di Lido's scientific blessings on romance. "The little packet contains a sleeping draught. You can get it into her somehow, empty it in her wine or her food."

Leonora's eyes went round but she struggled to keep surprise and doubt off her face. "Will it harm her?" she fretted.

"No, it will only make her sleep like a dead one. And with everyone at the church you can slip from your chamber unobserved. Leonora? *Querida?* I must speak with you alone, even for a few minutes. Please." And with a lover's desperation he demanded, "You must come."

For a second her expression remained unsure. Then her brown eyes went soft and she nodded, looking up at him affectingly through her lashes. With a smooth movement she slipped the packet under her tight belt, just as the measure signaled a change of partner. Then the line of women moved forward as the line of men moved back.

This particular step was performed twice, and then twice more in reverse, so that Francho resigned himself to losing Leonora to two more partners before he retrieved her again at the end of the dance. But he enjoyed dancing. The rhythms challenged him to display the beauty of the music in the grace of his step and bearing. His new partner turned out to be a warmly smiling lady in a butterfly hennin of gold and silver cloth, the Viscountess of something or other, he couldn't remember, but she stepped lightly and was pleasant to share a few words with. The measure signaled change again, the lady tossed her head coyly at his light flattery and moved ahead. He stepped back and bowed to his partner for the next figures.

A small shock ran through him as he found himself staring into Dolores's appraising gray eyes.

"*Buenos tardes*, Don Francisco," she murmured as she laid her hand on his arm. She was a shimmering vision of beauty. Her high-waisted gown was of heavy satin the color of almonds, as was her matching tall, jeweled coif and the net into which her reddish brown hair was thickly twisted and coiled. A flashing gold necklace with an amber drop pointed up the flawless beauty of her bosom. There was even, in fact, a smile curving her wide, lovely mouth. But it held no warmth.

"My lady." Francho coolly inclined his head, although he felt jolted by her unexpected nearness. Surreptitiously he

251

studied her as they moved, but her perfect and composed profile gave him no clue to her mood with him. Since he was determined to make amends with her, he had a feeling that his safest course was to totally ignore their wordless exchange last night about her card-playing habits and act as if it had never happened. So, there was nothing for it but to plunge in.

He cleared his throat. "May I presume you received my short letter in Seville, Baroness? I have hoped all these months that my sincere apologies were accepted."

"If you wish the truth, I thought it the apology of a coward."

"A coward? I do not take your meaning, *doña*."

"You saw fit to give your insults directly into my face. How craven that you could not do the same with your apologies."

They turned opposite shoulders to each other so his gaze was directly down at her lovely features, although she did not raise her eyes from a point at his shoulder. Somehow, in her ungracious reply, he heard a tiny echo of the Dolores he once knew and he felt more confident. In fact, he felt faintly amused. She was going to extract her measure of blood and he might as well prepare for it. "I was forced to make a written apology because time was lacking to me, yet it was a most heartfelt missive. Besides, I did not think you would wish to receive me again, Doña Dolores." He was carefully formal with her.

Again they brushed shoulders, but in opposite direction. The long smudge of lashes rose. She was attempting to keep her glance empty of expression, but for Dolores this was a struggle, and so he caught resentment—or was it exasperation —before she dropped her lids on her luminous eyes.

"It was not a matter of seeing you again, Don Francisco, it was a matter of hearing *directly* from you how abominable had been your greeting to me, a friend of so many years. I think in that way, and only that way, can we find a better footing for a courteous acquaintanceship."

Since he wished for them not to be enemies, he did not mind giving her the deference she exacted. Yet he had the feeling there was more to her demand than just to humble him; that at the least she did not find his company odious, and that at the most, she felt as dangerously drawn to him as he had been to her. The idea was intriguing, in spite of himself.

The figure, almost finished, called for him to take Dolores's fingertips and lead her around in a graceful arc. He did so, then watched her face, for he had to wonder, in spite of her fixed, flinty smile, if the hot fire launched by the touch of their hands that raced down his arm and now burned in his belly had assailed her too. Satan take the wench! She seemed to affect him as swiftly and drastically as a cup of poison. He would be wise not to go near her. But he owed her some courtesy and that was what he would deliver.

"If it is your wish that I bring you directly my most humble apologies, if that is what it will take to restore our friendship, then such will be my pleasure, *doña.*"

"As you please, *señor*. This time the arrangements will be in your hands." Her smile was a little warmer now, even though the profile she turned to him again was still haughty.

"So soon as the proper opportunity presents itself, my lady," he promised, ignoring the tingle of excitement that the idea sent down his spine. The figure ended and now he went forward and she, back, but first she turned her black-lashed, quicksilver eyes up to look into his for one devastatingly charged last moment.

The next morning Isabella insisted that she and her ladies be taken upon a complete inspection tour of the camps both north and south, excepting only the outposts where a revolving complement of commanders and troops acted as buffers against the frequent and fierce Moorish sorties. The tour was to be conducted by her own dear husband and co-ruler himself, and a good many noblemen and members of the Royal Guard came along as escort.

Isabella knew there were roses in her cheeks; she had not felt so energized in a long time. Her husband was sometimes a rough lover for he did not realize his own strength, but he obviously had missed her much and so what did she care for a few tiny bruises? To judiciously run the affairs of a sovereign state was exhausting. How often her ladies had finally tucked her up at night and offered to read to her to rid her weary head of buzzing problems, when it was not reading but the comfort of her beloved's strong arms she really longed for. Looking about her it amused her to notice, too, that the husbands and lovers who rode along with the tour that day were also unusually cheerful in spite of the early hour. She suspected so long, isolated, and uneventful a campaign had enhanced the charms of even the homeliest wife, and a conspiratorial smile lit her classic features.

Dolores had dressed very carefully that morning, hoping her face did not show the ravages of too much wine and dancing and only a few hours of sleep. But leaving nothing to chance she had tucked back her auburn hair into a green and silver turbanlike headdress that emphasized the sparkling beauty of her tilted gray eyes, and she had wrapped herself in a new, flowing cloak of silvery fur. Soon after the tour of the camp began she deliberately pulled up her horse so that Leonora's mount finally came jogging abreast of her. Leonora smile formally, then pointedly transferred her attention to the row of barracks they were passing. Dolores knew why Leonora even bothered to smile. The Duchess of Medina-Sidonia had been in very poor health all summer, and if she conveniently died, rumor had it that the Duke was thinking of marrying his beautiful, questionable Baroness, and in that case would give her a title and precedence to be reckoned with. And in Dolores's opinion Leonora de Zuniga was one of those who felt it best to play the game safe.

Dolores kept her horse at a walk beside Leonora's mount. "We have a magnificent day for the inspection, don't you agree, Doña Leonora?" she asked blandly to open a conversation.

"Oh . . . yes, it's quite brisk."

"The Queen seems intent upon seeing every stick and stone, I fear, although I would gladly change this saddle for a pillow before the fire. Her Majesty has a remarkable vigor; she led out almost every dance last night until far into the morning, and now she will not let us rest until she has poked into every corner." Dolores stifled a yawn.

Leonora glanced at her sideways. Mother of God, she thought, this gypsy-faced female is a shallow dish! But she responded, "The Queen feels a great responsibility in this campaign, Baroness, having done as much to secure it as any commander in the field. Surely her avid interest in the results of her tremendous endeavor is understandable."

Blood of a Saint, thought Dolores, this dimpled little paragon is completely bereft of a sense of humor. "Oh quite—of course. And how does the Infanta this matin? The vapors have left her, I hope?" She had noted that Leonora had had to leave the fiesta early the night before to attend to the Princess and her overgorged stomach.

"She is recovered, God be thanked, but the doctors enjoined her to keep to her couch in order to regain her strength."

Dolores smiled as if it mattered to her. The conversation lagged for a moment. Then Dolores remarked casually, "Poor Don Felipe was desolate when you had to leave the dancing so precipitously last night." She drew from her sleeve a flimsy kerchief embroidered with the antelope insignia of the de la Rochas and dabbed at her nose innocently.

"Indeed?" Leonora's glance was cold.

"But you needn't trouble about it, we had a long, long chat and I convinced him that you couldn't help your absence, and soon he was in fine fettle once more."

Leonora's color rose. "Most solicitous of you, Baroness, but I assure you Don Felipe needs no explanations of my behavior. I pray you leave my own affairs to me."

"Oh tut, perhaps I was presumptuous, but after all, he is the son of my dear friend the Duke, and I could not bear to see his face so gloomy. And I did you a good turn in speaking for you; Don Felipe was laboring under the impression you had—ah— another interest, and you know he stands above competition. But you see, I jested him out of it and we had a pleasant time—he is an excellent dancer—and now you need not worry that he is angry."

Leonora's face was stiff, haughty, her nostrils flared out with silent anger. "I do not worry about Don Felipe or anyone else, I assure you."

"Well, I would if I were you, if you care for his company." Dolores's smile was pure venom. "My Lord Perens brooks only so much injury to his pride and then he will look elsewhere for praise. But, since you indicate that you are not that interested in him, he will have even more need of my—ah—sisterly comforting. It puts the Duke in good humor to see his son happy; and I am infinitely interested in the Duke's good humor. . . ."

"You go to great pains to imply that Don Felipe is also attractive to you, in spite that you are—ah—a dear friend of the father."

"Ah yes, well that is because there is no spice in stealing coppers from a blind woman. It's too easy. . . ."

Pleased with the glimpse of distress she had raised in Leonora's eyes, Dolores smiled and nodded archly, then wheeled her horse out of line and trotted further forward in the train, the silvery fur of her cloak ruffled in the wind. Now, she thought smugly, *that* should confuse the little milksop's aim a bit. And she was hugely pleased with herself.

No sooner had she ridden away than Francho cantered up to Leonora. His charger was covered to the fetlocks with a velvet rig embroidered in the castle-and-bar device of the Mendozas crossed by the jagged red bar of the bastard. The hard, steely gleam of a cuirass showed under Francho's open cape, and he sported steel greaves and gauntlets and elaborate, gilded spurs on his boots.

He peered into her face, and for the first time Leonora noticed that his eyes, usually amused, could go cold and hard, and that the mouth that spoke such poetic and eloquent flattery could also square into a rigid, uncompromising line.

"What did she say to you?"

"Who? The Baroness de la Rocha? Why—why nothing."

"Does nothing always bring such a droop to your lips? Such lines to your brow? What happened?"

Leonora immediately rearranged her face and smiled sweetly at him. "Why nothing of import, Francisco. She merely made a remark on the Infanta's early departure from the celebration—a remark I considered very unkind, and I told her so."

"Oh. Was that all?" Francho's voice was gruff.

"Indeed it was. I have no interest in making chatter with her, I do not care for her type." Leonora's eyebrow arched. "But do you know her? I mean, more than just being merely presented? And why are you so anxious about what she may have said to me?"

Francho felt foolish to have let the sight of Dolores talking to Leonora undo him. He mustn't let himself suffer the fear that every time Dolores addressed a word to Leonora she was venting a spite on him. "I know little of her; we have spoken maybe ten words together. It was only because you appeared so disturbed that I wondered what had passed. I cannot tolerate the least unhappiness to touch you, don't you know that, *doña?*" Now the sapphire blue eyes had softened into the tenderness they usually showered upon her.

But perversely Leonora remarked, "I must say she is a beauty, certainly. But gaudy. She is much acclaimed by the troubadours of the Court, and Medina-Sidonia showers her with expensive luxuries."

Francho was anxious to drop the subject of Dolores, and so,

leaning over, he made a detailed accounting into his love's pretty ear of how much more exquisite were her own charms. And in fact, her creamy ivory face framed by blowing wisplets of honey hair escaped from her russet coif-and-wimple, her smiling cheeks stung a pretty pink from cold, was more complimented by the clear, hard daylight than Dolores's exotic allure. Francho set his mind to dwell upon how good Leonora's small, pretty mouth would taste to kiss in the fresh, cold air, would all the spying humanity around them simply vanish.

Coming to an isolated wooden building separated from the rest of the camp by a rushing and swollen stream, the monarchs reined in their steeds and halted the company before crossing the narrow timber bridge which crossed the flood. Even at that distance the stench which surrounded the edifice before them was nauseating. Many of the company quickly applied kerchiefs to their noses. The King rose in his stirrups and addressed the riders behind them.

"My lords and ladies, the structure you see before you was built upon the suggestion of your most excellent Queen, whose idea it is that all the disabled might be better cared for were they to be gathered in one place and not tended each to his own tent. We have many men suffering still the wounds of this summer's battles, and every day brings us fresh casualties from the outposts. Our physicians and chirurgeons are most able, and we have been able to recruit from the numerous civilians who camp with us attendants to help. It is reported to me that our novel manner of seeing to the battle-injured has caused more lives to be saved than otherwise—a tribute to my most honored Queen and lady."

Isabella wasted no time blushing. "I wish to inspect this infirmary," she announced to those who could hear her. "It will not be pretty. Only you who are hardy and with strong stomachs attend me. The rest may wait until we ride on. Who will go?"

Behind the building the members of the Court could glimpse large, grisly mounds of char and ash, all that remained of amputated arms and legs, of blood-ruined garments and noxious refuse, and there also, flapping away, was a long clothesline of stained bandages hung out to air. The somber structure itself seemed lifeless and silent at this distance, but it took little imagination to know it was surely filled with the groans and moans of human pain, of men dying with fever and infection and ghastly wounds which would not heal.

A number of the men and a very few ladies rode forward, and Dolores was among them. What was a few stinks and groans to a daughter of the alleys, she had shrugged mentally, and her reward, as she had hoped, was Isabella's surprised but visible approval. The Count of Cabra helped Dolores to dismount and offered his arm as escort into the hospital. She took it and did not look back, but she could almost feel the intensity of Francho's eyes following her determined, proud walk across the timber bridge. Good. She hoped he was impressed, the *bribón*.

Muffled in heavy cloaks against the damp cold that crept into the bones, the Count of Tendilla and his son took the night air to flee a raucous game of cards played by di Lido, Pulgar, and several knights of the Count's complement at a rude trestle table set up in Tendilla's quarters. The wind brought the pungent smell of damp hay and horses to Francho's nose, blowing from the huge, canvas-covered corrals in which the animals were sheltered, and it also scattered the glowing remnants of the fires on which the common soldiery had cooked their suppers before their huts. He heard, from within the tight dwellings, the chink of coins and the slap of cards, the plink of a guitar, an offkey voice, even a woman's laugh, a sound until recently just the camp follower's high-pitched giggle in this place of men, beasts, and killing weapons.

At various intervals along the paths fires burned in sheltered iron braziers where the watch on their rounds could stop and warm their hands. The two strolling men returned the sentries' salutes with casual nods.

"What ails you, Francisco? You were pacing like a caged beast this evening."

Francho hunched his broad shoulders. "The fact is, I feel like a caged beast, my lord. 'Tis the inactivity that grates my nerves. I have not even the comfort of fingering my lute, although after all these months I doubt I can yet play it."

Tendilla's voice was calm. "A true musician needs only a few days' practice to recall his art. And you are a true musician."

"I might as well be a true tailor for what good the knowledge of minstrelsy does me."

"Francisco, can you not control your impatience? We have discussed this all before. The longer we place you in Moorish territory, the more likely becomes the chance of your being uncovered before you can garner anything of value. Only when the approach to Granada is finally open to our armies can we plan our own strategy so that we emerge invaluable to the victory. Yours is the vital part; it must be played with delicate timing or not at all, and with consideration of any future turn of events." His tone took on an acid quality. "Our enemy, unfortunately, does not cooperate by surrendering on time; they care naught for our ambitions."

"My apologies for my impatience or for seeming ungrateful, Don Iñigo, but I am restive. Either I am a man of substance or I am not; and I am anxious for the trial to begin and have done. Sir, I was knighted under the name Francisco de Mendoza, a name it is my greatest pride to bear, but yet I am a fraud, an actor, an imposter. Can you understand?"

More than you think, my young lion, ran Tendilla's thoughts. I am not blind to your interest in Doña Leonora, but we will not discuss that now. Instead he replied, "You are your own worst enemy, Francisco, for you do not understand that the essence of a person is not written on a baptismal certificate, nor is the worth of his deeds. You were honored for your personal valor, not for your name."

"*Your* name, my lord."

The Count sighed. "Yes, withal; I understand you. I sympathize with your feeling of impermanence, but this is a bargain we have made and to which we have been and must continue to be faithful. I cannot, I will not jeopardize either of our aims by catering to your restlessness and sending you forth prematurely. For any reason."

Francho opened his mouth to mention his uneasy situation with Leonora and then shut it, changing his mind. One did not argue with Don Iñigo. Besides, Don Iñigo's original offer was to help him recover his birthright, not to woo the Count's kinswoman. He doubted that the cool, reserved Count would understand that love does not wait for convenience in order to happen.

He ventured a glance at his companion's aristocratic profile outlined against the flare of torches bracketed on the building walls. Still—he could be wrong. Doña Maria had once let slip that she thought her restrained cousin had been in love with Francho's mother, Elena de Venegas. In fact, she implied that

259

Tendilla still kept Elena's memory so bright that no other woman seemed to engage him, even after twenty years. Perhaps he *would* understand Francho's fear of losing Leonora to a more viable suitor and why he was suddenly so irked not to have his inheritance; for after all, the Count had supplied him, as a loan, ample funds to support himself pleasantly at Court. But the words to express this stuck in his throat.

Halting at a dark corner where no torchlight masked the awesome spangle of the black heavens, Don Iñigo called Francho's attention to certain formations of heavenly bodies and brought up new advances which had been made in astronomy and navigation. But although he spoke on one level his mind operated on another, considering again the complexities of his relationship with this young man. The blood always tells, he reflected. He doubted the possibility of taking any ragtag orphan off the street and creating a successful gentleman—not with that inborn grace and command that only the blood could carry.

And yet, his pseudo-son was not supremely noble; he did not look upon himself as a crusader fighting to clear a dead father's name, or to hold to waning ideas of old-time chivalry. He followed his early training in the alleys, where ephemeral honor meant nothing and self everything. Not that Francisco was not honorable, Mendoza corrected himself—the fact was he was admirably honest to admit that his efforts were to revive a name for himself, and only incidentally for his forebears. A representative member of the younger generation, this one, Mendoza judged, proud but realistic, romantic but not mystic, strong but not brutish.

Reluctantly he had to admit to himself that Francisco had become important to him—not as a mere instrument of his strategy more personal than the many other agents, high and base, who comprised the eyes and ears of his spy ring—but truly as himself. The son poor, mad Carlotta had never given him.

His eyes traveled over the younger man's shadowed form, tall and broad-shouldered, head tilted up as he studied the unwinking stars. Elena's son. She would have gazed at Francho with glowing eyes and overlooked his faults and foibles to smile with pride at his courage, his bold style and his talent. Elena would have placed her hand upon her son's strong arm and swept into the Court like a bright angel, gay and triumphant, inquiring up at him with cozening, startlingly blue eyes to bring her a sweet, thanking him with the lovely, two-noted laugh which damped out all the unimportant noises of the dissonant world. Elena would have . . .

Mendoza shook loose the thought and crushed it into nothing and let it blow away. Elena was dust. Elena was gone.

Francho brought his eyes down from staring at the planet Jupiter. "My Lord? Did you say something?"

"No. Shall we go on?"

They continued to walk. They spoke of the ambassadors who had just arrived from the Sultan of Egypt carrying barely veiled threats against the Christians dwelling in the Holy Land should Their Catholic Majesties continue to persecute the Moors with wars.

"What answer are we sending back?" Francho asked.

"A dissembling one, of course; whatever will placate them for the moment. It is felt that the rents and tributes the Sultan extorts from the Holy Land's gentiles are so huge that this alone will protect them from his revenge."

"Pietro di Lido mentioned that Charles of Naples warns that our wars will cost the Eastern Christians dearly."

Mendoza's smile, if Francho could have seen it clearly, was thin. "Our King discounts this pious interference from Charles as worry that once having conquered the Moors, Ferdinand might then have the freedom to assert his claim to the crown of Naples. But I believe he is right."

They went on discussing the vulnerability of the Christians in Moslem lands, and soon they turned back toward their quarters. Each would have rather had a more personal conversation, actually on the same subject, Leonora de Zuniga. But neither could speak. Tendilla could not break his habitual aloof containment. Francho feared rebuff from this man he so respected. The barrier of restraint still pervaded their relationship.

Later that night, the night of the mass, the meeting Francho had arranged had to be short for there was only half an hour before the guard was changed. Francho arrived first at the low-ceilinged shelter just inside the gate in the west stockade, pushing back his hood to identify himself to the posted sentries he had earlier bribed to go blind, deaf, and dumb. Entering, he saw there was some warmth at least in the hut, from a crude hearth where faggots burned in an iron brazier. An oil lamp with two floating wicks sat on a plank table. And there was a bench.

Flinging back his cloak he paced back and forth on the packed earth floor, hearing the deep and lugubrious multi-voiced lament floating on the wind from the church where his uncle the Cardinal Mendoza celebrated a mass for the Christian dead. His mind was in a ferment, wondering and hoping that Leonora would really be coming, but annoyed with the coarseness of the only meeting place he could quickly arrange where they would be safe from interruption.

Abruptly the door was pushed open and Leonora slipped in, shoving it shut behind her and leaning back against the rough wood as if she had been running. As Francho came toward her she threw back the hood of her enveloping cloak and regarded him mutely, her brown eyes wide and waiting, her expression so apprehensive that he stopped short a few feet from her. They lost several of their precious seconds, suspended, just looking at each other as the muffled, solemn requiem music penetrated the hut. Then Francho whispered, "I love you, Leonora!"

The spell was broken. With a little cry she ran into his arms for a hug, and then put up her mouth to be kissed. And kiss her he did, but gently, almost reverently, fearing to frighten her. And then he took her lips again, still lightly and tenderly, but feeling a happiness coming over him at this close communion of their souls. She was like a small, trembling bird, warm, untried, but willing. Slowly, slowly, he warned himself as he sternly reined in his passion, his will to crush her to him, she is yet a girl, an innocent. . . .

Her breath was coming shallow. She slipped away from him, needing to conquer her reactions to his gentle, loving touch, and he allowed her to go for they had to talk. To give them both a space to recover their wits—he felt still the pressure of her warm mouth upon his—he began by asking her if she would ride out with him the next morning.

A shadow passed over her face. "But I have already promised Felipe de Guzman."

"Then unpromise him."

"But I can't do that. It would appear peculiar."

"You were with him all this afternoon, and part of this evening too. Perhaps you would rather ride with him."

"Don't be cruel. Do you think it is for Don Felipe's sake

that I have probably poisoned my poor *duena?* The Count of Perens is a good friend, we have known each other since childhood and I like him, nothing more. But it is improper for an unbetrothed woman to give all her attention to one man."

"It tears me apart when you smile so fondly at him. Or at any of the other gallants that trail you," Francho said jealously.

The amber brown eyes grew troubled and dark. "And what would you of me? Shall I wait alone and cheerless then until you decide to declare yourself, *señor?*"

"I *have* declared myself. You know I adore the very ground you walk on, that I would die for you gladly, that I dream of you waking and sleeping. I wear your kerchief next to my heart where it hears how that besotted organ beats only for you. . . ."

He reached out to take her hand but she jerked away from him, having suddenly grown angry. "Oh, you great dolt! If you truly loved me you would demand to wed me; you would have already put your suit before my mother and my uncle. You only amuse yourself with beguiling me. And I—so stupid to have believed your casual protestations, to have risked my reputation by meeting you here. How could you mislead me so? Oh, I want never to lay eyes on your false-hearted face again—"

She whirled toward the door and, as she knew he would, with one bound Francho had hold of her. Although she struggled he carried her back to the bench, plumped her down, and held her there. He brought his face close to hers and stared directly into her tear-bright eyes. "Leonora, my sweetest love, I ask for your hand. Will you be my wife?"

A tear slipped down her cheek. "No! How much could you honor me if you have forced me to speak with such humiliating boldness. I hate you."

"No, you don't hate me. Just listen to me," he cried, tightening his grasp on her shoulders. "There are serious reasons why I have not been able to speak of betrothal. There is nothing in this world I want but to have you as my wife before God and man, and I would cherish and worship you for all of my life. But I have no right to ask for you—yet."

"I don't understand that. What do you mean you have no right? Your name is Mendoza, your sire the Count of Tendilla who cares much for you. And so does my mother . . ."

"And my fortune is nonexistent."

Now it is out in the open, Francho thought, and better this way, for what good is a future without her? God grant she loves me enough to wait. "Leonora, I have little of my own to offer you. I have no lands, no coffers of gold, no castle. I am only a poor knight. Where is my right to speak to you of marriage now?"

She wiped her eyes on her sleeve, her ivory brow wrinkling in confusion. "But—you are Don Iñigo's only son. Surely he will soon settle property upon you. And when he dies you will inherit all of his estates. You will be vastly wealthy."

He came, then, within a hair's breadth of telling her everything, who he really was and the true patrimony which he had to claim, and that, if everything were returned to him, he would be wealthy. If, if. For once he heeded the shout of caution at the back of his head and bit back the words that had jumped to his lips. "My—my father has said nothing to me of inheritance. Nor can I count on it that he will. He is not too old. If his wife Carlotta dies he may marry again and have legitimate children and wish to settle his properties on them. A young wife looking out for her issue can twist even a man like the Count around her finger. It has happened before."

Her frown deepened, but her eyes remained on his. "I don't understand. Has he not given you any indication at all of his intentions?"

"Are you not familiar with the inscrutable Don Iñigo? He keeps his own counsel, nor will he be pushed by casual questioning. I could not allow you to share a niggardly life with me, and therefore, until I am sure of my fortunes, I must make my own provisions, which will take time. If you will trust me, my heart, if you can love me enough to wait, I will come to you some day with the whole world as a pillow upon which to rest your lovely head."

"But why do you have so little confidence in Don Iñigo? I cannot fathom it. He is your sire and he is not a heartless man. And—if your grants would not come from him, then from whom else?"

"I cannot speak of it. Trust me, Leonora, for I cannot divulge my plans. It will take a while but the rewards will be worth the effort. Believe me, *mi corazón,* I do have a way to make my own fortune, independent of whatever the Count may decide. And then I will claim you, and I will allow no one to tell me nay."

"And you cannot give me any inkling of what you must do?"

"No. I have given my parole."

Her small, full mouth trembled. "May I ask at least the length of time you speak of?" She saw a look of pleading come into his blue eyes, so somber under the knit black brows.

"Perhaps—a year or two."

"Oh, Francisco!" Leonora slumped as limp as a rag.

He went to his knees before her. He pressed the palm of her hand first against his lips and then leaned his burning cheek against it, but he would not allow her to disengage her eyes from his own azure intensity. "I will tell you the truth. There is a chance that naught will come of my endeavors. And there is another chance that I will inherit little from Don Inigo; perhaps at most I will attain a petty title and a moldering keep in the mountains. But Don Felipe can ask your hand tomorrow and eventually make you a duchess, rich and powerful and honored. So if I speak like a fool it's only because I adore you so desperately, and that is why I dare risk your laughter and ridicule by asking you to wait, to prevail upon your guardians to wait, to give me the time I need to be worthy to win you." His short laugh was hollow. "And because I am a grasper at dreams, I dared hope that you would love me that well. . . ." Tautness had crept into his voice, the fear of rebuff, for who would blame her?

The feeble lamp behind Leonora misted her hair with a spun-gold halo and cast the shadow of her lashes upon her chaste, soft cheeks. He stood up. She raised her head and regarded him as he stood, erect and strong, his heart in his eyes. She rose too. She did not smile. There was a faint veil across her gaze, accusation he thought, or disappointment. But the expression upon her face became soft and tender and told him he had won.

"Sir. You are unfair. You ask more patience than a woman should have. It would seem unclever for me to choose to join my life with yours. But—I will marry no other. There is none I would have for a husband but you, Francisco. And so I will wait—for as long as I must. . . ."

He smothered the rest of her words in a rough, ecstatic hug, pressing her head against his shoulder in a possessive, protective gesture more eloquent of his feelings than a kiss or caress, telling her with all the strength of his arms the joy she had given him. And she clung to him the same wordless, needing way.

Muffled against his shoulder she said, "But why don't you inquire what may be Tendilla's plans of Pietro di Lido? He is the Count's closest friend and confidant. He knows Don Iñigo's mind. . . ." She pulled back her head and her look was coaxing, almost arch.

He took her face between tender hands and brought his mouth down on hers, stopping her questions with a melting kiss.

❧ *Chapter 11* ❧

"IF YOUR MAJESTY will give me leave, I have promised to attend a very sick gentleman whom I discovered in the field hospital, a former member of my father's household. He would be grievous disappointed should I not come."

"Yes. Indeed, *doña,* you may go. Such caring duty is valorous; God will reward you." Isabella looked up from the pillow cover she was embroidering for her son and cast a much more dispassionate regard over her young lady-in-waiting than she felt. She had earlier been surprised at the Baroness de la Rocha's display of backbone by entering the malodorous, horrible, and pitiful atmosphere of the war hospital, thereby showing up most of her squeamish ladies, this damsel of an ancient but withdrawn family. Isabella had to admit to herself she had not been overly warm in her initial reception of the girl, taking her into the intimate royal presence as a duty-favor granted a powerful and influential lord. In fact, to look at the young woman one would dismiss her as needing to offer the world no more than that radiant complexion and those exotic eyes. But it was soon apparent that Doña Dolores Ganavet was also intelligent and had an agile wit. Isabella liked her. She found the Baroness a lively addition to her circle of ladies, most of whom were of sterling character but often boring.

Now some of the ladies surrounding the Queen like a circle of flowers looked up from their embroidery to wonder at this paragon who would brave the field hospital again, a few pursing their lips at so obvious and pushy a way of impressing the Queen. Others simply cocked an ear for a moment and then went on with their chatter and gossip, which to them was more interesting.

Dolores's friend, Luisa, Countess of Zafra, stretching her back by the window overlooking the barren little court where the Queen took the air privately, noted with concern, "The sky is very threatening, Doña Dolores; it will soon rain."

Dolores smiled her thanks. "The sky has looked like that for days and it hasn't rained. And should it, I'll get a little wet, that's all." She shrugged one shoulder unconcernedly.

"Go then," the Queen nodded, "and I hope you find your gentleman faring better. But do not forget this evening's competitions. You have promised to vanquish the Duchess here at checkers, and that I should be interested to see." She glanced at Beatrix de Boabdilla and winked, for her dear friend was the most clever player at the gameboard among all her women.

"I will not forget, my Queen, although it comes to me I might have been too hasty in my challenge," Dolores answered with a short, rueful laugh.

The co-ruler of Spain, a woman withal, stilled a quick pang of jealousy at the tender seventeen years that lent so lambent a glow to the girl's beauty.

"I will withdraw now, Madam," Dolores murmured, and backed away with a brief curtsey.

Engracia, sitting unobtrusively at the lower end of the room and holding Dolores's plainest wrap, separated herself from the group of *dueñas.* She took her mistress's embroidery and helped her don the cloak. Pulling up the hood, Dolores led the way to the nearby Queen's Portal, where a hostler stood ready with her small mare already saddled and waiting at a mounting step. But before she allowed the man to help her sit her sidesaddle, she patted her companion's wrinkled face. "Don't worry so, Engracia, I go only to the infirmary. I will be fine. I am in the bosom of this busy camp, what could happen to me?" She fished in her purse. "Here is a coin. Beg yourself a little cake from the kitchens." Engracia smiled, gap-toothed, but her brow still wrinkled.

Dolores guided her horse along the dirt street leading to the hospital. She smiled back primly at the mounted gentlemen who greeted her as they threaded their way through the stream of soldiers and civilians going about their various affairs in this wooden city, and she even waved gaily at the bowing purveyor of furs, to whom she was in debt, standing at the doorway of his knocked-together log establishment toward the edge of camp. But she was upset.

What could happen to me? she thought grimly as her horse drew her closer to the noxious building (where in truth she dreaded to go). She could be recognized, called out, shown to be an imposter, that's what. And the hangman could happen to her, because she went to visit not a fictitious gentleman, vassal to the old Baron, but big Alfredo from the inn at Ciudad Real, formerly her father's hulking bulwark and partner, and her old mentor in the fine art of jewelry clipping. He lay now barely alive, his eyes and half his head swathed in dirty bandages. But she had recognized him anyhow during the Queen's brief tour of the facility and had suffered her heart going up in fright until she realized he could not see her. He was blinded, and from the wrappings she also surmised the poor man's jaw or face was broken on one side.

She had always counted him either imprisoned or hung by the Hermandad like her father and that horrible boy. But obviously he had gotten away by insinuating himself into the levies for the army that were marched south from Ciudad Real each year. As her first panic subsided pity took its place. She had stared in misery at the terribly wounded man propped on a heap of straw. He had been kind to her when she was little, and what harm could he do her now? Only a shallow movement of that big chest had showed he even lived. Moved by compassion to see his plight, she made a vow to return and see if she could ease his existence. And so in a drawstring bag hanging from her saddle was a special curing ointment for the eyes which she had purchased from the Queen's chemist, clean cloth for bandages, and a stoppered flask of warm beef broth.

She put the spiced pomander ball which swung from her belt to her nose as her horse clopped across the wooden bridge toward the grim building. A disheveled and surprised guard at the portal helped her dismount carrying her drawstring bag and deferently pushed open the heavy door for her to enter. Dread assailed her. She almost turned about to flee the long, dim, and windowless space that was surely an intimation of

Hell. It was certainly obvious that two days earlier chirur-geons and attendants had made special prettying efforts for the Queen's visit, sweeping up the refuse, keeping the over-crowded room as calm as possible, certainly muffling the cries of the worst sufferers.

Now the tormented sounds of men in pain shriveled her ears. The horrible smell of vomit and excrement and blood gagged her, the sight of such hopelessly maimed beings minus arms, legs, swathed in red and pus-filled wrappings, turned her faint. But she clenched her teeth and pressed her lips together until they turned white, trying not to breathe in the foul air. Big 'Fredo was among these unluckiest of humans, and she owed him at least a last goodbye and some share of her own good fortune, however minute. Quickly looking away as two attendants hurried by her with a wooden tub slopping bloody water with something else red and horrid floating in it, she collared a hobbling, dirty crone and pointed in the direction she remembered 'Fredo to be. The toothless one nodded at the coin Dolores shoved into her hand and led her along a narrow aisle, Dolores vainly trying to hold her skirts and cloak away from the vile floor and from brushing the filthy pallets on either side. She kept up her hood to block out the surroundings and began to pray very hard under her breath to shut out the hoarse calls for help and mercy from all sides. Her whole being was revolted, but she was even more afraid that if she did not make this visit of pity and succor, God might turn His eyes away from her.

She held the crone with her when she reached 'Fredo. Money would persuade the woman to apply the ointment to his eyes and to change the bandages. More money and a drop of honesty might move the old thing to give him special care until he died, for she could see now that he could not ingest more than a trickle of liquid through one side of his mouth. He could not see her, but he could hear, she thought. She knelt by his side and reached for one big and dirty hand to hold between hers. He jerked it away weakly, moving his head, a moan escaping his rigid lips. But she reached for his hand again, patting it to soothe him, gently rubbing the coarsened flesh, hoping he could feel her sympathy. She leaned over toward the one unbandaged, hairy ear, flinching at the lice she could see in his hair, and whispered to him, with a strange sort of relief, who she was, Papa el Mono's Dolores.

* * *

She stumbled from the field hospital so sickened at the pit of her stomach that she lurched past the man who held her horse and ran blindly to a corner of the building where, ignoring the curious stares of attendants and ambulant wounded who lounged outside the structure, she simply held on to the wood and retched with dry heaves until the tears ran down her cheeks. She had to get away from the noxious infirmary. She had to get out, she needed to run and run from the misery that was called life and the frightful pain man inflicted upon man, and the toll of the endless wars in which God, in his mystery, allowed men to break themselves. She stumbled back to the portal.

The guard helped her to mount, and she kicked up her mare, knowing only that she wanted to ride, to ride free and breathe free as she had learned to do at Torrejoncillo whenever the depression of her spirits became too much to bear. She made for the northern gate, which was the nearest, believing the guards would let her pass, for yesterday a surrender delegation had arrived from Baza and the desperate Moorish sorties were finished. But when she hauled up before the massive timber gate the soldiers on duty quickly lowered their pikes to bar her way. An officer approached, curious about the cloak-muffled lady on her caparisoned Arabian mare.

"Please allow me to pass the gates, sergeant. I must let my horse run. She gets no exercise, the poor beast." Dolores pushed back the edges of her hood and favored the man with her sweetest smile. He appreciated it, she could see from his admiring attention, but not enough to draw him away from his duty.

"I am very sorry, my lady, but no one is allowed from camp without authorization from an authority of rank or the officiating camp commander for the week. Do you have such a paper?"

"Why no, I didn't think it was necessary, since—"

"Then I will not be able to let you through."

"But I must get out, just for a short ride. It is not dangerous. The men on the ramparts will be able to watch out for me," she pleaded.

The sergeant's eyes showed mild suspicion. "And what is so attractive out there in the cold that you must ride from the camp?"

She held back her frustration, but barely. "Nothing. I don't know what you are implying. Sergeant, I have just come from

271

the infirmary and I am sickened. I must get some air into my lungs. Please."

"Plenty of air in here, my lady, and a lot safer. This is a siege camp, not a meadow for ladies to go cavorting. You are alone. Without a pass I cannot let you go." He grasped the horse's reins to turn the mare around, the pikemen and assorted loungers at the gate grinning at Dolores's discomfiture.

"Take your hands off my reins, man, I do not need your help to turn my horse. Where is your camp captain? I will get your damned pass."

"You needn't get snippity, lady," the soldier retorted, surprised by the young woman's huffiness, "I am only following my orders. 'Tis the Count of Tendilla commanding this week and you may find him in his quarters, if he is there. Or . . ." The man jutted his chin as a pointer to someone behind her, "you can bring your plea to his adjutant, Don Francisco de Mendoza, just there."

Dolores twisted about to see Francho and several breast-plated riders heading toward her along the wall of the stockade. Francho rode cloaked, but without cuirass or hat, the wind ruffling his dark curls across his forehead.

"What goes on here, Nuñez?" he inquired pleasantly as he trotted up, glancing sideways at Dolores.

"The lady wishes to ride out, *señor,* but she has no authorization to leave the camp. I have told her that I cannot let her pass."

Dolores met the inquiring blue eyes with a lifted chin. "Please, Fr—Don Francisco, I merely need to ride out a short distance and back again. I have just come from the Queen's hospital where I attended a man who is mortally wounded, dying. I am very sorely grieved, and suffocated by that terrible place. I must . . . I just want to get some air into my lungs and the stink off my clothes." She had not intended to wind up sounding like a supplicant, but with her pleading tone so she had.

Under the familiar half-frown he studied her face. A look of concern crossed his features. "You look quite pale, *doña.*"

"I think—it was too much for me," she admitted, and her back slumped of its own accord.

Francho turned toward the other men in his complement. "Don Diego, ride on with the others, for there is only the small northwest gate left to report." The fellow nodded.

"Check the moorings of the stockade bridge over the stream where the rains have been eating away at the banks. We want no accidents. I'll return in an hour." And to the guard he said, "This lady is the Baroness de la Rocha, one of the Queen's attendants. Let her pass. I will escort her personally."

The man saluted. "By your order, Don Francisco." And he signaled the pikemen to draw up the bar.

As the gate opened, the wide swath of cleared ground which surrounded the camp came into view, a break which guarded against sneak attack with oil-soaked fire arrows which could cause disaster to the camp. Beyond it in the valley to the north low brush and stands of trees crept over the small hummocks that were the foothills of the dun mountains looming behind. "We shall ride to that line of trees over there, bordering the banks of the stream; do you see it?" Francho pointed to a copse about a six-minute gallop away. "That will keep us still within view of the pickets on our scaffolds."

"Thank you, Don Francisco," Dolores murmured gratefully, lifting her head again as they jogged through the gate. "I thank you for your understanding."

"We all need to run sometimes, *doña,*" he rumbled. But he glanced at her with solicitude.

The gate thumped shut behind them, and the sound acted like a draught of strong wine poured into Dolores's veins. With an unexpected rapid movement she shook off her hood, pulled off her small, tiara-shaped hat, drew out the pin that held her hair knotted, and shook free her thick and glorious hair in a gleaming auburn flood. She kicked the mare hard and the animal leaped and flew forward along the road, body stretched, neck stretched, reveling in this chance to run free as much as her mistress, who clung to the pommel of the cumbersome sidesaddle with her hair streaming out behind her and her cloak billowing, face tilted up to be cleansed and rejuvenated by the chill buffeting of air.

She had heard a startled shout. There came the pounding of hooves behind her and she grinned. Francho's big stallion could outrun the mare easily, but her small lead was fun, and she urged her mount to greater speed. The rush of damp air was clearing her eyes and flushing the stink of the hospital from her lungs and her clothes. She swiveled her head and through the whipping of her hair saw him bearing down on her, a grin on his face too. Laughing, she faced forward again and prodded the willing animal, "Come on, Passinella,

273

lengthen your stride, girl. For just another few moments let those two males suffer our dust." She didn't care that she would never make it to the copse first. She knew only that she was away from the crowded camp and coursing through the open country, away from the sometimes stifling manners of the Court and free for a moment to be herself. And coming up fast behind her was, *mirabile dictu,* the insufferable, the alluring Don Francisco de Mendoza. She had not felt so atingle with excitement in a long time, and suddenly life was good again.

Their laughter mingled as he caught up to her and they pulled both steeds back out of the wide-open dash into a more comfortable canter. He let her lead the way as they plunged off the road and toward the tangle of leafless bushes and willow and birch trees that lined the high banks of the rushing stream. This was where they were supposed to stop, but Dolores continued to canter on along the line of the copse until she found an opening and scrambled down a small hill to the stream bank where there was a sandy clearing. She pulled her horse up at the edge of the stream and allowed the beast to drink the clear burbling water.

"This is farther than I said we should go," Francho reprimanded her as he came up beside her and let the stallion lower his head too. His face was stung as pink by the cold air as hers.

Dolores tried to sound quite innocent. "I was only looking for a place to water my horse."

"We can't be seen from camp here."

"Oh, can't we?" she answered, with an air of surprise.

Amusement gleamed in his eyes. "Where did you learn to ride so well? I mean, at least you didn't fall off."

She threw back her head to laugh, and she saw his eyes follow the smooth, lovely arch of her bare throat where it emerged from the brown wool cloak. "Well, it certainly wasn't in Ciudad Real, my friend. Remember—remember how Pepi wanted so much to ride a horse? It was his greatest dream, to steal a white one."

"And Carlos's answer, that the Hermandad would soon collar a beggar like him on horseback?" Francho chuckled along with her.

"In fact, I learned to ride on an old nag at Torrejoncillo. The old man Miguel was a good teacher, and there was a lady's saddle in the stable. He said I took to it very well because I wasn't afraid."

He didn't answer. He was studying her face again, but this time with a sort of wonder in his eyes. She knew the ride had brought the bloom back into her cheeks and given her gray eyes brilliance.

"I do feel better," she offered, to break the momentary silence, conscious now that her hair was disheveled and streaming down her back most informally.

"You do look better. In fact—" The words seemed to tumble out of his mouth before he could arrest them. "You are unbelievably beautiful."

It delighted her that he thought so, but she wasn't going to let it show. "Unbelievably? Was I so ugly then in Ciudad Real?"

"No. Of course not. Only young."

"Young? Now I am so old, then?" she teased.

"Certainly not. I just meant you're more—more—well, ripened. . . ." he stammered. "By the boots of the Devil, Dolores, you know what I mean." He finally hauled up, exasperated. "I could shake you."

Then, sensing dangerous ground, he quickly veered the subject. "But what in the name of San Antonio were you doing in the hospital? And by yourself. What possible business could you have had there?"

"'Fredo is there. You remember him."

"What? Of course."

"He is blind and badly injured," she reported sadly. "He is close to death. The chirurgeon tells me 'Fredo was on outpost duty—only just the day before the Court's arrival—and he was felled by an arquebus which exploded in his face when he tried to use it, although he was only a regular foot soldier. I brought him medicine and clean bandages and gave an old hag some money to try to ease his dying. I think . . . I think he realized who I was when I told him. Or perhaps he didn't. In a day or two it won't matter."

"I would like to see him too."

"No. Don't go, you could spoil my excuse. In order to attend him I told the Queen he was of the Baron's household. So what reason would you have to be seen at his bedside?"

Francho nodded slowly. Then he looked off into the distance with memories in his eyes.

To distract him and because she did feel grimy, she said, "My hands are not clean. Could you get me some leaves?"

"Of course, *doña.*" Coming back to the present he swung

275

one long leg over and dismounted. He found a broken branch with dead leaves still clinging to it, swished it in the stream, and then offered it to her, careful not to wet her clothes with the drops. She scrubbed at her hands with the wet leaves until they felt clean, and even rubbed a softer, still partially green leaf lightly over her face.

"You can imagine why I so needed to take the smell of death from my nostrils. I was very lucky it was you on inspection duty, Don Francisco."

The strong planes of his face softened with his white smile. "Luck was only part of it, my lady. I saw you come from the hospital, and even from a distance you seemed to reel in your saddle. You turned in a direction away from your quarters, and I was puzzled as to where you were going. And so we followed you, my men and I."

Dolores stared at him for a second. "You followed after me? But why?" It suddenly came back to her that he had never really apologized to her properly, and she raised her chin haughtily. "Why in the world would you care what was happening to me, Don Francisco? If I remember correctly, you were more anxious last winter to consign my soul to the Devil."

Riveting her with his intense blue gaze and half-frown he started to answer and then stopped. Instead he grabbed her horse's halter and led both mounts back from the stream to a hammock where the sand was hard and dry and the wind whispered through the dry reeds. He dropped the reins and came to face her, arms raised commandingly.

"Get down."

"No. I don't want to," she demurred, unwilling to be ordered about, unsure if his gruff tone was serious or not.

"I said get down. Now. Or I'll pull you down," he growled, and when she saw his eyes glisten with the charming thought of manhandling her, she decided to do what he wanted. Francho had two personalities. When he laughed and swaggered he was appealing. When anger darkened his face he could be almost frightening. Not that she was frightened of him, she told herself. She just wanted no arguments. She leaned into his arms and he lifted her off the horse, but set her down with a rough jounce. Indignant with such cavalier treatment she bristled.

"Señor!"

"I have never met anyone so stubborn," he railed at her,

hands on his hip bones. "Do you never forgive? Well, here we are face to face, as you wished, and here is the opportune time we sought. So now, lady, I humbly ask your acceptance of my apologies for boorish and untoward behavior to you last winter, and I wish to sincerely withdraw all that I said which was mean, cruel, or insulting, along with my assurances as a knight and a gentleman that no such calumny will ever be repeated." He jumped in surprise. *"Ay, caramba!"*

She had stamped hard on his boot. "And you expect me to accept apologies that you are shouting at me, *bribón!"* she cried, as he jerked his foot back.

He blinked. "Was I shouting?"

"Indeed you were. Like a louse-eaten Catalan faggot peddler! Scoundrel!" They glared at each other.

Dolores saw Francho's mouth twitch. She pressed her lips together on her own twitch. Then that familiar light came into his eyes, the warm, amused gleam that had always enchanted her, and she could no longer hold in her sense of the ridiculous. Her laughter just burst from her. His shoulders shook too. Laughing they fell into each other's arms, carried away with levity that came from understanding how ludicrously the two best pupils of Papa el Mono's school of cutpurses were acting toward each other.

"Oh dear, oh Francho, how stupid we are being," she gasped, her voice muffled against his broad chest and fine wool cloak. "Yes, I forgive you. We should have no reason to be wroth with each other."

"True," he agreed in a baritone croak, and fumbled in his sleeve behind her back for a kerchief to offer her. He released her then. "Dolores, ah—you are incredible. No one can make me laugh the way you do," he marveled, tucking away the kerchief after she had dabbed at her eyes. "It feels good. But Holy Mother protect us, we have been acting like children on a teeteringboard."

"I know." She giggled. "Either we are miserably fierce with each other or we turn helpless with mirth." She threw out her hands in a mock gesture of defeat with the situation, but in her mind she was thinking how handsome he was. The strong, masculine planes of his face showed an excited flush under skin beginning to go rough with a hint of dark stubble. Black lashes framed eyes astonishingly and brilliantly blue. His expression was both relieved and open.

She had turned so that the wind was behind her. In an

unthinking gesture he reached out with gentle fingers and brushed away the streaming, silky locks of auburn hair from where they blew against her nose and mouth.

His touch made her tremble. She couldn't help it. She cursed herself silently, hoping he would be the gentleman and turn away from her now, for he was in love with someone else and did not feel the earth shake as she did. She saw him stop as he realized what he was doing, and as he saw her reaction. If she dropped her eyes demurely now he would step back and, their fences mended, they would return to the camp, relieved to no longer be enemies, parting in friendship to follow their separate destinies.

If she dropped her eyes now, as would a dignified and true lady, they would have no further problem with each other. But she had a problem already. She could not drop her eyes from his, those amused, stern, bold, angry, tender, and compelling eyes that haunted her dreams; she could not drop hers any further than the hard, expressive mouth with its full, square underlip, which had once moved on hers so tenderly. Transfixed and betrayed by her own helpless desire she stared back at him, hearing the soughing of the wind through the bare trees above the barrier of brush that hid them, the snorting of the two horses as they ambled together down the small strand, the soft flap of his cloak as the wind rippled it back and ruffled his hair over his forehead.

Terrified she stood before him, aware that she was exposing herself to cruel hurt, aware that her boldness was open enticement to him, helpless to keep her lips from parting in a half-sigh.

With a groan he pulled her into his arms and held her close to him. "What do you do to me? Why can't I leave you alone?" he moaned into her hair.

Somewhere inside her a muted horn of triumph blew. Reckless now, she pulled her head back. "Just kiss me. Just kiss me, for that's all there is. That is all there will ever be; our lives are parted from each other. But if you will kiss me some of the longing will go."

"I don't think so, beautiful temptress, I don't think so," he answered, pained disquiet in his eyes. But before she could wonder how she had found the daring to ask what she did, he had dipped his head and taken her mouth. And she gave it, melting into his embrace, breathing in his breath with its strange, compelling, musky excitement, molding against his tall body and muscled thighs, her hair whipping about them both.

His warm hand tenderly caressed her face. He could not get enough of her mouth, tilting his own in this direction and that to claim her lips every delicious way he could, and she went with him, anything, anything he wanted—

His lips left hers and she felt their warmth, burning now, on her cheeks, the tip of her nose, her chin, and, as he brushed away her hair, pressed against her slim, smooth throat. She thrilled to his kisses, her eyes closed, her head thrown back, her heart beginning to pound. The sure, male strength of the arms encircling her, claiming her, poured joy into her veins. She tightened her grip about his neck and their lips met again and clung, hers parting helplessly under the onslaught of his fierce, unspoken passion, allowing his tongue to taste her own and to plunder her mouth, searching, searching, and the only answer she could give him was to willingly succumb.

Her whirling mind knew she should wrench herself away, resist, refuse, but her muscles would not comply. Her body thrummed and suddenly, shockingly, she was wild to tear away both her clothes and his so they could come even closer together, skin upon skin; she yearned to be locked into his naked embrace along the length of his body, so close and with nothing between them so that they would blend into one and he would finally understand that they *were* one.

The same desire must have taken him, for one arm slid inside her cloak and his warm hand moved imperatively up and down her velvet-clad back as if he would peel the fabric away, descending lower to rest on the curve of her rounded buttocks and pulling her tight against the demanding hardness in his groin. Shivers of fire raced through her.

He finally released her bruised mouth and buried his face in her hair, rocking her back and forth as a muffled cry escaped him, *"Ay, querida, querida . . ."*

Her hands unwound themselves from about his neck and plunged under his cloak to hug him about more tightly, her tingling fingers exploring along the length of his back, and feeling the dense, taut muscles move in pleasure at her touch.

He pulled her partly away from him, and now she could look up to see his handsome face open to her, darkened with desire, nostrils flared, breath coming hard. Without warning the heat of his hand slid up from her waist and cupped about her velvet-covered breast, one finger unerringly and defiantly caressing in just the right place, right against her nipple, which strained to rise against the fabric and meet him. Great delicious tendrils of shock ran through all her nerves. Keeping his hand on her breast and squeezing gently and rhythmically he raised her desire higher and higher into quivering wantonness. He reclaimed her lips as if they were his due, Dolores noted dimly, as if he were perfectly aware that God had molded their mouths to fit perfectly and hungrily upon each other. His lips moved on hers as if he were saying something, her knees trembled, and she felt a wetness glide down her stockinged leg. A little scurrying part of her brain questioned, "But where, how, here on the cold ground . . . ?" For she could not deny the moist surge of her passion, her terrible need for this one man. She wanted him to take her—

The sudden, startling brilliance of the sun flooding full upon them through a break in the clouds acted like the harsh stab of a great light invading the privacy of a curtained bed. Or perhaps it was like an explosive premonition of disaster. He ceased kissing her. She felt him abruptly freeze. A shudder ran down his frame. He straightened up and shoved her brusquely away from him, ignoring her pained gasp.

"Dolores, I . . ." His face was rigid with self-anger. "I beg you . . ." he strangled, shame clouding his eyes and robbing him of speech. "I am beyond words . . . I . . ."

With an effort born of grimmest pride and because she had been, in her deepest heart, wary of him, Dolores was able to force herself to a quick recovery, clamping shut, it seemed to her, the very blood that ran in her veins. She stopped his stammering by putting a quick hand over his mouth. Self-contempt was rising in her too. "No, do not blame yourself, Francho. It was my fault. One does not create a lady by adding a title," she declared bitterly. "I *asked* you to kiss me. You only did what I asked."

"Just as I would do if you happened to ask me to throw you over a cliff?" he answered angrily. "No, the fault is mine only, for I cannot seem to control my—my lusting for you. Like a barbarian." He ran a nervous hand through his hair and for a moment turned his gaze away, looking at the ground in embarrassment. "But I give you my vow, here and now, that you will not suffer my unjust advances again. I appeal to you to accept my word on it." Pointedly, he added, "My lady." And looked fully at her.

Dolores appreciated his effort to erase her harsh judgment

of her own actions, and she knew his scowl was not for her. But embarrassment and bleakness at his words flooded her anyway. Was that all he suffered, then? Just ordinary masculine lust? Would the other gentlemen who stared so longingly at her have folded her so possessively into their arms, would their fingers have held her face so lovingly? She ached to believe there was more in Francho's heart. Yet her mind jeered at such moony-eyed stupidity, at her need to see love where there was none. She regarded him, standing there like a huge, stricken boy, and wanted to hit him for his insensitivity. And for the throbbing ache of her body, which she hid behind a dredged-up dignity.

Her tone was brittle as she asked him, "And how will you proceed to protect me from your impulsiveness, *señor?*"

The line of his mouth hardened. *"We* will see to it, Dolores, by not being alone with each other again. It seems I cannot answer for my actions with you. But I can prevent the vile advantage I take of your trust by keeping distance and people between us."

"Is your character so weak, then, that you cannot simply exercise self-control whether we find ourselves alone or not?" Her lip curled.

Her attempt to sting did not touch him. "Yes, my character is that weak," he answered, his voice flat. A coldness came into his eyes. "Especially I would not wish to hurt you—to compromise your—your arrangements."

She felt very unhappy. She tried to keep her voice from quavering. "Francho. Please. Let me tell you about the Duke of Medina-Sidonia. He is—"

Now he in turn stopped her mouth, roughly. "No. I do not wish to hear about him."

"But, if we are friends . . ."

"And so we are, and I pledge you, lady, the strength of my sword should you need it. But of him I do not care to know; do me that kindness, *doña.*" He turned partially away from her, arms akimbo, his stare brooding on the horizon. "Dolores, I wish you well. And I beg you to forgive my unchivalrous, brutish actions. I don't know what more to say."

Neither did she. She wasn't even angry. Just empty. Sadly she understood that it had not even entered his mind that her eager, willing response to him was not just unmaidenly lust in her turn, but love. Because he was not interested.

"We should go back," she said stiffly and turned away,

drawing her cloak close about her for the day suddenly seemed to have gotten colder in spite of the fitful sun. But when she looked around at him he was squinting into the distance, across the opposite bank, where a clearing gave an unobstructed view of the plain and the mountains to the north.

"What is it?" she asked, sighting in the same direction.

Absorbed, he answered without turning. "One of our caravans, can you see? Descending from the pass, men and mules. Strange. The caravans have been suspended, so I thought. Our storage towers are filled to bursting. . . ."

Dolores observed tiny flashes in the distance, which she translated as sun glinting off the steel plate armor of a forward guard she could barely make out. "Perhaps there was just this one more remaining?"

He continued to stare, his half-frown deepening as he shaded his eyes, straining to make out the details of the column as it advanced. "We surely would have been notified," he muttered. "There seems to be too many more mounted men than pack mules. And the mules are not very heavily laden; the pace is too fast. Strange. I wish I could make out the leader's insignia."

"We should go. They will pass close to here and it would be more discreet for us not to be observed by the riders." All she had to fall back upon was primness.

"Yes, of course," he agreed absently, still absorbed. "How can they— *Caspita!*" She saw him start and stare harder. The column had arrived at a distant bend in the gently rolling road so his view of them was not quite head on. "That's not one of our caravans; those are Moors. Marauders!"

Dolores gasped. "How do you know that? They are still so far away." She strained her eyes into the northern distance, rising up on her toes as if that would help, grabbing on to his arm for balance.

"If I'm seeing right, only the first few riders are wearing steel plate, as do our knights. The mounted men behind are in Moorish chain mail and leather; it reflects little of the sun. And those mules must be carrying empty loads to confuse us. They think to come up on us from our less protected flank. . . ."

"But our pickets would eventually make them out."

"They hope only to get close enough for their longbowmen to rain fire arrows over our walls, which would do us great damage. The Moors have adapted our longer bow to achieve distance. They are coming this way and quickly . . ." But he continued to scrutinize the suspicious column, just to make sure. . . .

Suddenly he was sure. He grabbed her hand and pulled her toward the horses. "Come on, Dolores. We're going to have to run for it. They won't see us until we come from behind the trees, but when they do they'll realize we could give the alarm and their mounts are swift." Putting his hands around her waist he easily boosted her into her saddle and with a creak of leather swung up into his. He wheeled about motioning her to follow. "As soon as you gain the top of the bank, dig in your heels and ride," he commanded. His frown was gone. An aura of excitement, of a warrior challenged crackled about him. His eyes glinted.

But then he blinked and regarded her with reservations as she yanked up her hood to cover her hair and drew the string tight about her face. "Are you frightened?" he asked.

"Frightened? *Madre mía!*" She couldn't help the laugh that rippled from her in spite of their serious situation. "Is this the first time that I have had to run for my life, Francho? *Vámonos!*"

The amused light sprang into his eyes again, and admiration too, as he saluted her. And suddenly, enemy bearing down on them or not, her heart grew lighter.

He delivered his rascally grin. "You ride as fast as that little horse can go. I'll stay with you. We've tarried overlong. *Vámonos!*"

Dolores swiftly guided her mount up the stone-littered break in the bank and he followed; and at the top, scrambling past the dead foliage that lined the stream, she swerved the animal toward the road, kicking the fat belly as hard as she could. *"Vámonos!"* she cried to her mount and then clung on for dear life as the startled animal spurted under her. Francho surged from behind her, holding his big horse neck and neck with hers. Cloaks billowing out, they galloped thunderously toward camp.

She sneaked a quick glance at the strong profile of her companion. He wasn't smiling, the chiseled line of his jaw was set. But she knew the smile was there, the joy of a knight answering a flung gauntlet with his puissance—in this case, speed—and his arms at the ready. His sword belt, which he had turned behind him while they walked on the sand, was now returned so that the sword in its embossed scabbard was

directly under his hand. He must have felt her eyes on him.
The handsome profile turned, and he smiled encouragingly at
her from under his wind-whipped hair.

"What if they catch us?" she shouted.

"They might kill us." He grinned.

"Holy Virgin . . ." Dolores spurred up her horse again. But
she felt only purpose, no fear. She was with him and irration-
ally she felt safe.

As they came to the road at the end of the brush that lined
the upper banks he spurted ahead to take a swift look north
and she veered to join him, their horses' hooves drumming on
the packed earth. "Keep going," he yelled. "Now they've
surely seen us. And they're close. . . ."

She'd heard stories of midnight riders being chased like this
by hairy demons from Hell, and the breathless suspense and
pounding pace was all she'd imagined in spite that it was
daylight. Lips pressed together, she tightened the grip of the
one leg hooked over the sidesaddle horn and stiffened the
other leg in the stirrup to keep herself steady in the seat,
willing her limbs to take the aching strain. She had done the
same thing on the way out, but it had somehow been easier
when it was just for fun. She risked a quick glance back but
could see little because of the billow of her cloak. When she
faced forward again into the streaming wind she saw Francho
had gotten a few lengths ahead of her. He realized it and
looked back to reassure her, fighting to bring the charger's
pace down to hers.

And then, in the space of a breath, Dolores felt her mount
check, lurch, and swerve to one side. She heard the animal's
terrified shriek and knew a shriek issued from her own throat
as well as she lost her grip and catapulted over the falling
horse's head, the road and the sky and the world tumbling and
flying all about her. A great pang of pure horror lanced
through her. She was going to be killed! God, dear God! It all
came almost at once, the brutal impact of the ground and the
sharp crunch and crackling of dried branches, and the almost
instantaneous mercy of blackness that snuffed out her consciousness and erased her terror.

Aghast, Francho sawed his mount to a rearing, whinnying
halt and jumped off on the run toward the pitiful bundle lying
too still on the mound of dead leaves and branches which the
wind had drifted and held against the irregular rock outcrop
alongside the road. His heart pounded with dread, with terror

that she might have suffered a fatal injury, that she might be dead.

"Dolores!"

Just as he reached her he saw her move and slowly flop over on her back. Relief shook him. The Lord, the Savior and all the good Saints be thanked! "Dolores?" He knelt beside her, fearing to touch her until he knew where she might be injured. Her face was smudged, scratched, bruised on one cheek but otherwise unharmed. The wide, gray eyes opened, blank, unfocused. "Dolores, *querida,* speak to me, are you all right?" he implored, squeezing her limp hand.

Consciousness swam back into her eyes. She blinked and took a deep breath. "What . . . ?"

"Your horse went down and you flew over her head." He lanced a desperate glance over his shoulder. "Quickly. Can you tell me if you are injured? Try to move, little sister," he urged her, using the old name of affection learned from Tía Esperanza.

Now memory had reached her too. She lifted her head and tried to struggle up. "The Moors . . ." He watched her arms move stiffly and her legs; nothing broken there. He got his arm under her and lifted her up to her feet carefully, noting the pallor of her face. "Where does it hurt?" he asked as she winced. He pressed gently at her clavicle, her breastbone, for shock often hid the pain of broken bones.

"Here, here," she groaned, pointing under her breastbone.

"You've cracked a rib, maybe two," he muttered. "You'll have to bear it." He stepped watchfully away from her to see if she could stand. She did, swaying. Her face was drawn but determined. "Wait here."

Her horse was on its side, huffing and struggling weakly to get up. Francho needed only one quick glance at the splintered white bone jutting through the bloody hide of the bent leg to know the horse was through. The little mare rolled her eyes wildly at him as he strode up and struggled all the harder to rise, whinnying in pain. He snicked his sword from its scabbard and came up to the doomed animal from behind, calling softly to her to calm her and as the nervous head stilled for a moment, he plunged the point of his weapon with unerring aim through the terrified bulging eye and into the beast's brain. He heard Dolores's anguished scream but he had no time for such grief. Jerking his gore-dripping sword from the dead horse he swiftly wiped it on the turf beside the road, resheathed it, and in a second had brought his horse up to where Dolores stood.

She had hidden her eyes with shaking hands. Roughly he pulled them down. "If we don't ride now they'll be on us in a few minutes and they'll show no mercy. Pull up your skirts, you'll have to ride astride. If your ribs are broken I won't lift you, but I'll help you gain the stirrup and you throw your leg over. Sit forward up there. I don't want you falling off again."

In spite of her pain and the shock still gripping her, her chin came up. "I did not fall off. I was thrown."

He could hear the thundering hooves behind, he didn't need to turn around. "Do it! Now!" he roared, and she hitched up her skirts with speed. He grabbed her arm as she put her foot in the high stirrup and with that leverage and a hand under her rump practically threw her up on the lofty, cantled saddle. He vaulted on behind her, jerked the nervously prancing stallion about, and dug in his spurs unmercifully. A momentary glimpse back showed him the closed-visored forward riders, one flying a captured Spanish pennon on his lance, bearing quickly down on them. Drawn bows had appeared in the hands of the men following them, now riding with their knees only as they galloped. A few minutes and they'd be in range to let fly their deadly missiles.

Francho's stallion shot ahead, hooves striking sparks, uncaring of the extra weight. At that moment they spied the encampment gate ahead of them being flung open. A battalion of Spanish horsemen boiled out and rode rapidly straight for them. "Someone had eyes in their head, God be thanked," he yelled in Dolores's ear. "If luck is with us we'll reach them before the Moorish devils reach us."

She didn't answer. She rode before him in the necessarily tight grip of his arm, leaning against him as he bent into spurring up the horse. What he could see of her profile which was close to his own was distressingly pale and set. She bit her lip, a tear sparkled in the corner of her eye. He could hear her moan. His heart contracted, and a momentary picture jumped into his mind of this young woman lying in a still huddle on the leaves, tumbled up in her cloak and perhaps dead with a broken neck. His little sister of the inn. . . .

He put his cheek to her cold one to comfort her, feeling the dampness of her tears of pain. Dear Jesu, he could have lost her.

The great horse was becoming winded, he felt it lose speed

under the extra hundredweight and a bit more, although they still galloped just out of arrow's range from the enemy, who were now crying out insults and charging ferociously at the Christian forces riding to stop them. It would be a hair's breadth escape, Francho knew, hearing the whirr of arrows that were as yet falling mercifully short behind them.

And then they were surrounded by their own horsemen, *caballeros,* lancers, bowmen, shouting at them and waving them back toward camp, not stopping their own headlong countercharge but parting and pounding by on either side of the double-mounted riders as a rushing river flows around an obstacle. But as they rode Francho recognized one of the stragglers still coming up behind the main body and yelled out to stop him, a young man in the Count's company of fighters. "Ho, Canterigado, to me, to me," he shouted, sharply reining in the charger and gripping Dolores as the horse reared. He heard the man's horse neigh as he brought up short too, and in a few seconds the rider cantered up to where Francho's horse was standing and blowing, with heaving sides, flanks glistening with sweat.

"Greetings, Don Francisco. It seems we arrived at an auspicious time for you," the young man grinned, attempting a joke.

"So you did. Señor Gregorio, I would ask you to take my mount and bring this lady back to camp. Carefully. She was pitched from her horse and may have some badly injured ribs. Bring her immediately to the quarters of the Queen and see Her Majesty's physicians are alerted to her condition. I will take over your horse and join the battle."

They could both hear and see the nearby melee of men and horses as the larger Spanish force (some of whom had not dodged the deadly rain of arrows and already lay littering the ground) closed with the desperate marauders, who were still beyond their objective of getting close enough to the encampment to fire it.

"But sir, you have no cuirass, not even chain," the young man pointed, hiding his chagrin at being sent back, for this was the son of the lord in his district in whose complement he served and to whom he had pledged his arms. "Then take mine, *señor,*" he offered generously, "we are almost of a size. There was no time for me to don full armor."

"I will, and thank you, Canterigado, I am grateful." They dismounted and with nimble fingers Francho helped the man undo his breastplate hooks from the back plate. In turn Canterigado aided him to don the steel cuirass and to swiftly lace on the greaves, which would protect his shins. He even offered his helmet, which Francho refused, for a man's helmet was a most personal possession.

Canterigado swung himself up on the stallion, who backed and stepped, not sure he cared for a rider not his master. Francho talked soothingly to the beast and rubbed the wet nose. He tossed up his cloak to the young man and then turned his attention to Dolores, who had been slumped silently during the five minutes which the whole exchange had taken. She released her chewed lower lip from her teeth and looked down at him, eyes clouded with pain, the tip of her nose pinched and reddened with cold.

He was as grave and as silent as she was as he gazed up into her bruised face. He could say nothing because there was a miserable confusion of emotion inside of him. It was better for her that Canterigado ride her up to headquarters.

Finally she relieved the tension of their silence and his undefined feelings which he knew were mirrored in his eyes by smiling weakly and insisting, "I was thrown, Don Francisco."

He smiled back at her with grateful warmth, and somewhere inside him a pressure that had been building up went away. He kissed the gloved hand she held out, the glove soiled and rent from the life-saving soft pile of leaves and debris she'd been thrown into, and saluted her. "I pray you will soon recover your well-being, Doña Dolores. Go along slowly, Master Gregorio. The lady is in discomfort." He stepped back and slapped the stallion's rump to get it going.

As he vaulted onto Canterigado's patiently waiting horse, he heard Dolores's voice float to him, "God keep you in his hands, Don Francisco." Setting a breakneck pace toward the clang and clash of the battle raging raggedly over a stretch of the valley ahead of him, he thought one more thing about Dolores—that she was a remarkably indomitable woman. No, lady, for that's what she had become, just as surely as he had been turned into a gentleman.

Then she disappeared from his mind as he flashed out his sword and, yelling "Santiago and Mendoza for Spain!" plunged into the thick of the melee, hacking energetically through to relieve Von Gormach, whom he had spotted holding off two Moorish swordsmen at once.

* * *

After six months and twenty days of siege, on the festival of Santa Bárbara, patron of thunder, lightning, gunpowder, and explosives, the strategic city of Baza officially surrendered. Ferdinand and Isabella took possession of the city in pomp and splendor at the head of their armored cavalry and tramping legions, amid pealing bells, the triumphant blare of horns, and earth-shaking artillery booms. A bright red standard displaying a huge white cross was run up to fly over the ancient battlements of Baza as a stream of the proud banners and emblems of Spain cantered through the gates.

Cidi Yahye, leaden-hearted but determinedly gallant, had his troops drawn up to attention as Their Catholic Majesties rode to the city's Alcazar, to which he would soon bid farewell forever. The citizens of Baza, their empty stomachs growling, watched in hollow-eyed silence from window and street how the mighty Christian noose was growing ever tighter around the Moorish neck.

❧ *Chapter 12* ❧

"GREETINGS. DON IÑIGO." Ferdinand boomed from behind his writing table, the weatherbeaten skin around his eyes wrinkling in a smile as his commander was shown into the private study of the royal apartments in the Baza palace.

Tendilla came across the thick carpet bathed with patterned sunlight from the arabesque grills on the windows and bowed solemnly, hand on heart. "Your Majesties," he murmured. He did not remove his brimless felt hat.

"We trust the Christian captives have been taken care of? What were their numbers?"

"Five hundred and two, sire, counting thirty children. All were fed and their sores treated. The last of them were dispersed this matin, singing praises to their monarchs for the gifts of money to see them to their homes."

"Thank you, my lord." Ferdinand leaned back against the small, rolled pillow that protected his neck from the hard, high back of his chair. His wife, sitting to one side in a more comfortable chair, had her feet up on a small stool.

Ferdinand came right to the point. "My lord, what we must discuss now is the subject we could not take up before the rest of our advisors this morning. We are sore troubled by the lack of information from Granada. Have you received any more communications?"

"No, Sire, and the problem has become acute. My best source of information was recently removed from his post, having unwisely aroused the ire and suspicions of his enemies. In fact," Tendilla added dryly, "he lost his head. Quite literally. My other informants in the city do not have sensitive enough positions. The hard fact is it will take some time to fill so important a breach in my sources."

Ferdinand grimaced and slumped tiredly in his seat. He rubbed a smoothed and polished oval stone between impatient fingers. "That is not good, my lord. We must have adequate tidings from the Alhambra. It is our good fortune that the hatred between the various Moorish princes so far keeps them from uniting powerful forces to repel us. But the Grand Sultan Boabdil in Granada is our good fortune. His nature is weak, he is conciliatory. We strongly feel he will prove no obstacle in our path when we are ready to demand surrender of the capital city itself."

Isabella nodded. She wore a simple, unadorned gown which lent her the look of any ordinary matron, except that for three nights, along with Ferdinand and the royal ministers, she had been closeted until far into the mornings working to coordinate the urgent administrative affairs of the city, the prosaic lot which befalls conquerers. Now she sat wielding her embroidery needle and gold thimble, enjoying a short relaxation. But her blue eyes were as alert as if nothing had claimed her sleep the nights before.

Tendilla stood silent, waiting.

"This morning we reported in council that Cidi Yahye's response to the courtesies we have showered upon him is gratifying; he will go to Almería and beard El Zagal. He believes he can persuade the crafty old man that he cannot win against our superior forces and resources, that surrender is his own best hope and the salvation of his people."

"I find it hard to believe that wily demon intends to reach Allah's garden without his sword in his hand."

"Agreed, but we must try, for we do not have the strength remaining to back up our threats at this time. That is why we have thrown into the pot the huge bribe of vassalage title to the Barony of Andarraxa with its revenues of four million maravedis." Ferdinand tossed the stone on the table with a clatter. "No matter what, we must keep him so occupied with us that he has no mind to consider overthrowing Boabdil, for should he and the other rebellious warriors come to power

291

again in the capital city their united opposition to us would be violent. Weary years might be added to our crusade before victory came into our hands."

Isabella leaned forward, contemplating Tendilla with her clear blue eyes, her embroidery frame abandoned on her lap. "Up to the present, via our own sources and yours, we were aware of every palace rumble or mumble or chicanery behind Boabdil's throne, besides knowing to a man the strength of his garrisons and the state of his supplies. And now your own well has dried up. That worries us. We seem to be in the position of a hunter who can neither hear nor see, my lord Count."

"Not quite, Your Majesty. Only a very temporary condition, soon remedied. Perhaps by early spring. You have my assurances on this."

Finally. The waiting was over.

Ferdinand smiled, pushed his chair back, and propped his leg up on the table. "Ah, good. I knew Tendilla would not be found lacking a trick up his sleeve."

Tendilla offered his dry smile back. His features showed little of the excitement that ran through him at the vindication of his farsighted, detailed, and patient planning. "No one enjoys deafness less than I, Sire. I have kept in reserve an excellent, absolutely trustworthy agent specially prepared for just such emergency and will immediately put him into operation. Of course, at this late hour, his becomes the most difficult of missions and the element of chance may hinder his success no matter how thoughtfully we have prepared. Whether he can insinuate himself into the Granadan court remains to be seen. We will need patience."

"If you vouch for him, Don Iñigo, we are satisfied of his worth. Is it someone of whom we have knowledge?"

"No, Sire, this man is new."

Ferdinand nodded and pushed no further. Tendilla's sources were his own affair, and they had always proved worthwhile.

"Our own informants have been decimated and scattered by the civil riots that keep convulsing Granada. We are now wholly reliant upon your good offices, Don Iñigo," Isabella said. "And we shall have to be patient in any case, for this brave camp has totally drained us."

Ferdinand changed his position again, sitting up straighter, fatigue keeping him from comfort. "You remained fairly silent at the council meeting this morning, *señor.* What think you of Cadiz's plan to make use of this great army while we have it and help El Zagal to his decision by looming over him before he has time to think, or to realize how empty of real force might be our gesture?"

"It is a good plan, Sire; I had little to add beside what Medina-Sidonia already noted, that in this season it will be a most difficult and dangerous march. We will pay for such defiance of winter."

"We will pay, sir," Ferdinand agreed with a weary shrug, "but not Don Alvaro Suarez de Figueroa, whom we leave here to govern this city, nor you and your lieutenants. It is our decision, my lord Count, to give into your hands the command of the entire frontier about Granada. It will put you close to your informants, and your prior experience and vigilance in maintaining the dangerous outpost of Alcala recommends you to us."

Mendoza bowed deeply. "Your Most Gracious Majesties, I am honored by your trust."

"You have a free hand, my lord. Cidi Yahye and his delegation depart this day for Cadiz to present our terms to El Zagal in return for the surrender of all the cities and territories he holds. In a short while we will know our road." Ferdinand's shrewd expression softened, turned reflective. He smiled, hooded eyes crinkling again. "We have come a long, long way since Zahara, eh, Don Iñigo?"

"A long way, my King. The eyes of all Christian Europe are upon us. With astonishment."

"And those of Moslem Egypt and the Caliphates of Barbary with ire." Ferdinand chuckled. "Ah well, we shall have to spread some honey upon their unleavened bread this winter. But keep our gains in Granada safe from encroachment, my lord, and God will guide our hand in the rest."

Tendilla nodded. "My pledge on it, Sire."

✤ *Chapter 13* ✤

ABU ABDULLAH, THE Grand Sultan Boabdil, sat with glazed eyes, staring through his arched window at the majestic reach of the purple, snow-capped Sierra Nevada mountains in the distance. He thought of nothing. He willed his mind to be empty, empty and clear, aware only of the plaintive, unusually loud music performed by two turbaned musicians squatting in a corner across the rug-scattered mosaic floor, one fingering a haunting pipe, the other plucking at the horizontal strings of a twanging instrument.

The Sultan's body didn't appreciate the large, soft divan heaped with silk and velvet pillows upon which he was propped. His senses didn't rejoice in the perfect, perfumed day. His hand didn't notice the golden tassel it unraveled. He was using the music to shut out most of the sounds from the first plaza below, where seven of his courtiers were being executed.

The Sultan withdrew like this often. When the thousand cares and fears hidden in the crevices of his brain threatened invasion of his consciousness all at once, he just withdrew his attention and outwitted them. He would not think. It was a trick carried over from his persecuted childhood, taught to him by a slave, a strange holy man from Asia. It was only a temporary respite for he was not too good at it, but when finally he refocused his eyes he sometimes felt strong enough to cope with the problem threatening him. Such as now.

His Grand Vizier, Comixa, had argued him into ordering the death of seven aristocrats whose support of El Zagal had only been suspected and whom he would rather have spared and won to him with generous gifts. But: "O Sultan, do you sit upon the throne to rule or coddle? You must show your people you are strong, that they may be loyal to you above all others. Reward the treachery of these traitors with little measures and you reward yourself with little power!"

And already the tip of the executioner's huge blade had rung thrice upon the courtyard's flags. Boabdil refused to hear it. If think he must, he would think about the glorious past of his people, as he often did, and keep his ears stoppered to the present.

The Sultan dreamed with his eyes open, dreamed of warriors that had swarmed seven centuries earlier across the narrow strait from Africa to Iberia, a ferocious host of Eastern Arabs, North African Berbers, and Christian Copts from the desert, led by Tarik, a forceful general, whose name was given to the great mountain of rock standing between the two continents, Jebal Tarik. It took but seven short years for the clamoring warriors of the Prophet to overpower the native Visigoths and swallow up the whole of the peninsula, except for a stubborn knot of the followers of Christ who hid themselves in the grim northern mountains of Asturias.

But the conquered land became the conquerer, and Iberia absorbed the Arabs, as she had the Celt, the Semite, the Greek, the Latin. Those who came fiercely thirsting for water, for dark soil, for the luxuriant verdure of Andalusia, soon gentled under the spell of the land. The harsh, unbending spirit of the Arab, born of the hot desert, crumbled away in the fragrant gardens of southern Spain. The Moslems of Iberia became a different people from those of Baghdad and Damascus and Egypt. The stern rigor of their Faith relaxed, and Islam, whose name was war, desired peace.

As the centuries passed Moslem, Christian, and Jew mingled as one people in pleasant Andalusia. A golden civilization bloomed, far outstripping the rest of Europe in culture, in sophistication, in science. From all over the world travelers and seekers came to Andalusia, a mecca of knowledge and learning, wealth and refinement, and, especially, tolerance.

But to the bitter northern Christians backed into their tiny mountain kingdom of Asturias there remained only the desire for vengeance, which they sullenly nurtured and strengthened over the centuries. At last, having gathered strength, four centuries after they had lost their land, they came swooping down from their rugged and barren mountain strongholds and fell with astonishing success upon the gentled Moslems. Relentlessly, taking the role of barbarian attacker, century by century, the Cross pushed back and conquered the Crescent, retaking Burgos, Zaragoza, Barcelona, Toledo, Valencia; inching farther and farther south to at last strike at Andalusia itself, reconquering Seville and the glittering Caliphate and university city of Cordoba as well.

By the early fifteenth century, as reckoned by the Christian calendar, there remained to the Moors only the lush southern toehold of Granada, a kingdom over two hundred leagues long and sixty deep, with its decadent cities governed by unruly princes who often refused the orders of the Grand Sultan in Granada, the capital city. At this point in their history, however, the Christian Kings of Castile and of Aragon were embroiled in shoring up their own territories and required of the remaining Arabs on their peninsula only oaths of fealty and money tributes as the price for peace. The Arab princes, resentful, but caring only to enjoy their existence in this last bit of Allah's garden, complied.

There was peace in the years before Boabdil's birth, and for many years subjects of the various Iberian kingdoms came and went with impunity over each other's borders, students, merchants, farmers, artists, pilgrims, cavaliers, and aristocrats of both faiths. Even though the Granadan chieftains continued to harass each other, for most Moslems and Christians it was a glorious time of shared tranquility.

Boabdil's face darkened as the familiar scroll which he could cause to unroll behind his eyes came to the marriage of the Princess Isabella of Castile to Ferdinand of Aragon, the event which finally united most of Spain and brought political ease to the Christians. The covetous eyes of ambitious Spaniards had the freedom now to turn southward again, toward the tempting, green, and fertile vale still in the hands of the Prophet.

The Sultan stirred uneasily. To this point his thoughts had rolled over the familiar history smooth as water in a marble course, but now, as he came to his father, there was the usual emotional jar; he hated his father's very memory, for the man was instigator of all the woes that now beset the son.

The Sultan Muley Abul Hassan had ascended the throne of Granada in the year of the Hegira 869, or 1465 reckoned by Christ, coming to power in an era which had enjoyed a long peace at home and with the Christians. But Allah had imbued Abul Hassan with the ancient belligerence, and after several years of ruling he suddenly refused to pay the degrading tributes which had been exacted for a century by the Christian kings.

Abul Hassan had two wives whom he had raised to the rank of Sultana. The eldest, Ayaxa, held undisputed sway for many years. She produced two sons for her husband, the elder being Abu Abdullah, or Boabdil, but at the birth of this heir the astrologers, despairing over their charts, lamented, *"Allah akbar!* This child will one day oversee the downfall of our kingdom. It is in the hands of God."

From that day forward the Sultan regarded his eldest child with great aversion, and the boy grew up safely only because of the strong protection of his stubborn and determined mother.

When Ayaxa's youth and beauty faded the Sultan found another exquisite charmer in his harem. She had been born Isabella de Solis, the daughter of a Spanish noble, but she had been captured in childhood, raised and educated in the Moorish faith, and given the name Zoraya, Morning Star. The Sultana Zoraya also bore two sons, and these the aging Abul Hassan favored above all other of his children. There was, most naturally, a terrible rivalry between the two Sultanas and a mighty vying of ambitions for their offspring.

The nobility of the Court, siding with one Queen or the other, widened the rift with their jealous intrigues and dissensions. The Sultan himself, and his brother, the warlike prince called El Zagal, favored the beauteous Zoraya. The great, noble families of the Abencerrages and the Zegris, although feuding between themselves, distrusted Zoraya's Christian lineage enough to set them firmly in Ayaxa's camp. There was betrayal and plotting and cold-blooded murder, and the populace, nervous before these shudderings in high places, threatened riot.

Raging, feeling impotent to avert the disaster which these female feuds threatened to bring on his head, Abul Hassan looked for an outlet for his ire and decided on the fateful, terrible step of swinging his scimitar at the Christian city and fortress of Zahara, only feebly garrisoned because of the prevailing peace. Leading his troops at night in a sneak attack he exacted a terrible, unnecessary toll of lives, mercilessly slaughtering women and children in their beds and allowing his army to reduce the helpless city to charred rubble.

But when the triumphant Sultan returned to Granada, driving before him like animals pitiful lines of haggard humanity, his own people shook their fists with outrage and with the fear of what was to come. The terrible voice of an ancient, holy dervish, whose age had withered his body but not quenched the fire in his eye, daily harangued the people: "Woe, woe! Woe to Granada. Its hour of desolation approaches. The ruins of Zahara will fall upon our heads. The peace is broken and the sword shall inherit us!"

A rash of conspiracies broke out among the nobles to place a more reasonable man on the throne. In response, the Sultan clapped Ayaxa and her son Boabdil in a tower and ordered the executions of a number of their Abencerrages cavaliers. But nevertheless the royal refuges were freed in a daring rescue and carried away to a hiding place in the Alpuxarras mountains.

Desperately stoppering up his ears with the music to drown the clang of the giant scimitar on the flagstones below, Boabdil willed his scroll to move faster before his eyes, for he did not care to dwell on the homeless and often frightening years of his youth. The attack on Zahara was avenged by a Christian attack on the city of Alhama, where the Spanish repaid the Moorish atrocities by atrocities of their own, ravaging and plundering and enslaving any inhabitants whom they had not murdered. The two catastrophes of Zahara and Alhama were all the spark Their Catholic Majesties needed to ignite their crusade to free Spain of these ancient interlopers, Ferdinand craftily submerging his crass territorial ambitions beneath the loftier religious zeal of Isabella.

The horrors at Alhama so incensed the Moors that Allah removed his hand from their hearts; the old ferocity reclaimed them, and they sprang to arms with all the fervor of their ancestors. And so commenced, in 1478, the long and bloody wars for the last Moslem territory in Europe, the Kingdom of Granada—slow moving at first but gaining in momentum and captured territories for the Spaniards with each summer's campaign.

Sultan Abul Hassan held the west of the Kingdom of Granada, and his brother, El Zagal, held the east, including the rich cities of Gaudix and Almería. Both of these headstrong men were feared by disgruntled nobility, who favored the more manageable son of the Sultana Ayaxa, the prince whom the people called Boabdil the Unlucky.

Boabdil, pushed by his mother and the vengeful Abencerrages, finally rode at the head of a great, flashing army to join forces with the veteran marauder Prince Ali Atar of Loxa and then led the whole Moorish host in an attack on Lucena. He had no love for war or talent for strategy, but Boabdil knew no one could fault his personal courage once engaged, and his pride stirred to remember how he had led his men to such feats of bravery that Lucena was almost won— when down from the hills surged a relief of Christian forces including the infamous Donzeles, Ferdinand's elite corps of seasoned and fiery *caballeros*.

Boabdil the Unlucky was captured and for months languished in captivity, albeit a luxurious captivity, for the Catholic monarchs were chivalrous. Abul Hassan made overtures to ransom his oldest son, but Isabella was neither stupid nor heartless enough to give over her royal captive to a sure execution. Besides, as Boabdil realized later, the Spanish rulers had political reasons for wanting him alive, for he formed a center of contention which could pull Granada apart from the inside while the Christians gnawed at the outside.

Finally ransomed by Ayaxa, but forced to swear fealty and payment of annual tribute to Spain, and to offer his small son as hostage, Boabdil was released.

He was despised for the pledge he had made to the Christians. But when Abul Hassan died, some said from being poisoned, the young heir was helped by Ferdinand to soundly defeat his rival, the vicious El Zagal, in a bloody battle, and the populace of Granada welcomed him. Long live the Sultan Boabdil!

Boabdil shook his head to remember how his inconsistent people had cheered him, having forgotten for that moment his ordinarily passive nature and the oath of vassalage to Spain which he had taken and which he had hoped to observe. El Zagal retreated to Gaudix to lick his wounds, taking many discomforted nobles with him, but leaving enough at court to continue the plots and schemes against his nephew.

As Sultan, Boabdil had neither sent help to the besieged and prostrate city of Malaga several years before, nor now to Cidi Yahye suffering a siege at Baza, for he was terrified to reduce his forces and be attacked from Gaudix by his Uncle El Zagal. He hated the Christians; the unwelcome friendliness of Ferdinand and Isabella had become an albatross around his neck, for it offended his people. But, and with greater passion, he loathed and feared his uncle.

Boabdil brought his eyes and his attention back into the room. With a sharp gesture he silenced the musicians, tilting his head to listen. From below came only the sound of marching feet and the barked commands of the officer in charge of disposing of the bodies. But—rising from the city proper in the valley below the Alhambra palace came other sounds, the distant voices of the gathered populace, crying out and cheering. The words were not distinguishable but the excitement was wafted to him, high up on the hill. The Sultan cocked his head, listening to the noise of acclaim borne on the breeze, and it was gratifying music to his ears.

A bitter smile flitted across his face. He knew why he was a hero today. His Grand Vizier Yusef Comixa, an aging relic from his father's reign but a shrewd administrator whom he trusted with power second only to his, had probably ordered the bloody heads of the unproven traitors to be mounted on spears over the city gates, and for this sign of severity the citizens of Granada now applauded their Sultan. They still distrusted him as conciliatory. Even so small a showing as this seven-headed defiance of El Zagal made them happy, believing that Boabdil the Unlucky had become Boabdil the Lion. Ah well. The Grand Vizier had been right, as usual. Not merciful, but at least right.

Mercy? What was mercy? he mused sourly. What mercy that he was quickened in the belly of a sultana, a driving woman who instilled in him a will to rule, the maddening, ceaseless desire to be acclaimed Grand Sultan, yet had no way to imbue him with the cruel and forceful spirit necessary to hold his throne.

Boabdil el Chico, that was what the Spaniards called him. The youngster, the immature. Young yes, he was young in years but old in grief. Despised by his father, who would gladly have killed him, despoiled of his throne, captured by the Christians, and forced to leave his pride and his only son behind, distrusted and reviled by his people, who finally turned to him when there was no one else, hagridden by plotters and overruled by his counselors—there was no one so old as he.

And yet, and yet life brought some gifts that could release his foundering soul from dark and weary depths: Music and song, poetry, his favorite, loving wife, Morayama, these were his without travail. And only these brought him happiness without exacting bitterness and struggle in return.

The sound of cheering again rose from below; the Granadans were pleased with him for once. His heart warmed with gratitude. In spite of it all he loved this beautiful land, and for all their caprices he loved his subjects. Allah bestow great wisdom and strength on him that he might provide them with further causes for pride. He absently stroked the smooth red leather binding of a book of verse lying by his side but suddenly sat up, brightening with an idea. For his birthday he would announce a competition—a Tourney of the Poets—to choose the greatest versifier in all Granada. The subject would be—would be Loyalty, and a fat purse of golden dinars would be the prize, and appointment to the Royal Academy. . . .

An ebony-hued Nubian guard strode into the room, salaamed, and stood aside with arms crossed as the pantalooned Grand Vizier Comixa, spare and sour, entered behind him, followed by two guards and a stranger. Yusef Comixa crossed the wide floor with a stride admirable in a man of his age. A large sapphire gleamed in his spotless white turban as he made a sketchy salaam before his ruler. He was stern and unsmiling, but then the Vizier never smiled.

"We have tidings from Gaudix, O Sultan," Comixa announced, folding his lips in, the sign of a distasteful subject to come.

"Speak then, what is the news?"

"An unheard of disaster, my lord, impossible to believe." Even so the voice was curbed.

"Yes, yes . . ."

"El Zagal has capitulated! He has surrendered his arms and his territories to the Christians. And he has sworn an oath of vassalage to the Spanish Crown!"

Boabdil leaped forward from his divan as if thunder had

clapped in his ear. He grasped the Vizier by the arm. "What? In the almighty name of Allah, is this true?"

"True, every word. The news is rampant over the city by this time," Comixa answered dryly. "Prince Cidi Yahye was the treacherous instrument by which your uncle was wooed. He sought to convince El Zagal that it is Allah's will that Granada fall—though one needs not brains to realize that your uncle had already bethought himself of the advantages of friendly submission. Alone he knew he would eventually be taken, and rather would he cede his possessions to the enemy than place them, and himself, under our protection. They have given him the Andarraxa Valley and revenues from the salt mines there, and consigned him to oblivion."

Quickly Comixa held up a warning hand to halt the Sultan from reacting. "We have an eyewitness to the meeting, a disaffected Morisco," the Grand Vizier said. He jerked his head and the soldiers behind him pushed forward an exhausted, booted rider, still wearing the dirty, crumpled tunic and hosen of Christian Spain, the dusty cloak which had covered them crushed over his arm.

"Speak, man." Comixa's rusty voice grated.

The red-rimmed eyes blinked, the weary body and hand sketched a salaam. Then the man plunged right in. "O greatest of Sultans, the monarchs of the Spanish allowed their army neither rest nor recovery at Baza for they gathered their troops and followed on Cidi Yahye's heels, the King leading the army forth from the gates of Baza, the lady Queen herself riding with a few of her train to hold together the rear. The route along the spine of mountains and through the passes of the Sierra Nevada toward Almería is torturous in winter, many of the passes winding and narrow, hardly room enough for eight men abreast . . ." The deserter caught up his breath for a moment and then flung himself on his knees before Boabdil and cried passionately, "O Grand Sultan, if only a handful of our own courageous warriors had but earlier occupied the mounts above each of these high passes the whole Christian army could have been decimated, crushed by the hundred in deliberate falls of rock, showered upon by rains of arrows, bolts, and shot, we could have—"

Comixa impatiently jabbed him in the back with the toe of his shoe. "But we didn't. Therefore relate the facts. Do not waste our time."

The haggard rider hung his head, but continued, "Those peaks soar into the clouds, the valleys are so deep the sun scarce reaches there. The wind roared bitter cold down the ravines. The army rode through dense snowfalls and camped upon barren rock, and having started in fatigued condition many men as well as horse were benumbed and frozen to death, and many lost the trail in the whiteness of the storms and were only saved by the Marquis of Cadiz, who caused beacon fires to be lit and sustained from the loftier points about the main group."

"Yes, yes, but get to the point." Comixa scowled. "A few frozen infidels more or less make little difference."

The Morisco eyed the Sultan's unreadable face as if to gauge his state of temper, for innocent bearers of bad news sometimes suffered unjust consequences. But he went on. "Finally, outside of Almería, El Zagal and his *caballeros* met the Christian Monarchs and . . . and surrendered upon restatement of the lenient conditions offered to him and his people; and together, the victor and the vanquished, they entered the city. The Christians took some rest for a few days and then continued on, turning north to Gaudix, which also threw open its gates, and from whence I fled."

"And why came you here, since you had already lightened your captivity by serving as guide to the enemy's forces?" Boabdil asked in a tense, quiet voice.

The man was frightened and trembled, but tears stood in his bitter, tired eyes. "I could no more stand the shame of such defeat, O Excellence, nor bear the trampling in the dust of the almighty Koran. I ran away to bring you the true tale, to beg to be taken into the avenging army of the true Prophet. . . ."

The unsaid words— "which can be launched by you, Grand Sultan, the richest and strongest hope of repelling the invaders of our homes and land"—these words hung in the air, louder than silence as the eyes of Comixa, the Morisco, and furtively, even the guards, leveled upon Boabdil.

The Boabdil waved his hand in brusque dismissal. "Take him out. Give him food and give him over to serve with the leanest troop." He held tight control over his voice. The rider was hustled out by the guards.

The moment they were alone Boabdil bounded past Comixa with a shout of joy like a man released from a cage.

He ran to the grilled window and threw up his arms to the sky in a transport of delight, hardly remembering when he had been so happy. *"Allah! Allah akbar!* God is great, God is good. He has plucked from my shoulders the most venomous reptile of all. Rejoice with me, Yusef, the stars have eased their persecution; henceforth I am Boabdil the Fortunate, for Allah guides my destiny onto grassy paths." He swiveled back to Comixa. "Now I reign without a rival. Now there will be peace in our land, finally."

Boabdil stood there feeling puissant enough to tear apart boars, but he saw Comixa remained silent and stern. "Why do you not rejoice? Why does your face wear such gloom? Think, Yusef, we are rid of our enemy!"

Comixa shook his head. "We are rid of one enemy, Excellence, the greatest, 'tis true, but not the last. A troubled sea is still around us—"

"And can be smoothed now that the great djinn no longer roils the water. Listen to how the people below are acclaiming me! They have heard the news."

"Yes, but—"

Boabdil felt on sure and firm ground. "Gather all my nobles, Grand Vizier, and order my steed decked in his jeweled trappings. We shall all descend in pomp to receive the tribute of my people. Set the drums to booming, the horns to sounding, I proclaim this day of exultation a holiday, and there shall be dancing in the streets!"

"Harken to me, O Sultan, the time is not right for such a showing. Let my Sultan defer rejoicings until all has settled into a calm."

"Nonsense. Your cautious nature ill becomes a triumph, Yusef. We shall ride through the streets and accept the homage of our people while the cruel memories of El Zagal and their deliverance from him are still fresh in their minds. I wish them to see their victorious Sultan among them. . . ."

His heavily bejeweled mother, Ayaxa, swept into the salon, imperious for all her small stature and flimsy face veil, trailed by gloomy-faced council members. "What?" she cried out, hearing his last statement. "Are you mad, my son? Descend into that ravening horde? Don't you hear what they shout? They are in a ferment of grief, of indignation, they extol Abdullah El Zagal to the skies!" She watched the sensitive, weakly handsome face of the Sultan go pale.

"Extol him? Impossible. Didn't they abjure him? In hate, in disgust?"

"So they did, but that was several months ago. Their memories are short. Now it is you who draws their ire."

"No," Boabdil whispered in shock. "That cannot be true."

Ayaxa took his arm grimly. "Come. Hear for yourself." She led him out onto a balcony overhanging the city. Now the voices of the people milling in the streets below came to him clearly for there was a throng of them at the gates to the Alhambra, held in order by grunting royal guards flashing wicked scimitars. Boabdil could see them from where he stood at an angle to them and unobserved, shouting and shaking their fists at the palace.

"Come out, O Sultan, and show us the sword with which you helped El Zagal against his enemies!"

"El Zagal went to defeat as a warrior, not as a vassal to unbelievers!"

"Traitor, O Sultan, traitor to rejoice in the defeat of the faithful!"

White-lipped, Boabdil asked his mother, "What do they mean, 'not as a vassal'? But he has given his allegiance to the Christians. He did not even resist."

Ayaxa's scarves fluttered behind her in the breeze. "They do not wish to inquire into the particulars. Now they are safe from him they raise up El Zagal into a hero," she explained bitterly. "He always lived by the sword and that is what they remember and admire—so long as it is not directed at them."

Now they heard muffled thunks as vegetables and stones were hurled against the palace gates. "Boabdil el Zegoybi brings misfortune to Granada!"

"War upon the Christians! Let us succor our brothers."

"Down with El Rey Chico, friend to the unbelievers."

Shrieks and cries and groans arose as a detachment of palace guards poured from the gates and lay around them with scimitars and pikes. Silently the observers filed from the balcony.

Boabdil threw himself upon the divan, beating his fist upon a pillow. "Why do I break my heart for these savage people with a will like the west wind, blowing first hot, then cold. They love me for the golden advantages of peace I have brought to them, and then they revile me for not plunging them into disastrous war. What, O Allah be Merciful, do they want?" he moaned.

Comixa attempted to pacify him. "Illustrious Lord, the city is full of refugees, men ruined by war and existing only for revenge, and thousands of disbanded soldiers whose only livelihood is by the sword. These are the hub of the fury raging at the gates. And the nobles who plot against you, they too want war. The merchants, the civil servants, our ordinary householders, they find themselves so stirred up by these violent factions they know not which way to think."

As he had done many times before, Boabdil turned his eyes toward his loyal old counselor to relieve his indecision. "What shall be done?"

Comixa sighed. "We wait. Wait until the fury wears itself out. Once the first shock of the capture of Gaudix is past the clamor will subside."

"And if it does not," cried Ayaxa, "can we hold the Alhambra against the hysteria that surrounds us?"

Comixa shrugged. He was tired. A dispirited old man.

But Boabdil stood up with an angry show of determination. "Yes, by Allah, I shall hold my throne! And by the very means that those ingrates below despise. I am still allied to Spain. Ferdinand will come to my aid again if I request it; no one would dare to revolt against our concerted might. No more bemoaning my alliance with the unbelievers. For once I have accomplished a politic act which will prove our salvation."

"Or our ruination." Ayaxa glared at him, her black eyes burning. "You rely on them too much. Remember, the beetle may cross safely the chasm on the spider's thread, but the spider waits with gaping jaws on the far side! You can *yourself* unseat your foes. Here are your council members, ready to do your bidding. I say, we say, go to the factious warlords and the restless nobles and bring them to heel with the only gesture that will unite every true Moslem under their one Sultan."

Again Boabdil directed his gaze at Comixa. His mother always made him feel helpless and inadequate to the situation.

"War," agreed the Vizier with a stiff nod. "War against the Christians, lord, to gain back our lost territories, and over which you will be the only ruler. We have the manpower, we have the supplies . . ."

"We have the might and the courage!" Ayaxa grated.

"The Sultan of Egypt and the Ottoman caliphs will send us their aid now you reign supreme in Granada. With Allah leading us and our efforts and sacrifice, we can prevail. . . ."

"No! Speak to me not of war!" Boabdil shouted, backing away from the knot of tormentors standing before him. "That was the way of my father and that way is doomed. Of all Andalusia only Granada remains to the Faithful; only in this one small land can we walk in freedom. And the fates—the fates moan to us that not even that will be ours if we continue the bloody course set at Zahara."

"But what freedom is there in vassalage?"

"At least to remain in our land and in our homes. Do you forget the weeping fate of Malaga, whose reward for savage resistance was ruin and slavery and wholesale deportation of its citizenry? The fortune tellers say we cannot win. Shall we wander homeless in the barren hills of Africa and pine for our captured paradise? No, I say. Let us accept the half loaf they offer us and praise Allah for His Mercy."

One of the counselors asked timidly, "O Sultan, what of the frustrated revolts that may rend this kingdom? We might remain with only the mercenaries, the palace Africans loyal to us."

"I do not believe that. The people of this kingdom will walk close behind us for there is no one else to lead them. That is my word and so it shall be. Now go and leave me in peace; I wish to think."

Comixa and the Sultana Ayaxa exchanged exasperated glances. Comixa's scraggly gray eyebrows were drawn into a straight, stern line, but he shrugged. "May Allah bring light to your contemplations, Great Sultan," he rasped. Fingertips to forehead, the Vizier and the council members bowed and retreated from the Sultan's salon.

Ayaxa was the last to leave. "A mother's warning, O Sultan. Remember the spider." Stiff and straight she glided from the room.

Boabdil sank exhausted onto the divan. His head ached miserably. There was fear in his heart, a familiar emotion, not for himself but for his people and this lovely land of his forebears. Could one defeat the soothsayers and the wheeling of the stars after all?

He signaled to the forgotten musicians to resume their playing, and he lay despondent and upset, shredding the golden tassel hanging from a cushion. But the musicians were either incredibly stupid or stupidly brave, and chose the wrong ballade to sing, for which, moments later, the great

Sultan shouted them out of the room and banished them forever from his sight:

> *Friends, ye have alas to know*
> *Of a most disastrous blow*
> *That the Christians, stern and bold,*
> *Have obtained Alhama's hold,*
> *Woe is me, Alhama!*

> *Out then spake old Alfaqui,*
> *With his beard so white to see,*
> *"Good Sultan, thou art justly served,*
> *Good Sultan this thou hast deserved."*
> *Woe is me, Alhama!*

> *And from the windows o'er the walls*
> *The sable web of mourning falls.*
> *The Sultan weeps as a woman o'er*
> *His loss, for it is much and sore.*
> *Woe is me, Alhama!*

Tendilla chose for his frontier headquarters the site of his historic victory, Alcala la Real, an almost impregnable aerie whose ponderous stone castle, supported by great buttresses jutted from the side of the cliff, commanded the main pass through the rugged mountains surrounding Granada. But he kept the impatient Francho firmly on the leash because the most important part of their operation was still missing—a reliable communication line.

"A plague on these tantrum-prone Granadans," the Count inveighed to Francho. "Had not our excellent courier been killed in one of their typical riots you would have already been in their midst. Now it will take time to find another man who can be trusted to get your messages out."

"There must be numerous Moors of some Christian lineage who could be bribed to aid us," Francho muttered.

"Bribed, indeed, but think, Francisco, this requires a very special individual since we will one day be operating under conditions of war. This man must be entirely above suspicion and able to pass through the gates even during hostilities. My agent has singled out such a person in the city and contrived to engage his friendship, but he must be feinted with and cultivated before he can be approached safely."

Francho was aware that twice a hooded figure had given a certain password at the gates of Alcala and had been taken directly to Tendilla, and that this was one of the two agents who formed the outside half of the courier team, stationed beyond the city of Granada's gates.

"But God sees that when one leg is lame the other grows stronger," Tendilla continued, a long finger indicating a parchment on his table. "I have here a dispatch from di Lido. Their Majesties have requested him to undertake an embassy to placate the Sultan of Egypt, who is still threatening retaliation for Granada upon his Christian subjects and who might yet take it into his head to dispatch an army to aid Boabdil. The monarchs are trusting to the maestro's diplomatic turn of words to soothe the Sultan, and will also strengthen his argument with exquisite gifts. Di Lido adds here that the King bids him appoint a number of *caballeros* from our finest families to accompany him, to add the weight of the great houses of Spain to his. Do you see how this eases our path?"

A leaping tongue of flame from the freshly built fire crackling on the hearth gleamed the satin of Tendilla's fur-lined, knee-length tunic, encircled by a dropped belt of incised leather from which hung his jeweled dagger. It also pointed up the shadowy, baggy smudges under his sharp eyes, witness to the unceasing attention required to command so wide-flung and rugged a perimeter.

Francho nodded and looked up from the parchment, his gaze narrowed but eager. "It could account for my long absence from Court and from Alcala . . ."

". . . in very logical and satisfactory manner," Tendilla continued the thought with uncharacteristic fervor.

Francho grinned. He hooked one ankle over the other knee and teetered back precipitously on two legs of his stool. "When is this mission projected, my lord?"

"The end of February. Next month. If fortune smiles upon us and we have secured our courier by then, you will be attached to the mission to Egypt. Ostensibly."

Bold blue eyes met eyes of deepest jet, anticipation glittering in both.

Francho returned to the locked chamber which had been set aside for him and hung with several layers of cloth and tapestries to conceal the sound of his music. The room had no window, but one wall was an outer wall and tiny wind gusts coming through chinks in the ancient courses of stone stirred the hangings. He chose a guembri, a Moorish guitar, from among several types of stringed instruments resting on a velvet-padded bench. He put one booted foot up on the bench to cradle the sleek, polished guitar and sighed with impatience as his fingers thrummed a dark minor chord. He would give anything he owned and gladly, to bring that last man in their network immediately, solidly, into the fold.

❧ *Chapter 14* ❧

IN FEBRUARY THE entire glory of Spain gathered in Seville for the brilliant wedding celebration of Don Antonio de la Cueva and the French Countess Lysette de Moulines. Grudging time spent away from his headquarters, for Moorish marauders continued to strike at isolated fortresses in random pattern, Tendilla departed Alcala la Real at the last possible moment, so that his party of gentlemen who had been invited to the festivities plus their equerries and escort had to keep up a grueling pace to reach Seville the evening before the nuptials. They would stay only three days, for the ceremony and the tourney, and return to their duties at Alcala the fourth morning.

They arrived at the Count's Seville residence exhausted and hungry. Francho went to his chamber and was soon reclining against the high back of a shallow wooden tub while Esteban Ebarra sloshed ewers of warm water over his tired body. Bare-chested, and sitting in his undergarments, he ate his supper before the blazing hearth, for the nights were chilly this time of year in Seville. He had finished his meal, penned a short note to Leonora, and was eyeing the deep bed with longing when a soft tap came at the door. Esteban opened it to an apologetic lackey. "There is a gentleman demanding to see Don Francisco. Will you inform him?"

Circling one shoulder to relieve a cramp, Francho strode to the door. "At this hour?"

The compact bulk of Hernando del Pulgar appeared behind the anxious lackey, and the brash cavalier pushed his way into the chamber. *"Sí,* at this hour! And have you forgotten the custom of feasting the bridegroom on the eve of the wedding?"

They clasped hands, grinning. "But Hernando, we have just arrived and ridden hard to do it. My bones ache with fatigue."

"A pox on your bones, *señor.* Antonio would never forgive you if you did not assist at his last supper in freedom. Come, we're gathered at La Luna de Plata and he's sent me off to fetch you no matter what your condition. So let's be off. . . ."

Francho knew the inn, favored by the young bloods for unhampered carousing. He cast a glance at the bed with its turned-down coverlet, but it had suddenly lost its appeal. He pushed a carafe of strong wine and a goblet along the inlaid top of his table toward Pulgar. "Here, *amigo,* rinse the dust from your gullet whilst I clothe myself. I can't appear at the party without my hosen."

Pulgar poured himself a brave measure. "Well, don't take too many pains, my peacock. If we don't hurry all the comelier tavern wenches will have been appropriated."

Esteban was already laying out doublet and hosen, a short velvet cape lined with wool, and soft leather boots. Francho shoved the letter he had written into Esteban's hand. "This is very precious, Ebarra. See it is delivered first thing in the morning." He closed the man's fingers over the crackling parchment, for his heart was inscribed there in loving words of greeting to his lady.

Pulgar looked up, taking for granted he knew to whom the letter was addressed. His mouth turned down a bit. "Perens has been dancing attendance upon her like a pet dog."

"I know. So I expected," Francho responded grimly.

The bluff Pulgar struggled against prying and lost. "But why do you not approach Doña Maria and your father and demand her hand, Francisco? An official betrothal would certainly jam a stick up that cockerel's behind." Pulgar was not known for his delicacy.

"Because the Count of Perens is rich, titled, landed, and offers a powerful alliance of families. I've not much hope they would give her to me, even if it is her choice. At least not now. Perhaps, when I return from Egypt . . ."

"You accompany di Lido?"

"Yes, and who knows?" Francho said defiantly. "The Crusaders returned wealthy from the East. Perhaps I will happen upon some riches too."

Pulgar watched the broad, smooth chest disappear as Francho shrugged into his shirt. His friend's bravado didn't fool him. He was likely to return from Egypt with nothing but a few souvenirs. Pulgar's affection for his comrade and his curiosity outstripped courtesy again. "I don't understand, *amigo.* You are your father's only heir. Your prospects are considerable. If the lady strongly prefers you that could tip the scales in your favor. You should put forth your suit right now."

"Hernando, you don't think." Francho growled, annoyed only because he had been over this ground so often in his mind. "My father is not old. He could marry again, advantageously, and have legitimate issue to inherit his title and the most of his fortune. This is why he hesitates to declare me heir." He peered through his lashes to observe the effect of this excuse for his inability to move, pausing for a moment from tying the twisted cords that laced his doublet into an open V over his shirt. Looking into the wrinkled-brow face of his staunch friend he longed to confide the truth, his real name, and his desperate quest to redeem it. Frantic to overcome the strong temptation he threw himself back with a broad smile, to their earlier insouciance. "Come, Don Hernando, there is a revel going on and here we waste the night with serious considerations. I for one want a big flagon of ale and an even bigger wench to jounce on my knee so her breasts pop from her bodice; we live like monks at Alcala. If my equerry will find me my boots we can be off."

Pulgar's high spirits flooded back. *"Sí,* shake your tail, Ebarra, and get him his boots ere the poltroons Antonio numbers among his friends swill down all the drink." His big laugh boomed out. "Very well, Mendoza, you go to Egypt. And I shall command a troop against Lacalahorra this spring, so saith the King. But I hear those veiled Egyptian odalisques have devils which wink from their bellybuttons to enslave you. I'd have a care about jouncing *them,* friend."

Arms over each other's shoulders in camaraderie and anticipation of the drunken night ahead, they marched out to the wrought iron fenced court, where Francho's horse was already being saddled.

Francho remembered the rest as only a moment of revelry and noise, an ocean of drink, coarse jokes, and even coarser women smelling of sweat; and then someone was rudely chasing away kindly oblivion by jostling him insistently by the shoulder. He opened his eyes, winced, and Ebarra stopped shaking him. The equerry stood back, holding a large mug in one hand. "How go you, master?"

"Terrible," Francho groaned, struggling to sit up and squinting against the light. There was too much light. "What hour is it? Still morning, I pray?"

"*Sí*, just past nine." He shoved the mug into Francho's shaky hand. "Drink it, master, it will relieve your discomfort," he advised.

Francho's head felt like the interior of a booming drum, pounding with such vibration that his eyes squeezed shut in pain. Desperately he downed the tepid, smelly potion in one large gulp. "Aargh! What was that nauseous concoction?"

Ebarra calmly drew back the bedcurtains. "Merely a nostrum of egg yolk, goat's milk, bitter almond, linseed oil, rock salt, treacle, ground dragon's bone—very efficacious—and herbs. An ancient Arab remedy for overindulgence and headache."

"Fool, you have poisoned me." Squinting against the light that stabbed at his eyes he swung his naked body over the edge of the bed—Esteban must have undressed him upon his dawn return—wrapped the shirt his man handed him partially about him and tottered over to a chair. "Fetch me my breakfast," he moaned, "a slab of venison and enough bread to take away the taste of your ministering. And then attend me. I must go out." He felt the stiff stubble on his face. "In decent shape."

It seemed as if the whole city of Seville was whirling with the preparations for the wedding, and yet Dolores found herself clapped up in her house, sitting in a little room off her bedchamber, and staring with irritation at Lencastro's precise columns of figures marked in her small ledger, as if scowling at them would make them go away. Lencastro was the Medina-Sidonia's counting master, who, by the Duke's wish, was helping her to bring order to her financial affairs, for she did not handle numbers well.

She had to admit she had lost total control of what to her inexperienced eyes had seemed a vast fortune of money. Now she realized, in her second year at Court and after it was half spent, that the rent on her river land had only been a moderate sum in relation to the wealth surrounding her.

She owed the furrier, the seamstresses, the jeweler, the vendor of scarves, kerchiefs, and stockings, and various other merchants, a long list of debts compiled by Lencastro from bills she had accumulated in an untidy pile in a chest. The problem was that if she paid all these there would be little left in her small money casket, and no hopes of accumulating more unless she sold off Torrejoncillo, as Medina-Sidonia was maneuvering her to do.

Stupid. How could the daughter of the wily Papa el Mono have been so stupid as to react like a child with a glittering bauble, allowing her scramble into the ranks of privilege to trap her into such foolish spending? No wonder the Duke had paid her the entire sum on the ten-year lease of her river land all at once. He had judged her perfectly. He had known she would not be wise with the money but would spend it quickly on the seductive trappings of luxury.

However, the house she sat in—and she glanced around at the smooth, white walls and painted ceilings, Turkish carpets scattered across the tile floor, and the small, graceful hearth of the little room—was hers by his request and at his cost. And it was only leased, not purchased, as rumor would have it. Her eyes had been dazzled by the charming little house sited on this street of fine mansions when Don Enrique showed it to her. He proposed an agreement offering her exclusive use of the house for, if she wished, ten years. What he would gain of it was not mentioned in writing, of course, but it was in the same vein, the same prideful buttress to his ego as his other agreement with her. Hardly onerous, one would say.

She rose and wandered in a fog into her bedchamber, where soon Engracia would come and dress the wavy hair now tumbling below her shoulders and held off her forehead by a circlet, and would also carefully apply henna to her long fingernails with a small camel's hair brush. Dolores distractedly poked among the jumble of bottles, jars, and little pots of perfumed unguent with which she made her toilette, she picked up and put down her silver-framed mirror and her ivory comb (an expensive present from one of the lovelorns who pursued her), but all the while thinking furiously.

To sell Torrejoncillo was unthinkable, for it represented her dowry, and a greater one than she had believed, now that she realized the value of the fall of water in operating machinery. She had at least had the wisdom to protect her reputation by swearing Medina-Sidonia to greatest discretion in respect to her, for rumors alone would not tarnish her irretrievably. Gossip was a major pastime of the Court. Any courtier with personality or verve lived with rumors against him or her, and most of the hearsay was discounted in the long run in the absence of proof. But ego-sustaining rumor was just what the Duke was after. This house was his way of slyly feeding the rumors, although indirectly and discreetly, for the landlord collected the rent from her. But most clever of him, as she finally understood, it was another way of binding her to the taste of luxury.

It had all seemed so simple in the beginning as she stood uncertainly in the old Baron's tumbledown manse; so easy a way of adding legitimacy and stature to her purloined station by acquiring a grandee's personal sponsorship and patronage. But it was now becoming tiresome. The secret that she, and perhaps no other, knew was that the Duke of Medina-Sidonia, one of Spain's most victorious commanders, was impotent, having been made so by the groin wound which had also caused his limp. But once he had been a man of virile pride and needs and had counted some of the Court's greatest beauties among his conquests—most discreetly, of course, for Isabella was not tolerant of flagrant extramarital affairs—but never so discreetly that rumors had not abounded.

Don Enrique would not tolerate pity of any sort. His arrangement with the enviably beautiful, young, and impoverished Baroness de la Rocha, so little worldly at first, was an inspiration which suited them both. She was to act—discreetly, of course—as if there were a certain closeness between them, which discretion would even allow her to accept the homage of other gentlemen. And in turn he would introduce her to the Queen and guide her through the thickets of the Court. So great was his physical embarrassment and craving for the reputation of virility in his forty-seventh year that such deception was not beneath him.

Restlessly, her gray eyes darting and mirroring her turmoil, Dolores prowled about the room, finally raising the skirt of the silk robe she wore over her linen shift so she could step up to the arched door and small balcony overhanging her lovely little garden, green even in February.

In her first year at Court, because she was quartered with the Queen's ladies, she truly saw Medina-Sidonia only in public, even though the whispering abounded, and even what business he wished to discuss—it amazed her that a man said to have over sixty thousand ducats a year in rents would care about a mill to make paper—was done quietly in a removed windowseat of the public audience or reception rooms. But since she had accepted this house last spring, as a pleasant refuge when her shift of twenty-four-hour-a-day attendance upon the Queen was rotated to another lady, he had taken to occasional evening visits—very discreet, of course, entering by the door to the garden—because he liked to be with her.

If the Duke was not modest he was at least not boring, a man accustomed to command, although more celebrated for his patriotic bravery and the huge army he brought into the field from his own resources than for astute military strategy. His conversation revolved about the war and the accumulation of land and plunder; he shrugged at her questions about the Moors as people because he cared little about them, they were merely the enemy.

But she was not altogether naive. She realized if her polite reception of his campaign tales pleased him, her person pleased him even more. The bulbous eyes rarely left her face, he licked his smiling lips often as if in anticipation and held her hand overlong as he kissed it. He constantly touched her arm or her shoulder to emphasize a point. He had, not unreasonably, a proprietary feeling toward her, and although he battled with outrage and shame over his impotence, he was still a man with a man's desires. She often felt, under the restrained hunger of his gaze, like a forbidden sweetmeat on a plate.

Dolores was well aware of what guaranteed her safety from more vigorous advances on his part. It was her land. He wanted her, but he wanted Torrejoncillo more, before she could marry and perhaps put it forever from his reach. He had a clever method of finally levering it from her, she acknowledged ruefully, as the specter of the debit figures rose before her eyes. But he preferred to treat her most respectfully at the moment so she would entertain no other buyers.

Dolores had wanted so much to tell all this to that dimwitted Francisco de Mendoza, to tell him that she was guilty only of greed and not of whorishness, that she had never given herself to the Duke or to anyone but him, anyone. But the lout had refused to hear, he preferred to think ill of her. And his heart was elsewhere. Angrily she pulled away a yellowed leaf from the vine climbing her tiled balcony. To him, His Excellence with the real pedigree, she would never be anything more than a masquerading guttersnipe.

Her mind drifted back to Baza after that wild and painful ride from the Moors. Francho had visited her that same night after the Spanish forces had routed the marauders, striding into her chamber escorted by Pulgar and de la Cueva. She was reclining in her bed upon a great heap of pillows, fussed over by Engracia and some of the Queen's ladies, including Doña Luisa, who immediately commenced coquetting mercilessly with the bashful Pulgar. Francho's intention to keep people between them was hardly necessary that night since her ribs were bound up so tight she could barely breathe and only lying very still eased her, along with the potion she had been given that made her lightheaded. She was pleased, anyhow, to note the troubled concern behind his blue gaze as his eyes swept her buffeted face and the bulk of bindings about her middle, which her smocklike gown did not hide.

He stepped up to the bed and gallantly presented her with a pink, dethorned rose, which he must have bribed from the swift rider who weekly arrived with a great armful of southern blossoms for the Queen. "How do you feel, My Lady?" he inquired gently.

"Passable, sir, my thanks. I am just grateful my teeth were not knocked out. I must look—terrible." It didn't hurt to talk now, not since she had taken that foaming potion from the Queen's Hebrew physician.

His smile enveloped her. "You do look a bit battered and swollen, true. But at least you're alive and nothing worse than wounded ribs. With rest and time you will soon regain your feet."

"Did everyone want to know what I was doing out there?"

"Yes, and the truth sufficed, a need to regain your equilibrium after the horrors of the hospital. I was just not very wise to allow it."

"Nay, do not blame yourself, sir, you were being kind." Then she could not resist tilting her head and inquiring in a low, mocking tone, "Do you find your escort enough people to keep me in safety from you, Don Francisco?"

"Yes, enough, *doña,*" he answered evenly, but she saw his face stiffen and was immediately sorry for her ungraciousness. She breathed in the perfume of the opened rose and put her hand out to stay him, smiling, contrite.

"I'm sorry, forgive me, I have so intemperate a turn of words at times. Will you let me blame it on my fever? And oh, how lovely to have this blossom to erase the odor of that physician's vile unguents."

Francho nodded his head in a small bow, as Pulgar approached the other side of the bed along with Doña Luisa, but it was as if an opaque, stubborn veil had closed off the expression from his eyes. "Even injured your beauty yet outshines that of the flower, *doña,*" he intoned, the perfect, chivalrous knight mouthing harmless compliments, and she wished she could bring back that gentle, solicitous light that had been in his eyes when he first leaned over her. And she had continued to wish the same thing on his subsequent courtesy visit, just before the army broke camp. The rose was now carefully pressed in the small gospel which had once belonged to the old Baron. And she kept trying to expunge from her mind the thrilling memory of that wild and dangerous afternoon when his arms had been about her both in desire and in rescue.

Absently she sat upon her bed and jounced up and down a few times. Francho would certainly ride in from Alcala to attend his crony's wedding, in fact he was probably already in Seville. She would surely see him during the celebrations. It would be nice to pass a courteous word or two with him now her face had come back to its normal, unmarked state and her ribs had healed.

"La mentecata!" Dolores upbraided herself, annoyed at the blood beginning to course more strongly in her veins. "If you do not stop thinking of him you will ruin your life. Think of yourself, think of that pleasant Viscount de Capmany among your admirers whose interest in you seems most serious should you encourage it, think of the new gown you will wear to the wedding (unpaid for, her conscience grumped) and of the expensive tidbits of food the Queen graced you with from her own larder when you could scarce move, even angry as she was that you left the camp. Think of how she favors you more and more. . . .

"Think of the smooth-tongued, pale-eyed Don Felipe de

Guzman and his constant attendance upon Leonora de Zuniga and the damsel's mother—and the dimpled blonde's deft flirtation with the persistent Perens. . . ."

No! Think of how you can pay your creditors and not give up your estate! Dolores sternly brought her musings back under control. Moneylenders? How could she pay them back? Selling her jewels and furs? Oh no that would break her heart. She could enflame the Viscount de Capmany and finally marry well enough, ignoring his lightly pocked skin, but *ay mi madre,* he was so bland and boring. There had to be a way. Something would occur to her. Meanwhile she would have to sell at least some of her jewelry to pay each debtor a little. Don Enrique, of course, would loan her anything she needed, and more, but that would just be clasping his chains tighter about her. God would aid her somehow. Meanwhile she would try to live more frugally.

Tired of thinking she bounced off the bed and clapped her hands for Engracia. It was surely past nine; her stomach was growling, and she was due at the palace for the Queen's readings after chapel at eleven. She would put her mind on tonight's nuptials and the celebrations and how wonderful she would look in her violet, red, and white embroidered moiré gown with its pearl-trimmed, low neckline and cuffs dripping with fine voile, and her new Italian-style headdress, a small cap of violet velvet worn to the back of the head over flowing, center-parted tresses and fetchingly secured by a slim, jeweled velvet band flat about the forehead and tied in back in a bow. She even had one of those new, sensuous feather fans fastened to a handle of ivory to wave about. She would think of all that; those were pleasant things.

Two hours after rising, the shaven, scented, and colorfully attired knight who was known as the bastard of the Count of Tendilla, followed by his dark-skinned equerry, rode tall amidst the stream of pedestrians and mounted citizens on the wide street of fine houses leading up to Seville's Alcazar. His muscles had been loosened by a good, pommeling massage from Ebarra, his headache and queasy stomach were almost gone, and the fresh air of the sunny morning revived him further. The crowded city pleased the eye with its almost homogeneous architecture of Moorish simplicity and privacy, bright white walls gleaming under the red tile roofs and adorned along their smooth facades with the contrasting fussiness of black ironwork balconies. Each balcony and window sprouted a profusion of potted plants and brilliant geraniums, even in the crisp air of February, and along every wall small hanging urns dripped slim vines of green foliage to blow in the breeze and create graceful patterns of light and shadow. There was an alive, gay air to Seville and in the stride and glance of the Sevillanos that matched Francho's own carefree mood.

He was not only riding toward the Zuniga residence, where he would soon be meeting with his darling Leonora—and not even the inevitable presence of her *dueña* could mar his pleasure with that—but before he enjoyed this pleasure he was going to accomplish another mission. And, oddly enough, his final decision to do so had also raised his spirits. The raucous, riotous debauch the night before seemed to have done him a world of good, shaking loose any lingering depression brought on by his inaction at Alcala and especially from the imminent necessity of having to leave Leonora for so long.

He began to whistle under his breath a tune he'd heard in a gypsy camp. On this benign and happy wedding day even the birds darting overhead twittered back to him the uplifting message that no goal, even his own unpredictable, extraordinary gamble, was impossible. When he awoke that morning, done in by drink, he wouldn't have cared if they'd wrapped him in a shroud. Now he was glad he had dressed with care in his favorite shade of blue, with martin fox trimming the droopy armholes of his surcoat and a jaunty pheasant feather in his hat; and on his wrist, just below the tight cuff of his doublet, a new gold link bracelet and a dangling medallion showing his own red-banded device, a gift from the Archbishop Talavera in honor of his knighting.

Francho's whistle grew a little more attenuated as he came abreast of a narrow, three-storied residence he identified by the coat of arms over the grillwork gate in the whitewashed walls. Although the house was small in comparison to the large, white establishments on either side of it, proclaimed by coats of arms over their gates to be the residences of the Marquis of Moya and the Count of Feria, respectively, it was not insignificant with its arched and columned windows, portal of inlaid woods flanked by two great urns containing small orange trees, and an iron-hatted guard lounging inside the gate, his tabard and pike insignia scattered with embroidered antelopes.

She doesn't play at small stakes, Francho grumped to himself, almost losing his resolve to act the shining, chivalrous knight out of the old ballads. But to own such a house, if it was true, was one thing, a solid position; to merely be installed in it by a besotted admirer was quite another. He dismounted, tossed his reins to Ebarra, and took from his equerry a velvet drawstring bag whose contents was not light. Passing through the open gate he gave his name to the guard to be announced to the Baroness and was admitted and bidden wait in a cool anteroom with cushioned seats and colored tile outlining the windows.

He sat down, at first gingerly. Then as the minutes dragged on he jumped up and began to pace. He wondered if he weren't setting his affairs too scrupulously in order, and then called himself coward for the impulse to remove himself from the Baroness de la Rocha's disturbing aura. He felt that the impulse which had come to him one night as he had pondered the fact that his life might be lost in "Egypt" was the right thing to do and a generosity his patron in heaven, San Bismas, would approve of. It had to be the remaining effects of the past night's rowdiness that gave him the feeling that his heartbeat was in total suspension and his mouth dry.

He thought of Leonora and remembered how each sweet letter he had enjoyed from her helped to erase the persistent picture of Dolores's poor, bruised face from his mind. He was sure he had gathered enough moral strength from those precious letters to resist Salome herself. Salome. The temptress. Now why did he . . .

Francho whirled about at the sound of footsteps, and there stood the servant Engracia in an old-fashioned wimpled headdress, beckoning to him. In a tone none too cordial she said, "My lady will see you now. Please come this way."

Relieved to be finished with waiting, actually not too long he had to admit, he followed the woman through another anteroom and then across the square of a small interior garden and into what was the reception room of the house, carpeted with a huge, arabesqued rug from the East and scattered with carved x-chairs and small, round tables in Moorish style. Dolores stood before a tall hearth, where a small fire burned in spite of the temperate day and over which hung a painted wooden sculpture of the suffering Christ. A tiny dog jumped from its tasseled pillow to come forward with wagging tail as Francho entered the room, followed more slowly and fluidly by his mistress.

He would not be human if the sight of her did not take his breath, and he had no time to wonder what caused this: the ripe and radiant beauty of the young woman wafting toward him in a ripple of pale green brocade gown, a starched white coif with floating veil hiding the smoulder of her hair yet emphasizing her slender neck and tipping even more the wide, luminous, and lively eyes; or the surprised but warm and wide smile that lit up her face. But by the time they stood with only a few paces separating them she had drawn the smile together somewhat, into a more reserved regard.

"Well, it is good to see you at Court again, Don Francisco. I had imagined Don Antonio's nuptials would rouse you out of that eagle's nest." She offered a slim hand to be kissed.

"The respite is welcome, *doña,* I assure you." He realized his expression was tight and relaxed it as he bent to kiss her hand, then straightened to gaze calmly into the silvery depths of her eyes with their dark, thick lashes. His breathing seemed steady and he wondered if he might have finally broken her spell. It was possible, finally, that what he felt for her was nothing more than any man's normal appreciation of her loveliness and a certain warmth of affection, as one would have for an old childhood friend. Feeling safe and in control, his smile grew broader. "And how do you go, My Lady, although you look so—so well I need hardly inquire after your health," he declared, stopping a stammer just in time.

"I am admirable, sir, I thank you." She smiled back. "My poor ribs are healed," and she did a charming little pirouette to show him, "and so my face and other places that were bruised, and I intend to dance all night tonight. But my manners are lacking. Please, will you sit?"

He did so, not quite comfortably, the velvet bag balanced on his knees. He gazed about the good-sized chamber for a moment, taking in the intricately-wrought iron chandeliers, the inlaid wood tops of the tabourets, the delicate plates and pitchers displayed on a high rack running along the walls, the draperies adding color to the whiteness of the walls. "This is a very fine establishment, Dolores," he declared, meaning it as a compliment. But a sudden jealousy stabbed at him and he forgot to be polite. Looking her straight in the eyes he dropped

323

the courteous lady-gentleman pavanne they were doing. "But do you own it?" he demanded.

With typical directness she looked straight back at him and answered, "No, I do not." And then, with a lift of her chin, added haughtily, "Although it is mine to live in however long I wish." There was both bravado and challenge in her voice.

However long the *Duke* wishes, you mean, growled Francho, to himself. Now the business he had with her was all the more important. He was anxious to get it over with and depart.

Annoyed with his probing, she decided to tilt with him a bit. "And where are your escorts, Don Francisco?" Her eyes lit mockingly. "Did you not decide we were never to be alone together, at any time?"

He was not going to be goaded into losing his temper. "I assure you I am quite cured," he responded coolly. "At any rate, you are safe enough for I see you've asked your *dueña* to stay." He gestured with his head at Engracia who sat trying to be inconspicuous in a corner.

"Forgive me, I only meant to tease you." She laughed lightly. Now it was her turn to be impolitely curious. She pointed to the velvet-wrapped object he balanced on his knees. "And what is that, pray?"

"Doña Dolores, I have a favor to ask of you. It is brought about by the fact that I am embarking on a very long journey from which, it may happen, I might not return."

Her formal little smile wavered. Unconsciously her fingers tightened on the arms of her chair and a touch of concern crept into her eyes. The Moorish wars were hardly a long way from Seville and an ordinary seasonal occupation with Spanish nobility. She presumed he could not be referring to that. "A favor? Yes, of course. But where do you go so far away and so dangerous that you fear for your life, Francho?"

Her unthinking use of his old nickname warmed him as always, and so did the concern she could not quite conceal under her mantle of composure. "With Pietro di Lido and his party of gentlemen to Egypt, a very honored appointment— and I don't mind admitting that the thought of the trip to so exotic a land along with the delicate mission we have to accomplish really excites me. As why shouldn't it, eh?" He winked at her and for a tiny moment the expression they shared returned them both to lowly cutpurses again, plotting to get rich on a few stolen coins and never dreaming further

324

than a possible trip to Toledo in their lives. "But Egypt is not just across yon plaza. Things could happen. Pirates, slavers, brigands. The suspicious old potentate could imprison us and dance us a dance for several years before accepting ransom, or we could be accidently embroiled and killed in one local war or another on the long road between here and Alexandria, and there would be an end to us." He shrugged fatalistically. *"Que será . . ."*

The breath seemed to have left her. She sat back in her chair. *"Ay, mi madre,"* she lamented and stared back at him.

He had distressed her with nothing more than the truth, of course. He might lose his life on his venture and wind up with his head stuck on a pole like the Count's original agent. But—he stole a look at her face—why should it make him feel so mean to have made her unhappy? Yet it did, and so in order to rally her he let a grin chase the seriousness from his aspect. *"Por Dios,* Dolores, I have a charmed life. If the Hermandad didn't get me and the Count didn't have me hung and the Moorish fighters haven't yet sent my soul to beg place from San Pedro, what matter a few pirates and Janissaries? They will get short shrift from Spanish knights, I promise you. And yet, one must make provisions. . . ." Without further ceremony he began to unwrap the velvet bag on his lap. "There is in this casket notes and coins worth twenty thousand maravedis which I have been holding with one of the Jews on the Calle Ruy Gomez." He leaned forward over the box and frowned into her eyes to impress her with his purposefulness. "I want to leave this money with you. If I have not returned in three years from Lententide, it is yours. I want you to have it."

The wide, seductive mouth dropped open in surprise. She struggled to find her speech. "Are you mad?" she gasped, clutching at her seat. "That is a large sum. Why should you give it to me?"

Why? Because he somehow felt responsible for her, and for all of her few hectares of land in Extremadura she was still unprotected and defenseless against the lure of a philandering Medina-Sidonia, or at best a marriage to an impoverished courtier who was willing to ignore her suspect virginity and trade marriage for her beauty and small dowry. The money he offered her was what remained of the large amount (less a hundred ducats he had removed for travel expenses) loaned to him by Tendilla when he came to Court and which he had every intention of repaying if their plans grew to fruition. If not, if he did not reach the ultimate goal of his own name and estates, or if he was killed, then the money could be counted as wages for services rendered to Tendilla in a dangerous and unique enterprise. But by enabling Dolores to buy a place in one of the fashionable convents which gave refuge to gentlewomen who lacked family or protection, the money would provide her an honorable way out of the other alternatives. It was the best he could do for her if he never came back. And even at his return he was determined to find some way to make her a gift of the money without challenging her pride.

Although her face still mirrored the vestiges of surprise, she had collected herself enough to rise from her chair stiff-spined, her sleek, straight nose taking on more altitude. "If you think for one moment, *señor,* that I am in need of your alms, you are very mistaken and I suggest you leave your funds with the Jewish banker, who will pay you for it. Indeed, Don Francisco, you mightily overstep the bounds of friendship—how do you dare presume that I . . . that I . . . that . . . oh!" She fumbled to a halt and hastily stepped back in alarm, her eyes widening, for he had put aside the casket, unwound from his seat like a spring and now he loomed over her with his hand on the pommel of his dagger by habit, glowering down on her blackly as a thundercloud.

Francho had already resolved what he wanted to do and this female's stupid vanity was not going to upset his plan for her safety! "By San Bartolomeo and San Andres, woman, do you not recognize legitimate concern for you, you who are otherwise bereft of family and still unwise and young? You try my patience . . ."

With a little cringe she retreated backward some more steps but he advanced along with her. "Uh . . . I mean of course I do appreciate your solicitous and generous thought, *señor,* but . . ."

"Then accept my arrangement, Dolores, and do not start a quarrel," he ordered brusquely. "It isn't charity. It isn't even a gift, because I intend to return, whole and in one piece. Consider the money a bequest. From a friend. Just in case. A last wish. To be honored."

She reminded him of a bright and beautiful bird nervously deciding between staying and taking flight. She tilted her head a fraction as if to discern better was he teasing and what did he mean, and then her hands fluttered helplessly before her chest. "Well. Yes, I see now. Very well, then, if you put it that way."

He continued to scowl at her, trying to detect any tricks beneath her sudden capitulation, for it *was* sudden. But her expression was open, even gratified, as if the dawn of reason had truly overrun the darkness of pride. Mollified, his anger passed away quickly. So to lighten the atmosphere again he let a smile clear his face, "The fact is I have no other brother or sister, so to whom else would I leave these funds? Hadn't we agreed before that by virtue of our childhood together we are not just acquaintances?"

"But your sire? He is your family."

"He has great fortunes. This would be unnoticeable to him."

Glancing up through fringed and tilted eyes she turned away from him and glided toward a table in mid-floor. He forced himself to tear his gaze away from the lovely sway of her hips and the suggestion of rounded buttocks under the thin, clinging silk of her gown. In a merely curious tone, as innocent of malice as a child's, she asked, "But what of Doña Leonora? Surely she is not just an acquaintance?"

"True, but she has a great inheritance from her father. And I do not owe her a debt as I do to you, for look you, lady, you are the only representative present of the family that saved my life."

She turned toward him, bland as butter, her mouth curving up in a smile. *"Cielos,* you have so honeyed a tongue, Francho, you could talk the fox from his den. Very well, I will keep the money for you but you shall have it back the moment you return."

"Agreed," he growled.

A second of silence stretched between them and he wondered why he didn't leave. She picked up a small monkey made of brass from the table and toyed with it. "Presuming God keeps you in safety, will your mission then be long in Egypt?"

He relaxed his shoulders, shifting them under the blue velvet surcoat, which was becoming too warm in this house, noticing her eyes on them as he did so. Quickly he offered, "That depends on the Sultan's temper. We stop first in Rome to consult with the Holy Office and then in Constantinople, and if all goes smoothly in Egypt then eight or nine months will see us back. But Maestro di Lido warns we may be kept cooling our heels for a while. So then, perhaps over a year."

"A year. That's a long time, Francho." She glanced down at the brass monkey she turned in her fingers and just then he realized that for Papa el Mono's daughter this must be an amulet. "I shall miss you," she declared softly.

He should have been gracious enough to thank her but instead something drove him into a rather crusty "Not so. You have many—distractions."

"Ah, but I have only one friend. Only one who cares for me enough to try and assure my future."

A hot blush rose in his face, and in his chest so did something akin to panic as she set down the figurine and strolled toward him with that damnable hipsway. She fixed her exotic and subtly challenging eyes upon his, and he knew if he didn't leave now he would be testing his newfound control to the extreme. So he strode toward her aggressively and took one of her hands in his to say farewell. Still gentle and smiling, she remarked, "I don't see how Doña Leonora will bear your protracted absence; I know it would be hard for me if we were lovers. It must be trying to love a man who is often far away."

Her tone was so sympathetic he took no offense; in fact it came over him there was something he should say to her, to instruct her if he could. "When one loves, Dolores, even a small minute together can be an eternity of happiness. Distance and time become nothing, love can make even separation bearable for it stretches over leagues and years. I hope someday you will find such a love." But immediately as he got out the last word embarrassment engulfed him; and he became aghast with himself for braying like a pompous donkey. He braced for the deserved mockery surely forthcoming.

But she merely kept those limpid, hypnotic eyes on his and seemed to sway closer. "How eloquently you put it, Don Francisco. Yes, perhaps someday I will know such a love," she murmured.

He realized he was still holding her hand, quickly kissed it, and let it go. "With your permission I will take my leave, now. *Adiós* then, Dolores."

He inclined his head and saluted her. She stood still, the pale gown shimmering in folds at her feet, the filmy veil at the points of her coif stirring softly in a breeze from a window.

Her tempting mouth displayed what he thought, somehow disappointed, was no more than a polite smile. Turning on his heel he strode away, ignoring a peculiar sense of having forgotten something, for after all he had finished his business with her and said his goodbye. He was already at the door when she called after him "Francho! Wait!" and he heard the light rustle of her skirt as she ran toward him. Then, just as she reached him she caught her toe in the knotted fringe of the carpet and stumbled. He shot his arm out to steady her and restore her balance and as he did so caught the medallion of his bracelet in the sheer organdy puffed through the slashes of her tight sleeve.

With an uneasy chuckle and clumsy fingers he began to fumble at the delicate cloth. Her pleasant laugh took over as she pushed his hand aside to work at the caught threads herself. Helplessly he subsided and just stood there, content to allow her smaller hands do the job and to breathe the inspiring scent of her jasmine perfume. He gazed down at her as she concentrated, studying the rich and shining auburn triangle of hair revealed by her coif, the sweep of dark lashes against the satin of her cheeks, the slim, lissome body with its handspan waist and curved hips.

Only a fool lies to himself, the admission flooded through his mind. I do love her. In a certain way. Her beauty of face and body enflame me. I want to touch her. But I do not think of her as I do Leonora, and I will cut off my hands before I breach her trust again, like some swinish peasant. . . .

"*Caspita!* A stubborn tangling," Dolores said breathlessly as she successfully disengaged the two of them and looked up, just missing, he hoped, the rapid change of expression on his face. "There. You are free, *señor.*"

The distant cathedral bells began tolling the hour, followed by the higher-pitched tintinnabulations of the smaller churches. The morning was wearing on. She glided around him and opened the door partially. "What I wanted to ask was that you not say '*adiós,*' Francho, but rather 'until we meet again,' for at any rate our paths will surely cross again while you remain in Seville. And you will return, Francho, I am sure of it. Was not my grandmother supposed to be part seer?" She smiled.

Her attempt to reassure him and the friendly warmth in her eyes made him even gladder that he had left her his funds. "God keep you, Dolores."

"And God give you safe journey and swift return, Sir Knight." Swiftly she reached up with both hands, pulled his head down, and kissed him on the lips; but when his arm of its own accord went around her waist she pushed him away, a glisten of tears in her gray eyes, and quickly shut the door in his face.

He stood for a moment, rattled, staring at the closed portal, the impression of her soft, compelling lips still on his, battling the impulse to barge back in. The door reopened and a determined Engracia slipped out to herd him back to the front entrance. Straight-backed he strode after her, and yet even as he approached Ebarra and the horses the hollow feeling he had suffered for a moment before that firmly closed door, still lingered within him. Swinging up on the saddle he frowned into the sun and ordered himself sternly to pull himself together and lift up his heart, for the wonderful fact was that he was headed now to see his beguiling Leonora. And, in fact, as he concentrated hard on chasing Dolores from his head, his mood did begin to swing up.

Dolores subsided limply against the closed door and shut her eyes. Of a certain that azure-eyed, stubborn, scowling thickwit whom she adored would surely return from Egypt; he was only trying to frighten her and push her into taking the money. And why should she be so distressed, at any rate? He was not leaving her, he was leaving the dimpled Zuniga. But—a year? She would be getting old before she saw him again, and even then all he would want was his money back. Disconsolately she scuffed across the carpet to the money casket which he had left on the chair.

His chivalrous impulse to match in death the kindness her family had shown him in life was commendable. But why was his debt to be paid only by his death, the Lord forbid?

Why not now, when she needed it? It was a thought that had come to her earlier. She fingered the small padlock which secured the casket's lid; it could be easily broken by any smith to whom she appealed her loss of the key. The whole thing was simple, of course. She would borrow from him enough to calm her debtors and in a year she would replace the money, either by accepting some gentleman's suit if he would pay off her debts, or by selling her land.

An ironic smile played about her lips. In her heart she knew she would never chain herself to a man merely to pay off a debt, for surely at eighteen she still had a few years of youth to capture someone she truly liked. Nor would she sell her land, while she could sell her jewels. Anyhow, she would rather owe a debt to Don Francisco de Mendoza than to a passel of uncaring merchants. Him she could pay back. Somehow.

It was the first major fete of the new year, this marriage of the Duke of Albuquerque's heir, and a most important liaison between two great houses and countries. The Countess Lysette Marianne de Moulines was a widow even at the tender age of sixteen, having had as first spouse a crabbed but enormously wealthy French noble forced on her by her father. But after the old man's death her father had managed to have her declared "intacta" by virtue of nonconsummation, and here she was, again being married as a virgin in the eyes of the Church.

The jewel-encrusted coronet weighed heavy on her veiled head as the bride knelt before the magnificent golden high altar of the hugest cathedral she had ever seen in her life. Undaunted, relieved by her deliverance from the old man, she slid, throughout the lengthy and solemn ceremony, quick glances of admiration at the stalwart young groom kneeling beside her. Her heart swelled with thanks toward her father, cousin to King Charles VIII, for the gift of this kind and handsome young man.

For his part Don Antonio de la Cueva didn't even feel the heavy gold coronet pressing down on his pomaded brown hair. He was pale and sweating—if not from the fact that he was taking a wife, then at least from the copious drinking he had done in company with his lewd-minded friends the night before. He was aware of his chin, itching fiercely from unguent applied when his valet had nicked him with the razor, and of the huge, preening assembly behind him staring at his scarlet-sheathed back, rustling with whispers every time the mighty choir fell silent and the Archbishop again took up the ritual. With a dry mouth Antonio said the nuptial pledge, "I Antonio, Marquis of Santurce, eldest son of Beltran de la Cueva, Duke of Albuquerque, take thee, Lysette, Countess of Moulines, second daughter of Hubert Moraine de Valois . . ." He wished fervently it were still the night before when he was yet a bachelor unhampered by a wife. Albeit she was a very pretty one. . . .

That evening the light from a thousand candles blazed out from every window of Albuquerque's great mansion, with

music and dancing and hilarity to honor the brilliant marriage, to say nothing of a stupendous banquet. But this time
Francho had outmaneuvered his archrival, for being one of
the young gentlemen in the groom's honor escort, he was
seated far above the salt in this gathering of the rich and
powerful of two great countries, and he had asked Leonora to
sit next to him. It was his intention to enjoy the festivities to
the hilt, seeing it was the last he would attend for some time,
but even so he could not remember being so happy, for his
blond-headed love was at his side and pressed her knee
against his under the table, even when she smiled and chatted
with the other diners seated near her. He ate with great gusto
of the myriad rich dishes. He chose from the salvers the finest
pieces to lay upon Leonora's plate, which she devoured with
good appetite, her eyes sparkling at him as he carved with his
knife against his chest a round loaf of the whitest bread and
with mock ceremony handed her a hunk with which to sop up
the savory juices of the potted hare.

After the dance music began and the bride and groom were
each led out by a smiling monarch, Francho claimed as many
dances with Leonora as his proprietous lady would allow. In
fact, instead of standing and glowering as in the past when she
accepted Don Felipe's arm, he revealed the security of his love
by joining Pulgar, Gonsalvo de Cordoba, who was Isabella's
youngest and well-favored captain, and other *caballeros* in an
uproarious group downing cup upon cup in toast to the
flushed-faced bridegroom.

But needing to guard his sobriety he soon parted from them
to wander the crowded chambers, greeting this one and that
whom he knew, and standing for a while alongside Tendilla to
converse with several gentlemen before making his excuses
and getting away. Out of kindness he even engaged in a short
exchange of pleasantries with a shy, stocky Italian he had met
briefly at the encampment at Baza, an eccentric Genoese
named Cristoforo Columbo upon whose coarse features sat
the strain of those who wait with little hope upon royal
decision. When Columbo's sad face lit up at the approach of
Pietro di Lido, elegant as ever, Francho excused himself, glad
to leave the two gesturing Italians to their technical arguments
over geography. Francho understood that Columbo was looking for backing to find a passage to the Indies by sailing far to
the west, a risky and questionable business, but Francho's

mind was crammed with too many of his own thoughts to spare such doubtful adventuring much room.

Dolores was not hard to find. Strolling into a smaller chamber where banquettes around the wall held players seated at tables for intense games of checkers, chess, and beard-the-fox, he heard her laugh ring out to mark a particularly clever move, and there she was, watching Medina-Sidonia checkmate the dismayed Archbishop of Burgos while the knot of mostly male observers covertly eyed her with pleasure. He had no intention of going closer for it was almost time to reclaim Leonora from her admirers, yet he couldn't help standing for a moment on the fringes of the group to watch her, her eyes sparkling with the vicarious excitement of winning, the rise and fall of her half-exposed bosom carrying a garland of gems nowhere so precious as the flawless skin they rested upon, an alluring shine upon her lips. Somehow she seemed to feel his eyes upon her, and she unerringly turned her head to look in his direction. Did the music filtering from the great hall suddenly swell and sweeten, or was he imagining the heightened sound as her limpid gaze clung to his and her seductive smile began to draw him to her as inexorably as a magnetic stone attracted iron filings?

Doggedly he resisted and suddenly her smile appeared merely friendly, a polite greeting, and was there, perhaps, a touch of cynical amusement? He nodded a stiff acknowledgment and quickly exited the room.

By midnight he had managed to remark to a number of people that he expected to accompany Pietro di Lido to Egypt. At midnight, also, the bridal couple retired from the hall and were installed by their parents and friends into their chambers upstairs. After a carefully timed interval measured from the moment the couple was left alone, the entire company was silenced and the music ceased. In ancient days this period was reserved for the guests to listen for the bride's virginal scream as a signal that the marriage was truly consummated. In this case the idea was faintly ridiculous, and in any case too barbarous for these enlightened times. But the custom of the silence was still preserved and in a few minutes broken by the King himself, who shattered a glass against a wall as a sign that the marriage was considered joined. Having observed the bride's teasing ways with her betrothed and knowing Antonio's suavity with women, Francho imagined that his friend had about now only coaxed his new wife into taking off the linen and lace wedding nightrobe in which her friends had dressed her, and perhaps he held out to her as well a golden goblet of wine.

He watched a troup of entertainers spill into the great hall to begin a popular and elaborate spectacle with music, pitting the Devil (a hoary old man with an evil cackle) against a wavering angel (a too pretty, graceful boy), the angel soon to be bolstered up in his refusal to sin by a procession of martyred and bloody saints, eyes gazing devoutly toward heaven. Gaily everyone had gathered from all the chambers about and above to watch the play, leaving even the gaming tables abandoned. Francho moved toward an entranceway unobserved.

Watching for her chance Leonora finally edged away from the group surrounding the Infanta and slipped unobtrusively through the throng of guests. She spotted Don Felipe as he started to follow her, reading on his face the intention of cornering her in a dark alcove, and she shook her head, trying to look embarrassed. She was anxious neither to make him suspicious nor to offend him. He smiled his thin smile and let her go, for he remembered she had twice sipped her wine cup dry and must need be in a hurry.

Leonora held her skirts to her and hurried down the empty corridor. She wished she was feeling only the anticipatory beat of her heart knowing that she was hastening to a rendezvous with her handsome, importunate cousin, but uncertainty and annoyance crushed her excitement. She was not a mere girl anymore, and still her future was unsettled. Her mother, her guardian, was little help. Her mother said, "I was fortunate, daughter. I loved your father. As long as the match is in all respects suitable I will allow you to follow your inclination." Following her inclination she was indeed, and yet it might be no more than reaching for the mist on the meadow. Francisco was confusing, hard to grasp at times. And now he was going away. How awkward it all was. So messy.

Still, his sincerity and love for her was certain. She would not spoil this precious meeting, neither for him nor for her, by pressing him too hard with doubts. She passed around a corner to a narrower passage, counted two doors, and entered the third room.

Francho waited for her, half-seated on the edge of a wide

table, one black-and-silver-clad leg swinging impatiently, a habit he had picked up from Tendilla. She ran into his waiting arms and he enfolded her, both of them sighing with the relief common to lovers who must subdue their feelings before the world and wait for infrequent private meetings to let them free. Boldly he slid his hand down her satin-covered hip and thigh, and she snuggled against him. "Francisco, how shall I endure when you leave? Life will be empty—an inane posturing, a smile here, a curtsey there, and silly, vacant chatter— and all the while my heart will be longing for you. Ah, life is cruel. . . ."

"Ah, sweet heart, don't sorrow, you will take all my courage from me. Try to think of when I return—that we will be wed and our future assured, with a happy life stretching before us."

"But I still do not understand what might Egypt have to do with us? Is it that you hope to find a treasure on the desert? Or so please the Sultan he will shower you with riches? And why can't we at least claim betrothal? It is all very confused." She pouted prettily, her small, tender mouth beguiling.

"You promised not to ask questions of me, sweet. You said you would trust me."

"I do trust you; forgive me. But—but a year is such a long time."

Francho had not the courage to tell her that it might be much longer; in fact, when it came to her he refused to let the reality sink into his own mind that he would be gone as long as the war to capture all of Granada lasted. He would find some way to tell her later and pray she would be willing to cope with an extended separation. But now it was easier for both of them to part saying it was just for a twelvemonth. "Will the time stretch so long for you that you will forget me? The Court abounds with gallants who would claim your attention, especially since there are no contracts, no banns?"

"How can you utter such words? I am listless as an unstrung puppet when you are not nigh until I hear your voice and see you. And no matter how we observe amenities, think you the Court is blind? Oh, they may try to draw me from you, but they will not. Francisco, I shall never want anyone else but you, ever. Swear you will never doubt me," Leonora begged.

"I swear I shall always love you." He took her small face between his hands and stared deep into the guileless, velvety brown eyes. He found her so sweet, so unaffected. "You make me tremble. I yearn for you so," he whispered.

She saw in his eyes the longing and the question and put her fingers over his lips. "No, don't ask me, Francisco, for I will answer yes. Yes, yes, I want to be yours, to lie sheltered and happy in your arms tonight. But God help us both for then we would know the true sweetness of love and understand the terrible width of the ocean soon to be between us. It would be a torture beyond bearing and my heart would break with the burden. Do you love me enough to spare me that?"

She needed no answer and he gave her none; wordless, strained, he studied her poignant face, then put her away from him and turned his back. His hand was steady as he lifted a decanter of wine Ebarra had furnished for them, but he drew out the pouring process until he could face her more calmly.

"I am selfish," she whispered.

"You are wise."

"I love you." His voice was hoarse.

Gliding up to him she pulled from her index finger a small gold band inset with chip rubies. "I have had this ring since I was a child. Keep it with you always; it will remind you I am waiting and praying for you, counting every hour until you return." She kissed it and put it in his hand.

The ring hardly went over the tip of his smallest finger. He unbuttoned the neck of the doublet and dropped it into the pocket of his shirt, then took her hand and pressed the palm over his heart. "Do you see where it lies? Only you may take it away, and then you should have only the gold, but not the kiss."

She leaned against him, the top of her honey-colored head in its intricate, openwork cap of pearls and gold thread barely reaching to his chin, and he held her gently to him. "I shall truly be lonely, Francisco," she mourned.

"I go because I must, sweet heart," he tried to soothe her, "but afterward we shall never again be separated, I promise. By all the Saints in heaven I swear—"

"Very pretty. An eloquent tableau!" an intruding voice sneered from the doorway.

Francho whirled; he had not heard the door open. Don Felipe stood leaning against the jamb, pale eyes slitting, shoulders tensed under his short scarlet and gold cape. "But you should not give your trust to a man with so facile and flattering a tongue, Doña Leonora." He pushed away from the door and walked a few steps into the room, swaying.

For Leonora's sake Francho strained to hold his wrath in check. "You intrude, My Lord Perens. Get out."

The Count of Perens's face could be called handsome in a cold way; but his narrowed eyes of palest ice blue now rimmed with red glittered with his spiteful nature. "On the contrary, Mendoza, it is you who trespasses. Remove your distasteful presence from my lady's vicinity or I shall show you the way out with the point of my sword." The words were detectably slurred, the man weaved a bit as he stood, but the eyes fixed on Francho delivered a menacing message.

Leonora gasped as Francho's hand flew to the grip of his sword. "Francisco, he is drunken. He doesn't realize what he is saying."

Felipe leered at her. "Not drunk enough, my charming damsel, that I cannot see this lout has taken advantage of your trusting disposition to inveigle you into a private meeting. It seems I must save you from yourself. . . ."

"I am capable of managing my own affairs, Don Felipe," Leonora flung at him, "nor have you ever been given the right to interfere with them. You overstep the bounds of friendship, my Lord. As a gentleman you will withdraw."

Perens scarcely heard her; it was Francisco de Mendoza to whom he spoke. "Females are notorious for placing themselves in situations they later decry. Be thankful, *doña,* that I am here to see you do not succumb to the empty blandishments of a knave who only this matin paid a lengthy visit to my father's mistress."

Francho started. Did this viper have eyes everywhere? "You miserable, intolerable snake, what you insinuate is a damned lie," he retorted in the deadly, back-of-the-throat rumble of a glowering mastiff. His sword whipped from its scabbard.

Leonora caught at his arm. "Francisco, I don't believe him, I know he's lying. But you cannot attack him; he can barely stand up. It would be murder!"

Francho shook her off. "Save your sympathy, dearest heart. I've had enough of my Lord's meddling attentions and insults. I finally intend to teach him some manners."

"That is correct, my dear lady, your sympathy is misplaced," Felipe agreed, arrogantly strolling some paces forward and kicking aside a small chair in his way. His sword snicked out of its scabbard. "I could dispatch this fellow if I were blindfolded and one-armed. Come, Mendoza, or are you reconsidering . . ." He crouched, circling, arms wide.

"Francisco!" Leonora cried to halt him, but she backed away from the cold, calm, blue menace she saw glistening in his eyes, more frightening than any burst of fury.

"I only consider, Perens, whether to wound you or kill you. Or perhaps I will do both," Francho snarled and launched himself at the person he detested most in the world; and steel sword rang upon sword like the crash of cymbals. Francho fleetingly wished Felipe were sober, although the man's skilled swordsmanship seemed not impaired, for a dead Felipe's partisans would question the fairness of the fight, testifying he had been too drunk to draw sword. But there was no stopping now, the hate that burned in his heart for the posturing rival who wanted to own Leonora overpowered his reason. Fury to be forced to leave his beloved alone in the same corner of the world with Perens overcame his intelligence—edicts, the ire of his rulers, retribution be damned—his outrage came first. The man parrying his blows so proficiently was every insult, every fear, every scorn that had ever struck at him in his life. He sent his opponent hurling away from a closing-in that had brought the insolent, sneering face closer to his and knew as he sprang forward on the offensive again that only the bright spurt of blood from Guzman's throat would assuage the jealous rivalry that consumed him.

Hand to mouth and forgotten in a corner, Leonora watched with eyes filled with dread as the two duelists battling over her clashed, and ringingly clashed again, hacking at each other up and down the room with violent blows which were just as violently parried and turned, each pressing grimly for the other's small mistake that would produce a bloody victory. Backed up and arched against the heavy trestle table, Francho's bunched muscles repulsed the fierce weapon that would have cut him in two and knocked it to one side, the force of the stroke jolting up to his shoulder, then kicked out viciously so that Felipe jumped back and gave him the second he needed to swivel away from the untenable position.

Felipe recovered instantly and advanced with relentless aggression. Their swords engaged in a flurry of powerful strokes, steel ringing against steel. Grunting they rammed up to each other as one sword slithered upon the other. For an instant the hilts touched and they came face to face. Felipe

338

was pale, paler than usual, sweat trickled down the side of his face, the cords of his neck stood out with strain. "Drunken as I am I play with you for a while, Mendoza; it amuses me," he panted with a hot breath. "But soon I will put an end to this farce. I warn you, say your orisons. . . ."

But even as Francho snarled and shoved Felipe away a measure of cooler calculation descended upon him and he moved to set up his enemy for the unusual, Italianate method of skewering an opponent which di Lido had taught him. As Guzman launched another rain of slices and sidecuts Francho parried furiously; whirled away, dodged, and whanged at the Count of Perens's sword with the edge of his own, throwing the man momentarily off balance. This was all he needed. Crouching, flipping the sweat back out of his eyes, he flew forward with the lightning fast move called a lunge, the point of his sword aimed inexorably for Felipe's heart, and if the man's automatic reflex to leap back hadn't instead caused him to slip and fall under the level of the deadly, thrusting blade he would have been dead. Recovering immediately he scrambled back up to his feet, while Francho, surprised at the accident, for he had forgotten the man's condition, hesitated a heart-beat.

But suddenly Felipe's arm relaxed, his grip opened, and his weapon thumped to the floor. For a moment he stood rooted to the spot dead white and shaking, his hand gripping his stomach. Then his hand raced up to his mouth, his eyes grew wide in distress, and he made a dash for a corner of the room, where he leaned over the high back of a carved mahogany settle and noisily gave up the great quantity of aguardiente and sweet wine that had undone him. Helpless, retching uncontrollably, covered with cold sweat, the Count of Perens turned his unguarded back toward his mortal enemy and puked.

Francho's unbelieving stare turned into a whoop of laughter. He drove his sword into its sheath with a satisfied gesture and turned to Leonora, who, though just a minute before was on the verge of fainting with fear that her suitors would kill each other, now began to giggle hysterically. "I could run him through this very moment, *doña,* and be rid of him forever," he chortled, "but God help me I've always felt a kindness for the sodden." Even so, he knew that his amusement was mixed with just as great relief that he had not had to kill Felipe and surely ruin his own life by incurring the wrath of the King.

"Oh, the blessed Virgin, I have never seen anything so funny. He just collapsed like a pricked wine skin . . ." Leonora's chiming soprano laughter joined Francho's deeper tones as they made merry over Perens's gasping figure.

Francho bent to pick up Felipe's sword, a fine Toledo blade of the newest, lighterweight type, with guard wings of twisted gold and silver wire. "I might just keep this as a memento to hang over our hearth. A trophy of a bravo whose grip was too weak to hold it." Such an end to the raging, bitter duel was just too ridiculous. Another wave of laughter overcame him. He walked toward Leonora, holding out his hand to her. "I am sorry, my Lady, that I couldn't give you the—"

"Francisco! Look out!"

Striking with the speed of a scorpion's sting, Felipe had launched himself at Francho's back, putting his entire weight into the leap so that his unwary enemy found himself suddenly toppled to the floor, flattened with the wind knocked out of him as Felipe's body landed across him. A steel-hard arm swiftly encircled his neck and squeezed, forcing him to struggle for air. Francho writhed to shake the man off, grappling with the deadly arm, but he could not loosen the berserk grip. He heard Leonora cry out, he heard Guzman's thick snarl of victory, and the room began to darken and purple as he fought to keep Guzman from strangling him. Driven and beside himself with mortification, the man was using every ounce of his considerable strength to throttle his bucking, writhing victim. Francho was aware of a sour, panting breath that rasped in his ear, "Die, vermin, die!"

The arm that was choking him to death could not be pried off. Convulsively Francho reached back and grabbed a fistful of Felipe's hair, hanging on with all his might to keep the man's head pulled forward. Praying that God's mercy would guide his hand as Felipe jerked his head about in an effort to get loose, he jabbed back blindly with vicious strength and felt his thumb partially strike its soft mark.

With a yell of pain Felipe clapped a hand to his eye, loosening his hold enough for Francho to wrench out from under him and roll away and come up to one knee, gulping air into his lungs. He saw Felipe jerk his dagger from its sheath. One eye screwed shut in agony, teeth bared in towering fury, Felipe surged up with a powerful thrust of his thighs and launched himself upon his detested foe.

Springing to his own feet, and with a swift and agile twist of his body worthy of the finest Moorish bullfighter, Francho dodged the gleaming blade aimed at his heart, which instead ripped through his sleeve, plowing a gash in his bicep. Catching Felipe's arm on the downstroke, he used a wrestling hold of Von Gormach's, levering the raging man across his own body and with a masterful flip sending him crashing on his back to the floor. Without giving the dazed Count of Perens a chance to move, Francho pounced on the prone, gasping body and with two battering blows to the jaw knocked his tormentor into insensibility.

Enraged beyond thinking, Francho wrapped his hands around Guzman's throat. "Suffocate me, will you, you whore-master! I'll show you how to do it—"

"Francisco," Leonora cried out in terror. "Don't kill him! Don't kill him, I beg you, it will only bring trouble upon our heads. Listen to me, please," she pleaded, running up and tugging with frantic strength to pull him off Felipe.

"Why should I not send him to Hell, where he was spawned?" Francho demanded. "He would have finished me."

"Oh please, no, let him be." Leonora began to weep. "You have bested him before me. He will never dare to interfere with us again. If you strangle him the King will imprison you, execute you, his friends will say he was besotted, helpless. Oh my dear, don't throw away our lives on your hatred for Don Felipe, for then even in death he would be gratified. It isn't worth it."

Her words and her tears pierced through the fury that drove him. Francho's hands relaxed and the breath of life gurgled back in Felipe's bruised throat, the faint tinge of blue left his lips. Dazedly Francho stood and surveyed his unconscious enemy for a moment; then he turned and gathered the sobbing Leonora in his arms, stroking her hair to calm her. "It's all right, it's all right, *doña,*" he muttered. Silently he thanked God once more that her reason had reached him before he had squeezed away that malicious life and impaled his own upon the deed.

"Francisco, you're wounded!" She reached out, the sight of the crimson soaking his dagger-slashed sleeve stopping her tears. But he gently put by her hand.

"Do not bloody yourself, sweet heart, it's just a scratch. See, it hardly bleeds. Listen, Leonora, you must go back to the dancing now, before you are too much missed. My equerry is in the courtyard feasting with the townsfolk. I'll find him and leave so he can bind up my wound and I can clean up and change my attire. I'll return shortly and find you."

"What about Don Felipe?"

"Leave him here. If he is found they'll think it was just a drunken stupor felled him." Francho stepped over and righted the overturned chair and proceeded to erase other marks of the scuffle, wiping up flecks of blood on the floor from the cut on his arm with the flimsy kerchief Leonora held out to him. "After all, I would not like the gossip of a duel to mar my friend's wedding celebration," he wryly observed, in a weak attempt at lightness. He slid Felipe's sword and wiped-clean dagger into their scabbards and then mopped his own forehead with a clean part of the kerchief.

Leonora wrung her hands. "Now he will enter the tourney against you, he will somehow arrange the draw of opponents to fall out that way. But he will be sober and wild for vengeance. And Don Felipe has a deadly score of 'accidental' killings in the lists."

"Well, let him do so, that would give me much pleasure to skewer him on my lance in the presence of the entire Court. Drunk or sober he is not capable of overpowering me at anything," Francho assured her gruffly, picking up his feathered hat from where it had fallen during the fight. He took her by her dainty shoulders and smiled tenderly, flattered by the unconcealed esteem in her eyes. "And you may believe that, my Lady. You need never to worry on my account."

She said nothing, but gave him a tentative smile back.

He pulled open the thick door, which, along with the sturdy walls, had kept the sounds of their combat from becoming public knowledge. The passage was momentarily empty. "I'll leave you as the corridor branches," he told her in a low voice. You must find a tiring room where you can wash away the tear stains from your face." He looked down tenderly at her delicate, ivory face, the small nose tipped with pink from crying. "Weeping or laughing, you cannot help but be lovely, can you, *doña?*" he murmured, chucking her chin to strengthen her wobbly smile. Bending, he brushed her lips with his.

They set off, making sure the door to the chamber was firmly closed behind them. Holding lightly to his good arm, she looked up at him with anxious eyes. "Will you be back soon?"

"Of course, soon. Think you I would allow the other

gallants the remaining sets of dances with you when 'tis only on my arm which you belong? Not likely, my Lady." Her relieved smile removed the last of the black anger from his heart; that, and the thought that his good right arm would soon propel a steel-tipped lance straight into the Count of Perens's face.

Dolores came into the corridor just a few steps ahead of the chattering ladies in whose company she had visited the convenience chairs set up in a special chamber. She was just in time to recognize the two figures hurriedly stepping from a room down the hall. She shrank back to mingle with her companions, an unwanted pang of jealousy stabbing at her for the way Francho had pressed Leonora to him as they hurried off, the little Zuniga looking up into his face as if he were a god. Dolores's useless reaction irritated her, but not enough to stem her curiosity at why Don Francisco had held a kerchief pressed to his arm. Pretending she needed to return to the tiring room, she hung back until her twittering friends disappeared toward the main hall, then glided noiselessly up to the chamber Francho had just quit.

An intuition, a feeling, the stealthy way the two had exited, had piqued her interest. She listened first for any sound coming from the room, but the muffled music of drums and tambourines from the dancing was enough to hide anything faint. Shrugging at her own too lively imagination, feeling foolish, she pushed open the door and walked in.

The sour vomit smell that assailed her made her crinkle her nose. A quick glance around and with a muttered oath she ran to where Don Felipe de Guzman sprawled on the floor, seemingly dead. She knelt and put her ear against the stained velvet covering his chest, and a wave of relief washed over her as she heard a heartbeat. Sitting back she saw his sword was in its scabbard. There was no blood. He certainly smelled as if he were in a drunken faint. Then she noticed the blackening eye and bruised jaw, and the faint red thumb marks on Felipe's neck. And she understood Francho's arm. Of course. There had been a fight.

By her pulling up Don Felipe's shirt the narrow ruching on it hid the marks on his throat. She could do nothing about the purpling eye and jaw, but anyone finding him would suspect he had weaved into a door before passing out. She desired that

Francho stay free and alive, and so if he had attempted to cover this hostility—for the rooms showed signs of hasty putting-to-rights if one looked carefully—she would help him.

She was on the point of making a hurried exit when one of the candles burning in a wall sconce guttered and a metal object, partially hidden under Guzman's body, gleamed and caught her eye. Stooping, she drew Francisco de Mendoza's bracelet medallion from under the unconscious Count of Perens and held it reflectively on her palm. Then, smiling, lowering her lids on the gleam in her gray eyes, she dropped it safely in the pocket among the folds of her flowing skirt and glided out of the room, back to the dancing and entertainment, to the huge supper that would be served somewhere before midnight, and to the unctuous attentions of the Duke of Medina-Sidonia.

❦ *Chapter 15* ❦

URGING HIS FINE dappled gray up the steep path to the looming fortress of Alcala la Real, Pietro di Lido reflected on the luck that his mission's ship to Rome was being outfitted in Cartagena, making reasonable a stop at Alcala to pick up Don Francisco de Mendoza, who had returned to his post from Seville six weeks before. He knew the gentlemen riding behind him, followed by their escort guards and baggage mules, could use a night's rest as well. And he looked forward as much to the little game to be played out for them as to the sumptuous meal Don Inigo would surely spread.

That night he hardly had to interrupt his dining in order to display the requisite polite disappointment when Tendilla announced that his son was absent from the board suffering with some sort of gastric upset. And the next morning when di Lido joined the refreshed party waiting for him in the castle courtyard he had no trouble generating a look of concern as he announced to all that he had seen Don Francisco and that that gentleman was suffering a bad congestion of the lungs and a fever and could not join them immediately; however, as soon as he was well he would sail on his own and meet the party in Rome or Constantinople.

With a gracious bow he accepted Don Iñigo's salute and Godspeed and his wishes for a successful embassy and then

345

smartly led out his impressive little cavalcade, the bright banners of their houses fluttering proudly from the lances of their alert and armored escort.

"'Tis a pity Don Francisco has caught a fever and is too ill to ride," Don Diego de Cerda remarked to di Lido as their horses threaded their way down the mountain's steep slope. "He's a sharpling at cards. I was hoping on the sea journey to gain back some of the gold he relieved me of at Baza. Ah well, the opportunity is flown, now."

Di Lido flicked a bit of mud from his silken knee and smiled pleasantly. "I shall be glad to provide you with a chance to recoup, *señor*. Although I may not give you so good a game as Don Francisco."

From de Cerda's grin of acceptance, the amused savant knew that the Viscount did not realize from whom the young Mendoza had acquired his skill at cards. The months at Mondejar and Baza had been long and sometimes dull, and a bit of gaming always perked up the brain. His flat turban was secured against the wind by its own tail tied as a wimple under his chin. He pulled this closer about his ears and hunched into the fur collar of his fur-lined cape. "'Tis always cold in these high places," he grumbled to de Cerda. "I am looking forward to the civilized climate of the Eternal City. *E vero!*"

Granada

❧ *Chapter 16* ❧

STANDING AT THE lip of one of the high passes through the Sierra Nevada, the traveler imagined that if he but blinked his eyes the mirage that was the great, long valley of the Sultanate of Granada, laid out to right and left below him, might disappear, merely a creation of a brain weary of mountain dun and the somber green of pine and spruce. In most of Spain winter still hung on, and even in Andalusia the early spring rains caused chill. But in this lovely southern valley, protected on every side by humped ranks of towering mountains, it was astonishingly, eternally June.

As far as Francho could see on that crystal clear morning stretched a living mosaic of fields and forest, green, gold, and brown, alternating with flower-dotted, open meadows, where herds of animals grazed. The sun glinted from a vast cross-hatch of irrigation ditches netted across the land, carrying along the life-giving waters of streams, which descended like silver ribbons from the high snowcaps of the surrounding peaks. Growing up the flanks of these giant guardians were olive trees and neat fruit orchards, stands of frond-waving date palms, garlands of vineyards, and patches of purple gentian blooming wild and vivid. Below and hidden in the hearts of the rearing granite barriers—and especially coveted by their enemy—were the Moors' labyrinthian, slave-worked mines, which delivered to them the earth's riches: gold, silver, iron, lead, sparkling marcasite, and sapphires large as eggs.

Gleaming white towns and villages dotted the valley, each with a creaking water mill and a mosque tower rising above its red tile roofs. And in the distance, drawing the eye like the main jewel in a tiara, there rose behind its thousand-towered walls the fabled city of Granada, the resplendent dream of centuries of pashas, spread out on the plain and climbing in steep tiers along the creased, purple foothills of the mountains.

Every rising breeze brought the perfume of orange blossoms, of scythed grass and warm, moist earth to Francho's enchanted nostrils—as well as the smell of mules and donkeys as a caravan coming up behind him from the rocky defile crowded him close to the edge of the cliff. Pulling his eyes away from the view he settled his pack more comfortably on his back, filled up his lungs with the scented air from the valley, and set off on the descent down to the vega.

To the eye of anyone who beheld him he looked an ordinary figure in his white turban and flapping, long tunic; a tall, olive-skinned, black-bearded Moor with all his possessions in one small pack on his back, the only difference between himself and the other subjects of the Sultan who traveled along the packed-earth road to Granada being the lacquered and inlaid seven-string guembri fixed atop his bundle. He shared his route with local farmers driving produce carts, and with the owners and shouting boys attached to files of donkeys and camels heaped with bulging sacks of goods for the lucrative souks of Granada.

Although the warm sun forced him to halt several times for something to drink, his brisk stride ate up the leagues, and by noon the reddish walls of Granada were scarcely a league distant. He could make out the houses rising along the hillsides, dazzling white or pink or blue, a maze of buildings pierced by the gilded spires of minarets gleaming in the sun and separated by avenues and squares lined with trees and palms, an unusual amount of lush greenery for so densely inhabited a city. And high above all, in solitary splendor on its own peak, sprawled the palace-fortress called the Alhambra, renowned citadel of western Islam.

Francho had no doubt he looked his part. Two weeks of simulated illness at Alcala and two more weeks camping in

the hills with Ebarra had given him the beginning of a short
black beard which he'd shaped in the Moorish manner and
which he actually liked; he thought it gave his strong-nosed
face a more serious appearance. His dark hair was cut shorter.
His skin was naturally a pale olive, and his brilliant blue eyes
were no detriment; for after hundreds of years of intermar-
riage between Arab and Goth many Moors were blue-eyed,
with fair complexions and even blond hair. Only those Moors
of pure southern nomad stock had the dark skins and the
piercing black eyes of the desert dweller.

Francho wore the humble costume of the poor, an unbelted
brown tunic which almost covered the baggy brown breeches
secured about his ankles, and leather sandals. In fact, the
loose-fitting clothing had a liberating effect, for there was no
weight of a heavy swordbelt around his waist or any bother
with buttons or tangled points when he disrobed. In his pack,
around which he had wrapped the old cloak he had worn in
the mountains, he carried an extra cotton turban cloth and a
tunic, some food, a few handwritten pages of Arab verse,
some sections of the Koran bound with cord, a wooden bowl,
and a flint. Hidden under his garments was a filled purse. The
snake-headed dagger was stuck under the band of his
breeches, and, incautiously he knew, there was a tiny silver
cross sewn inside the waistband of his pants.

At one village, because he was close to his goal and in high
spirits, he unslung his guitar and treated his fellow travelers
and the delighted urchins about the well to a rousing ditty,
lifting his voice to sing it strong and clear—and for the first
time awarded his white smile to the enthusiastic applause of a
circle of grinning strangers and their cries of "More, more,
more!" But with a rakish bow and salaam he continued on his
way again.

His thoughts centered on his new identity as his feet carried
him along. He reflected that this was now the fourth time that
he had changed lives, nor would this be the last time, if
fortune ran with him. He had gone from monastery to tavern
to castle, and in each one he had felt comfortable but yet not a
true part. In fact, sometimes he envied men that he saw, not
merely noblemen but even common householders, because
they lived just one life with one name and suffered no
confusion about where they belonged.

If God—if Allah—willed it, however, he expected that this
recurring detachment, the vague feeling of incompleteness

that had always drifted with him, would find its peace as soon as he took his father's name and his rightful place as Francisco de Venegas, Marquis of the realm.

Thinking of his rightful name brought up the startling discovery he'd recently made, that the Moorish general Reduan, known for both the strategic cleverness and the ferocity of his attacks, was a Venegas! Both Tendilla and di Lido thought the other had recounted this to him but neither had, until Tendilla mentioned it at Alcala. It seems that Reduan's grandfather, Pedro de Venegas, who would have been Francho's granduncle, was captured as an eight-year-old by the Emir of Almeria, adopted, and brought up in the Moslem faith. Pedro made a fortunate connection by marrying one of the Emir's daughters and subsequently rose to great power and prestige. His son, named Abul Cacim Venegas, became Grand Vizier to the Grand Sultan Abul Hassan, Boabdil's father. And now the grandson, Reduan Venegas, was the second in command of Granada's forces—in spite of the fact that at one time he had been in league with Zoraya and El Zagal against Boabdil and the Abbencerages. How bizarre, Francho reflected, that this second-generation Moorish warrior was his cousin once removed.

The road as it approached the city was now lined on either side with country estates belonging to the wealthy citizens of Granada city, and through the trees Francho caught glimpses of fine houses, each with an airy and graceful pavilion set in a hedged garden, often reached by a delicate bridge crossing a narrow, silvery brook. Squinting up at the sky he judged it was not much past the hour of one; plenty of time to gain the city and search for a place to live. A growl in his stomach told him he was hungry; the enticing grove of willows he had just come to called to him to rest. But because the side of the road was already preempted by a peasant sleeping in the shade of a cart loaded with honking geese, he climbed the low bank and walked farther back into the copse, pleased with the springy feel of the tangled wayside grass under his tired feet.

The soft gurgling sound of water drew him on, and he proceeded further until he came to a brook which flowed crystalline over smooth stones and between tufts of shaggy grass, its bank decorated by a willow whose long, trailing withes dipped into the stream. Delighted, Francho sat down amid bobbing red poppies and there made a leisurely meal of bread and sausage from his pack, washing it down with the cold elixir from the stream, which he scooped into his bowl. Stretching his muscles with pleasure, for never had food tasted so delicious nor water so sweet as they did in this tranquil little dell, he was reluctant to leave. And so he detached his guembri from the pack and leaned back against the trunk of the willow. Fleetingly a memory of Dolores crossed his mind, which he thought was strange. He could picture her as a child, bare-legged, with tangled hair, edging along the dirty wall of an alley to peek out and see if all were clear, or, as now, displaying her beauty and jewels at a Court banquet, or even, although his stomach clenched with the thought, practicing her allure in Medina-Sidonia's bedchamber. But not here, not in such simple, pastoral peace. He sniffed, and in a minute it became clear what brought the perturbing young woman to mind—the air was heavy with the perfume of a jasmine bush growing nearby.

He laughed and stretched. The lofty Baroness de la Rocha, practicing her haughtiness, might not appreciate the simple pleasure of the sun shining warm through the lattice of willow leaves. Trying to blank out both the insistent floral scent and the tilt-eyed temptress from his mind, he forced up a picture of golden Leonora and imagined her sitting by his side, smiling and happy. Yes. He would mark this charming place and bring his love here some day. The thought soothed him.

Tightening the guitar strings, he strummed a few chords, trying to decide what song was just right for his mood. A blue-and-gray bird dove from a low branch to swipe at the brook, where a darting water insect had caught his bright eye; the tiny splash he made, along with the buzzing of a fat bumblebee around the field flowers, were the only background sounds as Francho's fingers caressed the guitar strings. His rich baritone was resonant and carried well, and he had a trained and elegant control. With almost no change in the volume of his voice he could deliver the ring of a warrior's pride or the soft yearning of a lover.

*In the valley sings a bird, O love, a fowl of snowy
  plumes,
And I shall silence him at once; the wildling bird
  presumes.
His song, 'tis not so sweet enough e'en though that it
  endears,*

*The nightingale alone, my love, is worthy of your
    ears.
Ay sweet, sweet, sweet, ay sweet.*

Twice he played the six stanzas of this lilting Arabic love
song to a squirrel that chittered at him from the tree, then he
changed keys and continued with "Melissandra," the ballad
of a maiden whose lover seeks her for seven years and at last,
after many a trial, finds her.

Becoming engrossed in his music and the mellow sound of
the guembri as it floated out in the open at last, not soaked up
by muffling drapes, Francho swung into the rousing "Bullfight
of Gazul": "Sultan Almanzor of Granada, he hath bid the
trumpet sound"—his guitar became a martial instrument,
decisive and compelling—"summoning all the Moorish lords
from the hills and plains around . . ." He went through the
whole colorful saga of the festive bullfight, changing the tone
of his voice to fit the various personages described and
thumping the guitar with the heel of his hand to represent the
bull, which was an effect he had invented himself.

When he finished, with a triumphant flourish and a rich
laugh and smiling broadly to himself, he paused to sip the
water left in his bowl and glanced up lazily at the blue sky
showing between the leaves. The sun had progressed but he
was still loath to go, unwilling to leave the bucolic glen for the
crowded hives of the city. A twig crackled behind him and he
looked around, thinking he had waked the peasant sleeping
under the cart who had come, scratching his beard, to see
what the racket was about.

Instead the branches of the willow were pushed aside by a
turbaned man of medium height, light-skinned, with a light
brown beard and sad brown eyes, and simply dressed in a
plain white tunic with yellow leggings and heelless slippers.

"Salaam," the Moor greeted him.

"Alecum salaam," Francho responded in his accent-perfect
Arabic, scrambling to his feet. "I beg forgiveness for trespassing."

"Stay where you are, minstrel." The man smiled. "You do
no harm. Your music has enhanced the beauty of the countryside. I have been listening to you from my kiosk." The man,
perhaps about ten years older than himself, Francho judged,
did not seem rich enough to own this fine property. Perhaps a
relation, or overseer . . .

"I am happy to have given you pleasure, *sayed.*" Francho bowed, touching the tips of his fingers to his forehead and chest.

Surveying Francho's dusty tunic and knapsack the newcomer observed, "You are not from the city."

"No, *sayed,* I am from Malaga, but recently I have lived in other towns. I have come to Granada to find my fortune."

"As a musician?"

"That is the only accomplishment I can offer to earn my bread. One hears there is already a surfeit of laborers and beggars in the city."

"Unhappily you hear the truth. People have poured in from every corner of our besieged land, the city walls bulge with them. But perhaps they will find a few coppers to spare for a minstrel who lifts up their hearts for a while."

Francho's unfeigned pride in his music asserted itself. He grinned and shook his head. "Allah provide I shall not have to play for coppers, my master. 'Tis not for the applause of the ignorant I have come; my training is too fine for their ears. I intend to enter the contest the Sultan holds every year on his birthday, and win a position with the royal musicians."

"Then the stars are not with you, minstrel, for the Sultan will hold no festivities this year; the times are too uncertain."

Francho's grin slowly disappeared. Without the Sultan's contest to gain him a royal audience his plans were seriously set back. "You do indeed tell me bad news, *sayed!* I had pinned my hopes on catching the Great Sultan's ear," he muttered from under his dismayed frown. The man would never know how true those words were. "Now what can I hope for except a place in one of the *kavah* houses, with only poverty and obscurity in return for my years of study." The personnage of Jamal ibn Ghulam was real enough to Francho for such despair to come naturally. With growing upset he bound the guembri to his pack and swung the knapsack to his shoulder. The whole of Tendilla's scheme would be a hundred times more difficult to carry out unless he could discover some other way of getting to the Sultan.

The Moor watched him for a moment and then asked, with mild interest, "Is the loss of the Sultan's contest such a blow to you that your face becomes a mask of distress?"

"You cannot understand, master," Francho answered, even though he was anxious, now, to go on to the city. "It means an end to my hope of reaching the eminence of a royal musician, for I have no friends or influence in Granada. And what laughter remains to a man who loses his dream?"

"Ah, but I do understand, minstrel, very well indeed. Yet—there are always next year's contests."

Francho shrugged and turned his hands up; already the fatalistic Arab gesture seemed native to him. "Who knows where we shall be next year, *sayed?* Perhaps in the belly of the Christian monster or in Paradise. Allah does not tell me his designs, and I have found it wiser not to anticipate him. I must resume my journey now. Peace be with you." He salaamed respectfully and walked away.

"Perhaps I can help you, minstrel. Wait for a moment," the Moor called to Francho's retreating back.

Francho turned. "Help me? And why should you? I am a stranger to you, just another unfortunate who has come to take refuge in Granada."

"I enjoy your music—and you have a sensitive face. Sometimes my judgments are based on less than that; I am prone to whims. So I will make a bargain with you, singer of songs. What is your name?"

"Jamal ibn Ghulam."

"I have some influence at the Alhambra, son of Ghulam. If you will come to my pavilion just beyond those trees and entertain me for an hour, I will see what I can do to bring you to the Sultan's attention. He is a great lover of music and will surely be very appreciative of my effort to introduce you."

Francho thought fast. The Moor seemed, now that they had had some conversation, a man of means who had little to do and was idly looking for someone to help him pass the time. He doubted this individual really meant to extend himself for an itinerant musician who could not return the favor. On the other hand, there was always the chance that this fellow really was hoping to earn a monetary gift from a pleased ruler, or even a connection to the royal ear that his own standing could not bring him. The man was likable in his mild manner, and the brown eyes held a hint of something more than dilettante interest. An hour, more or less, would make little difference to Francho's plans, already in disarray, and might bring something to help them along. It was a small chance but worth taking.

He shrugged again and nodded. "Fair enough, *sayed,* my

music for your influence. I had hated to depart this small bit of Allah's garden anyway. I am your servant."

The Moor led the way along the bank of the brook, past a grove of blooming fruit trees, and thence to a clearing of clipped, velvet grass bounded by beds of flowers. In the center stood a pink marble confection of slender columns and delicate, mitered cornices, open on three sides, and shaded by willow trees and trembling aspens. They walked across the soft turf past a round marble pool, where great waterlilies floated serenely, and mounted the three low steps that gave entrance to the square pavilion.

Water splashed in a low, carved fountain in the center of the bright mosaic floor. On a thick rug heaped with pillows Francho saw a leather volume lying open, abandoned when its owner had heard him singing. There were enamel bowls of dried apricots, fruits, and dates on a tray on the floor, along with a silver wine decanter and cup. A breeze brought the aroma of cherry blossoms from the trees about and ruffled the pages of the forgotten book.

There are some who do not lead such a hard life, Francho reflected with envy, looking about at the kiosk with its gilded ceiling. At the other's invitation he folded himself cross-legged on a fringed rug and tuned his instrument, while his new friend lounged on his pillows. Smiling, Francho looked at the Moor inquiringly. "You have only to request, *sayed,* and instantly the tune will spring to my hand."

"Just play, Jamal ibn Ghulam, just beguile me with whatever comes to your head and I will be content," the man said and smiled back.

Francho plucked his guitar and began a medley of short *canciones,* which he performed so well and invitingly that his host slipped easily into joining the choruses, his tenor voice pleasant but not quite true, a growing, unself-conscious pleasure lighting up the sad eyes. After a while the Moor himself suggested several ballads and Francho obliged. Then he asked would the *sayed* care to hear some original compositions, and when the man said he would indeed, he played several of the minor-key coplas he had composed in a flush of inspiration at Mondejar. He ended the concert with his rousing rendition of the "Bullfight of Gazul," finishing the last chords with an exuberant flourish, and looking up to see his host truly beaming in delight.

357

"Excellent, excellent, minstrel. You achieve sounds of a glory that would please the Prophet himself!" He tossed Francho a plump orange the color of sunshine.

Francho did not mind the praise. "I am the most skilled musician in Granada, *sayed,* nay, in all of Iberia," he boasted, mindful of the situation. "And that is why it would be a pity should the Sultan not hear me. Some talents are rarely come by in a lifetime."

The brown-bearded Moor threw back his turbaned head and laughed, genuinely amused. "By the beard of the Prophet, son of Ghulam, you are quite correct about your ability, but did your father not teach you the grace of modesty? It is not seemly for you to praise your own gifts."

"One cannot eat modesty, *sayed.* 'Tis the merchant who cries his wares loudest and with greatest vigor who attracts the buyers in the souks. If the Sultan understands fine music and lauds me as the most splendid artist in all Islam, I shall tell him he is right, for I am that." Francho thought the jaunty white grin he flashed through his dark beard would soften the conceit, for all it was true.

The affable gentleman's gaze drifted to the guitar in Francho's hands. "That is a very fine guembri you have. It is as elegantly made as the tones you coax from it." There was curiosity under his flattery.

Francho's African guembri was shiny black and differed from a lute in its flatter silhouette and straight neck. It was inlaid with coral bits and mother-of-pearl, and the frets were of silver. "You wonder how a ragged minstrel came by such an instrument, *sayed?* Well, I did not steal it, it is mine. My father was a city official in Malaga, a tax collector, and we had a fine home with private baths and slaves. My mother had costly jewels and I was gently raised and taught music; in fact I can also play the lute and the harp. While I was on a visit in Gaudix the cursed Christians besieged and captured Malaga, and when I finally got through I found my father and mother and sisters dead and our house in ruins. Everything had been smashed or looted. But as I walked through the ruins I tripped over a piece of canvas and found under it my guitar, barely scratched. It was all that was left to me, accidentally, by the vile infidel."

Francho was careful to keep his tone resigned. Belligerence was not in his role.

"You have my sympathy, minstrel. It was evident that you

were not just a common wanderer." He looked Francho over
frankly. "But you seem strong and healthy to me. Why do you
not join the ranks of soldiers, if you can? Or perhaps the
Sultan can find a place for you in his palace guard. He is
greatly in need of loyal men."

Francho allowed the corners of his mouth to droop in an
expression of pain. His eyes mirrored hopelessness. "No one
is the victor in war, master," he intoned with bitter fervor.
"Never again shall I lift a weapon in these hands. 'The ruins of
Zahara shall fall on our heads!' the old dervish wailed to Abul
Hassan, and for my family and me this prophesy has come
true. But in the charred remains of my home and my life I
found this guembri, whole and waiting, and it was as if the
hand of Allah touched me and a voice said, 'Here, here is your
weapon, to soothe and to charm and to beguile away the
deadly thoughts of war and of vain resistance from the minds
of your doomed and suffering people.'"

For the first time his listener's features were shadowed by
disapproval. "What? Would you allow the unbeliever to take
from us our land, our cities, our homes, and not lift a hand in
defiance?"

"I think only of beautiful Malaga that bravely resisted
against clearly superior strength and finally falling was burned
and sacked and decimated and her citizens taken as slaves.
And then I consider Gaudix, which El Zagal gave over in a
bargain and whose people are alive and still enjoying their
own hearths and families, their possessions and business.
Look you, master, we exist surrounded by the enemy and far
from our friends; it is my opinion that our position is hopeless
and that 'tis better to live than to die in vain battle. Do you
think me craven? I shall tell you I am not. But I do not wish to
wander the world like the Jews. Most important is to keep
what we have left, this beautiful kingdom, and live to enjoy
it."

The Moor had given close attention to Francho's pacifist
remarks. Francho did not expect him to agree, but in any case
he dropped the seeds of passivity as part of his mission. If they
did not germinate here, they would somewhere else.

"And how would you go about retaining this kingdom?"

"Pay whatever tribute is exacted and again pledge fealty to
Los Reyes Católicos, just as our Grand Sultan once did.
Which is why we are yet here to talk about it."

The mild face had smoothed again into a calm expression.

"Heaven is the reward for the warrior fallen in battle. Have you no desire to lie in the lap of Allah when you die?"

Francho laughed disarmingly and stretched. "Ah, but so I shall, *sayed*. The hosts of Paradise are fond of music, and there is a great shortage of excellent minstrels these days!"

The man chuckled. "You are a brash one, Jamal ibn Ghulam, but I like you. So I will caution you that if you fling about such philosophy you will make many enemies in Granada, for the people are in a warlike mood. In fact, I sympathize with your ideas and find them wise, but the citizens of Granada will abhor you."

"Then I shall heed your warning, master, and keep my thoughts to myself. I do not want to educate the people, I want merely to entertain them." Francho glanced at the sun and found the hour he meant to stay was long past. "I must go on to the city now. I will have to search for lodging for the night." He stood up and refastened his guitar to his pack.

Lounging on his pillows the Moor selected a fruit from one of the bowls and then regarded Francho amiably. "I believe you think I will overlook my part in our bargain. But you do not realize how you have brightened my day and dispelled the morose mood that was on me. Here, take this." He slipped from his finger a heavy silver ring hammered with the image of a fruit and held it out. "In four days, at this time of the afternoon, go to the Alhambra and present this ring to the Chief Keeper of the Second Gate. He will take you to an official of high position, whom I will have persuaded to allow you within earshot of the Sultan. From there on you will have only your own talent to rely upon."

Francho took the ring, searching brown eyes that held no guile. A certain shyness drew color into the man's face and he pulled his gaze away. "This is a valuable bauble, *sayed*. How do you know I will not trade it for coin and disappear into the Albayzin?"

"Then we will count it payment for your services. But I see you have determination; I have no fear you will show it to the gatekeeper to vouch for your appointment. Peace be with you, O singer of songs, and go on your way."

Francho salaamed and was turning to leave when a thought struck him. "But—if the Chief Keeper asks who sent me? I do not know your name, *sayed*."

"Only show him the ring and say it was given by Abdullah, grandson of Muhammed. That will be enough."

360

As Francho cut across the elegant lawn he noticed horses and a mule hitched at a distance from the pavilion and, behind a hedge, the turbans of the man's pair of servants. From a nearby village the faint voice of the muezzin called the faithful to prayer and the turbans disappeared from view as their owners prostrated themselves among the flowers. Francho lengthened his stride. The day was waning fast.

❧ *Chapter 17* ❧

MUCH OF GRANADA was built against two main hills divided by the deep gorge of the river Darro, one hill supporting the fine homes of the aristocracy and rich merchants and capped by the Alhambra; the other, called the Rabbad Albayazin, an opposing and noisome warren of the poor topped by a smaller fortress, the Alcazaba. Below, spread on the *vega,* was the Granada that encompassed the comfortable shopkeepers, lawyers, overseers, and petty officials, and the bazaars and businesses which earned them their livings.

Francho revised upward Mendoza's estimate of a populace of two hundred thousand souls by at least another hundred thousand; he had never seen such throngs of people, such huge and crowded markets, and so many homeless in the alleys.

The streets were narrow and crooked as in most cities, but lined with walled houses from whose gardens planted with flowers and blooming citron trees came a sweet fragrance which pervaded all the byways. The stepped rises and cobbles were swept clean and sluiced by gutters running down the middle of the streets, but what was a most unusual be-musement for one reared on the dry plains of Castile were the graceful carved fountains found at every corner with sparkling water jetting and splashing into their brimming bowls.

Water was important to the Moors. Descended from desert

nomads they had inherited a lust to see the life-giving fluid flowing in abundance around them. In addition, it was law for the religious Moslem to be clean before worship, to wash hands and feet, suck water into the nostrils, put wet fingers into ears and pass wet hands over hair, no matter where he happened to be when the call to prayer came, five times during the day. If no water was available to the orthodox believer, it was permitted to wash hands in sand or dust, but Francho could not imagine that anyone in this city of blossoms and greenery would ever have to resort to desert substitutes.

He had decided to live in the Albayazin in order to be close to his contact. After entering the city through a vast, horseshoe-shaped gate, he had been obliged to ask directions several times to help him navigate through the bustling maze of streets and open plazas. At last the road began to climb, but even so one couldn't miss the quarter of the poor—the streets were more narrow and tangled, ill kept, with crammed, almost windowless houses. A typical city stench rose from the littered gutters.

Painted harlots leaned from ramshackle balconies, where bedlinen and wash flapped like tattered ensigns. Barely veiled women in cotton mantles carrying water jugs or baskets on their head jostled past turbanned graybeards. Unemployed mercenaries gathered in grumbling groups. Urchins of all sizes and both genders darted between makeshift stalls, where vendors hawked their meager, second-rate wares. Alms-criers crowded around the slovenly public inns and shabby mosques. Faggot sellers and charcoal men shouted their presence, and boys with skins of goat milk knocked on each door. Now and then a decrepit donkey burdened with sacks of rice or old clothes and led by an abusive peddler would scatter the soiled tots playing directly in their path, and the children's shrill jeers and curses added to the incessant hubbub of people coming and going and living in the streets; Jews, humble in yellow turbans, penniless Moors from Ronda, Almeria, Malaga, Alhama, eking out precarious existences by day labor, glistening blacks prohibited from living elsewhere no matter how their purses jingled, citizens and freed slaves whose only crime was to be haunted by poverty, and the lees and dregs of the city—the thieves and pimps and whores—all of these, more than one hundred and sixty thousand souls jammed into the limited streets on the Albayazin slope.

Francho tramped the inclined byways, footsore and tiring,

inquiring at every scabrous lodging house, only to be told there was no chamber to let nor even dormitory space. He might have found room in a better part of the city, but that would have been out of character and taken him far from his contact. So continuing on doggedly he trudged from lodging sign to lodging sign, but none had even a niche left to rent him. It was after he emerged from the fifteenth hostel with the owner's curt, "We are filled to the rafters," still echoing in his ears that he realized that he had acquired a shadow, a little boy whom he had briefly noticed six inquiries back and who seemed to be deliberately trailing him. Francho put down his pack for a moment and slumped dejectedly against a building wall. Discouraged, fatigued, and hungry, he had just about decided to try another section of the city, be it however expensive and inconvenient, when the youngster he had noted sidled up to him.

"You seek a place to live, master?" Thin and dirt-streaked, with a shaven head and bare feet, the dark-skinned child was no more than six, his birdlike, reedy voice matching his skinny limbs.

Too out of sorts to be civil, Francho sneered, "And why do you think I trudge in and out of the hostels? To amuse myself?"

"Please, master, I know of a place to let. If I take you there will you give me a piastre?"

Glancing ruefully at his aching feet, Francho reshouldered his pack. The sun was going down and he needed to find a place to sleep besides the street. It would be dark before he reached the lower city. "I do not wish to scratch lice in bed with six other men. Run away, boy." He reached into his tunic and fished a few small coins from his purse. "Here. Now stop following me."

Great, limpid eyes looked up as the little boy put his spindling arms behind him. "No, master, I will not beg or take money I do not earn. Only listen please—there is a woman whose husband was buried today. I heard her say she wants to lease her house and leave the city. I will take you to her."

The fact that the boy would not take unearned money impressed Francho. He leaned down and asked more kindly, "What is your name, little grasshopper?"

"Ali Afsah, master."

"Well, Ali Afsah, I am sorry but I do not require a house, only a single chamber or a bed."

"Oh, but it is a very little house," the child declared gravely. "It is?" Francho's weariness stayed him to listen. "Well, we shall see. If it is cheap and what I require, then you shall have several piastres for your initiative. Lead on and I will follow."

With a grateful smile the youngster padded off, threading his way expertly through the hodgepodge of alleys. At a somewhat more prosperous-looking inn, the Golden Horn, he crossed a small square, rounded a corner, and entered a short, cul-de-sac alley, looking back to make sure Francho was still behind him. He stopped at the third building down the alley, a narrow, one-story shelter with a flat roof, wedged in between higher buildings which were leaning slightly, as if to hold the rundown little house together.

"This is the place, master," Ali chirped hopefully.

Francho rapped sharply on the splintery door. There were shuffling footsteps and the door squeaked open on rusty hinges. "What do you want?" The fat woman peered at them suspiciously, using the end of the cotton shawl she wore on her head as a casual veil over her mouth. "I have no money for creditors. This is a house of mourning. Go away." She started to shut the door but Francho put his foot in it.

"I want to inquire about letting your house," he said quickly.

She looked him up and down. "You do not have enough money. Rooms are hard to get these days and the landlord calls the tune. I will not lease my house for a paltry sum."

"I have money. Only let me see what you have to offer. If it suits me I am certain we can come to terms."

He could almost see the greedy wheels turning in her head as she stared at him speculatively. Then she opened the door wider. Francho stooped his head under the lintel and entered, smiling at her in his most charming manner, for she was merely fat but not old, and possibly susceptible to flattery. He had only just so much money and didn't want to part with an exorbitant sum to make her rich.

The woman gestured about with a pudgy hand, "I will leave the furnishings for the right price."

There were only two little chambers. The larger in which they stood boasted a blackened hearth with an iron cookpot and some cracked bowls and pitchers set on a crude inside ledge. There was a low table with straw mats for sitting, a rickety cupboard holding a few utensils and cups, a battered oil lamp, and a large market basket. The woman showed him a

365

pallet in one corner, and Francho was pleasantly surprised to note that the straw was fresh and the old blanket covering it, although threadbare and faded from many washings, was clean. The second room, through the doorway screened by a tattered cotton hanging, offered a wider pallet, also in good condition, and wall pegs, which now held the woman's few skirts and mantles.

The floor was swept clean and the house looked as if it might be fairly free from vermin and rats. Francho decided he would find no better shelter in this quarter and told the woman he would take it.

The woman eyed his guembri. "You are an itinerant musician," she sniffed. "Can you pay three dinars the month?" This was an outrageous price. A laborer earned perhaps one silver dirhem for a very long day, or two and a half gold dinars a month, but only if he worked steadily.

"Come, madam, the Sultan himself would not pay so much gold for such humble quarters," he chivvied her. "A musician's purse is slim and a man must eat as well as sleep. I can pay you twenty dirhams." He knew that in normal times the woman would have groveled at his feet for the offer, but these were not normal times.

"What?" she cried, dropping her shawl and revealing a double-chinned, pouty face with a large wart in the corner of her nose, "You are wasting my time. Only this morning the proprietor of the Golden Horn offered me a truly generous sum, for he needs extra lodging for his guests. It was only fear that my property would be defaced by the ruffians he caters to that kept me from agreeing on the spot. Now that my poor husband is gone to the pleasures of Paradise I am lonely and wish to return to my father's farm. But I have debts to settle; if you desire my house you must pay."

The dickering went on for a quarter of an hour, he offering a bit more each time, she coming down a bit, for the eyes behind the ragged veil marked well the sapphire gaze and white smile of this black-bearded haggler. Finally Francho shrugged and spread his hands fatalistically. "Ah, I had hoped to have a roof over my head tonight, but it seems the little money I have gathered is not enough." He let his eyes travel slowly over her heavy form, and her round eyes widened slightly. "I am sorry, madam, to have bothered you."

She regarded him stolidly and did not acknowledge his rueful smile. But when he reached the door she called out,

"One dinar and a half, and that is my last word, you robber. In advance." She extended a pudgy, steady hand.

He could tell from her tone she would go no lower. "So be it. If I go hungry I will at least starve sheltered."

He gave her the gold and silver coins, and she bit the gold one, then dropped them with satisfaction into her ample bosom. Her suspicious attitude relaxed. "Give me an hour to collect my belongings," she said, "and tonight I will stay with a neighbor. I shall come in the morning on this day every month to collect my rent. Make sure you are here." She told him her name and asked for his, then admonished him to take care not to break her pitchers or tear her blankets. "I could have gotten my price, I can tell you," she simpered with fluttering lashes behind the big shawl as she left, "but you have gentle manners and I have a big heart."

The boy was waiting for him in the darkening alley. Francho gave the child some coins and saw the liquid eyes widen with pleasure at the amount. Then he strode off to the Golden Horn to wait while his landlady packed.

The common room of the inn, reached by a short flight of stone steps, was below the level of the street; the wailing sound of a flute accompanied by a small drum rose above a babble of voices as Francho pushed aside a wooden screen and found himself in a sea of turbans bobbing in the purple gloom. He picked his way through the badly ventilated space to an unoccupied mat on a platform against the wall. Everyone sat cross-legged and Francho did likewise, grateful to be off his feet, placing his knapsack beside him. Not much light came from the lamps suspended from the rafters; only a cleared space in the center of the room boasted some bright lanterns in a ring around it.

The music could hardly struggle over the racket of the guests' chatter and the rattle of crockery as it was set or taken off the ankle-high table before each person. Some men drank tiny cups of thick, black and bitter *kavah,* some had mugs of *nabidh,* a fermented drink made from honey and dates, and some drank wine dispensed from bloated goat skins dangling from hooks at the rear—the Prophet's injunction against intoxicating beverages being commonly ignored in Granada. Francho called for some wine and a round flat of bread. He was too fascinated by the surroundings to give attention to heartier food.

The whitewashed walls seemed bluish-purple in the dim

light; the atmosphere was heavy, almost sinister in the murk, in spite of the loud laughter and talk. The whining music was heavily Arabic and was played by African musicians, dark and impassive. Here and there groups of unemployed soldiers could be recognized, for they still wore their fighting costumes: baggy, knee-length pantaloons, wide red sashes, and spiked metal helmets atop their turbans. The pungent, strangely appealing smell of the black *kavah* climbed above other odors in the airless place, hanging over the turbaned men hunched over the tiny tables, their bearded faces shadowed and indistinct.

A jingling dancer slid among the tables, deftly avoiding the hands that grasped and pinched, and the music quickened in tempo when she reached the cleared space. An unctuous, greasy man, his robe tight around his huge girth—the proprietor, evidently—announced the dancer's name and that she hoped to amuse and entertain the gentlemen, to which he got an eager chorus of "Aye!" and "Dance, let her dance!"

Francho had seen some Moorish dancers perform at the Spanish Court, but this girl danced with an aggressive, overt sexuality that was new to him. The several cups of wine he downed on an empty stomach was of poor quality, the bread was coarse, but he did not notice. His whole attention was riveted on the wriggling dancer, the fascinating tsing-tsing of the tiny metal disks attached to her thumbs and third fingers, the jingling of the bracelets and baubles adorning her bare arms and ankles. The wide, white pantaloons she wore, tight only over the hips and at the ankles, were slit from waist to ankle in four places so that as she swooped and whirled the audience got tantalizing glimpses of bare and pretty brown legs. Her short, sleeveless jacket left her undulating, rippling midriff bare, and in her navel there was set a flashing red stone.

The girl was small and infinitely sinuous; her graceful arms writhed seductively as the drum beat grew agitated and the flute wailed in a high-pitched frenzy. All that could be seen of her face was expressive black eyes rimmed with kohl over and under the lower lashes and painted indigo on the upper lids; the rest of her features and her hair were heavily veiled. As the drum beat more frantically and the flute shrilled, the dancer sank to the floor, leaning back against her heels, torso rippling, arms writhing above her, thighs wide open, the slit pantaloons giving glimpses of the soft brown flesh. Her eyes closed in ecstasy as her body arched tautly. The audience of panting men moaned as one, and gold and silver coins fell in a shower to the clearing about her.

Of one piece with the shouting, stimulated audience Francho watched the small body arch up again and again as the explicit dance heightened to a climax and he felt the heat of excitement in his groin, and his breath stuck in the back of his throat. As with every other man there he desired to embrace that quivering body and to pull the veil from the face of the seductive *houri*. The presence of the veil, in fact, was more than intriguing, it was unusual. In the relaxed mores of Granada only the most conservative of women hid their faces totally. Most, especially the upper classes, wore a *yashmak,* a small veil of quite transparent chiffon, an accessory of fashion more intriguing than modest. But public entertainers were seldom covered.

The woman rose up from the floor with the fluidity of a snake and circled her hips. As the drum ceased with a final thump and the flute trailed off, the dancer quickly scooped up the considerable number of coins, executed a clinking, low salaam, and backed out through a curtained door guarded by the smirking proprietor. There was a storm of calls and hoots and stomping, which the paunchy one finally quieted by shouting that his dancer would return after a while.

Slightly rocky from the wine and the dancer's effect on his nervous system, Francho paid his account and left, emerging into a street suddenly grown dark and quieter. The greasy smell of cooking rose from outdoor braziers. A few late denizens hurried past the blind beggar squatting below the single flaring torch fixed at the entrance to the Golden Horn whining, "Alms for the love of Allah, master, alms . . ."

Francho was annoyed to see light flickering through the one small window of the house he had rented. He was very tired; he wanted to fall on his pallet and mull over his plans until sleep overtook him. "Shaitan seize that woman!" he cursed under his breath. "Does it take her this long to collect her few miserable belongings?" Worried that perhaps she had changed her mind and he would yet have to sleep in a doorway, he quickened his step and pushed open the door. A small charcoal fire burned in the hearth and on a mat before the warmth lay Ali Afsah, curled in sleep like a trusting puppy. At the sound of the door closing the boy awoke, startled, then scrambled up rubbing his eyes.

369

"What are you doing in my house?" Francho demanded, just as startled.

"I . . . I have made you a fire, master," the youngster responded hopefully.

Frowning, Francho approached to loom over the child. "I asked for no fire. You must go home. I have no further need of you. A boy that pesters after he has been amply paid is in need of a beating."

The child blanched and Francho felt evil for deliberately frightening him, for the menacing expression showing on his face was really more surly than he felt. But he wanted the child to leave for good and not come back to cadge for more coins in the morning along with a gaggle of ragged friends who would swarm on the doorstep begging and whimpering.

"Please, master, but I have no home. Can I not work for you? See, I have made a fire and I have drawn water for you from the well, and I can sweep and scrub and wash your clothes, and—and polish your guembri?"

In spite of himself Francho laughed. "My guembri does not need polishing, grasshopper, and I can't afford a servant. If you have no home why don't you appeal to the preachers at the mosque? They will see you are placed in an orphans' home."

The small, shaven pate drooped, the thin shoulders slumped. "I have tried. But the orphans' houses are too crowded; there is no more room. Please let me stay with you, master," the piping voice quavered. "I will work hard and I eat very little. I will do everything you tell me and I am very strong." In the huge eyes there was a poignant gleam of hope.

Francho surveyed the fragile frame that claimed to be so strong, clucked in annoyance, and turned away, depositing his knapsack in a corner. Of all the things he didn't need it was to be burdened with a homeless brat, a baby, really. The child was so starved his tender ribs showed through the patched tunic. It was unfair of the boy to attach himself to the first good prospect he saw—people had their own problems, they didn't need new responsibilities. But—he too had once been homeless and not even so defenselessly young, and Tía Esperanza had sheltered him and loved him and given him the chance to survive. It would not kill him to keep the boy for a while and be on the lookout for a good home for him.

He looked the waif over and knew he could not be the one to erase the childish trust yet left in the boy, that eager, puppyish hope that all would be well. Ali waited silently, a pathetic little creature, aching to please. "Well," Francho grumbled, "since you are here you can stay the night. In the morning I will take you to the mosque and see that you are accepted."

With a happy grin the boy rushed forward. "Let me take off your sandals, master; I will wash your feet. . . ."

"I will take off my own sandals." Francho rummaged in his backpack and found a remnant of bread and cheese he was too tired to eat. "Here, if you are hungry. And you may rest on that pallet for tonight. It is softer than the floor."

"Thank you, master."

"Do not call me master. My name is Jamal." Irritated, Francho pushed his shoulder through the curtain to the second room and pulled off his turban and clothes in the dark, letting them lie where they dropped. He sat on the pallet to knead and rub his blistered feet, then lay down to plan for the morrow. But his eyes closed and in hardly a minute he had drifted off into deep, dreamless slumber.

When he awoke in the morning he thought he was back at Alcala and lay for a moment with sleep-fogged eyes until a vendor hawking eggs in the street penetrated his consciousness. His stomach growled its emptiness and he remembered he had given the last of his food to Ali. He would have to make his way to the food stalls with a hole in his belly. A plague on everything! Muttering, he dressed in a fresh tunic from his knapsack and pushed aside the cotton drape. Ali was waiting for him, bright-eyed and eager.

"Good morning, master."

"Don't call me master!"

"Good morning, Jamal."

"Good morning, then," Francho replied sourly, wondering why he had taken on this unwonted responsibility. Then he stopped in surprise. A cloth was set on the little table before the glowing brazier and it held a round loaf of bread, a wedge of cheese, a bowl of oranges, dried fruits and raisins in another bowl, and a small pitcher of foamy milk. There was a cracked earthenware plate, a knife and a mug, and a mat was already arranged on the floor upon which he might sit cross-legged. In a corner another mat held a jug of water and a bowl and a clean cloth from the cupboard. It was a heartening sight for a grimy, hungry man.

With a quick, noncommittal look at the boy, Francho knelt

371

and poured water into the bowl. He removed his tunic again and with a small bit of coarse soap from his backpack vigorously washed his hands, face, neck, chest, and underarms. Ali watched him cheerfully.

"Where did you get the food?" Francho questioned as he dried his refreshed face and upper body on the cloth, which was of a spongy material.

"At the stalls, with the money you gave me."

"That was your money; you should have saved it. I can pay for my own food."

"But you are my friend," the child said simply.

Pleased with the boy's competence and initiative, Francho fell upon the breakfast, giving Ali a part of the food and milk, which the boy would not have touched first had Francho slept the clock around. Afterward, through the back door and in a tiny, dirt court scattered with rubbish, he found the ramshackle and malodorous privy. When he reentered the house all signs of their breakfast had been cleared away, the table was clean, the dirty water thrown out. Ali had hung his second tunic on a peg and was busy slapping the dust from it with his hands.

"You don't want to go to the orphan's house, do you?"

"No, mas— No, Jamal. That is charity."

"But the Prophet had said that it is as blessed to receive charity as to give it."

"My mother once told me that it is a sin for an able-bodied man who can work to take the alms meant for the sick and weak. You would not want me to sin?"

But Francho had already made his decision, although for less pious reasons that had suddenly occurred to him. "How old are you, Ali?"

"I will be seven next summer."

"Well, you are a bright boy and you make yourself useful. You shall stay with me if you wish, but only as long as you are obedient and quiet, and keep out from under my feet. Do you understand?"

The quick joy that lit the sensitive little face was reward enough for his kindness. Francho gave the child his sandals to clean, and the boy took a rag and scampered out to work in the back court so as not to disturb his new benefactor, who now sat frowning in thought.

He still had three days before testing how seriously the Moor of the grove gave out his word and his ring. His other alternative would be to offer a large bribe to the official in charge of the Sultan's entertainment, but that still meant somehow reaching the man. Nor would it be wise to spoil a possible sponsored introduction with a premature offer to a possibly upright official. He decided it was best to wait the few days and use the time to familiarize himself with the city and with the tenor of the people; information thus gathered might suggest some way to penetrate the Alhambra's inner sanctums.

Strapping the guembri to his back, for that was the safest place for it, he summoned Ali to retrieve his sandals and then allowed the delighted boy to lead him to various parts of the city and point out the landmarks that the child knew, important streets and mosques, shortcuts between squares, communal buildings such as the solid and impressive public baths which could be found in every quarter, and hostels the child had heard commended for edible food and where they sometimes hired musicians. With Ali chasing behind or before him, Francho elbowed his way through the crowds strolling the great bazaars, or souks, of the lower city, where a vast variety of merchandise, produce, and goods from all over the world was still being offered in spite of the Christians' blockade of Granada's seaports.

Voices separated themselves out to Francho's receptive ears. Merchants wailed to each other the poor state of business and heaped blame upon Boabdil, as did the muleteers and camel drivers sitting idle for want of shipments and the clerk and talliers looking for employment as businesses cut down their overheads. "He is ruining us!" went the cry in this district. "Let him jail the elements of violence and make a secure peace with the Christians so our ports will be opened, or else let him beat the unbelievers from our gates. But let him do something!" And some just cried to the speakers haranguing in the squares, "Peace, peace, at any price!"

On the other hand the armorers, the famous weapons makers, the suppliers of uniforms and horses, and all those with something to gain from a large and prepared army railed, "Let us make war! Let the warriors of Allah sweep away the enemy and gain their secure place in Paradise so that as sovereign people we may sell to the world again."

On ensuing days Francho heard the peasants and farmers of the outlying districts who brought their produce to market grumble, "Our homes and fields will be burned, our mills, our flocks destroyed, our land ruined. Peace! Let us have peace and our lives and we ask no more." In a public bath which Francho patronized one afternoon, for he knew the Moors were modest and he could wrap his hips in a towel to hide his uncircumcized member, he heard the upper classes' vehement disgust with Boabdil's timid policies; they were angry at his placating relationship with a Christian king who had driven so many of them from their homes, and they heaped recriminations upon the Sultan's head for not sending forth the fierce fighting men now available to him. These prosperous citizens were humiliated, and in their extremity a reborn and aggressive desert spirit filled them with a rage to avenge their loses, no matter how costly a final victory.

And the preachers in the mosques thundered the fiery words of the Koran: "Make war upon those to whom the book has been given who believe not in Allah, make war until they pay tribute out of hand and be humbled!"

From his outsider's viewpoint Francho thought he could discern the real issue—neither war nor peace but decision, an end to confusion. If tribute were to be paid, let the Sultan root out and silence those who agitated against it. If they were to fight to regain their kingdom and be free of the Christian yoke, then let the Sultan ride on his war horse at the head of his armies, strong and belligerent. But let the Sultan do something!

What praises he did hear were for the General-in-Chief of the army, Muza Aben Gazul, and his second-in-command, Reduan Venegas, whose forceful, daring feats of courage had made them the idol of every Moorish youth at court and in the streets. These two, and the leaders of the Abencerrage and Zegri clans, were dangerous men who might finally seize the throne and somehow save the Granada Boabdil could only lose. These were Francho's true antagonists, more so than the contemptible Boabdil, who presumed to a throne without the capacity for firm decision and rule.

In the evenings he returned to his house to help Ali prepare their supper, for the child had cut himself several times slicing onions. The boy glided about softly as a shadow, speaking only when spoken to and so anxious not to displease that Francho gradually relaxed his arm's-length aloofness. When asked about his past the child had little to tell; he had been born in Antequera, where his father had been killed in a

Christian raid. His mother fled to Granada the year after, penniless, but made a few piastres a day sewing. She had died of a fever some weeks before, and Ali had slept in alleys and spent the few coins she had left him for food and went about begging for any work he could do.

Although raised in poverty Ali had been treated kindly and with love; that much Francho could see, for the loss of that love showed in the round, vulnerable eyes, at once so helpful and so uncertain. It was not hard to like the child, and Francho did not regret his decision to keep him fed and sheltered until a better home presented itself. After supper the first evening Francho had visited his contact to establish some emergency signals. And twice, in spite of himself, he went again to the Golden Horn, where the veiled little dancer held the leering, lecherous audience in her throbbing spell, making him hot and sweaty too, and inwardly cursing how long he might have to go celibate in this benighted kingdom because he was uncircumcised.

On the appointed day set by the Moor of the pavilion Francho carefully shook out and brushed his simple clothes and with the guembri slung on his back marched through the Albayazin to the bridge over the Darro, a Moor among other Moors, a big, black-bearded, turbaned refugee with the vivid blue eyes and pale olive skin of a mixed-breed and the stolid mien of the Moslem. If his proud bearing was reminiscent of the aristocrat, no one remarked it. If his jaw was clenched because he could not think of a sure substitute for the canceled birthday contest, no one cared. Only Ali, at home, had seen him staring into space, pondering and pondering.

He might contact one of the ensembles of musicians already on the royal roster and pay to join them, but this would give him small latitude to impress Boabdil, and impress Boabdil he must. The Sultan had been known to make confidants of artists he admired, and this was the crux of Tendilla's venturesome scheme. Bribery seemed Francho's only recourse, and if he did not have enough money he would have to steal the rest.

Since the Moslem had no hereditary nobility or landed titles, it was the families of traditional wealth and power and royal officials, high city functionaries, and men of professions who formed the aristocracy inhabiting the lacy palaces on the opposite hill from the teeming Albayazin. The breezy Street of the Gomeres was lined with rustling palm trees, eucalyptus, flowering shrubs, and jetting fountains, and along this way the mansions rose one above the other up the sides of the hill. No grim and gloomy Spanish palaces these. Their delicate cupolas and spires showed above their pastel-painted outer walls, which were inlaid with colored tiles and overhung with vines and rhododendron, and even from without the walls, judging from the Moorish-style villas he had seen in Seville, Francho could imagine the columned courts, airy balconies, and sunny chambers shielded only by lattices that these owners enjoyed.

These residences reminded him of Leonora, exquisite, delicate, open, and gay. And she would have the finest of these for her own if all his fervent hopes were realized.

The top of the mount was capped by the irregular sprawl of the Alhambra, called the "Red Palace" from the color of the ruddy earth beneath its heavy stone walls and boxy watchtowers. Along with a busy stream of citizens on foot, in litters or on horseback, Francho finally arrived at the palace-fortress' main entry, a huge, square tower with its Eastern-style arch shaped like a wide horseshoe. There was a gigantic hand graven on its keystone, whereas the keystone of the opposite arch of the barbican was carved with a large key of similar proportions. Francho had seen the hand and key symbol flying from Moorish standards during the campaign of Baza and knew its meaning: the five fingers of the hand designated the Mohammedan creed of fasting, pilgrimage, alms giving, ablution, and war against the infidel. The key symbolized faith and power, it was the key of David transmitted by the Archangel Gabriel to the Prophet Mohammed. It had become traditional for muftis to try petty legal cases beneath this entry arch, and so it was known as the "Gate of Justice."

People came and went freely through this gate and into the First Plaza, a huge square where merchants displayed their wares to the passing members of the Court, especially looking for the profitable visits of the ladies of the royal harem. Ordinary citizens loitered everywhere, anxious to collar this or that official and plead their business, and troops of soldiers clattered through from the inner courts. Francho strode to the far end of this plaza toward another horseshoe arch with massive closed gates, guarded by glowering Nubian sentries, which marked the entrance to the Sultan's palace.

"No admittance unless you have a pass," rumbled the

red-pantalooned African whose bulk and pike blocked
Francho's way.

"I wish to see the Chief Keeper of the Gate."

"State your business with him."

"My business is with the Chief Keeper, not with you. He is
expecting me. If you will not admit me, summon him here at
once." His peremptory tone did more to impress the sentry
than his appearance. Even though the black African curled his
thick lip disdainfully, he nodded to a companion, who disappeared through a small door pierced in the great portal, but
when Francho started to follow, steady crossed pikes barred
his way.

"That is, I pray he's expecting me," Francho thought,
imagining the ire of a Chief Keeper summoned by a poor
musician of whom he had never heard.

The Moor who finally stepped through the door was hard-
faced and stocky. His sash was blue as a token of rank, a blue
plume surmounted his turban, and his saber scabbard was
richly damascened. He surveyed this shabby caller with
irritation. "By what right do you claim my attention?" he
demanded. "I don't know you at all. Speak quickly or
begone."

"By this right," Francho responded, producing the ring.
"And by the request of Abdullah, grandson of Mohammed.
You have instructions concerning the minstrel Jamal ibn
Ghulam?" He braced, fully expecting a snarl and the gate
slammed in his face. But the Chief Keeper examined the ring
carefully, and then, with a glimmer or respect in his calculating eyes, nodded to Francho. "Very well. Come with me." And
the crossed pikes slithered past each other and withdrew.

Francho had not much time to gawk at the beauty of the
formally planted Second Plaza for the Chief Keeper hurried
him through. Still, he could hardly keep from lagging behind
as they entered the palace itself, for not even the glowing
descriptions from Tendilla and di Lido had prepared him for
the Oriental splendor of this royal dwelling. Slender, gilded
pillars supported archways wrought like fantastic gold honey-
combs whose interstices were colored in glowing vermillion
and lapis lazuli, their verges edged with carved pendants
which hung like golden stalactites. The walls, traced with
fragile and painted plaster filigree, blazed with multicolored
tile dados to the height of a man and with gilded moldings

adorned with flowing Arabic script in high relief. Everywhere there were tinkling alabaster fountains. And each fretted and airy gallery opened into another even more fancifully opulent.

Goggle-eyed, peering about and dazzled in spite of himself by the magnificence, Francho realized wryly that he hadn't come too far from the ragged child of Ciudad Real who had gasped at the grandness of hulking Mondejar. The breathtaking glory of the Alhambra so captured his mind that it was' only when he actually stood in the chamber of the appointer of royal entertainers that it struck him that his friend of the pavilion had truly kept his bargain.

The official, Mustafa Ata, glanced at the ring and wobbled his three chins. "Too early, you have come too early; the Sultan is with his council."

"I shall wait, so it please you," Francho smiled, deducing from the man's great pelf, soft face, and beardlessness that he was a eunuch.

The entertainment chief rubbed his cheek distractedly and squinted at Francho; his high tone was petulant. "I am told you are an excellent balladeer, Jamal ibn Ghulam. May I believe this?"

"Indeed, *sayed,* and even better than you have heard. I have had fine training."

"Eh? Oh, and from whom?"

"Hakim of Lucena was my instructor for many years, until the day he died." Francho had garnered the name from Nuñez, his own teacher.

Mustafa Ata raised his eyebrows. "The Prophet's Beard! You must be older than you look. And how did you ever get that old jackel to impart any of his techniques? Well, no matter, he was a master musician and I pray to the Prophet you are too." He hitched up the great belly under his sash and his black brows wriggled fretfully. "These days Shaitan himself would be easier to please than the Grand Sultan. I bring him dancers and singers trained at the Court of Egypt, magnificent each one; poets famous the world over, jugglers, acrobats, flame-swallowers, jesters, tens of harpists and lutists and rebec players; men who fondle poisonous snakes and lanky black freaks from the heart of Africa, painted and feathered and taller than two men together! And which of them catches his fancy to earn a word of praise for this earnest servant? None of them!"

Mustafa Ata put a thoughtful finger to his pursed lips.

"However, there used to be one who delighted him—a singer of ballads with a way of holding the ear—now dead, alas, from the blow of a falling roof tile. My good ruler seems always to be seeking another of his ilk."

"Perhaps I may please the Sultan enough to take this man's place," Francho ventured. "And of course, should I gain his approval I would give all credit to your astuteness in seeking me out."

"Ah yes, that would be wise of you, of course. And seven dirhams each month in appreciation, as well." Mustafa Ata heaved his bulk from his low seat and gestured Francho to a leather hassock. "Then let us trust your words are not bigger than your ability. Although I value the opinion of the man who sent you." A small chuckle escaped the cupid's bow lips. "You may sit here until the Sultan is free. I will call you." And the Chief of Royal Entertainments departed the suite to attend to his various duties.

Now the shock of coming this far so easily overtook Francho. It was incredible to think that for all his worrying and scheming the past three nights it was the quirk of a chance meeting on the road which had brought him to a private audience with the Sultan—even a better advantage than the contest would have offered. Mentally he begged pardon of the sad-eyed aristocrat of the pavilion for having doubted his word and connections. In fact, he realized he did not even know the man's abode in order to return the ring. Well, he could be found somehow, and thanked.

The minutes dragged by. He shifted about from one haunch to another. He got up to pace the chamber awhile and then sat down again. An hour or more passed and there was no sign of Mustafa Ata. As time wore on his elation faded, as always diminished by his lack of patience. Cracking his fingers nervously he considered it was only an audition he'd been granted, after all. The greatest hurdle was yet to come, for perhaps he and his cohorts were naive in thinking his musical ability could compare with the famed masters whose artistry had shaped Boabdil's tastes. Even though Tendilla, di Lido, and Nunez too had praised the highly personal renderings Francho gave his songs, the Sultan could turn out indifferent to him.

In the next few hours he would have the answer to all his years of study and preparation. The sluicegates of his life would open or close in his face, and all was hanging upon the whim of a man deemed weak and vacillating, and hard to please, as Mustafa Ata had complained, who might take a cranky dislike to his face or the timbre of his voice and relegate him to the anonymous pool of musicians on Mustafa's long list.

He stroked the strings of the finely made instrument Tendilla had made for him as a gift of good luck. "It is truly as I said to that man of the pavilion, that Abdullah," he whispered with bent head to the guembri, his only friend in this exotic and strange place. "If I conquer it will not be by the sword, but by you. Your tongue speaks sweet like an angel, strong like the trump of Gabriel. Do not disappoint me, good companion." When finally, after another miserable hour had passed, Mustafa Ata came to fetch him, he was so weary of waiting he was resigned. He would do the best he knew how and humbly accept the outcome as the Lord would direct it.

But, as the plump official waddled before him into the Sultan's private saloon, he could not help one last, fervent prayer: "Santa Cecilia, sweet guardian of musicians, put honey in my mouth, let silver flow from my fingers, do this and I will forever keep vigil for you on this day. . . ."

Padding past the small knots of turbaned courtiers scattered in conversational groups about the lavish, gilded, and arabesqued chamber, Mustafa Ata halted before a deep, pillowed divan canopied with great swags of shimmering silk. He made a low and reverent salaam. "O Great Sultan, I bring you Jamal ibn Ghulam to whom the pomegranate ring was given—a fine musician whom actually I had marked for my Sultan's services many days ago."

Sapphires flashed as the Sultan waved his ringed hand. "Ah yes, Mustafa, you are very discerning. I am sure somewhere in your reports there is mention of this minstrel and a future appointment for a hearing. It is not your fault I chanced to hear of him before you could present him."

Stunned, Francho could only stand and stare in shock, for he was looking at his erstwhile friend, the gentleman of the pavilion, Abdullah, grandson of Mohammed—or Boabdil, Grand Sultan of Granada. Entirely different did he appear now, in his cloth-of-gold pantaloons and brocaded tunic, a ruby shooting fire from one earlobe and a diamond the size of a walnut pinning a trio of white egret plumes to the shimmering gold turban. And in spite of the small, formal smile shaping the bearded mouth, the face that had seemed mild was now tense; the softness, the affability had disappeared behind the closed and impersonal gaze of a ruler of half a million people.

Two red-sashed Nubians, great arms akimbo, guarded either side of the divan. A kneeling slave kept the Sultan's wine cup full, while another waved a languid peacock fan over the royal head. The odor of precious frankincense from Yemen wafted from a jeweled burner, and Francho soon realized that the tiny flashes of silver light, as if hundreds of fireflies were flitting about in the delicate fretwork of the walls, were actually reflected sparks from a marble bowl of quivering mercury at the Sultan's side.

"Play for me, minstrel, and sing. I have need of your soothing offices," the Sultan ordered.

Francho salaamed, not recovered from his surprise. "I . . . I pray my humble efforts will please my Sultan," he stammered.

"Such modesty, O singer of songs!" Boabdil responded with some acidity. "And did I not hear you term yourself the greatest musician in all Islam? Well, we shall see. You may begin."

But Francho remained transfixed, confounded, poise shattered. His brain skittered about, unable to light upon one number in his repertoire. Nervously he plucked out a few chords but his heart skipped a beat; he could remember nothing! His mind was frozen as solid as ice and he frantically chipped at it to unlock at least one small song from its paralyzed grip. Mustafa Ata, seated cross-legged on the lowest step of the dais, stared daggers at him. Shifting the guembri he cleared his throat. He frowned and recleared his throat.

"Perhaps you know the 'Bullfight of Gazul'?" the Sultan prompted, noting his distress. "It is my favorite."

The ice vaporized. With gratitude flashing from his eyes Francho nodded. He struck a chord and then another, and expertly swung into the opening lines of the ballad, all the more vigorously for his relief at the passing of his stupor. The Sultan's smile spread and Mustafa Ata relaxed, lips pursed in pleasure.

> *"From Vegas and Sierra, from Betis and Xenil*
> *They have come with helm and cuirass*
> *Of gold and twisted steel,*

In gowns of black with silver laced,
Within the tented ring,
Eight Moors to fight the bull are placed
In presence of the King . . .

The heel of Francho's hand thunked the wood of the guembri to simulate the pawing of the crafty black bull. As the song progressed he let his voice sink to a whisper or rise to a shout as the sense of the verse demanded, and throughout the many stanzas his fingers kept up an insistent, driving rhythm broken only by loud staccato twangs for the shouts of the crowd and the snorts of the bull.

At the triumphant ending his royal audience jumped up in delight and clapped his hands, and there was also enthusiastic finger snapping from the listeners around the room. "You see, Mustafa Ata, have we not heard the truth? Is he not an excellent artist?" the Sultan exulted.

"Oh yes, indeed, O Great Sultan, so I have thought from the first I heard him. Oh yes, by the Holy Name of the Prophet, he is indeed, as you say, the finest artist in the kingdom," the appointer of royal entertainers babbled, his multiple chins folded into a fawning smile.

"Inscribe his name immediately upon your ledgers: Jamal ibn Ghulam. And it is my desire that he have the title of Head Musician of the Royal Entertainers. See that we pay him very well and that he is contented, for Allah has bestowed upon him a great gift and I am joyful in his presence."

"Yes, yes, Excellence, it shall be done as you direct."

"And you, good Mustafa Ata, may go to the royal treasury and select a few pearls for your perspicacity. In you I have a faithful and capable servant."

"Thank you, thank you, most Excellent and Greatest of Sultans," Mustafa cried, salaaming his great bulk, the top of his turban almost touching the floor in his happiness.

Boabdil raised his voice to the rest of the saloon. "And now leave, all of you. I wish to enjoy privately the fine talent of my new Head Musician. Begone!"

Swiftly the elegant courtiers bowed out, and even the slaves, fan bearers and guards melted away through a doorway heavily screened with clicking strands of lapis lazuli and quartz beads.

As soon as they were alone Boabdil's face underwent a

382

curious transformation: the tense and arrogant aspect of the ruler drained away, and in its place appeared the mild, sensitive face Francho knew from the pavilion, eyes and beard of a medium brown, small-nosed, gentle-mouthed, a face forever youthful, regardless of time. The gem-encrusted fingers lay relaxed on the silken knee; the furrows of majesty between the eyes had smoothed and disappeared.

"I think you understand my deception of the kiosk," he said to Francho. "It was an opportunity too good to miss. A Sultan seldom finds such easy occasion for playing pranks."

"I might have done the same myself, had I been in your position, Excellence," Francho smiled back, weak to think he had successfully leaped his first hurdle four days back and hadn't even known it. "But if in my ignorance of your exaltation I might have made statements of which Your Excellence disapproves, I beg that my outspokenness be forgiven."

"But that is your charm, Jamal." Boabdil beckoned Francho forward to sit on the top step, on the thick carpet spread before the divan. "You voice peaceful sentiments not often heard in the bloodthirsty circles about me. And I believe that you are honest. Are you honest?"

Francho's blue eyes looked steadily at this Sultan who had so quickly stepped out of his royal personnage and conversed with him as a friend. He saw a lonely, troubled man. But he was not unaware of the pitfalls ringing a ruler's request for honesty and did not let the Sultan's intimate tone prompt him into boasting. "I *usually* do not lie," he answered prudently.

Boabdil laughed. "Yet see, that *is* an honest answer. Had you protested complete honesty I would not have believed it. I like you, Jamal ibn Ghulam. I have honored you for your talents, but I also have need of a truthful man about me. Yes, my mother is truthful, but her words are flavored by her sapping ambition. My Vizier, Comixa, is truthful but his words lack the ring of passion; he has become old. All the others are dissemblers; they tell me what they think I wish to hear or they exaggerate to enflame my passions and I must hear the mutterings of the people through their mouths. But you are of the people, ibn Ghulam. Will you tell me truthfully what they are saying?"

The invitation was an invaluable opening. Caution would advance nothing. Boldness might. "Their words are not flattering, O Sultan," Francho responded, holding his breath that the reaction to this was not annoyance against him.

It wasn't. Boabdil rose, clasped his hands behind his brocaded back and moodily paced his dais. "And what news is this? If I thought they looked kindly upon me, minstrel, would I not go among them to hear their praise myself? I stay cooped up here in the Alhambra, hoping their passions will boil away where they will not fling rocks and mud at the sight of me, or perhaps hire an assassin to strike me from my horse. You found me at the summer kiosk belonging to Yusef Comixa, yet here in the Alhambra I have gardens and pavilions to delight the angels. But here I am a prisoner sulking in a golden jail, and so with a few trusted slaves I steal away to that little pavilion outside the walls where I pretend I am a free man, unencumbered with the woes of half a million faithful in a sea of pressing Christians."

Furrows returned to his brow; petulance and anger colored his voice. "Did you ever imagine, minstrel, that a Sultan could be caged in his own palace?"

"I have always thought rulers the very fountainheads of power, Excellence."

The Sultan's lip curled in self-disgust. "And what is power without men to do your bidding? My policies are unpopular; I cannot enforce them. If I butcher my enemies as some would have me do, in a trice others would spring up like *djinn* from the ground. I believe as you do, that peace is our only salvation, no matter what the tribute. And with peace I shall build Granada into a glory rivaling even ancient Cordoba. But my people have no vision; they want only revenge and blood spilled in vain to recover what is gone forever."

From his cross-legged position Francho came to his knees, sitting back on his heels, but careful that his head remained always lower than the potentate's. He spoke intently, with his habitual half-frown. "O Sultan, there are many citizens who hope for peace, many—in the souks, in the Albayazin, on the farms, in the shops. And their voices could be swelled to a roar if those who were uncertain what to do saw a firm power declare for peace, one who would keep all the bellicose under control."

Fists planted on his hipbones, Boabdil's diamond-clasped plumes trembled with his excitement. "Aha! See there? You already do me good service, Jamal. My advisors are men from the ancient families of aristocrats, firm in the traditions of honor, of noble heroics and courage and the blessed death of a warrior. My generals? They are itching to fight; it is their reason for existence. It does not behoove them to tell me of the people who see the wisdom behind the course I would choose."

Sighing, seeming to Francho for all the world like a child, petulant because he could not have his way, Boabdil filled his wine cup but left it to sit on the low table while he walked to a grilled window at the rear of the dais and, standing with his back to his new confidant, looked down at the troubled city he loved. The small table, within easy reach of the Sultan's divan, also held a bowl of fruit and a long, jeweled knife.

"Well. If it is a show of strength my partisans need to prop up their opinions for peace they shall receive it. Momentarily my ambassadors to Ferdinand the Catholic will set out for Seville, to return with the promise of an army of Christian warriors to aid me in securing my throne, for I have been faithful to the letter of my vassalage. And then, minstrel, those who urge war in the face of my edict of peace will either discover obedient silence or face execution."

He plays right into our hands, Francho thought, he *must* be kept on the throne at all costs! Yet instantly he tempered his jubilance, remembering that it was the weakest of the Moorish leaders who spoke thus conciliatorily, only the weakest.

As if reading his mind Boabdil continued, breathing in the fresh breeze from the neighboring hills framed in his window: "Fortunately my enemies are divided, each one jealously watching that the other does not become strong enough to usurp the throne. They would rather bear my shortcomings than face each other's murderous vengeance." His chuckle was dry and without mirth. "Ah yes, I am aware of my shortcomings, Jamal ibn Ghulam. But my hope lies in the hate of Yusef Abencerrage for Muza Aben Gazul, and in Muza Aben's venom for Reduan Venegas, and Venegas's spite for Samel Zegri."

There it was, Francho thought, some of the names of the powerful aspirants to the throne of Granada, the men he had been sent to observe and, if possible, thwart. And there were others just as dangerous. . . .

But Boabdil had finished his diatribe. He turned away from the window with a smile that softened his mien again. "And now I am satisfied of one thing more—that you, to whom I talk as we had commenced, man unto man, did not come here to make an attempt on my life."

Startled, Francho answered, "That is most certainly true, O Great Sultan, for I am your most loyal and obedient of subjects." He judged it would not be amiss to make this plainer. "But I wonder and fear that you would put such trust in a wanderer, unknown and unvouched for, for not in every instance . . ."

His voice trailed away as Boabdil laughed,—in fact, the Sultan was grinning; he opened one hand toward Francho with a slight snap of his wrist, and a skinny knife, a slim and deadly little sticker, slid down from his beaded sleeve. "Trust? You flatter yourself, O singer of songs. 'Tis not you I trust but the faithful black man hidden back of that hanging, whose sharp eyes have been on you every minute. And because you did not move from you place, nor send the paring knife into my back, nor poison my cup when you had every opportunity I could give you, you are still alive and I still like you. Well then, come out, M'jambana."

The draperies concealing a niche rippled and a huge Nubian wearing the conical cap-and-turban combination of the palace guards stepped out, resheathing his narrow, curved scimitar. He rolled his eyes fiercely and uttered weird, unintelligible sounds.

"M'Jambana lacks a tongue, but his eyes and ears and scimitar work perfectly. He was presented to me when I was a boy, a frightened savage whose father had cut out his tongue in sacrifice to some heathen god. Master and slave we grew to manhood together. He is never far from me."

One could see the black was no ordinary slave. He wore a sleeveless velvet jacket embroidered in gold thread from which his bulging black arms emerged in naked magnificence except for a wide gold band on one huge bicep. His grin was the grin of a tiger, teeth widely spaced and filed to sharp points. He stationed himself immobile behind the Sultan's divan, a barbaric Goliath with shiny hoop earrings adorning his distended earlobes.

"M'jambana is a loyal slave," Boabdil explained, reseating himself and reaching for a fruit and the paring knife, "but a very poor conversationalist. And my loving Sultana, Morayama, Allah bless her, is dutifully silent as a wife should be.

My son is in the hands of the devil Christians, who teach him their incomplete faith, and my little daughters know only of the harem. Of my courtiers, I trust few. Ah, Jamal, a ruler is a man alone, a veritable monk in the cell of government, a solitary sufferer." A wave of self-pity washed the fine-featured face. "But why do you smile?"

Forthrightness was what the Sultan seemed to want, and this he would receive. Boldly Francho observed, "O Sultan, you have a harem of women more beautiful than the sun, casks of jewels, a thousand slaves to do your bidding, entertainers to amuse you, and a palace of shining beauty. Some might mistake your 'cell' for Paradise itself."

Suddenly annoyed, Boabdil leaned forward, grasping the edge of the divan. "By what right do you speak? You look at all this through common eyes, with no inkling of my responsibilities. How dare you imply I complain without cause?"

Francho's gaze did not waver. "You asked me to speak the truth as I see it."

"I suppose in your wisdom you can tell me how a man can be happy in a nest of vipers?"

"No, Excellence, I am not that wise. But I can do my very utmost to keep the sound of their reptilian hissing from your ears and help to repair their strikes at your heart," he answered, disarming the moment. He took up the guembri in his hands and roguishly tilted an ear inviting a request.

Smiling again, Boabdil leaned back on his pillows and considered the brash commoner before him: a musician, but with an intriguing frankness and a certain commanding air; a man who addressed his ruler respectfully but spoke without ambiguity; a genuine artist, an aesthete, a virtuoso of sensitive and delicate refinement, yet hard-headed at the same time. This ibn Ghulam was a dual character, able to live successfully on two planes. Could he learn from him the secret of existing and working with bitter reality without crushing the sweet and fragile dreams in his heart? Was there still time to learn how to extract happiness from his life?

Boabdil tented his hands and placed them against his lips with friendly amusement. "So. You withdraw from the fray and use your instrument as a shield? Very well. Then you shall be *my* shield. Bring forth your music, Head Musician, and soothe away the angers of a day spent in argument with a hostile council."

Folding his long legs under him again, Francho played and sang his ballads, one following another, choosing only those about happier events, along with a few of his most eloquent love songs. The Sultan relaxed, his bearded mouth curved in a wide, childlike smile, transported, sometimes striking his hands to the tempo to make the background of a tambour. At the end of the love songs, which particularly delighted him, he would call out, "That one! Remember that one. It pleases me."

Francho showed his white teeth and answered, "I am fond of that one too. Our tastes are similar, Excellence."

When at last he was dismissed, Francho received Boabdil's instructions to obtain a pass from Mustafa Ata and to attend his ruler's pleasure every day at this time without fail. Then Boabdil put out his jeweled hand. "You may return my ring."

Francho took the ring from his pocket. The fruit engraved on it was not a persimmon or peach, as he had thought, but a pomegranate, of course—*la granada,* the pomegranate, what better symbol for the Great Sultan's ring. He gave it up, and Boabdil put it back on his thumb.

"You shall have others more costly, Jamal, do you continue to please my ears."

"It shall be my greatest wish to bring you delight, my Sultan," Francho murmured, salaaming and bowing out backward.

He emerged from the Gate of Justice just as the sunset cry of *"Allah akbar . . . echhed en la ila ella Allah, echhed en Mohammed rasou Allah, hai ala Elsalat. Hai ala Elfalah. Allah akbar, la ila ella Allah"* pierced the air from all the city's mosque towers in every direction, and he hurried to reach his little house before dark. He was famished and thirsty. And he was utterly incredulous. Not even the cynical whispers he had heard as the aristocrats attendant upon Boabdil had bowed themselves out—"The Great Sultan has found yet another pet"; "At least a good sight more entertaining than was that boring poet"—not even the knowledge that he wasn't the first favorite and might not even remain a favorite as long as the poet could spoil his elation or dampen the conceit that sent him humming down the road with his natural swagger.

Francho was becoming accustomed to the taste of the dark, acrid, honey-sweetened *kavah* that Ali boiled up for him. A mug of it steamed at his elbow as he squatted at the low table in the yellow light of his oil lamp and, with reed pen and a sheet of the thick, glossy-surfaced paper in whose manufacture the Moors excelled, composed another report of his observations to Don Inigo.

". . . has come my way, as I am in the Sultan's presence every day, often within earshot in the background as his courtiers converse with him." Francho shook his head in disbelief, looking at the simple sentence he had placed on paper, remembering the worry of his first days in Granada with his plans gone awry, still astonished with the breathtaking speed of his access to the halls of power; sensibly wary that the mercurial ruler whose aesthetic sensibilities he had captured might just as quickly tire of him.

"Granada is like a boiling pot. Peaceful citizens are upset about the failing economy, which has no foreign outlets, and the army daily parades its might before them as temptation to break the blockade. During the popular jousting tourneys on the Vivarrambla, Muza Aben Gazul fires up the cheering crowds by speaking from the Sultan's pavilion on the skill and daring of the Moorish warrior which should not be left to wither when it can reap great rewards. As the armored, beplumed knights rear up on their horses and whirl their scimitars about their heads, he exhorts the crowds to remember the carnage at Malaga, the ten thousand kinsmen and friends dead by infidel flames and sword, the fair cities of the Prophet waiting for release from bondage. He raises up a great, mailed fist to the skies and shouts, "Death to the Christian dogs! A cup of Christian blood for every tear we have shed over our captured lands. Allah so wills it!" and the spectators go wild acclaiming him. The growing power of this general, Gazul, is a most dangerous threat to Boabdil's throne, as I see it, my Lord.

"The Sultan hides from assassins by keeping to the Alhambra, hoping for Spanish troops to prop up his otherwise numbered days. I note daily great stores of weapons and supplies rolling through the streets from the foundries in the *vega* to the supply depots. Those reporting to the Sultan say the army is at peak, swelled by some fifty thousand men, with more recruits from the countryside available in case of war.

"I strongly believe that the people of this city abjure Boabdil not for his leaning toward pacification but for his vacillation—his lack of settled policy and power to uphold his decision. If the Sultan's arms could be strengthened and his orders enforced, I think the greater part of the citizenry would in the end choose to save their skins and fortunes through peace. I do what I can to stiffen his resolve not to fight.

"I pray for your continuing good health, and that of our King and Queen and of our friends, especially the Lady Leonora, to whom recommend me as soon as you deam fit.

"This night, 5 May 1490. F."

And the second to the last word in the body of this letter he misspelled, one of the agreed upon signs whose absence would indicate forgery.

He left the house quietly without waking the sleeping Ali and padded through the dark and narrow streets, his dagger close to hand in case the supine bodies snoring in doorways and niches might have aggressive ideas. He turned into a crooked alley that smelled of goats and excrement; rats scrambled away from hunks of refuse as he approached. After knocking on the low door of a rotting shack he waited and then pushed it open, stepping into pitch darkness.

"Who enters?" asked a sleepy, querulous voice.

"He who speaks with a golden voice." Francho responded with the identifying phrase. "Strike a light. I cannot see you."

There was a fumbling, a scratching, and finally a tinder spark jumped and flamed the wick of a tiny lamp. The man sitting on a heap of filthy straw turned the milky-white disks of his eyes toward Francho's voice, his grinning mouth displaying rotted stumps of teeth. "Light or no light, it is all the same to me, *raiss*. But you are welcome to my humble abode."

The blind beggar who could not see his face was Francho's contact, passing his messages on and receiving others in turn from a man whose frequent visits outside the city were required: a snow gatherer, who went out to the mountains with a string of donkeys and empty baskets and came back with hard-packed snow from the peaks, insulated with straw and mats, to sell in the markets for preserving meat and fish, for chilling liquids and making the iced desserts so dear to the Moors. The snow vendor would leave the message under a cairn of rocks at a certain spot in the mountains far from the Moorish patrol routes, and there it would be retrieved by another agent and rushed to Mendoza at Alcala la Real. Even in the event of war the preserving of foodstuffs would be highly important. Snow gatherers could still find unblocked paths behind the city and another cairn would be arranged.

Francho put his sealed letter in the blind man's gnarled fist. "This missive must depart the city as soon as possible, old man."

"Your voice comes from a height, master, and it has a deep quality. I have perceived that you are tall and strongly built."

"You are not paid to fathom my looks. You would be safer to make no conjectures but do your job well and keep your prattle to yourself."

"I only jest, *raiss,* forgive a lonely man. It shall be as you say; the message will go forward without delay." The blind gaffer cackled and stretched forth his other hand to receive three gold dinars in his dirty palm, for which he called Allah's blessings upon his generous gentleman.

The old man could be trusted to a certain extent; he was a miser who cared for naught but the coins he fondled with greedy fingers and probably buried in the dirt beneath his straw. The sum he was given with every visit plus the promise of further payment every third month had always ensured his silent cooperation with Mendoza's agents. But he knew neither Francho's features nor his name or lodging. The torture racks and dungeons waiting for a wretch suspected of treason could wring names and descriptions from misers and patriots and even the ignorant alike.

Francho returned to his abode and fell upon his pallet, satisfied with his progress so far. He lulled himself into a relaxed state with longing thoughts of Leonora—although flashes of the Golden Horn's hypnotic dancer intruded—and his sleep was dreamless and tranquil. Had he known it was to be his last untroubled sleep for many days he would have enjoyed it more.

"But the Sultan will be most angry. He expects me." Francho strongly objected to Mustafa Ata, his way into Boabdil's quarters having been barred by stolidly adamant guards.

"The Sultan has no time for you today, ibn Ghulam. He is closeted with his council. But wait here if you wish, should he call for you." The paunchy worthy perfunctorily waved Francho to a bench in his chamber as a man wearing the silver breast medallion of a minor functionary bustled through the beaded entrance.

"But . . ."

The newcomer held a short, whispered conversation with Mustafa Ata, who then nodded and followed him, hurrying past Francho and out the door, his waddle more pronounced by his agitated gait. He spared not even a glance in the Head Musician's direction.

Francho heard loud voices approaching, and peering through the beaded curtains, saw a group of white-robed officials crossing from the far side of the colonnaded court, arguing violently as they hastened toward the royal council chamber. A large troop of pantalooned guards, barked onward by a grim officer, quick-stepped by, headed in the direction of the outer plaza. Men of rank, their faces tense, crossed the fountained court in increasing numbers, some muttering angrily. It was plain that some dire occurrence was disturbing the composure of the entire Court. Torn between wanting to wait should the Sultan summon him and aching to find someone to question, Francho paced Mustafa Ata's office. He willed himself to patience in spite of his rising sense of trouble, passing time by absently fingering melodies on the new lute Boabdil had presented to him and hoping at least Mustafa would return.

But the Sultan did not remember him nor did Mustafa come back. The ebon sky over the open court was flung with a net of twinkling stars and an owl hooted in a tree before he admitted to himself that no summons was forthcoming and that he might as well return to the Albayazin. Wearily he left the chamber. As he trekked along the wide reflecting pool of the Second Plaza he noted the grilled windows of the council chamber bright with the glow of lamps. Bareheaded slaves passed coming from the kitchens with delayed suppers for their masters, whispering among themselves as they transported their heavy salvers. The First Plaza too was swept clean of people, as always at night, but the guards at the gates and on the palace towers had been tripled and the pickets walked in fours along the walls. Trying to question some of the guards got him nowhere. They stared sternly and hurried him on.

The streets which were his route from the hill of the Alhambra to his little house seemed quiet enough, filled with the ordinary number of ordinary people. Evidently whatever was the alarm it was still contained within the walls of the Alhambra.

But not for long. By the time Ali shook him awake just after dawn the next morning with the report that there were great shouts and turmoil coming from the bazaars below the bad news seemed to be in every mouth throughout the city. Throwing on his clothes he loped down the hill and arrived in a main square just in time to hear a news teller shout out from the beginning again the report that was causing such angry commotion among his turbaned listeners, and to the facts that were known to the news teller Francho added his own ideas of what had transpired.

Ferdinand El Rey Catolico, it seemed, had become fed up with gradual measures and had brought his wily game of cat-and-mouse to a resounding end by sending back with Boabdil's outraged ambassadors demands which left no doubt of what Spain wanted. He reminded the Sultan of an agreement made during his Spanish captivity, that in the event the Catholic sovereigns should capture the cities of Gaudix, Baza and Almeria, Boabdil would surrender Granada into their hands peacefully, accepting in exchange some small Moorish towns to rule as a vassal prince. Ferdinand now called in the promise. He demanded a complete surrender of the city of Granada with all its supplies and arms, in return for which he would be a lenient and indulgent victor, as with Baza and Gaudix. Otherwise the city would suffer the same merciless and ravaged fate as Malaga. The worst insult was Ferdinand's contempt for any defenses the city could muster; he grandly allowed the Sultan a month in which to make his decision and name the city's fate.

Francho hurried to the Alhambra. He demanded entree to the Sultan and again wound up sitting all day in Mustafa Ata's cubicle. The atmosphere of the palace was as tense as a drawn bowstring. He came the next day and the next and the next, each time more afraid that his luck had failed and that now, when Boabdil's leaning toward peace needed special advancing, the Sultan did not remember his existence. Bleakly contemplating the toes of his heelless slippers and his slipping fortune, he understood how very cocksure he had been that the Sultan would continue to confide in him even when events went sour. In such a setback to his policies Boabdil seemed to have need of anything but an amusing minstrel.

Francho wondered what had caused Ferdinand's mask to

slip. Perhaps it was that the powerful ruler of Egypt had
speedily indicated to di Lido that he would not interfere in
this local quarrel. But, like a tarantula with the juicy beetle at
last in its maw, Ferdinand had closed the jaws of his friendship with a terrible, final snap. And knocked the Sultan's
leisure time for minstrels into the less demanding past.

❧ Chapter 18 ❦

"IF SHE KNEW it was me behind her she'd not be turning from the font so jauntily to pass the holy water from her fingers," Dolores snickered to herself as Leonora turned around. Dolores had deliberately hurried her steps and pushed through the crowd streaming into the great Seville Cathedral as the sonorous summons of the bells in the square tower died away, smiling her apologies as she went forward so she might slip in right behind Leonora. She needed to talk to her.

Leonora wore a loose, quilted surcoat edged in gold braid and a puffed, heart-shaped headdress covering her honey-colored hair. The famous dimples acclaimed by the Court poets were winningly in evidence as she turned to face the person behind her, one of the members of the Infanta's circle she thought. That it turned out to be Dolores caused immediate evaporation of the dimples and left a blank expression. But to her credit Leonora recovered in an instant both her manners and a stiff smile, and she touched the water drops to the Baroness de la Rocha's fingertips as prescribed.

Crossing herself with lazy grace Dolores returned a bland smile of her own, but she told herself, "Now, my girl, you could simply mutter 'thank you' and walk on and not have to deal with her sanctimoniousness or your own embarrassment.

Do it and the day will be much fairer." Still, her overriding need to know drove her to stay with her plan. She said, "I thank you, Doña Leonora. And what good fortune for me that we have met. I need urgently to speak with you. A matter of importance."

Leonora hid her surprise behind a rigid carriage. The small, pretty lips pressed together primly. "I cannot imagine what business we might have together, Baroness."

Snob, Dolores scowled mentally. But outwardly she remained smiling. "I would be grateful for a few minutes of your time, *doña,* and I will explain."

"Right now?" came the reluctant response and Leonora turned her head to look toward the backs of the regal Infanta and her peacock-hued coterie retreating into the incensed gloom of the giant nave. "I shall miss the Mass."

"Only a few moments. I will release you before the Agnus Dei . . ."

Curiosity got the better of Leonora. She tilted her small head questioningly and then shrugged. "As you wish." And she allowed herself to be shepherded to the edge of the crowds pressing in through the Gothic arched doorways. Dolores looked about and indicated a wide, groined stone pillar in the bluish-purple shadows just beyond the vestry of the immense building. "Why don't we just step over to that column where it is quiet?"

Gathering up the short trains of their gowns to keep them from being trod on, they made their way through the knots of whining beggars and noisy vendors of merchandise whose transactions often competed with the services, and were soon separated by the girth of the huge column from most curious eyes.

Dolores turned to face Leonora, whose dubious expression already reflected regret for having been drawn into this association with a woman whom she regarded as indecorous, and began without ado: "You could be of help to me, Doña Leonora."

"In what way?"

"Just a bit of information, that is all." Dolores smiled with forced warmth. The warmth was as false as her offhandedness. She was anxious to hear any bit of news on Francho, for it was almost six months he had been absent from Court. She'd heard he had not joined di Lido's party but had been detained in Italy and that was the last word there had been. She had the feeling that he'd blinked out of sight as precipitously as the sun dropping behind a mountain ridge, one minute there and the next minute gone. She found herself thinking about him and thinking about him, going over in her mind the events of their meetings in Toledo, in Seville, and especially the wild, galloping escape from the Moors in Baza. She remembered the fright in his voice when the horse had thrown her and he'd called her name, fearing she was dead. She remembered the raspy warmth of his chin pressed against her cheek to comfort the pain of her cracked ribs as his horse bore them toward the camp. And the involuntary wince and crinkle of sympathy around his eyes when he first saw her bruised face as she lay in her invalid's bed.

Now it was her turn to fear that he might be ill, or dead. Even his best friends had had no word from him.

She saw Leonora fidget and hurried on. "I was merely wondering if you had received any recent news of Don Francisco de Mendoza, since you were, ah, particular friends. Surely he must have written to you."

Leonora's lips parted in surprise. Then her eyes narrowed slightly, slyly. "And how would such information 'help' you?"

"Why, it's a question of a gambling debt," Dolores murmured smoothly. "A large sum I lost to Don Francisco at cards before he left Seville and which I was not able to pay at the time. It has been on my conscience ever since—I am very scrupulous about paying gaming losses—and I have had the money for him for a long time. I thought I might send it by the Queen's couriers to Rome. If he were still there, that is . . ." Her voice trailed off in a question.

Leonora looked down and pulled fastidiously on her velvet glove. "Why don't you ask Antonio de la Cueva, who is close to him?"

"I did, but he could say—or would say—only that Don Francisco is in Italy on his sire's business. He was not sure where. And my lord Tendilla, who would know, is on the frontier." Dolores tried to sound easy and casual although she hated to have to come to Leonora. Yet it was all she could think of to help scratch her intense itch to know how Francho fared.

Leonora's expression turned smugly patronizing. "I am sorry to tell you, *doña,* that I have nothing more to add to Don Antonio's statement. I cannot help you." She started to turn away, but Dolores slid around her and barred her path.

"No, wait. Surely he would have written you some letters in all this time? Please, *doña . . ."*

An eyebrow arched up in the delicate face. "I have never seen someone so anxious to pay a gambling debt. But I think I will not breach the confidentiality of Don Francisco's letters."

"Then he has written to you? Recently? And from where?" Dolores hated herself for begging crumbs from Leonora de Zuniga, but she couldn't even sleep at night, she worried so that something had befallen him. "I do hope the gentleman fares well?"

From the depths of the church behind them one hundred and seventeen male choristers offered up the shimmering polyphonic tonalities of a chorale. Leonora's chin tilted in satisfaction. "You would like to know, wouldn't you, my lady? And not for any gambling debt either. Do you think I am foolish? It has not escaped my attention that you have a certain interest in Don Francisco which has nothing to do with cards. A useless interest, for it is obvious he does not care to communicate with you." Spite glowered out from the brown eyes.

Dolores's hand under her cloak was in her pocket, her fingers turning over and over an object there. "I admit nothing of the sort," she said, holding her temper but happy to drop her fawning attitude. "Until Don Francisco himself returns to Court there is no way to know what circumstances commanded his dispatching one letter over another. Still, I see by your jealous attitude that Don Francisco is at least well, even if he might not communicate with you often."

Stung, Leonora flared, "But so he does—often. And that is all you will hear of him from me." She tried to push her way past, but Dolores, taller and wider-shouldered, blocked her.

The month had been dull, full of cloudy weather and unusual chill and boring evenings with nothing special to fete, and Dolores had been occupied with her frustrated thoughts of Francho, to the extent that the idea of a bit of mischief to liven things up had appealed to her. That was why that bit of metal was in her pocket, although she'd not approached Leonora with any definite plan to use it.

Now she flung back, "I have a right to some concern. We were childhood friends together. Or didn't he tell you that?"

Leonora looked startled, like a doe caught in the light of a torch. Then her lips thinned. "I don't believe you."

"It doesn't matter whether you believe me or not. All I want to know is if Don Francisco will soon be returning from Italy."

"Shh, lower your voice," Leonora grated with a quick glance behind her, where an unseen priest was now droning the litany into a hushed church. Then she measured Dolores up and down with eyes grown hard and said in a harsh whisper, "Perhaps you knew him long ago, Doña Dolores. But he is obviously not interested in continuing the acquaintance, since you are forced to seek news of him. And I will not say more to you on Francisco de Mendoza. Now let me pass."

Dolores's frustration, her dislike of this false, mean little prig, made her evil. "Oh, but the acquaintance was renewed indeed, just before he left. In fact we discovered to both our satisfactions that we were no longer children. See, let me show you the keepsake he gave to me." She pulled from her pocket the medallion she'd found under Perens's supine body the previous winter and let the gold gleam balefully on her palm in the flickering votive lights under an effigy to one side of them. "It was to remember him by," she gloated, looking up from the corner of her eye to see the effect.

Seething, Leonora flung out, "A keepsake can be given to anyone, especially an old acquaintance. If you are trying to imply a close friendship here at Court, let me tell you, it makes no difference to me . . ."

"Imply?" Dolores widened mocking eyes. "But dear Doña Leonora, I am trying to *tell* you how close our friendship was. For instance, a lady of your unimpeachable character would not know that Don Francisco has a strange scar on his shoulder blade in the shape of a tiny dagger? Of course, you would not know that." Now Dolores not only stepped aside, smiling with satisfaction in her turn, but she turned and began to glide away toward the long nave, where the drone of a response to the celebrant did not cover the words she flung back over her shoulder at the tense, staring Leonora. "But believe me, it is true. Ask him when he returns."

Almost stumbling over a kneeling vendor who had spread a blanket of trinkets and souvenirs from the Holy Land on the Cathedral's stone floor, Dolores recovered herself and, because she felt Leonora's eyes boring into her back, directed her steps with great dignity as she headed toward a small side niche dedicated to the Virgin and brightly lit with supplication candles. She sank to her knees before the gilded statue with its painted, upturned eyes and sad smile, and there she prayed. Her temper subsiding, she finally begged for intercession with God for forgiveness of her lies and wicked efforts to manipulate Francho's life. It was so stupid. He would be furious when he heard of it. Her cheeks felt hot with shame over the smallness of her actions in view of his last kind gesture to her—but also with deep anger that Leonora had treated her with so little decency, had not made some courteous answer to her inquiry. Unfortunately she'd learned very little for her malicious innuendoes.

But at least she'd learned he was alive, he was well. Had something dreadful happened to him, Leonora would not have hesitated to scourge her with it.

❧ *Chapter 19* ❧

THE BARONESS DE la Rocha and Don Enrique de Guzman jogged along through the March-bare trees in companionable silence during the lengthy ride through Torredonpedro Castle's hunting preserve, heading toward the high, marshy grasslands, where partridge, quail, snipe, heron and hare abounded. The royal hunting party had split in two: a number to go farther into the forest with the royal couple, who enjoyed coursing on their large hunters after a bounding stag as it was pursued by fifty or seventy-five of the three hundred English-bred greyhounds and deerhounds kept at this ancient estate near Baena; the rest of the guests turning off at an angle to achieve the tangled meadows and fly their beloved hawks.

Dolores was grateful for Medina-Sidonia's attachment to his hunting birds. The strike of the feathered killers was deadly but neat, scarcely bloodying their victims' feathers or pelts, whereas the larger creatures hunted with weapons often bled copiously from grievous spear wounds and the teeth of the dogs who encircled them, and sometimes as many as five javelins pierced into their hides before they collapsed with a bellow or a groan, spurting their lives like fountains. Dolores shuddered, although she was ashamed of her squeamishness when it appeared so many ladies adored being in on the kill, not only to watch but to throw a lightweight spear themselves and further dispatch the dying creature.

She could not deny her fascination with the trained African leopard that sometimes rode on a perch behind the King's saddle and whose leash was slipped as soon as the dogs started the deer or roebuck they were after. The spotted cat's flashing speed and flying leap onto the rearing prey's back was a marvel of power and grace, beautiful to behold, and its fangs, sinking into its terrified victim's neck to sever the spinal cord, brought a quick and almost bloodless death. But even then one had to endure the gory, ceremonial slitting open of the dead animal's body to dip bread into the beast's smoking entrails to throw to the leaping dogs, while the hunting horns echoed the conquest around the forest and the leopard tore at his reward of a fresh-killed hare. Even now as she thought of it Dolores could hear the horns faintly in the distance, ta-ta-tada, ta-ta-tada, the particular call that announced sighting of a red stag.

The Duke, bemused with his own early morning thoughts, might have wondered why she threw him such a sweet smile at that moment, although he was aware she much preferred hawking to the chase. Last year he had made her an expensive gift of a trained peregrine falcon, and he and one of his falconers had patiently worked with her for weeks to teach her to fly the bird properly, to slip it, to call it back, to become master to what was essentially and forever a wild creature, capable of disappearing into the heavens forever should it wish. The compact, sharp-clawed, somewhat diffident peregrine and she had finally come to an understanding. She called the bird Dalila, and she would have liked to believe that the feathered huntress returned to her more out of friendship than for the piece of raw beef she received. The hooded falcon was now riding quietly on the cadge, a wooden frame mounted to the falconer's horse, along with Don Enrique's larger goshawk and gyrfalcons. Behind them and before rode other hawkers and their retainers and alongside rolled open wagons loaded with pointing and retrieving hounds and their handlers.

Although their styles of costume differed according to their fancy, all the company of ladies and gentlemen were dressed in the same colors: doublets, capes, hose, and gowns in either beige or brown or a combination of both, with stiff feathers of the same shades stuck in each hat and headdress. This was a conceit of the Queen's, copied from the Burgundian court, and one which would make the field banquet to follow the hunt most charming to the eye. But Dolores was not very chipper so early in the morning; she was rather glad for the tranquil ride and Medina-Sidonia's silence. She hoped the pale cream of her velvet gown did not drain the color from her face in the sharp early light—which was why she'd chosen to wear a simple hat of stiffened fabric with a rolled brim sewn with pearls that allowed her auburn hair to wave about her features and be tied loosely behind.

She suddenly had to stifle a yawn with her velvet-gloved hand, ending with an apologetic chuckle as the Duke rolled his eyes at her. She hadn't slept soundly the night before, although the Queen had decreed this stay at Torredonpedro, to which she had invited only her favorite courtiers or those newly favored at the moment, to be one of relaxation and rest and offered little in the evening except some serious music. Most were abed by nine. But Dolores had been restless all year, since the end of the excitement of last spring's celebrations of the Infanta's betrothal to Alonso, heir to the throne of Portugal. Little seemed to amuse her anymore, although only her sharp-eyed good friend Luisa seemed to be aware of it.

"You need to marry, my dear, and that will dissipate your humours," Luisa said kindly, patting her on the knee as they sat chatting together in a window embrasure of the small castle one of the first mornings at Torredonpedro. Luisa had been away from Court with her adored husband and two children visiting their estate in the north for a couple of months. Reunited now, the two friends had been happily having a good gossip when Dolores finally had confessed her discontent.

Dolores did not turn her head from contemplating the forest which bordered at a distance the great sweep of cropped lawn and gardens around the castle. "I can't imagine why you say that, Luisa. How little I really have to complain of. My life is quite full. . . ."

Luisa sighed in mock exasperation. "I say it because I am older than you and more experienced. Merely having a man to your bed does not make you a happy woman. It is the embrace of a man most passionately loved that gives one face so special a look, a sort of tender glow as if one has a delicious secret. Oh, you are more lovely to look at than ever, my dear, as luminous as a jewel, but there is not that particular halo that I can spy so easily. And *that* is why I say you must marry—see, I seriously take the part of your family since you have none—while you are still in your beauty and so many seek you out. First you must secure your life with a husband and children, and I advise this in the role of guardian." Luisa's round face suddenly creased in a grin. "And then—and now I speak as your best female friend—you would be free to take a lover if your husband does not please you enough."

"Why Doña Luisa!" Dolores grinned back.

"Oh, most discreetly, certainly, but you might be good at that." Dolores's companion laughed. And then she turned serious again, her dark eyes mirroring sincerity. "Of course it is none of my business," she admitted, but continued on anyhow, "but rumor has always had it that the Duke's heavy attendance upon you could mean you will be his next Duchess when the present one dies, God keep her. That would surely be a most advantageous liaison, dear friend, and such cause for celebration." Luisa's smile showed her slightly crooked teeth. "The Duke has changed, I can tell you, in the two years since you arrived at Court. I'm told he was sometimes surly and danced many a woman a fine tune, each for a short while. And now he smiles and greets one kindly. And seems quite content to be broken to your leash."

"But the Duke's Duchess is very much alive at this date, Luisa," Dolores noted, "and besides, I do not think the gentleman favors me in such respect." Her voice held a touch of asperity for she hated that silly rumor that Luisa quoted. Yet, faithful to her bargain, she would not even tell Luisa of her peculiar and platonic relationship with Medina-Sidonia, or that all he favored her for was her property.

"Oh, do not be angry with me, *amiga;* I mean you no harm." Luisa reached out her hands, and Dolores was very glad to take them in her own as a salve to the loneliness assailing her lately. She squeezed the plump fingers.

"I know you mean well, Luisa. It's just that— Well, you are right. I am listless and restless and somewhat sad, I suppose, for no reason. Or perhaps it was caused by the small congestion of the chest I recently suffered, although I am most fit now. But I do feel as if something has riven a hole in my life. . . ."

"More likely someone, you mean. Someone special is missing, you see." Luisa was visibly enjoying the small advantage her extra few years of age, married status, and children gave her over her beauteous friend, whose poise was usually so unshakable. "Do I not fully understand that languishing feeling? But first you must be practical and choose a husband. Gossip about an unmarried maid is more damaging than gossip about a married woman," she pointed out with a wink. Placing one forefinger to the pinkie of her other hand in a counting gesture, Luisa pressed, "What about Don Diego de Bernaldez? A lady whose description is certainly you figures in every verse of love he writes—and declaims to a fare-thee-well at every gathering."

"He is sweet, but dull. And a terrible poet."

"True, true. But then there is Don Alfonso Huelvar. He beams, in fact, were he a puppy he would wag his tail off every time you come into his sight."

"Oh, but he is but a baby," Dolores protested, "no more than fifteen. I would have to wipe his nose at every turning."

"We are here talking about husbands, not dreams of the heart," Luisa sniffed. "And he is a Marquis with several castles. Ah well. And the Queen's hero, the illustrious Don Diego de Cordoba? It often seems as if he would gladly push Medina-Sidonia into the moat."

"He is merely flirting. Nor would his family agree."

Luisa mentioned two other quite eligible gallants who often hovered about the coquettish Baroness de la Rocha and twice Dolores made a face. Luisa sighed and shook her head, as if defeated. But then she slyly slipped in, "And of course there is the dashing Don Francisco de Mendoza, who so gallantly saved your life at Baza. When he returns."

Dolores's chiffon-veiled head reared on her neck like a proud swan. "Well! Why in good Santa Catalina's name would you remark him for me, Luisa? The whole Court knows that he favors Leonora de Zuniga and that she and her uncle might even hold in abeyance Don Felipe's suit, if it is presented, until Don Francisco returns. The gentleman merely did me a courteous duty—"

Luisa snorted softly. "Hark, my friend, you have found occasion to mention Don Francisco's name at least one hundred times in the past months and recounted me the adventure with him outside Baza—although I suspect not all of it—almost as often. One would have to be insensitive as a stone not to conclude that the wonderfully handsome *caballero* had made some mark on your heart?"

Dolores momentarily held her indignant attitude, but then

with a sigh she slumped. It really would feel so good to tell someone how much she did think about Francho, how anxious she had been at the news of his ill health in Italy, how disappointed that he did not return home with di Lido, how lovelorn she was in fact, although his heart did not belong to her. It was nothing to be ashamed of. Men and women of the enclosed world of the aristocracy became enamored of each other all the time. The Court was rife with licit and illicit romances, and the gossip of who languished for whom put spice in the day. But, of course, she could never tell Doña Luisa the true dimensions of her bond with Don Francisco de Mendoza.

"You are right, *doña,*" she admitted with quiet despair. "I have fought so to hide my feelings, even from myself, for it is no secret the gentleman has eyes for no one but Leonora de Zuniga." Dolores dropped her lids and picked at a nail unhappily. "The dear Saints know I tried to distract him from her, but I was most spectacularly unsuccessful. My efforts turn now on forgetting him."

Suddenly she was enveloped in a cloud of attar of roses as the sympathetic Luisa impulsively hugged her. "Ah, you will get over it, Dolores, you'll see, it just takes a bit more time." The black eyes rounded. "It happened to me once, such an unrequited passion—before I was affianced to my dear husband, of course," she whispered. "I can assure you, God takes care to finally heal the wounded heart." She hugged Dolores again to her rounded bosom on which gleamed a lovely strand of pearls. But then practicality overcame her and the hug turned into a friendly shake. "But *doña,* you cannot allow a yearning heart to steal your life, you must smile with all your old brilliance and insouciance and pave the way for your future. Love will come again, but meanwhile you must choose a husband. And see, since you are orphaned, perhaps the Queen, who seems very pleased with you, might act as ex officio guardian and sign the betrothal papers!"

And the thought of such a signal honor to her friend lit Luisa's face.

A husband? *Madre de Dios,* she is right, Dolores decided. Why do I act as if I shall be forever eighteen? A pox on him then, my arrogant old playmate of the gutter. My care and attention shall now be upon myself. A husband is what I need and sweet children like Luisa's, and a fine manse in the countryside to have my own brew house and bakery, and a stable full of the best horseflesh. . . . As such bucolic reverie flitted through her mind a soft smile touched her lips which caused Luisa to sit back, relieved.

"There, you see? We each need a conscience to nag us, lacking dear parents to guide. So do not forget my counsel, Dolores: A young woman of birth must finally think seriously of the protection of marriage." With a last pat on Dolores's hand she rose, as did Dolores, for the Queen's Confessor must surely have made his exit by now, and they would be expected to join the small circle of attendant ladies. Smiling at each other, each one made warmer by her friend's caring, they sallied hand in hand from the deep window niche, but not before Luisa got in the advice still uppermost in her mind.

"Still, you should never discourage the Duke. The Countess Romana y Perez mentioned even before I left Court that she had visited the Duchess at the family seat in the south and that the poor woman looked as if at death's door."

"But I suppose my lady is not yet awake enough to fly her hawk, Master Encastro . . ." Don Enrique's voice drawled.

Dolores started and blinked her way out of her deep thoughts. She realized that they had arrived at the edge of the meadow and that her companion had been addressing her. "Oh, I am sorry, my lord, I was preoccupied," she exclaimed, smiling her apology. "And yes, I am very awake and just aching to let my Dalila fly, if it please you." Her smile grew wider because this was the truth; she did very much enjoy hawking.

The Duke's expression was amused, indulgent. His eyes slowly took her in and it was evident to her—and even to the two falconers quietly sitting their mules and awaiting orders —that what he saw greatly pleased him. "Very well, dear lady, so you shall. Send your lightning bird first after what fowl we find, and I will scoop up the remainder. I shall reserve my goshawk for hare. Put on your glove, then."

They had drawn up amid the bustle of the others of the hawking group getting ready for sport and the retainers unloading the dogs and the various gear necessary to transport the catch. Dolores pulled the heavy hawking glove onto her left hand, unfolding out from its wide cuff a leather protector for most of her arm. Leandro Encastro, a falconer widely regarded as a master trainer, passed on to her fist her obedient peregrine, quiet now because of the calming leather hood over its head embroidered with gold and pearls and surmounted with a small, pert spray of exotic feathers. Dalila was a broad-shouldered bird but not very big; a slate-colored, cream-breasted hawk with a hooked beak, wicked, sharp claws, and great long wings that when unfolded gave her unmatched speed of descent. Sitting so still as she was now on Dolores's fist she seemed mild, but once unfettered she became the unrelenting mistress of the aerial chase and the deadly swoop to the kill.

"It is too crowded here," the Duke complained. "We will remove to the other side of that pond." The Duke, now holding one of his speckled gyrfalcons on his large, gloved fist, wore a calf-length tunic of brown brocade edged with cloth of gold and a short cape. Atop his chin-length dark hair, sparked here and there with gray, he wore a low, big-brimmed hat of beige fur. On his breast lay a thick gold chain and his right hand flashed with a large ruby. He was a figure of power and privilege, this senior commander of the armies of Spain, smiling his heavy-jawed smile at the young noblewoman who had become entwined in his life.

He was not young. He was not subtle or graceful or especially charming. But he was a Grandee of the Realm. Dolores lifted her chin. Power. Position. Wealth. This was all that mattered. All the rest was Ciudad Real. She favored him with a teasing smile and bridled like a fine-stepping horse as she slid a coquettish glance at him. And she had the pleasure of seeing his bulgy eyes kindle at this unexpected flirtation.

The big, gray hound stood statue-still, his tense body stretched from tail to muzzle in a straight, stiff line toward a clump of high grass. High above, so high she seemed nothing more than a tiny W wheeling through the wispy clouds that drifted the blue sky, circled Dalila, waiting for her prey to be flushed, her incredibly sharp vision fastened upon the pointing dog.

"Wait, wait, the bird is still climbing and too far downwind," the falconer whispered to Dolores. "Wait a bit . . . until she gets a little upwind. . . . Now!"

"Hah! Hah!" Dolores yelled, clapping her hands sharply. The hound, released like a spring from point, dashed forward, and a covy of three terrified quail clattered up into the air and winged away. Instantly the soaring dot in the sky dropped headlong, falling downward with unbelievable speed, the wind screaming through the double bells on her legs and streaming out the jesses attached to her feet. Within seconds Dalila had overtaken her chosen quarry, coming up behind and over the fleeing bird to hit it heavily with her deadly hind talons—thwack!—and a cloud of feathers filled the air as the quail fell stone dead toward the ground.

Dalila curved through the sky gracefully, turned, and circled down to land light as thistledown on her kill. Instantly Medina-Sidonia cast off his gyrfalcon after the remaining quail winging frantically away. Swiftly the hawk clawed his way up at a sharp angle and then soared on the wind a quick second to take stock. Spotting his victim he launched himself like a hurled spear speeding flat out to catch up with it. Galloping off in the same direction to keep under the bird, the Duke and his second falconer rode away to attend the strike while Dolores, accompanied by Encastro, jogged over to retrieve Dalila. The falcon sat warily on her kill, beak open, feathers tight, anticipating the fresh-killed thrush Dolores would toss her so she would relinquish the fat quail in her talons.

Dolores waited until Dalila had crunched up her snack, beak, feathers and all, and then whistled three soft notes. With a flap the bird rose up and flew to her fist. "Good Dalila, good," Dolores praised the perigrine. The bird tilted her sleek head and stared at her mistress with a cold, black eye, even as she allowed Dolores to stroke her breast with a feather. In a moment she ruffled up her own feathers, blinked, and subsided calmly. Dolores, gripping the jesses in the fingers of her gloved hand, dropped the hood over the bird's head, using her free hand and her teeth to help pull the leather traces tight.

The dead quail safely in a bag, Dolores and Encastro pirouetted their horses and galloped toward the other two, who were riding to retrieve the two birds downed by the gyrfalcon, dogs bounding alongside them. In this way, working for hours with three well-trained birds of prey, five quivering-nosed pointers, and a couple of retrieving dogs, their small party bagged a number of quail, partridge, and three large hares to contribute to the kitchens before Dolores heard the horns in the distance announcing the hunt collation. Encastro rode up to take Dalila and by this time the Baroness de la Rocha was grateful; she hoped the crook in her right arm and the painful ache in her shoulder would not be permanent.

The hunters and their retinues, Dolores and Medina-Sidonia among them, were converging from all parts of the forest and fields as they rode toward the verge of the woods, where an army of valets and servitors were spreading long tables with silk cloths and setting out a feast on gold plates. But before they cleared the trees the Duke waved on his falconers and hound-handlers and beckoned Dolores in a divergent direction. She followed after him as he led the way a bit deeper into the forest and then behind a tangled thicket. She thought he merely wanted a few private words. It took her by surprise that he dismounted and held up his arms for her to dismount too. Her elbow was sore and she felt disheveled, but the fine weather and the activity had pumped up both her appetite and her good humor. So, smilingly, she allowed him to set her on her feet.

Suddenly the Duke's arms shot about her and she found herself almost smothered in his groaning, frantic embrace. She was so astonished that her eyes remained wide open as he pulled back and clamped onto her lips, and it took a few seconds before she could marshal resistance to his deep, damp kiss by shoving at him with muffled cries. Although his mouth would not be dislodged from hers his lips were not firm but soft and without shape, so the more she struggled against the hand that held her head the wetter the kiss became. Disgusted, she strained to get free, but his insistent arm held her clamped against his fleshy but strong body and her efforts were useless. When he finally released her she staggered as she recoiled backward.

"Don Enrique! This sort of behavior is not part of our contract!" she sputtered. She wanted to scrub at her wet mouth with her sleeve, but even in her indignation she did not care to insult him and settled for a discreet swipe with the back of her hand.

Medina-Sidonia's features were filled with painful passion as he sought to engage her hands in his. "Verily, Baroness, it is not in our contract. But I should like to make another agreement. One for which a loving embrace would be both a seal and a symbol. I wish to take you for my wife," he stated, a man accustomed to giving out orders and being obeyed.

Dolores goggled at him, her breath quite taken away. There were princesses and duchesses galore all over Europe who would happily give their hands to this prestigious grandee. It seemed impossible he would wish to marry her, a little Baroness from an obscure family and without influence. She thought her ears deceived her.

"I know I surprise you. I surprise myself. And I know there are serious problems we must talk about. But my dear, beautiful young woman, it is absurd for me to continue pretending my interest in you is merely your waterfall. Not when I am so pleasured by, so delighted in your presence, and in turn"—there was the suspicion of a crack in the intense voice—"so devastated. I did not think this could happen to me, not after my—wound. But you have accomplished it. You have rekindled my desire for the affection and love of a woman, which I thought I had forever banished in my disfigurement. You have set within me such a longing to be with you that nothing will do but that you shall be my Duchess and share my roof and my bed, such as it is, and my heart, forever." The ordinarily unbending Guzman, almost panting with the effort of his impassioned plea, stared anxiously into the startled wide gray eyes that had so enthralled him.

Dolores thought that if he were not holding her tightly by the wrists she would fall into the chasm that appeared to yawn under her feet. "But, but my d-dear Lord Duke," she stammered, trying to catch hold of her skittering mind, "how has it escaped you that you are already married? And that Doña Catania is very much alive? You cannot have two wives at once." She found herself distressingly close to panic and she prayed it didn't show in her eyes.

"But she is *not* very much alive," the Duke growled, not realizing that he shook her by the arms. "That is, the lady is mortally ill. The Jewish physicians who have been attending her say she has little time left in this world, poor suffering woman, God help us all. But you certainly are aware that I have not had a loving accommodation with her in years; I have told you that. Why, she isn't even cognizant how truly grievous I was wounded." The last was said with a scowl, whether for his wife's ignorance or at his own impotence it was hard to tell. "When the Lord takes her to Him I will mourn the bare requisite time to satisfy my sons and daughter —and our pious Queen. But a soldier is not required to mourn forever. Then I shall be free. To choose you."

So intently did he stare into her face, his lantern-jaw willfully set, that he forgot to hold her tight and she was able to free her arms. Whirling away from him, presenting him her back as she resettled her hat that had been knocked askew, she grabbed a few precious seconds to collect herself. Heavenly

Mother, what a shock. Luisa had been right. While her own eyes had been dimmed with yearning for that blue-eyed wandering swaggerer, the great Duke of Medina-Sidonia had fallen in love with her. Two reactions zipped through her mind. The first was a glittering vision of a mitered archbishop lowering upon her bejeweled head the seven-pointed coronet of a Duchess while a great chorus sang out a wedding triumphal. But the second, almost superimposed, was the memory of that loose, damp, spongy kiss, and now she almost gagged. Involuntarily her lips writhed. She thanked God she wasn't facing him, for whatever she did she must not make an enemy of him. The wrath of such a man, already humiliated in his affliction, would snap her existence as easily as a twig.

He walked up behind her and turned her about to face him, but she was ready. The expression she molded upon her face held nothing but wonder. Exuberantly he crushed her to him and rasped in her ear, "I know I cannot consummate a marriage in the ordinary manner or give you children. But I can make up for it in other ways that will please you. And you will be the queen of my heart, of my household. . . ."

His voice went on describing the riches and comforts he could give her as his bulbous eyes traveled covetously over her face. But she was barely listening. She was casting around through her numb mind to select some wise course. . . .

Finally, with a weak smile she held up a hand. "Please, My Lord, but I am overcome by surprise. It never occurred to me you would . . . you would . . . I need time to consider what you are saying. I have no one to speak for me . . ."

"Time? Of course you shall have time. I will be gone to the north for several months to settle a border dispute in Navarre, and you may take this time to think. But you must not say me nay nor feel that coyness would become you. I realize you have no parent or guardian to advise you, but you have your own considerable intelligence to tell you where your best interests lie. I shall rely on that."

With downcast eyes to cover her confusion Dolores murmured, "My Lord greatly honors me."

He responded quietly, "My delightful, lovely lady, it is you who will honor the house of Guzman. But will you not at least give some indication of your feelings toward me so that I may sleep with lessened anxiety?"

"Why, Don Enrique, you know how much I enjoy your friendship. But I have given little thought to marrying, howev-

er foolish that may sound from an eighteen-year-old woman."
She thought her brain must be smoking with the effort of
finding just the right words to handle the situation; she still
heard Luisa's prophetic voice echoing in her ear. But she said,
"I must collect myself and consider your stunning offer . . ."

"No, you are not one to simper or be coy, Doña Dolores;
you are a woman who knows her mind enough to answer me
right now, if you wished. I understand what is tying your
tongue. It is the normal wish to want children of a marriage,
and I tell you so shall you have them, you and I together." His
heavy jaw worked. "My most favored son Don Felipe has said
he thinks you very beautiful, as what man would not. If you
were to have a child by him it would be of my blood, you see,
and I would love it as a father. And no one would know the
babe was actually my grandson."

She gaped at him, both for such generosity and for his
inattention. Don Felipe! She felt a shriveling inside at even the
thought of making a child with the disagreeable Count. It was
hard to credit the astute Medina-Sidonia with such infatuation that he refused to notice her cold relationship with his
heir. Still, now was not the time to give any offense to this
mighty suitor. "I . . . well, it is a solution, certainly. But does
Don Felipe realize . . ."

"No, he thinks I yet perform like the buck I was." His thin
smile was self-denigrating. "But when the time comes I would
tell him. He would be a fool to refuse to cooperate, and my
son is no fool. So you see, in the respect of children, how easily
our little problem is resolved." Now he raised an eyebrow
significantly. "And any other problem can be taken care of as
discreetly, if you take my meaning. I am a fairminded man."

Dolores colored and hoped she was not dithering. "I admit,
my lord, you have relieved my mind, which believe me, holds
no prejudice against you of any sort. Yet I still must beg the
time you so kindly offered."

He looked deep into her eyes, a middle-aged, homely man
who was wildly smitten, craving the youth, freshness and
beauty of a lissome girl. "I love you," he declared roughly,
unaccustomed to the word. He tilted up her chin. "I know you
do not love me, but you will learn to, for you have before you a
lifetime of pleasures. Consider, if you must, but consider with
your head, and your heart shall follow."

Feeling her ground more securely now Dolores stepped
away from him, a slight flush still in her face. "Don Enrique, I

beg you, this is neither the place nor the time for so intimate a subject to be discussed." They could both hear muffled laughter and conversation; riders, retainers, dogs, and servants had been streaming past not far from their screened brake. "Do you not think betrothal is a matter better discussed in privacy? Indeed, I would be more comfortable, so, sir."

Now he flushed, but he was not displeased. "You are right, *doña,* it was impetuous of me but I could not contain myself longer. I have been thinking on us for many a month, as I hope you will now do. But you are—can I find the words to tell you how appealing this morning?—that my suit just burst from me and it had to be placed before you at last. I shall not let you forget it, Doña Dolores, as you have a habit of doing when you wish to postpone an issue. I shall be persistent. I have rarely not gotten what I wanted," he declared, but with a smile meant to be encouraging and warm. He held out his hand. "Come, Lady, I will give you a leg up to your saddle."

She gave him her hand and he led her to her mount. He pulled her close to his large body, looking down at her flushed cheeks and flustered expression. "I long to embrace you now, and again take those lips I have watched in hunger for so long," he murmured. Then, to her relief he added, "Yet you are right, 'tis too public here. So think on my proposition, *doña,* and I shall impatiently bide my time."

They rode onto the path behind the last stragglers going to the field banquet. She smiled at him mechanically. He gave her a searching look which mellowed into a confident smile. "In addition, Baroness, when we marry I shall make out to you a disposition stating that your father's property—all of it—shall be yours to do with as you wish. I will not claim it as a dowry. You alone are dowry enough." High spirits seemed to hit him at that moment. "Come now, Doña Dolores," he rumbled, "you have to admit we do get along splendidly well!"

For once Dolores blessed her ability to blush easily. It was a wonderful cover for her moiling thoughts.

If the possibility of becoming the next Duchess of Medina-Sidonia wasn't shock enough, an infinitely more upsetting situation awaited her late the same afternoon. The lively outdoor banquet, complete with the gay music of shawms, horns, pipes, and tambourines had helped her shove Medina-Sidonia's marriage proposal to the back of her mind; she would deal with it later in the quiet of her chamber. Her poise regained, pleasantly tired from the hunt and fresh, cold air, she rode by her benefactor's side back across the dry moat and through the castle gate into the courtyard, where there seemed to be much more activity than that which usually attended the bustle of dismounting hunters and the unloading into the kitchens of their mixed bag of deer, hares, squirrels, and fowl of all kinds. There was, in fact, a dusty train of baggage mules unloading, and saddlehorses and mules and empty litters were being led away by valets with white crosses prominent on their tabards.

"I thought this was to be a small group of courtiers, sixty or so, for a restful month," the Duke observed dryly to Dolores as he threw his reins to a hostler and then turned to steady her down from the dismounting steps she was using.

"And so it is, if one speaks of courtiers." Dolores shrugged. "But you should know the Queen; she cannot rest for long. Before we left Seville she had arranged a convocation of abbesses from convents in the regions hereabout to attend her for a fortnight and report to her about education, for she is not satisfied that young women are being offered the subjects which would qualify them as properly educated. Her Majesty says she wishes the mothers superior to inform her, but she, of course, is going to tell *them* what to do." Her admiring laugh fluted out.

"The fact remains a lady need only know how to please her lord. I do not see the case for educating women beyond that." Medina-Sidonia scowled and offered his arm to help her negotiate the uneven, ancient paving stones of the bustle-filled courtyard. Dodging men and beasts and dogs, Dolores tried to hold her beige satin skirts away from the grimy stones as they made their way to the portal. "Women read that misled Christine de Pisane and begin to believe they are equal to men."

Dolores arched her brow at this. She had read and reread the infamous *Treasure of the City of Ladies* and often turned over in her mind Pisane's contention that women possessed as much moral strength and intellectual ability as men. "But why is such an idea abhorrent to you, my dear Duke? Don't you think it makes us more charming companions to be able to converse intelligently on worldly subjects? And surely our children will be born with greater capacity to lead and to govern if both sire and dam are—" Her sentence broke off but her mouth remained open. In turning her head she had glanced up just above the portal to the single wide balcony which broke the smoothness of the old, square tower. There several of the newly arrived nuns had gathered, standing etched against the deepening blue of the sky like great, angular birds in their starched, stiff headdresses and dark or white habits. The rest of Dolores's words were swallowed in a stunned gulp as she instantly recognized the tiny sister with the severe face who stood silently among the visitors on the balcony.

O Holy Virgin! Her mind tried but failed to deny her eyes. Her stomach turned over sickeningly and a sourness rose in her throat. So solidly had she fitted herself into the place of the Baroness de la Rocha that—as if she were the real Blanca—she had not given one thought to the fact that the directress of the Convent of the Holy Family and Santa Rosa might be one of Isabella's invitees. She heard a booming in her head, like the drums whose slow measure accompany a wretched condemned going to the executioner, and along with this dirge of doom her heart began to pound. There would be no fooling the sharp-eyed Mother Ines. If that woman saw her—and the Queen would certainly introduce her ladies to her guests—the existence of "Dolores" of Torrejoncillo would surely be ended.

Quickly Dolores lowered her head, as if watching for her footing, and with an effort willed herself to swallow her panic. The Duke had noticed nothing, embroiled as he was in following up their conversation with acerbic remarks about overly instructed women. Fighting hard against the immediate urge to bolt and hide Dolores made it seem as if she were listening. In a few moments they were sheltered below the balcony out of sight of the nuns, and entering the castle. Dolores could lift up her head and breathe again. Stopping under one of the massive stone arches of the great hall she mustered up a smile for her companion.

Crinkling the lids of one eye almost together, a habit when he was concerned, Medina-Sidonia scanned her face and said to her solicitously, "But I think you are weary, Baroness. You must rest."

"First I must see to the Queen. And then I will rest."

"Of course, *doña*. But I insist that you will be my partner this evening at cards. Even if that old rascal La Corunna has wheedled you first. Will you honor me?"

416

Heart still pounding, she couldn't get away rapidly enough. "Gladly, my lord. I look forward to it," she promised hastily. She tried not to pull her hand from his grasp as he lingeringly kissed it, but she was fearful any minute the Abbess would appear and she would not be able to dodge her. However, a moment later, sparing him a last, falsely bright smile, she was able to withdraw and went hurrying toward the door which would take her to her chamber.

"Lord help us, my lady, what is it?" Engracia cried, startled out of her nodding doze in a chair as Dolores swept into the room like a maelstrom, banging the door, sweeping off her hat and muttering, *"Madre mía, madre mía!"*

"Ask no questions, Engracia, none at all. Just do what I tell you to do. See my laundry is collected. Pull out a good traveling gown and hat, and see my chests are completely packed, and your things as well. We must leave here by dawn tomorrow, without fail."

"Cielos! But where do we go? And in such haste? What has happened, the Holy Virgin preserve us?" The servitor gaped as she watched her mistress pace the room in agitation, biting on her thumbnail.

Where were they to go? That was a good question. What was not in question was that her only hope of escaping discovery as an imposter was to leave at once, to vanish into thin air, to flee. Ah—

Suddenly a measure of calm descended upon her. Here was something she knew, running from danger. One needed speed and surprise and nerve, all of which she had on her side until morning at least. Her mind began to function again, an emerging plan began drawing off the fever of panic. She could deal with this emergency. Was she not Papa el Mono's Dolores, after all, not the protected, helpless lady she pretended? In fact, she could face this active danger with a cooler composure than her earlier reaction to a grandee of the realm who had asked for her hand in marriage.

"The laundry, the laundry!" She shooed the blinking Engracia out and went to the window to watch the westering sun. Already the back of her mind had told her she could not go back to Seville for she would have no good reason to do so. Actually there was only one place she might have reason to hurry back to—Torrejoncillo, the de la Rocha ancestral estate. And the reason could be simple, the same as once before. Someone dear to her was expiring and she wished to say a last goodbye. But who could it be? Everyone knew she had no kin. An old nanny, perhaps? Ah yes, that was it, a beloved wet nurse and nanny who had raised her. She would somehow think of something to tell Engracia that would shut up her questions.

The plan of action began to take shape in her mind. She could safely go about her duties with the Queen this evening, for she was sure that the nuns, exhausted from their long journeys, would follow convention and rest and sup in their chambers. Then she would plead high indisposition as she did every twenty-eight days—as a truant if the truth were told—mainly to give herself some breathing space from attendance on the Queen since her monthlies caused her little trouble. She would leave letters for the Queen and the Duke, and Luisa too, explaining that a messenger had galloped in with news from home. And after a short stay at Torrejoncillo—for it would never do to have Don Enrique's steward report she had not been there—she could return to Seville in safety to meet the Court. The Prioress would be returning to Santa Rosa and it was not a rich convent; the woman would probably have neither the money nor the necessity to visit the Court again. The nun's face, stamped on her mind, had taken on the menacing aspect of a demon. Well, the woman's age was advanced. Maybe she would die soon.

Engracia bustled in lugging a basket of clean linen and chemises. Allowing the woman no time to ask the questions that were popping the faded eyes under the arched, scraggly brows, Dolores gave her instructions for immediate transmittal to the two men she kept as guard/valets, for them to stand ready to load the baggage mules in the small hours of the morning so they all might leave before daybreak. A hamper of food and drink needed to be prepared as well. "And all must be done as discreetly as possible and as quietly," she emphasized to the loyal serving woman. "And don't look at me like that. I promise you we are not accused criminals avoiding justice, if that's what you think."

"But where do we go in the cold and dark morning, my lady?" Engracia cried.

"To Torrejoncillo. And I will tell you why some other time."

"Torrejoncillo? But—how do we know how to get there? It must be a month of days from here," declared the astonished and dismayed woman.

"No, it is not that far. We need only follow the road to the northwest, at an angle to the lowering sun, and when we reach Cordoba we will inquire further. Someone will know which way to send us. Now don't worry. We have good mounts and I have money. Just see that my jewel casket is well hidden among the blankets."

Dolores's strong if baseless confidence communicated itself to Engracia. The serving woman took a deep breath and raised and lowered her shoulders in acquiescence. "Torrejoncillo, is it? Well, I suppose I will be glad to see my old home again."

"Leaking roof and all?" Dolores quipped acidly, for *she* would not be glad. She smoothed her hair and replaced her hat, preparing to hasten to the Queen to help along with the other ladies at the royal undressing and redressing and freshening of toilette for the few hours of quiet chatter and supping in the great hall before bed. A sensation like little bugs crawled up and down her spine as she considered the small possibility the Mother Ines might be about, to be bumped into in a passage or mayhap even conversing with the Queen. Perhaps it would be safer to plead sickness even now? No, it was too soon after her obvious good health on the hunt. She would have to take her chances and pray. She realized the Queen was going to be very angry with her for running off so precipitously without permission, but hopefully Medina-Sidonia would intercede when the time came to calm the royal ire.

Leaving Engracia lifting down gowns and cloaks and garments off hooks to be folded into the chests, she opened the heavy, carved door and slipped out. She hurried toward the Queen's apartments, head high but eyes alert even as she nodded at those she encountered, on the lookout for the merest flicker of habit and veil, ready to spin about and march the other way. Her heart had begun to pound again.

In spite of Dolores's confidence about making her way to Cordoba—or perhaps because of it—she found herself and her small party of three riders and half a dozen baggage mules lost by noon of the next day, which was overcast and windy. Without the sun to orient them, the choices they made at several forks in the road were guided by the directions of other travelers or passing locals. But at one lonely branching they could only select what seemed the more important road of the three, one which ultimately proved to have taken them too far to the south.

Dolores learned long after that the hard-riding guard of

eight armed men which an alarmed Don Enrique had sent after her as additional protection had chosen the correct road to Cordoba and then had doubled back after half a day without finding her, but finally could not fathom at which of several crossings the Baroness's party had branched off, nor could they find anyone who recalled her antelope device passing by. The men then rode back to Torredonpedro, in the end, their mission of safely escorting the Baroness de la Rocha to her destination unaccomplished.

It was not Cordoba Dolores reached the next day but Lucena, and there discovered that she would have to go even further south and out of her way to reach the road running northwest along the Genil River and through the Sierra Morena passes. But her relief at having avoided detection as an imposter was so great she did nothing more than mutter at the prospect of the extra four or five days' journeying, and at the next hostel she gave her valets a handful of coins to buy themselves extra flagons of ale in compensation.

❧ *Chapter 20* ❧

THE COUNCIL DISSOLVED in an uproar over Boabdil's third and most conciliatory communication yet with their bellicose Christian Majesties.

"Shameful!" cried out Yussef Abencerrage, the head of that family. "I would rather this grisled old head be struck off than it should bow in such cowardice before a Christian dog." He shook a trembling fist at Grand Vizier Comixa, who had just revealed the content of Boabdil's feeble rejoinder to Ferdinand's threats.

Another council member jumped to his feet. "Our Sultan begs King Ferdinand to be satisfied with all he has already gained in conquest? Does one thank a disease for consuming every part of the body but the head?"

"If the King will help him keep order, Boabdil promises to rule over Granada as an obedient vassal of the Crown and offers even greater tribute than before to honor his scurrilous masters! Is that not the same thing as surrender? Why does he not just open the gates and let the Christians sit upon the throne?" sneered a richly dressed advisor upon whose silver breast medallion a cannon was engraved.

"Do we speak into the empty air when the Sultan attends us? Does Boabdil think he can ignore his council and rule as an autocrat? We have placed him upon the throne, and we can as easily put him down for such calumny!" raged an apoplectic nobleman.

Yusef Comixa stood before the clamor in silence, his face more sour and inscrutable than ever. He had known what Boabdil's latest weaseling would bring, and privately he agreed with the council. All he could do for the Sultan now was not to add his own opinion to the hostility.

A new, big voice overrode the angry babble of the thirty or forty men pressing before the beleaguered Comixa. Muza Aben Gazul, his head bristling with a spiked helmet riding the folds of his purple turban, pushed his shoulders through the frenzied group and strode to the Vizier's dais. "We have stood enough, noble Moors! Now let us give our own answer to the Christian jackals, for they do not even treat with Boabdil as a true ruler. See here, this missive has just arrived from Ferdinand, and it is addressed to me as commander of Granada's armies, and to you as council for the city. The words are not new, but his appeal to surrender is now an outright ultimatum. And I say *Shaitan* take the Christian King and all his evil forces! Does he think that we are old and weak that threats of invasion will make us tremble? Or that we are women, to be content with the crumbs of grace our Sultan begs?" Muza Aben's slanted black eyes flashed defiance into the upturned faces of his audience.

"If such is the enemy's opinion, who can blame him? We have waited too long upon the decision of a Sultan shuffling before the need for action. Now let us take the bit of a fiery warhorse in our own teeth and charge to the victory! Let the infidel know to his regret that a Moor is born to the spear and scimitar, nurtured upon the bolt in the bow, given the javelin in his hand at puberty. If the Christian King desires our land and our city, let him try to take it, but at his peril. For he will pay in rivers of blood, in seas of tears for every league of our ground he covets. Courage, courage and arms, in the name of Allah, my sirs, will defend us and launch us to our own victorious attacks." Fists on chain-mailed hips, booted feet planted firmly on the gleaming tiles, Muza Aben's stentorian voice radiated power and confidence. He continued:

"For my part a defender's grave in the sweet soil of Granada rather than the easiest pillow in her palaces earned by cowardice and submission!" he cried. "Let us fight, I say, let us beat our drums and gather our men, let us awake from this shameful sloth and set every man and boy to defending our walls. Draw your scimitars, my masters, and show the presumptuous Spanish dogs the deadly fangs of our ancestors. Your army is strong and prepared, your commanders ready. Only shout the name of 'war' and we shall rekindle our fighting heritage. What do you say, noble Moors?"

"War! War!" the council responded, swept away by this fiery oratory and deaf to all reason. "War! War! War!" each man shouted, and Comixa fell back a step or two to disengage from the ferment surrounding the general.

Dewlaps trembling, a wealthy merchant and erstwhile supporter of Boabdil tried to voice an objection. "We take a terrible risk with the lives of our wives and children," he cried. "A warrior's grave is not their salvation or wish. And our commerce will be ruined, utterly ruined. Consider, I pray you—" But he was drowned out.

"I say down with the Sultan; he makes us sniveling women!" a younger man hooted, and several others even began a call to depose Boabdil. But most of the dignitaries were caught up in Muza Aben's military defiance, and the only desire they burned with now was to crush the enemy as in the old days of glory. Contemptuously they retracted Boabdil's conciliatory peace effort and honored the inspiring Muza Aben by giving him the right to draft their reply to Ferdinand: that they would suffer death before surrendering their city, and that all treaties and commitments between the Catholic rulers and Boabdil were hereby considered null and void.

High above the council chamber, hidden by a false grill which appeared as innocent as all the other gilt arabesques decorating the sumptuous chamber, was a small niche for the convenience of any Sultan wishing to eavesdrop on the doings of his advisors, or for the occasional Sultana who was interested in politics. The council members knew the chamber was there, although they could never tell whether or not it was occupied. But now they did not care; Boabdil's wrath was a weak thing.

As the meeting below began to disperse in a high fever of belligerence, Francho dragged his fascinated eyes away from the grill to observe the rebellion's effects upon Boabdil and Ayaxa. Ayaxa said nothing at all to her son but looked at him with hard, challenging eyes and a pressed mouth. Mutely then she turned her back and ramrod stiff stalked out to return to her apartments in the harem. Boabdil gnawed on his lip and exited silently. Francho followed him out.

But in the perfumed splendor of his private salon the Sultan vented a short, harsh laugh. "She warned me Ferdinand was not to be trusted and would never rest with mere tribute. Which, of course, I knew in my heart. She loathes me for a fool, and loathes herself for having borne me. And you, O singer of songs, she despises, for someone has told her you drip the poison of peace into my willing ear."

Francho nodded, aware that in the past six months he had garnered a haughty enemy, antagonistic to his influence on the Sultan and perhaps even mildly suspicious of his designs. In his presence Ayaxa acted as if he did not exist, but he could feel her sharp stare boring into him when his back was to her, as a mother lion eyes the biting fly that settles on her heedless cub. She seemed the only one aware to what extent the Sultan could be swayed by the opinions of an obscure musician. The other courtiers ignored his constant presence with the Sultan as one more example of Boabdil's feckless character.

His meteoric rise to royal favor still stunned him, and he often thought to pinch himself in case this was just a wild dream conjured by a youth in the boredom of Mondejar. It seemed only yesterday that Ferdinand's first ultimatum had forced Francho to wait in despair and declining hope for the Sultan to remember him, passing the days in a frenzy of frustration. Events were becoming crucial and he needed facts to pass on, not the wild rumors of the marketplaces. No one was certain what tack Boabdil would take. It was a delicate moment, when the impressionable ruler might be swayed by someone crafty reinforcing his reach for peace—and there Francho found himself, along with other languishing entertainers, moping in Mustafa Ata's antechamber unsummoned as the days flew by.

Once Mustafa Ata even ventured to mention the minstrel his Sultan had so enjoyed to a preoccupied Boabdil as he strode to the council chamber, but was brusquely ignored. The Chief of Entertainments returned to Francho and shrugged; then retired to his chamber to brood over his own fate if Boabdil was actually deposed.

And then one dark and silent morning at an hour after midnight a pair of burly palace guards sent by Mustafa Ata beat on Francho's door in the Albayazin and awakened him.

Sending Ali back to bed with a few reassuring words, Francho dressed and mounted the mule they had brought for him, slinging his guitar on his broad back, not allowing himself any more than a tingle of hope that his luck had prevailed. The large square they passed through on the way to the Alhambra was deserted, yet only a few hours before, hundreds of torches had bobbed and flamed, and Muza Aben Gazul had worked up the huge crowd into a chant for war. Francho had loitered on the fringes of the throng, watching the vaguely Oriental features of the stocky general work with passion as he railed against Christian treachery and the Sultan's cowardice. Francho remembered the warring reactions called up even within himself as the throng shouted approval for the general, for had he been truly born a Moor he would have reviled the Sultan too and looked upon this bulldog of a warrior as Granada's only salvation from peace at the price of liberty. With the stubborn Muza Aben Gazul on the throne, Granada might have a chance of flouting Ferdinand; with Boabdil there was none.

But Jamal ibn Ghulam had no business with personal preferences, he who fought his war on the field of hypocrisy and treachery. And so he had sternly reminded himself that he stood firmly for Boabdil.

The guards had escorted him through dimly lit courts and halls to the Sultan's bedchamber, where he found the ruler in a furred dressing gown moving restlessly about the room while a graybeard physician stirred up an odiferous potion in a silver beaker. The low couch on the dais showed a tangle of satin coverlets and pillows; the jagged shards of a large mirror smashed to smithereens lay on the thick carpet along with the gold cup the Sultan had hurled at it. There were dark circles under Boabdil's tired eyes, and the corners of his mouth drooped into his double-pointed beard.

A sleek, black leopard sat chained at the foot of Boabdil's couch, tail twitching, yellow eyes slit and ominous, made restless by the Sultan's nervous pacing.

The physician bowed and handed Boabdil the beaker. The Sultan threw back his head and gulped the liquid, then pitched the container into the heap of pillows on the bed. "Gahh! A city famed for its schools of physic, for its sages of medicine, and not one, not one can cure my aching head!"

The graybeard stammered, "N-newt's tongues, Great Sultan, dissolved in oil of beech, and a pinch of mercury—"

"Get out, get out, you poisoner!" Boabdil shouted, and a low rumble emerged from the throat of the great cat. Gasping, the purple-turbaned physician scurried from the room with as much dignity as his haste could muster.

Boabdil climbed the dais and sank onto the couch, edgy and despondent. "You may come closer, minstrel; I will not bite you. And Aswad eats only council members and assassins."

"With M'jambana at your door and Aswad at your feet, your sleep is well guarded, Excellence."

"From physical enemies, perhaps. But not from the anguish brought by the faithlessness of my enemy and the stupidity of my subjects. Or from the throbbing skull that has plagued me for days." He stared at Francho from eyes rimmed in red. "But what do you know of sleepless nights and heavy heart? You almost offend me, minstrel, standing there free, your brow smooth, your life unburdened by care or pain . . ."

"I was not always a rootless minstrel, Excellence," Francho reminded him softly. "The soil of Malaga is salt with the bitter tears of a man whose only flower of the heart lies buried in her tortured ruins." The raggedness of his tone, even constrained as it was, pierced the young ruler's self-absorption.

Boabdil made a helpless gesture. "That was unworthy of me, Jamal. But either my fulsome burdens have dulled my memory, or I did not realize. . . . You were betrothed?"

Francho nodded. "Yes," he said, thinking of Leonora and how he missed her, so that involuntarily a shadow passed over his face. "And I have also lost my family, my home, my friends, all perished with my city. If I seem detached from tribulation it is because nothing will ever touch me so terribly again. Such shock as I have suffered forms an armor."

"Then I should be walled about with such an armor at present, for all the shocks I have sustained in this bloody game of greed. What think you now, talker of peace? Now that Granada, your last haven, is threatened with the same fate as Malaga, will you stand to defend it with those who feel we can pinch to death the striding colossus? Or do you still hold your view that life in captivity is better than the finality of death?" Boabdil gazed at him bitterly, but in his voice there was an underlying appeal that nerved Francho to continue his stand.

He took the plunge. "The wheel of fortune turns slowly, O Sultan, but it turns true. I reason that peace as the wheel turns

426

under us will serve our ultimate victory better than the devastation of war. Once *we* were the colossus and bestrode all of this land and the Christians trembled before our might. And see, how in a few hundred years they have come from a tiny corner of the north to regain all they say was theirs. But the wheel grinds round and our turn will present itself again. And to what avail if our bones rot under the soil and our strength is smashed and ruined beyond recall?

"The Sultanate of Granada swarms with our people; no matter how many Spaniards Ferdinand brings with him to settle here, they will not outnumber us. Even as slave to the Christian yoke yet we will live, and there will come a day when the legions of Ferdinand will depart to fight other infidels, in France or Sicily perhaps, great wars which will sap their strength and drain their resources. Then will we have the opportunity to reward treachery with treachery."

Francho stopped in momentary confusion. He had allowed the persona of Jamal ibn Ghulam to carry him away, and the Sultan gave close attention to his words. His task was to see Boabdil clung to peace by reason of his own misty dreams as preserver of his people, not to give him concrete and terrible ideas for the future. But what other way was there to urge Boabdil into Ferdinand's hands? Peace now seemed to mean total surrender. Only a coward would choose it, and he did not believe that Boabdil was so craven. But peace that carried with it an aggressive hope? The impractical Sultan might cling to that.

Filling his lungs with the incense-sweetened air of the ornate bedchamber, Francho used every ounce of his ability to project strong conviction and continued to expound his argument that a calm surrender would be Granada's finest ally in the long run. After a while some of the strain eased on Boabdil's face. He leaned back on his pillows, visibly letting go his tension and requested Francho to pluck his guembri— no voice, just the soft, melodic, sweet notes of the instrument. And soon the miserable Sultan fell into a heavy-breathing sleep.

From that night forward Boabdil required Francho's constant attendance, even during important audiences, so that the blue-eyed, black-bearded musician who in public said little soon became familiar to the entire Court as the current royal intimate.

Boabdil told him, "You realize, Jamal, that my friendship may cost you your life? The Sultan's favorites are the first executed should their protector be overthrown." The smile was ironic, the soft brown eyes sad.

"You do not force me to serve you, Excellence." Francho shrugged, offering his insouciant grin. "If such disaster comes to pass it results from my own free choice. It does not frighten me away to know I will share in your fate, of good or evil."

"I have not many friends, minstrel."

"Nor has any man if he would count truthfully."

"But I shall count you among the few."

Francho's thoughts then were full of irony: He likes me because I echo back his own will but with a strength and conviction he does not possess. Yet by urging him to follow his dream of peace I am a greater enemy than any of his Moorish foes for I weave the Christian noose he places about his own neck. Within him there are seeds of tragedy—only water them and he will do the rest. I sneer at him, his weaknesses, his trust, at the very moderation of his disposition and the irresponsibility that allows him to put more store in the advice of a minstrel than in all the words of his experienced advisors. And yet—there is a sensitive depth to the man, a yearning for beauty, a gentleness and a generosity that is appealing. In a poet, perhaps, Francho remonstrated to himself sternly, pulling back from the pitfall of pity. But not in a person who insists on leading a nation.

Thus with his own sort of courage the Sultan had ignored the great processions around the city crying war and the rabid demonstrations of contempt for him just below the very walls of the Alhambra, and he drafted his pacifying response to Ferdinand. And today, as Francho had witnessed from the niche above the council chamber, Muza Aben Gazul and the council threw their sneering defiance in the Sultan's teeth. Now the great Sultan sat pale and gnawing his knuckle, sunk in self-loathing and anger, looking as if he wanted to retch up his last meal. Nor was the ruler any more distressed than his companion, who struggled to keep a composed aspect to shield the furious workings of his brain.

The acceleration of popular outrage with Boabdil's policies in the past months had prompted Francho to send a message asking Tendilla's advice on the course he meant to take should the situation get out of hand. But no clear answer had come.

And now the crisis was here: Boabdil's peace effort was lost, war seemed inevitable, and the people threatened to sweep Muza Aben Gazul onto the throne. Still, Francho reasoned, if Boabdil could be kept clinging to the throne, it might at least be a short war.

"Excellence, what action will you take now?"

The silence allowed faint cries and shouts from below to reach them in the moment it took Boabdil to answer. "The only action I can. I will let my offer of friendship stand with Ferdinand and prepare to fight off rebellion by holding the Alhambra. The city will fight but I shall not. When the conquest is a reality Ferdinand will be disposed to treat with me leniently and I can do my best to bind up the wounds of my people."

"The people would call Muza Aben Gazul Sultan."

"Let them. He will ultimately be killed or captured by the Spanish."

But Ferdinand did not want the stubborn and fiery Gazul to gain a power which could hold the Spanish to a long and expensive siege. Under Boabdil, on the other hand, with a taste of war to intimidate them, the spoiled citizens of Mohammed's last stronghold in Spain might allow their Sultan to talk them into a quick surrender.

"O Sultan, if you shut yourself in the Alhambra while your people battle for their lives you will be named to all the generations to come as the most reviled of rulers. The Christians will mock you, your people will despise you. You can count on only your palace Nubians to protect you, and twice their number would not hold the ravening mob, who would murder you as the goat for all Granada's tribulations. And if you live you will be as a leper, shunned by all, abhorred, spat upon."

Boabdil started and fixed upon his musician a disbelieving glare. "Say you I should turn about my face? Become a champion of war when I have always spoken peace?" he cried in indignation. "My subjects have disliked me through my whole life and thus Allah wills it. Now what cruelty is this that you measure the full misery of my fate to torture my ears?"

Francho did not hesitate. He could feel Boabdil's need to be directed. He made a deep and reverent salaam and dropped to his knees, a humble posture to mitigate his stern words. "I beg my Sultan to forgive my boldness, which is not impertinence but true concern. You must not allow degradation to fall upon your house. If a father warns a child to fear the rushing waters of the river that fill the nose and stop the lungs—if the father binds the boy to safety with rope and yet the child wriggles free and falls into the torrent—will the father stand upon the bank and hope the child learns to swim so that when he struggles to shore the father may kiss his face and wring out his clothes? If you were this father, would you not plunge in to save the child, without thought of his disobedience? If you drowned with him your spirits would meet together happily in Paradise. If he drowned alone his curses would follow you throughout eternity."

"But—perhaps there is time yet . . ."

Francho pressed on. "No time at all, Excellence; the boy is already leaping into the flood. That is the reality and it cannot be changed by closing your eyes and refusing to look. You have seen today another man who stands ready to take the place of the father. Will you allow Muza Aben to take your place? Or, now that the die is cast, will you lead your people and be with them in their destiny?"

Boabdil jumped up and stood over his kneeling musician, the anger of betrayal in his eyes. "This, then, is your secret of existence, minstrel, the 'armor' that sustains you in this violent world?" he grated. "You shift your convictions as easily as the wind!"

"Nay, I do not shift them," Francho retorted heatedly. "But when they conflict with duty and sense I must place them in abeyance. You are the Great Sultan of the country of Granada, the champion of the Hand and the Key, the Living Sword of the Prophet, praise Allah. You have a duty not to desert your people, be they wise or foolish, and you must perform it. You have done your best to lead them in the path of wisdom, but their eyes are blinded with rage and they are not able to see the future. Now you must stand with them in their trial and let the future rest in Allah's hands."

Boabdil blinked. The angry light slowly died from his eyes. "But it was you who spoke once of the revolving wheel and that a peaceful surrender would hasten our time for revenge."

"But now there will be no peace, Excellence, for in spite of your impassioned pleas to the council they have thrown off your hand from the wheel's laboring crank and cast longing glances toward Muza Aben Gazul, the man of war. What is written is written. In spite of your majesty you are only one man. If the people of Granada with the army at their back demand war you must hear them."

A heavy silence followed as Boabdil turned away, face slack, shoulders slumped under his embroidered silk coat, even the red plumes in his turban seeming to droop. It looked to Francho as if the man's ears were listening to silent voices, others who had spoken the same reason to him in less poetic words. Francho let out his breath. He could only pray that he would be able to convince Abu Abdullah where the others had failed.

A pang of sympathy ran through him. The man, after all, was a pawn, pushed this way and that by stronger, more clever people—even by Francho himself, a most unofficial advisor. A more venal and cruel ruler would never have trusted Ferdinand's promises; would have so coveted the riches of Gaudix and Almeria that at the surrender of El Zagal he would have struck like lightning and with untold bloodletting taken the cities for himself, pushing back the Christian frontier and letting Ferdinand fume over broken pledges. To have saved Granada would have required a leader of positive and wily action from the beginning, before the fall of Baza, and this was not Boabdil. Now no matter how he decided he could only lose, ultimately. His decision for war now would keep him on the throne, but would help only one future—a young Christian knight whose service to the Catholic rulers could win him back his name.

Francho got up and passed behind the Sultan, who stood staring from the fretted window, his arms folded so tightly against himself his knuckles were white. He was unseeing of the verdant, crowded city below him, so was he wrapped in misery. Francho went out on the balcony to calm his own nerves. He began softly to sing the "Lamentation of Don Rodrigo," knowing his words would be clear to the man at the window:

The host of Don Rodrigo were scattered in dismay
The Christians lost the battle, nor heart nor hope had they.
He saw his royal banners where they lay drenched and torn,
He hears the cries of victory, the Arabs' shouts of scorn.
He looked for the brave captains that had led the hosts of
  Spain

But all were fled except the dead, and who could count the slain.
"Last night I was the King of Spain, today no king am I;
Last night fair castles held my train, tonight where shall I lie?"

Several stanzas later he looked up to see Boabdil at the balcony doorway, the smooth face suddenly expressionless. "You are right. The wheel will turn, Jamal ibn Ghulam," the Sultan said with stiff lips. "The Prophet whispers to me that it will turn."

An hour later Boabdil stood before the reconvened council and in front of their eyes tore up the copy of his pleading capitulation to Ferdinand, causing a shocked silence both with the men who sat cross-legged before his dais and with the nervous group peering down from the screened niche, where Francho also stood discreetly in the background. He saw the giant ruby which tacked the Sultan's plumes to his turban shooting spicules of red fire as the ruler surveyed the suspicious faces turned up to his.

"I have been a man of peace," Boabdil declared in as ringing a tone as he was capable of, "but I am a man and I am a ruler. The gauntlet of aggression has been tossed at my feet. In my surprise I have hesitated a moment. Now, good sirs, I pick it up and fling it back—as the gauntlet of war. The hand of the Sultan Abu Abdullah upholds the Sword of Allah! Now shall we ride forth with the terrible cries and the ferocious might that once chilled the blood of our ancient foes. Los Reyes Católicos will go down to perdition where waits Roderigo the Goth to greet them. We shall vent our fury, we shall have our vengeance; the scurrilous enemy will now suffer our full wrath. The vengeance of Allah will be turned upon them. War upon the infidel, this I decree—Abu Abdullah, Great Sultan of Granada, Champion of the Hand and the Key! And thus let it be known in every corner of my realm."

From the astonished murmur of voices sprang a few shouts of approval, "Aye, Great Sultan, so be it!" And then, with a joyous outburst of relief the majority of the council members scrambled to their feet to cheer their ruler. With regal aplomb Boabdil stood before them calmly smiling, but Francho knew he was soaking up the unaccustomed sound of their approval like a man shriveled by years of rain allowed finally to bask in the sunlight. A few listeners in the back slipped out of the chamber to speed the news of the Sultan's declaration of war throughout the city.

Returning to his house somewhat earlier in the evening than usual to help Ali prepare the rice and meat for supper, Francho found the boy sitting on his pallet conversing with a mantled young woman who jumped up in frightened confusion as Francho stooped through the doorway. She stammered out that she was a friend of Ali's and was just leaving, but the boy quickly piped up in spite of her warning glance, "Azahra is my sister, Jamal."

"Your sister!" Francho exclaimed. "You told me you had no family, rascal."

"I said I had no one who could care for me," Ali wavered. "Azahra tried, but I was a great burden to her."

Clasping her hands nervously the girl glided toward Francho, moving with a natural, sensual grace that rippled the light mantle she clutched about her and that did not entirely conceal the lines of her short, supple body and her large bosom. Her features—why, she was only a child, Francho realized, abruptly terminating the tenor of his thoughts. Dark-skinned and pock-cheeked, with huge eyes, the irises black as jet in a sea of white, her plain face was that of an uncertain girl set upon the ripened form of a mature woman.

"Please, *sayed,* don't be angry with Ali." The lovely, liquid eyes held the same hopeful trust as her brother's. "It is all my fault; I shouldn't have come here. But I miss him. We have never been so long separated."

"And I suppose he has a mother and father somewhere about too?" Francho broke in sharply.

"No, sir, we have no one. Oh please, please, he did not really mean to deceive you. He had no place to live; that was true."

"Then where do you stay?"

"Where I am employed, at the Inn of the Golden Horn."

Francho frowned his displeasure. "What sort of sister are you that you could let your little brother roam the streets and sleep in doorways? Why don't you share what you have with him?"

Tears rose in the girl's dark eyes. Looking more closely Francho saw that beside pimples her face was also disfigured

by a thin scar that traced a painful white line from one ear to
the point of her chin.

"I did, good *sayed,* for as long as I could. But the proprietor
did not like Ali and beat him and kicked him, until I saw it
was better for Ali to find his own shelter than to have his
bones broken by that brute of a man. He used to grab Ali by
the arm and twist it and I thought surely one day I would hear
Ali's poor little arm snap—" The tears spilled out of the great,
black-lashed orbs that seemed to inhabit her whole face.

"Here now, girl, don't weep," Francho said in a kinder tone,
ashamed of himself as she wiped her eyes with a corner of her
mantle. He saw her suddenly become pale and trembly, and,
afraid she would faint, he led her to the pallet and made her
sit on it. Ali hovered about so anxiously that Francho directed
him to bring a cup of wine. "But why do you stay in the
employ of such a man?" he asked, immediately realizing how
foolish was such a question in a city overcrowded with
unemployed.

Azahra told him a sad tale of a mother too ill to work who
had sold her to Zatar of the Golden Horn as a bond slave for
seven years, hoping for a miracle to occur so she could buy
back her daughter from slavery; and whose hopes had ended
in the grave and left Ali alone to linger about the Golden
Horn, where his sister managed to pass him enough food to
keep him alive. "Oh, I beg of you, you have been so kind to my
little brother, do not abandon him now. He is a good boy and
very willing to earn his keep."

Pityingly, Francho soothed her. "You have no need to
become overwrought, Azahra. I have no intention of abandoning Ali."

"And that terrible Zatar beats her for nothing," Ali cried
out. "She showed me. He is a mean and cruel man. Show
Jamal the marks," he urged Azahra. "Jamal is very strong; he
will go there and punish him." The child's eyes glowed with
hero worship as he gazed at the tall friend who sheltered him
and who was so important he was sometimes in the very
presence of the Sultan as one of his musicians.

Azahra blanched with fear. "Oh no, you must not do that,
sayed. Ali is stupid. It is Zatar's right to strike me if he
wishes."

But Ali pulled down the mantle from her shoulders and
Francho quickly stayed her hand from drawing it up again.

She wore a sleeveless jacket. The flesh of one upper arm showed purple-greenish bruises, in the outline of cruel fingers. Both rounded arms and probably her back, Francho imagined, were covered with red welts, as if from a whistling willow whip. He pictured the weeping young girl cringing helplessly in a corner as the paunchy proprietor flayed at her with the whip and a dark frown appeared between his brows. "What is it that you do at the inn. Are you a cook?"

"I . . . I am a dancer."

Of course! Now he knew why the expressive eyes had seemed so familiar and the walk so undulating. "But you are a very good dancer. I have seen you; you dance with your face veiled."

"He makes me do that. It intrigues the customers and serves to hide my scar and the ugliness of my skin."

"If you do not misbehave, then why does he hit you?"

Azahra hung her head. "B . . . because he makes me lay with him and he hurts me and sometimes I just cannot bear it," she whispered. Then, with shamed eyes, she pulled the mantle about her and rose, trying tremulously to smile through the pallor that still lay on her face. "I must leave now, *sayed*. Zatar will be raging if he finds that I am gone."

Clenching his jaw against the swinishness of Azahra's master, Francho amazed himself by offering the dancer sanctuary. She could keep house and cook for him and share Ali's pallet, and he would give her a small sum for her services. Ali's face shone as if he looked upon a bearded god, but Azahra shook her head sadly. She was legally the property of Zatar, and prison awaited anyone who aided a slave to escape. And the innkeep would not sell her. Others had offered thrice what he had paid for her, so Zatar had gloated, but she drew hordes of patrons to his common room. "And above all," she added, tonelessly, "he lusts for me and he delights in tormenting me."

Francho tipped up Azahra's unhappy face. "Would you rather stay here with Ali? Well then, we shall hide you. Since you have danced with a veil no one on the street will recognize you, and you will make sure to keep away from the vicinity of the Golden Horn. If he looks for you he will never conceive that you are hiding so close, he will think you have fled beyond the city."

Still Azahra hesitated. "It is not for myself that I fear, I am but a worthless slave. But I do not wish to bring trouble upon you, *sayed.*"

Francho's laugh was a deep rumble. "I have a few friends at the Alhambra who will help me in case Zatar discovers where you are. Powerful friends. He can do me no harm, Azahra, be easy about that," he assured her with a certain pride.

"Jamal is a Royal Musician, Azahra, and sometimes he plays for the Sultan!" Ali announced to her proudly.

Azahra's midnight eyes filled again, this time with tears of gratitude. She clasped her hands. "Oh, you are so kind, *sayed.* Surely the blessings of Allah and the compassion of Fatima will follow you always."

"Good, then the matter is settled. Zatar has gained from your dancing many times what he paid for you. Your debt to him is ended." Francho brushed away her thanks in embarrassment. "Now tuck up your mantle, sister of Ali, and see to our supper. This has been a long, weary day."

He went through the curtain to his small chamber, feeling through his back the grateful eyes of the two orphans beaming upon him. Immediately, calling himself fool as he exchanged his turban for a more comfortable little skullcap and his heelless leather shoes for rafia slippers, he began to regret his impulsive offer. It was bad enough he had come to feel responsible for that scamp Ali, but now to bring a half-grown girl, a runaway slave, into the house was sheer idiocy. He wanted no fracas with the owner of the Golden Horn to spoil his anonymity in the neighborhood. It was known that he was employed at the Alhambra as a musician, but so were a hundred other trumpeters, drummers, instrumentalists, and singers. But since the Sultan had insisted he dress as befitting a Head Musician, he came and went from his house with a concealing mantle over his new tunics and narrow pantaloons. He expected his exalted position to be discovered eventually by his neighbors in the Albayazin, and then there would be a horde of beggars swarming on his doorstep, and his movements around the quarter would be more remarked. But he was safer to preserve his insignificance as long as possible, and having the Golden Horn's popular dancer hiding in his house was not the way to do it.

Still, in pity for the young girl's undeserved bruises and welts he had reacted by offering her haven, and now, even upon sober reflection, he hadn't the cruelty to withdraw it. He could only hope fat Zatar would give Azahra up as a bad bargain, or that at least he or his agents would not find out where she hid.

✥ *Chapter 21* ✥

THE SULTAN RECEIVED his Grand Vizier in the royal garden, a lush, grassy area with pink oleander bushes, iris, white roses and poppies, myrtle trees, jetting fountains, and a spoked wheel of tiled paths leading to a serene lily pond in the middle. Resting on silken pillows under a tasseled canopy the Sultan motioned the spare Comixa to another heap of pillows, lower than his own. Francho sat on the rim of the lily pool strumming a lute softly, with less interest in their discussion of the gala tourney and banquet to be held in honor of Gazul's continuing and successful raids on Spanish towns than in the sparkling blue water of the pool, where one of the floating gold-and-white lilies suddenly became Leonora's sweet face laughing up at him.

He didn't want to think of Leonora, it disturbed the "persona" of Jamal ibn Ghulam by reminding him of Francisco de Mendoza, an incautious overlay that might cause him to stumble. But he would have to be less than human to view the glorious pinks and golds of the drifting blossoms and not recall the delicate beauty of his lady.

He was living, in fact, as celibate as a monk and had done so all these months. He worked off his physical restlessness with daily long and vigorous swims—a concealing towel tight about his hips—in the great pool of the palace baths, then by getting pummeled and pounded and massaged, and often by finding a willing partner for a friendly, grunting wrestle on the carpeted area set aside for this. He assiduously ignored the female slaves around the palace who slid flirtatious eyes at him and politely avoided the bolder, diaphanously veiled ladies of the Court, who tossed provocative looks along with their roses when he performed at banquets and who begged the fortunately unwilling Sultan to lend his splendid balladeer to their houses.

He was often restive in his silken but solitary bed, yet he hoped to keep it so, even if the physical hunger for a woman's warm body sometimes drove him to late night pacing of the large and finely appointed chamber and private patio the Sultan had insisted he inhabit at the Alhambra so that he would always be near at hand. He did not want *any* woman. He would wait for Leonora.

But he could do nothing to control the erotic dreams caused by his necessary chastity, nor the involuntary physical responses to them that woke him in sticky wetness, breathing heavily and more aware than ever, in the flower-perfumed darkness, of his loneliness. What irritated him was that most of these dreams involved not Leonora but Dolores. He often dreamed he lay naked and powerful in the springy grass of the garden, drawing to him, then clasping to him with eager arms a woman's smooth, warm, silken body, a body that fitted its curves into him and moved so exquisitely against him that in a second his maleness had grown to bursting with desire and so had his heart. And finally, in his dream he rolled on top of her and with a powerful thrust into the secret, hot damp she opened to him, he possessed the writhing, moaning woman and moved over her so frantically that when the release came—in his dreams and in reality—he thought it would fling him across the room. But just before it happened he would look down triumphantly at the passionately gasping woman beneath him and the closed eyes were tilted ones, the waves of scented hair spilling across the pillow glinted auburn, the moist, delicious mouth that tantalized his dream was wide and full and pink-lipped. Over and over he dreamed it was Dolores his body craved; nor could he keep blaming it on deprivation, for there were close at hand graceful and pretty women—their flimsy veils hid little—and he deliberately pictured them unclothed when he relaxed just to force the seductive innkeeper's daughter from his dreams. But nothing worked.

Even when he allowed himself to think of Leonora, her small, white hand light as a feather on his arm and her melting eyes, even if he heard in his head over and over her soft voice saying the glorious words, "There is none I would have for a husband but you, Francisco, and so I will wait, for however long I must," even then flips and flashes of mocking, wide gray eyes swept by dark lashes, the turn of a glowing velvet cheek, of an arched neck thrown back in a throaty chuckle, and the taste of a hotly clinging mouth intruded themselves into his reverie.

Iridescent, fan-tailed goldfish darted up to try nibbling at his fingers. Could a man love two women at once? Physically desire them, yes, but not love, he decided. After all, what virile man would not want to possess the erotic beauty and spirited charm of the Baroness de la Rocha, captivated by the impudent glint in her eye that Francho knew was a legacy from the streets? He frowned and stared doggedly at a bobbing water lily until Leonora came strongly into his mind—the honey ringlets blowing over the alabaster fore-head, the limpid brown eyes shaded by curling lashes, the frequent gay music of her laugh accompanied by enchanting dimples he had ventured to capture with the tip of his finger only to have them disappear as she struggled to look solemn, and he knew that this lady was worth his very life. What was she doing now, he wondered forlornly, this very minute?

Pangs of loneliness caused him to flip his hand abruptly so that the water flickered with tiny, gleaming fish panicked away from tickling at his fingers like a litter of nursing puppies. He remained watching their aimless dartings, but suddenly, like well-trained servitors, his ears picked up a change in the tenor of the conversation going on under the shade canopy. It was almost as if his ears swiveled in that direction of their own accord while he still gazed at the water.

"But you are not going to send the maiden on this long journey in such perilous times?" was the shocked question from the Sultan's lips that had caught Francho's attention, for it was voiced louder than the murmur that had gone before.

"I must, Great Sultan, in spite of my own fears, for very soon it will be too late." The usual dour expression on Comixa's face was even more pronounced. "My niece's marriage has already been postponed twice, and I fear that the Emir of Tetuan will break the agreement altogether if he is made to wait longer for his bride. You realize how wealthy and influential this potentate is, an excellent political bridge to Egypt. I cannot allow such a brilliant match to slip away from my ward. It is my duty as her guardian to see her safely and advantageously married."

"But how do you propose that the Lady Fatima reach Morocco? All of our ports are solidly blockaded, Shaitan take the infidel dogs."

"The Emir has already sent a large vessel to fetch his bride; it is waiting off the fishing village of Almuncar. It will mean a roundabout journey for Fatima and her train and partially through territory under Christian sway, but the infidel will hardly expect such a cavalcade in the southeast. And we will turn their eyes in the opposite direction with heavy and concerted raids in the northwest from Mala to Moclin. If Allah so wills it, in ten days' time Fatima will ride safely through to Almuncar."

Because his throne was more secure than ever, Boabdil considered his longtime advisor with a compassionate gaze. The pinched look of misery had faded from his mild face, the dark smudges gone from under his eyes. "You will sorrow to see the lady go, is that not so, good Yusef? You keep your feelings hidden but I have known you many years. The more crabbed your face, the sadder your heart."

A grudging smile flitted across the old Vizier's face. "One of your noblest qualities, my Sultan, is your sympathy. Yes. I shall miss my elegant Fatima. She graced my house as a daughter with her soft laughter and obedience, and it comforted an old man's soul to watch her bloom into a lissome, rounded, and lovely woman. Well, I have done my best for her, and tomorrow she will leave. She is a dutiful maid. Allah will watch over her."

Francho had picked up his lute and was languidly strumming it, he was unconcerned outwardly but a ferment of excitement inside. A lofty Moorish noblewoman leaving Granada to marry the powerful Emir of Tetuan would certainly be taking with her a magnificent dowry, which meant a long train of mules laden to their tails with exquisite gifts, precious jewels, and money. What a prize of booty for Don Iñigo and the Crown!

The afternoon dragged on, for after Comixa departed

several others took his place, and then Boabdil asked to hear the ballad his acclaimed troubador was composing in honor of his Sultan's brave declaration of war. Approving of the finished stanzas, Boabdil finally gave Francho permission to retire. Flinging a cloak over his satin tunic, Francho hastily made his way down the Albayazin and with quick greetings to Ali and Azahra sat down in his old chamber to write an urgent dispatch. Leaving the house he told Azahra that he would return shortly, and she asked no questions but nodded silently and dumped his wooden bowl of spiced lamb and rice back in the pot to keep hot.

It was at the fete for Muza Aben Gazul that Francho finally caught more than a passing glimpse of Reduan Venegas, who spent most of his time in the *vega* whipping Granada's swollen army into fighting units and who seemed to have no patience for the intrigues and politics at the Alhambra. If Francho looked for a family resemblance in the Moorish-Spanish warrior, he was disappointed. Reduan was of middle height with a flat, undistinguished face, cold eyes, and a thin, humorless mouth surrounded by a scraggly, pale beard. He lacked the crackling vigor and brute strength of Muza Aben, but he had something else—a sharp, incisive mind capable of shrewd tactical planning. From his aloof manner and rigid bearing Francho guessed his men were more afraid of him than fond of him, a good reason why he remained in a somewhat secondary position to the inspiring Muza Aben Gazul.

Reduan's conversation, as Francho overheard it, was terse and laconic. He had a slight tic on the right side of his face, which grew more pronounced when he seemed to be bored. What communicated itself to Francho's covert study was that the man was an egoist, even more a lover of self and of power than an idealistic patriot. The unsupported impression was not productive for the moment, but Francho stored it away.

If the lavish banquet was a personal triumph for Boabdil, who for once was given the obsequious respect he craved— although Francho suspected this was because the lesser aristocrats merely followed the example of Yussef Abencerrage and Ahmad Zegri, whose superficial homage mirrored their relief to have the throne out of each other's grasp—it was also an artist's triumph for Francho, whose name was announced in the entertainments by Boabdil himself and later shouted out by the delighted guests sitting on low banquettes around the walls, who pelted him with flowers and money and did not allow him to resume his seat at the steps of the Sultan's dais for an hour. A flush of pleasure rose to color the strong planes of his face, and his heart squeezed with the impossible wish that somehow Tendilla, di Lido, Nunez, Leonora, Dolores, his friends and even his foes could hear the cries and loud finger snapping for his talent. If he grinned and swaggered back to his place, none could blame him, he excused himself.

The day after, a colorful tournament was held on the Vivarrambla, impressive with the experienced arms and caparisoned, trained steeds of the most daring of Granada's knights. But Francho's frustrated longing to lock weapons with them was somewhat mitigated later as he read a missive received from Tendilla: the Lady Fatima and her entire company had been waylaid in a short battle at Espinos and were now captive at Alcala la Real. The Count also mentioned laconically that the lady comported herself graciously and did not seem at all distressed at this interruption of her nuptual journey—or even with the loss of her considerable marriage portion.

Hardly a few hours later the Vizier Comixa, waving a message recounting the ambush, rushed in horror to the Sultan's chambers, where the ruler was relaxing with his wife Morayama and watching his Head Musician teach one of his little daughters how to finger the guembri. Salaaming to the ground until his old bones nearly creaked, the distraught uncle feverishly requested of Boabdil one hundred Christian captives from the Alhambra dungeons to add to the ransom of gold and pearls he was collecting to offer.

A secret smirk lit Francho's inner being, both for the feeling of power that coursed its way through him and also in behalf of one virgin given at least reprieve from an arranged marriage that had evidently chilled her heart.

Boabdil's anger with this Christian coup prompted a stern decree that in no case would any more Christian captives be ransomed, regardless of rank or circumstance. In the same communiqué informing Tendilla of this, Francho had also added: "I pray you, my lord, give up the enclosed letter into the hands of Doña Leonora de Zuniga. . . ."

The euphoria of his triumphs, however, did not last and soon a melancholy gripped him which he tried to keep to himself. To everyone about him Jamal ibn Ghulam was the same strapping, cheerful musician as ever, even a bit grander in fact as the Sultan's unending largesse afforded him more sumptuous tunics, bright leather shoes, big gold rings, and even a slave boy to bring his meals. But when he was alone in his own small garden he wandered about disconsolate, plucking idly at the leafy shrubs. He swam more fiercely than ever, and his wrestling partners complained he seemed to want to kill them. His moodiness did not escape the Sultan, who had an uncanny sensitivity to unhappiness and who believed for some reason that Jamal yet grieved for the sweetheart he had found murdered in Malaga. Francho did not deny it.

They were alone one early spring day, almost a year after Jamal ibn Ghulam's arrival in Granada, moving about huge ivory chess pieces on an inlaid gold-and-onyx board when Boabdil raised his head and regarded his companion, perhaps a decade his junior, with a paternal air.

"You ought to take a wife to you, Jamal. There is only one cure for the loss of love gone forever, and that is the love of another. In your position you can negotiate for a woman of decent upbringing and with reasonable dowry."

"Great Sultan, I just am not made to forget that easily. Some men love once and that is all." Francho stretched muscles cramped from sitting still and concentrating too long.

"Then you must have a concubine who you need not love but who will at least warm you at night and fill the empty hours. Come now, Jamal. Who can live like a hermit and be surrounded by the sensuous beauty of this, my glorious Granada? Whichever of my many palace women catches your eye, that one you need only ask for. You can glimpse them on their way to the outer court to buy their baubles and trinkets."

Not to seem ungrateful for Boabdil's genuine concern for his well-being, Francho first smiled and then looked thoughtful for a moment. "Well, perhaps you are right, Excellence. But I need a while longer yet to mourn, else I reproach myself for taking too lightly the tragic death of my lady."

Boabdil tossed him a golden-skinned Safary peach, the first of the season. "In a few months, then, singer of songs, remind me of my promise. For a man like you, to live without the affection of a woman is unhealthy."

But Francho did not want a concubine. He wanted Leonora. And thus he wanted the snow to fully melt in the high mountains so that the main Spanish forces could come through the passes and the final war could begin, the faster to get him home.

The Darro and Xenil rivers were already rising higher in their beds with the snow melt, and so a week later he was not surprised to see Muza Aben's ebullient troops returning with hundreds of booty-laden mules and donkeys and a long, wretched line of dirty prisoners. Francho was just returning from a visit with old Zemel, the hospitable artist who had fashioned the beautiful, crooked-neck lute whose tone had captured both the Sultan and the Sultan's guests, but this time he had gone to commission a gilded minstrel's harp, for the Sultana Morayama had shyly mentioned that she much admired the sound of that celestial instrument.

Bemused by the memory of Zemel's gossipy tales of the Spanish, Sicilian, and French families whose members had in the past purchased his famous instruments, Francho pulled the mule he rode into a cross street to allow Muza Aben's lumbering cortege to go through. From the number of burdened animals and the captured banners displayed upside down it was obvious that several large merchant caravans had also been waylaid in addition to the herds and goods and dwellers taken from raided towns.

And then one pennon struck his eye like a physical blow—a golden antelope on a field of blue—and he swung sharply around in his saddle to stare at it fluttering upside down from the lance of a chain-mailed Moorish knight. With a growing dread he turned his attention to the file of captives now plodding past and ran his gaze over the weary, frightened faces of the couple of hundred Spanish villagers, merchants, muleteers, guards, and peasants trudging along with bound hands, wailing children running along at their mothers' skirts. And then, as he hoped he wouldn't, he spotted Dolores at the very rear of the file of prisoners.

A susceptible, mustachioed sergeant had allowed her to ride on a baggage donkey, for the delicate leather shoes peeping from under her ripped skirt were in tatters. She kept the hood of her dusty velvet cloak drawn to shadow her grime-streaked face, and she cradled in her arms the rag-wrapped infant of the woman walking beside her, but she jogged along as erect as if the mule were a white mare with gilded hooves, and she stared out of proud, reddened eyes at the grinning, gratified

445

citizens of Granada, who lined the way, hooting. Oh yes, it was Dolores, indeed, and after the initial disbelieving shock of seeing her in such a plight an unreasoning stab of anger cut through Francho.

Idiota! How had she come to get herself captured? She must have been traveling near the border, and by herself evidently, since Medina-Sidonia's guards or banners were not to be seen. Francho's life, his mission was proceeding smoothly. Why had she to roll up a boulder into his path? At last, resignedly, he urged his mount to fall in with one of the soldiers bringing up the rear of the slow procession. "And do you take all these Christian scum to the Alhambra dungeons?" he asked, with mild curiosity.

The soldier glanced at Francho's long brocade coat and medallion of service to the Sultan and answered politely, "No, *sayed,* these all go to the Alcazaba. Now that none can be ransomed the palace cells are too good for them." The man snorted companionably and grinned. "But if you see one of them that pleases your eye, *sayed,* these are all the able-bodied and will be sold for slaves shortly. If I were a rich man," he winked, "there is one flame-haired wench up ahead I would spend some dinars for."

Francho smiled back. "And when will this particular slave auction be held, should I be in need of servants?"

"In a day or two, as soon as they are inspected by the slave masters and the best of the lot cleaned up and put in shape to bring more money. The sales of these captives go fast. 'Tis strange you are not aware of them. Most gentlemen are anxious to obtain a Christian dog, especially of some breeding, to wash their feet. Prices will rise higher now, now that the Sultan has forbidden ransom, and the 'betters' will be on the market."

Francho slipped a dirham into the brawny hand and rode off scowling down a side street leading toward the palace. The day, which had started so pleasantly, with no complications, was ruined. He certainly could not allow Dolores to be sold as a concubine or slave, or even suffer her to languish in the dripping and rat-infested cells below the Alcazaba. Most probably she had not been molested by her captors; she was obviously a lady of quality and the habit of treating the wealthy less roughly because of the ransom they would command was engrained. But now, once dragged onto the selling block, Dolores would no longer be a high-born lady—she would be reduced to a female of no rights, a property, a slave, a body to be used and abused if such was her owner's bent. That could not happen. He would have to purchase her himself, even if sheltering her involved taking her into his confidence, although he was sure there was one thing he could trust Papa el Mono's daughter not to do—not to rat.

Plague on the female, anyhow! Why couldn't she have stayed where she belonged, safely in Seville enjoying the largesse of her aging Duke. A jolting thought suddenly crossed his mind. Even in her dishevelment Dolores would draw the eye of every man who came to the sale, and many of them would be very rich, with many concubines already in their women's quarters. And even with the considerable gold he had accumulated in gifts from the Sultan and other admirers of his talent, he could never match these inveterate buyers of choice female flesh. Never. But there was Boabdil—

Stopped in midstride at the entrance to the Sultan's private saloon by the sinewy arm of M'jambana, Francho made out from the mute's hand gestures that Boabdil dined with the gentle Morayama this late afternoon and wished to be alone with his wife. Suffering an uncomfortable pang behind his breastbone, whether from annoyance to have to bide his time or jealousy of Boabdil's idyll, perhaps both, Francho asked M'jambana to bring word when the Sultan could see him, even if for a moment, no matter what time. He made his way back to his chamber, where a palace lackey had already lit his oil lamps, and picked up a volume of Jorge Manrique's *Coplas,* that great, sonorous elegy which he was rereading in Arabic translation. He tried to concentrate, to relax his taut facial muscles, but with little success. He knew that his excitement was not just because of his need to rescue Dolores from disappearing forever into some rich Moor's harem, but that it was caused by Dolores herself, her presence in Granada, and he remembered the peculiar skip of his heart and the palpitation of joy that had flooded through him at the sight of her on that donkey not twenty paces distant from where he sat his horse. He felt a shameful thrill of power humming through him now to know she was dependent on him for her freedom, maybe even her life.

Remembering his lascivious dreams his stomach muscles tightened again, and a heat began rising in his face as he wondered, not without more shame, how grateful would she be? Villain! Varlet! He slapped the book down in disgust for his baseness, growling and muttering to himself through his forked black beard, and launched himself across the couch at the brass table standing there in order to fill his empty innards with nuts and candied fruit and halava and give himself something to do. He had finally dozed off when, hours later, the huge mute tapped softly on his door to fetch him.

He found the Sultan sitting bare-chested, being prepared for bed by several servants softly padding about him. Boabdil's smooth, tan skin was stretched over a fine-boned frame that was well proportioned if a bit narrow in the shoulder. A scattering of dark strands on his chest ran down in a line to disappear into the broad silk sash wrapped about his waist. His brown hair was tousled by the unwinding of his cloth-of-silver turban. He looked boyish, relaxed, and more assured, as he had been ever since his defiance of the implacable foe to the north had gained him what he hungered for—greater respect from his subjects. He watched Francho approach with a mild expression on his face, and his eyes crinkled in a huge yawn as he suffered his valet to pull off his low, gilded boots. "What is it, Jamal? I told M'jambana I do not require you for tonight; you should take advantage of such freedom. Repose has not avoided me lately and I am tired from an—um—exalted evening." His smile was sleepily suggestive.

Francho immediately fell to his knees in a deep salaam. "A boon, a Great Sultan, I beg a boon," he cried. "I have come to remind you of a promise you made to me."

The urgency in his voice prompted a sharp glance of curiosity from Boabdil. Waving his valets away from his couch to keep them from removing his pantaloons, he complained, "Can it not wait until the morning, minstrel? Must what you wish be accomplished in the dead of night?" He yawned again, significantly, but anyhow in curiosity cocked an eyebrow. The self-contained ibn Ghulam had never asked for anything before.

"Morning might be too late, Great Sultan. I beg your indulgence now, Excellence." Francho's ordinarily resonant voice was muffled because his turbaned head was still touching the floor.

"Well, look up, look up, singer of songs. Since when are you so abject? This favor you crave must be no less than half my realm." Boabdil chuckled, amused and intrigued. He was in an expansive mood and wondering what his musician could so suddenly need.

"Excellence, today I saw the new captives brought in by Muza Aben Gazul and his cavalry. There was one among them, a well-born young woman, so she seemed by her dress and demeanor, who took both my eye and my breath. It's of her I beg leave to speak."

The Sultan leaned forward, more than curious, now, his hands braced on his thighs. "Is this a tall lady with hair of auburn and great doe eyes the color of silvered smoke?"

Francho blinked. "But—how does the Sultan know this? Have you already viewed the captives, then?"

The indulgent smile seemed to wipe itself from Boabdil's face, to be replaced with a petulant droop. "No, I have not seen this damsel. But not an hour ago this self-same female was described to me by another petitioner. It seems she is of the nobility, a Baroness de la Rocha, and she has made great issue that she is under the protection of one of Ferdinand's council, the Duke of Medina-Sidonia, who will happily pay a good ransom for her so she insists. As I am sure he would. But Tendilla's scurrilous refusal to release the ward of my Grand Vizier has sealed this woman's doom, and no matter her station or offer of gold, she will be sold as a slave."

"Indeed, Excellence, as is right, an eye for an eye," Francho agreed. "But in this captive my soul has trembled to see a woman whose attributes match that of my departed love. Excellence, I would have this Christian female as concubine. All prisoners are yours until they are sold. Once you offered me any slave in the palace. Now, O most generous of rulers, I beg you to sell this one slave to me."

Tranquility disappeared entirely from Boabdil's face; he threw up his hands and rolled his eyes to heaven in exasperation. "Allah have mercy, I would gladly give you the wench as a gift had I known sooner you desired her, musician. But I have already given my promise to sell her elsewhere."

Francho rocked backward on his heels, taken aback. "Promised her! To whom? When?" he demanded, unheeding of the impudence of his questions.

"Tonight, as I said. To my good general Reduan of the house of Venegas, whose request I cannot refuse. Tomorrow he will install her in his harem." Boabdil moved his shoulders uncomfortably under Francho's stricken expression and looked away, rubbing at the stubble of beard on his cheek. "I am truly sorry, my friend. But I am also happy that your heart is free of the grave at last. Perhaps there is another among the captives or here in my house that will please you as well, now your mourning has passed. A Moslem woman of soft voice, more obedient than those haughty Castilians. . . ."

"You promised my choice of your women when I was ready, Excellence," Francho answered bitterly, aware he sounded like a spoiled child but needing to maneuver in the desperate tug-of-war. "You tell me you are happy the veil of grief has been lifted away from my eyes. Yet the very female whose face has accomplished this you will not give to me."

"*Can* not, Jamal," Boabdil stated with a frown. He impatiently motioned Francho to rise from his knees and indicated he should sit on a pillow beside the couch. "I have given my pledge to General Reduan."

"Reduan Venegas has a harem bulging with women. This one will merely amuse him for a time and then he will forget her. And she looks so much like my poor Sobeida. I have great need of her to mend my broken heart, to comfort me and remove my loneliness. You have made a promise to me also, Great Sultan," he pressed on intensely, a proud man just on the threshold of pleading.

Chin jutted out in annoyance, Boabdil yanked the satin coverlet from his couch to wrap about his naked chest— although the valet knelt in the background with his linen shirt, not daring to approach—and stalked to a low table. He waved away the shadowlike servant who had rushed to pour him some wine and decanted it himself. "Well, what would you have me do, minstrel?" he asked. "Break my word to Reduan and thus anger him, a powerful noble and an officer of great importance to my army?"

"While I am of no importance at all . . ." Francho's voice trailed off morosely.

"Yes, you are important to me, personally. But Reduan is necessary to the freedom of Granada."

"And will the removal of one Christian wench from his grasp erase his loyalty to Granada, Excellence?" This was an insolence for which another ruler might have had him punished.

"Will the denial of the pretty-faced Goth ruin your loyalty

450

to me?" Boabdil demanded softly, locking his brown stare with Francho's relentless blue one.

Francho's gaze was unwavering. "Great Sultan, my loyalty was given, not bought, nor can it be sold along with a slave woman. Rather would I leave your employ than know you trust my integrity so little. I am neither slave like M'jambana nor an adoring dumb beast like that huge cat which stares so balefully at me from the foot of your couch. Perhaps I sometimes speak my mind with what seems disregard for your royal eminence, but I am your most loyal of subjects, not merely because you are my liege lord and the Sultan of Granada, but because through the love of the art of music there has been forged a bond of respect and friendship between two human beings. My Sultan, I ask you for the woman; I have been taken with her and I desire her. If I cannot have her I will be sad that my lord has broken his promise to me—and that is all."

Francho was the first to drop his eyes from the silent dismay that went between them. Distress that was very real showed in the line of his slumped shoulders and lowered head. Strangely enough, had he truly been born Jamal ibn Ghulam, every word he had uttered would have been true. For all Boabdil's incompetence and indecision, Jamal had come to like the Sultan and would have stayed loyal to him through every adversity, stupid as such blind friendship might prove. The musician Jamal, absorbed by his art, narrow in his needs, was a much less complicated man than Francisco de Mendoza, born Venegas. The sensitivity, gentleness, and generosity Jamal liked in Boabdil might have been derided by the harder, more ambitious Christian knight.

Visibly upset by Francho's dejected feelings, the Sultan clenched his jaw, considered a moment, and finally tossed down the last of the wine in his golden cup with a resolute air. "Very well. You shall have your slave girl, Jamal ibn Ghulam, but not as payment for your loyalty. As appreciation for your simplicity. You do not confuse me; black is black and white is white. You do not lie and I am grateful for that. I am also a man to whom the Great Allah has presented a wife of virtue and perfection, I know the joy of this. If you think you can gentle this tempestuous Christian to such a state, I will not deny your woman to you." He struck a small brass gong and the metallic boom vibrated through the room. "Reduan Venegas may be a powerful general but I am Sultan. I shall tell him I have seen the female in question and have decided to reserve her for my own harem. There is an unusual girl in my harem who was a gift from the Caliph of Smyrna, a slender female from somewhere beyond Trebizond, golden-skinned, with long, silky black hair and slanted eyes, and a mouth like the bud of a flower—and this one, with her pagan name, will I present to Reduan for consolation."

A secretary entered the room, salaaming, to attend the Sultan's call. "I shall have your Christian moved to my women's quarters this very night and spare her the lice of the dungeons. My women will instruct her so she will know her place and her duties. And soon you may claim her."

Francho struck his chest in salute, relief lighting up his face. He made a deep salaam.

The Sultan motioned him out.

"Now go and let me sleep. I am twice as weary as when you arrived."

With heartfelt expressions of thanks Francho backed away toward the door but before he could exit Boabdil called out, "Jamal!"

"Excellence?"

The Sultan was smiling wanly again. "Reduan was told by the examiners that she is without maidenhead. She is young but she is not virgin."

"No matter, Excellence, I want her still." Francho controlled the outrage suddenly constricting his chest at the thought of fingers poking and prying into Dolores.

"You are indeed an odd one, minstrel. One minute you are a completely contained man with a strong control of emotion which you deem 'armor'; and the next minute you cannot live without the company of a particular, unknown female who somehow has reached your heart."

Nonplussed for a second, confronted as he was with contradictions caused by his duplicity, Francho's mind yet worked. He pulled back his shoulders and grinned jauntily. " 'Tis simple to explain, my Sultan. I suffer the mercurial temperament of a true and most unique artist!"

Boabdil's appreciative chuckle followed him through the portal.

452

But once outside the bedchamber Francho's grin faded, he drew a deep breath for the first time in half an hour and nervously rubbed his sweaty palms on his brocade-covered thighs. He had managed to snatch Dolores away from a Moorish harem and Reduan's couch. Now what was he going to do with her?

❦ *Chapter 22* ❧

DOLORES JERKED HER shoulder away from the prodding hands of the two red-sashed black-skinned guards driving her along a columned, open-sided gallery, but she quickened her pace to keep them from touching her again. She was dimly aware of fantastic, arabesqued arches and ceilings overhead, golden-washed by the soft light of hanging oil lamps, aware that her purchaser lived in splendor. But to her the veritable palace was uglier than the cracked-walled tavern she was raised in.

She did not cry anymore. She had run out of tears on the long, hard trek through the mountains, when for warmth at each stop during the day she huddled together on the ground with the village women and listened to their sobs while she pretended a noblewoman did not weep. But she had wept later, silently, in the dark, with grief at Engracia's accidental death as they had fled from the Moorish patrol, from panic, from fear too, even certain as she was that Medina-Sidonia would ransom her and that the fiercely bearded, mustachioed soldiers would not dare to mistreat her as they were the shrieking country women who had neither the youth nor the comeliness to be considered for sale as concubines.

But on what proved to be the last night of the march, as she rubbed her blistered and painful feet and sat drooping, half-supporting and half-supported by the back of another

woman, a passing officer, scimitar and spurs clinking, stopped
to chuck her under the chin. His eyes mocked her in the light
of the small fire, and he delighted in informing her in
Castilian that she could forget her fine airs; didn't she know
the Sultan no longer ransomed prisoners? Her only value now
was as merchandise on the slave block. He and his fellow
officers only saw to her safety because they would get a share
of the good price she would bring. And with a contemptuous
laugh he went on, fading into the darkness. Tears started from
her eyes again, tears of despair, for he was not just tormenting
her, she fully understood. He was telling the truth.

The slave block! Was this how her life was to conclude, in
the degradation of a heathen harem? Was this where the hard
road from Ciudad Real to Torrejoncillos to her lovely house in
Seville was to end? She had heard the tales of Arab harems,
stolen women clapped up in them and never seen or heard
from again and all sorts of foul deeds perpetrated upon their
shrinking bodies. Was this her punishment for daring to usurp
Blanca Ganavet's place? Dear Lord, be merciful, she prayed
forlornly over and over with an aching lump caught in her
throat, do not abandon this penitent sinner. . . .

She could not run; the guards were alert and her feet and
hands were chained with just enough slack to allow her to
walk and minister to herself. She could kill herself, she
thought, hugging clasped hands hard to her chest, but with
what? The mountains where she could have hobbled to a cliff
and flung herself off were behind them. Did she want to die?
Oh no, no dear Mary, merciful Mother of God, she had hardly
yet lived. Frightened, she could find no peace in sleep that
whole night but slumped swollen-eyed, tears leaking down her
face that such fate could happen, that she was helpless and
entirely alone and destined to be sold like an animal into the
hands of who-knew-what degraded and pitiless slave owner.

Just before the guards came to rouse the captives and fling
them some bread and a small water skin to share, the rosy
light of dawn woke her from a half-doze, and she forced open
her eyes to the sight of a cloudless sky and a wheeling, piping
white bird making great, free circles on stiff wings high above
their weary columns. It made her remember Dalila and think
of the indomitable will and deadly strike of what was after all
just a small parcel of feathers and claws, and a trickling of
courage began to stiffen her depressed spirit. The cool morning breeze rippled across the fallow field where they had spent

the night, and even with her tear-stuffed nose she could sniff the scent of flowering vines from the bowers shading the white farmhouses beyond the road. She wiped her nose with the wide, bedraggled sleeve of her gown, poured a drop of water on a clean corner of it, and patted her eyes to refresh them.

The brightening light of a fine day seemed to reassure her that life was not over yet, dredging up her normal mettle. If it came to that, if she was offered and sold as a slave, no matter whether she was bound to harem or kitchens, there would always be an escape, a window to leap from, a pool to drown in, a sash to hang herself with. But a mirthless chuckle escaped her as her stubbornness reasserted itself: "Ay, mi madre, Dolores, you even have yourself believing you were born a lady. Noblewomen commit suicide. Common women, such as you, live." She pressed her lips together, and when a young officer approached her as they began the march she intensified her painful limping, showed him with a piteous look her lacerated feet, and hoped that greed to deliver her unmutilated would move him.

It did and she rode on a donkey through the double gates of Granada. She rode tearless and numb, as unmoved by pleasure at the sight of the beautiful city rising on its hills as any captive would be on viewing her destined prison.

With the main column of soldiers peeling off to their barracks, a smaller force herded the stumbling prisoners into the high-walled court of a forbidding edifice, lined them up, and made them stand as clerks moved down their ranks recording them and fastening numbers to their garments with sharp thorns. Raising her head Dolores saw the officer in charge salute a finely mantled Moor, the end of whose turban rose in a stiffened cockade above his head. Easily keeping in hand a prancing, head-tossing stallion, the Moor rode casually along the ragged lines of woebegone captives, looking them over. She saw him look directly at her, as if her eyes had called him.

Cursing herself for a curious ninny, Dolores ducked her head and tried to look inconspicuous as she stood amid the trembling women and sniveling children, but in a moment the rider had halted his mount before her. The man motioned sharply, and a soldier jumped to jerk down the hood that shadowed her face; she raised her head up to keep the soldier from yanking her hair to do it for her. She thought her face must be smudged and tear-streaked, and because she had lost her small hennin and hair pins her locks hung tangled and dirty about her face. She looked straight ahead, praying she was unattractive enough to discourage the attention of the flat-faced, sparse-bearded man who scrutinized her closely from his high perch.

But his grunt was low and meaningful, and the quick upward glance she stole was enough to freeze her heart. His covetous expression was not new to her, she had seen it on male faces before, surprised it even in the eyes of those old-fashioned men of chivalry who declaimed women as fragile flowers of innocence to whom they offered only purest thoughts. She had, in fact, reveled in the flattery of those lustful stares, when she was safe enough. Now, shrinking from the portent of it, she blurted out desperately, "Sir, I believe you are a gentleman. I am the Baroness Dolores de la Rocha; I am a lady to the Queen Isabella and I claim the protection of the Duke of Medina-Sidonia. I beg you to inform His Excellence, the Sultan, of my plight. If he will notify Don Enrique de Guzman through the Crown's couriers any ransom he asks will be honored."

The Moor continued to regard her without change of expression, his eyes moving over her like an insult. Finally the straight and humorless lips moved. "Woman, I have two Christian Counts, a Marquis, and a dozen lesser nobles slaving out their lives in my copper mine in the mountains. The followers of Allah do not pamper dogs of infidels who murder women and children and exile whole cities of people from their homes. But you may consider yourself fortunate. Comely women do not bend their backs in the mining pits. There are better uses for them." He spoke in Castilian so she would understand, but he need not have said anything; his flinty eyes and toneless voice told the tale.

He motioned again and the alert soldier yanked the entire cloak from Dolores's grasp. The hard eyes seemed to flick the clothes from her body, measuring her. Then, with a stiff nod and a sideways jerk of his head toward the building, he picked up his reins, turned the horse and passed on. Two soldiers came from behind him, grabbed Dolores by the arms, and marched her away from the rest of the captives and into the prison building. Up and down stone steps they dragged her until she found herself dumped into a dark cell with a tiny, high window allowing the feeblest blue glimmer of daylight. Overcome with despair because the grim-mouthed Moor had obviously separated her out for his own purpose, she sank bonelessly to the stone floor.

A whimper escaped in spite of herself as she huddled in the rank darkness. "Oh, blessed Mary, Mother of God, take me away from here. This cannot be happening to me. . . ." She tried to pray eloquently, but her captors had not even left her her garnet and silver rosary, and in her extremity she could call up nothing but the Pater Noster. Finally, in what seemed hours of fear listening to the heavy silence about her punctuated only by the scrabbling of mice in the shadows, the weighty door to her cell scraped and creaked back and a yellow circle of light bloomed to reveal a turbaned little jailer holding pike and keys and wearing a vest of heavy leather straps over his tunic. Behind him crowded two burly women with long plaits down their backs whose somber tunics swung over baggy pants and who pushed aside the obsequious jailer like a useless sack of beans.

Silently, with no ado, the matrons went sternly to their business. Dolores gasped as the larger one grabbed her and hauled her up like a feather, in one expert motion twisting her arm behind her back so that any movement would wrench it from her shoulder, pinioning as well her other arm and body close to her own mountain of flesh. The other woman methodically pulled off or ripped off what was left of the clothes from her flinching limbs until Dolores stood naked but immobile in the iron clutch of her great-bosomed captor. Goose-pimpling, she had no choice but to suffer the expert examination of the main matron. The woman's sharp eyes moved carefully over her. Squeezing Dolores's jaws together painfully the strong hands forced her to open her mouth and in the light of the two lanterns they had brought the woman scrutinized her teeth and the lining of her mouth for sores, and then examined her scalp for vermin. The questing fingers ran down her neck, pinched her breasts and her buttocks, pressed her ribs and upper arms, raised her hands and her feet to inspect them closely.

Then the fat, cold hands moved slowly over her thighs and hips, lingering, giving them small, suggestive squeezes that caused Dolores to look up startled into the dark, glittering eyes.

Unable to move without causing an excruciating yank on her arm, Dolores submitted to the rest of the examination, grinding her eyes shut through most of the indignity, managing not to squeal when the woman smiled and maliciously pinched her nipple hard between a rough thumb and forefinger.

With a sly smile on her face, the examiner then bent for the two lanterns and moved them to illuminate a mound of dank straw that evidently served as a pallet. Dolores grunted as her strapping captor clamped tighter the arm about her waist and lifted her bodily off the floor, ignoring her wild kicking to carry her to the pallet and toss her upon her back with a snort. The woman immediately flopped right across her, pinning her down but at least shifting her mass so that her victim was not suffocated. The other examiner knelt by her feet, grabbing her ankles, and forcing up her legs so that her knees bent. Suddenly she felt her thighs shoved roughly apart, in spite of her straining resistance, and the matron easily introduced her shoulder and a stiff arm between them to keep them spread.

"Do not fight us, stupid wench, and you will not be hurt. Goods to be sold must first be examined," the woman holding her down barked in her ear.

This was a nakedness so humiliating, so bereft of any humanity or grace, that Dolores's eyes leaked tears of shame, her skin shrinking in dread, as if her body were being spitted and rent in two. Her eyes, darting about in helplessness, caught the jailer at the edge of the circle of light as he licked his lips and grabbed excitedly at his groin. Humming hoarsely the examiner ran her fleshy hand down Dolores's quivering thigh, kneading the softness of it, and just as quickly the hand returned to Dolores's knee to keep her legs from closing.

Dazed with horror Dolores heard herself squeal in shock from the painful scrape of a nail as a long, fat finger was jammed into the tight opening of her female place, pulled back, and jammed farther in. For a moment the finger relentlessly forced forward against the resistance of the dry passage, stopped and then wiggled forward again slowly, cautiously probing. Gritting her teeth in hurt, Dolores squealed again as the ragged fingernail tore at her tender tissues.

"Hee, hee," the jailer giggled in the shadows, frantically pumping his hand up and down at his crotch. "Hee, hee . . ."

Dolores tried to move her buttocks. "Be still, wench, and you won't be damaged." The giantess holding her wheezed garlicky breath into her face. "We must see what price you'll bring. If you've got it you'll be worth more. Stupid Christian bitch," she cried, jerking away as Dolores tried to spit in her face, and in punishment she applied more of her considerable weight to the daintier ribs under hers.

Then the long finger suddenly rammed forward inside Dolores like a sword of fire, thrusting all the way into her as far up as it would go, and its tip touched for a second something so pristine and protected that a faintness passed over her and she thought she would vomit. The finger withdrew.

"Nah, she's broken. But she's very tight. She hasn't had very much," the examiner rasped, sitting back on her heels. She showed Dolores a gap-toothed grin that disappeared into hard cheeks. "Had a good time once or twice, did you, eh, Christian trull? It might cost you plenty. The best of them out there buy little virgins, twelve, thirteen years. You are old. You are a fornicator. You will go to a shopkeeper to be taken on the floor, or sent to the kitchen to scour pots."

The other sounded surprised. "But Gamala, the warder said—"

"Shut your mouth," Gamala ordered, harshly. "Can't you see this wench is cold." On hands and knees she stretched her bulk to reach Dolores's ruined wool cloak. She flung it over both her trembling prisoner and the arms of the matron pinning her down.

"You're worth nothing if you become sick," she explained to her victim. The dark, hawk-nosed face hovered again above Dolores's kneecaps and again her thighs were harshly shoved apart. With a laugh that was a low rumble in her chest Gamala asked, "Would you like some more fun, eh, little kitten?" The matron's voice had gone oily, but with an edge of excitement in it. "Like this? Like this, maybe?" Deliberately she held up the long third finger she had used to probe Dolores before, stuck it in her mouth to wet it and with an evil grin slowly reinserted the long, fat digit into Dolores's quivering body.

"Hee hee, hee hee . . ." The voice from the shadows shot up into an idiotic falsetto.

In spite of her eyes squeezed shut and shuddering knees Dolores could not keep from reacting and heard herself cry out in pain and mortification as the woman forced another finger inside as well. She heard the female holding her heave up to thrust a pudgy hand beneath her own voluminous tunic. Dolores cried out again and tried to writhe away from the rasping hurt.

460

She heard a great snort of laughter from the matron at her knees, and suddenly the fingers were pulled out. The woman who was sprawled on top of her gurgled wildly and then moaned.

Gamala sneered with wicked pleasure. "Ah, what's the matter? You don't enjoy it, Christian pig?" She got to her feet ponderously, wiping her fingers off on her stained tunic. "Too bad. For the joy of that you will have to beg your master's pleasure and kiss his feet. Christian whore! He will suck you up like marrow from a bone and then toss you forever away. The other doll-faced women in your harem will be your only relief—if you don't get caught making love to your own sex and your skin flayed away from your living body."

She kicked her lolling assistant in the shin and barked, "Well, let her up, Fatima, we're done with this rubbish." And she watched the heavy woman struggle to her feet. Then she picked up the lantern, turned, and pushed past the gaping jailer. "Gather up those keys, you pin-headed slobbermouth, and let us out. You've had your fun, worm." Although she glared as she ordered the concave, grinning jailer to move, he complied with little speed and with no concern about the wet stain on the lower part of his tunic. They all three trudged out silently in the bobbling lantern light, without a backward glance.

The dark that surrounded Dolores again was now blessed, for it hid her abasement. Slowly she sat up on the straw and huddled into her cloak, hugging her knees, rocking back and forth to dry, harsh sobs that rose from the bottom of her soul. The place between her thighs burned and pained like a raw cut. She felt hot, feverish, as she rocked herself back and forth devastated by shame. Violated by a woman! By fingers! Never had she heard of such a thing. It was vile, it was base. Back and forth Dolores rocked, back and forth, hating her body as dirty, defiled, sunk in humiliation.

At length her mind found the intelligence to whisper to her, "Of course. It is exactly the way that evil one wanted you to feel. She is no less a tormenter than any black-hooded wielder of burning iron, and just as experienced with cruelty. Will you hate your flesh for being flesh? Could you better withstand the boot or the strappado?" she implored herself. She stopped rocking and laid her aching head on her arms.

Finally, she calmed down, exhausted. The chill of the stone walls began to creep into her bones. She straightened her legs and crawled stiffly to where she remembered her clothes had been dropped. She felt around with a trembling hand, touched cloth, then sat up and slowly drew the garments on. Her sense of degradation began to ameliorate somewhat with the familiar feel and dignity of chemise, stockings, and gown to clothe her, torn as they were; her self-esteem as a worthy child of God trickled back. But the hateful memory of being restrained naked on the musty straw and of suffering the sexual insistence of the cunning, dirty fingers, lurked. She could not forget the sight of the matron's hawk-nosed, thin-lipped face and glistening eyes, leering, urging her to respond. . . .

Bruised and aching, she crawled back over the cold stone floor to the straw and lay down, bundling herself in her cloak. The silent blackness rang shrilly in her ears except for a muffled drip, drip of water coming from somewhere. She shivered in misery. What was going to happen to her? O Holy Mother, help me, she whimpered, I am repentant for all my sins. She sniffed and sighed and prayed, and at some point she fled into sleep.

She was torn away from the depth of her exhausted sleep by the clank and creak of the cell door opening and opened her eyes to see once again the lanky jailer appear in a pool of lantern light, but solemn this time and followed by four blank-faced, pantalooned African guards. Two of them strode forward, either to pull her up or help her up. In spite of her muzziness she scrambled to her feet first and stood stiff-backed in her cloak, warning them with her eyes not to touch her. Thus, with two guards leading and two following, she found herself exiting from the terrible cell, retracing the torch-lit way she had come before, and being marched into the prison courtyard, where a litter awaited. The guard held back the curtain for her to get in and watched her settle herself on the cushions. She felt the litter lifted on strong shoulders, and, swaying and bobbing, her conveyance was transported through the night-quiet city. To where she did not know, but to whom she was almost certain.

She believed she felt stronger; she must have slept for some hours in the cell, neutralizing some of the fatigue of a night without sleep and hours of tension and fright. Her mind was clearer. And firmly lodged in it was the determination to resist any further defilement of her soul, even if it meant death. She decided there was no use to try to jump from the litter as it

462

passed through the city, for an alert, scimitar-armed guard marched on either side. But she was not going to help them, like a lamb going meekly to the slaughter. When the litter was finally set down with a small thump she sat rigid and still until one of the men thrust in his turbaned head and a strong black arm unemotionally pulled her out.

Now, as they herded her deeper into the Moor's residence, she threw off their prodding hands with an angry jerk of her shoulder. The halls and plazas they traversed, overseen by silent, stationary guards, represented with their lavish, honeycombed traceries and Oriental arches an alien barrier between her and the world beyond Granada, and each confusing turn cut her off further from her past. A deepening sense of finality threatened to overturn her desperate bravado.

Her guards halted before a huge and ornately carved wooden gate, which looked to be blocking off an entire wing of her buyer's extravagant domicile. She did not understand the short exchange between her escort and the sentries guarding the portal, but her fear-sharpened hearing caught the word "harem," and a flare of panic made her whirl to escape, to run, to flee anywhere but forward, where a small door in the tall gates was at that moment flung open by a sentry. Two of her unblinking guards caught her by the arms, dragged her forward, and gave her a determined shove right through the shadowy square of the door so that she fell with a cry inside and landed on all fours. Before she could recover her breath and twist around the door had closed with a solid thunk and her fate was decided.

Getting to her feet she shrunk back against the heavy mahogany portals to see about her. She was in a roofed, fountained court festooned with many bronze hanging lamps, although only a few nightlamps by the gate were actually lit, casting a low pool of light at the entry. The mosaic floor under her feet was intricately patterned with vines that seemed in the gloom like writhing serpents. And from the shadows opposite someone was slip-slapping across the floor toward her. She put her hands behind her back to hide their shaking. If that cold-eyed Moor touched her she would scream loud enough to wake the dead.

But it was only a pantalooned woman, whey-faced and broad, who approached her in the dim circle of light from the hanging lamps. The woman halted and looked her over, arms akimbo, and then wordlessly moved to grasp her by the elbow. Twitching away Dolores growled, "If you so much as touch me, hag, I'll claw your eyes out!"

Thin eyebrows arched up in the fat face. "Foolish Christian goose! I'm not going to harm you," the woman wheezed in faulty Castilian. "I only want to show you where you can sleep." With her heavy arm she motioned toward a bead-curtained, horseshoe-arched doorway.

"I'm not going into that . . . that harem."

The woman snickered and crossed her arms again. "You are already in the harem, stupid, and the gates are barred, so make up your mind to that. These are the only locked portals in the wing; otherwise you can go where you wish and there is a comfortable couch awaiting you inside. But sleep on the cold floor here if you will, I don't care. It's your back, not mine."

"What . . . what are they doing in there?" Dolores could not keep the wary quaver from her voice.

"Are you crazy?" The woman's dark eyes squinted at her in disbelief. "Sleeping, of course. What do you think at this time of night? And so would I be, had I not been ordered to wait for you. Come along now and give me no more trouble." She turned and slip-slapped away, not looking back but muttering, "You Spanish females are all alike, fainting and fussing as if you were to be rent limb from limb. What fools!"

Dolores hesitated, but a despairing glance back at the closed and ponderous door in the gates convinced her she could not open them with only her bare fists. The woman thought she was a fool? Well, she would soon learn different. Meanwhile there was nothing to be gained by remaining in the entry plaza. So, with a leaden heart she followed after the stolid broad back wrapped in an embroidered shawl and passed through the clattering beads of a doorway. Then they went along an open gallery bordered by flowering shrubs and into a long, carpeted corridor lined with small, velvet-curtained chambers. The woman stopped before one of these and pulled aside the hanging, motioning Dolores in. The room was tiny, but it offered a low couch which was spread with a light woolen blanket and a round silk pillow. There was a small Persian carpet on the red-tiled floor and an inlaid tabouret, where a little oil lamp flickered.

The woman yawned hugely and with momentarily watering eyes announced, "I am the mistress of the harem. My name is

Sayeda Fawzia and my word here is law. If you obey and are
sweet and docile we shall have no problems. If you wish to
present a prickly exterior you will find we have many pinchers
with which to snip off your thorns." The dark eyes, stuck like
raisins in the pudding face, regarded Dolores unwaveringly
and with unmistakable authority. Yet Dolores did not feel
either malice or menace in that stare.

Fawzia wrinkled up her brown, oily nose as Dolores's tired
grip allowed her cloak to fall open. "Fagh! Do you Christians
never wash? Well, it's too late for that now, we shall have to
clean you up on the morrow." She bent at one wall to lift up a
low, carved screen on hinges and showed Dolores the porcelain pot behind it. "Now go to bed," she ordered curtly, and
turning her back on her new charge shuffled out, yawning.

Dolores's hands flew to her hips in a burst of high indignation. "How dare she!" she fumed to herself. "If she had slept
in the mud for four nights with a bunch of flea-ridden
peasants she would not smell like a violet either. The *puta!*"

Wearily she dropped her cloak and, removing the porcelain
pot from its niche, took care of an urgent need. She realized
her throat was uncomfortably dry, that she was suffering from
thirst, and at the same time noticed a small brass ewer and
cup behind the lamp on the tabouret. Relieving her thirst with
cool water she eyed the soft couch with a confused mixture of
longing and denial, unwilling to use anything belonging to her
captor. If she were clever and resourceful, she would now steal
from the chamber and find someplace to hide, someplace
where the dreadful Moor of the flat face would never find her.
But she was not clever tonight; she was tired and scared. She
needed the strength a good sleep would give her.

She rolled down her stockings and struggled off the remnants of her stained gown, remembering with a sad sigh the
solicitous ministering of poor Engracia. Sinking down on the
couch, she sourly eyed the narrow opening to her cubicle,
wishing there were a door with a stout bar instead of the velvet
curtain. But reason told her that there was little chance she
would be menaced at what was surely long past the midnight
hour. Sinking down, she lay back on the feather-filled mattress
and pulled up the blanket just for a moment before peeling off
her wilted shift, but her muscles simply refused to move
again. With a quivering sigh she closed her eyes to try to think,
and in moments unconsciousness took her.

* * *

Sunlight streaming through a narrow, grilled window awakened her as a barefooted serving girl with a nervous smile entered her cubicle to deposit a lacquered tray holding a round of flat bread, an orange, and a pungent hot drink. Dolores gobbled the bread and fruit. The drink she tasted warily and found too bitter. But the sleep, the food, the cheerful sunlight, and the cool air coming into her little cubicle lifted her spirits, and she felt her natural optimism flowing back. Maybe she would not have to forfeit her life to honor, crept into her mind. Somehow, someway, might she find a way to cheat this fate?

She was just picking her dirty gown off the floor to don it when the curtain was pushed aside by a healthy shove from Sayeda Fawzia. Behind her stood two attendants, arms akimbo but peering at Dolores with curiosity rather than threat.

"Allah preserve us!" the harem mistress cried out as she saw Dolores bend. "Don't touch that filthy thing." And she kicked Dolores's pile of ruined clothes into a corner. But a more friendly smile appeared on her fat, brown face when she noticed Dolores's frightened expression. "You needn't be upset, girl, you'll soon have other raiments, much finer indeed. Now come along with us; we must bathe you and get you clean."

Seen in the light of day the harem mistress seemed shorter and less imposing than the night before, although she now wore a fine orange damask tunic over white silk pantaloons and painted shoes with upturned toes and her dark hair was hidden by a beaded chiffon veil pinned at the nape and hanging down her back. The small eyes peering from the suety brown face were wide awake now, and they were bright with intelligence and shrewdness, but although they measured Dolores steadily, there was a certain sympathy within them that evinced to a disposition inclined toward tolerance if the lady were not crossed.

A bath? How could that hurt? Welcoming it, in fact, Dolores nodded in agreement, but did not smile back. She went with them without fuss into a nearby small and steamy bathchamber, which she later learned was one especially reserved for unwashed newcomers and women ending their week of bleeding. Her hope that she might be left alone to soak in a tub was immediately dashed, but she had not imagined such a scrubbing, rubbing, scraping, pummeling, and pounding as the two attendants gave her while Fawzia, seated on a stool, directed. She was made to step from marble tubs of hot water to ones filled with cold water, several times alternately boiling and freezing, and in between being soaped and rinsed and rubbed with cloths until her skin tingled. Then they wrapped her up in a type of fuzzy cotton cloth that swiftly soaked up the moisture clinging to her, and led her into another chamber, where she was made to lie on the pillows of an inclined wooden settle while her washed auburn locks were henna-tinted to a brighter red and combed out behind her to dry in the sunlight which poured through an arabesqued grill. The harem mistress, who had left after seeing her charge thoroughly parted from any vestige of dirt, now returned with several other attendants, these younger and chattering with each other. Smiling, they pattered in and busied themselves with beautifying the new arrival. They carefully slathered her with a slippery unguent and, wielding sharp razors which so intimidated her that she dared not move, scraped away every last hair on her body including that about her groin, which she was certain had to be a sin. The cuts and abrasions on her feet were treated with a stinging lotion, and with pumice stone they smoothed away callus from soles and ankles and roughness from her elbows. Her finger and toenails were carefully trimmed and cleaned, and to her astonishment the palms of her hands and soles of her feet were stained red and painted with white pigment in intricate designs.

All the while, droning from a high stool, a reader imparted to her from a scroll the iron-clad rules of concubinage, returning to the beginning each time the scroll came to an end and repeating. "Thy master is beloved of Allah, and thy master is thy lord. Thou shalt hear and obey thy master's every wish. Thou shalt anticipate his needs and fulfill them. Thou shalt crawl to his feet in thy abasement, and wash them gently in rose water and oil them. Thou shalt amuse thy master in one thousand different ways. Thou shalt answer thy master's desire upon the couch of love with thine own, and take him lovingly in thy hand. Thou shalt delight his eye with thy form and face, and his ear with thy soft voice, singing songs . . ."

At last Dolores stood upon her feet, still wrapped in her cotton cloth, to face Fawzia's critical scrutiny. Dolores felt that she virtually glowed from cleanliness, and to judge from the harem mistress's approving nods she probably did.

"Well, well, you appear a great deal more appetizing than

you did last night. You have beautiful hair, girl. Wavy and thick." Fawzia passed her hand lightly over Dolores's burnished mane cascading to the small of her back, and then stood back for a better look overall. "Your complexion cannot be faulted either—smooth and warm, like the blush of a peach. But you are too skinny." She looked down. "And your feet are too big."

"My feet are not big!" Dolores glared ungratefully. But she could not deny she felt wonderful, better than she had in weeks, the fatigue, depression, and panic scrubbed and massaged and powdered away by Fawzia cool-fingered assistants, the pleasure of being beautiful again restoring her pluck.

"Can you dance?" the harem mistress asked.

"No."

"Can you sing or play on an instrument?"

"No."

Fawzia heaved up a short laugh. "Well, you can be taught. But you better have other attributes, my fine Christian lady, or your lord will soon tire of you. There are too many women already here in the Alhambra who pine away their lives forgotten."

Dolores gaped at her. "Is this the Alhambra Palace, then? Have I been cast into the Sultan's harem?"

"Yes, but you are not destined for the Grand Sultan Abu Abdullah, stupid; have you heard nothing? The Sultan pays no heed at all to the women he already possesses. What would he need you for, untalented as you are? The Sultan has given you to his favorite courtier, Jamal ibn Ghulam. Though I would not understand why an ill-tempered Christian scarecrow as you should be so lucky."

"Lucky?"

"Yes, unbeliever, you will be the envy of the entire harem. The Sayed Ghulam is a virile, handsome man with eyes to cause the houris in Paradise to faint with delirium and a voice like a majestic lion." Fawzia crossed her arms over her ample stomach, causing her myriad bracelets to jingle. "But I do not know. It worries me to think you cannot—at least—excite and seduce him with the dance. You may not please him overmuch."

Dolores's eyes flashed; she drew herself up and put cold contempt in her voice. "Well, mistress Fawzia, he will have to find another to seduce him. I want none of him. He is ugly and vile and if he puts his horrible hands on me I shall kill him," she cried. The realization of why she was being so pampered hit her and lanced a spasm of nausea through her.

Quite unperturbed, with not even a frown on her face, Fawzia stepped closer and without warning forcibly swung the flat of her great palm twice to hit Dolores swift, resounding blows on both cheeks, almost knocking her off her feet and leaving her head ringing and her face stinging with red marks. Noting with satisfaction the stunned tears of pain welling in her insolent charge's eyes, the woman shook her once, impatiently, by the shoulders. "Perhaps you were previously a lady, but you are now just a slave and so shall you always be. You have no rights, you have no thoughts, you have only duties: obedience, subservience, and silence. Your master is your lord; you are his property. He may treat you kindly or strangle you if he wishes, and the sooner you learn that submission is your only recourse the better for you. Do you know what we do with unruly females?"

Dolores shook her head, dazedly.

Fawzia crossed to the window and pointed through the grill. "Come here then and look. And learn, if you are wise, Christian."

Outside, opposite their window and at the base of a rectangular, mosaic-tiled court stood a strange device, unshielded from the bright sun: a platform of planks on which rested a long block of wood and two upright poles supporting a heavy yoke that could be raised or lowered to any height. The platform was occupied. A mocha-skinned, raven-haired Berber girl knelt naked upon it, her hands captured by round holes in the block of wood, her shoulders and head pressed down by the yoke so that she suffered a painful, bent-double position. A group of brightly dressed women crowded around, laughing and giggling and pelting the crying girl with pebbles and rotten fruit. Some had long peacock feathers with which they tickled the soles of her feet and her belly. Some pulled her hair or reached up and slapped at her bare haunches while she wept and weakly pleaded with them to stop.

"The punishment yoke is just for minor infractions, where the girl's beauty is not to be marred," Fawzia noted. "That one has always been a troublemaker. She has been there a day and will be released tonight. But if she continues to misbehave she will earn the wire lash."

Horrified, Dolores whispered, "But why do those women torment her? Is she not one of them, one of this harem?"

Fawzia shrugged her fat shoulders. "They distress her because they are bored, that is why. But it would go worse for you. This quarter is for the Sultan's wives and women and his guests, as such you are. But some facilities are private, only for the royal concubines. Your master will have to make use of the punishment yokes located out in the open of the First Plaza, where any man that passes can see your shame and toss buckets of filth on you or spit at you, anything so long as you are not marked. So, if my noble Spanish lady does not want to kneel naked and covered with dung to amuse the loiterers in the plaza, I advise her to calm herself. And never, never speak of harming your master. For those words alone you could be blinded and crippled and sent to amuse the beggars in the Albayazin. But I shall be lenient with your ignorance—the first time."

She jerked her head sideways as an order to Dolores. With a last, subdued glance at the humiliated woman outside, Dolores stepped away from the window to face the callous grins of Fawzia's assistants. One of them gave her a pair of soft slippers and a wide blue silk robe to slip over her head. Her hair was left undressed, simply tied back with a silk ribbon.

"There, that finishes you for a while. New women are ordinarily trained for several days before being taken to their masters, but yours is in a hurry to assess his purchase," Fawzia mocked, her beady eyes still reinforcing the message that she meant to be obeyed. "Go where you wish, or rest in your cubicle. We will find you again later. The serving maids will give you food. They all know a few words in your language." She motioned to her assistants and turned to lead them out, but swung back again to where Dolores stood. "Oh, there is one more matter. Your past life is dead; you shall never leave here except to be sold or buried. Therefore you must choose another name. That is the rule. What shall it be?"

Dolores could no more utter another name she wished to be known by than she could stop the rigidity that took her muscles again at the harem mistress's casual words or the dread that plucked at her insides. She stood silent, nonplussed.

"Well then, I shall give you one, a good Moslem name to please your new lord." Fawzia squinted her eyes to study Dolores for a moment and tapped one fat ringed finger to her lips. A pleased chuckle issued from her creased throat. "Karima, that's what it shall be. Karima is your name, girl, and do not forget it." As she lumbered away Fawzia threw over her shoulder, "That means 'gentle.'" And there trailed back a chortle of mischief from her.

Dolores followed the women along the gallery and into a small, columned hall glowing with the brilliant colors of mosaic tile walls. The sound of women's voices could be heard from beyond its graceful, farther archway. Somewhat forlornly she watched Fawzia and her assistants disappear through an opposite curtained doorway without even another glance at her, and suddenly she stood alone. She looked at her red palms and raised her wrist to her nose to sniff the exotic oil they had rubbed into her skin while she thought. If they left her to herself like this they must be certain she could not escape the harem. Ha, perhaps not Dolores, the Baroness de la Rocha, but the Dolores of Ciudad Real's mean alleys and cul-de-sacs might. And would. In one manner or another.

She raised up her head, squared back her shoulders under the sensuous slip of the silk robe, and headed toward the garden which she could see framed in the archway. Her first task in the few hours she had was to study her surroundings and understand what a physical escape might involve. She stepped warily into the garden but immediately jerked herself back under the arch as she was almost run into by several laughing, shouting women in flying veils and jangling jewelry pelting along after another hooting girl who fled them holding something above her head. Dolores's ears filled with their laughter and the musical sound of female chatter, along with the splash of water and twang of a stringed instrument. She stepped from the cool shadow under the archway into the most beautiful garden she could have ever imagined.

Shrubs and grass and flowers marked off little lawns, each with its own splashing fountain and shady almond trees and complement of ladies of the harem, lounging in shades of apricot, pink, red, gold, pale blue, and lilac silk attire more colorful than the beds of huge roses and peonies surrounding them. The great, verdant garden, bordered by tall poplars and threaded with pebbled paths, centered upon a long, rectangular, azure pool of floating lilies and gliding white swans, its raised marble rim supporting at intervals brass pots of flowing shrubs. Iridescent peacocks sounded their raucous cries as they strutted between the lawns, birds chirped and sang in the trees, the voices of small children piped as they ran playing along the hedges.

Dazzled by the sunlit glory of the garden, Dolores at length strolled slowly up and down the paths, trying to observe without herself being observed, although she received many curious looks and even some polite nods and smiles. But none of the women stopped her or spoke to her, for which she was, for the moment, grateful. For her part she was also startled: surprised that the handsome, pantalooned women resting on the grass or sitting in groups on cushions, or trailing lazy hands in the coolness of the pool did not seem mistreated in any outward respect; confounded that they did not even act unhappy or fearful—although she thought she detected a note of petulance in their high laughter. There were not half as many of them as she expected from the fulminating tales she had heard, and only a few children. The women chatted together, did needlework, and listened to female musicians, and the younger ones played shrieking games of tag or threw a ball with seemingly light hearts.

She circled the garden several times but found no openings in the monolithic, high walls enclosing two sides. She pattered down the cool galleries which opened onto the garden but found only more sleeping cubicles, two large halls with cushions, gaming boards, and other objects for amusement scattered about, and, guarded by a eunuch and squatting female slaves awaiting summons, the private apartments of the Sultana Morayama, and Ayaxa, the honorable mother of the Sultan, so she was informed. She peered into the harem's main bathchamber, a vast, echoing space where women were laughing and splashing or lying languidly in the soothing rays of sun from the high windows. And there were other chambers she came to, of ordinary uses. The succession of galleries and halls, she found, either ended opposite the harem garden in small, walled patios, or debouched into the same entry court she had been flung into the night before, its massive gates still shut and silent. Fawzia had spoken the truth. This barred and guarded portico was the only way into or out of the Alhambra's harem.

Harem! She felt foolish in her disappointment at finding the fabled and dreaded harem of the Grand Sultan of Granada a peaceful wing of quiet halls and gardens peopled by pampered, indolent concubines attended by scurrying female slaves and bored eunuchs, who, although she had already seen one roughly separate two angry squabblers, seemed to smile more than they scowled.

In fact, she now really believed the attendant who had beautified her and gossiped in her ear about how lucky she was to have been given away to another besides the Sultan. The ruler neglected his women, the slave whispered in Castilian, calling so seldom for any of them except the Sultana that many wept day and night from the loneliness of their bodies and the barrenness of their wombs. The attendant was a gap-toothed, rough-handed peasant girl of Andalusian heritage, but her scornful, indignant tone shocked Dolores. Far from being the objects of lustful orgies and the cruel passions of the Sultan and his friends, these desirable women bound in concubinage to the throne were wearing away their lives in rejected seclusion.

Still, she could find little sympathy for such languishing, captured butterflies for she had stared into the brazen eyes of the Moor that bought her and seen his appetite rise for her, and her fate promised to be immeasurably worse than theirs. She sat drooping on a marble bench in one of the small, empty patios and tried to think what to do next. She scooped up water from the fountain to wet her dry mouth, but cared nothing for food as the warm sun slipped down the sky. And here Fawzia and her trailing assistants found her and reclaimed her, late in the afternoon, leading her back to the dressing room of the small bathchamber.

Forcing her down on the settle again, the slave women set to work rubbing heavily perfumed unguent into her skin, from chin to toes. They blended a scented, light oil into their palms and then passed these lightly over her hair to give it shine. They combed her hair back from her forehead and plaited it into one thick braid intertwined with green, gold, and silver ribands whose tasseled ends would bump gently against the small of her back when she stood. They smoothed her complexion with a fine powder and painted her lids with silver pigment, then outlined her tilted eyes with broad strokes of kohl and darkened her brows. To her pink lips they applied a greaseless ointment to make them look moist and inviting, adding a giggled warning not to lick them and spoil the effect.

In spite of her passive cooperation that far (for she had not forgotten the lesson of the girl on the punishment platform) they had to force her into the outlandish costume: wide, floppy pantaloons of silver cloth and a flimsy, low-necked gauze bodice separated by a sash of crushed purple silk wound about her slim waist. They gave her no chemise at all; only a short, sleeveless green jacket trimmed with gilt bangles to partially cover the almost transparent blouse and save her from nakedness. A green hat, like a little round box, was fastened to her head with a strap under her braid, and a spangled chiffon shawl was pinned over it with the ends left floating behind. She thought scornfully that they were negating most of their hard work when they settled across the bridge of her nose a little, cobwebby veil—Fawzia called it a *yashmak*—which covered her face from nose to chin. But when they held up a long, undistorted mirror to her she was chagrined to see how exciting and lustrous her eyes appeared underscored by the cosmetics and especially the subtly revealing, gossamer veil.

Fawzia rummaged in a large, ivory box and pulled out a silver band tinkling with bells, which was clasped about Dolores's ankle, and round silver hoops hung with tiny dangles, which were fastened in her ears. The harem mistress stood back, arms folded on her big bosom, and gazed at her with satisfaction. "There! Now you look like something. You may have the silver anklet and earrings, and if you are dutiful and pleasing your lord may buy you other trinkets with which to adorn yourself."

"And when do you clap on the iron slave collar?" Dolores demanded bitterly.

"Slave collar, so that your master must caress cold metal about your throat, stupid? There is no need for such caution, anyone can see you are a concubine. Wives and daughters wear more dignified attire, brocaded tunics and embroidered shoes."

Dolores looked down at her dainty, bare feet shod in purple-dyed, turned-up leather soles held to her feet by cords about the ankle and rings of gilded leather about each big toe.

"And be warned, daughter of the Cross," Fawzia continued without rancor, "no female of any rank, with the exception of the Sultana, is allowed to exit from the palace except in the company of her master or husband, or with a signed and sealed pass. The guards are alert, for it means their life if someone is missing. You will learn our ways," she finished, and the last was really an order, but softened by a slight encouraging smile.

Dolores was taken to her cubicle and left to wait there until she was sent for by her new master. She heard footsteps and chatter pass back and forth outside her drawn curtain, and soon there was the rattle of crockery and the smell of food being transported past her cubicle.

She felt primed, adorned like a pagan maiden going to the sacrificial altar. Panic was raising in her breast again, causing her to wring her hands until her fingers ached. She thought of the Moor with his hard, pitiless expression and his obvious power and wealth as a favorite of the Sultan's and shuddered. At the prison he had turned deaf ears to her plea for ransom; she felt certain he would do the same with any other plea contrary to his will. She paced the tiny chamber and cursed how tightly sealed was this harem quarter. Unless she found a chance to run and hide herself as she was taken to the Moor's chamber, to hide and hope to find a way out of the palace itself, unless she could do this she saw no way to shake her fist in the face of this enslavement and its promise of torture for obstinacy except to take her own life.

Cold fingers wrapped themselves around her heart as she tried to understand what it would be like to be no more, as she contemplated the end of her brief existence in a pool of her own blood or dangling from a scarf tied to a tree limb. Frantically her eyes swept the room, lighting on her old clothes, which had been shoved aside but were not yet disposed of; and in this pile she caught something glinting in the last rays of the sun from the window. With a few quick steps she stooped, and there, caught in the lining of her cloak hood, was the large, bead-headed pin which had held the coils of her hair in place. Joyfully she grabbed it up, seeing that the other amber bead which covered the sharp point of the sturdy, six-inch skewer was lost.

Here, the Creator be praised, was something she could defend herself with; she could drive the pin into her captor's hateful, steely eye until it reached his brain. And then she would plunge it deep into her own throat. No slavery, no defilement, no punishment yoke or wire lash for her. What terror did quick death hold for her now? She was a captive, her life was ruined, despoiled, she would end it in defiance, almost as it had begun. She concealed the long pin in the fold of her sash with steady fingers. Papa el Mono's Dolores did not lack for courage.

Deep reaches of shadow stretched across the floor of her cubicle before Fawzia returned with two big eunuchs in tow. Although Dolores set her jaw and refused to move from the couch it did her no good; the two Negroes calmly grasped her under the arms, pulled her up with no trouble, and propelled her forward. She stumbled out and down the gallery with Sayeda Fawzia's parting advice in her ears: *"Esmahee,* Christian fool, make the most of the pretty face and body Allah has bestowed upon you. Show your master affection, give him obedience, and he will shower you with gifts and money. You will be petted and pampered and the air in your nostrils will be sweet with incense. Otherwise his patience will fail and you will be sold to a laborer's doxy house, or metal barbs will be stuck in your armpits and your arms slammed down and your bleeding body bound and tossed into the river to drown."

Muffled from head to toe in the lightweight mantle Fawzia had thrown over her, Dolores padded along with her guards, having chosen the dignity of walking to being dragged. They passed through the small door of the harem's heavy gate, along a gallery and across several halls and courts, and she was glad for the mantle, which hid her brief and barbaric dress from the curious sideways ogles of the male courtiers and functionaries they passed. Presently her guard tapped on an ornate door beside which sat a slave boy whose round eyes judiciously rolled away from her enveloped form. A voice beyond the door called out something in Arabic, *"etfahdu-loo."* The slave boy pushed back the door and the impassive guards thrust Dolores through, and at the same time one of them, grunting something unintelligible, yanked away her mantle and cast it to the floor.

Just a few lamps warmed with their yellow glow the luxury of the chamber before her, across whose carpeted floor wafted the dry, enticing scent of sandalwood incense. Her first darting glance about told her there was no one present in the room, but then, at one end of the saloon where the light barely reached, a movement showed her where her adversary lounged. She attempted to calm the squeeze of panic that assailed her by remembering that he was, after all, only flesh and bone, a man, not a demon. He too could die, for if he touched her he would soon feel the deadly bite of her steel fang.

She had been instructed to prostrate herself upon the floor on entering her master's chamber and not to budge until he gave permission. Hah! She stood with fists clenched and her head proudly erect, glaring at the outline of the turbaned figure seated so confidently on the divan. His face was in shadow, but she could recall it in her mind as he had looked down at her from his mount, flat and lightly pocked above the scanty beard, cold and evilly calculating. She gritted her teeth to keep fright from making her heart fail.

In his toneless voice the Moor uttered something in Arabic. She did not respond.

"I allow you to approach, Christian slave. Come closer," he repeated, this time in Castilian, with an edge of impatience. And when she still did not move he droned, "Do you come or would you prefer I call my guards to drag you by the hair? For a so-called gentlewoman you lack dignity."

Dolores walked forward, but slowly, until she stood just a few feet from the divan which rested on a low platform. Her purchaser lounged with one leg tucked beneath him, Arab style. She could make out white leggings and the bottom of a patterned tunic, but the upper half of his body leaning at ease on a mound of pillows was still in the deep shadow of the canopy over the divan. Even so, she thought she could discern from the shadows the cold gleam of his stare.

"Stand there"—he stopped her just below a dim hanging lamp—"in the light where I can see you. Do not fidget." His voice faded away and there was silence for a moment. The Moor cleared his throat. When he resumed speaking there was a curious little catch in his monotone. "Lovely. Indeed, worth every dirham. A beauty to savor first with the eyes before caressing it with the hands."

Dolores lifted her chin higher.

"Ah, but you are haughty; that pleases me. There is zest in taming prideful women; you must know that of men. Such women are that much more grateful for any little favor tossed to them later."

Dolores shivered. The revolting brute. She was merely purchased flesh to him, to be used at will and for amusement broken to whimpering.

"So. Woman, you may speak. Have you nothing to say? Did they not teach you manners in your castle? Well, perhaps we do not need words for our pleasure tonight. That is just as well. Women babble too much. Perhaps you can win my approval—and your fate could be dire without it—with your silent talents: talents of the seductive eye, the coaxing hand, the seeking mouth . . ."

He was mocking her but a leashed excitement was deepening and adding color to his monotone.

Through lips stiff with aversion Dolores pleaded, "Sir, I offer you a fortune of ransom. Take it. Thousands of maravedis will buy you ten slave women to please your desires. Forcing me will not be worth your trouble, for I will not submit. I demand to be treated with the respect due my station, I demand to be released or ransomed, I demand—"

"Demand?" His sudden loud stridence silenced her. "Understand, woman, you are nothing but a slave, bought and paid for. You have no station. Your body and your soul belong to me. If I say live, you live. If I say die, you die. If I say fling yourself on the floor so I may warm my feet on you, you do so. I do not wish ransom. I wish you, and without a doubt I shall have you. Without a doubt, my Castilian peach."

The noble lady disappeared and in her place trembled Dolores of the tavern. *"Basta! Cabrón!* God grant you such a fever all your bones pour out of you like hot soup! You will have nothing of me but an inert body and undying hatred." Outrage against the unjust fate that had brought her such diminishment shook her. "I do not fear your punishments. God will help me endure them. And I am not your slave, you loathsome carrion," she cried with fists rigid and clenched at her side. Taking a step backward she spat toward him.

A deep growl came from the divan, and through a terrified rise of tears she saw the Moor get up, much taller and broader of shoulder than she remembered from her only other encounter with him. He strode swiftly toward her as if he were going to strike her to the floor. Quickly pulling the skewer out of her sash she ran full tilt at him, propelled by rage and fear, backing her raised arm with all her strength for a vicious slash at his eye. Instantaneously, as she fell upon him she was almost struck numb with horror: *Madre de Dios!* I have signed my death warrant, the terrible realization flashed through her cringing mind. Oh, dear saints in heaven, I don't want to die. What folly have I committed! I want to live!

But warned by the flash of the metal pin in the lamplight, the wily Moor had jerked himself out of the way of the deadly point. He grabbed her arm and twisted the weapon from her grasp in a second. She battled his relentless hold on her, clawing at him and kicking, sobbing hysterically.

But he swung her around, shook her, and, as if from a long distance away she heard a different voice, a familiar voice crying, "Dolores! Dolores!" She paused a scant second in her mad writhing under those cruel hands to listen to the impossible hallucination, for she thought it was the Moor himself pleading with her. "Dolores! Dolores, for sweet Jesu's sake, you almost murdered me. It's Francho, Francisco de Mendoza, can't you see? Look at me, wild one, look—"

Shuddering she stared at him, and although she realized it was not her buyer, for a moment all she saw was an olive-skinned, black-bearded, scowling Moor, whose cruel fingers dug into her shoulders unmercifully; a tall, white-turbaned Moor with a single silver earring glittering in one ear in barbaric splendor, with black brows drawn together over blue eyes, blue as the Andalusian sky—eyes she knew, filled now with concern and remorse.

"It was miserable and stupid of me to frighten you so," the voice she was imagining in her extremity pleaded, while the suddenly familiar, square-lipped mouth outlined by the beard formed the words, "but I only thought to tease you as you did me once when you first returned my dagger. It was a wretched prank—forgive me, little sister, please . . ."

Dolores's lip trembled. "F . . . Francho?" she quavered into his contrite smile. The fright, the panic, the shock, and the lack of food all day whirled up overwhelmingly inside of her. The blood drained from her head, the room turned purple and buzzing, and helplessly she went limp in his arms.

Someone was patting her cheeks too hard. Moving her head away from the insistent slaps, she opened her eyes and found she was lying amid the pillows of a divan, and Francho was alternately chafing her hand and gently slapping her face to arouse her. There was more light now, from an oil lamp on a stand he had moved over to the foot of the divan, and she could see him well, a man more handsome than ever in his cockaded turban and trim black beard, the flashing earring matching in brilliance the cerulean blue eyes now scanning her face anxiously.

She could hardly credit her senses. But it was true, it was Francisco de Mendoza leaning over her, dressed as a Moor among Moors and living in the regal palace of the Great Sultan of Granada. She tried to pull herself together in spite that her mind staggered. "Francho! What . . . how did . . . I don't understand . . ."

He pressed a cup of water into her hand and made her sit up and sip it. "In a minute, *doña.*" He stood watching her drink. "Tell me if they provided you with anything to eat?" At her headshake he raised a finger for her to be patient. He crossed to a large tabouret and returned bearing a bowl of what turned out to be a sweet pudding of rice and almonds, flavored with cinnamon, and a tray of aromatic fried cakes. Declaring she first needed her strength restored and that he would not utter one word until she ate something, he sat sternly with folded arms, but, as she noted from the corner of her eye, squelched amusement as he watched her gobble down the delicious dessert and some of the horn-shaped and twisted cakes. "It is only a small refreshment," he shrugged as she chewed. "I did not realize they would starve you."

"I do feel better now, although starvation is not why I fainted. How should I ever think to find *you* here? And . . . Oh, Francho, I almost murdered you! I thought you were the man who had me separated out from the rest of the prisoners, a cruel-looking man, very cold. *Madre mía,* I almost killed you!"

She struggled to get up further but he pushed her back gently. "Almost is a long way from having done it. An observer might say I almost deserved it, teasing you so. In any case, *hermanita,* when you attempt to stab someone you should not be sobbing so hard you can't see your target. Your attack technique would never have caught Reduan off balance either." He squeezed her hand.

"Reduan?"

"A powerful military leader into whose harem you were headed until I intervened and God—or Allah—helped us. Snatching you from under his nose has earned me an enemy, one both watchful and shrewd, but I'm hoping that time will deflect his ire."

"But I don't understand. You are supposed to be in Italy. How come you are in Granada? And to go bearded, like a Moor?"

He plumped up a mound of pillows and sat back facing her, one leg crooked under him. Soberly he said, "I'll tell you, of course, but it's a long story, and one you must guard in complete silence or we will both land among the severed heads stuck up along the city wall. . . ."

She listened closely to his tale, astonished. And yet, in spite of her rapt attention to him she was also aware on another level of a giddiness spreading warm through her veins that she could merely reach out and touch the one man who had ever engaged her heart, and that here they were, thrown together and isolated from their Christian world in a city of enemies, each dependent upon the other. A part of her brain whispered: Would I go through the terrors, the humiliations of the past days again just to be rescued and sheltered by this audacious knight in exotic raiment?

The answer was yes.

Francho had decided to tell Dolores only as much as she needed to know about his presence in Granada, and in the first few days, still recovering from the fright of her capture, she stared at him with a mixture of relief and awe and admiration that was undeniably heady. For his part, her unexpected entrance into his life rang like the peal of a silver trumpet amid the humdrum drone of ordinary days.

Even though he had known who would enter his chamber that night, seeing this lovely odalisque moving across the floor toward him in an undulation of veils and silk pantaloons and jingle of bangles, seeing the obdurate fire lance from her tilted eyes in brave, if foolish, defiance, hearing the familiar throaty voice, had made the pulse pound at the base of his throat; she was complicating his life and his mission, she intruded upon his concentration, and yet he was ravished to see her. And in spite of the chivalrous Don Francisco, Jamal ibn Ghulam had enjoyed a shiver of power. Jamal owned this woman as a gift from the Great Sultan, her face and form and will were dedicated to his pleasure, her yielding flesh to his hands. . . .

A powerful shame had overtaken him while he was trying to revive her from her faint, shame that his pent-up desires should see this Christian woman helplessly fallen into his keeping as a supplier of his needs. Cursing under his breath he vowed by San Bismas that never would he take advantage of either her gratitude or her proximity by assaulting her virtue in any way. And by the time she opened her eyes he had gotten control of, if not any understanding of, his wrenchingly ambivalent feelings toward his "little sister."

It wasn't difficult to arrange their lives. Dolores continued to live with the other palace women in the harem and after a while reported to him that she was amazed how pleasant was her life in the quarter she had so recently feared and despised, how she enjoyed the baths and the delicacies to eat and the ministrations of the attending slaves, and even the shy acquaintanceship of several Castilian-speaking beauties. Four or five times a week, to keep up appearances and because he enjoyed her company, he sent for her and she was escorted to his chamber to spend the night, sleeping on the divan while he gallantly took to the floor with a pile of pillows and an extra coverlet. If Boabdil dispensed with his services early enough they often ate together from trays brought by his servant Selim, and spoke and drank wine or *kavah* far into the night.

Her news and gossip of the Spanish Court was welcome, and nothing seemed to have escaped her attention. The Infanta had been betrothed to Prince Alfonso of Portugal amid brilliant celebrations in which King Ferdinand himself had taken the field against the visiting knights in the gala tourney and broken five lances. The Queen had ignored instructions from Rome and placed her choice of the Bishop of Oviedo at the head of the chancery of Valladolid, thus serving notice to the Borgia Pope, Alexander VI, that her piety did not extend to compromising her realm's independence. The Countess of Feria had been caught in adultery and shamed into a nunnery and her marriage anulled. The Grand Constable Haro had contracted a severe case of gout and suffered loudly. That peculiar Genoese, Columbo, to whom several nobles had shown occasional hospitality, was now desperately trying to coax the Duke of Medina-Sidonia into financing the dubious maritime venture over which Their Catholic Majesties hesitated. Don Antonio de la Cueva's French wife had presented him with twin daughters. It was suspected that King Charles of France would soon claim succession to the throne of Naples, dangerously threatening Ferdinand's own ambitions. The Jews were being squeezed to finance the coming war in Granada; those who did not virtually bankrupt themselves were accused of trying to convert Christians and handed over in chains to the Holy Office. Earl Rivers, the Englishman who had joined himself and his three hundred men to the Spanish cause, had been felled by a battleaxe. And so on.

Dolores wondered if Tendilla had informed Francho of the death of the Count's wife, Carlotta. "Ah yes," she told him when he pressed her, "last fall. It was a shock to see Don Inigo in mourning bands, so many had forgotten the very existence of the poor woman. She had, after all, been locked away with her broken mind for so many years." But when Francho shook his head in sympathy for Tendilla, she shrugged one shoulder. "Still, wouldn't you imagine your sire's mourning is more respect than grief, after so long a time of estrangement? And there is talk that he intends to marry when his period of mourning is over."

Francho's head jerked up. "Marry, you say? With whom?"

"Why, with the Lady Fatima, the high-born Moorish damsel you tell me you helped him to capture, and whom he has been harboring as a guest ever since. He escorted her to Court this winter, and I have to admit, she is as handsome and elegant as he, in spite of her youth. In fact, Ferdinand himself spent hours conversing with her, and if you don't think the Queen was annoyed at such heavy personal interest . . .!" Her charming laugh fluted out, teasing a smile from Francho too. "You know, it has always amazed me ever since I came to Court how many human traits a ruler shares with a peasant," she giggled, hugging her knees to her chest.

Enduring some of the sillier gossip Dolores found amusing, Francho finally asked, as casually as possible, "And what of Leonora de Zuniga? How does she fare?" He had written to Leonora, of course, several letters which he had asked Tendilla to transmit, which of course mentioned nothing of his whereabouts. She may have even answered, although the Count responded to his inquiries with a negative; perhaps she had sent her notes to Tendilla's Italian agent via the royal courier to Rome. But he had prepared her for a mystery, and his letters, at least, would let her know he was alive and still loved her dearly.

Ignoring the somewhat mocking light in the luminous gray eyes that slid toward him, he heard Dolores say, "She fares well, or so it seemed when last I saw her; we do not pass many words when we chance to meet. She has decided to accompany the Infanta to Lisbon for the Portuguese marriage and will remain there for a while. But she seemed a bit—oh—lovelorn is the word, I imagine. Does that make you happy, Francho?"

Why should he hide his love for Leonora from Dolores? "To know she may be thinking of me? Yes. Nor does she languish alone. I miss her desperately."

Dolores murmured, "Ah, but it is so different for a man. You can console your longing temporarily, at least with the physical needs men must satisfy. Azahra, for instance . . ."

He had seen no reason not to tell her about his little house in the Albayzin, and Ali and Azahra. From any other woman but Dolores he would have been shocked with her indelicacy. Now, as he thought back to another conversation, he realized mentioning Azahra had been a mistake.

Dolores had asked, at the beginning, "But if she was a bond slave of the proprietor of this wine shop, the Golden Horn, how came she to you?"

"He mistreated her. I offered to hide her from him, and someday when the wars are over I will see she and Ali find a good home."

"What is she like, this Azahra?" came the innocent question.

"Oh, a sweet, gentle child, not pretty but appealing in her own way. She was a dancer at the inn, a fine one, so uniquely skilled in using her body to hold the customers' eyes that the proprietor would not sell her."

"Oh?"

That was when it occurred to him he might have said too much. Dolores's "oh" was a complete indictment of his motives. "Don't be a ridiculous goose, *doña*. Azahra is merely a child, thirteen at the most."

"Children don't dance in public houses," Dolores observed sweetly. "And Moorish females mature quite early, I hear. Not, of course, that I am surprised you might take a concubine; one can be lonely surrounded only by enemies . . ."

He had gotten angry then. "Azahra is not my concubine— and if she were that would in no manner concern you. Ay, Maria, Dolores, when will you learn to mind your own affairs? Leonora does not need you to inquire into my constancy. Azahra is a friend, nothing more. And since you are so curious, learn then that the physical needs, as you put it, are easily controlled when the dearly loved woman is absent."

A shadow of hurt innocence crossed her face, and she stared at him wordlessly. He regretted his outburst and wished he could take back his last remark about controlling desire in the absence of love. *Ay de mi,* why did this woman always make him sound pompous?

Dolores was curious about the legendary Alhambra, and when Francho's time was free he enjoyed guiding his veiled and properly demure concubine through the public rooms of the palace, entertained by her grumbling at having to walk with eyes downcast and three humble paces behind him.

"This fine plaza is named the Court of the Lions because of

the twelve stone beasts supporting the basin of the fountain over there."

"Lions?" Dolores sniffed. "I hardly think much of Moorish sculptors. They look more like small dogs."

"The Moorish sculptors do not lack art, Karima," Francho informed her, calling her for practice by her Arabic name, which had made him grin appreciatively the first time he heard it. "It was deliberate that they carved only vague likenesses of the maned cats. The Koran forbids representations of humans or animals, which is why most Arabic decoration, as you see all along here on the walls and ceilings, is scroll work and arabesques and script." He smiled, pleased by her interest. "The Moors of Spain are very lax in following some of the Prophet's commands, but I think the artists hoped to lessen their sin here by avoiding a true likeness."

She tilted her head, the better to see an inscription. "But Arabic writing is so odd, it looks like chicken tracks. Can you read it? Then what does it say, this writing over the archway, for instance?"

He read it off to her. "Blessed be He Who gave our ruler a mansion that in beauty surpasses all other delightful mansions. On our ruler be the constant blessings of Heaven; may he restrain the extravagancies of his subjects and subdue all opposers!"

Her admiration was wide-eyed. *"Cielo,* Fran . . . master, I am astonished that you can really read those squiggles. And the expert way you play the lute and sing! I am truly amazed with you." It was obvious her praise was genuine and that his unexpected abilities intrigued her.

Francho looked down into her shining eyes and tried to keep his smile modest. "You flatter me, Karima. It is merely all part of my work. . . ." But in spite of himself his shoulders squared themselves back a bit prouder.

He exhibited to her the splendid Hall of the Ambassadors, where the Sultan held audiences, and the little garden of Lindaraxa, with its melancholy legend. They walked through the domed Hall of the Two Brothers used for state banquets and examined again, in the Court of the Lions, the brown splotches on the wide tiles which would not rub out, said to be the accusing bloodstains of the Abencerrage knights Boabdil's father had murdered there. They visited the zoo where the Sultan kept the wild animals sent as gifts by foreign potentates, and strolled amid the peacocks and crested African cranes in the gardens. And from the square-towered battlements they viewed the white and airy grace of the Generalife Palace situated upon a neighboring mountain, the cool summer residence of Granada's rulers.

Dolores listened with pleasure to the legends he repeated, able now to exclaim at the glowing, Oriental beauty of the halls and galleries and to enjoy from the battlements the breathtaking views of the tiered green, white, pastel and red-roofed houses below. Whenever they relaxed in the tiny, flower-scented garden attached to his chamber, he was both surprised and pleased at her intelligent questions on the history of the Moors and the Koran and the Moslem religion, and where was Damascus, and was it difficult to learn Arabic, and how did those funny waterclocks work? Although he twitted her that women did not have need of such knowledge, he found himself teaching her necessary phrases in Arabic and started to instruct her in speaking the language. He was delighted with her constant inquiry and quick comprehension.

As the weeks passed into late spring he found an unexpected and pleasurable release in reminiscing to her about Mondejar and his years of study in preparation for his present mission; about hearty Von Gormach and seldom sober Pedro Nunez; and about Pietro di Lido's fussy tutelage. She often asked him to play the guembri or the lute for her, and he was never too tired to comply, sometimes making her the first to hear one of his new compositions. She recalled to him the lewd ditties he had plunked away at in Ciudad Real, and merrily they remembered together old adventures and pranks, even touching briefly on the last moments they had together before he was taken away, but so lightly one could think that the boy and girl involved had been two other people.

There was no denying Dolores immeasurably brightened his life, filling the dulcet spring evenings with her vivacious presence and beauty, and dulling the ever present ache for Leonora. It was exciting and good to know that she would be waiting for him in his chamber when his duties were finished.

Good, and not so good, for constancy to Leonora and his determined words aside, he was a man, and to have the seductively clothed and perfumed Dolores/Karima constantly before one would have tried a holy anchorite. In Toledo and Seville he had already been exposed to her power to disrupt him; his solution then had been to avoid her. But now, since she was his responsibility, her days and nights were unavoidably intertwined with his. Of course, he had every intention of treating her with scrupulous respect, but she made it difficult to sustain an arm's length camaraderie, wafting under his suffering nose the jasmine perfume he had unwittingly supplied money for, reaching for a fig in such a way that the neck of her gauzy blouse gaped and disclosed the smooth, warm valley between her breasts, acting demure but gazing at him with beckoning cat's eyes and moist pink lips parted to show the gleam of even teeth . . .

To preserve the illusion of her concubinage, she slept in his chamber until the morning guards came to collect her. One soft spring evening she had loosed her thick hair from the confining braid and ribbands and was shaking her head to free the crimped auburn waves when she realized he was watching her from the garden portal. Her glance was artless from beneath her eyelids as she murmured, "Sometimes they pull the plait too tight and it hurts."

He continued to watch her as she combed through the long, thick strands with her fingers, her back arched, her eyelids half-shut in voluptuous pleasure, and he could not prevent himself from softly marveling out loud, "By Allah and all the Saints in Heaven, *hermanita,* how beautiful you are. It is no wonder the Duke so jealously guards you. Your hair recalls the reddish embers of a fire where bright sparks sometimes leap up. A man could yearn to twine his fingers in its thickness, and with no care of being burnt . . ." He broke off abruptly as he realized his thoughts were running away with him, and chewed the inside of his lip.

"Why, I thank you, master. I didn't think you had noticed," she answered demurely.

Hadn't noticed! But he was heavily annoyed with himself for allowing such words to slip out and giving her cynical soul another chance to gloat over the male susceptibility he had so virtuously repudiated.

She stretched luxuriously and then nestled back into the heap of pillows on the divan, the light fabric of her pantaloons outlining the alluring curve of her hips. She tilted her head playfully, as if she were contemplating him from several angles. "Do you know, Francho, strangely enough I like that forked beard on your face," she declared, complimentary in her turn. "Yes, it does truly become you. It is so strong-looking and as black as your eyebrows. In fact, you're very dashing as a Moor. All the women of the harem, poor slaves, are jealous of me. They ask me constantly are you a kind and satisfying lover, and they will not give me rest until I make up stories. . . ."

Desperate for peace from the subject he turned his back to stare scowling out into the fragrant garden. From behind him she seemed to have taken the hint and continued in a different vein. "Francho? Do you like it here in this heathen Court of the Alhambra, with all that you have attained?"

He moved his shoulders. "Yes, I like it. Temporarily. My position is pleasant enough, my duties are not onerous, I have had some successes in my mission. But it is not real. It is like the dream which comes between sleeping and waking, almost tangible but illusory stuff nonetheless."

"Well, I like it," she admitted softly. "I thought my life was over when I was driven through the gates of Granada. I was going to kill myself. Yet these past six weeks have been happy ones for me—full of so many impressions but—peaceful, I suppose. The quirks of life are so strange, aren't they?" He heard a fluid rustle, and she was padding over to him in her flat sandals, the little bells on her ankles tinkling. She stood close, looking out with him at the purple serenity of the garden. Her voice was husky. "For instance, it should have been Leonora who got herself captured rather than me, shouldn't it?"

When he refrained from answering she placed her hand on his arm as if to call back his attention, then seemed to change the subject again. Looking into the distance she called out, "Ah, see that great streak of lightning!" There was gay delight in her voice, "There must be rain in the mountains. I wonder shall we hear the clap."

He grunted a reply. Beneath the fabric of his flowing cotton robe his skin tingled under the pressure of her fingers on the muscle of his arm. Yet he did not move. She slid closer to him, and there was no mistaking the soft pressure of breast and hip and thigh against his side. He glanced down, wound tight as a spring, and she was smiling at him, lips parted, inviting, challenging—

Suddenly she was very transparent. He twitched away from her, his expression hard. "Does it amuse you to bait me, Dolores? Does it amuse you to see how long you must tease me before I reach out for you and breach my loyalty to Doña Leonora? You have no liking for Leonora and I know it, but not through me will you ever have the chance of wounding her heart."

She tried to look injured. "You have completely misunderstood my actions."

"No I have not. Who knows your ways better than I? Well, you need not trouble yourself, *doña,* I am not interested in your games or your kisses. No matter how you try you cannot reduce my constancy to my lady."

"Your lady!" she snorted. "Leonora is—" Her mouth snapped shut, biting off the words, and she shook her head as if warding off a buzzing fly. Expelling her breath she continued shrewishly, "Then how do you answer for the common dancer you keep so cozily in your house, my moral, parfait knight?"

"Be quit of Azahra, Dolores!" he flung out. "I've kept you from Reduan's harem, I treat you with the courtesy due a lady and shelter you so you may return to your Duke unharmed and inviolate, and you return my chivalry with mockery. Have you no gratitude?"

"But certainly I am grateful. And wouldn't one expect a gentleman of your birth to treat a lady with honor?" He saw she was drawing indignation around her like a shield.

"And so we shall continue," he ordered, turning and striding toward the divan, "with formality, and honor, whether you care for it or not." He extended the carved wooden screen behind which she usually disrobed and slept. "I'm going to snuff out the lamps. I need some rest."

Holding her head high and haughty with the insulted pride of one who has been falsely accused, Dolores stalked behind the screen.

The night was too warm. Francho could not sleep. He pulled his loose lounging robe over his head and lay barechested on the pillows, in his brief loincloth. He glared into the darkness. Why did she have the facility to irk him so? In fact, what was there about Dolores that set him to protecting his chastity so determinedly? He should have ignored her or laughed at her, ridicule would have put a spike through her game. Or even grabbed her and made her suffer the results of her despicable teasing and then indifferently set her aside to prove how easily disassociated is the flesh from the heart.

He shifted angrily as even the thought of possessing her caused a tightening in his loins. A fine way that would be to treat a helpless Christian woman he had chosen to protect.

But curse it, she knew he adored Leonora de Zuniga and that no one else mattered. Couldn't she respect that? If she hated Leonora for some slight or injury, enticing him was the wrong way to reach her. Women!

He heard rustling from the screened divan across the room as Dolores sighed and shifted her position. He squeezed his lids shut, desperately trying to get the image of her cozening, luminous eyes and glowing, satin-skinned visage out of his mind. Unfortunately, all that took its place was the way the clinging silk of her pantaloons outlined her round bottom as she sauntered with swaying hips before his helpless, starving eyes.

❧ *Chapter 23* ❧

Unused to riding, Francho shifted his haunches uncomfortably in the high-cantled Moorish saddle as his mount followed along in the strung out column of soldiers negotiating the rocky mountain path and silently cursed for the hundredth time the bad luck that had snatched away victory and plunged him into the depths of defeat.

It had appeared easy to foil the Sultan's feverish quest for heroics. But the continuing acclaim of the people acted like a powerful drug, finally dazzling Boabdil into suddenly ordering preparations for a surprise attack on Alcala la Real itself, in punishment for the marauding Christian squadrons that constantly swooped down, burned, pillaged, and left the *vega* a blackened, smoking ruin. And the Sultan was inspired to announce he would lead the vengeance strike himself!

As soon as he could get free from the royal presence, Francho had quickly headed to the Albayzin, where, ostensibly, as the palace snoops had contented themselves with learning, he kept another concubine, and there he sent off a detailed warning to Tendilla. Much of the Count's garrison would have already been added to the full army Ferdinand was gathering, but Francho felt confident his message would provide Tendilla with time to call in enough reinforcements from the other fortresses under his command even to launch a

491

counterattack. Accordingly, Jamal ibn Ghulam complacently strummed for his royal patron, on the eve of departure from Granada, one lusty ballad of Moorish victories after another and poured honey into the receptive ear by praising the masterful tactic that with one surprise blow would sever the head of the ravaging Christian beast from its body.

By this time Boabdil considered Jamal ibn Ghulam a human talisman, for surely the ruler's ill fortunes had reversed themselves when this great-shouldered troubadour with the rich voice and magic fingers had appeared. So now the Sultan cocked his head thoughtfully and commanded that his Head Musician accompany him on the foray.

Francho was not about to take sword in hand against his own people. "I shall delight to be present at your victory, if it please you, Excellence. But—I have made a holy vow which cannot be broken without sin, that these hands would lift no other weapon than this guembri, which Allah preserved unscathed in Malaga as a sign of His will for me."

Fondly Boabdil clapped him on the back. "Fear not to break your vow, ibn Ghulam, I have many capable warriors but only one fine minstrel. I would not allow you to go into combat. If Allah has willed you your music as a sword, he has also presented you to me as a buckler: a shield in the confusion and a clear voice to strengthen my resolve." The ruler's mild eyes smiled into Francho's own. "You shall ride with me in a place of honor, but when we reach our objective you will remain in the rear."

"O Sultan, I fear I shall appear coward to the others, and when the heat of battle rises my hand will itch to drive a scimitar into the guts of the Christian dogs who may have been those who murdered my kin." It seemed to Francho he would gain more by staying put in Granada so he could carefully monitor the rumbles of Boabdil's numerous enemies.

But the Sultan was not to be held off. "Pah, what do you care for the regard of others when the exalted Abu Abdullah of Granada calls you friend?" he insisted. The daring expedition was exciting him, so Boabdil shrugged and with good humor threw up hands shimmering with jewels. "And who can know the secret ways of Allah the Almighty? Perhaps one day your guembri shall prove more puissant than ten legions of swords."

Salaaming deeply in aquiescence, Francho enjoyed his

unvoiced thought: That is what I most fervently work for, O Sultan.

Some days later, with Muza Aben Gazul, who was recovering from an arrow wound in the thigh, remaining behind with the major part of the army to keep Granada's defenses strong, the great gates of the city opened into a rosy dawn, and through the soaring horseshoe arch rode two thousand armored horsemen, five thousand archers, pikemen, and arquebusiers, plus the necessary supply masters, surgeons, grooms, and flunkies for the officers, and seven hundred sixty pack animals laden with munitions and supplies. Noting the proud light in Boabdil's eyes as he rode smiling at the head of his army, Francho could not help feeling sorry for the man, setting out so confidently to build his prestige with a surprise attack that was already doomed.

Guembri slung on his back, Francho rode on the right of the Sultan's high-spirited white steed, just behind the Abencerrage officers; to the left cantered the spike-helmeted Reduan and the captain Abdul Kerim Zegri. Francho allowed himself a grimace beneath his black beard; he was an uncomfortably vulnerable Judas goat. The light shirt of chain mail he wore over his yellow tunic could prove little protection against a stray crossbow bolt, and noncombatant or not, the fighting would be heavy and desperate, and he wished he were encased in his own armor of heavy jointed steel plates and visored casque, with a hefty sword of Toledo steel to his hand.

More than half the day had passed and they were already deep into the mountains, winding along a high, rocky ridge, when riders from their advance guard thundered around an outcropping of boulders and galloped toward the column. Noting the urgency of their pace, Reduan halted the march and spurred forward with several officers to meet them, leaving Boabdil frowning and impatient until his impassive general cantered back to him.

"An unlooked for happening, O Sultan. It means our objective will have to be changed."

"What is it?"

"Our scouts came across a party of mountain dwellers who were bringing their families into safety in the city. They reported seeing a great force of Christians, about twelve thousand men, riding like the wind through the Elvira pass in the direction of Alcala la Real!"

"Shaitan take them, the dogs! When was this?"

"Yesterday."

Boabdil pounded on the high forward cantle of his saddle. "Allah defend us, is that commander of theirs—what is his name, Tendilla—is he a *djinn* that he divines our intentions so readily? How could he possibly conceive that we would dare to attack his fortress?"

Reduan's face showed no emotion, perhaps because, as it had been rumored in the palace, the risky attack did not have his wholehearted approval. "It could be merely circumstance that the infidel called in his outpost forces at this time. Or perhaps we have not yet uncovered all the spies he has burdened us with for years. The fact remains that we have no chance to win that fortress with so many soldiers at his disposal, especially if we have lost our advantage of surprise."

Francho's heart skipped. It was cursed bad luck that the reinforcements called in by Tendilla were seen by the few Moorish trappers left in the mountains who then, just as unfortunately, happened to meet up with Boabdil's scouts. The wild and rocky defiles in that area were barely inhabited, and there were several different routes and passes through the jagged terrain. It would not have been unusual for the Spanish troops to have gone through to Alcala undetected. But now even Boabdil would not be foolish enough to charge the eagle's nest with his smaller force. Yet, having come this far, would he just return home, crestfallen and ridiculous? Francho nibbled on his lip.

"Let my Sultan not be dismayed at such ill fortune," Reduan continued with toneless reassurance, and beckoned to an officer who handed him a rolled deerhide map, "the warriors of the Prophet have more than one sting to their tail." Dropping his reins he unrolled the map partially and jabbed at a specific location. "Here, Excellence, at the Alpuxarras pass, the fortress of Alhendin, reconnoitered recently by my scouts. It is commanded by a cavalier named Mendo de Quexada and garrisoned, my informant reports, by not over a hundred and fifty men. These jackals have been cutting off our convoys, pouncing down upon merchants and travelers, harassing our peasants in the *vega,* and burning their villages and fields. But see you, Great Sultan, the Spanish force marching to Alcala must have been recruited from everywhere close by, and Alhendin is surely left with few defenders." Reduan's eyelids flickered in his pocked face.

Boabdil studied the map, once more prey to indecision.

"But Alhendin is not Alcala la Real," he complained, disappointment adding petulance to his voice.

"We could do worse than recapture a powerful castle which commands the main route to the Alpuxarras valleys and a large part of our own *vega*," Reduan urged quietly. "It would be a tactically intelligent move. Now we know the border fortresses have been weakened of men considerably. If we use speed and surprise we can overwhelm several of these posts."

Boabdil considered a moment, eyes shifting restlessly over the map, then lifted his head. "So be it then." He raised an arm encased in chain mail enameled bright green, the color of the Prophet. "Let the Christian dogs fall to the wrathful warriors of the One True God. Let the fall of Alhendin prophesy our victories to come. Forward, together, servants of Allah!"

The column turned eastward, quickening its pace as it descended from the heights toward Alhendin. If the captains wondered at the speed of the Sultan's recovery from the letdown of Alcala, Francho did not. He suspected Boabdil's continuing present exhilaration marked secret relief and second thoughts at not having to tackle the formidable Alcala and its equally formidable commander.

The Sultan smugly smoothed his brown double-pointed beard as Francho rode by his side and glanced over at his minstrel with a self-congratulatory smile, inclining toward him slightly to keep his words private. "Astonishing, it is not, Jamal, how far we both have progressed since we met in the willow grove? You are Head Musician to the Great Sultan and ride a warhorse by his side; and I am beloved of my people, at last, and flash my scimitar under the enemy's nose. Muhammed, the beloved of Allah, has helped our petitions," he declared, his brown eyes filled with the unusual shine of pride.

Francho forced himself to smile back, even though the distress inside of him was rising almost to nausea. Because of his warning Tendilla would be waiting at Alcala with every available man that could be squeezed from the borders—but Boabdil would strike instead at Alhendin and continue to rampage among the other undermanned frontier strongholds. Tendilla would wait with his massed forces in vain, and Francho had no way to let him know where to dispatch his troops. Should the Moors actually retake the entire forward area about Granada, the Christian setback, bloody and costly, would be Francho's fault, however unintentional. Throughout the remaining length of the march, he mused blackly on his accidental culpability and suffered over his impotence, and deflected the Sultan's concern about his glum mood by blaming it on a bad stomach.

In spite of the stubborn and valiant defense by its outnumbered garrison, Alhendin was taken in a few days, mainly through the efforts of a huge taskforce of diggers. Reduan had observed that the castle was built on a packed fall of shale rather than the solid rock of the mountain and sent in sappers to undermine the walls, the men protected by wooden screens covered with thick, wet hides. Digging in constant shifts, the soldiers cut away the rock and earth base under the great walls and temporarily supported the stones with lumber props, which would be set on fire after the miners had gotten clear.

The small Spanish garrison showered down rocks and lances and heaved boiling pitch from the battlements, and many of the sappers, caught unprotected by the hides, died in a screaming agony of burns. But a greater and more important number of the castle's defenders also went down under the deadly volleys of Reduan's large complement of archers and arquebusiers. At last, seeing the burning torches being run up to the wall the hapless commander Quexada realized that even if he fought to the last man the castle was already lost, and so he chose to surrender. Boabdil ordered Alhendin totally destroyed so that the place might never again house a nest of vultures to scourge Granada, and so it was, the walls blasted into rubble by cannon.

Twice more in the following week, with a terrible aching inside his chest, Francho watched from the shelter of the Moorish camp the bloody downfall of other Spanish outposts, first the fortress Marchena and then the castle of Albolodny, watched as the Moslem army swarmed over the unprepared and undermanned bastions and left the ramparts draped with the dead and the dying heaped up upon each other. The exhausted remnants of the Christian defenders from both castles were carefully rounded up, chained and herded into groups, and immediately packed off to Granada, where the exulting populace would spit on them as they were dragged along behind their mounted captors.

In the cavernous main hall of Albolodny Francho lingered unobtrusively in the background while Boabdil and his commanders discussed their next moves. Since Boabdil seldom dismissed him, the others were as used to his inconsequential presence as they were to the mute M'jambana hovering always close to his master. But although he had been equal to the necessary display of joy at the Christian surrenders, a perpetual moist film rode his forehead as he burned out his brain trying to devise some way to let Tendilla know where Boabdil's forces were raiding.

He listened dully as Reduan labored to convince the Sultan it was time to return to Granada; they had captured three important strongholds, destroying one, leaving a third of their army to hold Marchena, and now needing to leave another third to garrison Albolodny. As reinforcement to his argument to withdraw, Reduan offered another plan. "Let us confound the enemy together by returning to Granada to renew our supplies and then quickly attacking in another direction—toward the sea. If we act swiftly and strike here"—Reduan's finger jabbed again at the map—"there is no possibility their border commander will anticipate us."

The dozen spike-helmeted officers in the surrounding group, their weather-creased, mustachioed faces stern, muttered approval. Now Francho had roused and found himself listening carefully, although he still held his appearance of nodding off. Boabdil, although unwilling to break up his triumphant campaign in the mountains in anticipation of the plaudits and new recruits his victories would bring, finally had the sense to listen to his wily general and reluctantly agreed with Reduan's plan. But on one point he was adamant.

The tall egret plume in his turban trembling, the huge sapphire fastening it flashing in the light of flaring torches bracketed on the bare stone walls, the Sultan announced firmly, "We now have an opportunity to avenge Vizier Comixa for the capture of his niece and her great dowry. The commander of this castle has spit out that a large convoy of Christian merchants and travelers left Jaen en route to Baza and will soon be somewhere about Quezada. Their escort is not large, they have no inkling we are in the vicinity. Tomorrow I want a part of our troops detached to go after this prize. On their return we shall depart here immediately."

One of the mailed and spurred captains spoke up. "Great Sultan, Quezada is dangerously close to Alcala la Real, where the enemy waits in full force and sends out daily patrols."

"True, but a small troop can avoid discovery, strike quickly as an adder, and disappear into the wilderness again. Tendilla expects a full army from the direction of Granada, not from the northwest. Surprise will again be on our side."

Reduan shrugged; he knew Boabdil had his mind set. "Very well, Excellence, it shall be done. I shall give the expedition into the hands of Captain Ahmed ben Fatar, and he shall handpick the men to accompany him. We will set a time limit for the detachment's return beyond which they will be left behind, so that the event of chance discovery will still not give the infidel time to reach us here."

"So it please you," ben Fatar spoke up, heightened color on his dark cheeks, "but I am not too familiar with the defiles and passes of that area."

Another officer chimed in, "That can be soon solved. With some coaxing the former commander of this castle indicated one of his men to be native to these parts. I removed the man from the prisoner convoys, and he is now languishing in the keep. To save his miserable infidel skin he has agreed to guide us along obscure but fast trails through the mountains."

Stretched out on a high-backed bench in the shadows Francho felt every nerve in his body tighten with tension. He had earlier thought of releasing a Christian captive to carry a message, but the vanquished had been chained together and removed so quickly from each fort that freeing one of them had been impossible. But now there was just one, and a prisoner who seemed so tractable he might not be under heavy guard. Attempting to get him away from the castle was a perilous risk, but at least it was the positive action Francho's conscience craved.

Therefore, just before dark, he took himself a casual stroll about the vast castle courtyard, sniffing the wind, greeting the guards stationed about with an airy wave of the hand, stopping here and there for a pleasant few words with the rugged soldiers cooking their suppers over small fires. The men treated him with respect because of his constant proximity to their ruler, and some because they had heard him perform or enjoyed the voice he raised to cheer them during the strenuous marches. Many gave him a friendly grin. He had made a habit of lackadaisical wandering about the camp whenever the Sultan did not require his presence, and the sight of the tall Head Musician in his long tunic stopping to watch the smith at his forge or to examine with a soldier a worn crossbow ratchet was not unusual.

Therefore no one wondered when he stopped before the iron-bound portal of the keep for a casual glance up at the first pale stars of evening, which covered his surreptitious study of the grim walls of the dungeon tower, topped by a crenellated roof and pierced by a few window slits.

The keep stood to one side of the court. Nearby, running around two walls, were the long, narrow, timber stables from which came the snorting of horses waiting to be fed. Across the great expanse of court stood a double-story barracks building that housed most of the Sultan's remaining army, with the rest of the soldiers lodging in tents pitched along the wall and in the center.

Francho cocked an ear at the offkey singing of one of the guards inside the keep, threw up his hands in mock indignation for the benefit of anyone who might be looking his way, and sauntered in the open portal, obviously to correct the soldier's pitch. A few minutes of pleasant banter later he emerged again, having gained valuable information. There were four guards on duty, their vigilance relaxed since they had only one iron-fettered prisoner to look after. The Moors had not found the keys to the keep, so the dungeon above was only barred, not locked. And the key to the prisoner's manacles was shoved into the sash of the pot-bellied guard who had been singing a coarse ditty as he pared his corns and who was now, in good-humored deference to the tender ears of the Sultan's favorite musician, only humming loud.

But reconnoitering the keep had only solved part of Francho's problem. It was at the sight of a troop of men carrying in water in buckets and jars before night fell that Francho's wild ideas for getting the Spanish captive out of the castle coalesced into a plan that had a chance.

The castle had no well. Water was brought from a mountain stream outside the walls and stored in huge brick cisterns. Since it was not their intention to leave their conquerers any comforts, the surrendering defenders had deliberately broken these storage tanks and allowed their contents to spill out, also smashing the great pottery vessels used to transport huge quantities of water at a time. The Moors had been working hard to repair the damage to the cisterns, but meanwhile five thousand men and hundreds of horses, mules, and camels depended on what water could be brought in several times a day by bucket and jug.

Sighing his thanks to God for this, Francho returned to the

castle to find the Sultan preparing to send a servant in search for him. Boabdil's finicky digestion worked better if he dined with music.

One minute a moonless midnight lay silent upon the darkened barracks and ranks of tents in the castle courtyard, a gloom punctuated by areas lit by guttering torches as guides for the watch; the next minute the stillness was broken by nervous whinnying floating from the stables. And in hardly the passing of another minute plumes of gray smoke puffed past the lantern at the stable entrance. The horses began to scream with fright, jerking at their halters and kicking at the walls as a hungry crackle of orange flame shot its way along the dry timber walls in several places.

A disheveled groom stumbled out as Francho watched, hiding behind a nearby tent. "Fire! Fire!" the man screamed. Two soldiers patrolling the area came dashing toward the growing flames, raising the alarm as they ran. "Fire in the stables! Turn out! Fire!" Bright, lurid flames raced upward to left and right, reaching for the stable's thatched roof.

Heads popped out of tents as the dread cry of fire went up and half-dressed men tumbled from the barracks, grabbing at the water buckets sheltered under a canvas beside their building. The portal to the keep tower, the closest structure to the stables, flew open, and two of the guards dashed out to see what the shouting was about. "Allah save us!" one of them yelled back, pointing to the sheds connected to the stables by a common roof, "The powder! The wind is blowing the flames in the direction of the powder stores!"

A helmeted sergeant ran past the keep followed by a hodgepodge of sleepy-eyed men. "Don't gawk there!" he shouted at the staring guards in the keep doorway. "There's water in the trough. Bring buckets, helmets, anything you've got, wet down those powder sheds, hurry." The guards ducked back into the keep, quickly emerged with what vessels they could find, and dashed off toward the stone watering troughs in front of the burning stable.

"The horses—cut the halters and let the horses out!" another officer bellowed as hideous screams and whinnyings came from the smoke-filled stables. Clapping wet turban ends over nose and mouth, soldiers and grooms ran through the stifling smoke and heat with knives to free the animals.

Fanned by a brisk night breeze, the leaping flames madly

consumed the dry wood and straw of the stable and threatened to spread to engulf every structure in the outer court.
Confusion reigned as men raced from the barracks and tents
and scurried from the troughs with buckets of water to toss on
the flames; others, led by an officer, began dragging the heavy
sacks of powder out and away from the conflagration; still
others dashed for the inner court, where they might get more
vessels and basins from the kitchens.

Leaving the shadows the bare-chested Francho became just
one more soldier running for water, coughing and masked
against the smoke. Looking back as if to see the progress of the
flames he deliberately collided with the pot-bellied guard
from the keep. Lowering his head with a snarled, "Watch out,
you oaf! Get your bucket filled!" Francho hurried on toward
the nearly dry troughs, where he shoved the bucket he carried
into the hands of a soldier who stood helpless, lacking
anything to scoop up the water with, and yelled at him, "Here,
take this, I'll go to the castle kitchens for a big caldron." He
disappeared through the milling, scurrying, and disorganized
firefighters into the semidarkness beyond the blazing stables.

But instead of heading toward the inner court, Francho
pulled up and flattened against the wall of the keep near the
portal. Hoping he would be unnoticed in the commotion by
the men pelting past with their eyes riveted on the blazing fire,
he faded inside the gaping doorway and out of view. Grabbing
up a lantern from the guard's table, and with the iron key he
had just removed from the portly guard's sash ready in his
hand, he bounded up a long flight of stone steps. A quick
glance down the corridor of the first landing pointed the way:
two cell doors were open, one was barred. He heaved the iron
bar from the two rings embedded in door and wall and shoved
open the door.

A startled and wary Spanish infantryman blinked up at him
from the dirty stone floor, his wrists circled by manacles
attached to long chains passed through a ring embedded in the
wall. Through the slit window of his cell the man had heard
the cries of "fire!" and the screaming panic of the horses, and
now he sneered insolently and muttered at Francho in the
slurred dialect of the mountains, "Don't think I'm going to
help you put out your fire, you accursed heathen." The coarse
face was derisive.

"You have harder work than that cut out for you tonight,
amigo; I hope they've left you in one piece." Setting down the

lantern Francho knelt and yanked the man's arm over to open the manacles.

The prisoner drew his head back suspiciously. "Eh? What's this? You're not the fat pig from below. What do you want of me?"

"I'm going to get you away from here. You must take a message to the Count of Tendilla at Alcala la Real as fast as your feet can carry you." The opened manacles fell off.

The soldier gaped, but he rubbed vigorously at his wrists and rose to his feet. Francho was relieved to see he was undamaged and steady. "What slimy trick is this?" the man demanded in a surly growl.

"I am a Christian," Francho snapped, "one of Iñigo de Mendoza's complement of knights. And it will cost our side dearly if you don't manage to get my warning to him. How fast can you make your way from here to Alcala? Is there a shorter route than through the Elvira pass?"

"Yes. A narrow chasm not wide enough for horses that goes northwest straight as an arrow. On foot, barely two days."

"If you succeed in two days there will be a gold ducat for you."

"You speak Castilian like a gentleman, yet you look a Moor to me. But just get me outside these walls, and if it serves the King I'll do what you require and with pleasure."

Wrapped around his waist like a hastily tied sash, Francho had brought the knee-length white shirt of a Moorish soldier. Whipping it off he tossed it to the man. "Here, put this on over your hosen, in the darkness you'll pass. But be quick about it. If the guards return we are both finished."

The masking flap of turban over his nose and mouth hid the grim smile with which Francho heard the thunder of hooves and the wild neighing of horses outside the slit window. He had counted on the fear-driven frenzy of the loose and unmanageable horses to create more diversion. Now, if the desperate need for water to save the other half of the stables and storage sheds would drive the firefighters to open the gates and form a bucket line to the nearby stream . . .

He handed a packet of food and a sealed paper to the soldier, who stuck the letter into his hosen, and then, in case the paper was lost, gave the man an abbreviated verbal message. And even with his lower face muffled he tried to stand with the dim lantern behind or below him so that if the runaway were caught he could not easily identify his accomplice. The two of them ran down the stairs and edged over to the door still unguarded by any of the keep detail. Outside there was pandemonium. Now almost the entire huge court was lit by the ravening fire that had transferred its writhing and swift flames to a number of tents. Wild-eyed bunches of horses ran loose, trampling the unagile, blundering into tents, knocking over the piles of sacks and powder kegs that a sweating squadron of soldiers were hastily transporting into the inner court, their terrified whinnying echoed by the brays of the pack mules in the corrals outside the walls. Trying to head off and capture the panicky steeds, panting men chased after them waving garments and lances, shouting directions to each other, but succeeding only in further frightening the stampeding animals.

With eyes rolling and nostrils flared a group of horses galloped just in front of the keep entrance, cutting it off from general view temporarily. "Now!" Francho yelled over the noise of their hooves, and he and his companion ducked out to slide along the outside wall of the tower, inches from the heaving sides of the alarmed beasts, and then smoothly joined the running, gesticulating stream of soldiers that followed behind the horses in an attempt to drive them into the inner court and away from the open main gate.

A wooden bucket rolled crazily on the ground in their wake. Francho scooped up the stray bucket and pushed his man into the dark of a deep arch built between the barracks and the wall. "Praise Mary, the gates are open and the guards have their hands full trying to keep the horses from bolting. It's up to you now, *amigo,* you are free. Take this bucket and run through the gates for water with the others, keep your head down and ducked into the collar of your shirt. If anyone shouts at you, just grunt. Once you get outside you'll find an opportunity to keep running; else you'll know what their finest tortures can do." Francho wiped the sweat from his brow with the back of his arm. "God go with you, *hombre,* and don't fail me." With his thumb he made the sign of the cross on the other's chest.

The soldier grinned toughly, nodded, crossed himself again, took a deep breath, and plunged out into the swarms of soldiers dashing about.

For good measure Francho traced a cross on his own breast. He flattened against the shadowed wall of the arch, straining to see the gates through the smoke. He thought he saw the freed mountaineer scoot before a bevy of horses and disappear under the raised portcullis gate amid a hurrying crowd of bucket carriers. In the darkness and confusion the man could slip behind the chain of bucket passers that had been formed and swiftly get away, Francho hoped, for now officers of higher command were taking charge in the courtyard and would soon restore a semblance of order.

He had to get back to his chamber, and without being noticed. Setting the fire had been easy—two small torches quickly lit and shoved through wide gaps between the planks of the old structures to ignite piles of straw had done it—but getting back into the castle now that everyone was up and about was another matter. He slunk through the melee toward the kitchen court, since the chances were that everyone was coming out the faster way through the inner court. Once inside, if he could scale the rough-stoned far wall unseen, he would land in a weedy garden where a tough vine gave him access to a window not far from his chamber.

It wasn't until he slid through the narrow gate to the kitchen court that he realized from the noise that they were corraling the captured horses in the inner court. And at that moment he came up full tilt against the cold-eyed Reduan and two of his adjutants. The general, fully attired, his sash carefully wound, his spiked helmet gleaming amongst the folds of his under-turban in the leaping light from the portal, stared at him for a moment. Then, as Francho stepped aside, Reduan strode on without further recognition. But Francho was not deceived; the Moor had recognized him and marked his presence half-dressed and sweaty and coming from the flame-filled outer court—the last place one would expect to find the Sultan's pampered musician.

❧ *Chapter 24* ❧

"IT'S...IT'S HARD to describe the . . . the elation that burst through me, especially since I had no certainty whether my messages had gotten through at all, either with the man I freed from Albolodny or the later one I sent from here."

"Well, try," Dolores urged.

They sat on pillows on the floor enjoying a light supper together. She leaned forward attentively, elbow on the low table, chin in hand, enchanted by the impassioned light in his eyes as he cast back in his mind over the past three weeks.

He chuckled, pleased with her eagerness. "Your wish is my will, *doña,* but I'll start from the beginning so you can feel the true pace of it. One has to credit Boabdil for moving fast. From the quick turn around we made here in Granada, off we marched with a fresh army and the cheers of the people ringing in our ears. We reached Salobrena, which perches on a cliff overlooking the sea, in remarkable time, but the worst of it for me, at least, was that it took only one day for Reduan's keyed up troops to overrun the outnumbered garrison and take over the port. And I . . ." Francho paused and grimaced, remembering, then took up his knife and fiercely speared a date. ". . . I was ordered to compose a ballad of triumph for the celebration that night. Ah yes, I sang and smiled and guzzled wine with all the rest, but I almost drowned in my

505

own bile, hating myself for having failed to prevent this catastrophe. The destruction of Alhendin still haunted me, every night in my dreams I struggled with the blame of having denuded its garrison. And now the Moors had captured the port of Salobrena and opened their gates to the world again. I felt that nothing I'd accomplished before could balance my ineffectiveness in preventing so crucial a victory. Boabdil, of course, lost no time in commandeering one of our merchant ships and sending off that fox, Yussef Abencerrage, to the Bey of Tunis to wrangle enough ships to keep Salobrena open."

"Would he have gotten it?"

"Probably. The Bey is greedy, even his own pirates must pay him heavy tributes. Granada was offering him a bounty of five hundred dinars per manned ship and requesting six of them. If they had arrived and stationed themselves in proper formation at the mouth of the harbor, they could have easily fended off a Christian naval force twice the size. And then . . ."

He paused for a moment to appreciate her nose. It was slim, the skin stretched over it so flawlessly a man might want to experience that warm smoothness with his lips. The tip was delicate, if not quite classic. . . .

Unaware of his drifting thoughts she urged him on, wide-eyed. "Yes, and then . . . ?"

He blinked, shook his head, irked with himself, and resumed. "Well, no more had this embassy departed, perhaps two days, when the watch on the fortress tower called out "Sails, ho!" and there, suddenly appearing out of the mist, were four great warships standing off the northern spit, each with great crosses on their sails and the glorious colors of Castile and Leon and Aragon whipping from their tall masts. What a heart-stopping sight! It was all I could do to keep from leaping into the air with joy. Except I wasn't sure that these ships had not put into Salobrena purely by chance and might sail themselves in jeopardy of the cannon on the cliff as soon as the tide turned. But something strange occurred. . . ."

He tore a hunk of bread off a flat, round disk, dipped it into his wine cup, ate it with gusto, and wiped the wine dribbles from his chin.

"Tell! *Madre de Dios,* how do you stop at such a point?" Dolores protested, bouncing on her pillow.

"Patience, woman, you want to starve me?" he protested in his turn, sawing off a slice of roast lamb. But he continued.

"What happened was the warships calmly hove to just beyond the reach of the castle's bombards and rode the swells for several days, neither attacking nor running for help. They seemed to be waiting. Nor was I the only one who suspected what they were waiting for. But the General Reduan could not convince the Sultan that his attack had been anticipated. Finally a courier, having sped first to Granada and thence to Salobrena, galloped into the gates with the news that His Catholic Majesty, Ferdinand, was in full march with a powerful army toward Salobrena. At that point Boabdil had to give in, for without help from Africa, which was not certain, a Christian pincers attack from both land and sea would cause great losses—and worse, would cut him off from Granada. And so we withdrew in haste and made a forced march back here not to be caught in the trap."

"What a triumph for you," Dolores said admiringly. "I mean, it was your warning alone that provided time for the warships to reach Salobrena quickly, before help could come to Boabdil from Tunis. And His Majesty was able to retake the area without a drop of blood spilled! Didn't that further lift up your spirits?"

"Of course, because it redeemed my credibility as an informer. But it also convinced Reduan even further that duplicity was the cause of our failures: the troops at Alcala, the rich caravan that never passed through Quezada, the lack of surprise when the Spanish ships found their port occupied, and the obviously concerted action between the arrival of heavily armed galleons loaded with troops and the marching of Ferdinand's army. Even Boabdil could not deny the enemy had to have acted on information. But he rolled up his eyes and told Reduan he had been surrounded all his life with spies and enemies who would rather have the Christians take Granada than accept him on the throne. How could he begin to know which of his myriad foes was selling information?

"Reduan strongly advised him not to take so many people into his confidence, not to give the council every detail of war plans, not to inform the lesser officers from noble families of delicate operations until they were in the field. But I could have told the general he pushed too hard. Boabdil is a man, but with a boy's thin skin. He becomes sullen, angry to be considered naive, and he closes up his ears."

Dolores caught her lower lip between her teeth. "Do you think there is a possibility Reduan suspects you?"

507

"Ay de mí, who can read that jackal's face? I admit his eyes seem to linger on me overlong when I catch him at it, but this might be merely hostility over losing you. At Albolodny I made sure to immediately explain to the Sultan that I had been taking the air and was impressed into helping put out the fire, and not even Reduan can accuse the Sultan's intimate of treason without having proof. Still"—he heaved a sigh—"I have learned an important lesson. In this dagger's edge business I cannot hope to win every battle. Now I must allow suspicion to subside even if it means some Moorish victories which I might have prevented. It would be wiser to minimize the risk of discovery by reserving my messages for major attacks, such as the one on Salobrena. That conquest could have become the entry point for huge Moslem reinforcements from Africa."

Dolores was trying unsuccessfully to crack a hard-shelled nut in the angle of a brass-handled device. He removed it from her hand, with an easy squeeze crushed the shell, and absently handed her the results.

"Do you think that even now King Ferdinand is marching on Granada?" she queried, picking out the nutmeats from the debris in her palm.

"Quite probably, with so large an army already in the field, but it might not be a serious attack. For one it is late in the season. For another, Granada is too fat with food and arms and defenders. He will come, though, just to serve notice, and to continue to burn off the planting and crops and ruin the earth, so that what is already stored here is the last to be gotten."

He yawned and leaned his elbow back on a pile of pillows, at peace with himself for the moment.

Dolores clapped the crumbs from her hands and rose in order to serve him more *kavah* from a long-handled little pot on a brazier. She saw him blink and look up lazily at her with a soft smile on his lips, and in that one unguarded instant the affection and admiration beaming from his smitten blue glance caused a joy that struck her like a blow. It was only a second's revelation, and then he blinked again, immediately recovering his usual amused but guarded expression around her, but it was enough to feed her determination to get him to realize the truth.

There had to be some reason why he hadn't already sued for Leonora de Zuniga's hand, something that was staying him from betrothal to the woman he claimed he loved. The reason was her, she was sure of it, beginning with Toledo and in spite of his battling against himself ever since. Toledo? No. Beginning in Ciudad Real. The face of the boy who had loved her superimposed itself upon the visage of the adult with little displacement. Her eyes lingered on the planes of his face, tracing the faint frown furrows, the strong cheekbones, the bearded jaw hardly softened by the gleaming hoop of earring, the strength and sensitivity of the square lower lip, and then leaped to meet his shining gaze. She loved him terribly. *Idiota!* Why did he deny what was real?

Smiling, she poured the *kavah* slowly so as not to disturb the sediment already in his small cup. Her thigh and perfumed veils brushed his shoulder. And then, ankle bells jingling softly, she brought him his lute and gracefully sank down across from him, eyes smoky and provocative in the light of the oil lamp.

"Play for me, Francho?" she asked huskily. "Sing my favorite ballad, will you not? 'My Sweetheart Pricks Her Finger.' I have truly missed your voice and your lovely songs."

Francho stubbornly clung to his composure, even though a vision came into his head of how she had run into his embrace with undisguised relief and joy at his return, and his arms felt again how delightful it had been to hug her in that brief moment. He realized it was lonely for her when he was away, although he had provided her with a permit to shop among the vendors crowding the First Plaza. Now he studied her thoughtfully. "I wish there was a way I could pass you on to our own forces when they come close, but it would be more than dangerous. You are much safer remaining here."

Her smile lost some of its spontaneity. "I will survive my captivity," she said dryly, "if *you* will."

The sarcasm was not lost on him, which was why he would not tell her that if and when she departed Granada his life would shrivel like a dried apricot; she would be sure to misunderstand. Instead he rose and stretched and rebuttoned the high neckline of his tunic. "Please forgive me, *doña,* I shall be happy to play for you tomorrow evening, but tonight I will spend in the city since Boabdil occupies himself with his Sultana."

She scrambled up too. "In the Albayzin? But I thought you said you would refrain from sending messages for a while."

Francho drew his eyebrows together. She had become much

too interested in the exact ways in which he spent his time in the city, and for her own protection he wanted her to know as little as possible. To make an innocent visit to his little house with trinkets and scent purchased in the First Plaza as if for a concubine, to stay the night and seem the industrious lover, was all the more important now as answer to any interest in his absences from the Alhambra. What was more, he had become very fond of the two youngsters there and enjoyed visiting them, hearing Ali's proud recitation of his lessons and exclaiming over Azahra's cooking, even delighting the girl and himself by requesting her to dance for him. He knew his casually explained visits to the Albayzin made Dolores unreasonably jealous, but her insinuations irritated him. He had no intention of accounting for his actions to her.

Her expression had faded from eager expectation of an evening together to an unreadable blankness that made him uncomfortable, and he suspected he had been too offhand in ignoring her obvious pleasure in his return—a clumsy but necessary ploy to keep distance between them, and to keep himself in check. But he plowed on, "I would prefer you leave my business to me, *doña*. Return to the harem tonight. In fact, study your lessons. I will be interested in your progress in Arabic. I shall return in the early morning to attend the Sultan, and if he finds my presence unnecessary in the evening, I will send for you."

Disappointment and insult tightened Dolores's chest to hear him order her about as if she were a little child, do this, do that, and she could do little but obey. That cursed, heathen dancing woman! A while back one of the harem ladies had slyly jabbed her with the information that the Sayed ibn Ghulam had been seen buying a Persian shawl in the First Plaza and if it was hers why did she not wear it? Why did she not wear it! Because it was not in *her* garment chest such a pleasant gift rested. Oh, why was it that men had such freedom to take just what they wished and women must do nothing but bide? "When I come back *perhaps* I will remember you," she paraphrased his last sentence to herself, making an invisible face.

Resentment churned behind her eyes, but she worked hard to hide it for a tiny bud of an idea had bloomed in her brain. To him she nodded slowly, tilted up her chin, and murmured with a thin smile, "As you wish . . ."

Feeling helpless, he thought she was angry as she salaamed

exaggeratedly and turned to go, but in a few steps she turned to face him again and seemed to have changed her attitude for her expression had smoothed and become more cheerful. In fact, as she faced him in her rippling pale green veils and pantaloons, saucy mouth curving under the gauzy *yashmak* she had just refastened, her provocatively kohl-outlined, dark silver eyes were wide with a hope. A shimmer of garnets hung from her earlobes, and golden bangles clinked when she moved her arm (since shopping amused her he supplied her with ample dinars to keep her occupied). She stood smiling before him with dainty bare feet in purple-painted sandals, impertinent, delicious, and desirable, and she knew it. He felt the muscles in his stomach tighten.

"Good *raiss,* would you be kind enough to order a litter for me tomorrow so that I may go down to the Grand Souk?" she asked sweetly. Francho raised an eyebrow. The kidnapping of beautiful female slaves was not unknown. Reduan, perhaps alerted by a palace guard, would not be past such spite, and once incarcerated in a household's harem a woman could be hidden forever. "But can you not find what you want right here in the First Plaza?"

"Oh, but there is not much choice in the merchandise. They do not care to transport a great deal up the hill. And I would so much like to find an unusual casket to keep my baubles in, something the other women do not have and would envy."

Her request was harmless enough, and he was probably being too jittery about the cold-eyed general. He finally gave in to her eager look of expectancy. "Well, go then if you must. I'll have a litter sent to you. But stay only in the souk and do not linger overlong."

"Why?" she jousted with him mischievously, head tilted. "Are you afraid I'll be stolen away?"

She was joking but he saw no reason to alarm her unnecessarily. "No. I just don't want you to fall into any trouble. Anyone who was unwise enough to travel close to the border when the passes were clear of snow must have a penchant for creating difficulties."

Her cleft chin rose haughtily. "When one is confronted with the face of doom one flees, helter-skelter or any other way," she protested. But her eyes were still alight with the thought of going down into the city to shop.

Francho accompanied her to the door and then called Selim in to attend him. A wry smile touched his mouth as he remembered, years before, the young Dolores's delight with the gaudy-stoned belts she had slyly maneuvered from unsuspecting waists in the crowd. A man would *have* to be rich to placate her love for adornment, but he had little to buy with the dinars the Sultan heaped upon him. It gave him pleasure to indulge her.

The Great Sultan could not have wished for more receptive, excited subjects than those who peered and craned from streets, balconies, rooftops, and trees along the path of his procession which wound down the petal-strewn Street of the Gomeres to the blaring of trumpets and clashing of cymbals.

The populace saw, closely following the heralds, squadron after squadron of cantering knights in glistening, spiked helmets, masses of horsemen under gold banners and Moslem crescent standards, riding with warlike frowns, lances erect and painted bucklers held stiffly, their light Barbary steeds covered with nets of coins and medals that flashed in the onlooker's dazzled eyes. The Royal Musicians in striped turbans and pantaloons and yellow sashes marched hard on the heels of the cavalry, led by the Sultan's favored Head Musician mounted on a black mule, tall, stern, and important in his embroidered mantle. The drums, fifes, horns, and tiny bells behind him sounded clear in air washed clean and cool by rain the night before.

Behind him Francho heard the crowd's pitch of excitement rise as they saw the Sultan approaching, preceded by an honor guard of splendid palace Nubians with glistening black faces fierce under their high white turbans, their naked scimitars shining as they marched. He heard a roar of approval come from section after section of the citizens of Granada as the smiling Sultan passed before them, stately on a white horse with gilded hooves. The Sultan's red banners with the motto "La Galib ile Allah," "There is no conquerer but Allah," were carried by staunch cavaliers on either side of him. But what pleased the populace most, Francho knew, was that Boabdil was dressed as a soldier, in gold link armor and spiked helmet crusted with jewels, a round buckler with a graven Hand and Key on one arm and a great war scimitar at his hip.

Other renowed personages followed in this parade to celebrate Boabdil's victories in the mountains: Muza Abdul, Reduan, the Grand Vizier, the Chief High Mufti, the Sharif Aamer, and the knights of Granada's powerful families, the red-plumed Abencerrages, the violet-plumed Gomeres, the Zegris in green-and-gold attire.

The procession wound down into the lower city and through the main bazaar, where the wondrous products from the ends of the earth engaged the attention and mingled odors filled the nostrils: spices, garlic, fried fish, incense, camphor, cinnamon, goats, heady smells as all-pervading as the cries of the vendors and the daily yammer and babble of merchants and their customers. In fact, Francho's heart sank as he contemplated how long a seige it would take to reduce such a fat city to starvation.

Still, as they paraded down a path of strewn rose petals enjoying the dappled shade of a tree-lined street, the exigencies of war seemed remote and far away, improbable on this balmy, fragrant day. A mild smile curved his lips, and his thoughts drifted loose as the mule carried him on in state to the inspiring, rhythmical martial music of the corps of musicians behind him.

But just before he rode past the West Gate in the city walls the great, iron-banded portals swung open to admit a bedraggled troop of Moorish cavalry, some of them riding double with wounded companions, their reduced number testimony to the blood-price paid in their constant attacks and ambushes against Christian strongholds in the mountains. The elite members of the procession proudly raised scimitars in salute as they rode by the weary, dusty soldiers, and the people cheered as they scattered to allow them passage, for the men were flourishing numerous captured Spanish emblems and the decapitated head of an enemy knight spitted on one of the pennon staffs. Suddenly, for Francho, the day turned to ashes. He recognized the tattered banner of the house of Pacheco and with horror realized that it was the gaping and bloody head of Don Alonzo de Pacheco, brother of the Marquis de Villena, which was so grotesquely skewered on the pike.

With a smile turned false and frozen he rode on, nor did his interior anger seep away until later that day when Boabdil, in vaulting spirits and careless of Reduan's warning of spies, triumphantly informed his entire council that an organized resistance had been formed against the Christians in both Baza and Gaudix and that when winter closed the northern passes both cities would be ready to overthrow their subjugators and open their gates wide to Boabdil's warriors of Islam. He spoke of the ringleaders of the insurrection with gloating for they had once been his hated uncle's followers, who now despised the defection of their leader. He made flowery promises of victory. Cries of *"Jihad! Jihad!"* rose from every part of the room, and in their approval of his Holy War Boabdil found such peace that toward evening he dismissed Francho and made ready to visit Morayama in her own quarters.

In an excited state Francho left the palace and rode across the bridge to the Albayzin, in his pouch a detailed missive on the Baza plot efficiently naming names that would draw a commendation from even the impassive Tendilla. He planned to send Ali off with it to the blind man, as he had been doing as a precaution in reaction to Reduan's hard stare at Albolodny.

But he found Ali sitting on the threshold step of the little house in the alley sobbing bitterly as one of his urchin friends tried to comfort him. Francho vaulted off his horse. "What is the matter?" he demanded, "Ali, what is wrong?"

"It's Az . . . Azahra," the boy stuttered through his gasps, tears streaming down his thin, anguished face. "Old Zatar found her. He came with city guards and took her away. Ahmed saw it and came to the school to fetch me. Oh J . . . Jamal, he will beat and whip her. He will punish her for running away," the child wailed. "I w . . . want my sister!"

Francho patted the shaking shoulders. "Here now, don't weep so, boy. Tears are for women. Save your grief, Ali. I'll bring Azahra back. How in the name of Shaitan did he find where she was?" He shook his head, angry at himself, for he had been negligent not to ensure Azahra's freedom long ago by using the pressure of his connection with the Sultan to buy her. Well, the swinish Zatar would have to give her up now, if not willingly then by force.

Then Ahmed, a tall, squint-eyed ragamuffin, spoke up proudly. *"Sayed,* I saw it. I was in the street not far from the Golden Horn when the woman gave me a dirham to take a message in to Zatar. And when he read it Zatar sent his servant hurrying for guards. I followed them to see what was going on, and when they came here and dragged Azahra away I ran quickly to tell Ali."

Francho grabbed the boy by the arm. "Woman? What woman?"

Frightened by Francho's scowl the boy stammered, "I . . . I

don't know, I swear. But she came in a rich litter with a royal crest. She hid her face behind the curtain, but I saw a silken green veil and her arm held many gold bracelets. And she pronounced her words funny, like an infidel slave."

Dolores! Shocked, Francho recoiled. How had she dared to strike at Azahra this way? And why, the incomprehensible virago . . . ?

He shooed Ahmed away and steered Ali into the house, coaxing the boy to dry his tears, and promising, if Ali would go on a mission for him, that Azahra would greet him on his return. The youngster finally collected himself and slipped out with Francho's message for the blind man's delivery to the snow gatherer. Francho then waited impatiently until complete darkness covered his rich garments and turban with a hooded mantle and strode off among the dwellers of the quarter toward the Golden Horn.

This time he did not descend into the murky common room from whence issued the wailing sound of a flute as it tootled over the din of voices but used the street-level entry reserved for lodgers. A barefoot slave wielding a slow broom in the passageway looked around and announced in a dull voice, "No more beds to let, *effendi,* our space is full—"

"Where do I find Zatar?"

"But there is no available pallet, master, I sw—"

Francho grabbed him by the front of his greasy tunic so that the stupid eyes bulged with fright. "Where is Zatar, filth, and don't tell me he is occupied. Point out his chamber!"

"B . . . but . . ." Francho twisted the dirty garment tight about the scrawny neck. "Arghh—Allah have mercy—down there, *effendi,* the last chamber—b . . . but he *is* occupied, he is very busy. Mercy, my master, he will kill me."

Francho spotted a tall cupboard with an ill-fitting door and hauled the choking menial along. He stuffed him into the dank space and threatened to return and slit his gullet if he so much as sneezed, then jammed the wooden peg into the latch.

Swiftly he went down the empty corridor and then stopped, listening, before the last door. The slave had not lied. He heard the angry voice of the fat proprietor and behind it Azahra's gasping sobs. He gently pushed at the door; it was not barred. From under his tunic where he always carried it he drew the snake-headed dagger and held it ready beneath his mantle just in case Zatar was unwise enough to be stubborn.

The slam of the door and instant noise of the bolt shooting

JASMINE ON THE WIND

home whirled Zatar around from where he contemplated
Azahra, slumped like a tattered rag in a corner, her face
battered, blood dripping from her nose and mouth, her cotton
tunic ripped in strips. A blood-flecked leather whip lay on the
floor where the panting Zatar had tossed it. The man's eyes
narrowed as he prudently backed away from the intruder's
advance. "Eh? What do you want? You have made a mistake;
this is a private chamber." His nasal voice held annoyance but
not fear.

Azahra forced open one puffed and purpling eye. "Jamal!"
she mumbled. "Oh, Allah is good, I prayed you would
come—" She cried out in pain as she tried to rise.

Francho wasted no time. He kept his voice low, but its cold
menace was not lost on Zatar, who was trying to edge toward
an inner door. "I am Jamal ibn Ghulam. I want to buy this
slave from you. Name your price, you vermin." With a quick
step he cut off Zatar from the other door.

Zatar scowled, his chins quivering. "So! You are the culprit
that sheltered a runaway slave from her lawful master." The
fat face glistened with sweat, but the piggish eyes gleamed
maliciously. "You shall suffer the darkest dungeon in the
Alcazaba for your thievery, knave. One does not trifle with
Zatar, you will find out, nor steal from his property—"

Francho threw his purse, heavy with dinars, on a littered
table. "That will pay you for four slaves. Now fetch me her
bond paper."

"She is not for sale. I do not wish to give up the pleasure of
teaching her to obey. No female scum makes a fool of Rashid
Zatar." With a lumbering lunge at the door to the corridor he
pushed past Francho shouting out, *"Haramay! Haramay!*
Thief, thief! Abdullah, Hamet, to me. . . ."

Francho jerked him away from throwing open the bolt and
swung the man's great bulk around. Then the muscles of
Zatar's flabby face tightened and his thick lips trembled, for
the sharp point of a knife was jabbing into his shrinking belly,
and his hamlike arm was in the grasp of iron fingers.

The voice of the antagonist facing him, though not any
louder, had become pure ice. "Bring out that paper, fat pig,
and be quick or I'll find it myself and dip it into your stinking
blood. Move!" The dagger jabbed harder and Zatar gasped.
"My sharp little friend will slit your guts open if you contemplate anything foolish."

Gulping like a bloated and beached fish under Francho's

516

rough urging, Zatar moved to the table, fumbled around, and finally drew a small document from under a pile of ledgers and papers. There was a reed and an ink pot on the table. With one hand Francho shook open Azahra's bond bill and scanned it quickly.

"Now write a transferral of ownership to Jamal ibn Ghulam and sign and seal it," he commanded, pricking the dagger hard enough into the side of the lardy stomach to draw blood. The pen was hastily taken up and his order complied with.

"May your bones rot, vile thief," Zatar cursed, finally hurling the pen to the floor in outrage. "I shall bring guards and haul you before the mufti and swear I signed her away under force. Zatar is not without powerful friends, you will see, to your woe." He flung his words at his tormenter, purple with anger, but careful not to stir under the deadly little blade almost piercing his belly.

Francho released him suddenly and stepped back, throwing open his mantle to exhibit to Zatar the silver medallion of office hanging on his breast. Zatar stared at it.

"Are your friends more powerful than mine, innkeep? Think you I jest when I warn you that I can whisper one word in the Sultan's ear and no more will you sit by your wineskins and count your profits? If you do not wish to have the river fish snatching pieces from your corpse, I advise you to take that purse and be happy I do not disembowel you right now for your cruelty to this girl."

Zatar gaped. "Of course. Jamal ibn Ghulam, the musician the Sultan smiles upon so generously. The name did not strike me at first. Of course." Like a wave washing over a wrinkled strand of beach a benign expression flowed across his fat face to smooth away the ugly wrath of a moment before. "But why did you not treat with me like a gentleman, *sayed?* Had I known you wanted my miserable slave so direly we could have come to an agreement without such—distress. Would that not have been simpler?"

"I do not treat with your kind, Zatar. I am taking this girl to my house. If you dare come anywhere near her again I will see the Sultan's torturers dip you in boiling oil before my eyes," Francho snapped.

Zatar scuttled to where Azahra stood weaving and propelled her forward. "See," he exhibited, "she is in good condition; I did not whip her very hard and her face will soon heal and look well enough under a veil. After all, what is a poor man to do when an expensive slave, his only dancer, escapes? Punishment is for their own good, is it not?"

"Leave hold of her, carrion." Zatar released the sinking Azahra, and Francho easily scooped her up in his arms, concerned about the amount of blood that still ran from her mouth and nose. But there was one more thing he had to know. "Who told you where to find this girl? Speak the truth or I'll see that your throat is slit!"

"Certainly, certainly, the truth, *sayed*. The truth is, I do not know. A boy brought me a note telling the location of a house sheltering my escaped slave. Fortunately I was standing by the door so I immediately ran outside and I saw, across the little square where the boy was pointing, a royal litter departing. It . . . it could have been one of the Sultan's own women. I thought it was strange, *sayed*."

Aching to kick the false subservience off Zatar's porcine face, Francho carried Azahra down the corridor, past two startled lodgers just entering, and out into the night. She leaned her head against his shoulder and moaned. When he reached his alley he kicked at the door of a neighboring hovel tenanted by an old crone who was skilled at midwifery and healing. "Come across the alley, old mother," he called to her when she hobbled to open up and see who was banging, "and bring your herbs and balms. There is a silver dirham for your services. Hurry!"

Ali was not there when he shoved open his own portal and it was just as well. The boy would have cried to see Azahra's beaten state as Francho laid her on his own pallet. She was barely conscious. Both of her eyes were blackened and swollen almost shut, her nose was surely broken, and he thought some teeth were knocked out. Her tunic and pantaloons were torn and stuck to the bloody welts left by the lash. With a wet cloth he wiped some of the blood from her face and neck. Very gently he cut away the tattered garments to expose her bruises and wounds, and a muscle in his jaw jumped. Had he not been so concerned for Azahra at the moment Zatar would have found himself facing the dagger again, with no mercy shown.

Mumbling toothlessly the old crone entered the house with her wooden box of jars and pungent herbs. She bent over Azahra, clucked. She glanced a question with rheumy eyes at Francho, who shook his head in denial and motioned her to get on with her task.

First she stopped the bleeding from the mouth by applying

a salve to the torn gums and forcing the groggy Azahra to clench her jaws on a small block of wood. Then the healer rattled through her medications and extracted several jars, croaking out what they were as lovingly as if each were her own child. She chose a vile-smelling ointment of theriac, which she rubbed into Azahra's raw welts, paying no mind to the girl's misery as her clawlike hands worked with determined energy. In a basin that Francho supplied her she formed a rag-wrapped poultice of wet thistle leaves, mint, chamomile flowers, and mustard seeds and then placed it on the girl's eyes to draw out the pain and take down the swelling.

The crone gingerly wiggled the puffed, broken nose, and Francho's heart hurt at Azahra's screech of agony, subsiding to weeping as the old woman, chomping her jaws and holding her patient's head still with one hand, used the other to plaster the nose with a white salve which would harden and hold the cartilege in place.

When she had finished her work and carefully looked the young girl over to see no other cuts or bruises had escaped her ministrations, Francho put a coin into her extended hand. "Let her rest as long as she likes," the hag advised. "If a fever comes on give her this. It is an emulsion of cowslip flowers and powdered dung to cool the brain." She handed him a vial of cloudy liquid. Seeing his concerned expression she cackled, "Don't trouble yourself, *raiss,* she'll fully recover. She'll not be a beauty with her crooked nose, but you look rich enough to buy many like her. Eh?" The healer shuffled out, still chewing her gums.

A faint cry came from the pallet. "Jamal, Jamal, he has made me ugly and now you will want me no longer." Azahra wept. "I want to die."

Francho took her hot hand and stroked it, all the while assuring her she would not be ugly, that her spirit was beautiful and so was her form, and her face would mirror her grace and gentleness; and that he would always care for her. In a while she lapsed into an exhausted sleep. He stood looking down at the young girl's pain-drawn, swollen face, and a terrible fury filled him. But not for Zatar.

An anxious Ali returned with word that the blind man had delivered the letter and had finally returned to his hovel with a missive for Jamal ibn Ghulam from the musician's lady in Malaga (so Ali believed). Viewing his sleeping sister with grief, the boy begged Francho to stay the night, but at

Francho's solemn word that Zatar would never come for Azahra again and that she was now free and her bond paper destroyed, the boy felt easier. Instructing Ali to call in the crone in the morning to change Azahra's dressings, Francho swung onto his horse and left.

Riding back toward the Alhambra through the night-quiet streets he blackly considered several dire methods of retribution, but in view of the only motive he could perceive behind this tragedy there was just one seemed fitting enough.

Arriving at the palace he threw his reins to a groom and stalked through the Second Plaza, reflexively nodding and touching a polite finger to forehead and chest as several late-leaving gentlemen he knew passed him. Incorrectly thinking he was out of earshot, one of them, a small man with a large black pearl nestled in his white turban, remarked, "The minstrel hurries like an advancing thundercloud. What storm is raging in the Sultan's chamber, I wonder, that he rushes in haste to halt?"

"Ahhh!" One of his companions shrugged. "The Sultan probably has a bellyache."

But the storm that was to break headed instead for his own apartment, where its victim surely waited. And she was there, amusing herself by picking the strings of his lute inexpertly, a new, wide gold circlet with green jasper and quartz stones shining on her arm. She had let loose her smoldering mane of hair, and it flowed back from her warm-skinned forehead, reflecting a burnished glow from the lamplight behind her. Her black-lashed, tilted gray eyes were long and languid, her moist lips parted. She lounged innocently on the divan, one white-pantalooned leg crooked under her. Smilingly she looked up to welcome him.

"Well! I was becoming lonely. I thought perhaps you were staying in the city again. Shall I send Selim to the kitchens for your supper, or do you want to rest and have wine first?"

He did not answer, only stared at her; the bare, pretty feet, the rounded hips, the pointed breasts that thrust up her tiny jacket; his gaze slid over her satin skin and slim nose and the bewitching silvery eyes, luminous and deep. And hiding guilt. Her langorous appeal was great, and that was her aim. But Francho carried in his ears the pitiful sound of Azahra's shrieks as the old crone manipulated her misshapen nose, and he had to clench his fists hard on the impulse to twist the slender, adorned neck before him until its owner screamed with a comparable pain. It was her mean spirit, however, not her neck that needed breaking.

Dolores laughed uneasily. "What ails you, Don Francisco?" Why did she call him by that name, which they had agreed never to use? To remind him of his real identity? Did she want him to shrug off Azahra as a human being only Jamal ibn Ghulam cared about?

"Have you seen a demon outside the door?" she asked. "Or a Moslem *djinn?*" Trying to appear casual she put aside the lute as he walked toward her. But now she could smell as well as see his fury, and she swiftly sat up, poised for flight.

"Shall I tell you what Azahra has suffered, Dolores?" he gritted through clenched teeth. "Shall I describe to you her welted thighs, her wounded face and split lips, her smashed nose? Or better still, shall I demonstrate to you the results of your evil on a timid young girl whose life was of no consequence to you?" He lunged and grabbed her wrist before she could move, jerking her to her feet.

"It wasn't I!" she cried in growing panic, fighting to be free from his grasp. "I didn't tell Zatar . . ." She gasped at her slip.

"Then how do you know what happened, female viper?" His fingers dug into her flesh.

Dolores understood lying was useless. She had thought her venture performed very discreetly, but that cursed proprietor must have glimpsed the litter, for all her speed in leaving. Even as she had watched the boy run off with the note to Zatar she had been suddenly rocked with the stupidity of her action and flooded with remorse. She had dispatched one of her bearers to bring the messenger back, but too late.

Now her eyes filled with tears of fright. "Oh Francho, listen to me, I . . . I didn't mean for any harm to come to Azahra. I didn't think he would— She was a dancer after all, an entertainer who made money for him. I just wanted her removed, taken away so that you would not scorn my company for hers, so that she could not beguile you into ignoring me. I just wanted her out of the way."

"Why?" he demanded coldly.

Dolores took a deep breath. The only thing that might melt his wrath now was the truth of the matter. Gathering her courage she looked straight into his furious blue eyes and told him. "Because I love you. So simple is it. And so puissant. Because ever since you took my maidenhead from me, ever since I gave it, I have loved only you. I held your memory in my heart for all those years I thought you might be dead. Francho . . ."

She started to reach out her hand to him, but his sharp laugh stopped her.

"Love me, vixen? You love only yourself, your perfumed, pampered, grasping self. Even a tender young girl stood in the way of your vanity. All men bow down before your beauty, do they, Dolores? And when I did not do that you struck out wantonly at an innocent child to preserve your self-esteem."

Dolores shrunk back from his intensity. "No, no, you . . . that is all wrong. I *do* love you. I merely never thought—"

"Well, let me give you something to think about, she-devil! I could easier love a sea serpent than you, you cruel bitch." The sensitive mouth under his black beard was set in a straight, grim line. His sun-darkened face held a black scowl.

But it was the frigid eyes that impaled her with their terrible portent, the eyes of a stranger, which scared her more than his words. He wouldn't, he couldn't clap her naked into the punishment yoke to suffer the torments of the palace loiterers! Or maybe have her whipped? No, not possible. In spite of the hate that consumed him now it was not in him to hurt her. She was his little sister. Alarmed nevertheless, she appealed to him.

"Oh Francho, believe me, I had no thought to really harm your friend. I am very sorry. Won't you understand that it was only because I love you, because you dallied with her so many nights and spoke of her so solicitously. . . . I was jealous, envious, deranged, call it what you will—I don't know why I did it. I thought Zatar would be grateful to have his entertainer back. I can't believe he beat her so hard." Half-hysterical she broke off, one hand trying to calm the heaving of her bosom.

He jerked her close up to him and held her there with cruel strength so that his icy gaze stabbed straight down into hers. "You besmirch the state of love every time you claim it, strumpet, mistress of Medina-Sidonia. Do not profess to love me, Dolores, for soon your lie will curdle in your mouth. You will grovel in humiliation for Azahra's pain. You wish to call yourself a lady? You are a concubine!" Deliberately he grasped the neck of the flimsy blouse she was wearing and pulled; the fragile fabric ripped apart down the front while Dolores stood rooted before him, her eyes huge with shock.

He swung her around roughly and whipped the little velvet jacket from her back and with it the torn remains of the blouse.

"Oh no!" she cried out, clutching her arms about her. "Oh please, no. Not this way—" Her throat threatening to close on her, she tried to run past him to the door, but he caught her about the waist. He yanked at the fastening of her sash, then hauled so she was forced to turn with it until it came away.

"Why don't you scream, Dolores?" he taunted. "Where is your conceit now? Go ahead and scream rape, my baroness of the alleyways, but don't imagine I will have any qualms about locking you in the yoke, where your cries will have more of an audience. It would be easier for me than this. I debase myself by touching you. Scream, I say!"

Dolores cringed, whimpering her shock and heartbreak at the sneer in that glance which she had dreamed would one day fall on her lovingly. His eyes raked along her half-naked body as if she were some dirty peasant woman to be thrown on the ground and used casually, churlishly. She tried to struggle away from him, but her violent movements to escape merely helped him partially rip off the pantaloons from her hips.

She gasped. The sharp, tearing sound pierced through her like a sword blade, a heartless, unjust, and cruel blade—in fact, a scurrilous one. The last thought acted like a flame to dry straw. Her temper flared, cutting through her mortification and loosing her tongue. She rounded on him like a snarling animal, eyes narrowed and flashing her anger and spat out, "Pig! Coward! Must you use your fury as an excuse to take me? Will that assuage your pious conscience and your duty to the simpering Leonora? Well, I shall not allow you that escape, *gusano,* that the noble Francisco de Mendoza could actually prefer a common-born woman to his aristocratic lady. I will not allow you to soothe your conflict of mind so easily, so righteously—"

His eyes remained hard, frozen with contempt. *"You* will not allow me! Medina-Sidonia's whore?" he lashed back. "You are laughable. You are pathetic. You are evil. You vent your spite on a defenseless child."

She felt herself scooped up and in spite of her clawing and kicking dumped onto the couch. Practically sitting on her, ignoring her writhing and the lunges of her head as she tried to bite his arm, he calmly ripped the pantaloons from her hips

523

entirely and then, by throwing a heavy leg over her, managed to squirm off his own tunic. His straight, Persian-style trousers had an easily opened front pouch.

Francho saw from Dolores's very panic that his instinct had been right: there was no punishment so bitter to this proud woman as treating her like abject flesh, the object of empty lust, a passionless rape, a callous violation. The accusations she had made against him only made him more determined to crush her conceit. He was acting as impersonally as the whip that had scourged Azahra, he told himself. Impatient with her wild writhings he dealt her a stinging slap to the face. She subsided suddenly, her body limp in his hands like a jointed puppet, her eyelids still and shut as if she had fled away somewhere.

He ran his hand over her smooth flesh, now as chilly as marble. He cupped a pointed, pear-shaped breast and felt the nipple rise under his thumb in spite of her limpness, rise hard and responsive and he laughed at her harshly. He clamped onto her inert lips with a hard mouth and took pleasure at the taste of tears there. He planted kisses on her luscious breasts and over the soft rise of her belly, and the anxiety he had felt that he would not be able to perform his will turned out to be baseless.

Dolores made only weak resistance as he forced apart her legs and relentlessly mounted her. She would not give him the triumph of vain protests and crying out against the pain. But although she lay motionless under his hard hands and let a whimper escape her only when he forced her limbs to his design, tears leaked silent and bitter from her eyes. Let him believe she wept from shame, from the vengeance of this joyless assault upon her body, from the humiliation of the methodical rape. But the tears that were flowing from the crack in her heart were for her fatal stupidity in believing that he might love her, no matter what he protested. Now he was proving he did not, nor ever would, and she could not bear to look at him, she could not endure to feel the heavy pounding of his heart against her like any ardent lover while she knew his eyes held the bitter truth: contempt and brute lust. Oh, sweet merciful Mother of God, not like this—not like this—

He deliberately squeezed her jaw painfully between thumb and forefinger, forcing her eyes to fly open, and although the lamp behind him threw his expression in shadow she nevertheless saw a mask of raw male power. Her swaggering, handsome knight, her solemn Moor, and the deep cerulean eyes that had glowed at her in her dreams now stared mercilessly, as cold as winter's ice.

She had turned numb against the hurt of his thrusting inside of her, which now grew fast and urgent. Finally he jerked, the arms on either side of her that supported most of his weight trembled slightly; and then quickly, silently, with only a single, muffled grunt and a small flicker of the eyelids to show any feeling, he pumped himself into her.

When he was through he squeezed closed his eyes and, chest heaving, rolled off of her, for a brief moment lying stiffly side by side with her. And a strange notion crept into her stupefied mind that he was feeling as violated as she. But then, with a rough push that almost tumbled her from the couch he growled, "Go. Get out."

Wincing, red-eyed, she awkwardly gathered up her torn raiment, donned what she could, and covered the rest of herself as best she could in her long, silk shawl. He lay on his back starkly, his big body rigid, staring at the decorated ceiling. "Since I purchased you as a slave, Karima, I wish you to return after dawn and I will instruct you in your other duties," he commanded her tonelessly. Wordless, Dolores barely nodded and slipped out the door.

She shuffled down the deserted gallery as if in a trance, staring at but not seeing the gaily colored mosaic falling away beneath her feet. She waited to seethe with hate for him. But there was nothing. No hate, no rancor, no shame surging up to fill the limitless void inside her. What does it matter, her thoughts echoed hollowly in her head, let him mete out his punishment, what does anything matter now? A commoner, a courtesan by rumor, willing the gilded knight to live by the girlish romance she had conjured? How stupid. How pathetic. She had listened to too many troubadours' ballads. And did she even know or want the man who had so miserably and crudely taken her in the guise of punishment?

Yet, a stubborn moaning from the very depth of her battered spirit insisted upon being heard. No, no, no it cried, I see behind his eyes where he will not look, I see the confusion of loyalties he labors to ignore.

With a groan she moved her dry lips, "O merciful Virgin, see my penance, O free me from these wishful illusions, from loving him," she whispered. Her heart lay like a dead, cold lump in her breast. She shuffled on, nor did the guard who opened the harem gate make any mention of her hanging head and abject condition.

The slave boy Selim was relieved of most of his duties. Under the threat of the First Plaza stocks, it became Dolores's job to bring Jamal ibn Ghulam's meals, clean his chamber, remove his shoes and wash his feet, and scrub his shirts and linen. She was ordered to prostrate herself upon entering the chamber, to address him as "honored master," to speak only when spoken to in what Arabic she had, to comb his beard upon command and expect a sharp whack on the behind if she pulled too hard. She was expected to back from his presence with eyes cast down and head bowed. And every night, whether he was present in the apartment or not, she was to lie on his couch and humbly await his pleasure.

Sometimes he dragged her to him with cruel hands, then barked out a laugh and shoved her away, but most often he stood above her as she lay supine and with a coarse epithet and sardonic eyes motioned with his thumb for her to get out. He never touched her in lust again.

Sayeda Fawzia had been instructed to remove her from her comfortable little chamber and give her a pallet in the airless dormitory where the harem attendants were crowded together. Fawzia did this with no more than a shrug and a shake of her head in reproof. Reduction to ordinary slave was one of the lesser punishments meted out to concubines who no longer pleased. It was sometimes rescinded after a while, although often the miscreant was left to live out her life as a drudge.

Silently Dolores did everything required of her, submissive to Jamal ibn Ghulam's every whim. Not once did she glare at him when he snapped at her for not getting something quite right, but kept her eyes lowered obediently; not once did she speak out without permission or curse at him, or show any revulsion with her servile position. The fact was, she had no will to do so. This was her penance to God for her sin against Azahra. It was also an abasement and humiliation she prayed would bring her to intensely despise him. There were times when she looked at her water-roughened hands, or rubbed a back aching from carrying the heavy food trays, or grimaced at the scratchy, coarse-woven tunic he made her wear as a domestic slave, and she hated him blackly. There were times when she wanted to rake the sharp teeth of his silver comb across his face. But it was obvious she had not prayed long and hard enough. She was still prisoner of a pride-conquering, unbreakable shackle. She loved him.

The miserable weeks dragged on, one dawn promising nothing more than another, and one day she realized the first flush of his wrath had passed. His attitude was the same, his treatment of her as crude, his occasional comment as sharp and terse. But when she dared to lift her eyes and briefly meet his stare she saw that the frowning blue gaze held less fury. She thought there was a hint of discomfort accompanying his harsh manner. But she believed her imagination to be misleading her again and continued to go about her menial duties and lonely existence as apathetic as before.

❧ *Chapter 25* ❧

"STUBBORN HYENAS! FOOLS!" the onlooker muttered, royal fingers drumming impatiently on the cold stone of the balustrade. "Silence will avail them naught but pain. Why don't they speak?"

The Marquis of Villena, following with vengeful joy the gory preparations being made below the landing upon which he stood, smiled mirthlessly. "They will speak, Majesty. Their false prophet will not sustain them much longer under our persuasion."

Ferdinand's high, angry brow glistened; the vast, arched chamber was extremely hot. "It will make no difference whether they spit out the names of the other conspirators or not, our mind is decided. Each and every heathen will feel our wrath, innocent and guilty alike."

"I do not believe they will betray their fellows," Don Iñigo de Mendoza murmured, gazing with detachment at the tortured wretches below. "To them this is the equivalent of the battlefield. If they die with honor their souls fly immediately to the warrior's Paradise, a deeply wished for fate."

The Catholic monarch glanced irritably at his most able of commanders, who had sent messengers from Alcala to reach him in the field and inform him of the projected calumny. Tendilla wore his burnished cuirass over a doublet of black

528

brocade; a black velvet rolled-brimmed hat shadowed his somber features. In the ruddy light from the open fire below he appeared the very incarnation of evil intent—were it not that his saturnine face reflected small interest in the bloody proceedings. "A plague of vermin on their false Paradise!" Ferdinand growled. "If those scum die my inquisitors will answer for it. We want them with enough breath left in their scurvy bodies so that they may be a living warning to any other Moslems who may think to embarrass our leniency."

"Yet we have their cache of weapons, the gold they collected to pay for arms and troops, and the main leaders. If any of the rest have escaped us they can do naught but starve in their holes. Their plan is already spiked," Tendilla pointed out quietly, knowing the King was entertaining a disastrous idea in his fury, and endeavoring by subtle maneuver to divert Ferdinand from his revenge.

"Do not plead the Moorish cause, my good lord. Baza has been the great example of what mercy and justice a Christian ruler could show to heathens who pledged loyalty and vassalage. Now it shall be a further example of the boundless suffering in store for any who dare to conspire against us and the Holy Church." Scowling, Ferdinand turned abruptly on his heel and strode out of the chamber. Tendilla, suppressing his distress with the stubbornness of his liege, who was about to perpetrate a terrible uprooting of innocent people with all its attendant economic repercussions, followed him out, face as unmoved as ever.

But the Marquis of Villena, eaten by the memory of his brother's dishonored and headless body flung like garbage on ripped Pacheco banners, remained on the landing of the stone stair overlooking the cavernous torture chamber and licked his dry lips in anticipation of the final degradation of the traitors.

Inferno heat rose from the great open furnace, where a stone crucible rested on a grate in the midst of sullen red coals, a white-hot liquid bubbling sluggishly in its depth. A flushed and sweating torturer, hairy body naked to the waist, knelt and worked a bellows through a hole low in the brick side of the furnace, urging up the temperature inside. Several of his fellows tied wet kerchiefs about their faces and worked over the four fainting captives who had been the ringleaders of the plot to wrest Baza and Gaudix from the hands of the hated infidel and open their gates to Boabdil's armies. Many of their subordinates had been rounded up too, and this very room had echoed to the creak of the rack and the terrible screams of the racked; and the floor was sticky where rivers of blood drawn by the iron-tipped knout had not been properly sluiced away.

But those inferior plotters could tell little beyond what Ferdinand had already discovered, and after punishing agony they were garrotted. These leaders, whose names the underlings had screamed out, would not name any others in high places who may have been involved. Their feet crushed and dangling, their shoulders pulled out of joint, their fingers bleeding and nailless, they had been brought back time and again from the point of oblivion by the clever timing and experience of the Chief Torturer.

Glancing up, this black-hooded personage was now disappointed that his royal audience had left the scene, especially since he had added to the next indignity, the blinding of the heinous traitors, the irony of using the Moors own method of passing seething liquid copper before the face to burn out the eyes. The hot pokers he usually employed were quicker and less trouble. But at least the Marquis was still watching and he would carry a report to the King of a job not only accomplished but most artfully done as well.

Above, in one of the sunny chambers of the governor's residence in Baza, Tendilla still tried to turn Ferdinand from his course. Toying with his jeweled dagger he leaned against a slender, carved pillar and watched Ferdinand mount the two low steps to a window bay to peer out over the city through the gilded grill. The Catholic King stood with his fists resting firmly on his hips, a posture which the Count recognized as his stance of definite decision. Shrugging, the Count hazarded one more point.

"Sire, Baza has been a rich center of commerce and a good source of taxes. To depopulate the city would in the end deprive the Royal Treasury of much revenue. Economically speaking, can we afford to wipe out such a potential supplier of gold for our coffers and products for our markets?" Not to mention, Tendilla added to himself sadly, the doctors, lawyers, skilled artists, and craftsmen who would be forever lost to the fabric of society.

"Bah! The monarchs of Spain could not afford *anything* they have accomplished in the past three centuries, and yet their feats have brought us to this triumphant present." Ferdinand turned and glowered at Tendilla; an old wound in his leg ached with the coming of rain and he felt suddenly tired. "You make too much of the value of these heathens to our well-being, my lord, although I subscribe it to your cautious instinct rather than any conscious sympathy for these benighted Moslems. Many of our northern people would happily remove south to Baza, I do not worry that the reins of commerce will be left slack. But I *will* teach El Rey Chico in Granada that his fomenting of conspiracies in my territories will only bring grief to his people and avail him nothing."

Smoothly Tendilla changed his tune; the situation could not be saved and he did not want to jeopardize his hopes of governing Granada by creating the impression he would be too mild in his treatment of the enemy. Idly he fingered his little pointed black beard where some glints of silver now shone, considering for a moment. Then he nodded his head. "Your Majesty, I bow before your great perspicacity. In the long run defanging the adder speeds our triumph and cuts our losses; I can see persnickity economics has no place here."

"Well, of course, my lord," Ferdinand grumbled, mollified by Tendilla's about-face. He valued Iñigo de Mendoza both in spite of, and for, his insightful and firm opinions, and seldom had the pleasure of seeing the man back down. To smooth what might be underlying ruffled feathers he said more heartily, "Good sir, I need not repeat how meritorious we consider your service to the Crown. But now I charge you reserve a purse of gold as extra reward for your agent in Granada. His informations have been timely and valuable and we want to keep him happy. The Devil knows how far that scabrous plot to assassinate my governor and storm Baza's walls from the inside might have got had it not been for his warning to you. How you manage to smell out these turncoats in the bosom of the Alhambra I cannot fathom, but pay the man whatever he requires to ensure his continuing dispatches."

"Indeed, by all means, Majesty," Tendilla concurred, concealing any sarcasm. The Catholic monarchs contributed not one penny to the cost of maintaining his spies; in fact, the frugal Isabella, realizing how much more efficient were Tendilla's informers, had dismissed as wasteful most of the Crown's own paid agents. But what chagrin the Count felt at how generously the fund-pinched Ferdinand allocated other people's gold was mitigated by the King's spontaneous praise for his excellent agent in Granada. Please God, in whose hands lay the future, it would cost the rulers of Castile and Aragon much more than just a purse of gold to eventually show their gratitude to him and to the luck-blessed, talented lute player in the Alhambra.

Tendilla quickly cut off the flush of optimism that threatened to rise within him. He was not yet in the Governor's Palace in Granada, Francisco could not yet own to the name of Venegas, and not yet could easily be never, so slippery were the building blocks of fortune he was endeavoring to pile one upon the other.

Ferdinand rang a bell on the table. "Call together the lords who have attended me here in Baza, at once," he ordered the lackey who entered, "and summon a scribe to attend me as well."

In the presence of his officers Ferdinand dictated to the secretary his punitive and harsh command to the Moorish populace of Baza: convert immediately to the Christian faith or be exiled to Africa.

For the majority of the Moslems this represented no choice and Ferdinand knew it. He was, in effect, ordering transplanted forty thousand men, women, and children whose families had dwelled in this city for centuries and to whom any other place would be alien. Warming to his work Ferdinand continued by dictating a letter to the Inquisitor Torquemada, bidding that cleric send a representative of the Holy Office in haste to Baza or come himself if he were able. Those Moslems who thought to feign conversion in order to escape banishment would think twice about insincere kissing of the Cross while the image of the tonsured saint painted on the dread yellow banner of the Inquisition fluttered above them.

❧ *Chapter 26* ❧

THE DAWN CRY of the muezzin on a nearby mosque tower—
*"Allah akbar . . . echoed en la ila ella Allah . . . there is no
God but Allah . . . prayers are better than sleep . . . come to
the best of work"*—awakened Jamal ibn Ghulam and set him
to sniffing the pleasant smells of the breakfast Azahra was
preparing. He dressed, then sat in his accustomed place by the
hearth and ate quickly, wanting to return early to the Alhambra; but not forgetting to praise the chewy, flat bread which
the girl had baked herself and for which she stood by anxiously and hopefully to hear his opinion.

The passage of six weeks had healed Azahra's body and
faded the bruises on her face, but her nose had a definite swing
to the side and she was left gap-toothed. She had taken to
wearing an opaque *yashmak* even about the house, to hide her
ugliness, she insisted, and her spirit, always timid, had become even more shy. But besides the visits of her benefactor,
to dance was her greatest pleasure, a way she could express
herself, and as soon as she had recovered she heeded to
Francho's urging and continued to dance to his guembri
accompaniment in the ancient, sinuous, suggestive Eastern
mode she had been taught. She danced for him as much as for
herself, bashfully trying to entice him, but her tender fourteen

533

years had totally erased his original prurient interest, and all that remained was his genuine appreciation of her talent.

Now he counted out his usual weekly allowance of money for her and Ali and hastily departed, for the foiling of the Sultan's ambition to retake Baza and Gaudix had left Boabdil in a funk, erratic and demanding. The Sultan seldom rose early, but it was better to be available.

He found Dolores sitting cross-legged outside his chamber as she did every morning, awaiting his summons. She followed him into the room, her eyes on the floor as became an obedient slave. He tore off his turban and unbuttoned the frogged closings of his tunic, shrugging the garment off.

"Sayed?"

"Well?"

"Late last night the Sultan sent a guard to request your presence in his bedchamber."

"Did you say I was visiting my house in the city?"

"Yes."

"I had no callers." Evidently Boabdil's recently reacquired headaches or nightmares or insomnia had not been so dire that he bothered to send someone to the Albayzin to fetch his minstrel.

Dolores stood patiently waiting for his orders, her head covered with a shawl. She wore a coarse, unbelted tunic loose over her pantaloons and no jewelry, no cosmetics. She was wanly beautiful, even though she appeared to his searching eyes to be drawn and very spiritless. He was still puzzled at her utter collapse in the face of his wrath; he had expected tantrums, curses. What had become of the Dolores who had scrapped with him over trinkets in Ciudad Real and pulled him up short in Toledo?

He had thought he would enjoy breaking the vanity of this pseudo-baroness. And he had, for a short while, when Azahra's misery was still fresh in his ears and the image of the whip-wielding Zatar standing over the bleeding young girl smote him. But as Azahra recovered with the resilience of youth, the first fury of his vengeful retaliation had drained away, leaving his mind open to an irrational shame through which whispered the distressing words, ". . . must you use your anger as an excuse to take me? . . . to assuage your pious conscience to Leonora . . . your mind and your heart conflict . . ." The heavy pressure of guilt galled him so much that he stubbornly would not consider relenting, at least not soon.

But Dolores was like some proud, wild mare who had been broken to a plow beast. Her uncomplaining subservience was disconcerting. Was she that much afraid of the punishment yoke, or was she truly repentant that she had not stopped to understand the harm that would come to Azahra? Had his cold brutality shocked her beyond recovery? Was she acting?

A fresh shirt dangling from his hand, he cleared his throat brusquely. "Dolores—I—"

At his gentled tone she looked up with dull, empty gray eyes. He dropped his gaze quickly, irked by both his pity and worry. Hadn't she deserved everything he had meted out? "Because I love you" came the recollection of her voice. Said to divert his wrath, of course. . . .

He muttered, "Go fetch some *kavah* to me, and be quick. And tell Selim to attend me in the baths. I shall steal a few minutes more from the Sultan."

Without a glance at him standing gruff and bare-chested and curiously nonplussed, she slid from the room.

Francho bent his head over the guembri, concentrating on the new and intricate melody he was picking out accompanied by fellow musicians on the harp and flute who listened closely to follow him. Suddenly the calm of the Sultan's noon repast was shattered by the frantic blasts of the alarm horns on the ramparts, staying the food-filled fingers of his guests halfway to their mouths. A panting captain of the palace guards rushed into the saloon and with a sketchy salaam informed his ruler that a Christian army was debouching into the *vega,* a vastly greater array than the motley troops who had been marauding all spring and summer in the valley, burning the fields and seizing the herds, filling the air with smoke and blackening the once green leagues about Granada. Startled, worried eyes met and locked, and then the members of the council who had been eating with the Sultan dropped their napkins and rose.

Beckoned to come along, Jamal ibn Ghulam hurried with Boabdil and his senior advisors to the highest square tower of the palace, where they were joined at the battlements by Ayaxa, a pale Grand Vizier Comixa, ailing ever since the capture of his niece, and various other council members in an agitated state.

Silently, grimly, Boabdil squinted into the distance toward the purple peaks, at what seemed like endless descending silver streams, actually mounted men in glinting armor pouring in proud order from several defiles in the mountains to join into a great, bristling column on the *vega*. His counselors, muttering nervously among themselves, stared at the enemy multitude debouching from the passes. Finally Boabdil grunted, "I do not understand this. The summer is far advanced and yet the Christian comes with all his might. We will not be drawn out into full-scale pitched battle with him, that he knows. And our walls are too high to be breached and too thick to be pierced, the flaming arrows of our bowmen massed enough to repel rammers."

"He begins a blocking siege, then," Comixa responded through dry, stiff lips. "One suspects he is determined to vanquish us this year."

"He is a fool," Boabdil frowned. "We have stores enough for three cities."

Below them they could see tiers of rooftops filled with excited spectators. Francho could imagine the merchants banging to the shutters of their stalls, the mothers dragging off their children, the mass recitations in the schools cut off in mid-sentence, the streets and marketplaces emptying as if by magic as people reacted to the alarm horns and the cry "The Christians! The Christians!" rising from every side, some running to hide, others racing to the mosque towers for a vantage view of the full enemy force. Looking tiny below, the squadrons at the city gates were being faced with an incoming stream of frightened villagers laden with whatever belongings they could lay hands on, escorted by mounted men sent to hustle them in faster. Carts rattled in crammed with children, oldsters, flapping chickens and geese, sacks of seed and teetering family heirlooms, threadbare prayer rugs and embroidered pillows. Ram's horns blasted out along the thoroughfares clearing a path for troops of mailed soldiers jogging from their barracks to reinforce the walls and for supply wagons loaded with the ammunition, cannonballs, crossbow bolts, arrows, and pitch needed for repelling any assault upon the great, keyhole-arched gates.

Standing next to the Sultan the old Sharif Mohammed Aamer cried out through his fluttering white beard, *"Izmahu!* And to what avail will be all our provisions? Do we forget the siege of Baza? Once his fang is in the fruit the Christian dog will not lift his siege until he sucks our juices. We cannot depend on our citizens to suffer want bravely. They are arrogant when the enemy is at a distance, but when he thunders at our very walls they will weep in misery at their empty larders and turn on us as their tormentors. I say, O Sultan of Greatness, we would be wisest to sue for honorable terms."

A loud murmur of protest went up, but not from all of the counselors.

At the sound of heavy footsteps, Francho turned to see Muza Aben coming from the stair followed by several lieutenants. The mailed and helmeted general approached scowling at the words he had just heard. "Shame to you, honored Sharif, for such craven thoughts, you who are called Sharif because the very blood of the Prophet flows in your veins!" he bellowed, heedless of the old man's dignity. "O Great Sultan Abu Abdullah, your fighting men salute you. We have nothing to fear. Our cavalry is fleet and courageous, and we will harass the enemy troops to their deaths. Our walls are defended by endless relays of archers and arquebusiers deadly sharp of aim, and most significant, our food depots are full to bursting. The Spanish king will have to sit before our gates double a twelve-month to starve us, and consider, the Baza siege lasted only five months. Then where in such a long, weary time would our enemy gain his own supplies or find the money to keep so great an army in the field? The fall rains will soak his flimsy camp and wrack his men with fever, with disease; illness will decimate his ranks as relentlessly as will our own fierce sorties." Now the heavy, black gaze transferred to the old counselor again. "I say calm yourself, Sharif Aamer. We are not helpless or intimidated. My masters, if we remain staunch, if we remain as stubborn and brave as our conquering ancestors, the power of great Allah will not desert us."

Even those counselors who had paid attention to the Sharif's wavering gave heed to this bull-necked, snorting warrior and quickly regained their balance, murmuring assent. Francho too regarded him with grudging admiration. His very physical presence could imbue a mouse with courage.

Fearing to be forgotten, Boabdil took up his general's ardor. His jaw shot out in an unconscious imitation of the general. "Well said, gallant soldier. Are we women, sirs, to cringe before the enemy? Is it not on our heads to avenge the deaths of our kin and our friends, the insults to our faith, the sorrow brought on our land by this treacherous aggressor?" The murmur of assent was even louder now. "We all know our duties. Muza Aben commands the cavalry, ordering and leading all sallies. Reduan Venegas and his adjutant Mohammed Sayde will defend our walls and gates. Abdul Kerim Zegri"—and his glance fell on a young captain who had accompanied Gazul—"has charge of the walls of the Alcazaba and the Alhambra. Sharif Aamer, we have placed the allocation of foods and provisions into the capable hands of Ali Hamet Gomeres, who has sworn to find us at least two years of plenty from within our full storehouses."

The elder dropped his head and his gray brows in withdrawal. A page in striped pantaloons who was holding a tasseled silk umbrella on a long pole over the Sultan's head forgot himself and shouted with excitement, "They pass by the village of Maras. This time they are coming up to the very walls!"

"Allah, Allah, let not the feet of the Christians' curse defile our dear valley," the pious High Mufti prayed aloud, raising his fine, soft hands. "Strike them down where they are, O Worker of Miracles," he cried.

With poise Boabdil studied for a moment the glittering Christian forces riding out the shadows of the moment onto the *vega*. He turned to his chief commander. "I order every gate to the city now closed; no one, neither master nor peasant, shall be admitted or allowed to leave except those I authorize and your cavalry. That is my decree."

Muza Aben bowed heavy shoulders in a salaam and backed away from the royal presence. "It shall be done, as you say, O Sultan," he barked. Wheeling, he thudded back down the stairs with his men.

Francho's gaze grazed Ayaxa, who had said nothing since she had arrived on the tower but who stood there, small and thin, her back as stiff as her iron will. Her eyes, however, were shining to see, at last, her mild-faced, silver-turbaned son acting the worthy successor to his bellicose father. But Francho turned toward the *vega* again, for he could not keep his own eyes from the glorious spectacle of the military might of all Spain united as it bore down upon them steadily, and now the breeze brought faintly the sound of drums and bells. He had coaxed to his dark, bearded face as angry an expression as the rest of them, but in his heart there was leaping joy to see the masses of bright Christian banners flying in final challenge to the crescent standards of Mohammed that fluttered from the towers of the city.

Still, the order to close the gates to everyone worried him. Did the edict mean that even those with important services, such as the snow gatherers, would not be allowed in and out of the city? Meat could be slaughtered only as needed, fish from the Darro sold as caught, the luxury of iced drinks and sherbets could be dispensed with. It was more than possible his line of communication would be cut.

In his exalted mood Boabdil allowed his attention to be heavily claimed by siege preparations and defense demands from all sides. Thus as soon as Francho was dismissed after the evening meal he rode across the bridge to the Albayzin, and when darkness set in he sent Ali off to inquire the situation from the blind man. In a while the boy returned with word that the blind beggar had reported that the snow gatherers yet came and went on their business in the mountains to the northwest unhindered; whether this would prevail remained to be seen. Bonfires had been lit throughout the city and around these, large crowds of young people had gathered to shout and gesture their defiance of the besiegers until they dropped with fatigue. Just as the last of these boisterous groups wove past the shadowed mouth of his alley, Francho's own drooping head was brought bolt upright as he sat in his doorway getting some air. Several tall, silent figures stalked toward him and he looked up to the black faces and stern expressions of three palace guards. Five minutes later, his turban rewound, his shoes donned, he remounted his horse to ride back to the palace with them because the Great Sultan was urgently requesting his presence. Stopping at his own apartment to pick up his lute, which the Sultan found more soothing than the guembri, Francho followed the guards once more and was admitted into the Sultan's bedchamber.

"A nightmare, musician, a most terrible vision," Boabdil croaked out to him and shuddered, propped among his silken pillows as hollow-eyed as an old man, unashamedly anxious to see his private chaser of bad dreams. He passed his hand before him in a wide swath as if painting the background for the apparition. "I saw before my eyes, under the light of a red sun, my very own throne, the proud and ancient throne of all the sons of Nasr, and it was covered by dusty spiderwebs and haunted by yellow-eyed bats and owls. And under the moldering cushions of this throne there was a skull—my skull with a lonely river of tears flowing from the gaping eye sockets. And everywhere around there were bones, broken, bloody bones. And the dead white skull wept and wept, somewhere beyond the heavy crimson sun a fearful voice boomed out wild laughter. . . ."

Boabdil turned over and buried his face in the pillows with a muffled groan, the body under his loose robe twitching.

Puzzled that the same man who had stood so regally on the ramparts that afternoon and gave courage to his counselors, a ruler whom he had seen ride to the attack with his troops and lay about him with his jeweled scimitar as bravely as any of his warriors, could yet be left so terrified by a bad dream, Francho unslung the lute, approached the divan, knelt, and sat back on his heels.

"A too rich supper, perchance, Excellence? Always the cause of bad dreams."

Boabdil's head moved back and forth in a despairing negative. Francho was put in mind of a hopeless child. He raised the lute and picked a soft, random melody. "Such dreams are the work of Shaitan to confound your course, Excellence. They are best forgotten."

Boabdil pushed himself up slowly and peered at his Head Musician with ghost-haunted eyes. "No. It is an omen. I shall call the Royal Astrologer to define it."

"That may not be necessary, O Sultan. Why do the evil one's work for him? Your own work calls you in the morning, and the joyful light of Allah's day will cleanse away this demon's poison from your mind."

"I am afraid," Boabdil muttered wanly. "There was a prophesy when I was born. . . ."

Keeping silent, the Sultan's minstrel let his ruler talk about the cruel prophesy, about his treacherous father and his hunted, fearful youth, and about his love for his people; for Francho had early realized what the lonely Sultan most needed was a sympathetic ear in which to pour his torments. But finally he took an opening to veer the subject away from the morbidities that weighed down Boabdil's soul and engaged the Sultan's ears in praise of how solidly fortified and prepared the city was, how excellently organized the army and the resources, how loyal to the throne seemed the people crowded into the stout-walled city. Color came back into the royal face, the lines began to smooth from the brow. In fact, his tension eased, Boabdil belched raggedly three times. He looked at Francho startled, and then laughed outright.

"A bad digestion, did you not say, minstrel?" he quipped, his mental relief as great as the physical one.

The Great Sultan of Granada lay back gratefully and closed his eyes. It took a long while, but he finally found the sleep neither wine nor his physician's potions could give him, soothed into it by the skillful, gentle hands of the musician, Jamal ibn Ghulam, moving upon the lute strings.

Francho judged it near to cock's crow when he finally padded through the silent, dim galleries to his chamber, yawning hugely and wearily, but pleased. He had once more demonstrated the worth that gave him intimate proximity to the Sultan and in the process even gained some fresh and important information on the unwillingness of foreign caliphs to help Granada as Boabdil had slumped shredding the tassels of his pillows. Francho's tired facial muscles fell into a brief but lupine smile.

But as he crossed a flower-planted court where a fountain bubbled softly into the tranquil silence a whiff of jasmine caught him, and there suddenly returned a heavy ache of guilt in his heart. He compressed his lips together hard as if that would erase it. He wondered if anything would ever erase it.

Dolores had fallen asleep on his couch. Even in the yellow light of the lamp her face was pale; there were dark smudges under her eyes where the lashes lay so still. She looked sad and so vulnerable, curled in a lonely huddle. He stood looking down at her, loath to wake her to send her away, ascribing to flinching conscience the mix of exasperation and tenderness that flooded through him and made him want to kneel down beside her and ask her forgiveness. He gazed at the sleeping woman and saw again the girl-child who had shared his youth, dirty-faced, bare-legged, sharing with him the comfits she had snatched from a vendor's tray, giggling in gamine delight at his vulgar verses insulting the pompous Alcade, oaths like a muleteer issuing from her pink lips when he teased her. He recalled Toledo and with what sorrow she had told him of Tía Esperanza's death—Tía, the only person who had ever cared about her—and how she had turned to him for words of comfort. He considered her startling beauty, her pride in the station she had so capably assumed, her fluting laugh, her courage. . . .

He squeezed his eyes shut. Well, he could no longer flail her for being Dolores. He had humbled her more than he had thought possible. The sin of his presuming to be judge and executioner of her spirit was finally confronting him, lay heavily on him, and he knew he would someday have to pay for it.

Without bothering to put out the small flicker of the lamp, he undressed and lay down beside her, wakeful, one arm behind his head, the quiet breathlessness before dawn allowing the events of the day and night to revolve through his head like a giant wheel. After a while he shifted his position slightly and accidently touched her hand, for she now lay on her back. Dolores sighed and withdrew her hand, then, obeying the prompting of some yearning dream, rolled over in her sleep toward his warmth, so close he felt her even breath on his arm and her leg pressed lightly against him. Filled with contrition and—no lying would help it—desire, he turned on his side and put his other arm about her gently so as not to wake her; and helplessly, humbly, kissed her smooth cheek. He hoped his beard did not tickle her awake. He just wanted to fall asleep like this, holding his impossible, alluring, sorrowful *"hermanita"* without strain or guilt or blurring of goals, just happy to lie next to her, his strength protecting her vulnerability.

But she did wake up. She woke up smoothly, without warning or start, he knew it by the sudden falter in her breathing. Slowly she drew her head back so that the tiny flame of the oil lamp on the stand was reflected in gray eyes, wide and questioning and forgetting to be blank, and he was pierced through by the fear he read there. Silently he lifted his hand and stroked the tiny tendrils of hair off her brow, off her face. Then his sensitive, strong fingers moved to trace her eyebrows, trailed down her temples to linger along her velvety cheek and then to tenderly outline the wide, full, parted lips. He was unable to hide the latent affection in his touching or ignore the tingling joy that came to him through his fingers, he was unable to tear his eyes away from the sheer disbelief in hers.

Dolores was certain she wasn't dreaming. She wasn't dreaming but yet she couldn't wake up. She felt the heat of his breath as his face came close to hers, but the brief kiss he brushed her lips with had only the weight of a feather. She lay as still and limp as a doll, only her eyes moving as she looked up into his shadowed, strong features. It came into her befogged mind that she must be paralyzed. Although she had stolidly endured the brutality she thought she deserved, she wanted now only to flee from this strange reversal, and yet she seemed to have no connection to her muscles.

"Dear God," she heard him groan, and he suddenly buried his face in the soft hollow where her neck joined her shoulder. "Dolores, Dolores," came his anguished whisper, and thoroughly startled, her eyes widening, she thought she felt the damp of a tear against her skin. The muffled, miserable voice mumbled, "How can you know my true remorse if I can hardly tell of it? I've treated you with unspeakable bestiality —and yet, I plead with you to forgive me. Forgive me, forgive me, Dolores, God help me, every word you flung at me was true. I wanted you and so I took you . . . ." His voice broke off into a groan again, the guilt-stricken pain of the man whose cruelty and contempt had cast her into limbo these past weeks. Her lips began to tremble. He went on, "Shaitan take the dainty lies of chivalrous troubadors. The word is not wanted, but want." The baritone became stronger. "Carnally, with every nerve and muscle in my body. And I am helpless to know how to apologize for it, to know how to atone for my brutality, helpless to control my hunger for you. Don't hate me, don't hate me, *hermanita,*" he begged against her neck with desperate fervor, "don't hate me—"

A sob caught in her throat, for she was as miserably helpless as he. She pushed his head up, pushed him back until she could see his eyes, and even in the shadows she beheld the suspicious glistening that matched the tears welling in her own eyes. For a moment her gaze moved over the planes of the handsome, abject face above her, dark curls falling over the forehead, strong, proud nose, the stubborn line of the bearded jaw where a muscle twitched, the mouth set in a grim line, the Adam's apple jutting from the strong neck, bobbing. Then once more her eyes met his. Neither of them breathed nor spoke nor moved, existing only in this moment of wordless communication with the private longings of their hearts held naked in their eyes. And then the spell woven of intimate silence and unuttered meanings deepened into movement.

Sighing, she slid her arm about his neck. He bent forward

and found her mouth. They kissed with so soft and exquisite a tenderness that the glory of the dreaming moment was forever impressed into the infinities of their memories.

And then the tranquil prelude was gone, and swept away with it was all the rancor, all guilt, all proud emotional dams. She clung to him, hugging him as fiercely as he was hugging her, and then she threw back her head to laugh shakily. He gathered her to him, kissing her throat, her chin, her lips; he tasted her lips with small, deep kisses as if he were savoring the sweetness of ripe fruit, and then forced them open with his thrusting tongue to explore the space beyond them, his arms tightening about her convulsively as she met him with her own questing tongue, timidly and then finally passionately.

Dolores gloried in the joy coursing through her. Nothing else mattered, she was doing what her heart wished and her body craved. With her own hand she helped him to find the simple fastenings of her garments and draw them quickly off until her flesh was as naked as his, and then went easily and naturally into his arms, molding her body to the heat of his, enfolded by him and pressed hip against hip, thigh against thigh, reveling in the ripple of muscles in his back, the tight, smooth warmth of his skin, the masculine smell of him as she buried her nose in his neck, the strong hand that carressed her buttocks. His groan this time was of sheer delight, and a deep pleasure flooded through her, and what was more, a bold need.

Her sudden move to withdraw surprised him enough that she was able to break from his embrace, but only to push him down on his back so she could crawl further up on him, acting by instinct and a powerful love to press quick and burning little kisses on any of his face not covered by hair, and then working down, over his broad, hard chest, his flat belly, hearing his breath catch in astonishment and then come quicker, feeling his heart beating strongly under her lips . . .

He pulled her up to fit his mouth on hers again and kissed her ardently, one hand slipping up and down her body in heated answer to her, then he rolled them both over so that now she lay on her back, and in the first blue light of morning from the window grill she saw that the hot azure gaze devouring her also held wonder and tenderness and perhaps even love, and it was her turn to give a small moan of pure happiness.

His warm palm caressed her hips and belly in sensuous,

possessive circles, and then his hand slid up to cup one pear-shaped, pointed breast. She closed her eyes helplessly against the voluptuous tremors that rippled through her body. His lips closed around her erect nipple and he tickled it with his tongue and sucked and drew at it, summoning her very soul to the site of his mouth, and also to the moist place, far away, where his other hand was beginning slowly to touch her and move. She gave herself up to the ecstasy he was creating, opened her legs, let her hips keep rhythm with the skillful hand where now her whole life and being seemed centered, her heart skipping as his tantalizing lovemaking seemed to lift her off the bed.

The hard, insistent lips sought her mouth again in a deep, lingering, tonguing kiss, and now that mysterious, musky male scent filled up her nostrils and set her body trembling, set it on fire. Deliberately he removed his mouth from hers and in a second she felt his lips close around her other nipple. The pace and movement of his fingers in the wet warmth below her triangle of hair increased feverishly. She was riding his finger, riding, mounting to a delirious pitch, her breath coming in gasps, her open mouth dried, she did not know where she was or care, she only wanted something, wanted, wanted— Frantic, she sunk her teeth into his muscled shoulder and heard him laugh. He discontinued for a very brief moment, and just when she thought she was going to kill him for it he was above her, he entered her, and there was no pain, only the most exquisite rapture spreading from between her legs through her whole body as she accepted him and surrounded him with her warmth, and finally moved frantically with him. He gasped out her name as the surge of his desire overtook him and also overtook her, like a burst of white light—he was her love, her passion, her only desire—and she experienced so nameless a convulsion she thought she was dying and cried out in ravaged shock.

Later, for there was a later and she did not die, she knew that they lay quietly side by side, drained, in an island of time that held only them, beyond the reach of anything else, even reality. His eyes were closed, his breathing regular; he rested with his hand relaxed upon her belly, relaxed and yet possessive.

Tomorrow was her nineteenth birthday, Dolores thought. But the number was meaningless for today was the first day of her life. Her body seemed emptied and full at the same time.

She wanted to laugh, to sing, to shout her triumph, but she felt too languid, her limbs felt too voluptuously heavy. She looked over at her supine knight, her master, her tormentor, her love. The future was veiled and imperfect, but for the present, still remembering the stirring heat of his kisses and then the wild excitement of his touch, she had only a grateful smile.

The wail of the muezzin from the palace mosque brought Francho's eyes open, and he saw the brightness of day peeping through the window grill. He had not been dozing, not really, just thinking. He turned his head toward Dolores and saw she was up on one elbow, her gray eyes soft, and she was smiling at him, a small, shy, and wondering smile, like a bride, he thought, on the first day of marriage. And she was very beautiful.

With a lazy arm he fished up from the floor the puffed silken coverlet to ward off the morning chill from them and with a satisfied grunt pulled her into the curve of his shoulder and gently pressed her head down.

"Sleep now, *querida*. A few more hours. Sleep."

Snuggling into him blissfully she did just what he told her to.

When she awoke she was alone. For a moment her heart skidded and dropped as she thought it had all been a dream. But no. Her breath came again as she took in the mussed couch where her love had lain and the pressure outline his head had left upon the soft pillow. The air was heavy and still in the room, perfumed by the flowering bushes beyond the bead curtain to the garden. She wriggled over to lay her head where his had been and closed her eyes, trying to breathe in his essence. She smiled langorously and idly stroked her own belly, appreciating its slight roundness and the sensuous smoothness of her flesh, remembering as little thrills ran up her backbone the sensations of being physically loved, of being caressed and kissed and sucked and entered and— Her eyes popped open and she struggled to stop her thoughts. *Madre de Dios,* her hips had begun to move in that way again, her body to yearn, she was intemperate, wanton, debauched. How would she get through the day?

Forcing herself to action she bounded up into the patterned rays of sunshine streaming from the window (which made it almost noonday) and drew on her pantaloons and tunic. She splashed water upon her face from a ewer and basin behind the screen, smoothed her hair and long, thick plait with wet hands, and opened the door. She intended to go to the slave quarters to wash more thoroughly and to find a fresh tunic, then to the kitchens for whatever she could scare up to fill her complaining stomach, and then back to put Jamal ibn Ghulam's chamber to rights, trim the lamp, and bring in some flowers from the tiny garden to decorate the room.

She found Selim sitting outside the door. He blinked at her sourly. "Well, finally. Does the Sultana deign to get up?"

"What is it to you how late I sleep if the master lets me?" she flung back.

"Because I have my orders. Clean up, he says, sweep, fresh sheets, fill the incense burners, bring wine . . ."

"I do not do that anymore?"

"No, he says. It's back to work for you, Selim, he says. And he sends me off to fetch his breakfast to the baths and take messages here and there. And he walks off humming and whistling as if Allah had showered the pasha's wealth in his lap."

"Well, you needn't grumble, it's the work you were doing all along before he punished me."

Selim pulled a long face to show what he thought of going back to work. He picked at a pimple on his chin. "Master also says he will go down to the city tonight." He looked up under his brows to enjoy her fading smile and then slyly added, "But he says he will be back not too late, for you to attend him, as ordinary. Yach! Women get too many privileges," he complained, and followed up with an adolescent smirk as Dolores flounced off.

The guard at the harem's slave dormers sent her to see Sayeda Fawzia. "Well I see you have been reinstated," Fawzia remarked. "I had a message by your master's slave boy this morning."

Dolores said nothing but stood with her chin elevated in her old proud manner. Fawzia's bright eyes missed little. They studied the high color warming the velvet cheekbones before her, the clear luster of the eyes that had so lately been dull, the cheerful smile sweetening the Christian's wide mouth. "Hmmmm. I see you have been more than reinstated," the fat harem mistress noted with dry satisfaction and a hint of curiosity. "Finally. It certainly took you long enough to please him. I wondered at his patience. If you are smart you will take the experience of the slave quarters as a warning, my girl, and remember my words: they seldom forgive twice." She wrinkled her broad nose in her usual habit. "Fah! Look at your hands! And your hair, so straggly. And your eyes are naked. Your old chamber has been restored to you this morning and all your belongings. Go there and I'll send some attendants to you." A smile warmed the pudgy face.

"I thank you, Sayeda Fawzia," Dolores said softly, and meant it. The dark misery of the past weeks had faded into the distance like a nightmare retreating on muffled hooves. The new day was brilliant with sun; in fact, it was the most beautiful day she had ever experienced. Everything stood out sharp and clear as she crossed a little plaza on her way to her room, the air was more wonderfully scented, the birds were more sportive and singing more sweetly than ever before. She was happy to have her clothes and jewels back, and some shreds of her pride. And beyond that she was just, very simply, happy.

That afternoon, once again bathed, plucked, tweezed, powdered, and perfumed, she begged to climb to the battlements atop the harem to dry her hair in the sun and meanwhile to peer out through the screening grill at the vast Christian camp of thousands of striped and patterned pavilions which was jumping up on the plain like a field of exotic mushrooms, but too far away for her to make out any of the individual insignias streaming from their tentpoles. She had always expected to be thrilled beyond measure to see Ferdinand's army finally swarming before the city of her captivity, promising with its might eventual freedom for her and victory for her side. But now she stared with a somewhat jaundiced eye at the brisk activity about the Christian encampment, where a palisade of stout logs was swiftly going up, and only felt annoyed. It was—it was an invasion of her privacy! Why didn't they go home?

She had the grace to burst out laughing at herself, drawing the curious gaze of several other women who had been peering through the grill at the enemy's number and twittering to each other. What disloyalty to wish her own people transported to the other side of the world! She clearly understood, after all, that her life—and Francisco de Mendoza's life—were anchored in the fabric of the Spanish Court and in Seville,

Madrid, Valladolid. And she further realized that the Catholic rulers would have to sit there and wait for months on end and their army fight many a bloody skirmish before Granada might weaken. But she was greedily jealous of this wondrous obsession which she and her love had at last bowed to, and she wanted no interference, not yet, not from Leonora de Zuniga or Medina-Sidonia or Tendilla or Felipe de Guzman, not yet. Still amused with herself, she chuckled. As if his dear Leonora or her own patron the Duke were capable of leaping the leagues separating all of them and flying over the walls! Yes, she could allow her heart to soar for a while, and this was her consolation. God would not begrudge her the joy of adoring this man, her dashing, parfit knight, her black-bearded Moor with the lyrical voice, the exciting lover who hungered for her too, if only for a while. Whatever befell her, should she live to be an old, old lady, nothing would ever surpass the profound joy of being with him in this wondrous place.

Looking about quickly to see that she was unobserved, she saucily thumbed her nose and crossed her eyes at the Christian encampment. Then, smiling widely, her cleft chin lifted high as her spirits, she flapped down the tower stairs in her loose slippers to have her hair brushed into a coppery sheen.

She waited for him that night, the hours passing so slowly that even the beadwork she had brought with her to pass the time became a bore. She looked up eagerly at every footstep passing outside the portal, every voice approaching, but no hand touched the latch. Even eavesdropping on the cavorting voices beyond the high hedge of the little garden, apparently several men and a giggling dancer chinking finger cymbals, grew tedious. Finally she put down the scarf she was embellishing and wandered about the room, but with an ear out for the right footfall.

She had donned her finest garments. Her wide pantaloons were of the most gossamer cotton, her little jacket was of weighty blue satin closely embroidered with arabesques of silver thread and tiny glass beads. There were shiny brass coins dangling from her purple silk sash, and her henna-soled feet were encased in green sandals trimmed with softly tinkling little bells. Her burnished hair cascaded in waves down her back, her eyes were rimmed with kohl to emphasize their tilt, her eyelids and lips had been touched with a shiny tint. The scent of jasmine had been artfully applied to her skin, her neck, the inner side of her elbows, between her breasts. Even Fawzia had approved of her.

She couldn't get her heart to stop bouncing around in her chest even as the wait grew longer and longer. What would he say to her? Would they both feel embarrassed? Would he regret the whirlwind that had swept them up? Every now and then panic would flutter in her stomach alternating with excitement. Finally she occupied herself for the fourth time with rearranging the flowers in a big brass vase. And suddenly she looked up and there he was, just coming through the door, tall and olive-skinned in his white turban and close-cut tunic.

She stood there frozen, hugging several of the long stalks of pink blossoms against her, her breath caught in her throat. He closed the portal behind him quietly. The intense blue eyes roved over her. She opened her lips to greet him but no words came out. In silence they stood and stared at one another, and yet the silence rang with meaning. Dolores felt her knees go wobbly.

He drew his dark brows together and his voice was gruff, almost accusing. "I heard nothing anyone said to me all day long. All I could think of was you."

She gulped and unlocked her throat. "The . . . the mistress of the harem seemed to be able to tell that I had—pleased you. Now she likes me better."

"So do I." He nodded solemnly.

She wondered at the childish bashfulness she was feeling, it was not at all like her. But she found something to say. "W—will you not step in? It is your own chamber."

For a moment longer he stood at the door, and then moved a few paces toward her and stopped, unslinging his guembri and lowering it to the floor. He unbuttoned the tight neckline of his tunic, not taking his eyes off of her. "You are more lovely than those blossoms you hold, *doña*. You are very, very beautiful."

Dolores felt the blush rise in her cheeks, yet she could only continue to stare at him, enmeshed in the virile charm that drew her and bound her. "I thank you, sir," she whispered.

Tongue-tied they both stood a moment longer, motionlessly yearning toward each other. And then, with a twitch of his lips that suddenly became a wide grin he flung open his arms in invitation. With a little cry she dropped the flowers and rushed into his embrace and he picked her up and whirled her around in a paroxysm of delight, both of them laughing in the back of their throats. She threw her head back, and he dipped and scooped her up in strong arms and carried her toward the divan, already spread with silky sheets for his evening repose. He covered her face with little kisses as he strode and then plumped her down in a nest of pillows.

Suddenly she felt nervous again. She sat upright. "Uh . . . have you already dined, *raiss?*" She smiled but one hand was twisting the fingers of the other.

"No."

"Then I shall immediately send Selim—" She made a half-hearted attempt to get up but he held her firmly in place.

"No. It is not food I am interested in . . ." Slowly he lowered his face to hers till the tips of their noses touched and then he pecked her parted lips briefly, several times, kisses so delicious and teasing they started her heart pounding. Then he straightened and moved his shoulders to loosen them. "But I could use some drink, a little wine for a gullet dry from wailing Arabic modes all day and evening to usher in Ramadan. No, you stay, I will fetch it."

He poured out and carried back to the couch two brass goblets of pale, straw-colored Andalusian wine. Smiling he tipped one goblet up to her lips. "Drink, *hermanita,* it will heat up your blood."

"I don't need it," she said and looked up at him through her long lashes. Nevertheless she took the goblet from him and drank a few gulps. He drained his quickly, his cerulean gaze never moving from her over the rim of the glass.

Then he chuckled. "You don't need it? Lady, where is your modesty?"

"'Twas never my saving grace, modesty," she said with a shrug, a chuckle in her voice.

He swiftly set down his goblet next to hers and with a rumble low in his throat launched himself at her and pressed her down on the pillows. He swiftly opened the rest of his tunic and cast it aside, then pulled off his turban. The eyes that scanned her face grew serious then, and into her breathless silence he said her name, said it so reverently and wonderingly that she quivered inside. "Dolores," he breathed. "Dolores . . ."

She reached up to smooth back from his brow the dark

tumble of hair, then slid her hand slowly down his face and put her fingers to his lips. She saw his vivid eyes deepen to indigo and darken with his urgent need. His hand fumbled with the waistband of her pantaloons. She helped him and kicked off her sandals as well. The little jacket and low-necked bodice came off too, hurriedly, and so did his leggings and embroidered shoes.

He took up her slim hand and kissed the henna-red palm and then the inside of her wrist. He kissed the tender inside of her elbow, breathing in the jasmine scent there. He pressed his lips to the glimmering valley between her breasts where an enameled charm dangled on a gold chain, the only jewelry she wore besides her ear drops. His lips moved up her perfumed skin to kiss her throat where the pulse hammered and then reached her mouth. But he did not kiss her, for first he drew her to him, molding her against the muscled length of his body so she could feel the strength of his chest, belly, and hard thighs and his male desire, and then his lips were close to hers again—barely touching as they lay facing each other, but touching enough so that their breaths mingled sweetly, and the firm smoothness of his mouth just brushing hers raised the sensitivity of her own lips so exquisitely that shocks of excitement raced through her.

He was arousing her even more quickly than the night before, for now she knew what she wanted, that wild, pulsing, delirious convulsion that seemed to shoot her body through the eye of a needle to leave her gasping and emptied and joyous on the other side. Feeling her response he kissed her more deeply, using the tip of his tongue to invade her mouth with his passion, and she welcomed him, her heart bursting with love. She wanted to melt into him, to become one with his bone, blood, and tissue so that nothing could separate them.

Her ears knew he made the same hungry, urgent, enraptured, soft noises that she did. Her nipples yearned toward his touch and his mouth, and when the heat of his hand covered the wet throbbing between her thighs her breath was propelled from her in a strangled gasp. Now he loomed above her, his half-closed eyes devouring her, and she strained up to meet him. She offered her body with wild abandon and he took her just as desperately, thrusting his manhood deep into her again and again until, in a frenzy of excitement, quivering taut as a bow, she released her soul and at the same time so did he, and they rode out the storm of their passion together.

When their breathing finally quieted they fell apart. She was damp with a thin film of sweat, whether her own or from his she couldn't tell. He turned on his side and threw a possessive arm over her and she snuggled her face into his chest, kissing the warm, damp skin. She loved him achingly.

Later she woke from a light doze and found him leaning on his elbow and gazing down at her. The lamp was behind him, his expression was shadowed.

"You think me wanton," she whispered into his silence.

"I think you magnificent," came his immediate, soft response.

"I am your concubine," she mourned.

"You are my—*querida,* my darling."

"I am not a lady."

"You are a passionate, beautiful woman, which is more."

She longed to say, "I love you," but she forced the words back. He could not answer in kind and she could bear his disdain more than his pity.

He took her silence for regret and with his strong, warm fingers stroked back the tendrils of auburn hair that clung to her cheek. "You have nothing to reproach yourself for, *querida mía,"* he gruffly soothed her. "It is I who am the sinner, I who have seduced a young woman under my protection. *I* will have to answer to God. In His eyes you are innocent."

It was not God's eyes she cared about at that moment but his. Nevertheless she couched her need in his terms. "Do you not think that God would bless us in the joy we have of each other, Francho, even without sacrament? Is not the tenderness of lovemaking more worthy of His name than the blood and clangor of battle, or the terrible fires of the Inquisition?"

She could feel the somber intensity of his gaze even before she looked up into his eyes.

"Do you wish to discontinue, *doña?* I will honor whatever you wish."

Unwilling to allow the least annoyance to spoil the moment, she ignored a tickle of irritation at such acquiescence and asked, in a small voice, "And where would I go to forget what has happened?"

"You have the shelter of the harem. We need never see each other further."

Never. She threw her arms about his neck in distress at even the thought of being separated from him and told him in a fierce whisper the naked truth, "I only want the shelter of your heart. If you will cherish me for what time there is, then that is all I want and I am content."

With a great sigh he hugged her to him. *"Querida—"* For a second she thought he was going to say more, but he did not. They had nothing to eat that night. Nor did they crave any food.

It was the cat who really deserved the credit for the coup, a scrofulous beast who bespoke his misery in carrying yowls that broke into Dolores's reverie as she sat in the blossom-strewn verdure of Zemel's garden. She was waiting not too patiently for Jamal ibn Ghulam to conclude his business with the instrument maker, for then he was going to take her to the Grand Souk, where they would watch the snake charmers, hear the speechmakers, and wander along between the stalls still filled with marvelous wares. She was excited about the outing; the Sultan's intimate was seldom given time to himself during the day, but when he had it he had no objection to transporting her out of her gilded prison and taking her about the city for a change of atmosphere.

She had, as was proper, a voluminous but lightweight peach-colored mantle thrown over her head to conceal her body and a *yashmak* to hide her face below the eyes, but the exhilaration of leaving the confines of the palace for a while canceled out the discomfort of going so warmly shrouded in summer. With nothing to do but lounge on the tiled garden bench and wait, she let her mind drift along. It was so pleasant to be out in the city. Although she yet had lessons in Arabic and embroidered and gossiped with the harem ladies, the small orbit of her life between the harem and Francho's chamber sometimes caused her boredom. Not that she wished to change it. Her lips curved in a smile. Without fail her boredom always disappeared the moment Francisco Jamal strode into the room.

She stretched out her feet in front of her and looked up lazily at the sun dappling through the waving branches of the myrtle tree above, and it suddenly recalled to her the little courtyard at her father's inn, where she had bathed in a barrel under such a tree, with her aunt standing guard against any incursions by her brothers or that young thief with a devilish grin and a battered lute.

Francho. Now *she* was his lute; his hands stroked her and tuned her and drew such harmonies of passion from her body as she had never imagined. Perhaps, as he insisted, she inspired his mastery, instructing him by her response, but she was sure she was merely the ecstatic instrument to his soaring inventions.

The warm summer, cooled by breezes from the surrounding white peaks, had passed swiftly, leaving a polychrome riffle of happy memories. They played chess and checkers, at which he often caught her cheating; they read to each other from manuscripts in Spanish he brought from the palace library; and he repeated to keep her amused the gossip and ripe intrigues of the Sultan's circle. For her part she listened carefully to the blind storytellers sitting cross-legged in the harem and then retold the exotic tales to her bemused lover. And she saw always that Selim obtained from the kitchens the tastiest dishes for the meals Francho took with her. They teased each other. They found almost everything a source of gay laughter (except for some of the storyteller's tales which ended in tragedy and caused her mouth to droop), and he allowed her to attend the many banquets at which he performed for the Sultan and the ruler's delighted guests, and where she sat with other of the favored women from the royal harem and smiled with pride. They stared often at each other, warm pleasure, pain, and wonder in both of their eyes, and they made frequent and ecstatic love.

But in her heart she knew the unreality of it.

She saw the envy flare in his eyes as they watched from the battlements the miraculously swift construction of a permanent Christian camp, a flag-flying, palisade-protected city of wooden buildings and towers that was so much larger and more solid than the siege camp at Baza it was even given a name by its army: Santa Fe, so it was reported. In spite of it being two leagues distant, one could see squadrons of knights pouring from its gates every day to clash with Muza Aben's hectoring forces, to prevent them from rolling up bombards. As she stared at him Dolores knew Francho was hearing the noise and clangor of the bloody melees in his head; it was evident he longed to sit astride a charger again and lower visor and lance in a furious, straightforward charge at the enemy, to earn his glory with a knight's weapons rather than with the treachery of guembri and lute. Although he spent time every day at wrestling and swimming, often in company with the Sultan, who took pride in his own athletic ability, yet the inaction of doing little otherwise but performing and lounging about at the Sultan's beck and call was beginning to chafe him.

And, in spite of his careful silence, she could easily interpret his occasional faraway preoccupation. Sometimes he fingered a blossom with such abstraction she knew he was not thinking of her. Leonora de Zuniga dwelt deep in his heart, she knew that, as surely as she was painfully aware that never did he utter the word "love" to her.

Francisco de Mendoza was as much a prisoner of the Alhambra as she. The difference was he longed to be free, and he cursed the strength with which Granada defied her attackers. "And so, too, must I wish for freedom from these walls," Dolores thought sadly, "for the longer we are together the less I will remember that in spite of his delight in me, he did not choose me. He chooses her. If this idyll will end I must escape it now while some vestige of awareness and pride is left to me." Now? Her head drooped. Granada could hold against siege for more than another year, Francho had said.

She heaved a sigh. What a miserable confusion, to fiercely desire one thing with her heart and the opposite thing with her head.

A clinking as she shifted position made her pat the pocket in her pantaloons to feel for the two glass vials inside. The Andalusian attendant in the harem had earlier given her the location in the Grand Souk of a maker of nostrums, and this worthy had prepared for her a potent preventative of pregnancy, two white powders mixed and taken with wine, which so far had proven successful. The vials she would now refill at the market—a preparation to keep the skin unblemished she had given Francho to believe. A pang clawed at her heart as she thought of the sweetness of bearing a child to this man, a boy baby with bright cerulean eyes and a lusty voice, the child a part of Don Francisco de Mendoza that would be forever hers to love, Leonoras and the unitings of great families be damned. She suffered loss because cold reality and care for her own future snuffed out her heart's desire.

Her life was in alarming disarray, having been suspended in

a void from the moment she fled the hunting castle at Torredonpedros. She'd learned that Medina-Sidonia had been informed of her whereabouts and that she was held safely and that he had made a difficult and unsuccessful attempt to ransom her. But much could happen to the Duke's interest before a future Christian victory finally released her, and he was, she could see now, her greatest bulwark against the world's cruelties. If it could be helped she would not further complicate her future with Francho's bastard child she had nowhere to hide. She bit her lip and distractedly brushed a fallen leaf from her mantle and wished she could so easily brush away the heavy thoughts that assailed her.

And then, from a nearby bush, a warbler poured forth his rolling song, and the lilting beauty of it helped her to throw off her mood. No. No, it was too lovely a day and much too soon for considering reality. She would concentrate on anticipating Jamal ibn Ghulam's imminent exit from Zemel's workshop and how soon they would both greedily enjoy the little honeyed cakes he would purchase in the market, and the gifts he would buy her of fine perfume and fabrics. . . .

It was then the racket began. She sat up straight, turning her head about at the loud, frightened mewling emanating from a very distressed cat. Believing the animal had caught a paw in something, she jumped up and began to search among the hedges and bushes in the garden to release the poor beast. But it was Francho, emerging onto the gallery to join her while Zemel repaired his guembri, who, finding her wandering perplexed on the paths among the flower beds, stood frowning and listening for a moment until his more sensitive ears found the direction. Pushing through a cluster of tall acacia bushes they discovered that part of the wall surrounding Zemel's garden had been built on a low earthen mound now thickly overgrown with creepers, and it was at the base of this mound where the frantic meows sounded loudest. Tearing away the stubborn, leafy vines Francho brought into sight a wood and iron hatch of respectable diameter whose handgrips were secured by a strong-looking iron lock.

"What is it?" Dolores questioned over his shoulder as Francho squatted on his haunches to examine the port in the earth bank.

"I don't know. But see these smooth ceramic bricks rimming the edge? I think the cat has somehow got itself into an old tunnel, mayhap one of the irrigation conduits for which the Moorish engineers were renowned."

"Can we get the poor creature out?"

Francho gave the hatch a hard pull by the secured handles. "It's fitted very solid, but the hinges are sound and made of wood. In spite that it must be ancient I think it would open if we could remove the lock."

"Do you think Zemel would have a key?"

"Possibly." He stood up, brushing off his hands and eyed this closure to some sort of burrow under the wall speculatively, brows drawn together; there was a tense set to his stance that started a tingle in her scalp.

"What is it?" she asked. "What are you thinking?"

"Dolores, listen, this garden is perhaps a hundred paces from the city wall, which here overlooks the banks of the Xenil, and there is no more than two or three hundred paces of brush and reeds between the walls and the river. If this is an old water conduit, it must surely have an opening on the river, forgotten but in some way passable, since the flea-bitten beast got in there in the first place without drowning." He turned to face her, eyes glinting with excitement above the trim, dual-pointed beard. "I have long been planning a venture which would drastically reduce Granada's food supplies, but I had no help to implement it. Now I am sure God has sent us a messenger in the form of a cat to demonstrate a way to bring in aid. My plan could wreak enough damage to force open the city's gates to our army in six months! *If* the tunnel has not collapsed somewhere."

Wide-eyed, intrigued, she could only stare at him, hardly hearing the cat's wailing anymore.

"Stay right here," he instructed her. "And pray Zemel has a key to this lock. A heavy bar could break it, but he might value keeping the lock intact more than rescuing that miserable animal."

He strode away toward the house. Dolores hunkered down meanwhile, trying to comfort the cat by tapping on the hatch and crooning to it. Quicker than she expected she heard two sets of footsteps returning down the flagged path and got to her feet. In a moment Francho insinuated his bulk through the small break in the high bushes, followed by Zemel, a bent but agile little Moor whose wrinkled cheeks formed two rosy mounds atop his white beard and broad smile. Settling his tipping turban straighter and totally ignoring Dolores as was courteous, the old man exclaimed, "Dear me, what a racket. How good of you, *sayed,* to have heard the creature's pitiful cries; I am a touch deaf and might not have noticed until too late. Allah bless us, how did he get in there?"

Over Zemel's head Francho winked at Dolores. "Master Zemel fortunately has a key."

"Yes, yes, this place was handed down from my grandfather's father and according to his nature all his descendants have been taught there is a place for everything and everything in its place, and never throw anything away." Zemel pulled a clinking pouch from his sash and, dipping into what sounded like a collection of several keys, proudly produced a plain and surprisingly small rusty iron key. "In my ancestors' time the city was not so crowded. They and their neighbors owned more land and were able to grow considerable onions and turnips here, as well as some rice. This conduit brought them river water when they needed it. When I was a child I was aware it was here; children, you know, find everything. But in the years I had forgotten." Clucking his tongue at the renewed cat yowls he drew a small flask from his sash, pulled the stopper with his brown-tinged teeth and liberally doused the rusty keyhole with olive oil. He inserted the key, turned it, and grunted with surprise when the bar on the lock creaked open then and there. But his tentative tugs on the iron handgrip, once he had removed the lock, were not so successful. "A younger, stronger arm, perhaps? This cover seems solidly set," Zemel admitted with a rueful, wrinkled smile and backed away with a gesture to his willing guest.

Picking up a stone Francho pounded heavily along three edges of the hatch to bring loose some of the crumbling brick that hugged it tight. He deliberately poured some oil on the hinge joints, and then, grabbing the handle with both hands and bracing one foot at the base of the mound, gave a mighty heave from the shoulders. With a loud creak the hatch swung open on its hinges, and Francho had to leap back as a terrified, angry yellow cat flew spitting from the tunnel and streaked past them to disappear through the hedge, accompanied by their startled laughter.

The cover was fitted back on, the lock put in place and secured. Zemel took the pouch again from his sash and slipped the key back into it. "Thank you, *sayed,* you have saved the life of one of Allah's small creatures." The old man showed his bad teeth in a smile.

Dolores saw Francho's eyes follow the man's hand as it tucked the pouch back in the sash over his belly, and then his stare bored into her as she stood behind Zemel; and as the instrument maker creakily bent to retrieve the olive oil flask from the ground with his turban falling askew again, she realized Francho was urgently mouthing the silent word "key" at her and sliding his glance toward Zemel. Her eyebrows raised in momentary confusion. And then sudden comprehension widened her eyes and set off a delighted grin under the *yashmak*. She winked at him and was rewarded with a jaunty wink back just as their host straightened up.

Zemel took his client by the arm and said warmly, "Come, *sayed,* honored ibn Ghulam, a man of your virtuosity should not have to bear with a slipping tuning screw. It will take but a moment to finish the new one I have carved, this time with a narrower thread to grip tighter. Let me give you some refreshment meanwhile. My servant brews a *kavah* black and bitter as the evil one's imps."

"I shall be delighted," Jamal ibn Ghulam answered and allowed himself to be led back to the gallery, where several doors led from various rooms of the house into the garden. Over his shoulder he called casually, "Come, Karima, it is cooler inside."

Francho pushed through the bushes first and then came Zemel. Dolores, head bowed modestly, followed just behind Zemel, but she was crowding him, in fact, and just as he reached the path she pretended her foot had caught on a root and she stumbled forward into the elderly craftsman in such a way that he was forced to swivel around to protect himself from her clumsiness, which had almost knocked him down. As Francho quickly untangled them, Dolores cast down her eyes in shame and tried to produce an embarrassed blush.

In an annoyed tone Francho said, "I humbly apologize for my servant, good master Zemel. She is stupid and looks not where she walks."

"'Tis all right, no harm done," the old man wheezed, setting to rights his orange turban again and looking askance at Dolores. "It was an accident."

Dolores hung her head and stared at her toes. She trailed

behind dejectedly as the two men resumed their path, the pouch she had deftly slid from Zemel's sash clutched tightly in the folds of her mantle to keep it from clinking. Stealthily she felt in it with her fingers. She could discern three keys, but one was too long and thin and one had an ornamental head. Fishing out the third key she dropped it into the pocket of her pantaloons.

Entering Zemel's spacious workshop where several apprentices labored with large chisels carving out soundboards, Francho stood back to allow Zemel access to his bench. Dolores brushed closely by him and with a swift and barely noticeable movement transferred the pouch to his waiting hand, then glided to the shadows of a corner, where she stood meekly by. She struggled to keep from showing the triumphant glee she felt, and she was sure Francho was doing the same, solemn as he seemed as he watched the old man's tough, hard fingers use a carving tool to delicately refine the pitch screw. How handily they accomplished the transfer of the pouch, she exalted proudly, as elegant and precise as a dance step, undetectable even if someone in the room had been staring at them. Once a pickpurse, always a pickpurse, she laughed to herself.

The chamber, with tools and braces hung in neat profusion about the room, was redolent of the spruce and rosewood from which Zemel fashioned his instruments and from the fish glue bubbling on a small brazier. With a bow a servant with a tray offered Francho a small steaming cup, which he accepted and sipped from while Zemel worked and lectured. "See you, *sayed,* a master carver forms a relationship with a piece of wood, as knowing of its character as if it were a person. Without that sense—the "feeling" of each piece of wood—an instrument maker might as well be a furniture maker. His guembris will have no individual sound or soul." He turned the brass-headed screw in his hand and blew away the wood dust. "Ah, now I think we have it. I will give it a hardening bath and then we will try it." The old man rose purposefully to dip the screw in a container of liquid on a nearby table covered with various unfinished lutes and guitars, and as he did so there was a loud jingle as something hit the floor. Looking down in surprise Zemel saw the pouch of keys at his feet. "Dear me, how careless of me. And how good of you, *sayed,"* he thanked his illustrious client, who had politely stooped to retrieve it for him. "I'd almost forgotten to return this to its place, for which my great grandfather in Paradise would be wroth." Smiling and shaking his head, he hung the pouch by its strings amid a dusty cluster of others on pegs above his bench.

At last Francho's business was concluded amid effusive goodbyes and an invitation to return sometime soon for one of their pleasant chats and a repast in the garden. Dolores silently followed Francho out and silently allowed Zemel's servant to help her onto her donkey while Francho slung his repaired guembri on his back and mounted his big mule. But as soon as they plodded around a concealing corner the twinkling blue eyes met her own dancing eyes and they both burst into laughter.

"Well, my fine Baroness de la Rocha, I see you haven't lost a certain delicate talent," he teased her.

"Nor have you, august sir knight," she admired back. "One ought to warn the poor Sultan to look to his gold." She dug in her deep pocket and handed him the key to the conduit hatch. "Well, have I earned my sweet cake, master?" A passing breeze fluttered the *yashmak* against her mouth and delicately outlined the shape of her jaw.

"More than that, *querida*. You shall have an ice with pomegranate syrup all to yourself, as well."

To her surprise, and in spite of curious glances from passersby, he impulsively leaned from the saddle, captured her hand, and kissed the palm. His glance held affection and pleasure. "You make a charming accomplice, *hermanita,*" he murmured warmly.

Two hungry-looking men had lately moved into a rotting shed in Francho's alley, sullen and penniless but repelled enough by the vile smell of the only shelter they could find to spend much time outside it, sitting up till all hours on a tattered blanket and brooding. That night, to avoid their eyes, Francho prudently used the roof trap in his house, clambering silently and unseen over the neighboring roofs to drop into the next alley, and thence lope on foot the long distance to Zemel's residence. Finally reaching it he scaled the uneven stones of Zemel's garden wall at a point he judged close to the hatch, jumped, and landed on his feet in the soft turf of a flower bed. The garden was tranquil and silent, illumined only at its edge by a weak torch from the gallery, and in the house

Zemel and his staff slept the deep sleep of the just—Francho hoped.

He had no problem finding the hatch by the light of a starry sky and a calm, pale cream half-moon. The oiled lock opened to his key, and with a soft grunt he heaved open the port again, which creaked, but softly. His mantle would hamper him; he dropped it to the ground. From his sash he drew a tiny oil lamp, its spout tightly stoppered, and a flint and striker, and in a few moments he was shielding the lamp's small flame from view with the bulk of his body. Squatting down he took a deep breath, and holding the lamp before him with an outstretched arm telescoped his body and crawled into the uninviting squeeze of the musty conduit, going forward on his hands and knees. His broad shoulders scarcely cleared the round brick sides of the tunnel. He kept his eyes squinted against the brick dust he was stirring up with his passage and pulled the tail of his turban over his nose and mouth. Cramped, able to see only a few paces ahead, he shuffled ahead on all fours through the damp silence of the tunnel, grateful for the gloves shielding his hands from the rough, crumbled brick. He knew with a trepidation he could not quell that he was moving further and further from the open air of the garden with no idea how long the tunnel continued and whether it might constrict into impassability. And worse, he suddenly realized that if the cat's point of entry proved too small or blocked to let him out he would have to crawl backward all the way.

Still there was air to breath, and in a while the lamp flame began to waver from a slight draught when he stopped to rest, which gave him hope that his uncomfortable journey might soon end. He labored along for what seemed miserable leagues until his heavier breathing made him aware that he had been dealing with a gradual upward slope of the tunnel. At last a cool gust of air hit his perspiring face and he heard the rustle of dry foliage whipping in the wind and the gurgling rush of the river. He thrust his lamp forward and saw the smooth glimmer of ceramic brick lining the deteriorated mouth of the conduit, which was only loosely blocked by a waving mass of tall reeds and grass. Snuffing out his flame he inched forward, blind until he touched the rattling stalks and then with anxious haste shoved them aside and scrabbled through them until he emerged and stood on damp ground, gulping in grateful breaths of river air.

When his eyes adjusted to the weak moonlight he saw that a peninsula of silt and mud had built up below the conduit mouth and that the river lapped a good fifteen paces from the irrigation inlet it had surely engulfed a century ago. The tunnel was passable, the ingress unblocked and located outside the city walls. What more could he ask?

But where was he? The tunnel might not have run straight from Zemel's house but obliquely; he could not get a sense of it during the claustrophobic crawl. Night hid the opposite bank of the river, and on the high bank behind him there was nothing but the black silhouettes of scrub bushes and trees. He could see beyond that Granada's walls, hulking and featureless, the occasional firefly of a bright torch bobbing along with the battlement patrol. Nothing stood out that would mark this spot so that men rowing across the river at night could find it easily. But the curve in the river had to be upstream; if the party started from there and went with the current, he could set out a lantern to guide them in.

Jubilant with his discovery he lit up his lamp again and, resetting the pads he had foresightedly tied on beneath his pantaloons to protect his knees from sharp shards, he began the long crawl back to Zemel's garden, the unnerving feeling of suffocation much ameliorated this time by knowing where he was going and how long it would take. Emerging in the garden and retrieving his mantle, he went over the garden wall without incident and slipped off through the quiet streets, avoiding the guardian patrols by fading into doorways. He stopped at a deserted fountain to wash the grime from his face and at last reached his house by the same stealthy way he had left—through the trap in the roof. Anyone by chance spying at his door would have to swear he had been inside all evening, and Ali and Azahra, fearing his cold stare, would ask no questions about the river mud on his soft shoes.

Weary from the tenseness of the squeezed, creeping journey, he flopped down on his bed for a few hours' sleep. But not before he muttered a short thanks to San Bismas for helping him find this hidden flaw in Granada's tight defenses.

The map crackled as Tendilla smoothed it out before his Queen, whose alert blue eyes quickly scanned the small square of parchment. His long, thin fingers tapped at several X-marks circled on the map. "Here, here, and here, Majesty, my agent has marked the sites of the main depots sheltering not only most of the wheat and rice and ground meal for Granada's sustenance but also great stores of cheeses, roots, onions, and dried beans." His voice was tight with controlled excitement; he had to clear his throat to continue. "If this vast quantity of food were lost in a great conflagration, both Moslem bellies and Moslem defiance would shrink within six months. Only the smaller storage sheds in the Alhambra and Alcazaba would remain, and whatever private stocks the merchants had put by."

"Good, my lord, most excellent!"

"Fortunately the depots are neither heavily guarded nor widely separated, for the fires will have to be set almost simultaneously to create the greatest havoc and confusion. My agent advises he can wreak this heavy damage with only twelve men, counting himself."

"Is there a chance to get these men out again safely?"

Tendilla shrugged. "Yes. If they are not trapped in the flames themselves, if the guards do not catch them, if the ancient irrigation tunnel does not collapse upon them. The men I have chosen for this venture bring superior abilities, Lady Queen. They will go in groups of four, each group to be led by a man who has some acquaintance with the city's byways. In fact, since it seems that I myself as a youth spent much time in Granada, I beg to ask relief from my duties and your permission to go along on the foray."

His ruler refolded the map carefully and handed it back to him. There were elements of both sympathy and impatience in her tone. "Well, you do not have our permission. We do not wish you to depart Santa Fe, my lord. This encampment has too much need of your command. Surely there are others of courage as familiar as you with Granada?"

Although he had anticipated her refusal, the Count persisted, for such an adventure did not often present itself to a gentleman of his rank—and age—and the thought of it quickened his blood and kindled his imagination. "But Your Majesty, how should I propose so risky a journey to my subordinates and refuse to share with them the hazards?" he protested.

"You should, as their superior, and surely you will." She waved away his objection. "Your valor is unquestionable, Don Iñigo, but we cannot allow one of our most capable commanders to chance his life in a bravado sortie better left to younger men."

"You wound my vanity, Majesty. I had judged my fleetness and agility equal to the situation."

"Ah, Tendilla, do not twist our meaning in your usual manner just to have your way; be assured we meant no insult to your physical prowess. This provident means to help put an end to this stalemated siege is welcome, without doubt. Here we sit a few leagues from those cannon-larded walls, careful not to venture closer and expend lives uselessly, and that demon Muza Aben scourges our camp, fills our hospital and burying ground, and then races to the protection of those bristling walls without so much as a handful of his own dead left behind. And those heathens that crowd Granada's battlements to cheer their champions in these skirmishes are as well fed and cocky as in peacetime." Her voice was rising, for the months of solid siege were beginning to cause problems with certain necessary supplies. But she cut off her tirade, astutely reading the disappointment Tendilla sought to hide.

"Attend me, Don Iñigo, our reference to your years dwelt more upon the uniqueness of your services and experience. Experience in leading your troops to victory. *And* invaluable experience in governing captured territories." Her eyebrows rose significantly in her smooth, white forehead. "Surely, my lord, you can see the possible import behind our refusal to allow our good commander and friend to risk being roasted alive in a grain depot?"

Her words insinuated enough to cause a momentary silence and an exchange of glances between them. Tendilla was human enough to rejoice behind his suave countenance. He realized Isabella could make no commitments now in view of the valid aspirations of the Marquis of Cadiz and the Duke of Medina-Sidonia, but her indirect indication that she was prepared to strongly back his eventual candidacy for the governorship of Granada was encouraging enough to take the sting out of obeying her orders not to join the raids. In any case, if God would see those Moorish food repositories leveled to the ground, the Catholic monarchs would count yet another outstanding victory accomplished through him.

He bowed his head in deferral. "It shall be as you order, my Queen. I will delegate another in my place. A younger man," he added dryly.

She gave him an amused smile. "Good. Now, when will this brave sally take place?"

"Within the fortnight, in the darkness of the moon. Meanwhile I shall rehearse my men in the detailed plan my agent has submitted."

Now Isabella blinked and sat back thoughtfully as she contemplated him, absently twisting a gold ring on her finger. "My lord Tendilla?"

"Majesty?"

Her steady blue eyes signaled they would brook no evasions. "Where is your son Don Francisco, my lord?"

So! The time had come. With the hint of a smile on his long, narrow lips the Count stood more erect and in an even voice told her, "In Granada, at the Sultan's court. He is the agent you have so graciously praised these many months."

"Ah. So we thought. You are a remarkably taciturn man, Count. Would not paternal pride lead you to inform us of his valuable offices? You are too much the prisoner of compelling modesty. We had thought it strange that you detained your offspring in Sicily while there was such honor to be earned here in the field."

"A convenient fabrication, to turn aside loose conjecture. My Queen is aware that scurrilous ears hear unguarded conversations, even at her own noble Court. To what avail alert the Moors that a Christian knight might be disguised and concealed in their midst?"

"Quite true," Isabella conceded. She threw up her hands in mock exasperation. "But must you extend your mantle of secrecy to exclude even your monarchs?" Yet she chuckled. "Ah well, we are not wroth with you; your reserve is ingrained and 'tis the results, not the method that counts. We shall not even inquire the whys and the hows until Don Francisco's work is done. Then tell your scion to continue excellent information to us, and we shall not forget we are his much in his debt." The co-ruler of Spain inclined her head. "Go now, good Count, and send in to us again my ladies and the Archbishop of Valencia, who wait without."

With a sweeping bow Tendilla backed from the room. He flung his cape over his shoulder and strode away from the royal abode toward his own timber-and-tile quarters located on a long, straight street of similar solid barracks and houses.

He reflected, "Your generous words will indeed be remembered, Isabella, for there is yet another, deeper secret to be unveiled. I will pray, my Queen, that time has mellowed your grudge-bearing heart." He wasted no time wondering when to offer up the last confession about Francisco to Los Reyes Católicos. The time would reveal itself.

❧ *Chapter 27* ❧

ELEVEN MEN IN dark clothing hunched down in the stolen fishing boat that drifted silent and unnoticed down the Xenil with the current, straining their eyes into the dark to catch the least glimmer of a lantern along the lonely further bank, glancing now and then at the towering ramparts of Granada outlined against the starry sky, where alert guards patrolled and scanned the river. In the prow crouched the two men Francho had asked Tendilla to assign as leaders, his two feckless cronies, Hernando del Pulgar and Antonio de la Cueva.

"There!" Pulgar whispered finally, nudging his companion. "On that small jut-out ahead. Do you see a spark of light?"

De la Cueva grunted assent. Pulgar turned around to the other shadowy figures in the boat. "Man your oars, and softly, do you value your lives. Pull us into that small point we approach."

The oars dipped quietly into the water and the boat swung its prow toward the nearby shore. Jumping out, Pulgar helped them quietly beach it on the narrow point, then led off cautiously toward a bright wink of light glimmering among the reeds. The light snuffed out. Pulgar whistled softly, the three characteristic notes of the whippoorwill, and a second later the signal was returned. A figure rose from the weeds, barely outlined against the spangled sky, and waved them forward. Muttering "Stay" to the men crouched on the shore, Pulgar and de la Cueva slipped forward to meet their host.

"Give you welcome to Granada," the figure whispered.

Pulgar approached, peering to see what he could of the man's features. "Jesu, Maria, Mendoza, is it really you behind that beard?"

"'Tis not Mohammed, you great ox. Is that Antonio with you?"

"*Sí,*" de la Cueva answered, clasping the hand the figure stuck out. "So here you have been, rogue, and not in Italy as we supposed. Don Iñigo first swore us to secrecy and then informed us you were most intimate with the Sultan. A fine bosom friend for a Christian knight!"

"So it leads to such signs of friendship as we will perform tonight, spare me such other relationships," Francho chuckled.

"And how does your harem these days, noble Moor?" Pulgar leered from the dark. "Lucky fellow . . ."

"I regret, old friend, but I haven't an houri in this world to lend you," Francho disenchanted him. A fish splashed in the water, making all three jump. Francho became serious. "In approximately one hour from now the guard on the storage towers will change, and this will allow us our best chance, as you've been told. On inspection tours with the Sultan I've noted the roof traps are bolted from the inside and only unlocked for the few minutes when the guard shifts change. We must look sharp and be on our way."

"We have the details of your plan well in mind, Francisco," de la Cueva assured him. "But Hernan here is entertaining a hare-brained stunt in his head that will get him killed."

"I have a little love note to leave behind," Pulgar grunted, patting something concealed in his tunic. "My assigned route looks to pass very close to the Grand Mosque."

Happy to be in action with his good friends again, Francho nevertheless sternly ordered, "No side trips, Pulgar, there's too much at stake here to risk any nonsense. I'll go first into the tunnel. Let the men follow me, and one of you bring up the rear."

For the fourth time Francho crept through the suffocating dusty narrowness of the conduit, leading the coughing men behind him, finally helping them to emerge with muffled gasps into the welcome night air of Zemel's garden. He huddled with them behind the acacia bushes, a tight group of sinister shadows in dark tunics and cowls, with naked daggers stuck in their belts and pouches carrying flint, short torches, and combustibles slung over their shoulders. At a muted command from de la Cueva three of the men moved to Francho's side, doubtless taking him for a renegade Moor he thought, which didn't matter so long as they took his orders. The raiders had all studied the map and memorized the course of action. There was no need for further discussion but there was a need for haste, not to miss the midnight change of the guard. Francho clasped Pulgar by the shoulder.

With a whispered "Santiago!" Pulgar took his men in a muted scramble over the wall first. Then went de la Cueva's group, and finally Francho's men clambered over, dropping into the cobbled alley on the other side. He took them at a lope through the crooked streets and deserted little squares without incident and without sighting the others, who had swiftly struck out in different directions. They avoided the occasional late horseman or pike-armed watch by melting into doors and niches or flattening against a dark wall. Presently they approached their objective, one of the three huge towers which remained from a former city wall, now stuffed to their battlements with grain and hay and enough foodstuffs to feed the city through any possible siege. Francho detoured through a handy back passage in order to come up on the rear of a scalable building which he had noted abutted a motley of structures hemming in the old, square tower.

Gaining the top of the flat-roofed building by pulling themselves up from a lean-to shed roof, Francho and his soft-shoed cohorts flitted from roof to roof until they stood above a narrow alley separating them from the looming bulk of the tower. One of his men now performed a fancy gyration and unwound from his body a long length of rope, his vague silhouette shrinking perceptibly about the middle. Much shorter ropes from the other men's pouches now served to lower Francho and two of his companions to the top of a low, one-story building adjacent to the taller structure, where the first man waited.

Using the second rope the two men with Francho slid to the ground, but remained hidden in the deep shadow of an angled wall. Francho stayed on the low roof, crouched and tense, giving his attention to the lantern-illuminated entrance to the alley a short distance to the right, where the guards who were supposed to be patrolling the tower base lounged at their ease. Presently he saw them jump up with a snap to attention, for the sergeant of the guard had just appeared. The sound of sharp scolding drifted to his ears and the guards were replaced with fresh men.

In his sash Francho carried a long, sharp dagger, one which he had eased from the sheath of a Moorish courtier trading next to him at a crowded stall in the First Plaza, the man unaware that his device-engraved weapon had been transferred from the sheath on his hip to under Francho's mantle. He readied the dagger impatiently. Finally the new guards strode out of the circle of light and approached down the murky alley, one holding up a small lantern. Francho drew back, waited until the footsteps were just below him, and then leaped out and down upon an unsuspecting back, bearing the guard to the ground and jamming his dagger between the man's shoulderblades before the stunned man could cry out; while his two lurking companions at the same time jumped the remaining guard, jerked back his head, and with a crack and a grunt dispatched him.

Swiftly they hauled the dead guards into the shadows and waited with indrawn breath to see if anyone had heard or taken heed of the lantern tumbling to the ground. Nothing seemed to stir. Francho now glanced up. His man still on the upper roof, one of the skilled mountaineers from the Asturian levies that had been assigned to each group, was supposed to have twirled his rope with its specially weighted loop to snag one of the outlined battlements of the tower, praying that the guard up there did not hear the small thud of the rope. From small noises that his ear had made out Francho could imagine the man expertly lancing the loop—and failing. It would take a magician to settle that rope over the jutting stone in the dark of the night. Tracing himself with the cross he hissed upward as a signal that the alley guards had been secured. To his amazement he heard the soft smack of the loose end of the rope against the side of the tower, and as he groped for it heard the Asturian slither down the other rope to join them.

With a leap Francho began a swift hand-over-hand assent of the stout rope, bracing his feet against the tower's thick stone wall, and his system was so keyed up that the climb seemed easy. Reaching the battlements he first peered through the crenelation and made out the vague form of the guard, evidently impatient to be relieved, leaning over the opposite parapet to see what transpired with the sergeant at the main portal below. As quietly as he could Francho pulled himself up and over the ledge to then slither rapidly into the angle of an abutment where he froze into an amorphous shadow. But the guard had heard the light, scraping noise of his arrival and now straightened up to peer curiously into the dark, showing no alarm at what he took to be just a rat gnawing at the old timbers of the roof from underneath. Yet—he sauntered across the roof.

Francho let the guard approach perilously close to where he was hunkered, then flipped a bit of crumbled mortar off to the side and tensed the muscles in his thighs. The man whirled toward the sound, crying, "Who's there?" and in that second Francho launched himself forward like a missile from a catapult. The long dagger plunged in an arc toward the man's unprotected throat, there was a gurgled cry and a gag, and the guard's body slumped, his pike thumping on the timbers. Francho eased the body down.

The raider who had followed hauled himself up and over the ledge and looked down to urge the two others on. In a few moments they all heard a muffled, cheerful hail from inside the tower, and Francho hastily pushed his companions to a position behind the hinged lid as the stout bar that secured the trap from inside the tower thunked aside. The new guard lifted the trapdoor back and began to climb out. "Ho! Kassim! Thought you were forgotten, eh? That misery of a sergeant stopped to *aaarrgh—!*" The Asturian rammed the dead guard's pike into the replacement's back with such force that it easily pierced the man's leather armor. With a quick lunge Francho and a cohort grabbed at him and kept him from tumbling back down the ladder to the floor below.

Now it was a matter of minutes before the off-duty guards waiting to return to barracks wondered what was taking Kassim so long to descend.

Francho stayed on the roof. The sergeant below would surely call up from the outside impatiently, and a muffled promise of immediate descent might delay his suspicions for a short, precious time. But the other men, well briefed, disappeared down the trap and dashed from the short ladder to run down the tower's stone steps as it spiraled against one wall, drawing short, oil-soaked torches from their pouches and igniting them from the lanterns which hung at intervals along the stair. In a few minutes, having delivered his delaying response, Francho dropped through the trap to join his men. They were working swiftly, one to each floor, touching the flaming torches to left and right behind them as they ran between the long mounds of sacks and bales, throwing burning wads of oil-wrung rags into the huge, open bins of grain, tossing packets of gunpowder into the farthest corners. He knew their steps would be made fleeter, as they raced from the crackling and flaring at their heels, by the knowledge that they had to finish their task and get up the stairs before the flames and smoke on the floor above cut them off.

Wielding a torch of his own on the dry wood of bins holding lentils and beans, Francho started from a far corner of the top floor, anxiously eyeing the smoky staircase as he criss-crossed the aisles. After what seemed like an eternity, with the flames licking at his own heels, he saw the first man leaping up the stairs as if all the devils in Hell were after him, coughing in spite of the kerchief over his face, and behind him pounded the second man. Throwing his torch at a far cluster of barrels of cooking oil Francho dodged away from the explosion and scrambled after them, and to his relief all three of his men made it back to the roof, gasping and choking.

Already there was a commotion below as the guards opened the main portal and fell back before rolling clouds of smoke. Francho swiftly pushed his panting men over the battlements one after another. They practically slid down the rope, swinging away from the side of the tower to avoid bright flames licking from slit windows and dropping to the ground in a dead sprint to get across the alley. Francho went last, descending as quickly as his men, but just as he was almost down a running guard spotted him in the lurid light emanating from one of the narrow slits.

The guard hauled up and then made a dash at him, hurling his pike inaccurately and shouting loudly to his comrades for help. Dangling in the air above him, Francho let go and dropped, landing in front of the guard in a crouching position. He sprang at the startled man and knocked up the arm that brandished a curved knife, then surged forward to drive his own wicked blade deep into the bearded face. The guard shrieked, a gush of blood obscuring his twisted features as he fell. Leaving the jammed dagger, which he could not pull out, Francho darted to the rope and was hauled up on the low roof by the Asturian as more guards ran into the alley carrying flares.

Amid a hail of furiously hurled pikes that clattered against the wall of the low building whose roof they quickly quitted, they clambered higher and fled the same way they had come, trailed by the shouts and curses of the soldiers, who could not follow because the mountaineer had cut the ropes, and the frightened cries of householders peering out their windows. Even though they were slowed up by one of the men, who gritted his teeth on a bad ankle, Francho nevertheless managed to spirit his group out of the area before the guards could scurry through the disjointed maze of alleys below to intercept them. Descending unseen in the sleeping streets they flitted back along the direct route Francho had chosen, happy to hear the cries and yells of "Fire! Fire!" dying away behind them. One of the men plucked at Francho's sleeve and pointed to the left of them where a garish orange glow was climbing the night sky. With a gleeful grin hidden beneath his black beard Francho hastened them on, rejoicing that Antonio de la Cueva had been successful too; and where two groups had succeeded surely the third would not fail. The muffled explosions and ugly crackling were waking even Zemel's quiet quarter by the time they reached his wall.

In fact they found de la Cueva waiting alone behind the acacia bushes in Zemel's garden, the young Count having already sent his men to safety through the tunnel. "Thanks given to God," de la Cueva breathed as Francho dropped down before him. "But Pulgar is not yet here, and your tower was further distant than his. He should have gotten back by now."

"If something has gone amiss there is nothing we can do for him," Francho whispered back, urging his own men to hurry as they scrambled into the tunnel. "Return to the safety of the boat, Antonio. If he and his men don't get to you within the quarter hour you'll have to leave without him."

"We can return along his route. Perhaps they've been cornered and a diversion would free them."

"No. We have no swords, and any citizen with a weapon is alert for us now, for the guards saw us departing. Reduan will turn out his best squadrons to find us. Look you, Pulgar is indestructible, Antonio, no cause for worry," Francho calmed his friend, although he was worried himself. "They may have been forced to take a longer way around or are hiding to avoid the chase. Now go on."

"And leave you to go after him alone? Oh no, *amigo,* I know that elaborately bland tone in your voice. I suppose you are chivalrously considering my wife and babies, eh?" The shorter nobleman thrust his face toward Francho's indignantly. "Since when have I ever run from a fight?"

"It wouldn't be a fight, it would be a massacre, you stubborn—"

His argument was interrupted by a low chuckle, and Hernan del Pulgar dropped from the wall behind them. "Report victory, *señores,*" he panted in a low voice.

In great relief both friends smiled at this puffing apparition as Pulgar's men swarmed over the wall behind him. "You're late," Francho accused in a whisper.

The massive frame struck a swaggering pose. "A little private errand," he shrugged, grinning and dusting off his hands as if he had just won the war by himself.

Nevertheless, Pulgar had lost one of his men, who, probably overcome by smoke, had never emerged from the fiery tower. With no time to ask whatever else Pulgar had been doing, Francho hustled the remaining men and his two friends into the conduit with hardly a farewell because he still had to close and lock the hatch, go over the wall, and return to his little house the same way he had come, and then, apparently awakened by the growing hubbub of aghast citizens rushing to see the fires, make a swift return to the Alhambra. Left alone in the dark he put to rights the hatch and again made the mark of the cross on his breast, willing his luck not to desert him now, now that the miraculous feat was accomplished. He pulled the hood of his mantle over his turban and putting one toe into a crack between the stones of the wall boosted himself up to the top, pausing just a second to view the angry flaming red sky outlining the buildings ahead and then pulled himself over.

Haggard, Francho would describe the drawn faces of the upset, hastily dressed officials and citizens packing the square audience chamber, haggard with the realization that the terrible smoking ruins in the lower city presaged catastrophe, or perhaps, as in Francho's case as he slumped wearily on a dais step to the rear of the throne, merely from lack of sleep. Only Boabdil's countenance showed some spirit, and that was because he could assuage his shock with rage; a rage that was focused upon a group of men coming toward him, parting the sea of spectators like a wedge. The front officials pressed back and aside, and Muza Aben and his men now reached the cleared space before the throne, where the Grand Sultan's choler was hardly cooled by the two Nubians waving peacock fans above him.

The grim general jerked a half-dressed prisoner from the grip of his guards and flung the man sprawling to the ground. "Great Sultan, I bring this traitorous vermin to grovel before your judgment. To him belongs the device on the dagger found protruding from the body of the depot guard," Muza Aben's voice vibrated with passion.

"Mercy, mercy, O most benign of Sultans, I am innocent!" the man wailed, raising his head, his voice high but clear against the threatening silence of the throng, and Francho recognized him as a shy member of the wealthy Rasoul family, a clan already in disgrace for the execution several years before of one of its members for spying for El Zagal. The slim, long-nosed young man who raised a terrified face to his ruler was popularly admired for the sad poetry he composed, some of which Boabdil had requested Jamal ibn Ghulam set to music. Now the Sultan glowered so angrily at the captive that the man commenced to tremble. "Yes, O Excellence, the weapon is mine but I did not use it. Yesterday it was stolen from me, or perhaps lost, I do not know . . ."

"You do not know?" Boabdil retorted, and it was clear to Francho that the Sultan had found a scapegoat for the impotence and the grief that assailed him. "Do you expect me to believe that, dog? You are of a family of traitors who have conspired against my throne before. Who is there who can swear you were not lurking about the towers this past terrible night?"

"M . . . my wife, my servants . . ." ibn Rasoul stuttered.

"Hah! His wives and servants! Ordered to lie for him, Excellence." Muza Aben bellowed.

Francho spotted a few of ibn Rasoul's relatives in the crowd of courtiers, but they, ashen, made not a move to step forward in their kinsman's behalf.

"Too long have I lived by a believing heart only to find that my reward is this loathsome assault behind our walls. Now I will believe no one," Boabdil stormed, a tinge of hysteria in his tone, grasping the edge of his silk-draped divan in a white-knuckled grip. "Your blade drips the gore of foul treachery, ibn Rasoul. Had not Allah in His mercy sent rain, the whole city might have burned to the ground. Who are the other curs who aided you in this cruel plot? Speak out while you can!"

The shaken poet, precipitously dragged from his bed and accused of a heinous crime, could not collect his wits. "No one, there was no one," he gasped. "I . . . I mean, I do not know. I am innocent of wrongdoing, my Sultan, I am your faithful servant," he wailed.

"Liar! Liar and traitor!" Boabdil shouted, pointing an accusing, shaking finger. With the other hand he grabbed up a sheet of parchment lying by his side and brandished it at the culprit. "And I suppose you know nothing of this foul desecration which was found fastened with a bloody Christian dagger to the door of our Great Mosque?" He held up the parchment and displayed it carefully all around the room, causing gasps and roars of shocked protest from his audience, for, as Francho saw by craning his neck, upon it was written in great red letters, "Ave Maria!"

Francho averted his eyes hastily, fighting to erase the grin threatening to reveal itself. What had Pulgar casually noted at the commencement of their raid, the rogue? "My return route comes close to the Great Mosque."

"Muza Aben Gazul, remove this evil odor from my audience chamber and see he spits out the names of the others involved in this infamous crime against the people of Granada. I sentence them to pay the forfeit before the whole city and let my people, whose bellies will now suffer hunger for this treachery, curse them in Allah's name."

Screaming of his innocence, pleading for mercy, the doomed ibn Rasoul was hauled away amid a hubbub of cries of abhorrence for him and approval for the Sultan. But some of the spectators in the sea of turbans only murmured nervously, for men who were tortured finally shrieked out names to stop the pain, any names at all. The Sultan surveyed the unquiet faces before him with bitter distrust. "If any of you that stand before me as loyal subjects have betrayed your people along with ibn Rasoul, we will soon surely know it," he threatened. "Now go, all of you, go, get out!"

The disturbed throng of ministers, council members, community leaders, and aristocrats backed away with no further urging, for none had ever seen the Sultan so enraged. Quickly they funneled out through the portals into the Second Plaza.

Francho sat downcast and still for a moment, suffering from a deep regret that he had unwittingly lifted the dagger of the talented and amiable ibn Rasoul, a man whom he would have preferred alive to many others in the Sultan's Court.

"You too," the Sultan turned and snapped at old Comixa, who stood silently, with turned-down mouth. "I need no officious advice this morning. I need to sleep." He rose from his throne and walked slowly, almost stumblingly, toward the wall of airy archways leading to his personal apartments, followed by M'jambana, who held the straining Aswad on a brass-link lead. With negative gestures he prevented several lingering, solicitous courtiers from accompanying him, but he looked back at his musician and nodded.

As padding servants undressed the slumping ruler in his bedchamber, he said nothing. Francho sat cross-legged on some pillows near the divan, industriously plucking out a favorite plaintive but soft and soothing air. Glancing up with a quirked brow he saw all the anger had drained from Boabdil's weakly handsome face, and that now it was weary and lined with pain. An image of a stained glass portrait he had once seen of the bearded, youthful, strained visage of Christ in His Passion flitted blasphemously through his mind.

At last, garbed in a flowing robe and with screens pulled up in front of the fretted windows to block the morning light, Boabdil let himself be led to his divan. "Give me sleep, friend Jamal," he groaned as he stretched out on the pillows. "Find for me the peace of sleep and then go to your own rest, minstrel. In a few hours we will consider how to bring calm to my subjects."

The exhausted Sultan's light snore came quickly this time, and Francho was grateful. He wearily picked himself up and shouldered his guembri, but instead of leaving the chamber he walked out on the ruler's balcony to view once more with tired but triumphant eyes the calamitous damage he had caused to happen, the three smoking areas below where the blackened towers gaped roofless amid the ruined char of surrounding buildings. The morning air, still damp from the unseasonable and sudden heavy downpour which occurred just before dawn, was still heavy with the miasma of burnt wood and roasted grain, a sadistically delicious odor, as if hundreds of loaves of bread had been blistered in a giant oven. In his mind's eye he could see again the jagged tongues of orange fury leaping against the dark sky, hot flames from the three blazing towers and the buildings they had showered with sparks erasing the light of the stars as cries and screams and shrieks rose from those who were fighting the fires and those who were fleeing them. He imagined again the rejoicing in the Christian camp as the raiders returned victorious and victory beacons were lit to signal an end to Granada's smug invincibility. And it was he, he who had placed the enemy within Ferdinand's grasp.

The unease which lately assailed him brutally wedged its way in again. The enemy? Ali and Azahra? Old Zemel? The hard-working Mustafa Ata? He would not even allow the thought of the amiable and generous Boabdil to cross his mind but frowned it away, irritated with such sentimental folly, hardly suited to a knight fighting in the King's service. Better think of the bellicose Muza Aben, of Reduan and the brutal Zatar, the selfish Abencerrages and Zegris, dour Comixa, bitter Ayaxa, the dungeons filled with Christian wretches. This was the enemy, the revilers of Christ, alien dwellers on the sweetest leagues of Christian soil; the ancient foe. But alien dwellers? After many several hundred years? His restless mind discomforted him.

His right fist clenched and unclenched. His jaw tightened. How long had it been since he had grasped the cold, sure hilt of a sword, a sword, naked, forthright, openly raised and openly wielded, unhidden. So much in his life was secret, hidden. He looked down and noticed mild abrasions on the palm of his hand and shook his head at the folly of running with the arsonists when he could have waited safely in the garden. Had he suffered a grievous wound or bad cuts and scratches he couldn't explain he would have had to flee with the raiders to the Christian camp and leave his mission here unfinished. And Dolores would have been left alone, unprotected, perhaps sold finally. . . .

He forced his purpose back in focus, for today was his triumph, and behind the face of a false mourner he was going to revel in the results. For a moment more he stared out at the rising, thin smoke and the tiny figures of people picking through the remains of Granada's pyres. Then he turned on his heel to seek his own couch for a few hours. His dry lips stretched in a small smile as he imagined describing the adventure to Dolores—his most rapt and admiring audience.

The ordered pace of Dolores's life was disturbed that week. The ladies inhabiting the royal harem were allowed an "en masse" outing to view the executions on the Vivarrambla from their gay array of curtained carts and litters. This rare privilege turned the violent deaths of Nuri ibn Rasoul and the eight others whose names he had screamed out, along with the delinquent tower guards, into an exciting entertainment for them.

But Dolores, accustomed to more freedom, had little stomach for the horror of a field of tortured and broken men tied spread-eagle on the ground and ponderously trampled into boneless gore by huge royal elephants in jingling harnesses. She was unnerved by the ugly, brutal mood of the spectators, who hurled their curses even at the bloody and mangled remains. She could not shake twinges of guilt for the suffering of the innocent victims, although their tragedy had only indirectly to do with her. Looking for Francho she glanced up at the raised royal platform and viewed the Sultan's glittering presence as he sat under a striped kiosk and peacock fans, surrounded by his counselors. The royal concubines' conveyance in which she rode was pulled up close enough that she could see tense strain on Boabdil's face under the plumed, cloth-of-gold turban and note that the royal gaze seemed to rest on a point just above the carnage.

But these dreadful public executions, which temporarily unraveled the fabric of her tranquil days, were wiped from her mind a week later when, in answer to an outraged protest and challenge from Boabdil, Ferdinand agreed to formal battle on open ground and the first clash of two great armies she had ever seen took place within her view from the harem roof. Details were not clear, of course, but the day was fine and she had no trouble making out the line of thirty thousand Moslem warriors (Francho had said) ranged in bristling opposition to the much larger Christian force drawn up to face them.

Turning her head she could see that every high tower and balcony in the city was jammed with the people of Granada, eyes riveted on the battlefield, and they seemed to her uncharacteristically anxious and subdued, and even the women crowding at the grill to either side of her did not chatter or giggle much. Everyone was mesmerized by the immobility of both armies—doll-like at this distance—separated by a scant five hundred feet. And the hushed, expectant silence, where even a bird did not twitter in the city or swoop in the ruined fields, lent an air of chimera. A breeze rippled the rainbow plumes and pennants on both sides. The sun flashed sparks off Spanish plate armor and visored casques and Moorish mail shirts and spiked helmets and reflected from painted shields and the shining flanks of pawing chargers. Amid the stiff forests of raised, steel-tipped lances, she could see the green-plumed Grand Sultan facing an armored Christian King from whose lance flew the pennon of the Cross. Moorish cavaliers returned the scowls of Spanish knights, yet not a man moved among the rigid file upon file of horsemen and infantry glaring at each other across the divide.

Then there was a silent glitter as Boabdil suddenly raised his mesh gauntlet. There sounded a blast of a deep-toned horn, and the Sultan's arm fell. Immediately the silence was dissolved as immobility broke into spurting action and a muted thunder of hooves rose to her ears as the opposing armies galloped into each other with a cacophony of trumpet calls and wild rallying cries, inexorable waves of death melding and mixing violently so that the deadly clang and clash of steel upon steel easily rose to the ears of the onlookers on the city walls. Choking dust sprang up around the fierce battle lines and was billowed by the breeze into the cerulean sky. In twenty minutes the blackened earth of the *vega* was heaped and strewn with broken, fallen bodies, the cries of both living and dying warriors, and the screams of wounded horses wafting back to the city with terrible clarity.

Trying to follow the confused fury of hacking blades, flying bolts and balls, of crushing hooves, swinging maces, and viciously flung javelins, Dolores could soon see that the Moors were being pushed back, yard by bloody yard, toward the city. But now, and the women grimaced and covered their ears, the big cannons on Granada's walls thundered out, expertly aimed to hurl their murderous missiles of stone shot and iron shrapnel into the rear of the pressing enemy lines, leaving big, tragic gaps in the ranks of Spanish foot soldiers and bowmen. She heard the tiny sounds of trumpets blowing in frantic recall above the clangor of the melee, and, following their gesticulating commanders, the Spanish forces turned and retreated out of the range of the bombards, immediately pursued by platoons of saber-swinging, howling Moors.

Now what had been one huge battle broke into numerous pockets, every inch of ground disputed with bloody valor. Dolores could make out some of the Christian banners, and the main leaders were not hard to spot. There was no mistaking the great iron-encased, orange-and-black-plumed figure of Ferdinand of Aragon, who laid about him steadily, a succession of nobles and knights at his back wielding their own bloody swords. Muza Aben's bright green helmet popped up at various points on the field as he urged forward his cavalry in a charge upon the most desperate contests and waved on faltering Moorish foot who were visibly suffering from fatigue and wounds. Once, the women about Dolores gasped with horror to spot Boabdil on his white Barbary steed suddenly left dangerously exposed as his soldiers fled in panic from a charge, but the Sultan reared his white horse and galloped to meet the attack alone. At the last minute an alert Moorish commander—Dolores thought it was Reduan—pounded up with a flying wedge of cavalry weighted with purple Abencerrage plumes, and the Sultan was safely flanked again as he engaged his foes.

Even though Ferdinand's forces were greater, the Moors were fighting for their lives and held the enemy from coming close enough to use their cannon on the city, although the Moslem ranks were tattered by the bursts of shot and shrapnel. For two hours the battle went on and on along the undulating line, and the outcome was uncertain. Servants brought food to the roof, and Dolores sat with the other women in the shade of silk awnings to eat date and lamb stew and rosewater pudding. Nevertheless she picked at her food, upset. She was afraid God would smite her where she sat as a faithless traitor, for she wanted the Christians to retreat, to go away, to leave her alone.

"See, see," a plump, pretty Arab girl with eyes big as black pearls gasped where she watched from the grill. "A catastrophe is happening. The infidel warriors have circled behind our army, like two great arms of the evil one. They will cut our warriors off from our gates!"

Fifty women at once rushed to the grill to stare out into the distance, where large units of Moorish cavalry desperately chopped and hacked at the pressing Christian forces, who were forming a relentless pincers that threatened to trap the entire Moslem army. A few moments later the women cried out, for, with a desperate shout that was audible to them, a line of Moorish foot soldiers wavered, broke, and turned tail before the enemy's vigorous onslaught, fleeing in ignominious confusion for the city walls. A panic started that spread like a contagion among the outnumbered and heavily battered

Moorish pikemen and archers, who also broke and ran. A universal gasp of disbelief and shame rose from the hand-wringing throngs on the city's roofs who viewed the rout.

A flurry of cavalry led by Muza Aben and the Sultan himself galloped along with the troops, attempting frantically to stem the tumultuous retreat of the beaten infantry, but the mindless surge of disengagement could not be stopped. The decimated ranks of horsemen were forced to flee as well, and even their valiant defense of the backs of their vanquished soldiers against the rampaging Christians did nothing to lift the sinking hearts of the citizens on the walls.

The Spanish cavalry broke off pursuit as the city's bombards began speaking again and squadrons of crossbowmen on the walls let loose a curtain of deadly flights of steel bolts to allow the gates to open and admit the defeated army. By straining her eyes Dolores could recognize the tabard colors of some of the hundreds of shouting, jubilant Spanish knights caracoling their horses and brandishing triumphant swords just out of range of the cannon.

Much subdued the women of the harem returned to the food bowls arranged on a fringed cloth under the awning. Sayeda Fawzia planted her ample form before Dolores and pointed to the untouched morsels before her. "Do you not wish to eat a celebration meal, Christian?" she demanded acidly. "Waste not the food, for even the Alhambra will soon yearn for bread. All of you," she warned the dispirited women around her who stared at the floor or clung to each other bewildered by what they had just seen, "do not leave what you have chosen to eat to be given instead to the animals. Each morsel is precious to our survival. The longer we resist, the greater the enemy too will feel the pinch of siege."

Hands on portly hips, the patriotic harem mistress tried to rally the spirits of her charges, but the luxuriously garbed ladies retrieved little appetite. Many of them suffered their own private fears of a Christian victory, as Dolores was aware. Those from distant lands feared freedom amid strangers; others feared being sold into a worse bondage than they suffered; some, the old ones remaining from Muley Abul Hassan's days, feared dying in poverty. Dolores feared too, and her heart was sad. She feared the end of her sweet and happy dream.

* * *

"I miss the flowers," Dolores sighed into the night. "These on the bushes have no scent."

"The roses will bloom again," Francho murmured, rubbing an itching shoulder blade against the bark of the young cypress tree they leaned their backs against. "In January it all begins afresh. At least the rain has stopped."

"*Sí.* We could not have sat out here last week, it was so wet."

"Still, it is much too warm and close. Unseasonable for November."

"But pleasant," Dolores crooned lazily, rubbing her hand in absent fashion up and down his thigh. They sat companionably silent for a moment, listening to a nightbird warble somewhere in the little garden. But she gathered her wandering thoughts and looked over at him, his face alternately in shadow or palely lit by a huge, creamy moon filtering through the dark, moving branches. "Are you hungry?" she asked him softly. The rations of thin stew, turnips, and bread Ali drew from the kitchen, sometimes supplemented by gifts of cheese and dried fruit from the Sultan, were not very filling over a long day. She thought his face seemed thinner, the cheekbones sharper.

He looked back at her. "Me? No. Just pensive."

She smoothed the coverlet they'd carried out to lounge upon. "And content?"

His half grunt, half ironic chuckle reflected his worry. "Ay, *querida,* how could anybody be content who must attend the Sultan's agony day after day? Each day he rides through the city and sees the miserable, pinched faces of the adults, the children's dull eyes and bony frames. Even the well-to-do have used up their caches and walk about gaunt. And yet the people disdain surrender and shout at him, "We will not give in!" Their courage surprises him, he admires it, but he knows it is useless suffering. He wakes by night sweating and in terror."

"And that is when they come for you."

"That is when they come for me." He nodded, stretching his arms up and then lying down so that his head was pillowed in her lap. "But not tonight anymore. I hope." He turned his head to face her. "It is past midnight. When I returned I thought surely you would be asleep, but I'm glad you weren't. I am too keyed up to sleep."

"Tell me about the council meeting."

He sucked in a deep breath and blew it out wearily. "The

meeting was tempestuous. Even men who were most adamantly opposed to surrender are now for it as their stomachs shrink, yet Muza Aben will not soften. I told you of the secret delegation Boabdil sent to Their Majesties? They returned this evening with extremely liberal surrender terms, which Boabdil laid before the council. The cadis, the muftis, the aristocrats and officials listened gray-faced, hopeless, some wiped away tears. But not Muza Aben. Ranting that Allah would sustain them, he swore that his army would hold closed the gates of Granada to the death of the last man and stomped from the chamber, followed by Reduan and the rest of his officers. The Sultan sat helpless and so did the council, left as they were with a signed surrender document but no means to implement it."

"But if the citizens want to surrender?"

"They don't! The perversity of the people of Granada defies all understanding. There is something in the Arab mentality I just cannot fathom. Mostly it is Muza Aben; he harangues them daily, he lifts up their spirits with tales that help will yet arrive from Egypt and the pashas of Africa, he whips them into indignation at the council, castigating the members as wailing women. He shores up their pride so that they feed on anger. You have heard them screaming defiance at the Sultan until the Nubians drive them away from the Alhambra gates."

"But for all his ferocity Muza Aben cannot nourish them. From where do they draw their strength?"

"I don't know. Desperation, maybe, and the unyielding preachers in the mosques. They grow weak on small rations and yet they cling to their bitter, unyielding general. Groups prowl the streets in search of the last crumb, the stray cat. I bring food to Ali and Azahra in small packets lest some neighbor grow jealous of a large bundle and steal it. And now that there is little to preserve, even the snow gatherers are not allowed out. I wish it were all over. Without couriers I have little purpose here," he said morosely.

Silver bracelets glinting in the moonlight, she caressed away the locks from his forehead, and he nestled his cheek even closer into the comforting curve of her silk-clad belly. She would have been content just to smooth the faint frown lines between his brows with her fingers and sit stroking him, but both curiosity and the fact that she knew he wanted to talk drove her on.

"What says the Great Sultan to all this?"

586

"He secludes himself and agonizes. For his people's sake he has signed a treaty which exiles him forever from his homeland, and yet they revile him and reject his sacrifice." He suddenly put aside her stroking hand and sat up, and by the brooding hunch of his shoulders she saw his reluctant sympathy for the tormented man who somehow drew moral support from him. "He has terrible dreams. He believes Allah is punishing him for his rebellion against his father. He is bitterly jealous that the people acclaim Muza Aben but he has not the power to arrest him and rein in the army. Only the hope of protecting the city from Malaga's fate sustains him."

Francho stared up at the little diamond points of light spangling the velvet sky, but he saw instead the Sultan slumped and staring at the brilliant pattern of his Persian carpet and then raising a worn face to Jamal ibn Ghulam, his candid companion, his honest bulwark, the talented killer of his pain, only to see his musician staring at him with stricken eyes, eyes which the Sultan did not realize hid culpability and a heart that could find no comforting words which would not be false.

Boabdil had grimaced sadly. "We make a fine pair, my minstrel, you with your guembri and songs of old triumphs and heroes, and me with my dreams of ruling a peaceful land. We battle the dragons of reality with too fragile staves." He turned his head away from Francho, staring emptily into a corner of the dimly lit salon where M'jambana dozed lightly. "I had somehow hoped Los Reyes Católicos would accept my allegiance and whatever they demanded in tribute and leave me the pretense of my throne for my lifetime. But they are adamant. I and my house are to be sent into the shame of exile. You, however—you are a man whose artistry makes him truly the solace of kings, and you could surely find yourself a place with the Christian Court. You are free, friend ibn Ghulam, to follow the fortune of your talent; I release you from all obligation, and I urge you with my kindest heart to go your own way."

Francho's throat was dry. He had no choice but to lie, both out of the cowardice of affection and because he could not bear to bring further hurt upon the luckless Boabdil, whose rigid set of shoulders under the rich tunic seemed to brace him against the strain of one more loss. "I will come with you, Excellence," he said huskily.

Boabdil's eyes moved toward him slowly, the tragic gaze

finally locking with his. "You are throwing your life away, Jamal. There is naught before me but degradation and oblivion."

Francho shook his head as if doggedly determined. "I will follow you, my Sultan, that is my wish. There has been much pleasure for me in your service." This much at least was true. "I will go where you go. My mind is set." The gratitude in Boabdil's eyes shamed him, made him bite the inside of his lip even as he smiled at the man.

Now, frowning out into the warm November night with Dolores beside him, he was pursued by the image of Abu Abdullah, almost surely the last of Granada's Sultans, clasping him by the shoulder and uttering a simple, "Gramercy, ibn Ghulam." When, in the end, Boabdil and his train rode away from Granada, he would finally know his cherished minstrel had deserted him. Perhaps he would have even been told by then he had harbored a Christian spy who had constantly betrayed him. War was war and could not be made less ugly, Francho understood, but he hoped he could give himself the privilege of not being present to view the Sultan's last degradation.

Dolores resolved not to question Francho anymore about the Sultan, for it was plain he was suffering for his part in the downfall of a ruler for whom he held affection as a man. To break the heavy mood of his last utterance she shrugged, pretended insouciance, and loosed a trill of laughter. She tugged at him until he unfolded himself and stretched out again and then playfully rolled on top of him, giggling loudly to hear his fake grunt as if her weight were too much for him.

"Shh, little wanton, you'll wake the palace."

"Shh, yourself. I see you no longer care that I am your faithful slave woman to do with as you wish." She looked down at him, and her loose, jasmine-scented hair spilled silkily to either side of his face. She wriggled her hips on his provocatively, shamelessly, and the hard, solid feel of his body under her ignited her. "It seems all you wish is to talk and talk."

"And who says this?" The muscular arm that went around her pressed her closer against him. In the flickers of moonlight she caught a glimpse of his white smile and a hunger for her sparking the dark sapphire depths of his eyes, and she experienced the joyous little leap of her heart that always answered it.

"I do," she responded lightly, flicking the barbarous silver hoop in his ear with her finger. "I say it."

"Not true. I have no desire to talk. In fact, all I wish right now is sleep."

"Oh!" she squealed and tried to break away, but the other arm came about her and he rolled on his side so that she was tenderly cradled in his arms. After so many months of lovemaking he had no doubts as to how to fuel the fire that raced ever hotter between them.

He nuzzled her nose with his, and the warmth and intimacy of his breath, the soft tickle of his beard aroused her. She especially loved it when they went slowly, he murmuring to her, drawing out the excitement, both of them discovering refinements in the senses of touch and smell and taste that made the inevitable plunge into rapturous abandonment all the more exquisite. But sometimes, as now, when overwhelming and blind desire engulfed her artful lover, the hot-blooded maleness of him intoxicated her and swept her along with him, and she was joyous just to give him what he sought.

His hot kiss consumed her as he gathered her to him, his arm purposefully pressing up between her legs and giving wings to the physical love that opened her heart and her body to him.

"Not here? On the grass?" she gasped as he freed her lips for a moment.

"Yes here, why not? There is no one but us. . . ."

But us and God, she thought, both shocked and titillated at the thought of coupling in the open, sheltered only by a tree and the warm, shadowed night. In a hurry he yanked off over his head his long, loose shirt of white cotton. She waited, for he liked to undress her. With quick, knowing hands he drew off her jacket and bodice and laid her down on the coverlet, passing one warm hand in a brief caress down the side of her throat and along one breast, teasing the sensitive nipple a brief moment.

She lifted her hips to help him as he pulled off her pantaloons—and then inhaled sharply at the intense pleasure that streaked through her, for holding her hips elevated, he had applied his mouth to her woman's place, drawing her soul there with hot, luring kisses, his tongue flicking out to lick and play with her until her body began to shake and she thought she would go mad. He moved up her quivering form, kissing and licking her all the way, whispering "darling, darling" against her skin, kissing her breasts from their fullness to their pink nipple tips, encircling each nipple with his lips so that she moaned and convulsed and engulfed his head with her arms so that those lips would never stop, never stop loving her, wanting her, never stop opening the gates of Heaven for her—

"You belong to me," he whispered fiercely, passionately, "you belong to me, Dolores. Here, in the open, in the view of God . . ."

He invaded her welcoming body with so driven a need to possess her that her breath was expelled in a great gasp, but in the next moment she was matching his ardor, making little cries of arousal, moving with him more and more urgently, her exaltation in joining this one man in the supreme act of human love, finally delivering her into the delirious explosion that was a small dying just as he fastened frantically onto her mouth and shuddered through his own great release.

Waiting some moments for his panting to subside, he finally raised his head and muttered, "You are insatiable and a wanton. You will kill me with your siren's spell." He bit her ear gently and flopped on his back beside her.

"Not yet," she promised, floating in a ravished happiness. "Not yet, *mi alma.*"

They lay still for a while, letting the mild breeze cool the fever of their bodies. She settled her head into the hollow of his shoulder, and his arm went around her to hold her there. But in a few minutes it slid away, and his breathing turned deep and even in sleep. She raised herself up on one elbow and looked down at his finely cut, handsome features, the olive skin drawn over cheekbones shadowed by his dark lashes. Sleep smoothed out the rugged alertness from his bearded face, the constant mild frown. He looked younger. "I love you so much," she whispered to his unhearing ears. She remained gazing at him, but as the seconds passed the joy of their loving seemed to seep away, to be replaced by a pervading sadness.

Silently she got up, gathered her garments, and, after covering his big, sprawled body with his shirt, padded back to the chamber. Sitting on the divan she pulled the sheet up about her and hugged her knees.

Papa el Mono's daughter was not stupid. She would not fool herself into thinking this happy eight months of intimacy, the light-hearted days, the passionate nights, were more real to him than his yearning for Leonora de Zuniga, the love of his

590

heart. His very inability to utter the word "love" to her made it easy to interpret the absent look in his eyes, his removed air as his gaze followed a swallow winging east toward the Christian camp, or the occasional sigh he tried to hide.

Yet, unless he had iron compartments in his heart, there were times when he touched her face and body with such sweetness and reverence that she could swear he loved her too. She shook her head in sad bewilderment. Still, even if she could give the people of Granada the strength to endure another year of hunger, she would not. If this was to him a mere fleeting attraction of time and place and warm flesh, then let it be over as it would and let her suffer the pain and be done with it. Although she dreaded to live without him, her love, her lover, her dearest heart, nevertheless she had a pride in herself, and when the world reappeared on their doorstep she was determined to accept the end every bit as controlled as he.

Lost in her melancholy thoughts she did not realize he was standing in the shadows by the door studying her profile until he clucked softly.

"Such heavy musings, *doña,* so late in the night? It must now be Dolores, for Karima would be soundly sleeping."

She looked over her shoulder and smiled. "And so she will be in a moment. What awakened you?"

"The lack of you. I suddenly knew you weren't there." He came toward her, unself-conscious in his nakedness, just as she unself-consciously allowed her eyes to wander adoringly over his sinewy physique. He sat on the edge of the divan and reached out to trace a finger along her forearm. "What were you thinking?" he asked in a gentle manner, and his very tone told her he knew.

She shrugged. "I was just thinking how like a dream it seems, everything that came before Granada. The Court, the Queen, Seville, the Duke, Torrejoncillos . . ." She smiled in order to keep it light.

His response came with as light a note. "I imagine you will go back to Medina-Sidonia once the surrender takes place."

The very casualness of how he disposed of the months of shared life between them caused her heart to lurch; if she had been standing she would have staggered under his cruelty. As it was she quickly lowered her eyes so he would not see her shaken reaction to his offhand admission that the future held nothing for them. "Yes, I suppose I will," she finally got out.

"If he still wishes. He has always been very kind. A woman without family needs a protector."

"You could marry instead," he said mildly.

She had never told him that her relationship with Don Enrique was purely platonic despite the gossip, nor of the Duke's offer to her of marriage when death removed his wife, for these facts formed a shred of independence from him to which she clung. "And whom would I marry?" she asked slowly, careful to keep her voice steady.

"There are fine men, respected knights or even younger sons of the nobility who would be eager to court you if Medina-Sidonia's obvious patronage did not discourage them. It would mean security for you and a position of respect." Now he had the grace to begin to look uncomfortable.

She could not control the brittle snap to her tone. "Ay, Maria, Don Francisco, for one so anxious to see me safe, you do not aim very high for me. Please do not trouble yourself over me. I have managed to survive successfully and alone, so far, and I will continue to do so."

"Don't be angry. Do you think me inhuman? Of course I trouble about you, Dolores."

Finding her balance again she smiled coolly and laid the tip of her finger on his lips to silence him. "Then you must not. I truly don't want you to. When we leave Granada I have plans of my own. We will do our best to put this—lovely interlude— behind us as quickly as we can."

But he gripped her arm and pulled her face closer to him. "Can you think it will be that easy, heart of stone? Are we nothing more to each other than just lustful strangers thrown together by fate? Yes, Leonora de Zuniga has my love, this you have always known, and she awaits me for I have begged her for her hand. But—" The blue eyes glittered under his frown, his fingers hurt her arm. "But there is a strong bond between you and me which was always much greater than just the affection of a shared past—a kind of love, perhaps, and this has given me much happiness. How you fare will always concern me, whether you welcome my interest or not. I want to see you safely guarded by an honorable man who will give you a name that is real."

She fought the aching lump stuck in her throat with sarcasm. "A small country gentleman, of course, who will take me far away from Court, mayhap? So that the good Leonora's dear lord will have no reminder of his dalliance and betrayal of her in Granada, of his ardent months spent making love to another woman?" She pressed closed her lips and jerked her arm away from him.

"I ought to slap you for that." He glowered. His open hand swept back.

Bridling, she sat straight up, daring him. "Go ahead, sir knight, slap me, but the truth is the truth. And I owe you no more submission. You'll find I've finally remembered how to fight back." Her threat and her stubborn chin and clenched fists were absurd, but defiance was all she had to counter his wounding rejection of whatever kind of love it was he thought they shared. But her preparation for battle broke the shell of his anger. His mouth relaxed and a slow grin spread over his face. For a moment his irreverence with her wrath ruffled her further, and then she realized he was not laughing at her but because even in her anger she was beguiling him. She could not define the emotion she saw in his eyes, but somehow she was embarrassed and confused by it. She pouted, discomfited, and felt the heat of a blush stain her cheeks.

Launching himself at her he bore her down on the pillows, and before she could pull away passionately kissed her brow, the tip of her nose, and both corners of her mouth. The corners of his own mouth still quirked; he murmured to her, "Please, *querida,* let us not quarrel. Let us take the joy of what we have both created while it still exists and not drag in the future. Futures have a strange way of confounding every plan . . ." He stopped in mid-sentence, unsure, his smile fading, his eyes wandering over her face.

Her lips parted under his wondering gaze—it was the smitten gaze of a man who loves, her heart cried out to her before she could smother such wishful thinking. *Diantre!* She was a grown woman, she had fallen deeply in love, and in the way of women she had followed her heart. That was all there was to it. So leave him be. She laid her palm on his cheek. "You do not regret?"

"No, *mi cara,* not ever. Will you?"

"Never," she whispered.

He lay silently by her side, and she fitted herself against him in the way they usually rested. A breeze had blown up, and there came the rustling of the hibiscus bushes outside. In her mind she imagined the waning sliver of the moon shimmering and drowning in the carved marble bowl of the small fountain in the garden, much as she was drowning in the fleeting joy of her love's presence.

> *My dame is a rose, a wild red rose,*
> *Red rose bloom perfect and joy to my heart*
> *But pluck it I cannot to hold to my breast,*
> *Sharp thorns are the nature that holds us apart.*
> *Dolores, Dolores, ay, cruel bright flower,*
> *Bloom sweet for me, lovely, if only an hour—*

Crossing the quiet Second Plaza toward his chamber, Francho yawned and shook his head to clear it of tedium. He hoped Selim had filled a tub for him, and what was better, he hoped Dolores might rub the knots from his neck and back with some oil. He had little time anymore to attend the baths. With the populace close to insurrection over Boabdil's attempt at capitulation and Muza Aben a real threat to the throne, the Sultan sat in his apartments alternately sputtering with rage or depressed; he demanded distractions of every sort, running Mustafa Ata ragged, and requiring Jamal ibn Ghulam's constant attendance. No matter. Francho had not visited Ali and Azahra for almost a month, and although he sent food by Selim and was told they fared well, he was determined to visit them on the morrow and let the distracted Sultan send in vain for him.

Occupied by his thoughts as he opened his portal he did not see until too late the soldiers that sprang at him from either side of the chamber and gripped his arms.

"What is this outrage? How do you dare enter my apartment in my absence," he roared, noting with some surprise the orange turbans and sashes that marked the men of the regular army. He shook off their grasping hands. "The Sultan shall hear of this unwarranted trespass."

The leader of the three scimitar-armed soldiers made a sketchy salaam and handed him a sealed note. "Apologies, *sayed,* but we have our orders. You will please read the letter."

Glaring at each of them in turn he broke the seal and scanned the paper. The message was brief: "To he who speaks with a golden voice: if you value your life you will follow my guards immediately and without protest. We have much to discuss. I have taken the liberty of removing your Christian slave woman to attend you here—or to be forfeit in case of your absence." The note was signed tersely, "Reduan."

Francho felt the blood drain from his face and a wave of alarm raced through him, but in a second he had got hold of himself; the guards saw nothing but narrowed eyes.

"You will come with us," the leader ordered and motioned him to the door.

Numbly he shrugged in the face of their drawn scimitars. And even if he could get away from them, Reduan had Dolores and evidently enough information to warrant torturing her for whatever crumbs more she might divulge. The game seemed to be up.

He allowed one of the soldiers to toss a hooded mantle over him to conceal his face, and he let them lead him along a little used gallery. The few passersby prudently averted their eyes not to be involved in these tense times; the obviously bribed palace guards along their way did not seem to notice the unauthorized presence of the army regulars. Groping about in the turmoil of his brain Francho decided he would barter his full confession in exchange for Dolores's freedom. He cursed himself for a selfish oaf for having involved her in his hazardous business when he could have left her in safety and perhaps even in ignorance of his very presence once she reached the royal harem.

They loped down several galleries and through archways, finally passing around the kitchens and into an obscure back court, musty with disuse, rimmed by tall, old storage bins. With a large key the leader unlocked the door of one of these, and in the weak light of the man's small lantern Francho could see there were narrow steps leading down. Francho knew the Alhambra was veined with secret escape hatches built by centuries of Sultans fearful of being trapped in the palace, and this was obviously one of them. A push in the back sent him forward down the long flight of gritty steps, and they silently filed down a close, narrow stone passage, which he presumed led under and beyond the palace gates to debouch somewhere among the mansions of the aristocrats along the hill.

At last a solid wall blocked their way. The guard fumbled at a stone and sprang the hatch of a hidden door that creaked outward. They emerged through the opening into a large, luxurious salon, and there, alone, sat the commander Reduan, cross-legged at a low, inlaid table. Casually Reduan motioned with his knife for Francho to sit on a cushion opposite him, at the same time with a jerk of his head dismissing the guards. Suspicious of the Moor's lack of caution with a man he

knew was in a desperate position, Francho remained stiffly
standing. "You wished to see me, *sayed?"* he asked in an even
tone, maintaining his role.

Reduan's cold eyes flickered over him briefly, then returned
to the dish of cooked beans he was eating from the point of his
knife. "Yes, Jamal ibn Ghulam. Or whatever your name is. I
have a proposition to put to you."

A muscle twitched in Francho's jaw. "A proposition?"

"Just so. I have had my suspicions of you since that
Christian prisoner escaped during the debacle at Albolodny.
You have been observed since then but you have been clever.
Now you are fortunate that I finally have my proof of your
perfidy at a time when my attitude is much softened."

"I have no idea of what you are accusing me," Francho
stated. "But I ask you to remember the Sultan holds my
person dear."

Reduan glanced up sharply, putting down his knife with a
clatter. "Don't waste my time and yours with denials, minstrel! I know you for what you are, an infiltrator and a spy. I
could easily, secretly dispose of you here and now if I were so
minded, or force a confession from you and give Granada
another gory execution to rejoice in, and the powerless Abu
Abdullah could do nothing to stop it. So spare me your
pretense of innocence and allow me to get to the point." He
jabbed his finger at a seat opposite him, a surprising invitation
in the situation.

Francho sat down on the indicated cushion and asked
warily. "What makes you so certain I am a traitor?"

"You think I am trying to bluff you into admitting more
than I am really sure of?" Reduan asked. "Not necessary. I
took a circumstance from here and a circumstance from
there—would a performer with delicate hands fight a fire, or
inhabit a rich apartment in the Alhambra yet spend much
time at a house in the stinking Albayzin, or be unknown to
any who came from the city he claims as his birthplace? The
incautious Sultan allowed you to be privy to every military
move we planned, many of which were shortly and inexplica-
bly subverted by the untimely arrival of Christian forces, a
result of obvious connivance."

"Your pardon, *sayed,* but you build a deadly accusation on
a base of air," Francho retorted. "The facts are I did not need
to be a public performer in Malaga, I maintain a concubine I

do not treat lavishly, and I dared to damage my hands by burns at Albolodny. Your circumstances mean exactly nothing."

"Exactly," Reduan agreed, calmly wiping his lips with a damask napkin. He rinsed his hands in a gold basin. "And that is why you sit here tonight and not in a dungeon awaiting execution. For by the time the instrument craftsman Zemel gathered his wits and came to me with a tale which confirmed my suspicions of you, our food stores were already destroyed, our army decimated, and Granada's fate sealed, it seemed. Which immutable situation causes me to let you live." He filled a wine cup and pushed it toward Francho and then poured one for himself. "You are lucky the old man was brought to me and not to Muza Aben. The morning after the depots burned the old craftsman wondered why an ivy bed in his garden was badly trampled and why there were many footprints before the hatch to an ancient conduit there leading beyond the walls. But it was not until yesterday, several months later, when the doddering imbecile discovered the key to this tunnel was missing, that he put the rumor that the arsonists were not traitorous Moors but Spanish together with his discoveries and came to me at once to report it. He had no knowledge at all of the unlucky ibn Rasoul, but he indicated that only you had known of the old tunnel in his garden. You will admit I now had reason to observe you very closely?" Sarcasm twisted the pocked face into a sneer for a brief moment.

Francho shrugged, admitting nothing. "What is unnatural about a musician frequenting the abode of an instrument maker? Had you another lutanist on your list of possible traitors Zemel would have known him too."

Reduan answered with a thin-lipped smile. "You struggle but the hook is through your gills. Allah be praised, just lately I have had another visitor, minstrel. It seems with lack of food in the city the snow gatherers had no incentive or permission to venture forth and risk capture. You lost your line of communication several weeks past, did you not?"

A muscle jumped in Francho's otherwise stolid face, and Reduan gazed at him with hard-eyed triumph. "When you deal with the avaricious, ibn Ghulam, it is not wise to let them lack the smell of money. For an exorbitant price and promise of pardon—which he will not live long enough to enjoy—a blind beggar spit out an ingenious plan whereby secret messages had been passed from the city to the Christian commanders. He knew the agent only as 'he who speaks with a golden voice' but sensed he was a tall man and that a lad who carried most of the messages had slipped up once and said the name 'Jamal.' You see how it all comes together?"

Reduan leaned back and sucked the shreds of his dinner from his teeth. Francho understood there was no evading the icy certainty in those eyes. He squared his shoulders. He had acquitted himself very capably in his mission. Now he would do just as nobly with the certain death that was the consequence of his unmasking. But first he must bargain for Dolores's safety.

Keeping his eyes steadily on the shrewd commander's face he asked, "You mentioned a proposition? What did you have in mind?"

"First confirm a little observation of mine. I have watched you salaam. You touch your fingers to your forehead and chest in the usual manner, but on occasion your hand automatically continues to the right before you catch it—in the habit of the Christian gesture of faith. It is a little thing, unnoticed by most eyes unless one were looking for such slips. You are not a Moslem. Perhaps not even a Copt of Arab blood. Who are you?" The demand was quiet but it seemed to ring in Francho's head like an iron gauntlet, and for a second he imagined the man's reaction if he announced that he too was a Venegas. Habit and caution stayed this confession, but a pulse pounded hard in his temples.

He smiled as he set down the goblet. "Very well, *sayed,* it is obvious my only choice is to cooperate. I am a Castilian. Don Francisco de Mendoza, knight of the realm."

Reduan's flat features showed some slight surprise. "Ah! But you make a most convincing Moor, Mendoza. Except for the slip of the hand I was ready to believe you are not only a spy but a filthy betrayer of your own people. I congratulate you on your successes. And I despise you for the harm you have brought upon this beautiful city. All of which is now in the past. You will now become a liaison between the Spanish monarchs and myself." Ignoring Francho's quirked eyebrow, he continued. "We have lost most of our provisions; we cannot beat your forces back from our gates. Let Muza Aben delude himself about help from Africa, I know this will never

598

come about. I have done my best for Granada but I am not a fool. Cynical, an opportunist if you will, but unwilling to die or suffer exile for a lost cause."

He pushed away from the table and rose, the caustic glint in his eyes the only life in his inflexible face, a glint as cold as the white sapphire in his cockaded turban. "Tonight I shall free you, infidel, to take an urgent warning to the Spanish camp, a deed which will surely earn you the highest gratitude of your rulers. In return you must give me your solemn word as a knight that you will inform them of my help to you and that I now place my hand at their disposal and my sword in vassalage. There is Castilian as well as Moorish blood in my veins, I bear a proud Spanish name. I have served one heritage well, only to have it come to the present chaos. Now, tell them, Reduan Venegas will serve the other. What small recompense I shall ask for my loyalty will be spoken of later. Bring me back their assurances and you may continue to operate unimpeded."

Taken aback with this shameless defection Francho stared for an unbelieving moment. Then he nodded. "Your message will be clearly delivered, *sayed,* and you will receive all credit for your aid, my word on it. But further, I would like to deliver the Baroness de la Rocha from Granada by taking her with me."

"Ah yes, the beautiful Christian lady you snatched from my harem's hospitality, ibn Ghu—ah, Mendoza. I did not take that too kindly, for indeed I knew to whose bed she was finally delivered, but I had more important matters at hand. The woman stays here. She acts as my hostage for your good offices. She will have the protection of my house and she will be treated with every respect and kindness. My word on it. Do not quibble, you have no time."

Urgency was apparent even in Reduan's colorless voice and so Francho closed his mouth on his protest. "What is the warning you wish me to ride with?" he asked.

"Your Queen habitually goes late to her private chapel for prayers before she sleeps. Tonight, when the moon sets, an assassin will murder her in cold blood," Reduan stated bluntly.

Francho had to wait only a few minutes in a small chamber off Reduan's salon, but the delay caused him to chew the edge of his thumbnail. Soon he heard a tiny tinkle of bells and bracelets and Dolores slipped through the beaded curtain, pale and anxious.

"Oh, Francho," she cried softly and ran to him, veils billowing. He clasped her tight, stroking her back to quiet her trembling, and then held her away from him.

The tilted gray eyes searched his fearfully. "What is happening? Have they found you out? Are we to die?"

"Listen to me carefully, *querida,* I have precious little time. You are fine, you are safe. The General Reduan has switched sides. He sees the eventual end to this conflict and offers Their Majesties fealty. He has given me some vital information and I must leave Granada tonight. You will stay here."

"Here?" Dolores gasped. "With him?"

"He would not dare to touch you now. His plans are big, and he is aware you are one of the Queen's ladies. You are safer being here in secret than returning to the royal harem, where, if I am discovered, the guards will come looking for you. Reduan will keep you in his women's quarters in comfort until we take the city."

He could see her throat move as she swallowed. "Will you come back?" she asked in a small voice.

"Yes. If the Lord will allow."

Visibly she tried to stop her lips from trembling. "But will I see you when you come back? Francho—I have a terrible feeling that we will not meet in Granada again. That . . . that we are saying goodbye."

She would be safer with Reduan from now on, even when he returned, and knowing this struck at his heart too, but he thought it better not to tell her. "Of course we shall see each other, *hermanita,* I shall return here in time to avoid any suspicion that I was ever missing from the palace. Don't be afraid."

"I am not afraid. I am—deeply sad."

He pulled her to him and pressed her head into his shoulder, and the faint scent of jasmine filled his nostrils. He closed his eyes in pain for a brief moment, not knowing what to tell her or to tell himself.

From without Reduan's toneless voice warned, "You must leave, Mendoza."

She raised her head to him and he kissed her, hard, tasting salt mingled with the sweetness of her mouth. The memory of the happiness she had brought him whirled up in him, the reluctance to know it was ending plucked at his heart, and in alarm for the acute sense of loss that threatened his composure he put her firmly away from him.

"Adios, querida mía. Sleep peacefully tonight."

"God go with you, Don Francisco. Always," she whispered. He turned on his heel to erase the image of her proudly held, stricken, tear-stained face.

❧ *Chapter 28* ❧

THE EVENTS OF that night seemed to Francho in retrospect to
have rushed by like the wind, so much was crammed into the
few hours between midnight and dawn. Reduan and a small
escort rode with him to the same seldom-used gate in the wall
that Boabdil's secret peace ambassadors had used. Accustomed to recent spurious comings and goings, the guards
obeyed their commander's request and quickly swung open
the portal to let the muffled rider through, having been given
the passphrase, *"Le Galib ille Allah"* to readmit him. Francho
trotted out, trying to keep the noise of his passage at a
minimum, and headed his mount down the hill, picking his
way slowly through the loose stones that littered the old path
down the slope. Finally gaining the level fields, he dug in his
spurs and sent the animal into a headlong gallop toward the
winking torches on the timber walls of Santa Fe two leagues
distant.

He believed he would make the camp with time to spare
before the moon set, if only the angels were watching over
Isabella and saw that she did not retire early. With the dry
comment that his sources of information were often efficient,
Reduan had told him that in lieu of stained glass the window
of the simple chapel was covered by a heavy parchment. A

candelabra within threw the shadow of the Queen kneeling at her prie-dieu upon the parchment, and anyone lurking outside could see her silhouette clearly. This night, Reduan's uninflected voice had droned on, a crossbow bolt was going to pierce both parchment and Queen before anyone could prevent it, accomplished by an assassin hired by Moslem fanatics.

Francho bent low and spurred his horse on unmercifully, the muffled hoofbeats on the turf accompanied by the racing of his thoughts. He was riding not only to save the precious life of the Queen of Castile but also the lives of the Alis and Azahras and the other ordinary Moslems he had met and whom he had grown to understand and like. The death of Isabella would be a fatal blow for them, for their eventual conquerers in their grief would rend every Moor in the city limb from limb. His mantle whipping about him, he lay along the horse's neck and urged her on. The Barbary stretched her legs and flew across the wastes of blackened fields and stubbled orchards, only by some miracle avoiding holes and trip-ups.

Presently, with the winded horse blowing and flecked with foam, Francho reined in before the stout gate of Santa Fe and shouted up at the guards who had heard him coming from their battlements. In what seemed like a year the ponderous gate finally opened and he rode through. A grim escort of soldiers awaited him, and although their leader eyed his Moorish cape suspiciously and refused to take him directly to the Queen, he was willing to escort the midnight rider with the urgent command in his voice to the Count of Tendilla. As soon as the Count had responded to the knock on his chamber door Francho pushed aside the guard who opened it and hurried in, followed by several guards. "My lord Tendilla," he blurted out, briefly saluting hand to chest, "I come to warn about a plot to take the Queen's life. Tonight. In her chapel. She must be immediately detained from going to her devotions. Immediately, my lord."

Tendilla asked no questions. Without blinking an eye in the face of Francho's surprise appearance and ugly announcement he coolly clipped out several orders to his adjutant and made short work of drawing on his boots. "Come with me," he instructed Francho and the guards behind him. "No time to get a horse saddled." And they set out in a fast run toward the nearby royal edifice, which loomed taller and bulkier than the buildings surrounding it. With Tendilla leading the way they burst into the audience hall, and the Catholic monarchs and several courtiers gathered with them over a stack of documents looked up in surprise. Tendilla hung back now that he could see the Queen was safe, but motioned Francho forward. Francho, who had almost skidded to a halt, made a low bow and after being given permission panted out his story again.

Except for Isabella's initial startlement to being confronted by a winded, turbaned, and scowling Moor, she kept her composure admirably, Francho thought. But Ferdinand rose up so precipitously from the table where they all sat his chair overturned backward. "What!" he barked, amid scattered cries of shock from the group. He leaned forward angrily, his knuckles on the table. "Have these ears heard you correctly, courier?"

"If the Queen will preserve her life, she will not enter her chapel this night." Francho rapped out again. "There is a plot to assassinate her at her devotions."

"In fact, I was just preparing to bid my tireless consort and advisors good night and repair to my prayers along with His Grace Talavera," Isabella affirmed. "God help us—"

"Do they dare? How do they dare!" Ferdinand railed. "Murder my wife? That villainous Sultan of vipers would murder the Queen of Castile and Aragon?"

"Not Boabdil, Majesties," Tendilla quickly put in. "Not the Sultan. An organization of fanatics."

"I will catch their assassin and hang him up with a hook through his Moslem testicles! What o'clock is it?" At the answer of "near to midnight" from one of the dismayed group, Ferdinand nodded. "Good. We have some time. Yet another hour, I believe, before the moon goes down. Cadiz! See a squadron of soldiers are immediately hidden in the area about the chapel, not too close, we don't want to scare the vermin off. And be discreet, my lord, no noise, no obvious movements."

"It will be done, Sire." The leonine Cadiz bowed briefly and hurried away.

But Isabella had been openly studying the tall courier whose midnight arrival had prevented her demise. Francho looked straight back at her and stretched his lips in a smile. "Is that you, Don Francisco?" she asked him, wonder in her voice.

He broadened his smile and bowed. *"Sí,* my Queen. It is."

Isabella gave him an intrigued look. Her gaze took in his cockaded white turban, the single gold earring gleaming against his pale olive skin, the forked black beard. "You have a barbaric look about you, indeed, sir. Not altogether unbecoming . . ." she remarked softly, a certain female admiration plain in her glance.

Ferdinand raised his eyebrow at her. Then he pointed to where Francho's mantle had fallen back. "And what is that you wear on your breast, Don Francisco."

"A medallion of office, Sire. I am Head Musician to the Sultan."

"Ah. Is that so? That explains much. Astonishing. You must not forget to demonstrate your musical expertise to us, *señor,* when the time allows." The King now transferred his heavy-lidded gaze to his wife. "My dear, you will retire to the safety of your quarters. I will have the guard tripled. Doña Beatrix, will you see that the Queen's windows are shuttered and barred?"

Isabella demurred. "My lord does not take into consideration that if my shadow does not appear in its usual place the murderer may not show himself."

"Your shadow will appear," Ferdinand said flatly. "We will get a substitute for you."

"No we will not. I cannot allow one of my ladies to take the risk that the killer might get past your ambush."

"A disguised man might do," Tendilla spoke up.

Ferdinand agreed. Francho was about to offer himself as bait, but Ferdinand saw his volunteering gesture and forestalled him. "Not you, Don Francisco, you are too big. Someone small and light."

The Count of Cifuentes offered, "One of your pages perhaps, Sire, in a woman's robe?"

"Indeed. Cifuentes, choose one of the pages cooling their heels without, and then find the lady who is mistress of the Queen's wardrobe. Make haste, my lord."

"I do not think it is wise to return to my apartments and alarm my ladies," Isabella declared. "I shall wait in the chamber beyond the chapel with Doña Beatrix and my confessor, and there the guards can attend me. I will be very safe, my husband."

One look at her set jaw, and Ferdinand took no time to

argue. "If you wish it, Lady Queen. Gentlemen, the windows of the dining hall overlook the rear of the chapel. From there, in darkened silence, we can see an end to this calumny." He pushed aside his fallen chair and stalked out, followed by the male members of the group.

From the unglazed window embrasure where he took up watch along with Tendilla, Francho saw little but the shadowy potted trees and plants which softened into the likeness of a garden and the empty little plot before the chapel. But he knew there were armed men deployed in the shadows of the adjacent buildings, each with his eyes alert for any unusual movement or flitting shadow which would indicate a trespasser. A quarter hour passed, and suddenly light flared in the long, yellow square of the chapel window and the shadow of a woman fell on it who in a moment knelt down in prayer, bowing her veiled head devoutly. An owl hooted mournfully in the distance; the regular guards were heard patrolling their usual route about the perimeter of the royal enclosure. A few minutes more and the wan light of the moon faded.

Suddenly, as if sprung from the ground, a dark bulk detached itself from other night shadows and crouching, silently slipped between the big clay planters. Finally, from Francho's line of sight, the killer obliterated the woman's form on the parchment with his own sinister silhouette, heavier at one shoulder from a crossbow which pointed its deadly snout at the victim.

There was an urgent shout "Get him!" and a concerted rush of men from the dark crannies where they had hidden, but in spite of the pikes suddenly whizzing past him the assassin stood fast and with a sharp snick sent his bolt crashing through the parchment. The next second the Marquis of Cadiz who was in the lead of the soldiers cut him down. "Allah be praised, Allah most powerful!" the man shrieked out and then was silent under a rain of pikes and swords which cut him to ribbons.

Gleams of light sprung up from surrounding buildings as the noise of the ambush roused part of the camp. Racing through the inside chambers just behind the King and those with him, Francho arrived at the chapel entrance in time to see the Count of Cifuentes help the shaken young substitute for Isabella to his feet, unharmed because, listening with desperate keenness, the volunteer had thrown himself sideways to the floor at the first wild shout and thereby saved his own life. "Thank the Good Lord," the King muttered at the sight of the gowned boy. "It is de Soto's son and a fine youth. Gramercy, young man. Let the gratitude of your monarch bring the color back to your face." He braced the pale lad by the shoulders. "Your courage is much to be commended."

Isabella swept in with her confidante, Beatrix de Boabdilla, and an agitated Talavera. She went immediately to examine the splintered shaft of the prie-dieu, where a long iron bolt was embedded six inches deep. "Merciful God!" Isabella muttered, "I would have been mortally impaled!" Talavera creaked down on his knees before the large silver cross on the wall, and his Queen joined him, hands fervently clasped. She prayed, "Dear God, we beg that we may please Thee in all Your works, for Thy mercy has shielded us from evil." Her clear voice rose to the wooden rafters, and those in the chapel bowed their heads. "With humility we pledge to continue to do Thy will, for we will not rest until each and every heathen and Anti-Christ is chased from this land. This, O Lord, do we pledge to Thee in gratitude for Your merciful protection."

Those who listened muttered "Amen" and crossed themselves. Ferdinand helped his wife to rise, and for a brief moment they embraced. The Queen looked about, and Francho realized she was looking for him as her gaze met his. "There was not time to thank you for foiling this frightening plot, no doubt at your own jeopardy, Don Francisco."

"My reward is your smile, Your Majesty, and your royal person safe from harm."

But the Queen's appraising eyes did not leave him. "You have changed much since we last saw you, sir knight."

Francho smiled. "'Tis the Moorish beard and robes, Majesty."

She shook her head. "No, 'tis more than your costume. There is that in your eyes, a certain tempering of experience and a quieter confidence in your bearing that was not present before. As a result of your perilous service in—"

She was interrupted by the vigorous entrance of the Marquis de Cadiz and his lieutenant.

"What of the assassin, my lord?" Ferdinand asked. "Who was he?"

"One of our most loyal Morisco guides, or so we thought, sire, gone to roast in Hell with the rest of the Devil's evil spawn. Do you see now, my Liege, how they lie, how little these Moslems can be trusted? They must be dealt with like the soulless heathens they are."

"Yes. The Sultan will soon know our wrath for this terrible treachery—to treat with us for peace and yet plot to murder our Queen? He is guilty, no matter what you say, Tendilla."

"It was not the Sultan Boabdil, Sire," Francho stepped forward to interpose boldly. "I am certain he had no knowledge of this plot, for he is a man of honor. Most likely it was the General Muza Aben Gazul who arranged the contact by which your Morisco was subverted. Muza Aben not only controls the army but he is stubborn and defiant of the throne. He foments a fanatical resistance among the people and leads them to despise Boabdil's efforts to concede. From my observations we do not battle a city now, my Liege, but the force and personality of one man."

Ferdinand's eyes narrowed and he thought for a moment. "Then by the same stealthy means he sought to employ against Queen Isabella let us rid ourselves of this human blockage. On your return to Granada, Don Francisco, emulate that vermin of a Morisco. You will see that Muza Aben is disposed of before the time limit of our surrender terms runs out."

"You set Tendilla's son a most unreasonable task, my Liege," Cadiz objected, staring at Francho from under his heavy brows and unable to hide his sourness for the respect his rulers showed for this young knight. "After all, a wary commander is more difficult to murder than a defenseless woman. It is my opinion that a heavy attack on the walls would be a surer and quicker method of shaking the Moors loose from their adoration of Muza Aben."

Francho snorted to himself. The old Marquis could see the luster Francho's success in this would add to Tendilla's petition for the governorship of Granada, and he was upset at being thus undercut. Francho opened his mouth to speak, but Ferdinand was quicker.

"For such an attack to be successful in the face of their defenses, we would have to give up half of our forces to destruction, my lord. If the assassination of their defiance-inspiring general saves us that, we will thank God."

"But young Mendoza may need to wait months for his chance at the man, who is after all guarded and not stupid.

Our walls have ears too, and he may be aware how depleted
our coffers, and that the specter of hunger may stalk our camp
as well. Many of our nobles have so wearied in these long
months that they have left part of their contingents and gone
home to tend to their affairs. War is war, my liege, and as I
have stated, if we do not strike now while we still have our
might we may not have the power to do so later. I submit that
we are staking our opportune moment upon a murder most
difficult, even improbable, to perform."

Always willing to consider well-taken points, Ferdinand
contemplated Cadiz's advice. Then he swung his hooded gaze
to Francho and put the problem to him. "Ill-conceived heroics
which do not succeed may harm us, sir."

"You may leave the task in my hands, Your Majesty, with
certitude that it will be done, and swiftly. Perhaps I may calm
my Lord Cadiz's doubts with the fact that we have a powerful
ally in Granada—the commander Reduan Venegas."

He could hear their breaths suck in. Even Tendilla, who had
been standing silent by the King's side, narrowed his black
eyes in surprise.

"What? Reduan, the perpetrator of so many bloody ambush
attacks upon our garrisons and towns? Turned traitor?"
Isabella was incredulous.

"It was Reduan who warned me your life was in danger, my
Queen, and helped me to speed the warning to you. He leaves
the sinking vessel and begs me to inform Your Majesties that
he is ready to act in your behalf in any measure to help depose
Muza Aben and end the war. He pledges vassalage and his
loyalty on the soul of his Christian-born grandsire."

"And what does he want in exchange for his allegiance?
And for rescuing me from a premature tomb?"

"He sends this letter."

Isabella broke the seal of the heavy parchment he handed
her and scanned the lines written there. She handed the
missive to her husband, who read it quickly.

"He wants the former Venegas lands and estates, as the only
remaining blood member of the line." Ferdinand threw Isabella a querying look, adding, "It may not be a price too high
to pay if he can help us to quickly end this interminable war."

Francho's stunned glance at Tendilla caught the lean face
darkening. Near him Talavera's hand groped for the silver
crucifix on his breast.

"Reduan indicates there would be numerous ways in which he could affect just such a service, Majesties." Francho went on in a strangled tone, keeping to the letter of the bargain in which he had unwittingly traded the Queen's life for his own future. But Tendilla seemed to have come to a quick decision, and now he moved firmly to stand at Francho's side.

"Most gracious of Majesties," he began, and for once there was a nervous tension in his voice. "As your most loyal and devoted servitor of many years I beg the boon of a private audience with you. Right now, if my lords and lady will allow?"

"Now, Tendilla?" Ferdinand rumbled. "It is late—"

"A matter most urgently involved with this current subject and most sensitive. I humbly plead your indulgence, Majesties."

Isabella searched the face of her valued advisor for it was rare for him to show any agitation. "Very well, my lord, but we will retire to the audience hall; secular business has no place in an edifice dedicated to the Holy Spirit. My lord Cadiz, our grateful thanks for the swift apprehension of the Morisco traitor, and bid you a well-deserved rest tonight. Doña Beatrix, inform those who have been awakened by the clamor"— she indicated the half-dressed, craning courtiers kept outside the open chapel door by the guards—"that we are safe and unharmed. And good Bishop, attend us. We keep nothing from your ears." She picked up the short brocade train of her furred surcoat and both monarchs exited, Isabella resting her slim hand on Ferdinand's arm.

In but a few minutes Francho stood at the foot of a dais in the tapestry-adorned audience hall along with Tendilla, both of them facing an impatient Ferdinand, whose face sagged with fatigue, and a tired but curious Isabella. Talavera settled in his chair to one side of the dais. Tendilla spoke, in his suave and elegant voice. "Gracious Majesties, we throw ourselves upon your merciful justice. I beg you, do not in the following minutes turn your face against me your eternal loyal servant, nor grow wrathful with Don Francisco, who has but followed my advice."

Isabella cocked an eyebrow. "Grow wrathful with the daring knight who burned Granada's food stores and this very night snatched me from Death's scythe? 'Twould be strange reward, Count."

Ferdinand added, "We had in fact marked Don Francisco for special honors after our final victory. Tonight's warning, regardless of the cooperation of that renegade Reduan, has served to deepen our gratitude." He glanced puzzledly at Francho and back to Tendilla again. "We are at a loss for your meaning."

Tendilla took a deep breath and began, quietly but clearly. "My meaning is that Don Francisco and I are guilty of perpetrating a falsehood. Not to dupe Your Majesties, I swear it, but to serve your greater glory. This man"—and he turned to face Francho, a solemn pride and a shadow of pain deep in the black eyes—"is not my son at all. His name is not Mendoza but Venegas. Don Francisco de Venegas, issue of Elena de Lura and Juan de Venegas—whose name my Queen will remember." The last was said in a respectful but deliberate tone.

Blue eyes widening in disbelief, Isabella jerked further upright in her chair and clutched at the gilt arms. "My lord Tendilla! You confound us! What you declare is most improbable. The infant son of that murderer Venegas was never found and was reported dead."

"He had been hidden in a monastery leagues from Toledo. Eight years ago pure accident gave the youth Venegas into my hands, and I spared no effort to secure every proof of his identity. My Queen, forgive me, but fearing the rancor you might have still borne his name I acted to give the innocent boy a chance to deserve your mercy, and so I brought him to Court as my natural son. Here he stands before you, the knight honored as Don Francisco de Mendoza, who has done a remarkable service to prove his undying loyalty and devotion to your throne. And we humbly beg your forbearance and your understanding of our deception."

Francho felt both pairs of royal eyes boring through him askance, as if he had turned into something not quite human. It was not as he had pictured this final dénouement as happening, he in his alien Moorish attire covered with the dust of his ride and everyone in the room wearied from the hour and the events. The necessity to reveal his birth here and now was an unexpected jolt, and yet what better time than when both rulers were still indebted and relieved that there were yet two of them and not just a single grief-stricken one. The sweat broke out on his back and under his armpits and trickled down his sleeve. Falling to his knees before the powerful monarchs of Castile and Leon, he prayed that his eloquence would not desert him and that he would remember some of the thoughts he had composed against this moment.

"Gracious Majesties, I was a swaddling babe when my sire was judged to have committed the atrocity against the Infanta. I have little knowledge of either of my parents, but I have their blood and I am a gentleman born. For the rest, I am what my soul and spirit and Don Iñigo have made of me, and by your own hand a knight, Sire. But there is deep despair in my heart that my name, the once highly honored name of Venegas, should die of a blight which attacked only one shoot of the tree. To be born a bastard with a lefthand name can cause confusion enough for most men. But to be born with an ancient name one cannot admit is an agony of the blood and a torment of the mind. Perhaps the way Don Iñigo and I chose to prove to you that the blight of disloyalty had not been passed on to me was wrong, but we could think of no other. Whether or not you see fit to restore my name I pray God I may always serve you. But I ask for your mercy and justice, and as a knight of the realm I petition for permission to bear my ancestor's name in pride, my father's titles in honor, and to inherit his lands and estates in right. And failing this, I humbly beg a greater boon upon the small service I have rendered in Granada: that your beneficent pardon go out to Don Iñigo de Mendoza, whose only sin was the charity of sustaining an orphan child in the hopes of adding one more worthy and steadfast knight to your train. If there is blame to be placed for deceiving you, I beg you, let me and the unfortunate legacy that curses me bear the burden."

Francho's Adam's apple bobbed up and down convulsively, and he bowed his head. It was done. His life either went on or it was finished, and in spite of his apprehension he was relieved.

There was a trenchant silence. Ferdinand rubbed his jaw and scowled. "A fine kettle of fish," he muttered almost to himself. "Two Venegas popping up on the same night, and both claiming lands that for years have been adding their revenues to our royal coffers." In the face of Isabella's continued, stoney silence he continued, more loudly, "We are displeased that our consort shall have to bear such shock to her memory after the earlier strain of the evening. However, since this—collusion—has been revealed, it must be addressed. Rise up, Don Francisco, and if there is more to your story say it solely to your Queen, for we have little knowledge of the case. We will concur in whatever the Queen's decision."

Isabella—now that her husband had washed hands of the business—seemed to come to life. With cold eyes and lips white with anger she said rigidly, "What more can they have to report than they have made a mockery of our vengeance. We swore to crush Don Juan's branch of the Venegas family and slept easier because we thought we had. And now the subject we most trust and admire has harbored a scion of that murderer under our very nose."

"Dear Gracious Lady," Tendilla pleaded, his voice projecting sincerity, "I beg you to understand that I harbored only an innocent boy. If, almost a quarter century in the past, you took an oath under the fresh grief of your brother's death, none could blame you. But surely after twenty years and more your great sense of justice must have risen above your woe and you will not demand that Don Francisco suffer from actions not his own. As a foundling you might have rejected him, but as Don Francisco de Mendoza he has earned your praises and promise of grace. What is in a name, Lady Queen, but pride and continuance and the means to identify one's blood. Loyalty resides not in a name but in a man's earnest heart."

"Do not presume to lecture me, Don Iñigo. And what is in an oath but the purpose of fulfilling it?"

"My daughter!" With mouth turned down in his round, ruddy face, the Queen's confessor Talavera broke in. "Do you visit the sins of the father upon the son? It ill becomes a pious woman who loves God to chastise a blameless soul, even though the babe is now grown to a man's estate. 'Vengeance is mine' saith the Lord. Do not place your state of grace in jeopardy with unmerited reprisal. 'Go ye and sinneth no more' were the words of our blessed and merciful Jesu, and this man has not sinned against you at all. Therefore, can you say less?"

Isabella's high, white brow seemed stretched to transparency as she strained to reconcile the anger of a Queen with the duty of a Christian. Tendilla, standing solidly beside Francho, projected a solemn and calm confidence in Isabella's scrupulous justice. Standing just as erectly, Francho could only pray that she would credit the sincerity of motive behind their deception.

At last with an explosive outlet of breath, Isabella's white-knuckled grip on the arms of her chair relaxed and the ire cleared from her eyes, leaving them nevertheless wary. "It passes through our mind that if the virulence of a young Princess against her brother's assassin was honorable, the forgiveness of a Queen for his issue is noble. We shall have the courage to admit to you that for all these many years we have borne a certain guilt for the life of an infant we thought we had destroyed. But before us now is an issue we cannot decide tonight. We will need time to weigh the shameful falsehood involved against your intent and your deeds, sirs, so that whatever our decision it will be in full and clear conscience."

She engaged Francho's eyes. "Francisco de Venegas," she intoned, and Francho's eyes flickered at her use of his rightful name. "You ask of us the right to your sire's title and estates, which have been confiscated to the Crown since our Lord's year fourteen hundred and seventy-eight?"

"That is my plea, Your Majesty."

"And if we refuse to grant your petition?"

"Venegas is my father's name. I shall cleave to it and pray that in any case I may be allowed to serve my monarchs as a proud and loyal knight. If not, I stand ready to accept whatever punishment the name deserves. But I cannot any longer sustain an identity not my own."

"You have tonight rescued us from an assassin's bolt—do not think we forget that. But we must examine our thoughts, and we ask that you remain totally silent about this matter until our decision is made." An intruding thought caused her to grimace in annoyance. "There is also the petition of Reduan Venegas to consider. He is valuable as an ally and cannot be ignored. On your return to Granada you will inform him his request is being taken under advisement at this moment, but that he has our solemn word that he will not suffer in serving us."

She leaned back in her carved chair and closed her eyes momentarily with a heavy sigh. "My lord Tendilla, you, sir, will attend us in our chambers on the morrow promptly after morning mass. Now we give you both leave to go."

Francho saw a subtle nod of encouragement from the somber-faced Talavera. Don Iñigo bowed deeply and backed away, but Francho dared to say one more thing. "Your Majesty, if you please? Don Iñigo informs me that Doña Leonora de Zuniga is now among your waiting ladies. May I have your permission to speak with her briefly before I return to Granada?"

The Queen's plucked eyebrows raised. "Leonora de Zuniga?"

"We planned to be betrothed when my duties in Granada were finished, my Queen. We are much in love and it is almost two years since we parted."

Isabella's eyes flicked to Tendilla a few paces behind him and then centered on Francho again. "She promised to wait until your mission was over and then marry you?" Isabella asked. "And in two years you have had no word from her?"

"Unnecessary messages could not be transmitted," Tendilla explained, stiff-necked.

Isabella frowned and addressed a dry rebuke to Tendilla. "There are some 'unnecessary' messages, my lord, that most obviously should have been sent." Knowing that Isabella was much enamored of her own husband, Francho was grateful for her understanding. "She may be already abed, Don Francisco, but we shall have her sent here. Without informing her of your presence."

"I am most appreciative, gracious Queen," Francho murmured and bowed very low. Isabella rose, took Ferdinand's arm, and the two rulers descended from the dais. As they swept past him Ferdinand stopped for a moment and considered Francho from under heavy brows. "You have been charged with one more vital task to perform in Granada, Don Francisco, and we ask you to dispatch it with all speed. We shall pray for your success."

Los Reyes Católicos continued on to find their rest, followed by Talavera, who made the sign of the cross in the air before both of his friends as he passed them.

Curiously reticent to meet Francho's gaze, the Count nevertheless took him by the shoulder and grasped one hand. "Well done, Francisco. We must rely now upon the good Bishop to further our cause with his special flock, and I cannot believe that this scrupulously fair Queen will deny us. I will await you, along with your mount, at the gate through which you entered. Be warned. There's little time before dawn." Tendilla whirled on his heel and strode from the hall, back still straight as an iron rod even though the anxiety of the interview must have been sapping for him too.

Francho threw off his dusty cloak and paced up and down before the empty thrones on the dais. Although the fateful dice were cast, he still had nothing but hope to offer Leonora. Yet, fortune or not, he would not give her up. Consent or not, they would marry, they would elope, they could flee to Italy and he could hire his arms to the house of her sister's husband—so went his wild thoughts as what seemed an interminable wait stretched on. His heart pounded. Her name throbbed in his head, over and over, Leonora, Leonora. Nervously he smoothed his long tunic of painted and embroidered silk and raked through his beard with his fingers, wishing he had a bath, a comb, and some pomander. He polished on his sleeve the huge amethyst ring the Sultan had given him and made sure his silver medallion with a guembri and the Sultan's symbol engraved upon it hung straight.

At last a small door opened and Leonora stood on the threshold. Francho sucked in his breath. She wasn't part of a lotus-scented daydream but a reality, just as he remembered her—fair, sweet-eyed, and delicate, a chiffon veil and circlet covering her loose amber locks and a pea-green velvet robe hastily tied about her small body. Since she probably expected to find only the Queen in this room, her dimples flashed and the charm of that well-remembered smile caused Francho's breath to catch. He stepped forward eagerly, but on seeing him she uttered a startled yelp, her smile fled and she backed away.

Of course. What was she seeing? Francho laughed to himself. A turbaned, black-bearded, hulking heathen in an exotic coat and white pantaloons, with a barbarous hoop hung from one ear and what could be taken as a sinister smile if one did not know it was merely anticipatory.

"Has the time been so long that you do not recognize me, my sweetest heart?" he called out, hastily stepping forward and putting out a hand to keep her from fleeing.

Poised to withdraw she took a moment to stare into his glowing eyes. Her jaw dropped and he saw the shock of recognition leap into her own eyes. Leonora's hand flew to her throat. *"Madre de Dios!"* she gasped. "Francisco. Is it you?" She stood rooted to the spot.

He strode to her and took both of her hands in his.

"Leonora!" he breathed, anxious for her to get over her shock and welcome him home with her heart.

"But you look like a Moor," she whispered numbly, "a Moor. Have you been in Granada, then? Not Egypt and Sicily?"

"Yes, in Granada, in the service of Their Majesties. Ah sweet heart, I thought this moment would never come. Do you love me still, my Leonora, do you? Tell me, so I shall know whether to live or die, tell me that all this weary separation hasn't changed your heart." He squeezed her hands unmercifully. Her lips parted as she stared at him. To be finally and in reality looking into the startled, amber-brown depths of her eyes, at the tender planes and creamy skin, cheeks touched with palest pink, of that dearly remembered face was causing him to stand a handspan off the floor with happiness.

But as her shock waned her reaction was not what he expected. Suddenly she stiffened and averted her face from him, pulling her hands from his grip with such determined force that he was taken by surprise and let her go.

"Leonora! What is the matter?"

"A good deal is the matter, Don Francisco de Mendoza. How dare you utter the word love in my presence."

It was as if she had rammed a knife into his belly. Hostility hardened every sweet line of the face she now turned back to him and her eyes were filled with accusation.

"Wh—what are you saying? What has happened that you recoil from me thus? Leonora, my dearest, I love you. I have not changed. . . ."

The beloved voice that had wrapped his dreams with its sweet, bell-like tones came chilly and disdainful from her pursed lips. "Ah, but I have. I am no longer so naive as to listen to you, so you may save your lies. Nor have you even the right to speak to me thus, for I am a betrothed woman, soon to be married. To Don Felipe de Guzman." The knife in his belly twisted.

But he didn't grunt or yell, he just stared at her in disbelief. "You are playing with me. This could not be true."

"Oh but it is true." Her voice lifted, as well as her chin. "In January I shall become the espoused of the Count of Perens, and I am very honored and happy."

If at first he thought it was a bad joke, the defiant coldness that darkened her eyes and stiffened her back told him otherwise. In sudden fury and in fear he grabbed her by the shoulders. "You cannot do that. I won't let you. You don't love him, you love me. You said you would marry no other, remember, that you would wait for me. And when I left . . ."

"Ah yes, when you left!" she broke in and now her voice gathered some heat. "Such promises you made me, such vaulting promises. Everlasting devotion, fortunes to be found on the desert, the world a pillow for my feet—and at that very same time you were dallying with her, that de la Rocha woman, and making great sport of me. Next time choose a more secretive paramour, because just before di Lido was expected back from Egypt she came to me and revealed the sordid affair between you. And as much as I despised the hussy, for she broke my heart, there was naught to do but believe her."

Into the turmoil of Francho's mind came a wisp of Dolores's conversation, interrupted at the time by something or other. ". . . and Francho, there is something I did, a wicked deed before I came to Granada, that I am very ashamed of now . . ." In misery he appealed to Leonora, "But did you love me so little that you would believe the falsehood of a spiteful woman? Why couldn't you have trusted me, Leonora?"

"Felipe himself told me he saw you leaving her house in Seville early one morning. And she showed me the medallion from your bracelet that you gave to her as a keepsake. She told me—" In spite of her distress a faint blush climbed Leonora's pale forehead. "Do you have a birthmark shaped like a dagger on your shoulderblade?"

"No. I mean yes, but it is a scar."

"You see? Even your closest friend, Antonio de la Cueva, didn't know or remember that; I asked him in a roundabout manner. But *she* knew it."

"Very well, I should have told you about Dolores de la Rocha. I've known her many years—we were children together—that's how she knew of my scar. If I went to her house in Seville it was to greet her as an old acquaintance, not to meet a paramour. And I most emphatically did not give her my medallion; it was ripped from my bracelet during that business with Perens the night of Antonio's wedding, and she must have found it."

"You have clever excuses, but she was more to you than just

an acquaintance. I saw it in her eyes and women are not mistaken about these things. On a journey south she disappeared into Moorish hands, it seems, and although Medina-Sidonia tried several times to ransom her he had no success. Tell me, sir Moor—for once tell me the truth—was your old childhood friend in Granada with you?"

"Of course I will tell you the truth. Yes, she was in Granada with me, but only because—" With a violent movement of her hand she cut off his desperate explanation and glided toward the door.

"You have no more to say to me, *señor*. I bid you farewell and pray you not to disturb me further or I shall have to inform Don Felipe."

But he slipped before her small figure and stood blocking the door, not letting her pass. He reached out and swung her chin up so that he could rivet her eyes with his. "No, you will not go with your head filled with such swill. Leonora, listen to me, I swear you are the only woman I have ever loved or ever will love. If only you will believe me! Don't throw away both our lives in a jealous fit over a woman who means nothing, nothing to me. No—look at me. You still do love me, I know it. You must!"

But even in his frantic despair and secret guilt he was jolted by the hardness momentarily revealed in her eyes, amber-brown eyes now narrowed and spiteful as a cat's, calculating, a glimpse of a woman he had never seen before.

"Yes, Francisco, I do, and that is the tragic part of living, I suppose. I love you more than I care for Don Felipe. But there is more to life than love, even when families might allow us to think of it. There is the prominence of wealth and position to consider. A woman has a brief youth to flower, and much time to think in two years. To waste one year of youth is sentimental, to waste two is stupid. I could not expect Don Felipe to dance attendance forever while I waited for this mysterious plan of yours to succeed. I had already turned eighteen and there were younger women coming to Court who were taking his eye. So when you did not return in a year as you had promised I saw I must accept the excellent match that was offered and reject fragile fantasy."

"Leonora, now you know where I am and why. I shall return for good soon. The war is drawing to a close and—and from the spoils I hope to give you the wealth you deserve—"

"Ah, you hope, that is what I suspected. But Don Felipe does not hope, he can and will make me a Duchess someday and even now will present me with a small castle of my own for a wedding gift and a casket of the finest jewels. And even your prediction about Don Iñigo has come true. Carlotta is gone and my good cousin intends to marry his Lady Fatima. And their legitimate issue will surely get the bulk of his inheritance and his title." If she saw his bitter shock it did not soften her words. "I am sorry, Don Francisco. I once thought I could marry an impecunious knight because I loved him, but I was wrong. Love would soon disappear in the wake of hardship, even my gentle mother knows that. Only regret would be left."

Anger climbed hot into Francho's face. "But you never truly considered following your heart, did you? You've always kept Felipe de Guzman somewhere about just in case your first choice did not inherit the station you wanted. Even the year you managed to wait was not for me but for the treasure in the desert you thought I might bring back. How convenient your jealousy of the Baroness de la Rocha, an excuse to get out of marrying a mere knight, a moneyless bastard."

For a moment his intensity seemed to take her aback. She protested, "But I did love you, with the love of a silly young girl, perhaps. Nevertheless, if I could have both you and position and enough to maintain it and my children, I would be more content than I am. But since the choice must be made now, it must be Felipe. Surely you can understand." Her voice took on a softer, pleading tone.

He stepped away and left the door free. His voice too had come down in pitch. "Only too well, *doña,* you are very clear. But when the day comes when you would exchange all your castles and jewels for one kind word from Perens, you can remember that I loved you. I still do, for all your cruelty to both of us. I should hate you for leading me to believe you were mine when you really belonged, as a dutiful woman of your rank, to the highest bidder. It doesn't matter. I love you, and you love me. If you can go to your rich marriage bed knowing that, and in spite of it, go then. I won't stop you."

There was a terrible pain in his heart. He wanted to fall on his knees and plead with her, to see the delicious dimples flash into being once more and hear her tell him it was all a bad joke, to seize her and ride off so far from the world that all the mercenary resolve would melt from her and she would be his sweet Leonora once more. But his pride was crushed, his dreams shattered. He could only bow rigidly and step further aside.

She had the grace to lower her curved lashes over her eyes, where he used to imagine a blithe and innocent spirit peeped, but she held her small head high. "Fare you well then, Don Francisco. I wish you every happiness," she said with a quaver in her voice, and in a flutter of veil and swirl of velvet robe she was gone, shutting the door softly behind her. He took a few minutes to compose himself, and then, mouth in a grim, straight line, set off quickly for the gate.

Tendilla, waiting under a flare of torches, studied his fixed and bitter face and walked him away from the guards. "I am sorry you had to discover Leonora's ambition in so crushing a manner. I did not think it was my affair to inform you."

"If you had not reserved her letters from me I would not have lost her," Francho lashed out. "I would have sensed her impatience and come back to tell her the truth of my hopes, given her something real to hope for."

"There were no letters," the Count answered bluntly. "The one short note she sent to Alexandria finally came into di Lido's hands; he returned it to her with some excuse. After the embassy came back without you she did not even seek to inquire your specific whereabouts from me. Do not judge her too harshly. Doña Maria is anxious for her to marry, and your prospects are not certain."

"Well, it doesn't matter, any of it. I still want her and if I can give her what she desires in time to prevent her marriage to Perens then I will be happy. You may not understand this, Don Iñigo, you and I are of much different temperaments. But if I do not have Leonora de Zuniga I will have nothing." His misery, his sorely wounded pride, emerged from him in an agonized growl.

The Count's thin nose was pinched, his voice intense. "I am not so iron-hearted as you imagine, Francisco. I felt the same way about Doña Elena, your mother. I loved your mother very deeply and she loved me—but she was Elena de Venegas and the wife of my friend. So young she was laid in her grave and my dead heart went with her; and until the time that the flesh of her flesh reached out for my purse in Cuidad Real I had nothing." The Count stood stiffly in his pleated maroon velvet

doublet slashed with silver at the elbows, a fine sword and
jeweled dagger adorning his waist. His noble face was long,
stern above the small pointed beard he affected, his dark hair
was heavily silvered at the temples, but his was the erect back
and slim waist of a man ten years younger. For once the
piercing black eyes lacked veiling, and looking into them
Francho saw the aching void of Tendilla's lonely existence, the
disillusionment, the unfulfilled dreams of a man past his
prime whose armor against the failings of life was his withdrawn reserve.

"At the moment my influence with the Queen is at its lowest
ebb, but I will do all in my power to see your own name and
patrimony restored so you may achieve the happiness you
seek," Tendilla said quietly.

Moved but not surprised, somehow, by the revelation of the
intimate, hopeless bond between Don Iñigo and Elena, his
shadowy mother, Francho put out his hand. "My lord, forgive
me. You honor me greatly. I hope the day will come when I
can show you the full extent of my gratitude for the friendship
you have extended to me. To carry your vaunted name is a
privilege I could have hardly dreamed of. But as soon as the
Queen releases me from silence I shall claim Francisco de
Venegas as I was christened, whatever the consequences, a
dungeon or a pardon."

Mendoza shook his head. "I commend your courage."

"If I can put an end to Muza Aben and remain alive, I beg to
consider my work in Granada finished. I will return to Santa
Fe immediately and take up my place as a Castillian knight.
And await the Queen's decision."

Tendilla said nothing in the face of this declaration.

A guard held his mount's bridle as Francho swung himself
up. The stout timber portals swung open. Francho looked
down at Tendilla's saturnine face, where the line from the
narrow nose to the unsmiling mouth had grown deeper this
night. He saw respect in the piercing eyes and something
more—could it be a certain regret that Elena de Venegas's son
was not his own? By God, he liked the man, taciturn,
unemotional, and all. One could trust him, and in the melee
of surviving the world this was to be valued above gold. The
warmth Francho put into his wry, parting smile was real.
Tendilla saw it.

"Go with God," Tendilla called out, his tone as dry as

straw. "Good luck." Then he dealt the dappled Barbary a sharp smack on the rump and the horse got away like an arrow from the bow toward the torch-dotted bulk of Granada flowing up the dark hills. There was no hint yet of morning light, but the breeze had begun to die down as usually it did just before false dawn.

❧ *Chapter 29* ❧

"But the sack of rice you sent from the Alhambra is still half full, Jamal, and anyway there is little food to be bought. We don't need all this money," Azahra protested.

Francho handed her the heavy bag of dinars. "Then keep it for me," he insisted. "Hide it behind the loose bricks in the hearth and use it when you have to. And should anything happen to me it is yours. It is more than enough for a good dowry and to buy Ali an apprenticeship in a trade."

Azahra's nose was crooked to one side, and when she smiled she had formed the habit of putting her hand to her mouth to hide her missing front teeth. But her lovely, liquid dark eyes were worried, and she pressed her palms together nervously. "What do you fear will happen? Do you mean you will not come back here?"

"No, no, there is nothing wrong, girl," he soothed, affectionately smoothing the wisps of hair back from her anxious face. "It is just the times are so uncertain—one can never tell." He passed it off with a vague shrug. Turning to Ali, who was shooting up like a wiry-limbed sapling, he added, "You will, of course, mention to no one the messages I was able to send to my lady-love so far away, eh, grasshopper? It would bring trouble upon the couriers. Your lips are sealed?"

"Forever, Jamal, it is forgotten." The boy sensed the

tension Francho was trying to cover. "But you'll come back soon, won't you, Jamal? Please? You don't come here very often anymore."

Azahra bit her lip and hung her head at the last remark. Francho knew she had developed a young girl's infatuation for him, but she believed that since Zatar had marked her up her benefactor came less often because he could not gaze too long upon her ugly face. Now she blushed as the tall musician's long, strong arms went about both of them as they stood before him.

"Of a certain I will come back; does one abandon one's family? But perhaps it will be a small while. Ali, I charge you to continue your school studies most diligently, and Azahra, continue to learn from Ali to write a fine script."

"He is a very unjust teacher. He has no patience," Azahra complained.

Francho chucked her under the chin. "Neither do most teachers," he smiled. "And do not forget your dancing, at which Allah has given you such excellence. It will someday delight your husband and you will be beautiful in his eyes."

"Will you remember that you have promised to teach me to ride a horse?" Ali piped in irrepressible optimism.

"I shall remember everything," Francho swore and squeezed the eight year old's thin shoulder reassuringly. "And now I must leave. I have other matters to accomplish and the Sultan soon wakes from his midday nap."

He bid them a falsely cheerful goodbye and rode back toward the Alhambra, the setting sun behind him, with one more mission left to accomplish. It would not be the last time he saw that humble little abode, if God watched over him, but the many contented evenings he had spent there as Jamal ibn Ghulam would not be repeated. Azahra would find in the money sack the deed to the house which he had purchased from a cousin of his landlady, who reported her killed in the burning of her father's farmhouse. He had done what he could to ensure the future of the two children who had so unwittingly helped him, and later, if this night did not claim his life, he would continue to watch over them.

Not only the parting from his little friends weighed down his heart as he cantered up the tree-lined street against a tide of workers and palace petitioners returning to their homes. There was Dolores. And Boabdil. In a way Dolores and he had said their farewells two nights earlier, and what would a further meeting produce for both except strain while yet they were entangled in the shimmery mirage of Granada. When they faced each other again at the Spanish Court, she on her duke's arm in her furred gown and pearled headress, he as a knight once more, with cuirass and sword, the heavy intrusion of reality would fade the passions—even the tenderness—that had joined them together here. As for Boabdil, what could the viper he had harbored unsuspectingly offer in regret for his fatal bite? Tonight he would attend the Grand Sultan, converse with him, soothe him, play for him more movingly than ever before, and finally leave as he had come, a fraud and an enemy. With no farewell.

Stonily he successfully blinked back the burning behind his eyes. A warrior loved not his enemies.

On the third evening of Dolores's residence amid Reduan's two wives, five concubines, and subdued children in the women's quarters, a husky woman servant entered her small chamber and with a grunt set down upon the carpeted floor a carved chest, an odd-shaped padded bundle, and a small, locked casket. Tears sprang into Dolores's eyes, although in her heart she had already known Francho would not let her return to the Alhambra again. In immediate succession there came a polite knock on the plastered grill separating her cubicle from the women's garden, and outlined against the parchment inlaid to keep the cool breeze from her couch she could see the taut silhouette of the master of the house, scrupulously awaiting her invitation to enter before breaching her chamber.

At her word he came through the velvet draperies, the lack of expression on his pocked face still causing a tiny shiver up her spine. He indicated the objects just delivered. "Our friend informed the mistress of the royal harem that you were sold and told her he would cause your raiment and jewels to be delivered to the new owner. His slave boy just brought them. He also asks you keep his lute for him."

The house servant bowed out. Reduan did not stir. He eyed her dispassionately. His hand rested casually upon the intricate hilt of his scimitar, but she thought he seemed disposed to talk.

With a sadness she could not dispel she asked, "And what of him?"

"He saved the life of your Queen the night he brought you

here by riding to Santa Fe with a warning. He has returned to Granada with but one more mission to accomplish, a very dangerous one. Tonight. If he succeeds the hostilities between your kingdom and mine will soon cease."

Dolores's lips parted. The news that issued from that thin, straight mouth upset her. Her mind tossed together circumstances and facts and up popped one idea. "The Sultan. He will kill the Sultan," she whispered, but Reduan's face told her nothing. She studied the powerful officer's face, the colorless eyes that challenged her and harbored unwelcome suggestion held in check only by expediency. "No . . . Muza Aben Gazul," she breathed and by his bark of a laugh she knew she was right.

"You are lucky to be here, lady. The general's partisans will go mad with grief. Should he succeed and escape, by the morning anyone who had more than brief contact with Jamal ibn Ghulam will be arrested and grimly persuaded to scream out his whereabouts. But, if Allah gives him his life, by my pass our friend will be already gone from the city. For good."

A thought stabbed through her fear for Francho and the bereft pain that gripped inside her. "How will they know with whom he was close? He kept mostly to himself."

A cruel smirk sat on Reduan's lips. "Each one will implicate another. Even the Sultan, of course, will be suspect. I will have my own men reinforce his palace Nubians until the terror dies down."

But it was Ali and Azahra that had occurred to Dolores. She stepped over to him in an agitated jingle of bangles and flutter of the *yashmak,* behind which hid the unhappy droop of her mouth. Lightly touching his arm she cried, "General Reduan, I appeal to you, there are two innocent children who were very dear to Jamal ibn Ghulam and who inhabit a house in the Albayzin where he went often. They must be brought to safety here, or given at least the chance to flee for their lives."

At his downward glance she hastily removed her fingers.

"Yes, I know of those two. The boy carried the messages."

"He knew nothing of what was in them, he thought them love missives to a sweetheart beyond the walls. Such mercy as you may show to save his life and that of his sister will put Don Francisco forever in your debt."

"He is already in my debt," Reduan intoned, losing interest. "Peace be with you, lady," he brushed off her plea, and his long, embroidered mantle rippled as he turned to leave.

"No doubt you are aware that Don Francisco's sire and commander is the powerful Count of Tendilla, Don Iñigo de Mendoza?" Dolores called in desperation to his retreating back.

As if her words were a cast fishhook the Moorish commander whirled about in his tracks, and the glitter that invaded his colorless eyes rivaled that of the jewel in his turban. "No. This I do not know. But of Don Iñigo de Mendoza, of his triumphs and his ultimate aspirations, I am well aware. Then perhaps you are right. One more show of cooperation, minor as it is, costs little if Tendilla's son so values the lives of two Moorish peasants."

Dolores let out her breath in a small puff.

Reduan reentered the room and faced her, irritation in his folded-arm stance. "And yet I dare not send my own soldiers to warn them. Things have not coalesced, and it is not my habit to uncover my own flank prematurely. I believe I shall have to pass up this good deed. My regrets, lady. And to Don Francisco." The curl of his lip said otherwise than regret.

"But I can go." Dolores detained him by the arm again. "I know the house." She swallowed to contain her distress. "Please let me go for them. All I need is a donkey for me and one for them. I will dress as a simple slave woman, no one will even note me." She saw his objection in the jut of his chin and forestalled him. "I know I am your hostage but where would I go, *sayed?* I know no one in the city. I cannot go back to the Alhambra. I do not wish to be taken either. I must return here, for my own sake."

"That is intelligent of you," he said. "Very well, go if you must, but with one of my guards with you dressed as a servant, who will allow you to do nothing foolish since I have guaranteed your safety. You may not go tonight but at the first light of dawn, and only if I know that Muza Aben is dead."

"That may then be too late," she pleaded.

The glitter that had given some life to the depthless eyes was long gone. "That is the best I can do. If Allah wills it you will be in time." It was hard to tell if it was a twitch that moved a muscle in his face or the hint of a sardonic smile. "Be ready." There seemed a subtle shift in the tenor of his thoughts as he stared at her. With insulting directness he asked, "You risk bodily harm yourself to succor Mendoza's friends. Do you love him?"

Dolores's chin came up.

The general mused, "The minstrel's beautiful Christian lady, a gift from his overgenerous ruler, was indeed his concubine. And yet it is common knowledge that the Duke of Medina-Sidonia sued for your release several times, which petitions the Sultan ignored. You must have many suitors, lady. A man seldom encounters so enticing a face and form." Some of the glitter had returned to the Moor's eyes. "Perhaps, Baroness, when I claim my Christian heritage, you will consider me also among your suite of sincere admirers?" he asked insinuatingly.

He pushed aside the velvet drapes and left her standing in her fanciful concubine's veils and chiffons, her half-bare bosom lifting and falling with her angry breathing.

Reaching the foot of the Alhambra hill, Francho rounded the illuminating flare of an oil bowl on a pedestal and turned up another silent road whose residences backed on the rocky gorge of the Darro River. It was not hard to spot the general's enclave up ahead, its walls lit by torches, and there would indubitably be guards inside the portals. In his bed was the only time Muza Aben was not surrounded by zealous officers, aides, and assorted cavaliers, and Francho's first thought had been that to dispatch the man in his bedchamber was the surest way, and one where he would have a better chance of escaping with his life. Yet high walls, an unknown layout, and guards everywhere made such a daring plan impossible.

Reduan, although anxious to avoid any overt brand of traitor to his people, had not turned a hair over collusion which would rid him of a man he had always despised. He reminded Francho that the blustering Muza Aben scarcely hid his desire to rid Granada of Boabdil and ascend the throne himself, for in such case the general was certain the Barbary caliphs would send help to rescue Granada, this most precious jewel of the one true Prophet. Yet even the charismatic leader of Granada's still formidable army did not dare to make a frontal military assault on the Alhambra yet and depose the Sultan. And Boabdil's intimates seemed incorruptible, his Nubians, more than one thousand of them, were alert, his food he had taken to feeding first to a pet monkey.

It had been Reduan's suggestion to assault Gazul by using his thwarted ambition for the throne. "Send Muza Aben a message smacking of disaffection and greed and hint that you wish to approach him for instructions. He will believe you;

why should he not? Disloyalty is woven into the Moorish nature. If you can effect a meeting after he dismisses his staff and retires, you have your chance."

Thinking it over for a minute, Francho had finally agreed. "It sounds viable. In fact the idea that my visit would be impromptu and at an odd hour makes sense. Everyone knows what state of nerves the Sultan suffers and how he clutches at my presence. If I tell him the Sultan gives me little time to myself and *that* only when he sleeps soundly, therefore I must come when I can, no matter how inconvenient."

"Have you a trustworthy messenger?"

"No. I have a slave boy but he would wonder at my business with Gazul and he talks with the other servants."

"Leave the message with me," Reduan had instructed. "I shall see it is discreetly delivered and an answer and a safe conduct returned, without implicating either one of us."

"My other problem is getting a weapon past his guards," Francho admitted morosely, having racked his brain on how to do it to no avail.

"I can help you with that, too. . . ."

Francho pulled up his horse behind a roadside shrub and waited, nervously moving his shoulderblades against the sheath of the long Moorish dagger ingeniously slung between them. There was a very narrow halter strap about the base of his neck and one running immediately under his left armpit, both well masked by his loose tunic and bunched mantle. The thought of committing cold-blooded murder was ugly to him, but a fair duel would allow the general time to yell for help; it would thwart his purpose and probably claim his life. As it was, even a frontal assault against the burly and dangerous man was chancy. Muza Aben would have to do Francho the favor of turning his back for an instant. The odds for success, unfortunately, were against him. Breathing deeply of the clean, dry night air, he glanced up at the unwinking stars, as alone as he had ever been in his life. The harsh expectation that he might never live to see the sun again drove the pulse to thumping in his throat like a drum.

And then, with a ghostly, amused smile he considered that he had already risked the Alcalde's dungeons and the slaughter of the battlefields with the very same expectation. And he was still breathing.

Muza Aben had the regular habits of a soldier. At the faint

cry of the watch calling the hour of midnight, Francho judged his victim would surely have retired. He spurred his horse into motion and continued up the hill, and no dog barked at the sound of his passage because Moslems abhorred canines and did not keep them. He reined in at the general's residence. Taking one foot from the stirrup he kicked at the oaken gates in the long, blank wall. A grilled panel slid back and suspicious eyes peered up at him.

"Who knocks at this hour?"

"I wish immediate interview with the General Muza Aben. The matter is urgent."

"He has gone to bed. Come back on the morrow."

"Then wake him up. He is expecting me. The matter is urgent, friend, this is not a social visit. I shall pass you a safe conduct. Hurry up!" Francho cracked his voice like a lash to get the soldier to move, never mind that it was not in keeping with the mild personality of ibn Ghulam. The man took the paper and the panel slammed shut. Francho waited, keeping his face muffled; he knew there were eyes on him from peepholes hidden about the gates. Finally he heard the bar shoot back. The heavy portal swung open and he guided his mount in.

Surly-looking soldiers surrounded him as he dismounted in the leaping flares of hanging oil pots. The guards understood that the nameless visitor with Muza Aben's pass wished to keep his head down and in the shadow of his deep hood, but his mantle was opened and rough hands ran down his body feeling for a weapon. A whisper came down through the years and he heard di Lido's sibilant voice bouncing from the stone walls of Mondejar, "It is the military mentality, Francisco. If they are not used to something they will never, ever think to think of it." Surely not a dagger slung down the back. Nevertheless he was grateful for the dark cloth that hid the sweat beaded on his forehead as he sturdily withstood the examination.

Suddenly a searcher's sleeve came into accidental contact with the edge of his hood, pushing it partially away from his face. Francho found himself eye to eye with a spike-helmeted, hook-nosed soldier as tall as he. The man barely blinked, said nothing, and quickly pulled the hood forward again, but Francho had seen the instant flare of recognition in his eyes. Jamal ibn Ghulam was, after all, a familiar and distinctive figure in the Sultan's train. Francho spent no time worrying over it now. Whether he succeeded or died in the trying, his Moorish identity was spent coin from this point on.

Having turned up nothing threatening, the guards gave him over to a sleepy house servant, who led him into the dwelling. Like most Moorish mansions it consisted of a series of arched and columned suites connected by roofed galleries and fountained courts, and Francho concentrated on remembering the route they took, in the dire and hopeless event he had to make a run for it. Orange-sashed, pantalooned guards impassively crossed pikes and opened them again in front of the general's portal. The servant flung open the door, showed Francho in, and then backed away.

He stood alone for a minute in a multi-arched, heavily carved little salon, evidently adjunct to the sleeping quarters and used as a study by Muza Aben. There were documents and papers strewn all over a low table and nearby several tall baskets of rolled maps. But Francho's gaze was caught and held by the glittering, singular paperweight which lay atop the pile of reports on the table—the sharp and unsheathed curve of the general's huge scimitar. If Muza Aben sat at the table, at the first false move the hilt of the damascened weapon would spring to his hand and put a bloody end to his visitor's precarious plan. Having hoped that bringing the general from his bed would also bring him without a sword, Francho could only clench his jaw at this circumstance and accept it. Kill him with his own sword, flashed through his mind.

But before he could move, the curtains on one of the archways stirred as if the general was first peering at him, and then they were pushed aside and Muza Aben strode through, scowling darkly behind his mustaches at the interruption of his rest. Yet, even in a long velvet robe, hastily wound turban, and turned-up Turkish slippers his powerful bulk was intimidating.

Francho salaamed deeply and pushed back his hood. "A thousand pardons, honored General, for this late visit, but there are few convenient times when I am dismissed from the Sultan's presence."

"I need my sleep, minstrel, let us come to the point." Muza Aben briskly seated himself cross-legged at the writing table, pushing aside the papers with careless disregard. "I am informed that you are willing to perform a certain difficult task for a suitable fee."

Taking on the retiring coloration of ibn Ghulam's personality Francho eyed the curtained archways uncertainly. "This is a very delicate matter. May I assume there is no danger of eavesdroppers?"

"You may," Muza Aben grunted. "Those with no knowledge can tell no tales is my belief. The guards cannot hear a low discourse through the door. Speak freely."

Diffidently approaching as close as he dared to the general's table, Francho began a rambling account of his relationship to the Sultan, using the digression to buy time to come up with a circumstance that would get the man away from that scimitar and give him reason for one brief moment to turn his back; force him away from that scimitar, get him to turn his back ran through his mind so desperately he thought the directive must be burned across his brow.

Fed up with the preamble from this self-centered sycophant, Muza Aben rapped loudly on the table and leaned forward, bracing his beefy hands on his crossed knees. "I am already aware of the Sultan's limitless regard for you, ibn Ghulam. Enough chatter. Just tell me why you are so suddenly willing to turn against him."

Francho delivered an indignant but glib pastiche made up of the offended patriotism of a man whose family had been murdered by the Christians and, more convincingly, his present lack of financial aggrandizement. He complained angrily that the Sultan's listlessness had cut off the flow of gifts which had augmented his minstrel's niggardly wage and that an artist could not live on melancholy sighs and tragic moans alone. He even dropped a hint that he was thinking of going to Italy, where it was said the Duke of Mantegna showered his artists with silver and gold. "If we can come to an agreement, honored General, I could find perfect occasion for, say, a pinch of powder in his wine cup, or when I play him to sleep, a pillow pressed forcibly to the face. The deed is not difficult for one in my intimate position?" He turned the statement into a question as a form of false modesty, and added unctuousness to his smile as he had observed of several of Boabdil's courtiers.

The black Asiatic eyes bored into him. "But what of Abu Abdullah's huge Nubian slave? That suspicious mute is constantly in his presence."

The oily smile became slyer. "So trusted is the musician Jamal ibn Ghulam that many times when he is present the

Sultan dismisses M'jambana to stand guard outside, or to lead the black leopard out for an airing. Alone I soothe him to sleep often. If I take care to arrange the body to appear sunk in slumber I can be far away from the palace before the corpse is discovered." His speech flowed smoothly, but Francho's nerves twanged. Get him away from the scimitar. Get him to turn his back—

The general was direct. "Name your price."

To one side of the table there was a large, gilded chest upon which rested a heavy hammer used to strike a polished brass gong hanging nearby. There was a good possibility Muza Aben kept money locked up in that chest.

"One thousand dinars." Francho said flatly.

"Your greed is fantastic, minstrel!"

"But the risk is vast and a dead man cannot find pleasure even in one dinar. My price is in accordance with the delicacy of my service and its uniqueness. And I must have it all now. You will understand, I have made arrangements for my own escape and I cannot come out of hiding to claim a remainder." Or to be killed in my turn, were the unspoken words that hung in the air between the two bargainers. Francho raised his hands in a depreciating gesture. "You may trust me, my General. I cannot get out of the city."

Eyes narrowed, Muza Aben contemplated him silently for a moment, one hand absently rubbing the cold metal hilt of the scimitar. Finally he growled, "Very well. I have no time to dicker with you."

Get up and go to the chest, go, go.

But Muza Aben merely shoved away a sheaf of loose papers and uncovered a flat iron box which he unlocked and pushed toward his hired assassin. "There are six hundred dinars in this box. That is your fee. Take it or begone. I will give you three days to accomplish your task. If your tongue wags or I do not get full value for my money, my cavaliers will have a living target upon which to practice their aim with the lance. Be assured of this, ibn Ghulam: if you dare cross me you will never escape my vengeance."

"You will be satisfied, my master. Allah hear me," Francho promised, stalling again with a shallow salaam and casting about in despair for another lever to get Muza Aben off his pillow. As his eye caught the basket of rolled maps in the corner he improvised, "To show good faith I can indicate to you a secret passage into the Alhambra from a residence outside the palace walls, by which the Alhambra could be infiltrated when the Sultan is dead." He thought he saw a stir of interest on the dark, burly face and added quickly, "However, to show you which outside residence is the terminus I would require a chart of the Alhambra." Surely if Muza Aben had plans to seize the palace he would have a chart. "I could trace the path of the passage and perhaps you would recognize the exit?"

Go, go to the basket of maps, Moor, take your eyes off me, leave the safety of that scimitar.

"I know of many tunnels into the Alhambra," the general said coldly. "Men must go in single file and few could get through before being discovered. Your job is to destroy the defensive purpose of the palace Nubians by removing its object. I will take care of the subsequent events."

Francho smiled hastily. "Of course, honored sir. I was just attempting to be helpful."

Muza Aben waved him out, barely disguised disgust on his face. "Go. In three days we will know whether your own life is forfeit for Boabdil's."

Sweat dampened Francho's brow. What now? The interview was over and the general sat facing him as stolidly as ever. There would be no other chance. Could he whip out his dagger, dive across that glittering scimitar, and make a deadly strike before his agile target dodged away from the blow and yelled out an alarm? He would surely die trying it, he knew, but even so, subtly shifted his weight so that the whole of his force would drive his arm. His desperate peripheral vision noted the chest again and one last gambit to help his chances flashed into his mind.

He pressed both palms together in a fawning bow. "Sir General, one request I beg from you. A sum such as this"—he indicated the heavy box of dinars he was about to take from the table—"can be kept safer in my house in the Albayzin than at the Alhambra. However, at this late hour the Albayzin crawls with voracious thieves, and as you know I do not carry any weapon. Would you most generously send one of your men to escort me through the quarter and see I am not beset by a gang and meanly relieved of my wage? I beg my General's indulgence to his loyal servant?"

Muza Aben's sour look spoke of distaste and the doubts he had always had of the virility of singers of pretty songs. But sending a guard along with the craven musician was little enough to do to keep him alive long enough to perform his function. The general shrugged an assent.

Get up, get up, don't bellow out for a servant, Francho agonized at him mentally through his clench-jawed smile, go to the gong, Muza Aben Gazul.

With a light movement unexpected for a man of his thickset proportions Muza Aben rose and walked the few paces to pick up the gong striker. He turned and raised the mallet to strike the large, flat disc. Francho's long dagger flashed out and its soft snick was almost simultaneous with his desperate, flying lunge. The shimmer of silent movement was reflected in the gong's burnished surface and whirled Muza Aben about, and in a split-second defense the hammer, with a decorative, deadly spike projecting from its head, came down in a whistling arc as Muza Aben's mouth opened to roar for help. But Francho's terrible blade, aimed for the back and by fortune plunging directly into the heart beneath the velvet robe, robbed the great lungs of life and breath before the voice could be willed, and the dagger drove up to its hilt into the formidable chest. The slanted, brutish eyes glared fury a tiny second and then glazed over. Blood spurted from the open mouth and the legs buckled.

With a grunt Francho grappled with the heavy body before it fell. He lowered it noiselessly to the thick carpet and dragged it behind the table. Stunned that he had accomplished this critical murder with his own life still remaining to him, he put his hand over the corpse's open mouth to make sure the formidable Muza Aben was really dead. Dulling, lifeless eyes stared up at him accusingly: would you have dared meet my scimitar in honorable combat? "Yes, I swear it. Sooner that than this," Francho muttered miserably.

For the first time he realized that blood was dripping into his beard from a bad rip torn down the side of his face by the spiked hammer, and he realized how he was blessed. Given a second's more warning and a longer reach, Muza Aben, even as he was dying, would have smashed his assailant's face. He took a moment to swab away the blood from his face with the hem of the dead man's robe, pressing on it to try to close the wound, then pulled his hood over his turban and as far forward over his face as possible. He took a deep breath to steady himself and opened the door to the chamber, still guarded on the outside by stalwart, unmoving sentries. He stepped out quickly, closing the door behind him, and forced himself to walk unhurriedly back the way he had come, tense to hear any minute the pinioning cry of "Murder!" It had to come; it did not seem possible that he could stab to death the great Muza Aben and yet escape in one piece.

Someone fell in step with him and his head jerked in alarm, but it was only the sleepy-eyed servant who glided from the shadow of a huge bronze urn to guide him to the entry. The few vulnerable moments this took were blown into hours by strain before they arrived at the gate and Francho was able to swing onto his steed. Blood was trickling down the line of his jaw and soaking into the dark folds of the hood about his neck, but he forced himself to wait silent and patient for the guards to open for him, his heart pounding in dread of the shout, "Hold that man! Muza Aben is murdered!" The gate yawned wide but neither did he gallop away from the residence. He rode at an unworried trot, his back prickling, his cheek and neck sticky with blood, until he came to the foot of the hill, out of earshot of Muza Aben's men.

Then he kicked the horse unmercifully and galloped west through the cobbled streets, ignoring two city guards who yelled for him to halt and identify himself, rounding jogs and corners with so little speed sacrificed to margin that his calves scraped against building walls. At last he reached the same city portal he had reentered a few days before. As he pulled up he gritted his teeth to hear the thunder of urgent hoofbeats behind him, but, watching the unmoved face of the guard who held up a lantern to read the pass he presented, he realized it was only the pulse hammering furiously in his ears.

The man was not the same sentry as last time. "This is General Reduan's pass but it is irregular. Our orders are now that only the Sultan may pass a man out of the city. Here, let's have a look at you." The soldier raised the lantern, and Francho knew the dark stain spreading along the neckline of his dark mantle would need explanation. Delay, fatal delay.

The lantern was grabbed from the conscientious guard by a higher-ranking companion, who used it to reexamine the pass and assert his own authority. "General Reduan's pass is good enough for me," he said. "What is the passphrase, traveler?"

"La Galib ile Allah," Francho muttered.

"He's all right. Let him out," the soldier ordered, and the thick iron bars were drawn back.

Suddenly Francho found himself outside the gates and free. Urging his horse with careless haste down the broad, stone-strewn hill, even though it didn't seem likely that God would abandon him at this late point, he would not feel safe until he reached Santa Fe's walls. What he had done seemed incredible. Muza Aben was forever silenced, and the next powerful commander of Granada's forces was a turncoat. Boabdil would surrender to save his people and his city. And Dolores was safe with Reduan. Dolores . . .

Granada was behind him, finished. The left side of his face, laid open deeply, was now giving him intense pain, but the cloth of his hood stuck to the wound and kept the cool night air from the raw gash. He strained his eyes into the darkness that held him close and did not turn his head to look back at the silhouetted minarets and domes of Granada, nor pause in his flight home to whisper a last farewell to Jamal ibn Ghulam, Head Musician to the Grand Sultan Abu Abdullah, or to the houri, Karima.

Sleepy-eyed, Azahra opened the door a crack in answer to the imperative pounding and found a mesh-shirted soldier standing there, scowling in the pale light of early morning filtering through the clustered rooftops.

"Jamal ibn Ghulam?" the man barked. She saw by his uniform he was not an ordinary palace guard but a cavalry officer of the army.

"Jamal?" she hesitated. "He . . . he is not here now. Perhaps tonight—"

"Good, then we shall be here to welcome him, the carrion!" He punched open the door, throwing her back, and four more sullen-faced men appeared behind him. Scimitars drawn, they strode swiftly through the two chambers of the house and the little littered court behind. Stunned, Azahara gasped and begged of the leader, "Wha . . . What are you doing? Jamal is not here. What do you want of him?" She could see the curious of the neighborhood beginning to congregate at the mouth of the alley, drawn by the noisy and precipitous arrival of this squad of grim soldiers.

"He will answer for the foul murder of the General Muza Aben," the officer snarled in response. He grabbed her by the arm and menaced her with his long, curved blade. "Look you, girl, the verminous cur you lay with is as good as dead, for we are combing the city to flush him out. Tell us where he is hiding or the worms will feast on your eyes too!"

A faint shouting and wailing seemed to rise on the breeze

from down the hill, and more gawkers were crowding into the alley. Too bewildered to feel fright yet, Azahra cowered in the man's grasp and looked desperately from one soldier to another. "I don't know where he is, I—"

"You do know! You female jackal!" He shook her and shoved into her face his own bearded visage, now twisted into a mask of grief-driven rage. "Shield him and you are as much assassin as he. Speak up or I'll cut your throat open."

It was dawning terror for Jamal, not herself, that set Azahra's body trembling like a leaf, for she saw on the fury-dark faces of the soldiers a hatred that spelled out certain doom for the man they sought. She could not believe that what they said was true, that the gentle artist Jamal, the Sultan's Head Musician, had murdered Muza Aben Gazul, but she finally understood that these wild-eyed men would give Jamal no chance for his life if he left the Alhambra and rode here tonight.

Through the open door she spotted Ali returning from the fountain, carrying his water jug through the knot of spectators, a puzzled look on his face, the little ditty he always whistled dying on his lips. The soldiers had spotted him, too, were evidently aware he belonged to the household, and they flattened along the wall, scimitars at the ready. The man holding her swung her around to face the door and act as a lure. A frantic sense of now or never blotted out all considerations in Azahra's mind, all fear except for the terrible danger looming over her innocent benefactor. With a desperate wrench she lunged away from the officer's grasp and cried out, "Run, Ali, run away! Warn Jamal at the Alhambra, they want to kill him! Run, run—!"

With black fury the officer's blade slashed out and caught her in the back. Azahra's breath gasped from her and she staggered, her eyes opening wide at the horrible blow. An immediate dizzying dark whirled down upon her. "Run to Jamal—warn him . . ." she croaked hoarsely with the last of her strength, and then she felt cold, dimly aware that some of the onlookers in the alley were screaming in shock. The world fell out from beneath her, but her last blurred sight was of Ali dropping his earthen pitcher and darting away.

The hand clamped over Dolores's mouth was almost suffocating her to forestall another scream as she stared in horror at the terrible blood-covered figure almost cut in two lying across the threshold of the grimy house. "Shut up, woman.

Don't bring attention to us. We have arrived too late. Let's be away," ordered Reduan's servant-disguised guard.

Rigid with shock, nevertheless Dolores vehemently tore the hand from her veiled mouth. Her eyes bulged at the murdered girl collapsed on the doorstep, the small body trampled over by the boots of the soldiers giving hasty chase after a boy who must surely be Ali. And who had just scampered past her as she stood pressed against the alley wall.

People dodged aside to let the running soldiers through and then raced behind them to see what would happen. With a cry Dolores darted away from the servant-guard who was holding their donkeys, and ran too, blindly, propelled forward by the momentum of the onlookers now rushing to meet the shouts and yells coming up the hill. "Muza Aben is dead! Muza Aben is murdered!" and although the people from the alley had no idea what a neighborhood boy had to do with it, such terrible cries had them ravening for any blood to assuage their shock.

Dolores saw Ali race up the street leading to an open square, but a mounted soldier with drawn blade rode around the corner and blocked him. "Stop that boy, Ahmed, stop him!" the pursuing officer yelled out. For a second the boy skidded to a halt as the arriving soldier spurred up to meet him. Thin legs pumping, the boy feinted, making a dash to the left of the street, and suddenly, almost as the armed men on foot were upon him and joining the horseman, he veered right, dashing into a short, narrow passage between buildings. But the passage was a dead end, and he popped back out from between two other buildings.

Shrouded in the peculiarly bright purple mantle she had been furnished, Dolores was carried along pell-mell by the people pressing from behind and debouched in the square in time to see the small figure of the child skid to another eye-blink stop as a troop of cavalry entered the far end of the square followed by a rabble of shouting, grief-stricken mourners who jogged along behind them. The chasing foot soldiers yelled, "Stop that brat!" The boy turned back desperately, and Dolores caught a brief glimpse of his small face, white and terrified, eyes darting, mouth sucking air as he ducked a thrown javelin and darted sideways toward another narrow alley where horses would not fit. The crowd closed up in front of her. "Ali! Ali!" she screamed out in anguish, for the petrified child was Francho's Ali and here she stood, hemmed in, powerless to help him, and he couldn't even hear her. . . .

Alas, the contest between dodging child and fast horses was unequal. Before he could make the alley the original zealous horseman caught up with him, leaned out from his saddle, and with a triumphant cry and a violent swipe of his long, curved scimitar spattered the street with the child's crimson blood, so furious to avenge his beloved general's murder he refused to hear his frantic officer's shout of, "Don't kill him! He knows where that offal is hiding!" Thwarted, the angry officer and his men ran up, yelling, to where the mounted soldier gazed hawkishly at the boy's sprawled and twitching body, his mailed fist still brandishing the stained blade that had totally severed the eight-year-old head from the thin neck.

"Ay, Allah preserve us," wailed out an onlooker from the growing throng packing the small square. "Muza Aben leads us no more. We are defenseless, we are finished!" And a loud groan went up.

Dolores, darting desperately about the perimeter of the tightly packed backs of the mostly male crowd straining to see what had happened, tried to squeeze her way through, half-gasping, half-whimpering at what little she had seen.

A turbaned head poked from a neighboring window to goggle at the proceedings and yelled, "What? Was he murdered by a child, then, you donkeys?"

The scar-faced officer jabbed cruelly at the small corpse with the tip of his sword. "Not by this wretched sprat, graybeard, but by his stinking kin. He can thank the dog of an assassin ibn Ghulam for his execution." Brusquely shoving his underling off his horse, the officer mounted instead and raised his weapon to open a path for himself.

"Will you leave the poor boy to rot in the street?" an aghast female voice demanded.

"Why not?" the officer snarled back. "Do you think his taint of treason will poison your cobbles?" As the crowd hastily parted to let him and his men through, Dolores got a clear glimpse of the tragic scene behind them—too clear a view of the splayed young body untouched except where the horrible, dripping arteries protruded from the headless neck. The ghastly, small head had rolled a few paces away with goggling, sightless eyes staring pitifully up at the sky.

Uncaring, unthinking what she was saying she wailed distractedly, *"Ay, Madre de Dios, Jesu, Jesu,"* but fortunately it was against the babble of the crowd and muffled by her veiling. Concentrating on shoving past the backs before her, she began unwrapping her mantle to at least throw a cover over the mortal remains of the poor, executed child and hardly heard the commotion behind her. But suddenly, like the lightning outlash of a whip, an arm clamped about her waist and she felt herself lifted, kicking, her gasping body hoisted onto the edge of the saddle of a wheeling horse, and then she was being borne away by a member of a heavily armed squad in Reduan's orange-and-brown-striped colors, trotting away from the square in grim, tight formation in the opposite direction from Muza Aben's men.

"Sorry, *sayeda,*" a deep voice growled in her ear as the tight grip holding her precariously to the saddle threatened to cut her in two. "The general does not wish you to come to bodily harm. Your purple mantle was easy to spot."

She hung limply in his support, not caring for the pain, feeling a burning sourness rise into her mouth. Her eyes squeezed shut against the vivid horror of the two brutal murders she had just witnessed, but no pressure of hot tears would wipe away the sight of the carnage that was indelibly stamped upon her eyelids. And Francho, *Dios mío,* Francho too—perhaps he too was lying somewhere on the cold stones, sprawled as grotesquely and irretrievably dead, blood congealed in his wounds, glazed blue eyes staring, eyes from which the soul of the man had forever fled.

In hysterical dread her constricted stomach heaved and she threw up, befouling her veil and mantle and part of the guard's mesh sleeve, but caring for nothing except that most of her heart may have died on this day too.

❧ *Chapter 30* ❧

TENDILLA PATTED HIS horse's shining neck to quiet him as the animal reacted nervously to the unnatural silence of the mounted nobility spread in a glittering semi-circle before the deconsecrated little country mosque, renamed San Esteban, where the official surrender of Granada would take place. A cool January wind rattled the tree branches of a little patch of woods left unburned, and he heard from beyond it the usually muted flow of the Xenil River rushing louder than usual over its eroded rocks. The road, once a broad and lofty avenue of elms before the siege, had every eye fixed on it and on the gate of the red-walled city rising dreamlike against the white peaks of the *sierras* from which the Sultan's cortege would issue.

But Tendilla found his own attention more drawn by the packed masses of the Spanish forces standing along the road as far as the eye could see, ranged behind the stiff-backed, mounted figures of their monarchs and leaders. This was an army of gnarled and steadfast veterans of horse and foot and artillery standing proudly under their forests of lances and crosses and fluttering plumes and pennons, standing silently as if overawed by the imminence of the hoped for, prayed for, bloodily paid for end to their ten-year struggle.

The regal queen sat her richly caparisoned white jennet arrayed in warlike half-armor, yet the jeweled coif which formed a coronet around her head glowed no less than the pious glory shining from her face. Beside her a fully armored Ferdinand, whose helmet supported massive, blowing white plumes, could not fully master the triumphant gleam of power in his eyes, a power now evident to the world. Mounted on their right sat the younger Infanta, Caterina, the thin Infante, heir to the combined thrones, and the majestic, red-robed Cardinal Mendoza. On their left, along with Tendilla, waited the colorfully beplumed and steel-clad commanders whose valiant efforts had won this war, Cadiz, Medina-Sidonia, Cabra, Gonsalvo de Cordoba, and other honored leaders keeping their impatient, bedecked warhorses in line.

A murmur ran like a great, rustling wind across the ranks, and Tendilla turned his head and squinted toward the city. The gate had swung open, and a slow, sad cortege was starting on its way toward the bridge.

The Sultan himself was in the lead, riding alone on a black charger before an honor guard of his Nubians, a somber mantle dimming the brilliance of the embroidered tunic beneath it but a superb crown of gold and jewels set atop the folds of his turban. Behind, in open litters, were borne the Royal Household, and as they came closer Tendilla could see that the Dowager Ayaxa sat rigid, stonily, in coarse robes of mourning dabbed with ashes, while Morayama, looking bewildered, hugged one of her little daughters to her breast; and Yusef Comixa swayed, ill and old, in his litter. Beyond came in a long, cheerless procession squads of palace guards, the royal concubines in their gay carts, some aristocratic families who felt it safer to go into exile, slaves, servants, syncophants, and long wagons in which, Tendilla was sure, had been packed as many royal treasures as possible, gold vessels set with pearls, precious hangings stripped from inlaid walls, robes and rugs and scarves of gold and silver thread woven on Persian looms, and unknown, unimagined accumulated rich objects hidden for centuries behind the harem walls.

Viewing the lumpy mountains of goods hidden under the lashed coverings of the wagons, Tendilla mused that the Sultan would at least not live rudely in his banishment to a remote castle in the far Alpuxarras Mountains, although, interestingly, the baggage train was not as long as he expected. He was certain many priceless, rich, and historical objects must still remain in the Alhambra and Generalife palaces, abandoned or overlooked because of haste, of distracted grief.

If only they could be protected from looting and dispersement.

Abruptly he turned his gaze away from the mournful column approaching them and tried to glimpse Francisco, who was somewhere in the ranks of specially honored *caballeros* fanning out behind him, his now clean-shaven features shielded by his helmet and the herb-plaster bandage tied to one side of his face. The man had returned several weeks ago from his unique and risky mission in Granada covered with glory, and yet his mouth seldom stretched into the insouciant grin of several years ago, and his stride, although firm, had lost the careless swagger of the cocky. Someone else might ascribe the knight's somberness simply to maturity, but Tendilla was too sensitive for that. There was much that weighed on the heart of his erstwhile protégé and spy, and while he could guess at some of it, there seemed to be other distresses, unspoken and maybe even unrecognized, that robbed the startling cerulean eyes of their remembered clear and open brilliance.

Accompanied to within speaking distance of Los Reyes Católicos only by his Nubian honor guard, Boabdil the Unlucky reined in his horse face to face with his conquerors, the grief of seven centuries of fierce ancestors written in the grooves of his young-old face and in his beaten, tragic eyes. Fingers to forehead, fingers to chest, he bowed his head in a humble salaam. Nothing sounded or moved in the heavy silence except the snuffle of horses and the whipping rainbow of plumes and insignia.

At that moment the Infante Juan, delicate, small-boned, encased in embossed armor almost engulfing him, led forward on a white mule a dark-eyed, handsome youth in a rich Spanish doublet and a cloth-of-silver turban. A wan smile spread over the Sultan's haggard face as the slim young man rode up to him with shining eyes, and even the unemotional Tendilla surprised himself by lowering his gaze for a moment, for so fierce and unspeakably sad was the embrace between the Great Sultan and the son whom he had given up for hostage as a little boy that only the most hardened could have watched unmoved.

Recovering himself, Boabdil rode forward, withdrew from his golden sash two large keys, and for a moment weighed them in his hand. Those in the forefront could see Morayama in her litter softly weeping, although the dowager Sultana

Ayaxa and Grand Vizier Comixa stared silently straight ahead. But Abu Abdullah had been born a Sultan, and his dignity did not desert him. His voice was not loud, but it was unwavering as he spoke out. "We greet you, O conquering monarchs of Castile and Aragon. In surrender we greet you, and to you we offer our fealty. We give unto your hands, herewith, the keys to our beloved Granada and to the Royal Palace of the Alhambra. They are yours. Take them, and may Allah grant you the greatness to be as merciful and just to his people in peace as you have shown yourself to be strong in war. In this you will have the blessings of Heaven and the gratitude of your servant, Abu Abdullah." Only at the last did grief quaver the timbre slightly.

Tendilla expected it would be Isabella who answered the simple farewell speech of the deposed ruler, her tact with words being greater than her consort's, but Isabella deferred to her co-monarch. And so, as the Chamberlain carried the proferred keys to him, Ferdinand's great baritone boomed out, "Your submission, O Sultan Abu Abdullah, has been timely and wise, for by this you have earned our respect and the sanctity of our solemn promise. Hear, you all gathered here, that we declare that in justice and in mercy our loyal Moslem subject shall find equality with our own."

Ferdinand handed the keys to Isabella who threw back her head and raised the gleaming gold symbols up toward the heavens for a moment of victory and silent dedication. She then passed them on to the heir of this conquered territory, the Infante.

Tendilla braced back his shoulders and took a deep breath, the green-and-white plumes waving from his helmet and affixed to the brow of his horse. Followed by a mounted squire holding the white castle and bar standard of the House of Mendoza, he rode forward before the young prince and slapped a mailed fist to his heart in salute. The Infante's pale face was alight with welcome as he handed the keys over to the new Governor of Granada, and it was this unexpected excitement from a boy who had always seemed timid before him that cracked Tendilla's poise and elicited from him a full smile. The saturnine face of Don Iñigo de Mendoza flooded with a pleasure much deeper than any realized.

The deep boom of a bombard on Granada's walls rolled across the ravines and river, and in the clear morning light tens of thousands of jubilant Christian eyes turned toward the city to catch the sun glittering from a great silver cross just raised over the Alhambra's main tower, carried in the night before by the Bishop of Salamanca and an advance group of Christian knights and men-at-arms. And, as the Prophet's crescent banners sadly descended, the red-and-yellow flag of Spain was run up to fly triumphantly beside the Cross.

Amid wild artillery booms a great shout of victory burst to the skies from the assembled army. "Santiago! Santiago! For God and for Spain!" the cries rang out, weapons and banners waving and brandished joyfully. A large company of Dominican brothers standing back from the road holding crosses and croziers and church flags began a deep Te Deum, soon joined by the fifes, flutes, and bells of the army, the whole delirious racket unquestionably penetrating into the deep recesses of Moslem homes where the followers of the Prophet had retreated to nurse their despair.

The meeting place at the mosque had been chosen carefully for it was located on a crossroad, and Boabdil's party would be able to veer away immediately to make their progress across the mountains. Boabdil's tragic gaze very briefly met Tendilla's as they moved past each other in opposite directions; the ruler into exile and disgrace, the new Governor riding proudly beside his monarchs toward the exotic, beautiful, and coveted prize of the Prophet's Granada. Nothing was conveyed in that tiny exchange of human emotion. Nothing and everything, the Count reflected—which could as easily be said for the fact of living and dying.

❧ *Chapter 31* ❧

"No, no, my lord, not so somber a costume, I pray you; something brighter, like this blue-and-gold velvet? 'Tis not a funeral, after all, but a triumph. The blue velvet with gold hosen and a feathered russet toque would be elegant, quite in the mood of the ceremony."

Francho made no objection as his erstwhile tutor di Lido instructed Ebarra to repack the brown costume into the chest of new clothes and lay out another brief doublet instead, as well as a fine lawn shirt, Francho's steel cuirass, and a short cape to fasten over one shoulder with a gold silk rope. Instead he stared bleakly out of the window at January's threatening sky. His thoughts jumped from Boabdil to Leonora, who by the time this day was over could be his, to Dolores and the note she had sent him about the terrible deaths she had witnessed—only a note, because since being reunited with the Queen's circle she mostly kept to the chamber assigned her "to recover from her arduous captivity"—and to avoid seeing him, he was sure. He did not want to think about Ali and Azahra. By the greatest will he was blocking off contemplating his complicity in their tragedy until his most vital road was fully traveled.

It was the ache of his bandaged face, perhaps, that so compressed his spirits. He put his hand up to pull listlessly at his beard before he remembered he was clean-shaven again, for over a month. No more the perfect image of a Moslem courtier, no more the acclaimed Head Musician.

"Come, my lord, the time approaches. You must dress," di Lido stirred him up. "This will be the greatest appearance of your life, and you cannot take too many pains with your toilette. Say now, did this day not seem improbable scarce eight years ago? How the time has flown! Do you remember the rivers of ale we quaffed at Mondejar to stave off the boredom? I daresay it did my liver no good nor does it still, but I am beginning to think that malt has a property which restrains the graying of hair. 'Tis a theory which will take more time to prove, of course." The fussy Italian picked up a hand mirror and critically surveyed the pomaded, scarcely streaked dark hair that rolled about his ears and was so exactly arranged under his brimless velour hat. In spite of his constant complaints about his health, di Lido seemed as wiry and fit as when Francho had first met him. In fact, for several weeks after their happy reunion the maestro had repaid Francho's hours of time spent detailing the events in Granada which di Lido wanted to include in his war chronicle by serving as dueling partner and sternly brushing up the returned hero on his swordsmanship.

"You're too early in addressing me as 'my lord,' Maestro," Francho muttered, pulling on his hosen. "I am yet only Don Francisco de Mendoza."

"Poof. What do a few hours matter, or formal ceremony? The day we rode into Granada the Queen informed Don Iñigo and you of her happy decision to reinstate you. And, to me at least, it was then you became the Marquis of Olivenza."

"The Marquis of Olivenza," Francho repeated.

Di Lido's sharp nose twitched. "Whatever ails you, Francisco? In a few hours the prize you have struggled for will be publicly conferred upon you. The rumor of your spectacular advancement is already spreading, and the Court is abuzz with conjecture. What enemies you have will soon be confounded by the honors descending upon you, and your friends will be pleased. You should be overjoyed, but instead you stare with a grim frown and seem beset by woe. 'Tis a strange way to welcome this day!" The savant peered intently at the silent Francho, sighed, and added dryly, "But I could have almost expected this, so well do I recognize your character. Look you, my young lord Venegas, let your old teacher console you. There is no kind of happiness that is pure, that hasn't been bought by someone else's tears and strife. There had to be some less than saintly measures on your part, some repercussions that others suffered, almost like the heavy travail of birth, to effect such miraculous transition from foundling to Marquis."

"I don't feel like a Marquis."

"One doesn't feel like a Marquis. One merely acts like one," di Lido snapped, out of patience. "Such childish doubt is unworthy of your position. Having so handily earned your title you should be spilling over with confidence." But di Lido's sympathetic understanding rose to the fore again. "Come, my lord Venegas. The Grand Sultan Abu Abdullah, Muza Aben, your two unfortunate young friends—will you debase their contributions, erase their worth in your life, by not at least rejoicing in your victory? Take a deep breath then and put on your conqueror's raiment."

Once more Francho trod across the decorative tiles of the Alhambra's resplendent Audience Hall, but now the royal dais held two high-backed throne chairs, and to the side a gilded seat for Cardinal Mendoza. He found a place among the men on a row of cushioned benches set up at the foot of the dais and reserved for those to be specially honored. The day would represent a high moment in the lives of many of the younger, outstanding heroes of the ten-year conflict, with knighthood, higher rank, or purses of gold among the honors to be conferred upon them.

The hall was brilliant and packed with the ladies and gentlemen of the Spanish Court and even, in more somber robes and turbans, some of the high-born Moslems who had been selected to serve in civil capacities to effect smooth governmental transition. Looking along his bench Francho nodded briefly at those he knew, all the while noting that Reduan Venegas, whose troops had stood at silent and obedient attention as Los Reyes Católicos rode through the key-and-hand barbican, but who had not received exactly what he demanded, was absent from the ranks of onlookers.

Trumpets rang out and the excited chatter halted in midsentence, heads swiveled, and a path swept apart for a stately procession of dignitaries led by Their Majesties, the scarlet-robed cardinal, the purple-hatted archbishops, including the newest archbishop, Talavera, and a complement of chanting, pacing prelates in embroidered surplices holding aloft golden crosses. And in their midst but not to be missed in his humble cassock and rope belt like a sparrow among preening peacocks, the heavy-shouldered, omnipotent Inquisitor Torquemada, walking alone with clasped hands, pious of bearing and ruthless of face.

Francho's wound throbbed dully. He touched the smaller dressing that had been recently applied to the healing gash on the side of his face and grimaced at the memory of the agonizing searing-iron the camp chirurgeon had used to stop the bleeding. At one time he would have been vain enough to have worn a curving plume in his hat to hide the inelegant bandage, but today it didn't seem to matter.

Looking over his shoulder he searched through the near crowd for a glimpse of Leonora, but she was hidden behind the front ranks of the most privileged peerage. She was present, though; he had seen her when she entered with her mother and Felipe de Guzman, her soft, creamy blond beauty supported on the arrogant arm of a man whose eyes were constantly narrowed. She was in for a shock, his dimpled, mercenary girl, that would make the arm she clung to so proudly suddenly less than necessary to her. For he believed what she had told him that night the Queen was almost murdered: "If I could have both you and a proud rank then I would be happiest." It was something like that she had said. Well, he would let her stew in the juices of her own selfishness for a few days and then, when her regret was the deepest, he would seek her out.

He caught a glimpse of Don Enrique, Duke of Medina-Sidonia, large and bucktoothed and resplendent in satin and a diamond chain, but his lady de la Rocha was not at his side for the moment. His mouth twisted into a small, ironic smile as he wondered if it were because she considered she had nothing becoming to wear in public until her boxes arrived from Seville. He was acutely aware that only time would enable them to meet face to face with the casual aplomb the situation called for, but the sharpness of the disappointment that he felt thinking she might not be present to see his elevation, seemed to him unreasonable.

The solemn chant of the Deo Gratias ended, and there was an expectant murmur from the audience which included the grand masters of Santiago, Calatrava, and Alcantara blazoned with the distinctive crosses of their orders; the craggy, disappointed, but resigned Marquis of Cadiz; the haughty Marquis of Villena; the dukes and duchesses of Albuquerque, Medina Celi and Infantado; the youthful Captain Gonsalvo de Cordoba; the Mendozas, the Pachecos, the Zunigas, the Silvas, the Cardenas; the distinguished foreign envoys, the counts, viscounts, lord justices, *hidalgos,* knights, and all their ladies—the spectacular secular and religious personages of the united kingdoms of Spain rustled and whispered and peered at the men who sat full of pride on the gilded benches.

A liveried herald, reading from a linen scroll, called out the names of the great war commanders, who were in the audience because their deeds had already been honored privately by their rulers, although now the herald read out ringing praises to them from a grateful Ferdinand. The reserved Count of Tendilla, as all knew, had received the greatest laurel wreath, appointment as Governor of Granada, while his rivals the lords Cadiz and Medina-Sidonia had been appeased with vast tracts of invaluable property about Baza and Almeria. However, courtly etiquette abounded. If these grandees and the other commanders begrudged Tendilla his prize they were careful, in this celebratory moment, to keep their jealousies hidden.

Then the herald called out, "Don Diego Fernandez de Cordoba," and one of the men rose from the gilded benches to receive the commendations and rewards of Los Reyes Católicos. Following, the Lord of Palma was called and then Don Xippio of Batros. And then the high voice intoned, "Don Francisco de Mendoza."

Thanks to the confused rumors, Francho felt all eyes swivel to examine him as he rose and advanced, bowing and then sinking to his knees before his king and queen—a sober, broad-shouldered knight in a gleaming cuirass, with a large amethyst ring winking on his thumb. That he had performed the vital service of informant in Granada, with a position there close to the Sultan, had become titillating common knowledge, and the Moorish earring he still wore as a defiant memento of this service had proved an exotic lure to many a damsel, now that Leonora de Zuniga had chosen otherwise. But the flying rumors (which Francho suspected were di Lido's gleeful work) had it there was even more to his story, a mysterious secret involving the Queen, and so, when Isabella suddenly stood up and began to speak, her voice could easily be heard throughout the breadth of the hushed hall.

Her blue eyes, so calmly certain of rule and right, swept the throng of subjects before her. "My lords and ladies, hear us," her firm soprano rang out. "A quarter-century ago our beloved brother, the young Infante Alfonso, was foully murdered by a nobleman turned traitor to us. This villain's name was Don Juan de Venegas, Marquis of Olivenza. In the grief and wrath of a prostrate sister, Olivenza's subsequent death and our confiscation of his patents and estates did not satisfy us, but that we also branded his sole issue, a newborn babe, as enemy of the Crown and declared his name outlawed in our kingdom. We neither sanction nor decry the action of a maiden Princess alone in the world with her grief. But in the maturity of our years we now wish to rectify a misstep of justice done to the innocent infant, the Venegas scion.

"Our herald has called the name of Don Francisco de Mendoza, and this knight who kneels before us has stepped forward in pride. And well might he be proud, for many a Christian life and much distress of struggle and fortune has he saved for us by the informations gleaned during his daring masquerade in Granada. Additionally, if not for this person's opportune interference your queen would have given up her mortal life to an assassin's bolt. And, 'Go and rid of us Muza Aben' was our next difficult request of him—and this task he performed with both deftness and dispatch, to the result we entered Granada in this New Year 1492 and not in what might have been an exhausted six- or twelve-month hence.

"Can we doubt the loyalty, the bravery, the true heart of this right gallant knight, no matter what the name he bears? In the necessity to prove himself to us he has been a credit to the adopted name of Mendoza all these years and shown himself to be worthy of our regard. Now, with our gratitude and by our royal decree, shall he bear with pride the true name of his heritage, and also another, to designate the refounding and renewal of his house. So we hereby remove our sanctions from the name of Venegas, and so let it be."

Her gaze rested upon Francho with the assurance of one who had conferred with God. She took the jeweled sword offered her by the Royal Chamberlain and lay it thrice upon Francho's right shoulder. "You may rise then, Don Francisco de Granada-Venegas!" she called out with ringing affirmation.

The open-mouthed silence of the audience behind Francho

was broken as he stood up by a whispered hubbub of astonished comments, from which some louder words floated to him: Venegas? impossible! . . . Elena de Lura, she had . . . supposed to have been killed . . . Tendilla's type of dramatic intrigue . . . name was anathema for . . . always thought he did not much resemble Don Iñigo . . .

Isabella raised an imperious hand, for she was not finished. Into the silence she continued, "Now, by the sublime right of disposition vested in us do we also assign to Don Francisco de Granada-Venegas the patents and estates held by his forebears, including the Marquisate of Olivenza, to which by our royal favor he is henceforth secured, along with his heirs and future line." She nodded and a royal secretary standing below her read from a legal document in a stentorian voice a list of estates, castles, villages, and revenues being returned to the Marquis of Olivenza by the Crown.

Trying to ignore the itching between his shoulderblades caused by so many sets of eyes skewering him, Francho watched the curled parchment unroll without even listening. He already knew the names and attributes of his eleven estates, even minus the three the Crown had awarded to the disgruntled Reduan, which included an added fiefdom carved out of Granada's lower *vega*. When Isabella had informed them of her decision, he could hardly contain his excitement and triumph. The ground became a cloud upon which he capered, the melancholy Granada turned once more into an Eden of marvelous beauty, the very air he breathed became sweeter. Something like jasmine. That this had come to pass, had happened to him, product of monks and thieves, of cloisters, taverns, and Mondejar's hard lessons, most accomplished cutpurse, troubadour, and poseur, most talented trader of life's paths! And now he was *he,* Granada-Venegas, the excellent Marquis of Olivenza, the real and true, the baptized, the blooded noble gentleman with a solid base of true patrician ancestors set under his name. At that moment, at that moment of rebirth, vindication had washed his soul clean of all guilt.

But now, in spite of the stirrings behind him, the surprise, the admiration, the undercurrents of envy and awe, of hearing the secretary proclaiming his *ricos hombre* worth, and realizing that King Ferdinand and Queen Isabella, the noblest monarchs of all Christendom, were regarding him with steady approval, one week past his initial jubilance and he could summon up no other reaction than a creeping panic that this was too much, the pompous royal secretary was making him too much a Marquis, too much a Venegas, too far from the rest of him. Suddenly he swallowed and bit hard on his lip to stifle a wild desire to laugh.

But he repeated the set response in a confident voice, swearing to uphold Church and monarchs, swearing loyalty, obedience, and service of arms, swearing good faith in the upholding of the responsibilities of his patents. He went to his knees again as the Grand Cardinal rose and blessed him, extended a jeweled cross over his head, and then, taking a ten-pointed coronet from a pillow held by a page, passed the crown three times over Francho's head, chanting in Latin. The coronet was returned to the pillow.

"Rise, my lord Granada-Venegas of Olivenza," Ferdinand rumbled. "Not many have the privilege of bearing two illustrious names during their lifetime. We charge you carry out the noble promise of both, and your monarchs will be well pleased. God preserve you."

Francho made a low and sweeping bow and then backed away. He felt a terrible urge to disappear, to get out of the too-familiar Audience Hall and far from the curious assemblage. The ceremony continued as he turned and strode toward the door through a path of whispers opening for him. He saw Tendilla and di Lido from the corner of his eye but did not look toward them. He also caught Haro, the Grand Constable, with a face white as the belly of a fish, but that one could wait for another day. The visage of his good friend Pulgar came into his line of sight, grinning in amazement. But he kept his own face closed and intent, and his brief cape billowed out as he hurried through the door, hastening only to be by himself and try to calm the nameless upheaval the ceremony had triggered.

He thought of the peace of the willow glen where a carefree minstrel had strummed to the fish in the stream and eaten his simple meal; a greensward, alas, now just part of the bitter, scorched earth about Granada. He wanted back the fine, small chamber and garden off a certain gallery here in the Sultan's palace where waited Selim and Dolores. Dolores—

Grinding his teeth in anger at such useless memories, he paced through the Second Plaza and started across the sparsely populated breadth of the First Plaza, where stood the strange intrusion of a temporary wood-and-stone chapel which had been swiftly erected, and it was then he heard Leonora's panting hail and realized she had been running to catch up with him.

"Francisco! Wait. Wait for me—please!"

He waited and she arrived, breathless, holding up her skirts, her pearled headdress catching in its satin sheen the thin reflection of a sun struggling through an overcast. He offered his arm to steady her and she clung to it. The troubled golden brown eyes sought his.

"Why didn't you tell me? Why didn't my mother tell me?" she cried. "How different everything could have been if only you'd taken me into your confidence."

"I had taken an oath not to reveal my name. Nor was I confident the queen would even reinstate me. I wanted to save you the torturous suspense I suffered and the disappointment if fortune ran against me. I was trying to shield my sweet innocent lady from ambition raised by suggestion—a laughable tenderness in view of events."

"Not so laughable as misguided, Francisco. It would have given me the courage to wait for you for two years—five years even . . ."

"Is there a set schedule, then? A lady waits one year for a knight, two for a viscount, three for a marquis, and as much as five for a wealthy marquis? And does it add a few months to each allotment if she waits for her heart's beloved instead of a man chosen solely for his rank? Your mother gave you no hint because it was her duty to see you as highly connected as she could arrange. It was only up to you to refuse, or to at least drag your feet."

Her mouth drooped. The tip of her pert, small nose seemed to redden. Anxiously she pressed closer to him. "Francisco, I beg you not to be cruel. That very night that I told you about my betrothal I realized the depth of my mistake, for when I saw you again my heart almost leaped from my chest, and I knew I had given up love to embrace unhappiness. But it was too late to withdraw, I thought. The contract was being drawn and my promise had been given. I . . . I was even afraid Don Felipe would seek your life and so I sent you away." Her eyes searched his hopefully for a moment, and then their soft, deep amber depths filled with appealing warmth. "But that is all in

656

the past. What is done is done and obviously irredeemable. I merely wanted to be the first to offer my felicitations on your elevation—my lord."

She dropped her gaze modestly and made him a deep and deferring curtsey, which displayed not only respect but the lovely round curve of her white bosom pushed to swelling by the low neckline of her fur-edged gown.

He found it almost funny how deftly she had changed the tenor of her attitude at their last meeting from disdain to sacrifice. Ah, Leonora, little calculating one, your haste is so unbecoming. What struck him was his realization that, for all her failings and his own immature and romantic flights of fancy that had turned a woman into an angel, after all was said she probably did love him, for Perens was still heir to a dukedom, by any measure a cut above marquis, and also to a vast fortune. And what struck him harder was his peculiar lack of feeling anything more than the boost to his ego. Her fawning lifted his spirits. But where was his heart? He did want her, didn't he?

"Doña Leonora!" They both swung around to see Felipe de Guzman, hand on sword hilt, stalking up to them. The Count of Peren's hail had been so harsh that the guards stationed at the plaza gate glanced furtively from under their iron hats at the stiff trio. "Your behavior enrages me, lady. I do not take kindly to the public insult of having my betrothed leave my side to pursue another man. Return to the ceremonies at once!"

Francho stepped in front of Leonora, placing himself eye to eye with the fuming Perens. "My regrets for your tender sensibilities, Don Felipe, but do not dare to again command this lady in so cavalier a manner. She is not yet married to you; she owes you no obedience. I strongly suggest you yourself return to the ceremonies."

Felipe's pale features arranged themselves into the snarl-smile of the baited wolf. "Ha! The new lord Olivenza takes much upon his hero's shoulders today—a name, a title, and a damsel already promised to another man. Best enjoy the gains you already have, Granada-Venegas. Trespassing on my grounds will remove you from them with a blade through your belly. Do you come, *doña*?"

Pulgar and de la Cueva had arrived in the plaza hoping to find the new lord Olivenza and bear him back to the ceremonies and the festivities that were to follow. De la Cueva hastily pulled his companion up and they halted a bit away, warily eyeing the scene before them. The players in the tableau stood for a moment like wooden statues against the backdrop of the flamboyant arabesque traceries carved on the red walls and the incongruous, rough-hewn little chapel. A wind smelling of rain blew up, swirling dust about the plaza still bereft of its former throngs of merchants and strollers, riffling the feathers adorning Francho's felt toque, fluttering the chiffon draped over Leonora's headdress, flattening Guzman's doublet against the long muscles in his thighs.

Leonora looked helplessly from one to the other of the grim men glaring challenge at each other. "Don Felipe . . ." she began, "I . . . I don't quite . . ."

"You don't quite understand, but I do, *doña.* You underestimate me. You shall not make me look a fool before the entire Court. To me you are betrothed and to me you shall be wed. After that you are welcome to a long, lonely time to regret the fairweather dance you have led me."

Other courtiers straying in knots from the long ceremonies in the packed hall to get a breath of air drew close, fascinated.

Guzman flung out an arm and shoved Leonora back from the space between him and Francho. She managed to gasp out a placating, "Felipe, please, you don't . . ." but Guzman was smiling thinly at Francho. "Your father was a scabrous, craven traitor, an assassin. No royal proclamation can wash that stink from your name, and no grateful rewards can obscure that you have inherited that same talent—for murder." Two red spots burned on Perens's pallid cheeks.

"This time we'll finish it, dung," Francho exploded, his rage mixed with a corrosive relief for the deliberate provocation. He yanked at the gold cord and ripped off his cape as Perens leaped back, his weapon half out of its elaborate scabbard. But Francho was having none of it. Shaitan take the rules of gentlemanly conflict. He wasn't practiced enough yet with the sword; Perens could best him and he didn't feel like dying. He whirled the cape and flung it out violently, and saw it envelope his opponent's head like a huge, flapping bat, staggering him back and stifling his yell of rage. Francho lunged right after it and with a vicious, long-legged kick at the arm that had managed to draw the sword free sent the weapon flying as Perens clawed frantically with his other hand at the tangled cape. It finally came away, but Francho was already on him, caring nothing for the shocked cries of the spectators, who took his rapid and unorthodox action to mean he was going to skewer the man while he was blinded.

Together they went down with a great animal grunt of breath, the steel across their chests clashing together, rolling over and over on the tiles. Perens recovered quickly and Francho found himself pinned down under a face pulled up into a rictus of hatred and grappling with hands that were straining to meet around his windpipe. But Francho was more prepared to wrestle than he was to duel. Slowly his superior strength forced apart the demoniacal, quivering grip laboring to strangle him. Grabbing some air into his starved lungs he heaved up, bucked Perens over, and flung him to the ground, achieving the superior position and at the same time manag-ing, with a quick twist, to pin one of the bucking man's arms beneath his body. This gave him the vital moment it took for him to draw back his fist, and with a hammering double wallop to the jaw that banged Felipe's head against the ground he pummelled the man into senseless oblivion.

Francho got up, first on one knee and then to his feet. He stood for a moment frowning down at the blood leaking from the mouth and nose of a man who would never rest now until he had repaid him this humiliation, not until one of them was dead. People rushed up, some to inspect Felipe's condition and his own friends to lead him off a small distance, one of them furnishing a kerchief and urging him to swab at a small cut under his eye.

In a swirl and swish of stiff silk Leonora ran up to him and grasped his arm in relief. "Oh, Francisco! Oh, how terrible. You might have killed him and then the queen would have punished you, and I would again be . . ."

Breathing heavily still he looked down at her and suddenly felt drained by indifference. Was this the face he had once considered open, appealing? It was as if he could read written on her white brow the vacillating self-interest which would have mourned the death of either one of her cavaliers with equal intensity. Now the chastely fair, dimpled face just seemed empty. With a quiet tone that even surprised him he told her, "Go to Don Felipe, Doña Leonora. He is your betrothed. If he wakes with his head in your lap he will understand that all his suspicions and jealousies are groundless. Go to him, that is where you should be." Gently he removed his hand from her arm.

"What?" B . . . but I don't understand," she stuttered, astonished. "I thought you wished me to break my betrothal. You fought Don Felipe for me."

"Could I allow any man to insult you, *doña?* Even the one you are to marry?"

Pique darkened her brown eyes, a willful tightening of the mouth stiffened her features. "I think you have played with my affections, Don Francisco. You have made me certain promises. I will not tolerate such behavior."

"What affections, my lady? Those that led you to draw a marriage contract with another man?" He knew the lack of color in his voice was bewildering her but he couldn't help it. He really did not wish to hear her answer, he wished to be gone, to draw different air into his lungs, to leave behind this sad, accusing city and its discordant memories. "Fare you well, Doña Leonora," he said stiffly. "God give you happiness, cuz." He turned on his heel and, firmly waving away Pulgar and the others who had drawn apart to allow them a private conversation, he stalked toward the gates of the keyhole arch, rubbing at his swelling knuckles, disliking himself.

Dolores had not seen the whole of the fight. The hall was so overcrowded and stifling she had only come outside to fan herself for a moment. But she moved quickly forward as soon as she realized who the protagonists were and stationed herself at a distance but where she could see, her fingernails unconsciously biting into her palms, her teeth clamped on her bottom lip. The combatants writhed and rolled and then, with a loud crack of knuckles smashing into bone it was over and she saw Francho stagger up, his shoulders humped, his chest heaving for breath. She watched his friends pull him away from the supine Perens and then fall back themselves to allow him to receive Leonora de Zuniga's plaudits.

Her lips trembled and pressed together to see them speaking so intently together, the tall, mussed man with the wind blowing back the damp, black hair from his brow bending over to rejoice with his small and exquisite lady whom the Count of Perens had obviously just lost. Not that she was not happy for him. She had been first shocked and then elated to hear the incredible saga the queen had revealed about Don Francisco de Mendoza who was thenceforth Don Francisco de

Granada-Venegas; for all that, he was and had always been Francho to her. What ballad or epic could the minstrel Jamal ibn Ghulam ever sing more astonishing, more romantic than his own story. And now he had won his lady too. She imagined that perhaps Tia Esperanza and Ali and Azahra were looking down from their separate heavens and smiling. For they had loved him, just as she had.

It was so hard to stand in this haunted, richly tiled plaza, to remember how, not so long ago, he and she had ridden out from here together, master musician and not so humble slave woman, on an outing to the bazaars; lovers, friends, grinning at each other, touching fingertips surreptitiously whenever they could because they had to touch. . . . A tiny whimper of hurt escaped her but she firmly forced back tears. No more crying. What was over was over.

She was about to slip back to the Audience Hall when, to her astonishment, she realized that Francho had wheeled away from Leonora and was striding toward the gate with a stiff, angry set to his shoulders, nor did he stop when Zuniga ran a few steps after him and called his name, her face a mask of dismay.

Francho was making for the palace gates, which meant he was coming directly toward her but without seeing her. In fact, as she stood accidentally rooted in his path in a borrowed gray brocade gown, her auburn hair swept into a green satin Turkish coif, he was suddenly upon her. Her chin went up automatically to help her sustain the impact of looking again into those familiar, intense, devouring blue eyes.

Francho stopped short, his consciousness finally registering Dolores. In silence they stared at each other. Perhaps it was for a year Francho stared into the wide, luminous, tilted gray eyes that spoke so much so silently. And perhaps his own eyes spoke silently too. All sound, all sight, all the world disappeared around them. They gazed at each other in pain. He saw her lips part. He felt his heart constrict, his throat close up, he wanted to say, "I miss you." He wanted to say "I love you." But whispers of words he had said to others seemed to rattle in his head, lies, broken promises, evasions, they wanted to choke him and he had to escape.

In a hoarse, hurting growl that was his only caress for that cinnamon-flower face whose dreams he had often watched over and yearned to share in the morning light, he grated,

"There is no honor in me. God keep you always, *hermanita.*"
He slipped around her and in a stride that was almost a run
disappeared through the arched gate.

She stood there still and erect for a moment, staring straight
ahead, not really seeing them lift Perens from the ground.
Then her bosom raised in the first free, deep breath she had
drawn in weeks. She did not smile, but the pulse was beating
hard at the base of her tear-choked throat. Nothing was over
yet.

Andalusia

❧ *Chapter 32* ❧

There was crying in Granada when the sun was going down,
Some calling on the Trinity, some calling on Mahoun;
Here passed away the Koran, therein the Cross was borne,
And here was heard the Christian bell, and there the Moorish
  horn.
Down from Alhambra's minarets were all the crescents flung
And arms thereon of Aragon they with Castile's display.
One King comes in triumph, one weeping goes away.
Farewell, farewell, Granada, thou city without peer . . .

It was hot going across the high little meadow between the two great peaks, and Dolores was sorry now she had chosen to wear so heavy a gown. But it was one of her best, worn in honor of the reunion with her brothers. Ahead of her, Pepi's big, black mule seemed to know the route by memory, and her own mount placidly followed along.

Pepi called back, pointing, "Do you s—see that outcrop there and the one opposite? L—lookouts are posted on them. B—But they won't b—bother us. Even their s—scabby eyes can t—tell its me."

The pretty, flower-dotted upland meadow narrowed as they reached the outcrops, and Dolores could see they would have

665

to ride through a very tight passage leading to the heights again, and she wondered if her poor horse could take another sharp ascent in the heat. "I must say for Carlos he has chosen a good retreat," she declared, patting her forehead with a lace-edged kerchief as she urged her mount up to Pepi's. "Only an eagle could find him. It is like a jail without bars," she sniffed.

"Forty-two blackguards with p—prices on their heads, with their women and children, you want them to live in the sewers of the city like rats? Here they eat and s—sleep easy. *Sí*, it's c—cold and lonely in the w—winter." He shrugged his narrow shoulders. "I w—would m—miss my noisy little taproom, b—but then, the constable is not scouring the countryside looking to hang me—"

"Ho! Pepi! Who is it you bring with you?" a deep, disembodied voice yelled, making a menacing echo that bounced and rebounded off the rocks.

"Who knows? The king's constable, maybe," Pepi yelled back, shaking his fist up at the outcrop. "You see the great army behind us, sloptail?" Out of the side of his mouth he hissed at Dolores, "S—see why I m—made you l—leave your escort in Boleita?"

"Ride in," another deep voice approved from the opposite overhang.

Their mounts plodded up the stony defile, rounded several sharp switchbacks, and after the last one trotted out onto a level and broad clearing before a rock slope pierced by natural caves which rose along a rugged little trail like the coops in a birdhouse. Some of the alerted brigands waited in the clearing to see what had brought their outside contact up the mountain in the middle of the month; they shouted out rough greetings to Pepi and got back as good. Dolores had to smile at the raisin-eyed, stubnosed Pepi; he was Papa el Mono all over again, but with the fortunate addition of a sense of humor. She was really happy to be seeing her brothers once more. None of them had welcomed the fate that had forced their parting.

"Look here, Carlos! S—see, I've brought you a s—surprise!" Pepi bawled, and out from the gathering group of rugged mountaineers stepped a thin, hard man with a dark cloth tied over one eye who squinted with the other unreceptively at the elegant damsel before him in the cut-velvet gown and jeweled and veiled coif. But in a moment recognition flared in the one good eye and one side of the slash of a mouth rose in a smile.

"*Diablo!* By the sweat of the Saints, if it isn't my little sister Dolores!" the amused voice rasped. Accompanied by a few appreciative if crude remarks from the grinning men circled about, the rangy leader of the bandit band took a few seconds to look her up and down. A chuckle escaped him. "But from what part of God's good earth did you spring from of a sudden, sister dear?"

"From a less rocky place than you inhabit, brother." She laughed and held out her arms. "Here, help me down. 'Tis a sore ride up these mountains."

Carlos reached up his long arms to her and then set her down on the ground. She glanced around at the hard, sinister faces leering at her and the slovenly woman who had shoved into the circle to stare at her suspiciously and then brought her attention back to her brother. The somber black kerchief obviously hid a blinded eye, but in spite of deep grooves between nose and mouth the long face still showed the austere composure she remembered. "You are looking well, Carlos," she smiled at him. "A bit damaged, mayhap, but well."

His lopsided smile recalled the old, arm's length affection between them. "And you are looking astonishingly prosperous, little tavern wench. You have grown into a beautiful woman. I salute you, Dolores. You evidently have been more clever than any of us."

"S—she is p—prettier than any of us." Pepi grimaced. "How rich could I get in a c—coif and girdle?"

Carlos swung around to still the loud guffaws and yeasty murmurings of his men. *"Hombres!"* he barked. "This damsel is my sister, Doña Dolores. Find what scurvy manners you have and treat her with all respect. Any villain who makes a boorish mistake will hang by his toes for it, that is my warning to you!" He motioned to a full-bodied, disheveled woman with wild gypsy eyes and pushed her before Dolores. "This is my wife, Caratid. She has given me three strong sons, one you see here"—Caratid nursed a black-haired baby at her big breast—"and the other two are off in the cliffs hunting birds' eggs." Now he regarded her with curiosity. "And what brings you to visit our humble camp after all these years?"

"Two things, brother. I suddenly had the desire to see how it went with Pepi and you; are we not kin, after all? And . . . and I came to speak with someone Pepi had already admitted you harbor here."

Carlos's uneven teeth showed as his slow smile turned sly. "Aha. Who? Him?" He jerked his chin up, indicating someone behind and above her.

Dolores swung around. She had to shield her eyes against the sun, but the man lazily lounging against the edge of a shallow niche, one booted leg swinging off the ledge, was undoubtedly Francho. He gazed down at her from his perch, his azure eyes seeming to blaze even more brilliantly in his sun-darkened face. But the left corner of his mouth was slightly drawn up by the still pink, wicked scar that jagged down the outer edge of his face from ear to jaw. Muscled brown arms bulged from his sleeveless leather jerkin secured by a wide leather belt which acted as a sheath for a long knife riding his hip. An incongruous rolled-brim hat slanted rakishly on dark hair, which fell to his shoulders. She had just enough time to decide, with annoyance, that if anything the slightly sinister expression caused by the disfigurement of the scar only added to his potent appeal when he discontinued his survey of her and jumped lightly to the trail.

He sauntered right up to her, ignoring the envious grins of the other men. "What could you possibly want to talk with me about, *doña.*" The white smile she remembered was stiff, unwelcoming. "We can't even speak the same language, a soiled brigand and a noble lady. I might forget my tongue in front of you, and I don't relish hanging by my toes."

Dolores hoped huge disdain was showing in her eyes and not discomfort, for to have him suddenly standing before her again was causing her trouble with her breathing. She tried to steady herself. "Nor do I relish what conversation I am forced to have with you—sir—but that is what I have come for. And you will listen to me. Will he not, Carlos?"

But Francho quickly interrupted with sardonic impoliteness. "Accept my regrets for your long journey, *doña,* but I didn't ask you to come here. I have no wish to know anything but my own untrammeled and untroubled existence in this place. Do me the favor of leaving me in peace."

"Hombre!" Carlos's low rasp held a warning, and his hand rested on the black muleteer's whip wound about his shoulder and under his arm, a weapon he used with murderous ease. "My sister desires to speak with you. I suggest you honor the

lady's small request. And keep your mouth civil while she is in your hulking presence." He turned back to Dolores, who raked the discourteous ruffian who had dared reject her with a triumphant smirk. "But not now, *hermanita*. You will confer with this rogue later. Now come along with Pepi and me and tell us of yourself."

Having made up her mind that this tawny beauty, scented and powdered and riding a fine mare with velvet reins was no threat to her, Caratid added hoarsely, "Will you enter our cave, lady? I have good wine and cheese to offer to my husband's sister."

For thanks Dolores inclined her head regally but graciously, ignoring the glint of amusement in certain blue eyes for her airs. "I will be happy to accept," she murmured.

Carlos's large, dimly lit, dirt floor cave was furnished with fine rugs, chairs, and even a curtained bed in one corner, the spoils of raids on trading caravans. They sat at a carved table, and Dolores unfolded her tale, relishing Carlos's narrow-eyed smile and the awe radiating from Pepi's and Caratid's rapt faces.

"S—she arrived at my place with an escort of t—ten men-at-arms, her own guards!" Pepi interrupted, less to corroborate Dolores's story than to communicate his excitement. "A b—baroness! And the men w—wear her emblem."

Dolores dropped her gaze to her lap in false modesty. In fact, she was paying for the guards from the money Francho had left with her and never claimed back.

She swept them up in her narrative, digressing here and there to describe this or that castle or personage until finally she came to her capture by the marauding squad of Moors and her sale as a slave, the fate from which Francho rescued her. Her voice faltered then and she stopped, not sure she wanted to go into Granada. She took a sip of wine and as if to catch her breath she asked casually, "And what of him?"—inclining her head to indicate the member of their small fraternity still outside.

Carlos casually teetered back in his chair. "He has told his story, too. But to Pepi and me only."

Heat climbed in her face. "All of it?"

"All of it." Carlos still did not strew words about freely, but he regarded her flushed cheeks and made the decision to continue. "I suppose you mentioned to him sometime where Pepi had settled. He arrived at the tavern and Pepi brought him here to us. I was surprised, but I was glad to see him. I didn't ask many questions. The others did not trust his fine speech and bearing and at first he was not very sociable; he kept to himself. But after he laid a few of them out they bound up their wounds and located some respect. El Moro, they call him, because of that earring and because when we attack the caravans passing from the north to Cordoba he orders the Moorish merchants about in their own language." Carlos chuckled his dry chuckle. "He is a good man, El Moro. When we divide in two groups to surround our marks I have begun to give him the lead of one. He has a way of scaring the caravan guards so badly that they turn and run before his sword."

"And h—he plays his g—guitar a Devil's sight b—better than he used to."

Dolores looked from one to the other of her brothers. "Did he tell you . . . of his rank and family?" she said guardedly.

"Didn't I say so? Finally he spit out his whole story to me. Are we not Papa el Mono's little brotherhood, the four of us together?" The dark eyes regarded her sagely. "What do you want me to know, Dolores? That of all of us El Moro hides in the mountains from no one but himself?"

But she had regained her composure and tossed her head. "That no longer interests me. I only came here to bring him a letter from the lady to whom he has pledged his love."

Carlos pursed his lips, nodding. "That is very good of you, *hermanita*. Such a long trip . . . !"

She added a bit lamely, "And to see you, of course; the time has been too long."

"A lady to the queen!" Caratid husked in wonder, hitching up the slipping shoulder of her bodice. With her other hand she shoved behind her skirts the two little boys who had slipped quietly into the cave, already warned there was a momentous personage visiting.

"No, no, let me see them," Dolores begged, holding out her hands. "They are my nephews, after all." Two urchins, dirty, in scuffed sandals and rubbed tunics, came out from behind their mother, the little one about four, the huskier one about six, not shy and grinning broadly at the stranger.

"This is your *tía,* my sister Dolores, a fine lady. These rascals here are my sons, Antonio and Bernardo." Carlos made the introduction with quiet pride.

670

"'Bernardo the bad,' we call him," the mother added, giving the older boy a gentle cuff which he gaily dodged.

But Carlos turned a serious mien to Dolores. "They are good sons. I do not want them growing up here too long. Listen, my rich and noble sister, will you care to take them into your household, to employ them? They are blood, they can be trusted . . ."

Caratid's head jerked up, her eyes flashing alarm.

". . . when they are older?" Carlos finished blandly, as if he hadn't seen his wife's scarcely swallowed upset.

Dolores smiled soothingly at Caratid. "It would be my pleasure, Carlos. But when they are older, of course."

"You must stay the night," her brother ordered. "I will not let you go so soon, and I want you to see how well we eat, like kings and queens—almost," he chuckled. "You will sleep in our bed; it is clean and has draperies for privacy. We will stay with the children, behind there." He indicated a curtained off space. "Do not say me nay, Dolo."

She giggled to hear his old name for her. "To you? Where would I find such courage?"

As the sun lowered and shadows cooled the air, they moved their chairs to the mouth of the cave to trade more stories and news and to admire the view, looking across a deep tumble of rocks and a screen of evergreens below to the jagged, high peaks of the *sierras* touching the sky with lofty, white tips. Dolores's nose twitched happily at the buoyant aromas blending in the pure air: pine, wildflowers, roasting meat, and wood smoke, mixed with the faint animal smell of the belled goats roaming the camp.

From above she heard the strumming of a guembri and looking up the zigzagging path saw a plump woman emerge from a cave to call up to the next level, "Ho, El Moro, by all the imps and devils, sing something happy for a change instead of that constant dirge to Granada. How about a lively one, one of those fancy dances the rich folk like. You do those good."

The guembri strummer looked down at the women below his perch and spat to the side. "If you do not like my repertoire, Tula," he bantered, "pick yourself up and move. There is an empty hole above Baldhead's cave you could squeeze your haunches into, with even some room to spare for your husband."

"Eh, eh, listen to him," Tula laughed, raising a finger in a lewd gesture. She brandished the wood paddle she had been using to remove the rabbit meat pies for supper from her crude stone oven. "If I move over there who will sweep out your dirty cave for you, eh ungrateful, answer me that? And don't tell me Teresa. She has given up on you, she gets nothing for her pains but a pinch on the behind. Is that a way to cheat a pretty young girl?"

Since she made the business of all the members of the camp her own, Tula waited for an answer and got what she expected —a hoot and a loud thrum on the guembri. "Laugh if you will, you wretch," she called up, chuckling, "but it's not good for man to live alone. Not one that's got his stick and stones, that is." She glanced down and shook her fist at the general mirth of the men sitting around below, then disappeared back through the dark mouth of the cave.

The musician leaned back with a grin against the edge of his cave and thrummed a loud chord and then another, searching for inspiration. His fingers of their own accord seemed to finally find an air that squeezed Dolores's heart, and although he did not sing with it now, he had done so many times before:

> My dame is a rose, a wild red rose,
> Red rose bloom perfect and joy to my heart.
> But pluck her I cannot to hold to my breast,
> Sharp thorns are her nature that hold us apart.
> Dolores, Dolo—

The tune broke off with a discordant twang, startling even Carlos, who, Dolores realized, had been covertly watching her as she listened. He swung around and yelled up, "Hey, *amigo*, the lady here wishes to converse with you. Be polite and oblige her."

"*Sí*, Jefe, *de inmediato!*" came the sardonic baritone. Conversations around the cook fires and cave mouths broke off again, heads turned.

There was a scrabble of loose gravel and Francho leaped down the last few feet from the path to land lightly before her on springy, muscled legs. He planted his hands on his leather-clad hips and waited, coolly, and she could read nothing in his eyes but false amusement.

She began to fume inside as she considered his impertinent

attitude. He was the villain, not her, and here he was doing her a favor to listen to her. Whoreson dog!

To Carlos she said smoothly, "Not here with the whole camp listening, pray. This is a private matter." She thought her brother would be good enough to offer his cave, but instead he answered, "Very well. There is supper to prepare here anyhow." His tone became peremptory. "Take her up to your place," he ordered Francho.

Dolores started and widened her eyes at her brother and opened her mouth to reject this idea, firmly and haughtily, but Carlos brought his dark, quietly threatening eye to bear on her too. "Go with him," he ordered softly. He wasn't smiling.

Francho's unwillingness was evident too, the square under-lip grinned in annoyance, but he shrugged and gestured stiffly up the path. Dolores set her nose to the loftiest heights of condescension and swept past him. She started confidently along the steep path, but her disdain soon turned to discomfort as the rough ground bruised her feet through the light soles of her shoes. But when he pushed past her and offered a hand to help her negotiate the climb she ignored it, picking her way over the pebbles and stones in stubborn independence, shutting out the muffled guffaws she heard from various sides.

She paid no attention to Tula either, whose fleshy arms were covered with flour as she grinned round-eyed and curious at this bejeweled apparition, but wobbled past her and finally reached the cave above, which was Francho's. He stood back to allow her to enter into the dim recess. But her patience, never the best, had worn thin, and she immediately turned to lash out as he followed her in, ducking his dark head.

"My lord Marquis of Olivenza, your paucity of manners is only exceeded by the baseness of your condition!"

"Who told you I was here?" he glowered.

"No one. It just occurred to me you might be, since it seemed you were nowhere else. And I made certain by prying it out of Pepi before he brought me up here to this goat's roost."

"I want to be left alone, can you understand that, Dolores?" he muttered irritably.

"No, I can't, but as far as I am concerned you may jump off that cliff and smash into a million pieces for all I would stop you. However, there is something I want to clear from my conscience and that is why I am here. I want to discharge my debt to you."

"Debt? How would you ever be in my debt?"

She contemplated him stonily for a moment, but independent of her will her eyes also studied the jagged scar that pulled at one side of his mouth, making permanent the flat laughter circles that had always attracted her. They took in the dark frown that hung like a ledge over the deep blue eyes, and glimpsed to the strong, bronzed neck where a moving Adam's apple gave away his tension. "I am more in your debt than you think," she answered with an insouciant flip of her shoulder. "However, you will change your mind about my arrival in a second. I've brought you a message—from Leonora de Zuniga."

He stared down at the square bit of paper in her hand as if it were an arrest warrant and then blinked at her, uncomprehendingly. *"You* carried *her* letter?"

Dolores shrugged. "Evidently she had made many fruitless inquiries for you. I had once told her we were children together, and when she grew quite desperate she dropped her pride and begged me to say if I might think where you were; in fact, that was what popped the idea into my head that you might be with Carlos. At one time I had gladly wounded her with certain—uh—tales, but now I pitied her. And I owed you. So I agreed I might be able to find you and deliver this message."

"Is . . . is she well?" Francho asked numbly.

"Well enough. Oh, her betrothal to the Count of Perens still holds"—Dolores arched her neck so that she was looking up at him from the corner of her eye—"but it seems she secretly prefers you." Now she righted her head and looked him up and down pointedly. "As she knew you last winter, of course. Not the desperado you have become in five months." She shoved the letter into his hand.

Recovering, he stuck it into his belt. "Thank you, *doña,* for your Cupid's offices," he said with sarcasm.

"Think nothing at all of it, my lord," she mimicked his tone.

He stalked to a rude log table, unstoppered a flagon of wine with his teeth, and looked back over his shoulder casually. "What news of the honest world, *doña?"*

She was glad for a moment to leave the bitterly personal for the general, although she had to lift an eyebrow that he cared. "Are you really interested? Much has happened." She began to drift around the nearly bare cave as she talked, as if she were interested in this bit of rock or that bit, but it was motion for its own sake, merely to soothe her nerves. "Finally the queen has decided to finance Columbo's insane voyage to the Indies—you remember him, the peculiar Italian from Genoa who went about begging for money for his expedition? Her Majesty almost had to pawn her own jewels, but the Aragonese treasury advanced the sum and three ships are departing Palos in August, westward—to their destruction, probably. The most unsettling event was the edict of expulsion against the Jews which Inquisitor Torquemada posted in March, signed, of course, by Their Majesties. So many of the Hebrews had acted as lenders of money, it caused quite a furor and panic among the bankers and those who had accounts with them, but nevertheless the Holy Office is being most diligent about sweeping the country clean of them. I have seen them on the roads in great, long, crowded masses from all over Spain, plodding toward ships to take them to Africa." Dolores had wandered the circuit of the cave, and now she stood before him again. She could not help the pity that softened her voice; she could not help wondering what he might think of the deed, this product of the tolerant Tendilla and di Lido. "They took along what they could, the young and the old, women and children, rich and poor, weeping for their Spanish homes, their ancestors, their lives. It touched the heart with sorrow."

He said nothing and so she shrugged. "For the rest the tidings from Portugal are good; the news from Sicily is bad. And the brave Marquis of Cadiz whom we all thought so indestructible died of lung fever not a month ago."

He had listened to her while he slowly poured the wine into clay mugs, with his back turned to her, brooding, she thought. But now he faced her with his mask of unconcern stubbornly in place and offered her a mug. "You were right," he shrugged. "I have no interest that Columbo will founder in the unknown wastes of ocean, that the Israelites are banished, that Ponce de Leon is dead. Good Valdepeñas wine, *doña,* a toast to the humble life. 'Tis much happier to be simple and not choke the mind with worries."

Never in her life had she felt so bewildered. She looked into the stubborn face, the eyes that met hers with such an effort that a vein pulsed at his temple, and she did not know what to think, nor how to reach this formerly vital man who was balking away from the mainstream of his life.

"You are despicable!" she flung at him, turning away the cup. "Not were I dying of thirst would I drink with so great an oaf." She turned about sharply to run from this dislikable stranger who was tearing her heart into shreds, but after a few steps stopped, damning pride. She swung around, her skirts whispering on the packed earth floor. "Francho, for the dear Virgin's merciful sake, what are you doing here?"

"Leave me, Dolores. You could not understand."

"You had more than a man could wish for—honor, wealth, the wreath of a hero. Why did you leave it for this disgrace?" She moved closer to him and pressed, "Do you know, they think you disappeared because you fear Felipe de Guzman's vengeance? You understand if you come back he will never rest until one or the other of you is dead sometime, somewhere, so deeply have you humiliated him. They think you fled . . ."

He almost choked on his mouthful of wine and spat it out. "Because I fear Perens?" he finished for her in an incredulous growl. "They say that!"

She refused to shrink before the gathering storm on his face. "Some say that, yes. What else can they think? And your friends are so mystified they might almost agree."

Francho hurled his mug to smash against the far wall. "Shaitan take them all, the stupid . . . I should have killed that dog with his own sword and had done with it." The dark curls clung damply to his forehead. "Show a bit of mercy and one is labeled not a man."

"Well, what was it made you run? Doña Leonora, then? Did her choice of Felipe hurt you so much?"

With a short bark of laughter he snapped, "Her choice of him, lady? The last time I saw her she had decided a wealthy Venegas was better than a Mendoza bastard. She came out to offer to break her betrothal. If that whoreson Perens is alive it is because I *gave* him to her." He slammed an angry fist into his hand. "Ah, Jesu, what is the difference. I don't want it—any of it."

But she watched him smolder at the suspicion of cowardice clouding his name at Court and jumped as he slapped his hat to the table with violent irritation. Her heart began to lift a little to see she had yanked up an edge of the barrier he had erected between himself and the world. She remained silent, mentally willing open that little breach for what might leak out. But it did not leak, it gushed. . . . He rounded on her.

"Three ugly deaths were the price of my honor and wealth!" he burst out. "Two innocent children paid for my title, an admirable general I murdered, I stabbed him in the back for my estates. I betrayed the trust of a ruler—a man—whom I found gentle and sensitive, whom I liked, maybe even loved. I broke the jaw of my damsel's almost-discarded suitor only for rage with her meanness of character. And you—I took it upon myself first to punish you with cruelty and then to make you my mistress and leave you. My birthright was so dearly bought it was ashes in my mouth when I had it. To Doña Leonora I was merely the new Marquis of Olivenza, to Tendilla a boost into the Governor's Palace and a votive offering to the memory of my mother whom he had loved. To the queen I provided expiation for her conscience. To you? To you I should have been a protector and instead I was a rogue. And to myself I became a torment and a fraud."

He sat on the table and pulled one leg up with his arms hooked around it so that his chin almost rested on his knee. The brooding eyes stared at her, but most of the fury left his voice. "So—am I truly Francisco de Granada-Venegas, upholder of the ancient house, lord of manors and overseer of tenants' lives?" Sarcasm took over from the spent anguish. "Or am I a figment of necessity, Tendilla's necessity and the queen's necessity and the war, with a new name as fragile as any of the old—Francho or Mendoza or Jamal ibn Ghulam? I went away to find myself. To go back to Francho the cutpurse who was sure and untroubled and search out the way I could have gone for myself without the advent of Tendilla. I must know in my own heart what I am."

Dolores stared back at him. Was this the man she thought she had adored? Hadn't she too bought life from death, which, if not murder, had anyhow laid poor Blanca in a grave not marked her own? She had not asked God to take Blanca, but she did not consider herself evil to have accepted the circumstance. And by using the sad dissolution of one life to build the vital substance of her own, was this not at least a small resurrection for the spirit of Blanca Ganavet? And here was this great hulk, a bold warrior with sword strapped to hip who would waste the terrible heedless deaths caused by war by wallowing in their tragedy and obliterating their meaning.

Her words came out clipped and scornful. "I will tell you what you are; you are a coward!" She sneered at the small, automatic jerk of his hand toward his knife. "You did not leave Granada, you ran. You always run when life becomes unpleasant, as you fled the monastery when polishing candlesticks bored you, as you welcomed the Count's arrival in your life when his offered pleasures outdid those of Ciudad Real, as you refused to recognize the feelings you had for me because it would complicate your life." She flung at him, "What's the matter, Don Francisco, you want to go back to being Francho the cutpurse, the simple, ragged boy, because it is too difficult to be obligated to a man like Don Iñigo who put the world in your hands, to owe a queen of easier conscience your utmost service for her generosity, to be responsible to your estates and tenants and to the reputation you established of a brave Christian knight? Must you always have another existence to try on like a new doublet while you discard the rub of the old?"

It was hot in the dim rock confines of the cave, oddly. Or maybe she was just hot. With an angry gesture she pulled off the Turkish-type coif and whipped it about as a fan, for sweat was trickling between her breasts under the heavy velvet of her bodice. Since he said nothing, just stared in silence at her from under beetling brows, she simply hurtled on, her anger outweighing the fact that she really didn't care anymore. He was not anyone she had thought he was. "You found much to admire among the Moors, do you remember? It was your hope that Don Iñigo would indeed be appointed governor for he alone among the candidates could be trusted not to despoil the city or vent a conqueror's fury upon the innocent. I was merely casually talking to Pietro di Lido—he looks at me so shrewdly, I do not think he believes I spent all those months as a hostage in Reduan's house—and he mourned to me that you would have been a great service to Tendilla now, helping him administer with a good knowledge of the Arabic mind. Anyone can see Tendilla needs adherents to offset the jealous men who think his policies too lenient. And the Archbishop Talavara in his saintly way has slowly garnered thousands of converts to the Cross, but not fast enough for the Holy Office, who would prefer the stake and the rack to make conversions. You loved Granada once, for all it was a heathen city. Now you sit here in the mountains when the time cries out for men of liberal view to prevent the tragedy of Malaga, of mass oppression and banishment for the Moors as happened to the Jews."

"Where did you absorb such politic philosophy, *doña?*" he jibed with half-closed eyes. "I thought you were interested only in jewels and gossip and fancy gowns."

"Where?" she flared. "Do you not recognize it? Much of it is your own, as you told it to me in the Alhambra. So many hours I listened to you, and I learned—" She choked to a stop and swallowed. Hot tears suddenly stung at her eyes. If he had meant to hurt her by demeaning her intelligence he had.

In a slick movement as lithe as the spring of a leopard he bounded the few paces toward her and grabbed her wrist, as if the charm of the sudden white smile on his face would sweep away her mood and stop the words that were jabbing their truth into his brain. He looked down at her. "Is that all you remember of Granada, the high-idealed talks we had? Have a drop of wine with me, Karima, and let's remember all the rest. *Ay, Dios mío,* how much more there was. . . ." He drew her to him. She felt his arm encircling her waist with a familiar, possessive warmth, and at first her astonishment with his utter insensitivity turned her to jelly. She saw a glint of excitement flare in the depths of his eyes. "I miss you, *querida.* I often long for you, I wake and yearn to put my arms about you . . . like this . . ." The other arm went about her and she could feel his breath on her face, knew his lips were lowering slowly to hers.

She jerked away from him, drew back her arm, and slapped him across the face with all her might, the tears in her eyes no brighter than the fire of her rage. "You vile monster, get your hands off me. I remember nothing from Granada, nothing, for it was nothing but carnal sin. Once I loved you so much that I finagled and lied to have you. But now I'm free of you, the Holy Spirit be thanked, and you can rot in this hole the rest of eternity if you think that will relieve you of life. For my part I will have a man, a man with the courage to carve his own image from the fortune he is given. I make the dainty Zuniga a present of you. You are a sniveling coward and . . . and . . ." She panted for breath. "And a cad!"

In spite of his half-hearted move to stop her she slipped under his arm and fled stumbling down the uneven trail, scrubbing away the tears from her eyes so she would not break her neck, passing the cookfires orange in the twilight without even seeing them, until she reached the safety of her brother's cave. That she had ever come at all, she seethed to herself, made her a greater fool than that rascal above shrugging over her rebuff, counting it as little as he had counted her love. She prayed for the night to pass swiftly as she smoothed out her face to enter the cave. She went in finally and with a small smile accepted the seat Caratid offered at her table.

Francho flung himself down on his pallet, cradling the earthenware flagon and in lugubrious silence began to drink himself into insensibility. Why, in the name of all the weeping angels in heaven, had he done that, insulted her attempt to befriend him with a vile sexual assault? Miserable, feeling the sting of her scorn and her fingers against his face, he quickly finished off the wine in the flask. Then he found a full leather bottle of aguardiente. He stared at the round flanks of a white unicorn adorning a plundered tapestry hung on one of his rough walls and drank, steadily, in wretchedness. And when the bottle was empty he hurled it into a corner and tried to rise to find some more or call Tula to bring some, but he lurched back onto the straw. Curiously an obscure memory pricked at his spinning brain: "Salute, you *bobiecas!*" an erstwhile cut-purse had greeted the liveried guards at Mondejar, "Salute, for yesterday you would not spit at me."

Yes, yes, they shall all salute, his mind wobbled, for I am the Marquis of Olivenza and that is what I was born. I am not a fraud. No—not fraud. Coward, she said.

Voices seemed to dart out at him from the dark recesses of his lair. Carlos's voice, dubious, "Can you forget the years of training that made you a gentleman?" Di Lido's voice, "A Marquis merely acts like a Marquis." His own voice as it roared in his head, "Tell the truth, scum, do you not really disdain these crude and ignorant bandits you have been emulating?" "Why don't you stand before a mirror," some voice or other said to him, "your reflection will not reveal the weaknesses that you feel, only those which you show." "Weakness?" babbled back another whisper from an opposite cobwebbed corner, "is it weakness to suffer from the knowledge of one's own stupidity, cupidity, duplicity? And to be tormented by a great sadness?"

A little glow seemed to creep from the furthest corner of his cavern. No, it was *not* weakness, and this was what Dolores was trying to make him see. It was reprehensible only if such human regret turned into the only meaning for life. Now it was his own voice that hollered out to keep that warming light from fading. "No, no, I am not craven, that's not it, Dolores, my tavern witch, my angry beauty, *querida mía, querida. . . .* I was stupid. I hated myself. I was ashamed. . . ."

Spin, spin away, head, he yelled mutely at the drunken physical paralysis that kept him pinned to his bed. I am not your prisoner anymore, he railed. And tumbled into a whirling spiral that sucked him down into darkness.

The barking of the camp dogs woke him up as he lay curled atop the pallet in a defensive ball. A bleary-eyed glance showed him sun already slanting along the ledge outside his cave. But the problem that precipitated him stumbling out of the cave and further up along the ledge, bare-chested and just in his hosen, was physical, and he just reached the great boulder and rounded it in time. Having accomplished his urgent task he shook his head to clear it, then trotted across a little plateau to where a thin fall of water from the melting snow at the top of the peak came over a cliff and descended like a tattered ribbon to form a little stream. He yanked off his hosen and with a whoop to keep up his courage, for the water was icy, waded under the sparkling fall and stood there letting everything wash away, dust, dirt, bad head from the spirits, yesterday . . .

Vigorously revived he loped back to his cave and found a loaf of bread and a pan of rabbit stew had been left outside in a niche too high for the dogs. Goodhearted old Tula. He'd have to search all of Castille for a talented baker like her to put in his kitchens. He took the food inside the cave but stopped for a moment, his head coming up, for there was a hint of jasmine perfume still remaining in the air. He smiled, his mind cleansed by the cold water and cool, dry air of the mountain morning, and sat down to fill his growling stomach.

His kitchens? What? Somehow, while he had soddenly slept off the wine and brandy, God had opened his inner eye to the truth of Dolores's words. He could not always take the best and avoid the worst. He must choose and forever decide, or forever be an interloper, an impermanent shadow on life's stage. So be it. He had been recognized Francisco de Granada-Venegas and so he would stride in the world.

It would hardly be a miserable existence, he thought, sardonic with himself. Honor and wealth. And a noble wife? Now something else clicked into place in his head. What was Leonora from the first moment but a charming part of the goal he had once set, a matching piece to the rest of the pattern? His sons would have rightfully carried the ancient Zuniga quarter on their arms and he would have had a dimpled blond lady to wife. One who might love him for this or for that, but who knew little of him and whose love was conditional, liable to vanish under stress. Did he want that? Had he ever wanted that, when the tilted gray eyes and responsive lips of a gallant, make-believe baroness had answered the every need of his heart?

Belatedly he pulled Leonora's letter from where it lay forgotten under his leather tunic and held it up to catch the light from the entrance. His eyes moved over it quickly. ". . . of what use is a woman's pride when a beloved remains absent? Return to me, Don Francisco, for I suffer the results of my selfish vanity and now know the values to cherish. Do you remember the words I spoke when you first left for Granada: I will have not other than you for husband? And so the promise remains in my heart although I am forced by your disappearance to continue my betrothal to Don Felipe. I beg you to return soon, before it is too late. . . ."

He crumpled up the letter and laughed softly, a clear, free laugh. "It *is* too late. You will have to make do with your heir to a dukedom, my lady Zuniga. If your man stays away from me and thereby continues to live—"

Loose pebbles on the ledge crunched and Carlos appeared, ducking his head to enter the cave. He dropped down beside Francho with a somber face reddened by contact with the cold water of the stream. "I haven't heard you laugh like that since you arrived here. It sounds good, *amigo,* it sounds more like the rascal I knew as a boy."

Francho grinned. "Carlos, I'm returning to my own world."

The lifelong outlaw shrugged. "I expected it, sooner or later. You don't belong here in this barless prison. You didn't belong at Papa el Mono's either, you who could read and write and recite in Latin and sing the chants along with the monks at the church. 'Tis not the worst thing in the world to be called 'my lord' and bow to the queen. If knavery were not so ingrained in me I would almost envy you." And then, with a sly and casual air he added, "See, sir nobleman, if you ride fast enough you may catch up with Dolores and have company on your journey back."

"Is she gone already?" Francho gaped.

"At the first light of dawn. And she did not seem happy." He stolidly contemplated his friend.

"I love her." Francho said.

"I know. She loves you too. But you have hurt her."

"I'll fix that," Francho muttered, jumping up to shoulder his way into the leather jerkin and knot the thongs that closed it.

From his sitting position Carlos punched him in the calf. "Wait. Sit down, *hombre,* I have something to tell you," he rasped, "and a few more minutes won't ruin your life. It might help it. She swore me to secrecy but what honor does a robber have? And my sister has grown a peculiar sense of pride, one she thinks should go with her title. I don't agree with her."

Francho obliged him in spite of his sense of haste. In this place Carlos was obeyed, and besides, he had rarely heard the man say so many sentences all at once.

"My sister was not mistress to the Duke of Medina-Sidonia. He is impotent from an arrow wound received in the battle for Ronda. She made a business arrangement with him, something to do with the lands she took over, and also, because there was land but no money, she agreed to ornament his arm and salve his pride by suggesting proof of his continuing virility, and for this she was paid well. He never more than kissed her hand, in public or private, she insists. A wild tale. But I believe her." Carlos slipped a small dagger from his belt and began cleaning his fingernails with the tip of it, avoiding Francho's rapt stare for the moment. "She says she has lain with no one in her life but you, no one, and that if she was mistress to anyone it was to you." Now he looked up to meet Francho's gaze with his own hard one-eyed stare. "I believe that too."

"Then why didn't she tell me? All the time we were together in Granada, sharing everything, not just passion . . ."

"She says she wanted you to love her so much nothing else mattered. Women!" Carlos spat sideways. "They think crazy. Sure. Can you imagine her running here after you, when even before she was dragged to Granada the great Duke had begged her to marry him when his sick wife died?" A lascivious chortle accompanied his half-smile. "She has the man lusting for her even though his dong doesn't work. But she doesn't choose him, more the fool, she, to give up a Duke! Now she is traveling back at all speed to accept the honorable marriage proposal of a younger man, I do not recall his title, not a memorable one, but he has much money and all his teeth . . ."

Francho had had enough. "The Devil she is!" he swore, jumping up again to collect his guembri and stuff a few items into his saddlebag. "She loves me," he muttered adamantly.

"From her parting remarks it would seem she hates you."

"If she hates me she'll have to prove it another way than by traveling a hundred leagues to call me a cursed fool."

Carlos scrambled to his feet, scooped up from the floor a belt on which hung a huge and ugly sword, and handed it to Francho. He watched him feverishly buckle it on. "Pepi says she's got a dozen guards with her. Take enough of my men with you to handle them while you handle her; you'll have plenty to do to convince the wench you aren't the rascal she makes you. And I hope you'll not forget to keep a strap handy in your house, my lord Marquis."

They clasped hands strongly. "*Adiós,* Carlos, my friend, and gramercy," Francho said huskily. "If you ever need a favor of any kind, you know whom to find. Of *any* kind. And you will come to the baptismal of your first nephew even if you have to sneak in dressed as Caratid's mother." They both chuckled. "San Bismas keep the path smooth under your feet."

"Go with God, *amigo.*" The angular highwayman smiled. He turned to cry down to the bandits scratching before their caves, "Ho, Julio, Manuel, I want twenty men to follow El Moro on an urgent mission. See they're saddled and ready in ten swings of the gallow's rope. Move!"

He watched Francho lope down the path to the clearing where his horse was tethered and saw him turn back and look up for a minute. "Give Teresa the loot in my cave," Francho called out and then spied the tousle-haired girl coming from her den. "Use it for a dowry," he bawled at her.

"Cut around to the Slitnose pass," Carlos shouted. "If you ride fast you can come around and get ahead of her, catch her just below Pepi's."

He watched the little troop, bristling with plundered weapons, ride off into the pine belt, Francho in the lead. "And I would never have told you what I did had you not first said you loved her, Marquis," he grunted. "She is my sister. *I* care for her, too."

Below, the road made several twists before plunging into a dense wood that marked for a number of leagues the edge of the plain before Montero. Dolores was glad they had made such good time for she would be happy to be out of the shadowy forest and well into Montero before dark. She was looking forward to the comfort of the good inn there to raise her spirits a little. If anything could. It was strange how one could breathe and see and hear and yet be dead inside. Everything inside her was eaten away, leaving a hollowness so empty even the hurt was lost. But not the anger. The anger seemed to sit on the surface of her skin like a sheen of perspiration; it at least gave her the appearance of being alive, she thought.

Her sergeant of the guard rode at her side; the other men, outfitted in antelope tabards over leather armor, rode in double file behind them, pennants attached to their lances, and a baggage donkey plodded along in the rear. From time to time the sergeant glanced sideways at his employer from under his metal casque as if measuring her inclination to a little conversation. A stocky, Andalusian-born mercenary, he liked to talk, but his lady seemed more withdrawn coming down the mountain than on the trip up.

Dolores dabbed at her face with a bit of lace. It was cursed hot for June in these highlands. She had donned a more appropriate gown of embroidered linen with a low, brooch-clasped neckline that left her shoulders bare under the minimal covering of an airy scarf, and the wide skirt of her gown was draped over her sidesaddle and the horse's flanks. She wore no coif except a cool, circlet-bound square of floating pink chiffon which, although it contrived to shade her eyes, allowed the sun to shine warmly on the auburn coil of hair at her nape. She comforted herself by thinking that just this one more bend and they would enter the coolness of the forest, and in Montero she would certainly buy one of those straw hats the peasants used in the fields.

Confidently they cantered around the blind curve. "Hold!" her guard yelled out, and she found herself yanking on the reins, sawing at the horse's mouth to pull him up hastily, as did the soldier at her side. A lone horseman sat firmly astride the road, deliberately blocking them from going forward. The heart Dolores thought beat no longer jumped to her throat. So did her anger.

The sergeant barked out, "You there! Fall back and let us pass."

Ignoring the order the rider spurred up and silently advanced toward them. The sergeant reached for his sword. Dolores knew what he saw; a broad-shouldered brute in yeoman's leather wearing a heathen earring, a broadsword, and a smile menacing for its insolence. He was carrying a long, heavy staff. Swiftly she placed a restraining hand on the sergeant's arm, causing him to stare at her in surprise. She hoped the guard noticed there was no warmth in her narrowed eyes. "Let him come, sergeant. He's only one man and we are ten."

"But my Lady . . ." the man objected, and was ignored.

"What do you want?" Dolores challenged Francho curtly.

The white smile broadened. "You."

Her back stiffened. "Give way and let us go on, brigand, before my men run you down."

"I'll have a word with you first, *doña*—"

"I do not speak to common louts. Do you give way?" And when Francho's grin never wavered nor did his stance barring their progress, she ordered grimly, "Sergeant. Clear him away."

The soldier went for his sword, the guards behind him lowered their pikes, but at that moment the scoundrel reared up his horse and yelled, "Santiago and San Bismas!" and from the close quarters of the high boulders squeezing the road on either side twenty menacing bows and arquebuses, cocked and aimed and ready to sing death sprang into view, topped by twenty surly, weather-beaten faces. Dolores's hired guards froze, knowing the cutthroats above them had the advantage and would not hesitate to kill.

But the sergeant proved he was worth his pay. He dug spurs into his mount, swung his sword about his head, and launched a courageous attack upon the leader of the scurrilous bunch, not even hearing Dolores's weak cry. But his valor was greater than his skill; nor had he ever dueled against the staff the highwayman used to defend himself.

Francho parried several of the man's sword cuts with his stout pole, the vigor of the guard's blows shooting pain down his arm and shoulder. Then his opening came suddenly and swiftly; he reversed his grip and cracked the lengthy pole against the sergeant's helmet with just enough force that the man tumbled stunned from his horse. Francho tossed the pole to the ground.

"You've killed my guard, you villain!" Dolores screeched out. He cantered quickly up to her and avoiding her hands that were trying to claw his eyes out dragged her kicking onto his mount. Grunting, he dumped her face down across the front of his saddle and whacked her hard on the rear to stop her squirming. "Dungpicker! Filthy whoreson goat-headed swine!" she screamed, beating on the horse's withers.

"Softly, my noble lady," he laughed. "Your muleteer curses will shock the ears of my men."

To escape the bitter scowls of Dolores's helpless guards and the leering interest of his own men, he galloped forward along the road a way and into a thick stand of trees that thoroughly screened them from prying eyes and ears. He swung off the horse and lifted her down, holding her steady as she recovered the breath that had been jounced out of her—and caught by the wrist the furious slap that, breath or not, she swung at him. In fact she took his own breath away standing before him with her dignity disheveled, pin-bereft locks of hair tumbling wantonly over cheeks the high color of a sun-ripened peach, a disarrayed scarf displaying the moist, gleaming smoothness of her clefted bosom heaving now with spite and the rough handling. Her eyes flashed silver lightning at him, her wide, lips were pulled back stiffly over gleaming teeth as if she wanted to bite him, and in the middle of everything it occurred to him that she was not only beautiful, she was— infinitely interesting.

"*Ay, gatamontes,* stop battling," he shook her by the shoulders. "I'm not going to rape you. I just want you to listen as you made me listen yesterday. I am returning to Granada, here and now."

"That concerns me not the least bit! Take your hands off me, ruffian," she spat out, struggling.

"Listen to me, hear what I am saying. If you love me come with me, help me to build afresh, Dolores—"

"I despise you! I've already found a gentleman who will give me a contented life and I'm going to wed him. He isn't handsome, he isn't dashing; he's a petty nobleman who is kind and selfless and he loves me dearly. He is all I want and you can find some other foolish woman's heart to wring. Now let me go!"

"Not while I live will you marry such paragon as that, *hermanita.* I won't allow it."

Her hands gripped into fists. "You won't allow . . . and just how do you think you are going to stop it?"

He grinned down at her because she was so transparent. "Simple. I will tell the gentleman in whose bed you were warming your backside—and other things—for so many months in Granada."

"Oh! You vilest of vile dogs! You would not, you could not do such a thing."

"Oh yes I could and would. Because you love me."

"I don't love you. I never did. You just seemed better than Reduan and I was a helpless woman trying to survive."

"Helpless?" he choked back a laugh.

"I don't love you. Make your mind up to that."

"You do. And if you marry it will be only to me."

"I don't love you, I don't, I don't. And if you drive away all my suitors and force me to marry you I shall never again speak to you!"

"Good. Do you promise that?"

"Oh!" Dolores cried, exasperated beyond endurance with this lout whose only aim in life seemed to be to humiliate and torment her, and she pushed fiercely at his chest to escape his hard grasp. Then suddenly something seeped through into her addled brain. She stiffened and left off her struggles. "What did you say?" she gasped. She lifted her head, finally seeing beyond her battered pride into the intensity of his gaze, where amusement and tenderness fought for precedence, emotional currents visible in the blue depths that bathed her with a warmth she had thought she would never feel again.

"I said I love you, Dolores. I love you, I love you, I adore you, and you are absolutely right, I am an *estúpido* who betrayed his own heart by not wanting to hear its song. Forgive me. Some way, somehow I will make it up to you."

"B—but Leonora?"

"She has nothing to do with this. She had become merely a symbol to me—probably from the moment I first laid eyes on you in Toledo. See, I brought her letter." He pulled the crumpled paper from his jerkin. "Read it. She wants me to return to her. She is as charming of face and form as when I thought I loved her, and her name still as proud. But I do not want her. My dreams as I gathered my thoughts together here in the mountains were haunted by your face, not hers. The happiest months of my life I spent in Granada with you, and they were happy because of you, *mi alma.* You loved me once, Dolores; love me still, I beg you. I offer this blind and witless soul for what it's worth and I humbly ask you to be my wife and to marry me. And to forgive my incredible wrongheadedness."

She suddenly felt overwhelmed. "You are a lord of the realm. You want me? Daughter of a rascal tavernkeep? A bogus lady whom the Court will always suspect was the mistress of Enrique de Guzman? And whose brother is a common highwayman wanted by the Crown?"

"Papa el Mono's daughter is as much a lady as I am a Marquis, my love." He cupped her face in his hands and turned it up to him. "I want her for her beauty and intelligence and spirit. Her father and brother and the entire Court can chase their tails. I'm not marrying them."

Dolores tried to catch hold of her dwindling sanity. "Indeed, sir, you take much for granted," she protested. "I have not said I would be your wife. I have other plans, you forget—"

"I didn't forget . . ." he growled, and his mouth came down on hers, hard at first as if to make an irrevocable imprint, his fingers slanted across her cheeks, and then, as she didn't stir, his lips softened and moved on hers. He raised his head, his heart in his eyes, and then tenderly, lovingly, once, twice more, he kissed her.

She thought little birds were fluttering on feathery wings inside of her. She opened her eyes as he slowly dropped his hands. She raised her own and with a trembling fingertip she traced the smile circles that edged the corners of his mouth and the thin, rough scar that ran to it, traced the strong, square underlip and curled her finger back quickly as he nibbled at it. "You could have lost me," she whispered. "I might have married without even seeking you. You would never have known."

"I may be stupid and craven, but I'm not quite crazy." He

smiled down at her. "Estaban Ebarra knows where I holed up. The least little public move you made I would have known it in time."

"You would have?" she breathed, eyes widening with child-like wonder.

For answer he pulled her to him and wrapped his arms around her, holding her tight against him, burying his face in her loosened hair and inhaling as if he were breathing her in, holding her that way long enough so that she could feel his heartbeat accelerating through the rough, heavy leather of his jerkin, clamoring as hard as hers was. But he made no move to claim from her any further embrace commensurate with the limitless passion they had shared. With wonder again she realized he wouldn't, for now he understood he loved her; now she was precious, fragile as jade.

Shaitan take that. She flung her arms around his neck and pulled his head back by the dark, thick hair at his nape. "Well, I don't believe you," she laughed in a flutelike trill, although she did, but she pulled his mouth down to her and fastened her own onto it, joyously thrusting her tongue against his startled lips until they opened and let her in, searching his mouth, clinging to him, kissing him deeply and thoroughly and passionately and intimately until her breasts swelled and her legs turned to butter and she smelled on his breath the exciting musk of his desire that drove her mad. She pressed her body erotically against the tensed muscles of his, and she didn't care if he pushed her to the ground and took her then and there with the throbbing male hardness that she loved, that was hers and that she craved. She squirmed, she wanted him; she was lost, he was all of her world, had always been—

But with heroic strength he peeled her off of him and jumped back, holding her away with one arm. In spite of the blue flame of desire burning in his eyes his face had gone pale under its tan as he fought against himself. "*Pecaminosa!*" he laughed shakily, restraining her. "Wanton tease! You are trying to seduce me. You offend my virtue, woman."

"Francho . . ." she began.

"No! Not without sanction," he roared. He saw the direction of her gaze and her shoulders begin to shake. "At least not until we reach a proper bed," he added helplessly, looking down at himself.

Laughter spurted out of her, exploded out of him, and, mirth drowning out their frustration, they staggered against each other weak with happiness, knowing the wait was not long but that their love was.

Presently they mounted his horse again and cantered back to where their men waited, she sitting haughtily before him. What was even funnier to both their eyes was seeing both brigands and dispirited guards, wilted in place like heat-melted statues, struggle quickly to alert stances as their employers came upon them. Dolores held her hand up to keep her guards in place while, with a few quiet words and a salute, Francho dismissed his companions and they disappeared behind the rocks. When he came back to her she was smiling at him and together they wheeled their mounts and rode on most serenely to continue the journey. This time it was Francho's signal that ordered the guards to follow behind them.

The sergeant at arms, nursing a headache, scratched his sprouting shadow of a beard. He was still struggling to accept that the baroness, missing her head kerchief and showing signs of hasty putting-together, seemed to have invited the blackguard who surely had violated her to accompany her on her way. His men were still goggling at the two of them, riding up there before them as dignified as if the rogue had been the Duke of Infantado, whom the sergeant had once served.

An errant breeze carried back their words to him. They seemed to be politely arguing. "I didn't say I still loved you . . ." the lady protested, but swaying toward her companion as if drawn by an invisible cord.

"Can you say you don't," came the rejoinder. "Come then, say it and say it clearly so I will know whether you will walk before the good Talavera with me or whether I shall have to truss you up like a goose and carry you to your wedding."

"You are the most high-handed, infuriating, arrogant . . ."

The rest of her speech was lost as the little breeze went on its way, but there was a delighted trill of laughter, and the sergeant spied his lady gladly suffering to put her hand in the paw of the common blackguard who was flashing white teeth at her in an arrogant smile.

691

The sweating soldier shrugged and entertained in his mind a good-natured, envious wink and a few bawdy thoughts. *Ay, mi madre,* what puissant, brute charm these illiterate bandits from the hills had for simple-minded women, eh? It scarcely paid, in any terms, to be an honest man these days. Scarcely paid.

Historical Note

The gate through which Boabdil left Granada for the last time was, at his request, walled up and never used again. Pining in the barren mountain land to which he was exiled, Boabdil sold the domain back to the Spanish monarchs. He took his family and few followers to North Africa and soon after fell in battle in the service of a princely cousin. "A wretched man," wrote an Arab chronicler, "who could lose his life in another's cause though he did not dare to die in his own. Such was the immutable decree of destiny."

The solemn surrender guaranteeing to Granada full religious and civil liberty was abrogated in 1502, when Their Catholic Majesties, pressed by the Church under Cardinal Cisneros and by pockets of Moorish rebellion, issued an edict forcing their Moslem subjects to choose religious conversion or exile.

Those who chose to convert then became subject to the attentions of the Inquisition.

Author's Note

In addition to King Ferdinand and Queen Isabella of Spain, and Abu Abdullah, Grand Sultan of Granada, called Boabdil, many of the characters in this book are based on historical personages, among these Don Iñigo de Mendoza, Count of Tendilla, the Bishop of Talavera, the Marquis of Cadiz, Hernan del Pulgar; and the generals Reduan Venegas and Muza Aben Gazul. A scholar named Pietro Martire, Queen Isabella's secretary, historian, and tutor to her children, served as model for Pietro di Lido.

Francisco de Granada-Venegas and Dolores de la Rocha were drawn from those exciting, passionate, and spirited lovers found in every century, everywhere.